A Choice of Kipling's Prose

Also published by Faber

A CHOICE OF KIPLING'S VERSE
Selected with an introduction by T. S. Eliot

by Craig Raine
THE ONION, MEMORY (OUP)
A MARTIAN SENDS A POSTCARD HOME (OUP)
RICH
THE ELECTRIFICATION OF THE SOVIET UNION

ff

A CHOICE OF KIPLING'S PROSE

Selected with an introduction by
Craig Raine

faber and faber
LONDON · BOSTON

First published in 1987 by
Faber and Faber Limited
3 Queen Square London WC1N 3AU

Printed in Great Britain by
Mackays of Chatham Ltd Lordswood Kent

British Library Cataloguing in Publication Data

Kipling, Rudyard
[Prose works. *Selections*] A choice of
Kipling's prose.
I. Title II. Raine, Craig
828'.808 PR4851.5

ISBN 0-571-13735-0
ISBN 0-571-13850-0 Pbk

To
Joyce Tompkins
a great Kipling critic
to whom we are all indebted

Contents

Introduction

WE need to think again about Kipling. He is our greatest short-story writer, but one whose achievement is more complex and surprising than even his admirers recognize. When the talkies arrived in Hollywood, Charlie Chaplin ruefully considered the future: 'It would mean giving up my tramp character entirely. Some people suggested that the tramp might talk. This was unthinkable, for the first word he ever uttered would transform him into another person. Besides, the matrix out of which he was born was as mute as the rags he wore.' There is no evidence that the patchily-read Chaplin ever glanced at Kipling. If he had, he might have realized that Kipling, in his different field, had already wired a silent world for sound. The centre of his achievement is that he made talkies out of the mute matrix he shares with Chaplin. He is our greatest practitioner of dialect and idiolect – a writer whose ear for inflection and accent is not just ebullient technique, a prose virtuosity, but the expression of a profoundly democratic artistry, however eccentric that claim may appear to those for whom his politics are repugnant and his transcriptions of demotic speech condescending.

In his best work, Kipling extends the literary franchise to the inarticulate. The mute are given a say in things – and this generosity extends even to those machines which Henry James found so distressingly preponderant in Kipling's later work. In *Ulysses*, Leopold Bloom meditates in the typesetting room of a newspaper: 'Sllt. The nethermost deck of the first machine jogged forwards its flyboard with sllt the first batch of quirefolded papers. Sllt. Almost human the way it sllt to call attention. Doing its level best to speak. That door too sllt creaking, asking to be shut. Everything speaks in its own way. Sllt.' In Kipling, too, everything speaks in its own way, not just people. *Kim* gives us 'the sticky pull of slow-rending oilskin' and 'the well-known purr and fizzle of grains of incense'. In 'Through the Fire', there is the charcoal-burners' fire: 'the dying flames said "*whit, whit, whit*" as they fluttered and whispered over the white ashes.'

Kipling's eye was extraordinary right from the beginning. There is no shortage of brilliant local detail in his work. One has only to remember the corpse in 'The Other Man', 'sitting in the back seat, very square and firm, with one hand on the awning-stanchion and the wet pouring off his hat and moustache'. One thinks of the water in 'At Twenty-Two' which floods a coalmine – 'a sucking whirlpool, all yellow and yeasty'. Or of the unforgettable, bloated, two-day corpse of Hirman Singh, from 'In Flood Time', which the hero uses as an improvised life-jacket. Kipling's ear, though, was initially less perfect – in particular the sometimes excruciating Irish of Mulvaney, which isn't properly perfected until '"Love-o'-Women"' in *Many Inventions*. This faultiness is detectable, too, in the narrator's voice of *Plain Tales From the Hills*, where it is occasionally unclear whether Kipling endorses the tough moral pokerwork with which several stories begin. In 'Beyond the Pale', Kipling clearly uses the story to ironize the flat fiat of his opening sentence: 'A man should, whatever happens, keep to his own caste, race, and breed.' The tale illustrates the dangers, but the Kipling who interprets the object-letter of Bisesa so ably cannot possibly underwrite the statement that 'no Englishman should be able to translate object-letters'. (An object-letter being a collection of objects by which the illiterate communicate with each other since they cannot write.) On the other hand, there is no indication that Kipling dissociates himself from the repeated notion that callow young men are like colts who need violent use of the bit. Indeed, his last work, *Something of Myself*, reiterates the advice *in propria persona*.

But Kipling's own voice, over-confidently confident, is always less plausible than the alien voices he chose to assume. The latter make a long list. 'The Dream of Duncan Parrenness' is a faultless pastiche of Bunyan's *Grace Abounding*. 'On Greenhow Hill' is narrated in Learoyd's Yorkshire accent, '"Love-o'-Women"' in Mulvaney's Irish, 'Dray Wara Yow Dee' in Indian–English, 'The Wish House' and 'Friendly Brook' in broad Sussex. The prose of 'The Bull that Thought' is delicately tinged with French idiom and 'The Judgment of Dungara' and 'Reingelder and the German Flag' exploit the German accent and word-order, perhaps a trifle crudely, but comedy is always Kipling's least successful mode: '"We will him our converts in all their by their own hands constructed new clothes exhibit".' As Kipling reaches maturity, his mastery of dialect comes to depend less on orthography. Fenwick, the lighthouse-keeper who narrates 'The Disturber of Traffic', is given a circling delivery that is naturally conversational. His prose isn't good in the conventional sense, but it is dramatically appropriate: 'those streaks, they preyed upon his intellecks, he said; and he made up his mind, every time that the Dutch gunboat that attends to the Lights in those parts come along, that he'd ask to be took off.' Kipling's ear at this stage was perfect. And later, like Joyce's 'Clay' and 'Counterparts', Kipling in 'The Gardener' deploys disguised interior monologue for a story which appears to be impersonally narrated. Just as Joyce's leaden, ponderous style in 'Counterparts' mirrors the mental process of its alcoholic protagonist, so the Home Counties accent of Helen Turrell informs 'The Gardener': 'She learnt that Hagenzeele Third could be comfortably reached by an afternoon train which fitted in with the morning boat, and that there was a comfortable little hotel not three kilometres from Hagenzeele itself, where one could spend quite a comfortable night and see one's grave next morning.' Those three 'comfortable's' in the same sentence, like the three 'that's' in Fenwick's, are artfully calculated to convey to 'one' the stifling propriety of Helen Turrell's protective carapace. They are designed to make 'one' feel 'uncomfortable' about her version of events – and to show that her lie has infected her very thought-processes. She doesn't just act a lie – that her illegitimate son is her nephew – she *thinks* a lie even to herself. And Kipling conveys this without external, explicit comment.

'"The Finest Story in the World"' explains why Kipling chose to use such a bewildering number of different narrative voices. In it the clerk, Charlie Mears, like Jonson's Dapper, has literary aspirations: 'He rhymed "dove" with "love" and "moon" with "June", and devoutly believed that they had never so been rhymed before.' His confidant, the narrator, is necessarily sceptical until Charlie tells him the fragment of a story about being a galley-slave. The details are extraordinary and vivid: '"When that storm comes . . . I think that all the oars in the ship that I was talking about get broken, and the rowers have their chests smashed in by the oar-heads bucking"'; '"he's on the lower deck where the worst men are sent, and the only light comes from the hatchways and through the oar-holes. Can't you imagine the sunlight just squeezing through between the handle and the hole and wobbling about as the ship moves?"' These details are, in fact, not imagined at all. Charlie is merely remembering, in a completely unliterary way, two previous existences – a hypothesis Kipling somewhat clumsily corroborates by a fortuitous meeting with Grish Chunder, a Bengali acquaintance with whom the narrator can discuss metempsychosis before he is dismissed from the story as summarily as he was introduced into it. The baldly functional Grish Chunder isn't the story's only flaw. There is also the melodramatic detail of dead rowers being cut up at their oars before they are 'stuffed through the oar-hole in little pieces' – evidently, but unconvincingly, to terrify the living remainder. Here we feel Kipling's design on his reader. He means to shock us, but we can see the electrodes in his hands.

More vivid, and more germane to Kipling's preference for dialect, is the description of seawater topping the bulwarks. Here Kipling offers us two versions of the same event – the educated and the demotic, the cooked and the raw. Charlie's version ('"It looked just like a banjo-string drawn tight, and it seemed to stay there for years"') is far more graphic than the more decorous alternative ('"It looked like a silver wire laid down along the bulwarks, and I thought it was never going to break"'). '"The Finest Story in the World"' is, in its way, an expression of Kipling's artistic credo. It explains his commitment to dialect – largely by its frontal attack on the conventionally literary: when Charlie Mears gets his head into Literature, his power is fatally diminished, his memories become tarnished and second-hand. 'Again I cursed all the poets of England. The plastic mind of the bank-clerk had been overlaid, coloured, and distorted by that which he had read . . .' Kipling knows that Charlie Mears could never do justice to his own story, because he is incapable of telling it in his own words. Only a genius like Kipling could do that, the most unliterary of literary men.

'"Love-o'-Women"' makes the same point – makes it initially in exactly the same way as '"The Finest Story in the World"' – by a considered use of quotation marks around the title. Here the story is given to Mulvaney, his brogue tuned down just the requisite fraction from its earlier appearances in *Soldiers Three*. It is still broad, but acceptable – an evocation rather than a phonetically pedantic transcription. The art, of course, is there in the powerful frame, which parallels the sexual vagaries of Larry Tighe, the gentleman-ranker, with those of Mackie (who is shot by a distressed husband) and with those of Doctor Lowndes, who 'ran away wid Major – Major Van Dyce's lady that year'. That hesitation over the name is typical of Kipling's prodigious attention to detail: it is less flamboyant than the justly famous description of Mackie's blood on the barrack-square, dried 'to a dusky goldbeater-skin film, cracked lozenge-wise by the heat', but it carries weight all the same.

Larry Tighe is suffering the final stage of locomotor ataxia brought on by syphilis: 'Love-o'-Women' was cripplin' and crumblin' at ivry step. He walked wid a hand on my shoulder all slued sideways, an' his right leg swingin' like a lame camel.' By the end of the story, Tighe has 'shrivelled like beef-rations in a hot sun' – and one cannot read this distressingly powerful simile without recalling that banjo-string of Charlie Mears. The demotic opens on reality like an oven door. We feel the unmitigated blast, rather than a literary effect. Mulvaney is no Gigadibs. When Tighe is being diagnosed by the army doctor, Kipling carefully prepares for his boldest stroke in this non-literary milieu – a quotation from *Antony and Cleopatra*. He establishes Tighe's superior social status and, therefore, the likelihood of such a quotation, by what might seem a gratuitous detail: '"Thrate me as a study, Doctor Lowndes," he sez; and that was the first time I'd iver heard a docthor called his name.' The immediate gain in verisimilitude is enormous: Mulvaney, Tighe, and the social gulf between them are measured as if by a micrometer screwgauge. But this detailed record of Tighe's *sang-froid* and social politesse also means that we are able to accept his final words to the woman he has ruined: '"I'm dyin', Aigypt – dyin'," he sez.'

Dialect, the filter of Mulvaney's accent and ignorance, is crucial here. Kipling uses it to distinguish between the effect Tighe intends and the one which is achieved. It is a gesture towards the tragic, which is typical of the man, yet the reader is left with a more bitter, less literary effect – the desperate pathos of Tighe's borrowed gesture, denuded of its false nobility by Mulvaney's coarse rendition of the line. As a straight quotation, it would have been sentimental. In dialect, it is redeemed, rough and powerful. Kipling manages to keep the force of the words and to place the literary gesture.

'Dymchurch Flit' is one of Kipling's greatest stories. Largely told in Sussex dialect, it bears comparison with Frost's 'The Witch of Coös' and probably surpasses it. Again, the use of dialect is crucial. Both Frost and Kipling renew the ballad tradition where the kind of supernatural subject matter they treat would have naturally found expression. The alterations are simple but profound. Both abandon rhyme and literary dialect-equivalent, Frost choosing real American and a flexible blank verse, Kipling going to prose and authentic Sussex speech. When Wordsworth wanted to renew the ballad, he chose to eliminate the sensational event that had been its staple. Kipling and Frost retain the macabre event, but naturalize the form.

In 'Dymchurch Flit', Widow Whitgift is a psychic and, therefore, a possible channel of communication for the fairies or Pharisees who have been driven into the Romney Marsh as Henry VIII's Reformation gets under way, tearing down 'the Images'. The Pharisees wish to escape to France where the atmosphere is more congenial, where they will be less 'stenched up an' frighted'. After a typically oblique and powerfully elusive exposition of the groundwork, much like Frost's sidling approach to his narrative subjects, the tale suddenly simplifies and accelerates:

> Now there was a poor widow at Dymchurch under the Wall, which, lacking man or property, she had the more time for feeling; and she come to feel there was a Trouble outside her doorstep bigger an' heavier than aught she'd ever carried over it. She had two sons – one born blind, an' t'other struck dumb through fallin' off the Wall when he was liddle. They was men grown, but not wage-earnin', an' she worked for 'em, keepin' bees and answerin' Questions.

Has any writer ever used capital letters with more authority or to greater effect? Kipling not only reproduces the dialect exactly and with complete conviction, he also, as it were, reproduces an authentic dialect of thought – which barely distinguishes between the relative importance of 'man or property' or between 'keepin' bees and answerin' Questions'. Picasso once said that Van Gogh invented boots: 'Take Van Gogh: Potatoes, those shapeless things! To have painted that, or a pair of old shoes! That's really something!' In the same way, Kipling extends the literary franchise. To the speaker, Tom Shoesmith, himself a covert Pharisee, bees and Questions are equally natural and the reader is persuaded by his matter-of-factness. Without dialect, there can be no entrée to his mind and the story is literally inconceivable, except in the terms in which Kipling frames it. The voice provides its own inherent conviction. Its accent and tone brook no questions.

In almost every way, Kipling is the opposite of Henry James, his devoted but not uncritical admirer – and not only in the way he so frequently opts for dialect. The sophisticated author has the burden of explanation, the transcriber of dialect has the different burden of accuracy, however much both are, finally, inventing. T.S. Eliot, in his essay on Milton, brilliantly observed that 'the style of James certainly depends for its effect a good deal on the sound of a voice, James's own, painfully explaining'. Kipling never explains. He asserts. On political and moral issues this assertiveness is often irksome to contemporary taste, but in matters of description Kipling leaves James agonizing at the starting line while he has breasted the tape. 'Deep away in the heart of the City, behind Jitha Megji's *bustee*, lies Amir Nath's Gully, which ends in a dead-wall pierced by one grated window.' In fictional terms, the place-names mean everything. They are authoritative and unarguable. Contrast the beginning of *The Spoils of Poynton*: James sets out to establish the vulgar tastelessness of the Brigstock family seat. As often, he is fabulously wordy and relies on the transmitted opinions of Mrs Gereth rather than on direct evocation. The tone is comprehensively Jamesian. We take on trust the fiction that Mrs Gereth is the actual source:

> What was dreadful now, what was horrible, was the intimate ugliness of Waterbath, and it was of that phenomenon these ladies talked while they sat in the shade and drew refreshment from the great tranquil sky, from which no blue saucers were suspended. It was an ugliness fundamental and systematic, the result of the abnormal nature of the Brigstocks, from whose composition the principle of taste had been extravagantly omitted. In the arrangement of their home some other principle, remarkably active, but uncanny and obscure, had operated instead, with consequences depressing to behold, consequences that took the form of a universal futility. The house was bad in all conscience, but it might have passed if they had only let it alone. This saving mercy was beyond them; they had smothered it with trumpery ornament and scrapbook art, with strange excrescences and bunchy draperies, with gimcracks that might have been keepsakes for maid-servants and nondescript conveniences that might have been prizes for the blind. They had gone wildly astray over carpets and curtains; they had an infallible instinct for disaster, and were so cruelly doom-ridden that it rendered them almost tragic.

There is a pleasing, if tasteless, asperity in the reference to the blind, but essentially this is James painfully explaining kitschiness in the abstract. What *are* 'strange excrescences'?

This style is wonderfully adapted to the exploration of intricate cul-de-sacs in the minds of his 'super-subtle fry', but it is frankly embarrassed by anything more concrete than a perception. Kipling, however, can arrest kitsch in a sentence of brisk description: 'Besides fragments of the day's market, garlic, stale incense, clothes thrown on the floor, petticoats hung on strings for screens, old bottles, pewter crucifixes, dried *immortelles*, pariah puppies, plaster images of the Virgin, and hats without crowns.' This isn't one of Kipling's great lists like the remorseless, tragic inventory of childish things to be burned in 'Mary Postgate', but it serves to show how little Kipling needed to explain. To the objection that James has the more difficult task of describing *expensive* kitsch, as opposed to

Kipling's vulgar kitsch, one might cite James's evocation of the butler, Brooksmith, fallen on hard times:

> There was a great deal of grimy infant life up and down the place, and there was a hot moist smell within, as of the 'boiling' of dirty linen. Brooksmith sat with a blanket over his legs at a clean little window where, from behind stiff bluish-white curtains, he could look across at a huckster's and a tinsmith's and a small greasy public-house. He had passed through an illness and was convalescent, and his mother, as well as his aunt, was in attendance on him. I liked the nearer relative, who was bland and intensely humble, but I had my doubts about the remoter, whom I connected perhaps unjustly with the opposite public-house – she seemed greasy somehow with the same grease . . .

Certainly, this is better, but there is something desperate in his reliance on the adjective greasy. You feel that James made seeing difficult for himself by allowing himself to wrinkle his nose so floridly.

But, then, James was a natural novelist and suffered agonies of introspective dieting when *The Spoils of Poynton*, promised as a short novella, proved after all to be a novel. With James's tirelessly greedy appetite for complication, every snack turned out to be a banquet. Kipling, on the other hand, was a natural short-story writer, whose inborn instinct was for economy and limitation. Even in his most successful novel, *Kim*, he doesn't explain. Take Lurgan, the healer of pearls: we hear of him first, not by name, but by his title. When we meet him, Kipling is both intensely specific and ultimately baffling. Having created in the reader an itch to know what a healer of pearls *is*, Kipling successfully refuses to scratch the itch properly. Just as ghost-daggers are mentioned but never explained, so the healer of pearls meditates on his art:

> 'My work is on the table – some of it.' It blazed in the morning light – all red and blue and green flashes, picked out with the vicious blue-white spurt of a diamond here and there. Kim opened his eyes. 'Oh, they are quite well, those stones. It will not hurt them to take the sun. Besides, they are cheap. But with sick stones it is very different.' He piled Kim's plate anew. 'There is no one but *me* can doctor a sick pearl and re-blue turquoises. I grant you opals – any fool can cure an opal – but for a sick pearl there is only me. Suppose I were to die! Then there would be no one . . . Oh no! *You* cannot do anything with jewels. It will be quite

> enough if you understand a little about the Turquoise – some day.'

It is a brilliant sleight of hand. Kipling has done what the short-story writer must do: he has convinced us that *he* knows, so that, for a moment, we believe we do, too.

Kipling, of course, *could* explain the arcane. He explains the way an object-letter works in 'Beyond the Pale':

> A broken glass-bangle stands for a Hindu widow all India over; because, when her husband dies, a woman's bracelets are broken on her wrists. Trejago saw the meaning of the little bit of glass. The flower of the *dhak* means diversely 'desire', 'come', 'write', or 'danger', according to the other things with it. One cardamom means 'jealousy'; but when any article is duplicated in an object-letter, it loses its symbolic meaning and stands merely for one of a number indicating time . . .

And so on, until the meaning is spelled out and the reader has learned something he never knew before. It is a process which is instantly gratifying, but it is also deliberately misleading: it promises explanation everywhere, whereas Kipling's point is that the whole tale is exactly like its setting – a blind alley leading nowhere. So that, when the denouement comes and Bisesa displays her 'nearly healed stumps', Kipling refuses to enlighten us: the circumstances remain unclear and 'one special feature of the case is that he does not know where lies the front of Durga Charan's house. It may open on to a courtyard common to two or more houses, or it may lie behind any one of the gates of Jitha Megji's *bustee*. Trejago cannot tell.'

The balance, in this early story, between the rigorously specific and the rigorously withheld, is a mode which Kipling discovered right at the beginning of his career and maintained thereafter. The short story is like Iago – whose final words are: 'Demand me nothing: what you know, you know:/From this time forth I never will speak word.' 'Beyond the Pale', is, in its way, as difficult as any of the more notoriously obscure late stories.

'The Wish House', for example, is described by Eliot as a 'hard and obscure story'. To Eliot, every reader of Kipling owes a great debt. Most of us came to Kipling via Eliot's finely judged recommendation. All the same, I think cautious dissent is the appropriate reaction in the case of 'The Wish House'. The meaning of the story is never in doubt for a minute: Kipling allows one of the inarticulate to speak, Grace Ashcroft, a widow who, for love, has taken on the burden of her ex-lover's physical pain. Kipling's theme, as in much of his late work, is the undying, secret passion which persists even in old age and which is prepared to sacrifice its life for another. This is the theme, too, of 'A Madonna of the Trenches', in which the disturbed Strangwick pretends to be haunted by memories of thawing corpses in a trench-wall. In fact, their creaks terrify him less than the proof he has had of an all-consuming passion between his 'uncle', John Godsoe, and his aunt Armine – 'an' she nearer fifty than forty'. It is a passion for which death is no obstacle, merely the opportunity to meet freely at last beyond the grave. The force of the feeling is achieved by Kipling's judicious contrast, by which the corpses facing the trenches are as nothing, and by Strangwick's struggle to express the inexpressible: '"It was a bit of a mix-up, for me, from then on. I must have carried on – they told me I did, but – but I was – I felt a – a long way inside of meself, like – if you've ever had that feelin'. I wasn't rightly on the spot at all."' The broken speech is at once banal and brilliant, like Charlie Mears's banjo-string.

In 'The Wish House', Kipling again rejects a conventional literary treatment in favour of something more authentic. The supernatural machinery is fantastic, but the details sustain our belief – from the adolescent sapphism of Sophy Ellis ('But – you know how liddle maids first feel it sometimes – she come to be crazy-fond o' me, pawin' and cuddlin' all whiles; an' I 'adn't the 'eart to beat her off . . .') to Grace's 'waxy yellow forehead' and her cancerous leg with the wound's edges 'all heaped up, like – same as a collar'. All this, and more, is rigorously specific. It is only the Token which is unexplained and, therefore, 'hard and obscure'. Even here, though, Kipling volunteers the information that a Token 'is the wraith of the dead or, worse still, of the living'. In this case, the Token is a wraith of the living – which is why Sophie's and Grace's accounts differ, each being a version of the teller: a 'gigglin'' girl and a 'heavy woman' who walks with difficulty. This partial explanation, of course, did not satisfy Eliot, nor does it satisfy us. But I do not think Kipling means it to. He knew that the Token's potency in the story is dependent on its precise obscurity.

> I turned into the gate bold as brass; up de steps I went an' I ringed the front-door bell. She pealed loud, like it do in an empty house. When she'd all ceased, I 'eard a cheer, like, pushed back on de floor o' the kitchen. Then I 'eard feet on de kitchen-stairs, like it might ha' been a heavy woman in slippers. They come up to de

> stairhead, acrost the hall – I 'eard the bare boards creak under 'em – an' at de front door dey stopped. I stooped me to the letter-box slit, an' I says: 'Let me take everythin' bad that's in store for my man, 'Arry Mockler, for love's sake.' Then, whatever it was 'tother side de door let its breath out, like, as if it 'ad been holdin' it for to 'ear better.

Should Kipling have given more information than this unaspirated, compelling, methodical account?

The answer must be negative. In fact, the hypothesis can be tested: 'In the Same Boat', a tale of drug addiction, shows two protagonists haunted by appalling hallucinations. They exchange horrors. Conroy's involves 'a steamer – on a stifling hot night'. Innocuous details – like rolled-up carpets and hot, soapy swabbed decks – are interrupted by the hooting of scalded men in the engine room, one of whom taps Conroy on the shoulder and drops dead at his feet. It is a powerful scenario, but perhaps less so than Miss Henschil's: she walks down a white sandy road near the sea, with broken fences on either side, and men with mildewy faces, 'eaten away', run after her and touch her. For a time, these horrors retain their undisclosed power and rank with Hummil's vision, in 'At the End of the Passage', of 'a blind face that cries and can't wipe its eyes, a blind face that chases him down corridors'. One thinks, too, of 'A Friend of the Family', in which we hear briefly and inexplicably of 'the man without a face – preaching' on the beach at Gallipoli, before and *after* his death. It is a parenthesis which lurks in the mind long after the rest of the revenge tale has been forgotten. And it remains there because Kipling never explains. 'In the Same Boat', however, provides a joint explanation of the scalded engineers and the mildewy faces: their respective mothers, while pregnant, have brushed against an engine-room accident and a leper colony. Under the influence of their addiction, Conroy and the girl relive these traumas which have penetrated the womb. The pat psychology is an artistic blunder, and the tension in the tale, palpable as a blister, leaks away uncharacteristically. The reader is left with the thing that Kipling, miraculously often, managed to avoid – mere writing, Wardour Street psychology in which the mystery is plucked, trussed and oven-ready.

Normally, the exigencies of the form prevent anything more than necessary assertion. Soon it will be over – the secret of the short story is known to everyone. From the moment it begins, it is about to die and the artist knows that every word, therefore, must tell.

Digression is a luxury that must pay its way ten-fold. As it does in 'The Gardener', when Mrs Scarsworth begins her confession with the observation, '"What extraordinary wall-papers they have in Belgium, don't you think?"' It is bizarre, yet convincing psychology – a last-minute reluctance to proceed with her embarrassing disclosure. But whenever Kipling is literary, he falters, as in the self-conscious reference which flaws 'The House of Suddhoo': 'read Poe's account of the voice that came from the mesmerized dying man, and you will realize less than one-half of the horror of that head's voice.' This is a rare failure.

Kipling, more than any other writer, except perhaps Chekhov, mastered the stipulated economy. His openings are packed: 'The house of Suddhoo, near the Taksali Gate, is two-storeyed, with four carved windows of old brown wood, and a flat roof. You may recognize it by five red hand-prints arranged like the Five of Diamonds on the whitewash between the upper windows.' In 'The Limitations of Pambé Serang', Nurkeed is instantly established as 'the big fat Zanzibar stoker who fed the second right furnace'. In that 'second right', what might seem an embellishment is actually a stringent economy. Chekhov outlines the principle in *The Seagull* when Kostya Treplev complains:

> The description of the moonlit evening is long and forced. Trigorin's worked out his methods, it's easy enough for him. He gives you the neck of a broken bottle glittering against a weir and the black shadow of a mill-wheel – and there's your moonlit night all cut and dried. But I have a quivering light and the silent twinkling of the stars and the distant sound of a piano dying on the calm, scented air. This is agony.

Or painful explanation.

Because the short story is always haunted by the sense of its ending, there are things – convoluted plots, ambiguous motivation, extended histories – which it should not attempt to tell, as well as those it must retail with the maximum efficiency. In the course of a long writing career, from 1890 to 1936, Kipling both abides by this principle and subtly violates it. The *oeuvre* of any good writer exhibits two opposite, but perfectly consistent tendencies: certain features will persist throughout ('in my beginning is my end') and there will also be a trajectory of change and development. So far, we have considered Kipling from the first point of view – that of consistency. His arc of change more or less follows the development of the short story itself. This can be roughly summarized by the difference between, say, Maupassant's 'The Necklace', with its notorious trick ending, and, say, Hemingway's 'The Big Two-Hearted River'. Admirers of Maupassant claim that 'The Necklace' is untypical of him, but actually even his best work is essentially anecdotal: 'Boule de Suif', despite its length, has little particular characterization and is designed merely to expose the hypocrisy of the French upper and middle class; 'The Trouble with André', 'The Piece of String' and 'My Uncle Jules', to take a broad sample, are all anecdotes. 'The Piece of String' is the story of a peasant who is unjustly accused of theft, exonerated by the facts, yet sent into a rather implausible decline by the refusal of the community to believe him. He has parsimoniously picked up a piece of string, not the wallet he is accused by an enemy of taking. Maupassant's talent is to dress up this amusing but thin tale with a vivid opening that describes the Normandy peasants going to market. 'Boule de Suif' shows a prostitute sharing her food with her fellow passengers, whose hunger conquers their moral repugnance. Yet when, to oblige them, she has slept with an occupying Prussian officer who is holding up the coach till she complies, they refuse to share their food with her. The irony is typically pat and not unlike that of 'The Necklace', in which the lost diamond necklace, replaced after years of scrimping, turns out, after all, to have been paste. Hemingway's 'The Big Two-Hearted River', on the other hand, avoids this fearful symmetry by abjuring plot: Nick Adams goes angling, but does not feel able yet to fish in the swamp. In terms of plot, a meal is a big event. The story's power resides in its brooding implications which, though never made clear, involve the attempt to regain the simple life after the trauma of war, symbolized by a fire which has razed the whole area about the river. In other words, the short story moves away from anecdote, the neat tale, to a plotless genre of implication. This, of course, is a generalization and Hemingway's 'Fifty Grand' shows that the anecdote, if brilliantly enough handled, will always continue to have a life. There the Irish boxer has to lose a fight because he has bet on his opponent. However, in a double-cross, his opponent has bet on him. The upshot is that, in order to lose, Jack Brennan is forced to call on enormous reserves of courage by going on after he has been hit low. The narrator, his trainer, puts this down to Brennan's meanness in money matters, which he over-emphasizes throughout: Hemingway, though, is more interested in the paradox by which Brennan's cynical decision to throw the fight has to be sustained by brute heroism. The 'cowardly' route proves to be its opposite.

'Fifty Grand' is an exception. More typical of the short story in this century is 'The Killers', in which two gangsters take over a café in order to murder a customer, who doesn't in fact appear. The dialogue we hear is full of menace, but we never discover why the men are after Andreson. The modernity of the story can be gauged when you consider how like Pinter's *The Birthday Party* this dramatic vignette is. (Some day, incidentally, the influence of Hemingway on Pinter will be properly assessed.) 'The Killers' is a classic story in its open-endedness, culminating with Ole Andreson stretched on his bed, resigned to his eventual fate for some undisclosed offence.

Early Kipling is often anecdotal in the Maupassant manner, but whereas Maupassant felt constrained by the form and eventually did his best work in the novels *Bel-Ami* and *Une Vie*, Kipling made a virtue out of the limitation imposed on him by the form. By employing narrators, he was able to squeeze more into the story. *Plain Tales from the Hills* employs a catch-phrase that finally becomes irritating – 'But that is another story' – yet it serves as an index of Kipling's awareness of the constraints of his chosen medium. Late Kipling, however, circumvents the difficulty. M. Voiron, for example, in 'The Bull that Thought', narrates a story which takes place over a number of years, but because he is a character he is allowed to edit his material openly: 'And next year,' he says, 'through some chicane which I have not the leisure to unravel . . .' An author could not permit himself this transition which amounts to the phrase, 'to cut a long story short'. Kipling's narrators allow him, without breach of decorum, to ramble, to re-cap, to circle, to back-track, to anticipate, as real people do, and therefore to deal with long periods of time over a short space. The narrators, too, permit Kipling to avoid explanation, where necessary, because the responsibility for the story appears to rest with them, the author's role being that of auditor. In this way, Kipling crams into the short story the substance of a full-length novel, while the privilege of occlusion is retained.

'Mrs Bathurst' is probably the most notorious example of these techniques at work, though '"The Finest Story in the World"' employs them too. The narrative in the latter is, as the Kipling-figure remarks, 'a maddening jumble'. Charlie Mears can remember not just one previous existence but two, which, in his mind, are inseparable. In fact, as the narrator finally realizes, each tale told separately would be banal: 'The adventures of a Viking had been written many times before; the history of a Greek galley-slave was no new thing.' The details are luminous because they are deprived of a coherent setting and context. They exist in the dark – inexplicable and end-stopped – hence their potency. 'The Dream of Duncan Parrenness' further illustrates the point: for most of its length, Kipling re-visits the theme of self-haunting. (Despite his often-repeated determination never to repeat himself, he had already touched on this in 'At the End of the Passage': 'the first thing he saw standing in the verandah was the figure of himself.') After Parrenness has donated his trust in men and women, and his boy's soul and conscience, to the dream-presence of his older self, he is left with his reward – 'When the light came I made shift to behold his gift, and saw that it was a little piece of dry bread.' Perhaps this piece of dry bread alludes to Matthew 4:4 ('Man shall not live by bread alone, but by every word that proceedeth out of the mouth of God'), thus illustrating the nature of his transaction, the swap of morality for materialism. Perhaps it alludes to 'the bread of affliction'. Either is possible. Reading the story, however, the image is strangely satisfying in itself. It tells, and tells profoundly, without explaining itself. It is the man, this shrivelled piece of bread, and hardly needs the Bible to underpin it.

At the centre of 'Mrs Bathurst' is another famously baffling image, which once read is never forgotten: two tramps, one squatting, one standing, by the dead-end of a railway siding in South Africa.

> 'There'd been a bit of a thunderstorm in the teak, you see, and they were both stone dead and as black as charcoal. That's what they really were, you see – charcoal. They fell to bits when we tried to shift them. The man who was standin' up had the false teeth. I saw 'em shinin' against the black. Fell to bits he did too, like his mate squatting down an' watchin' him, both of 'em all wet in the rain. Both burned to charcoal, you see. And – that's what made me ask about marks just now – the false-toother was tattooed on the arms and chest – a crown and foul anchor with M. V. above.'

When everything has been said about this story, it is this image which continues to grip the heart and squeeze it. Like the piece of dried bread, it never relaxes its hold on the imagination. Is any explanation, then, possible? Kipling approaches this *coup de théâtre* by a very circuitous route, using several narrators, and yet each apparent digression contributes to the whole.

Most readers see 'Mrs Bathurst' as an obscure tale of elective affinities – the core of which is the passion of a middle-aged warrant officer called Vickery for Mrs Bathurst, a widowed New Zealand hotel keeper. What has passed between them is only guessed at by the narrators. But they agree that Mrs Bathurst is something special. She has 'It', hence Vickery's obsession which manifests itself suddenly and feverishly when, in Cape Town, he sees her for a few seconds on film. She is arriving at Paddington station in search of Vickery. Night after night Vickery watches her – then deserts. Another narrator, Hooper, supplies the grisly denouement above, at the point where the other two, Pyecroft and Pritchard, break off. Vickery's tattoo shows up white, like writing on a burned letter. There is some dispute as to whether the other body is that of Mrs Bathurst: Pritchard plainly thinks it is, but critics have differed, myself included.

Though the rambling narration has been denounced by both Kingsley Amis and Angus Wilson, the story is as precise as a Swiss watch. Everything fits, but the reader has to wind it up. The theory of elective affinity stems from the narrators. They fit Vickery's story to their own experience: sailors, they know, constantly desert for reasons of the heart. Moon has jumped ship in the South Seas for a woman, 'bein' a Mormonastic beggar'; Spit-Kid Jones married a 'cocoanut-woman'. Hooper agrees that some women can drive a man crazy if he doesn't save himself. Hence the theory. Kipling, however, is careful to show the observant reader that his narrators are unreliable, and to tuck away the truth of the matter. The credulity of Pyecroft and Pritchard is established in the framing story of Boy Niven who dragged them off on a wild goose chase through the woods of British Columbia. In addition, there is a persistent motif of unreliable machinery – trains derailed on straight lines, a gyroscope that goes on the blink, a brake-van chalked for repair, damaged rolling stock, sprung midship frames, ill-fitting false teeth, and so on. It is a broad hint that the machinery of this story is also unreliable.

Moreover, on ascertainable facts, the narrators are shown to be wrong. Hooper hears a clink of couplings, '"It's those dirty little Malay boys, you see."' It isn't. It's Pyecroft and Pritchard. Similarly, Pyecroft gets an expert to 'read' the captain's face – wrongly as it turns out. Further, Kipling makes Pyecroft employ a variety of foreign phrases, all italicized, adding an extra one to the magazine version – *moi aussi*, *verbatim*, *ex officio*, *status quo*, *resumé*, *peeris* and *casus belli*. Taken with other Biblical props from Acts – the beer ('Others, mocking, said, These men are full of new wine') and the strong south-easter ('a sound from heaven like a rushing mighty wind') – these phrases add up to a parody of the gift of tongues.

In other words, Pyecroft speaks more than he knows, trusting to erroneous inspiration, as when he compares Vickery's false teeth to a 'Marconi ticker', hinting at strange communication with Mrs Bathurst. Hooper's tic of dialogue is to say 'You see', a total of sixteen times. The point is that his companions don't see at all.

The truth is concealed in the words of 'The Honeysuckle and the Bee', sung by some picnickers on the beach, words by A.H. Fitz, music by W.H. Penn. They tell us what Vickery only hints at in the phrase 'my *lawful* wife', namely that he has married Mrs Bathurst bigamously, in a Moon-like way. A 'lawful' wife implies an unlawful wife and the song confirms this suspicion:

> As they sat there side by side,
> He asked her to be his bride
> She answered 'Yes' and sealed it with a kiss.

Vickery's eventual fate, death by lightning, tells us what happened after the bigamy, for it is paralleled in the framing story of Boy Niven. 'Heavy thunder with continuous lightning' is, according to Pyecroft, the punishment for *desertion*. Vickery, then, is a double-deserter, from Mrs Bathurst and the Navy. We don't know much about Mrs Bathurst, but we know enough to understand why Vickery is afraid, 'like an enteric at the last kick': first, 'she never scrupled to... set 'er foot on a scorpion'; secondly, as Pritchard's anecdote of the beer-bottles demonstrates, she never forgets. After five years, she remembers Pritchard's name and his 'particular' beer, unlike the servant girl who chucks him a bottle in mistake for someone else. The contrast is telling.

Vickery has committed a crime, bigamy, and that presumably is why the captain connives at his absence without leave – desertion being less of a disgrace than legal proceedings from the Navy's point of view. The element of criminality also explains why Vickery watches the film so compulsively, yet with such dread: in the oldest of traditions, he is revisiting the scene of his crime. The film explains, too, that Vickery, unlike the others, has found Mrs Bathurst forgettable. He takes Pyecroft along for confirmation – so much for their romantic interpretation.

In 'Mrs Bathurst' nothing is wasted. Every digression contributes to the total meaning. It is like a closed economy, as parsimonious as a city under siege, despite its air of beery reminiscence. In 'The Wrong Thing', Kipling makes it clear that his art had no place for guesswork. Though he believed in his Daemon, as any writer must if he is not to force his talent, he was conscious and critical after the

Inner Voice had played its part: 'Iron's sweet stuff', says Hal, 'if you don't torture her, and hammered work is all pure, truthful line, with a reason and a support for every curve and bar of it.' Though one can scarcely imagine any child grasping this piece of aesthetic theory from *Rewards and Fairies*, it is a plain warning to adults that nothing can be skipped, that every detail is relevant – as it is in 'Mrs Bathurst'.

Does this affect the status of the charcoal figures? Ultimately, it does not. Are we to assume an accident? Or an act of God? Clearly, the fate of Vickery carries an element of poetic justice, but we cannot speculate beyond that point. The reader untangles the thread of the narrative only to discover that Kipling, at the crucial moment, has deliberately snapped it in order to preserve the shock at the heart of the tale. There is no insulating context, only raw voltage.

The same thing, though less strikingly, is true of 'Dayspring Mishandled', when Manallace draws on his black gloves at the crematorium. The gesture has a power and solemnity which are unaccountable. This story illuminates one difference between Kipling's early work and his late work. In *Something of Myself*, Kipling dilates briefly on his art: 'The shortening of them, first to my own fancy after rapturous re-readings, and next to the space available, taught me that a tale from which pieces have been raked out is like a fire that has been poked.' Kipling, rightly in my view, never deviated from this prescription. Yet there are those who have argued that, whereas in the early work excision creates intensity, in the later stories it merely creates obscurity. However, in the later work, the reader is often expected, as in 'Mrs Bathurst', to reinstate what Kipling has eliminated. Links are suppressed to involve the reader in the tale: close reading implicates the reader as he deciphers the encoded text. In Henry James's formula from *The Golden Bowl*, the writer forgoes 'the muffled majesty of authorship' – in order to compel us to 'live and breathe and rub shoulders and converse with the persons engaged in the struggle'. 'Dayspring Mishandled' is a case in point.

The plot is as neat in its way as the resolution of Tom's antecedents in *Tom Jones*. Alured Castorley has, in his youth, been a member of a literary syndicate which provided pulp fiction for the undiscriminating mass-market. Manallace, another member of the group, decides to ruin Castorley's carefully nurtured reputation as a Chaucer expert by getting him to authenticate a planted forgery of a previously unknown Chaucer fragment. While Castorley has risen in the world of letters, Manallace has made a reputation of a different kind in 'the jocundly-sentimental Wardour Street brand of adventure'. Manallace's income goes towards nursing 'Dal Benzaquen's mother through her final illness, 'when her husband ran away'. For about half the length of the tale, Kipling conceals the revenge plot so that, like the narrator, we believe that when 'Dal's mother dies, 'she seemed to have emptied out his life, and left him only fleeting interest in trifles'.

Part of our pleasure resides in the simple realization that the series of apparently pointless hobbies are, in fact, related to each other and have a profound purpose – that of revenge. Each step is lucid and mesmerizingly technical – Kipling's impersonation of the insider with special knowledge was never put to better use. Everything comes together - the experiments with ink, the medieval paste, the handwriting, the early Chaucerian tale – as if Kipling was demonstrating to his readership that, in his work, the diversion is always in fact central and germane. In this tale of revenge and literary hoax, where the avenger is finally compassionate, Kipling is careful not to explain two things – the motive for Manallace's subterfuge and the reason why he finally forbears. Castorley's careerism, his lack of generosity, his 'gifts of waking dislike' – these are all inadequate reasons for a scheme which is designed to kill its victim. The narrator is told the real motive, but we are not: 'He told it. "That's why," he said. "Am I justified?" He seemed to me entirely so.' Most readers assume that Castorley grossly insulted the mother of 'Dal Benzaquen, in conversation with Manallace during the war, because she had turned down his proposal of marriage: 'He went out before the end, and, it was said, proposed to 'Dal Benzaquen's mother who refused him.'

That parenthetical 'it was said' carries its own charge of doubt and, taken with the warnings against passive readership that are scattered through the story – like Manallace's reiterated 'if you save people thinking, you can do anything with 'em' – it should put us on our guard. The truth about Castorley and 'Dal's mother comes out under the influence of illness and Gleeag's liver tonics. (Kipling was always willing, perhaps too much so, to use drugs as a way of speeding up necessary disclosure, as in '"Wireless"' and 'A Madonna of the Trenches'.) The fuddled, dying but truthful Castorley begins by saying that 'there was an urgent matter to be set right, and now he had the Title and knew his own mind it would all end happily.' His rambling monologue concludes with his naming 'Dal's mother. The crucial words are '*and knew his own mind*'. Castorley, then, is the person who *didn't* know his own mind. The phrase would be meaningless if Castorley, as 'it was said', had proposed and been refused. Clearly, he proposed and was accepted – only to desert her in order to better himself and get on in the world. Like Wilkett, in 'The Tender Achilles', he opts for career rather than caress. Manallace's motive, then, is that Castorley has rejected 'Dal's mother and perhaps boasted of it – a thing hard for Manallace to bear because he has 'adored' her.

Castorley is such a repellent character, so bereft of redeeming features, that this may seem implausible. We find it almost impossible to believe that 'Dal's mother actually loved him. Kipling, though, has thoughtfully provided an analogue – in Mrs Castorley, who, if equally ghastly, is having a passionate affair with the surgeon, Gleeag. It is obvious enough, yet Manallace doesn't realize for a long time: '"But she's so infernally plain, and I'm such a fool, it took me weeks to find out."' The heart has its reasons – reasons which transcend mere appearances and unworthy personalities. Castorley may be snobbish, selfish and bellied – but neither is Vickery such a catch, or the 'unappetizing, ash-coloured' Mrs Castorley.

Once we have grasped that Castorley has loved and left 'Dal's mother, the story falls into place. For instance, the scrap of Latin, which incorporates an anagram of Manallace's name, now has its full significance. The text is not simply a vehicle for Manallace's device to prove the fragment is a forgery. Translated, it reads, 'Behold this beloved Mother taking with her me, the accepted one.' We are never told 'Dal's mother's name. She is, as it were, 'this beloved Mother' and the words 'the accepted one' refer to Castorley's proposal. The Nodier poem, which provides the story with its epigraph, now makes fuller sense: 'Dal's mother is 'la fille des beaux jours', the old Neminaka days, whose memory is now poisoning Castorley's system like mandragora. The Chaucerian fragment, too, with its account of a girl 'praying against an undesired marriage', slips into place. 'Dal's mother is forced to marry someone else, by default. When she is enduring her fatal illness and is 'wholly paralysed', we are told that 'only her eyes could move, and those always looked for the husband who had left her'. Clearly, if this was her legal husband, the obvious candidate, Manallace would have been better employed in mounting a campaign of revenge against *him*. In fact, 'the husband who left her' must be Castorley. Kipling again resolves the doubt by another careful parallel. At Castorley's cremation, Mrs Castorley's eyes turn, like 'Dal's mother's eyes, to her real passion, her illicit lover, Gleeag.

Dowson's 'Non Sum Qualis Eram Bonae', glancingly alluded to by Manallace, also finds its true place in this structure. The poem is an account of sleeping with a prostitute, while actually being sick with love for someone else – Cynara, who comes as a vision in the grey dawn:

> But I was desolate and sick of an old passion,
> When I awoke and found the dawn was grey:
> I have been faithful to thee, Cynara! in my fashion.

Dowson's poem is yet another example of dayspring mishandled, like Nodier's poem. Kipling's text is so richly worked that one wonders finally whether it is totally fanciful to see the motif of the grey dawn punningly reiterated in Graydon's name.

Graydon's factory, which produces pulp literature for mass consumption, makes its contribution to the whole. Kipling seldom wastes a frame in any of his stories. Here he is warning us against literature which does not require the reader to think, as well as touching on the idea of forgery, fakery and substitution: 'So, precisely as the three guinea hand-bag is followed in three weeks by its thirteen and sevenpence ha'penny, indistinguishable sister, the reading public enjoyed perfect synthetic substitutes for Plot, Sentiment, and Emotion.' The single word, 'sister', alerts us to the parallel between literature and women: Castorley, instead of marrying the real thing, has chosen an ashen-faced substitute, who has never believed him 'since before we were married'. As a consequence, Castorley has to endure a concealed, corrosive passion. It is *this* that Manallace finally takes pity on. Like many another in Kipling's work. Castorley is compelled to eke out his emotional life on 'perfect synthetic substitutes' for sentiment and emotion.

One last detail of 'Dayspring Mishandled' remains to be accounted for – the twice-repeated phrase, 'for old sake's sake'. This comes from a poem in Kingsley's *The Water Babies*, which describes a doll lost on a heath and rediscovered:

> I found my poor little doll, dears,
> As I played in the heath one day:
> Folk say she is terribly changed, dears,
> For her paint is all washed away,
> And her arm trodden off by the cows, dears,
> And her hair not the least bit curled:
> Yet, for old sake's sake, she is still, dears,
> The prettiest doll in the world.

The paralysis of 'Dal's mother and Castorley's sick-bed declaration of love are encapsulated and underlined by Kingsley's poem. The gloves so mysteriously donned by Manallace continue to hoard their meaning – as so often in Kipling's work.

For those to whom Kipling is merely a crude jingoist, the almost Joycean meticulousness of his art will come as a surprise. But his abiding concern with love, in all its desolate manifestations, will come as a revelation. Love in Kipling's *oeuvre* isn't often happy: in *Plain Tales* it is mainly adulterous or disappointing or competitive; in 'Without Benefit of Clergy', it is tragic, with Ameera and the child dead, the mother greedily acquisitive and Holden's home suddenly wrecked by the rains: 'he found that the rains had torn down the mud pillars of the gateway, and the heavy wooden gate that had guarded his life hung lazily from one hinge. There was grass three inches high in the courtyard; Pir Khan's lodge was empty, and the sodden thatch sagged between the beams.' What had once seemed secure and solid is wiped out virtually overnight, the house mirroring the frail relationship – a symbolic scene possible only in the tropics. Desolation, sacrifice and waste are the words that present themselves when one considers Kipiing's treatment of love.

There are, of course, moments when sacrifice isn't entirely negative. Even 'The Wish House' has its positive side – grim and thankless though Grace Ashcroft's sacrifice is. She may herself be doubtful, for all her toughness, and seek reassurance from her friend Liz Fettley ('"It *do* count, don't it – de pain?"') but there is something movingly tenacious in her emotional commitment which Kipling captures in one sentence: 'The lips that still kept trace of their original moulding hardly more than breathed the words.' If Kipling had added the indefinite article – and written 'the lips that still kept *a* trace' – how much weaker this statement of willed beauty in the face of old age and imminent death would have been. If we compare 'The Wish House' to Chekhov's great story of old age, 'A Dreary Story', the power of Grace Ashcroft is evident. Chekhov's hero, Professor Nikolay Stepanovitch, is the incarnation of Yeats's summation of age – 'testy delirium and dull decrepitude'. The Professor's sense of mortality infects his entire life, empties him of profundity, interest and affection, even for his ward Katya whom he loves. 'Farewell, my treasure!' the story ends, but these are the hollow words of a man recalling the memory of emotion, not the thing itself. By comparison, Grace Ashcroft isn't such a desolate figure.

The sacrifice in 'Dymchurch Flit' is difficult and touching, too. The Pharisees ask for a boat to take them to France 'an' come back no more'. There is a boat but no one to sail it, and so they ask the widow to lend them her sons: 'Give 'em Leave an' Good-will to sail it for us, Mother – O Mother!' The conflict is then between her own delimited maternal feelings – 'One's dumb, an' t'other's blind . . . but all the dearer me for that' – and her mother's heart which goes out to the invisible Pharisees and *their* children: 'the voices justabout pierced through her; an' there was childern's voices too. She stood out all she could, but she couldn't rightly stand against *that*.' Finally, she consents, shaking 'like a aps-tree makin' up her mind'. She is rewarded for her charity by the return of her sons and by the promise that psychic gifts will run in her family, but Tom Shoesmith makes it clear that her sacrifice was not made for gain: 'No. She loaned her sons for a pure love-loan, bein' as she sensed the Trouble on the Marshes, an' was simple good-willing to ease it.'

Kipling's stories return ceaselessly to the nature of parental love, its ability to expend inexhaustible passion on apparently worthless objects. There is Wynn Fowler in 'Mary Postgate', 'an unlovely orphan of eleven', who repays Mary's devotion 'by calling her "Gatepost", "Postey", or "Packthread", by thumping her between her narrow shoulders, or by chasing her bleating, round the garden, her large mouth open, her large nose high in the air, at a stiff-necked shamble very like a camel's'. Kipling, artistically generous as ever, doesn't reserve strong feeling for the handsome. Nor are the recipients of this love perfect. In 'Friendly Brook', Mary, the adopted Barnardo girl, garners no praise from Jabez and Jesse; '"It don't sometimes look to me as if Mary has her natural right feelin's. She don't put on an apron o' Mondays 'thout being druv to it – in the kitchen *or* the henhouse. She's studyin' to be a school-teacher. She'll make a beauty! I never knowed her show any sort o' kindness to nobody . . .' For this plain, vinegary girl, whose 'Maker ain't done much for her outside nor yet in', her foster-father, Jim Wickenden, is prepared to commit murder – loosening a plank so that her real father is drowned on one of his visits to blackmail the foster-parents. Eliot, understandably in wartime, chose to read this story as a kind of pagan celebration of England, with the brook as a tutelary deity. It isn't. Jim Wickenden's relationship with the brook is made clear in the implicit pun with which Kipling ends the story. Wickenden is happy when the brook floods and takes a snatch of his hay because that represents hush-money: 'The Brook had changed her note again. It sounded as if though she were mumbling something soft.' His secret is safe with the brook.

In the same story, there is the Copley family and their 'Bernarder cripple-babe', whom they foster, but not for the financial inducement: 'It's handy,' says Jabez. 'But the child's more. "Dada" he says, an' "Mumma" he says, with his great rollin' head-piece all hurdled up in that iron collar. *He* won't live long – his backbone's rotten, like. But they Copley's do just about set store by him – five bob or no five bob.' For Kipling, this isn't an extreme case. It is a human constant he can effortlessly empathize with.

It is this knowledge of parental love, too, which produces some of Kipling's most savage stories. He knows it can be murderous if threatened – as it is, most obviously, in 'Mary Postgate', where the wizened old spinster stands over a German airman with a revolver, luxuriating first in his death (from injuries sustained in a fall from his aircraft) and then in a hot bath. This act of barbarism, her refusal to fetch a 'Toctor', Mary knows, would not gain Wynn's approval were he alive. Nor does it, I think, elicit Kipling's approval – only his understanding. The same theme is examined in 'A Sahibs' War', where Kipling's attitude is less ambiguous. The narrator, Umr Singh, is a Sikh who is a kind of adopted father to a Sahib called Kurban: 'Young – of a reddish face - with blue eyes, and he lilted a little on his feet when he was pleased, and cracked his finger-joints.' How carefully Kipling implies, in the first three phrases, this young man's virtual anonymity, and how carefully he conveys the immense emotional investment of the narrator in the last two descriptive touches, singling out characteristics invisible except to the eye of love. In this story, the narrator attempts to revenge himself on a treacherous Boer family who have killed his 'son', Kurban Sahib.

They are not prepossessing: 'An old man with a white beard and a wart upon the left side of his neck; and a fat woman with the eyes of a swine and the jowl of a swine; and a tall young man deprived of understanding. His head was hairless, no larger than an orange, and the pits of his nostrils were eaten away by a disease. He laughed and slavered . . .' When the Sikh narrator plans his revenge, he intends to be exact, a child for a child: 'and the idiot lay on the floor with his head against her knee, and he counted his fingers and laughed, and she laughed again. So I knew they were mother and son . . .' He means to hang the son in front of the mother and Kipling accurately records her anguish: 'The woman hindered me not a little with her screechings and plungings.' Umr Singh, who has taken opium to sustain him, is deflected from his purpose by a vision of the dead Kurban Sahib who orders him to refrain, telling him that this is a Sahibs' War. Mary Postgate has no such assistance back to civilized values and the rule of law – only her tortured instinct, in its full atavism. Nevertheless, though the Boer family survive, Kipling makes us know the force of parental grief. If it is the eye of love that isolates and cherishes that habit of cracking the fingers, it is the same eye, hideously inflamed, that registers the wart on the left side of the Boer's neck.

In his stories, Kipling often measures love by its opposite, and *O Beloved Kids*, his letters to his children, also shows how deep this habit of thought and expression went. His expressions of affection are rarely straightforward. Except for two occasions ('You see, I love you'), Kipling prefers the ironical mode: 'Mummy is better I think every day than she was (perhaps because two yelling pestiferous brats are away)'; 'she says as long as she hasn't you two horrid brats to look after she can stand most things'; 'I regret I have not kicked you enough'; 'if it had been you I should have chastised you with a cricket stump.' Examples of this knock-about stuff would be easy to multiply. Clearly, they conceal an almost embarrassing concern and tenderness, a passion more single-minded and obsessive than the sexual. Despite the tough front, Kipling is evidently infatuated and showers gifts on his son while the letters keep up a saving pretence of sternness. Squash courts are built, there are treats at Brown's Hotel followed by music halls, motor bikes are bought, gramophones, and finally a Singer car. There can be no question – Kipling was a sugar daddy.

With this, and the death of his beloved daughter, Josephine, in mind, we come to Kipling's most tender story, '"They"', which unfolds in a way that gives new meaning to that old cliché: its progress is as grave, delicate and measured as Mrs Bremmil, in 'Three and – An Extra', 'turning over the dead baby's frocks'. Kipling's treatment of the theme of bereavement is simple and reticent. There is none of the bravura prose with which 'The Gardener' ends, when Helen Turrell confronts the military cemetery: 'She climbed a few wooden-faced earthen steps and then met the entire crowded level of the thing in one held breath. She did not know that Hagenzeele Third counted twenty-one thousand dead already. All she saw was a merciless sea of black crosses, bearing little strips of stamped tin at all angles across their faces.' This difference granted, to the detriment of neither, '"They"' and 'The Gardener' are intimately connected. Behind each lies the death of one of Kipling's children, Josephine, and John who was lost in action during the First World War. Both, too, share the theme of reticence. Helen Turrell is prevented from expressing her grief by the threat of social exposure, the narrator of '"They"' by an emotional fastidiousness, which is clearly related to Kipling's own personality – as we see it in his ironic letters to his children and in the very title of his autobiography, *Something of Myself*. Kipling was shy about his emotions, shy indeed about using his own voice, preferring to speak through others or adopting the bluff clubman's tone of his caste and its grating air of worldliness: 'for he did me the honour to talk at me plentifully' and 'it is not always expedient to excite a growing youth's religious emotions'. '"They"', however, has none of this ponderous archness, except deliberately.

The narrator is, at first, in marked contrast to Miss Florence, who is blind and therefore openly sensitive as an exposed membrane: '"we blindies have only one skin, I think. Everything outside hits straight at our souls. It's different with you. You've such good defences . . ."' The defences are apparent in the narrator's response to Miss Florence's question, '"You're fond of children?"'; 'I gave her one or two reasons why I did not altogether hate them.' This is recognizably the Kipling who told his children he loved them by brandishing a cricket stump. And, of course, the narrator's shyness is more than matched by the elusive children, 'the shadows within the shadow'. The narrator's attitude to Miss Florence is one of straightforward pity, without a trace of condescension: like her, he accepts that he is more capable, less vulnerable. To the other parents who have suffered bereavement, he is less neutral, more superior: 'I saw the Doctor come out of the cottage followed by a draggle-tailed wench who clung to his arm,' he coldly notes, and we are reminded of Helen Turrell's refusal to meet the hysterical, 'mottled' Mrs Scarsworth on equal terms.

By the story's end, everything has been reversed. His grief is such that Miss Florence pities him: ' "And, d'you remember, I called you lucky – once – at first. You who must never come here again."' The narrator is included in the democracy of grief, but when his heart is opened the pain is so great that the consolation provided by the children of the House Beautiful is, after all, no consolation but an unbearable torment. The unseen touch of *his* dead child is just not enough – and therefore too much. Finally, Kipling's attitude is there in the inverted commas which surround his title, '"They"': the children are wraiths, necessary to some, but they do not exist, and it is this which the narrator finds impossible to endure.

Kipling's poem, 'The Road to En-Dor', specifically warns against dabbling in the supernatural and in *Something of Myself* he is equally firm: 'I have seen too much evil and sorrow and wreck of good minds on the road to En-Dor to take one step along that perilous track.' Still, '"They"' is an exploration, even if Kipling does turn back: the tallies which feed Miss Florence's fire are an example of a more ancient form of communication; both the narrator and Miss Florence know about 'the Colours' and 'the Egg which it is given to very few of us to see'. Kipling doesn't explain what either is, though the Egg may be the Egg of the Universe, deposited by the First Cause from which Brahma came. It isn't important: the mere mention is enough to open up possibilities about the potential of the human mind – a theme Kipling considers in '"Wireless"'.

There, a consumptive chemist, Mr Shaynor, is in love with a girl called Fanny Brand, 'a great, big, fat lump of a girl', who distantly resembles 'the seductive shape on a gold-framed toilet-water advertisement'. Shaynor, weakened by TB, takes a drink prepared by the narrator from random drugs and goes into a trance. Once under, he stares at the advertisement and writes snatches of 'The Eve of St Agnes' and the ode 'To a Nightingale', occasionally lapsing into the deadest prose. The poetry (Shaynor has never heard of Keats) is inspired by his surroundings – vulgar druggist's dross, a hare hanging up outside *the* (Kipling's use of the definite article is always superb) Italian warehouse next door and so on. The narrator, desperate for an explanation, tries analogies with radio waves and faulty receivers, since the story is framed by some early broadcasting experimentation. The frame, however, is completely ironic, though the jargon of Cashell, the enthusiast, comes so thickly that Kipling's deflating irony is easily missed in the welter of Hertzian waves and coherers. '"That's all," he said, proudly, as though himself responsible for the wonder.' How much more wonderful, Kipling implies, is the transmutation of life's pitiful fragments into art – Spinoza, falling in love, the noise of the typewriter or the smell of cooking. Eliot's comment on his list might have been Kipling's: 'When a poet's mind is perfectly equipped for its work, it is constantly amalgamating disparate experience; the ordinary man's experience is chaotic, irregular, fragmentary.' Kipling prefers a description closer to Yeats's rag-and-bone shop of the heart: 'Followed without a break ten or fifteen lines of bald prose – the naked soul's confession of its physical yearning for its beloved – unclean as we count uncleanliness; unwholesome, but human exceedingly; the raw material . . . whence Keats wove the twenty-sixth, seventh and eighth stanzas of his poem.' Beside the miracle of the gifted human coherer, that rare occurence, stand the pathetic transmissions achieved by science – '*Signals unintelligible*'.

This fascinated respect for the miracle of the mind isn't logically opposed to a disbelief in the supernatural. But perhaps the more exact word for Kipling's position would be distrust. Clearly, he felt it dangerous to meddle, as we can see from 'The Disturber of Traffic', where the lighthouse-keeper, Dowse, is driven mad by his ceaseless contemplation of 'the wheel and the drift of Things'. The prefatory poem pleads, 'Lay not Thy toil before our eyes', and in the story itself Kipling touches in the same message, alluding to I Corinthians 13:12, as the narrator is lent 'a pair of black glass spectacles, without which no man can look at the Light unblinded'. As often in late Kipling, the narrator, Fenwick, is unreliable: he takes Dowse's account more or less at face value, though Challong, with his webbed hands and feet and the ability to survive being tipped into the sea from the Light, is patently a figment of Dowse's imagination. Challong is, we are told, an 'Orang-Laut' – that is, a man of the sea. The epithet points us towards the old man of the sea, Proteus, the god renowned for constantly changing his shape. Dowse's madness takes the form of a fascination with shapes and patterns: when he is finally rescued, he is barely able to speak because 'his eye was held like by the coils of rope on the belaying pin, and he followed those ropes up and up with his eye till he was quite lost and comfortable among the rigging, which ran criss-cross, and slopeways, and up and down, and any way but straight along under his feet north and south.' Once Dowse is absorbed in the changing shapes of things his mental stability deserts him. The Protean world doesn't bear looking at, any more than the Light.

Kipling's attitude is similar to that of Stephen, the abbot in 'The Eye of Allah', who takes the decision to destroy the microscope – even though his mistress is dying of cancer. The possible benefits are outweighed by the immediate dangers – inquisition and execution ('"You can hear the faggots crackle"') and the longer-term threat to the Christian religion, whereby the war between Good and Evil would become merely an endless struggle between two morally neutral forces of creation and degeneration – without any hope of a final outcome. The short-term danger of 'more torture, more division' is clear enough, a transparent conclusion, but the route to it is subtle and any reading must account for the details of the story.

'The Eye of Allah' groups itself naturally with 'The Manner of Men', a story in which Kipling describes the progress of St Paul (described by one of the narrators, from his limited viewpoint, as 'a Jew philosopher') by sea from Myra to Rome, with a shipwreck at Malta *en route*. Like Browning's Karshish, who witnesses the raising of Lazarus by one he describes as 'a leech', Quabil and Sulinor are witnesses whose testimony is reliable as to fact, but perhaps unreliable as to interpretation. Sulinor is the more sympathetic to Paul, who has nursed him through dysentery and, more importantly, intuited Sulinor's life-long fear of the Beasts in the circus. As an ex-pirate of dubious status, Sulinor is justifiably leery and the Beasts are a grumbling presence through the story: even the '*hrmph-hrmph*' of the oars in a trireme reminds Sulinor 'of an elephant choosing his man in the Circus'. The story poses the question: who has saved the ship? From a Christian standpoint, Paul is clearly responsible - with God's help. From the seamen's position, it is finally their skill which brings off the safe beaching of the boat. Kipling, I believe, doesn't express a bias, unlike Browning, and the reader is left to adjudicate between the rival claims of miracle and pragmatic technique. Either way, Paul's fearless calm, whether justified or not, plays its part in the operation. If, at the story's outset, Kipling appears to incline towards Paul – since Quabil mistakes Paul much as he himself is mistaken for a land-lubber when he is actually a master-mariner – the finale's emphasis is on technique, pure seamanship, as Sulinor and Baeticus indulge in a war game.

The theme of miracle versus the purely natural explanation of phenomena is central to 'The Eye of Allah', taking the form of medicine or metaphysics. Despite the monastic setting, sceptics are well represented. John of Burgos, the artist, is an unbeliever, although he is attached to St Illod's: '"*Thy* soul?" the sub-cantor seemed doubtful.' Roger Bacon is a freethinker: '"*Every* way we are barred – barred by the words of some man, dead a thousand years, which are held final."' Roger of Salerno also resents Church interference. The infirmarian, Thomas, won't be other than a lay-member of the community because he fears his heresy: '"I confess myself at a loss for the cause of the fever unless – as Varro saith in his *De Re Rustica* – certain small animals which the eye cannot follow enter the body by the nose and mouth, and set up grave diseases. On the other hand, this is not in Scripture."'

The story shows, however, that the 'certain small animals' *are* in Scripture, since they now form part of John of Burgos's illustration for the Gadarene swine. How does Kipling want us to interpret this? Are we to believe that scientific discovery is inherent in the gospel once it is *illuminated*? After all, in a glancing reference to Colossians 4:14, Stephen reminds John that Luke is a physician. Similarly, when Roger of Salerno sees John's picture of the devils leaving Mary

Magdalene, he immediately recognizes what has been depicted – not a miracle but '"epilepsy – mouth, eyes, and forehead – even to the droop of her wrist there. Every sign of it! She will need restoratives, that woman, and, afterwards, sleep natural."' He pays the artist a physician's compliment: '"Sir, you should be of our calling"'. This reconciliation of the theological and the physical is matched by another profound pun, however, to set against that of 'illumination': John's great Luke begins with the Magnificat and he has literally *magnified* the Lord, using the microscope, so that what, when unexplained, seemed miraculous, becomes part of the natural world. The Lord is no longer outside his creation: he *is* his creation, a position which is theologically untenable. Christ – if this line of argument is pursued to its conclusion – is nothing more, or less, than the gifted leech identified by Karshish. Stephen seems the only person to reach out towards this possibility – and he destroys the microscope, to save a system which, however imperfect, ensures a necessary order against chaos. The chaos he fears is not purely social. He fears, too, 'that man stands ever between two Infinities' and I think Kipling shared this fear.

The impersonal scale of things and the smallness of the individual made him flinch, as Kim's crisis and breakdown show: 'He tried to think of the lama – to wonder why he had stumbled into a brook – but the bigness of the world, seen between the forecourt gates, swept linked thought aside.' And at last the outcry of the threatened ego is heard: '"I am Kim. I am Kim. And what is Kim?"' Mental breakdown interested Kipling. He himself was twice afflicted as a young man and his sister was troubled for most of her life. He treats the subject directly in 'The Janeites', where the shell-shocked Humberstall is restored to a sanity of sorts by Macklin, who persuades him to memorize the works of Jane Austen, by pretending that they will give him an entrée to a quasi-Masonic society of 'Janeites', with attendant perks. It is, of course, a gentle conspiracy of a different kind – to exercise and re-educate a mind which has been disturbed by trench warfare and experiences that are the more horrific for Humberstall's insouciant Cockney re-telling: '"then I saw somethin' like a mushroom in the moonlight. It was the nice old gentleman's bald 'ead. I patted it. 'Im and 'is laddies 'ad copped it right enough."' *I patted it*. Kipling didn't flinch from much.

Eliot, Orwell, Edmund Wilson, Randall Jarrell, Borges, Kingsley Amis, Angus Wilson, and the most gifted Kipling critic of all, Miss J.M.S. Tompkins, have all spoken out for Kipling – without success.

His work remains ignored by the literary intelligentsia, largely for political reasons. Yet his politics are more various than their reputation. It isn't difficult to find attitudes in his work which are unpleasant and one could compile a damning little anthology. There is the anti-Semitism of '"Bread Upon the Waters"', where McPhee remarks, '"Young Steiner – Steiner's son – the Jew, was at the bottom of it"' and the prejudice is reinforced by McRimmon's '"there's more discernment in a dog than a Jew"'. Sometimes it is possible to write off remarks like this as elements of characterization. For instance, the racial prejudice of Curtiss in *The Story of the Gadsbys*: 'Hang it all! Gaddy hasn't married beneath him. There's no tar-brush in the family, I suppose.' Kipling's 'Lispeth', 'Without Benefit of Clergy', or 'Beyond the Pale' show clearly enough that, though he saw the difficulties of mixed marriages, he was disinterested enough to register disapproval of the 'white' position: the clergyman in 'Lispeth' is exposed as a mendacious hypocrite. Similarly, Ortheris's prejudice is undermined by Learoyd's report of it: '"Orth'ris, as allus thinks he knaws more than other foaks, said she wasn't a real laady, but nobbut a Hewrasian. Ah don't gainsay as her culler was a bit doosky like. But she *was* a laady.'

All the same, there is, for example, Kipling's anti-Irish prejudice to consider. In *Something of Myself*, he asserts: 'the Irish had passed out of the market into "politics" which suited their instincts of secrecy, plunder, and anonymous denunciation.' There is, too, a callous Darwinism which is hard to accept, a sense that some life is acceptably cheap: 'the weakest of the old-type immigrants had been sifted and salted by the long sailing-voyage of those days', he writes, deploring the imperfection of later immigrants to America who were preserved by the shorter steam voyage. And in 'Without Benefit of Clergy', he is cool about the function of cholera in this Malthusian aside: 'it was a red and heavy audit, for the land was very sick and needed a little breathing space ere the torrent of cheap life should flood it anew. The children of immature fathers and undeveloped mothers made no resistance.' Perhaps Kipling intends his tone to be stoical. *Tant pis*, it comes across as simply callous.

But if there is no difficulty in mounting a case against Kipling, it is also worth pointing out that his opinions are by no means as stereotypical as biased accountancy can make them. In *Something of Myself*, he also deplores the extermination of the American Indian: 'I have never got over the wonder of a people who, having extirpated the aboriginals of their continent more completely than any modern race had ever done, honestly believed that they were a godly little

New England community, setting examples to brutal mankind. This wonder I used to explain to Theodore Roosevelt, who made the glass cases of Indian relics shake with his rebuttals.' The Boers, too, are seen clearly and prophetically by Kipling: 'we put them in a position to uphold and expand their primitive lust for racial domination.' He blames the white man for the importation of disease into Africa, ruining a 'vast sun-baked land [that] was antiseptic and sterile'. And for an establishment figure, Kipling is capable of savaging the highest, as in this plea for regulated prostitution as a way of controlling venereal disease: 'visits to Lock Hospitals made me desire, as earnestly as I do today, that I might have six hundred priests – Bishops of the Establishment for choice – to handle precisely as the soldiers of my youth were handled.' This isn't the predictable voice Kipling's detractors would have us expect, and if it doesn't excuse other lapses into illiberalism, it certainly complicates our picture.

'The soldiers of my youth' is a significant phrase. We know that Kipling didn't mean 'the officers of my youth'. For preference, Kipling always took the part of the inarticulate, the anonymous, the helpless – and it is typical that his version of Browning's 'The Bishop Orders His Tomb' should be 'The Mary Gloster', a poor relation but full of passion and coarse pathos. And written in the demotic. It was a mode that Kipling consciously gave himself over to, as we can see from the poem which follows 'The Manner of Men', spoken by the St Paul whom Quabil mistrusts because 'he had the woman's trick of taking the tone and colour of whoever he talked to':

> I am made all things to all men –
> Hebrew, Roman, and Greek –
> In each one's tongue I speak . .

There is something of himself in these verses, and in the plea with which the poem ends: 'Restore me my self again!'

Browning expresses a similar pang in 'One Word More':

> Love, you saw me gather men and women,
> Live or dead or fashioned by my fancy,
> Enter each and all, and use their service,
> Speak from every mouth – the speech, a poem.
> Hardly shall I tell my joys and sorrows,
> Hopes and fears, belief and disbelieving:
> I am mine and yours – the rest be all men's,
> Karshish, Cleon, Norbert and the fifty.
> Let me speak this once in my true person . . .

Whatever the regrets, the achievement, in both cases, is bound up with the artistic choice 'to have gathered from the air a live tradition'. Pound's words apply to every writer engaged in the endless rediscovery of the oral and the liberation of literature from the tyranny of the classical, the received, which was once itself 'language really used by men', in Wordsworth's famous phrase. Isaac Bashevis Singer adapts the Yiddish folk tradition, with its generous allowance of formulaic phrases, old-fashioned omniscience and Biblical directness. Whitman revels in his 'barbaric yawp' and the escape from European habits. Twain's fiction introduces the drawl into American prose: 'you don't know me, without you have read a book by the name of *The Adventures of Tom Sawyer*, but that ain't no matter.' Almost exactly a hundred years later, Saul Bellow, after a false and frigid beginning, has fought the literary until he can confidently begin 'Zetland: By a Character Witness' with the words, 'Yes, I knew the guy'. We should see Kipling in this company of essentially oral writers who insist on talking in the library – and then remember how many more voices he can command. Kipling deliberately chose to work with 'unpromising' material, just as his allegorical artist, the bull Apis, chooses ordinary Chisto, rather than Villamarti – the result, for both, is immortality.

I have quoted freely in this essay, frequently from work which I haven't selected for inclusion, in the hope that readers will be encouraged to explore Kipling further. *Kim* in particular should be read and I had to fight the temptation to extract from it. Let me conclude, then, with one last quotation from that work. 'The sullen coolies, glad of the check, halted and slid down their loads.' It seems an ordinary sentence, doesn't it? But how different it would have been, how much lighter their load, if Kipling had written 'set down their loads,' instead of 'slid down their loads'.

Craig Raine
21st April 1985

A note on the text

NO selection could do justice to Kipling's prodigious variety. His *oeuvre* encompasses science fiction ('With the Night Mail') and imaginative historiography ('The Church that was at Antioch'). There is travel writing, violent knockabout farce, myth. There is the animal fable: 'A Walking Delegate', an exercise in American dialects, derives from Mark Twain and probably fathers Orwell's *Animal Farm*.

I have, therefore, simply chosen the best Kipling, wherever it occurs. Accordingly, some volumes are ignored, while others are heavily drawn on. There are two exceptions. Kipling's writing for children is inadequately acknowledged here by the inclusion of 'The Elephant's Child'. The autobiographical 'Baa, Baa, Black Sheep' is included for the invaluable glimpse it gives us into Kipling's psyche. Otherwise, nothing is merely representative. Merit is the sole criterion.

I have chosen nothing from the novels. Only *Kim* was a powerful temptation, in any case, and extracts are always an unsatisfactory compromise. My aim has been completeness. With this in mind, I have included poems whenever they accompany the stories, either as prefaces or pendants. Their relationship to the prose – sometimes intimate, sometimes distant – differs in every case, and it is for each reader to determine Kipling's intention. In 'Friendly Brook', the verse explores a perspective which is scarcely explicit in the story. The Rahere verse with 'The Wish House' offers a dense, concentrated parallel. The verse accompanying 'Mary Postgate', on the other hand, is a crude summary which misrepresents the subtle prose tale. Often the poems are integral and mined with significant clues: 'Gertrude's Prayer' is one example and the 'extract' from 'Lyden's *Irenius*', which precedes 'Mrs Bathurst', may explain the anonymous status of Vickery's unfortunate travelling companion.

I considered adding notes to this selection of stories. For instance, one could explain that Kipling's reference to Edgar Allan Poe's 'mesmerized dying man' alludes to 'The Facts in the case of M. Valdemar'. Or explain that the 'marring fifth line' of Miss Florence's song in '"They"' is 'Listen, gentle – ay, and simple! listen, children on the knee,' from the opening verse of Elizabeth Barrett Browning's 'The Lost Bower'. Or one might list every Masonic reference in 'The Man who would be King' and comment redundantly that these are secret Masonic references – adding, perhaps, that Kipling was a Freemason himself, admitted in 1885 to the Lodge, Hope and Perseverance, No. 782 E.C. at Lahore.

On the whole, however, I am inclined to think that these three examples show that Kipling has already provided the necessary amount of information. The point of the allusion to 'The Lost Bower', for example, is to impair the atmosphere surrounding the House Beautiful, to *suggest* something mysterious and perhaps grim. A note would short-circuit Kipling's finely calculated effect and the subtle suggestion harden into flat statement.

Of course, the stories have dated in some unimportant particulars – we no longer use 'tickey' for threepenny bit, or 'Bradbury' for a pound note, after the name of the Bank of England signatory. Yet, even here, the context makes things clear enough. A note would only exaggerate their significance, and a cumbersome *apparatus criticus* suggest, falsely, that Kipling's work needs a life-support machine. In time, it may, like all literature. At the moment, the stories are vigorous and hale. When they are indirect and difficult, they are meant to be so. Dr Johnson said of notes: 'the mind is refrigerated by interruption, the thoughts are diverted from the principal subject'.

In the House of Suddhoo

A stone's throw out on either hand
From that well-ordered road we tread,
And all the world is wild and strange:
Churel and ghoul and *Djinn* and sprite
Shall bear us company to-night,
For we have reached the Oldest Land
Wherein the Powers of Darkness range.

From the Dusk to the Dawn

THE house of Suddhoo, near the Taksali Gate, is two-storeyed, with four carved windows of old brown wood, and a flat roof. You may recognize it by five red hand-prints arranged like the Five of Diamonds on the whitewash between the upper windows. Bhagwan Dass the grocer and a man who says he gets his living by seal-cutting live in the lower storey with a troop of wives, servants, friends, and retainers. The two upper rooms used to be occupied by Janoo and Azizun, and a little black-and-tan terrier that was stolen from an Englishman's house and given to Janoo by a soldier. Today, only Janoo lives in the upper rooms. Suddhoo sleeps on the roof generally, except when he sleeps in the street. He used to go to Peshawar in the cold weather to visit his son who sells curiosities near the Edwardes' Gate, and then he slept under a real mud roof. Suddhoo is a great friend of mine, because his cousin had a son who secured, thanks to my recommendation, the post of head-messenger to a big firm in the Station. Suddhoo says that God will make me a lieutenant-governor one of these days. I daresay his prophecy will come true. He is very, very old, with white hair and no teeth worth showing, and he has outlived his wits – outlived nearly everything except his fondness for his son at Peshawar. Janoo and Azizun are Kashmiris, Ladies of the City, and theirs was an ancient and more or less honourable profession; but Azizun has since married a medical student from the North-West and has settled down to a most respectable life somewhere near Bareilly. Bhagwan Dass is an extortioner and an adulterator. He is very rich. The man who is supposed to get his living by seal-cutting pretends to be very poor.

This lets you know as much as is necessary of the four principal tenants in the house of Suddhoo. Then there is me of course; but I am only the chorus that comes in at the end to explain things. So I do not count.

Suddhoo was not clever. The man who pretended to cut seals was the cleverest of them all – Bhagwan Dass only knew how to lie – except Janoo. She was also beautiful, but that was her own affair.

Suddhoo's son at Peshawar was attacked by pleurisy, and old Suddhoo was troubled. The seal-cutter man heard of Suddhoo's anxiety and made capital out of it. He was abreast of the times. He got a friend in Peshawar to telegraph daily accounts of the son's health. And here the story begins.

Suddhoo's cousin's son told me, one evening, that Suddhoo wanted to see me; that he was too old and feeble to come personally, and that I should be conferring an everlasting honour on the House of Suddhoo if I went to him. I went; but I think, seeing how well off Suddhoo was then, that he might have sent something better than an *ekka*, which jolted fearfully, to haul out a future lieutenant-governor to the city on a muggy April evening. The *ekka* did not run quickly. It was full dark when we pulled up opposite the door of Ranjit Singh's Tomb near the main gate of the Fort. Here was Suddhoo, and he said that by reason of my condescension, it was absolutely certain that I should become a lieutenant-governor while my hair was yet black. Then we talked about the weather and the state of my health, and the wheat crops, for fifteen minutes, in the Huzuri Bagh, under the stars.

Suddhoo came to the point at last. He said that Janoo had told him that there was an order of the *Sirkar* against magic, because it was feared that magic might one day kill the Empress of India. I didn't know anything about the state of the law; but I fancied that something interesting was going to happen. I said that so far from magic being discouraged by the Government it was highly commended. The greatest officials of the State practised it themselves. (If the Financial Statement isn't magic, I don't know what is.) Then, to encourage him further, I said that, if there was any *jadoo* afoot, I had not the least objection to giving it my countenance and sanction, and to seeing that it was clean *jadoo* – white magic, as distinguished from the unclean *jadoo* which kills folk. It took a long time before Suddhoo admitted that this was just what he had asked me to come for. Then he told me, in jerks and quavers, that the man who said he cut seals was a sorcerer of the cleanest kind; that every day he gave Suddhoo news of the sick son in Peshawar more quickly than the lightning could fly, and that this news was always corroborated by the letters. Further, that he had told Suddhoo how a great danger was threatening his son, which could be removed by clean *jadoo*; and, of course, heavy payment. I began to see exactly how the land lay, and told Suddhoo that I also understood a little *jadoo* in the Western line, and would go to his house to see that everything was done decently and in order. We set off together; and on the way Suddhoo told me that he had paid the seal-cutter between one hundred and two hundred rupees already; and the *jadoo* of that night would cost two hundred more. Which was cheap, he said, considering the greatness of his son's danger; but I do not think he meant it.

The lights were all cloaked in the front of the house when we arrived. I could hear awful noises from behind the seal-cutter's shop-front, as if some one were groaning his soul out. Suddhoo shook all over, and while we groped our way upstairs told me that the *jadoo* had begun. Janoo and Azizun met us at the stair-head, and told us that the *jadoo*-work was coming off in their rooms, because there was more space there. Janoo is a lady of a free-thinking turn of mind. She whispered that the *jadoo* was an invention to get money out of Suddhoo, and that the seal-cutter would go to a hot place when he died. Suddhoo was nearly crying with fear and old age. He kept walking up and down the room in the half-light, repeating his son's name over and over again, and asking Azizun if the seal-cutter ought not to make a reduction in the case of his own landlord. Janoo pulled me over to the shadow in the recess of the carved bow-windows. The boards were up, and the rooms were only lit by one tiny oil-lamp. There was no chance of my being seen if I stayed still.

Presently, the groans below ceased, and we heard steps on the staircase. That was the seal-cutter. He stopped outside the door as the terrier barked and Azizun fumbled at the chain, and he told Suddhoo to blow out the lamp. This left the place in jet darkness, except for the red glow from the two *huqas* that belonged to Janoo and Azizun. The seal-cutter came in, and I heard Suddhoo throw himself down on the floor and groan. Azizun caught her breath, and Janoo backed on to one of the beds with a shudder. There was a clink of something metallic, and then shot up a pale blue-green flame near the ground. The light was just enough to show Azizun, pressed against one corner of the room with the terrier between her knees; Janoo, with her hands clasped, leaning forward as she sat on the bed; Suddhoo, face down, quivering, and the seal-cutter.

I hope I may never see another man like that seal-cutter. He was stripped to the waist, with a wreath of white jasmine as thick as my wrist round his forehead, a salmon coloured loin-cloth round his middle, and a steel bangle on each ankle. This was not awe-inspiring. It was the face of the man that turned me cold. It was blue-grey in the first place. In the second, the eyes were rolled back till you could only see the whites of them; and, in the third, the face was the face of a demon – a ghoul – anything you please except of the sleek, oily old ruffian who sat in the daytime over his turning-lathe downstairs. He was lying on his stomach with his arms turned and crossed behind him, as if he had been thrown down pinioned. His head and neck were the only parts of him off the floor. They were nearly at right angles to the body, like the head of a cobra at spring. It was ghastly. In the centre of the room, on the bare earth floor, stood a big, deep, brass basin, with a pale blue-green light floating in the centre like a night-light. Round that basin the man on the floor wriggled himself three times. How he did it I do not know. I could see the muscles ripple along his spine and fall smooth again; but I could not see any other motion. The head seemed the only thing alive about him, except that slow curl and uncurl of the labouring back-muscles. Janoo from the bed was breathing seventy to the minute; Azizun held her hands before her eyes; and old Suddhoo, fingering at the dirt that had got into his white beard, was crying to himself. The horror of it was that the creeping, crawly thing made no sound – only crawled! And, remember, this lasted for ten minutes, while the terrier whined, and Azizun shuddered, and Janoo gasped, and Suddhoo cried.

I felt the hair lift at the back of my head, and my heart thump like a thermantidote paddle. Luckily, the seal-cutter betrayed himself by his most impressive trick and made me calm again. After he had finished that unspeakable triple crawl, he stretched his head away from the floor as high as he could, and sent out a jet of fire from his nostrils. Now I knew how fire-spouting is done – I can do it myself – so I felt at ease. The business was a fraud. If he had only kept to that crawl without trying to raise the effect, goodness knows what I might not have thought. Both the girls shrieked at the jet of fire and the head dropped, chin-down on the floor, with a thud; the whole body lying there like a corpse with its arms trussed. There was a pause of five full minutes after this, and the blue-green flame died down. Janoo stooped to settle one of her anklets, while Azizun turned her face to the wall and took the terrier in her arms. Suddhoo put out an arm mechanically to Janoo's *huqa,* and she slid it across the floor with her foot. Directly above the body and on the wall were a couple of flaming portraits, in stamped-paper frames, of the Queen and the Prince of Wales. They looked down on the performance, and to my thinking, seemed to heighten the grotesqueness of it all.

Just when the silence was getting unendurable, the body turned over and rolled away from the basin to the side of the room, where it lay stomach-up. There was a faint 'plop' from the basin – exactly like the noise a fish makes when it takes a fly – and the green light in the centre revived.

I looked at the basin, and saw, bobbing in the water, the dried, shrivelled, black head of a native baby – open eyes, open mouth, and shaved scalp. It was worse, being so very sudden, than the crawling exhibition. We had no time to say anything before it began to speak.

Read Poe's account of the voice that came from the mesmerized dying man, and you will realize less than one-half of the horror of that head's voice.

There was an interval of a second or two between each word, and a sort of 'ring, ring, ring,' in the note of the voice, like the timbre of a bell. It pealed slowly, as if talking to itself, for several minutes before I got rid of my cold sweat. Then the blessed solution struck me. I looked at the body lying near the doorway, and saw, just where the hollow of the throat joins on the shoulders, a muscle that had nothing to do with any man's regular breathing twitching away steadily. The whole thing was a careful reproduction of the Egyptian teraphim that one reads about sometimes; and the voice was as clever and as appalling a piece of ventriloquism as one could wish to hear. All this time the head was 'lip-lip-lapping' against the side of the basin, and speaking. It told Suddhoo, on his face again whining, of his son's illness and of the state of the illness up to the evening of that very night. I always shall respect the seal-cutter for keeping so faithfully to the time of the Peshawar telegrams. It went on to say that skilled doctors were night and day watching over the man's life; and that he would eventually recover if the fee to the potent sorcerer, whose servant was the head in the basin, were doubled.

Here the mistake from the artistic point of view came in. To ask for twice your stipulated fee in a voice that Lazarus might have used when he rose from the dead, is absurd. Janoo, who is really a woman of masculine intellect, saw this as quickly as I did. I heard her say *'Asli nahin! Fareib!'* scornfully under her breath; and just as she said so the light in the basin died out, the head stopped talking, and we heard the room door creak on its hinges. Then Janoo struck a match, lit the lamp, and we saw that head, basin, and seal-cutter were gone.

Suddhoo was wringing his hands, and explaining to any one who cared to listen, that, if his chances of eternal salvation depended on it, he could not raise another two hundred rupees. Azizun was nearly in hysterics in the corner; while Janoo sat down composedly on one of the beds to discuss the probabilities of the whole thing being a *bunao*, or 'make-up'.

I explained as much as I knew of the seal-cutter's way of *jadoo*; but her argument was much more simple – 'The magic that is always demanding gifts is no true magic,' said she. 'My mother told me that the only potent love-spells are those which are told you for love. This seal-cutter man is a liar and a devil. I dare not tell, do anything, or get anything done, because I am in debt to Bhagwan Dass the *bunnia* for two gold rings and a heavy anklet. I must get my food from his shop. The seal-cutter is the friend of Bhagwan Dass, and he would poison my food. A fool's *jadoo* has been going on for ten days, and has cost Suddhoo many rupees each night. The seal-cutter used black hens and lemons and mantras before. He never showed us anything like this till tonight. Azizun is a fool, and will be a *purdahnashin* soon. Suddhoo has lost his strength and his wits. See now! I had hoped to get from Suddhoo many rupees while he lived, and many more after his death; and behold, he is spending everything on that offspring of a devil and a she-ass, the seal-cutter!'

Here I said, 'But what induced Suddhoo to drag me into the business? Of course I can speak to the seal-cutter, and he shall refund. The whole thing is child's talk – shame – and senseless.'

'Suddhoo *is* an old child,' said Janoo. 'He has lived on the roofs these seventy years and is as senseless as a milch-goat. He brought you here to assure himself that he was not breaking any law of the *Sirkar*, whose salt he ate many years ago. He worships the dust off the feet of the seal-cutter, and that cow-devourer has forbidden him to go and see his son. What does Suddhoo know of your laws or the lightning-post? I have to watch his money going day by day to that lying beast below.'

Janoo stamped her foot on the floor and nearly cried with vexation; while Suddhoo was whimpering under a blanket in the corner, and Azizun was trying to guide the pipe-stem to his foolish old mouth.

Now, the case stands thus. Unthinkingly, I have laid myself open to the charge of aiding and abetting the seal-cutter in obtaining money under false pretences, which is forbidden by Section 420 of the Indian Penal Code. I am helpless in the matter for these reasons. I cannot inform the police. What witnesses would support my statements? Janoo refuses flatly, and Azizun is a veiled woman somewhere near Bareilly – lost in this big India of ours. I dare not again take the law into my own hands, and speak to the seal-cutter; for certain am I that, not only would Suddhoo disbelieve me, but this step would end in the poisoning of Janoo, who is bound hand and foot by her debt to the *bunnia*. Suddhoo is an old dotard; and whenever we meet mumbles my idiotic joke that the *Sirkar* rather patronizes the Black Art than otherwise. His son is well now; but Suddhoo is completely under the influence of the seal-cutter, by whose advice he regulates the affairs of his life. Janoo watches daily the money that she hoped to wheedle out of Suddhoo taken by the seal-cutter, and becomes daily more furious and sullen.

She will never tell, because she dare not; but, unless something happens to prevent her, I am afraid that the seal-cutter will die of cholera – the white arsenic kind – about the middle of May. And thus I shall be privy to a murder in the House of Suddhoo.

Beyond the Pale

Love heeds not caste nor sleep a broken bed.
I went in search of love and lost myself.
Hindu Proverb

A MAN should, whatever happens, keep to his own caste, race, and breed. Let the white go to the white and the black to the black. Then, whatever trouble falls is in the ordinary course of things – neither sudden, alien, nor unexpected.

This is the story of a man who wilfully stepped beyond the safe limits of decent everyday society, and paid for it heavily.

He knew too much in the first instance; and he saw too much in the second. He took too deep an interest in native life; but he will never do so again.

Deep away in the heart of the City, behind Jitha Megji's *bustee*, lies Amir Nath's Gully, which ends in a dead-wall pierced by one grated window. At the head of the gully is a big cowbyre, and the walls on either side of the gully are without windows. Neither Suchet Singh nor Gaur Chand approve of their women-folk looking into the world. If Durga Charan had been of their opinion he would have been a happier man today, and little Bisesa would have been able to knead her own bread. Her room looked out through the grated window into the narrow dark gully where the sun never came and where the buffaloes wallowed in the blue slime. She was a widow, about fifteen years old, and she prayed the gods, day and night, to send her a lover; for she did not approve of living alone.

One day, the man – Trejago his name was – came into Amir Nath's Gully on an aimless wandering; and, after he had passed the buffaloes, stumbled over a big heap of cattle-food.

Then he saw that the Gully ended in a trap, and heard a little laugh from behind the grated window. It was a pretty little laugh, and Trejago, knowing that, for all practical purposes, the old *Arabian Nights* are good guides, went forward to the window, and whispered that verse of 'The Love Song of Har Dyal' which begins:

> Can a man stand upright in the face of the naked Sun; or a Lover in the Presence of his Beloved?

If my feet fail me, O Heart of my Heart, am I to blame, being blinded by the glimpse of your beauty?

There came the faint *tchink* of a woman's bracelets from behind the grating, and a little voice went on with the song at the fifth verse:

Alas! alas! Can the Moon tell the Lotus of her love when the Gate of Heaven is shut and the clouds gather for the rains?

They have taken my Beloved, and driven her with the pack-horses to the North.

There are iron chains on the feet that were set on my heart.

Call to the bowmen to make ready –

The voice stopped suddenly, and Trejago walked out of Amir Nath's Gully, wondering who in the world could have capped 'The Love Song of Har Dyal' so neatly.

Next morning, as he was driving to office, an old woman threw a packet into his dogcart. In the packet was the half of a broken glass-bangle, one flower of the blood-red *dhak*, a pinch of *bhusa* or cattle-food, and eleven cardamoms. That packet was a letter – not a clumsy compromising letter, but an innocent unintelligible lover's epistle.

Trejago knew far too much about these things, as I have said. No Englishman should be able to translate object-letters. But Trejago spread all the trifles on the lid of his office-box and began to puzzle them out.

A broken glass-bangle stands for a Hindu widow all India over; because, when her husband dies, a woman's bracelets are broken on her wrists. Trejago saw the meaning of the little bit of glass. The flower of the *dhak* means diversely 'desire', 'come', 'write', or 'danger', according to the other things with it. One cardamom means 'jealousy'; but when any article is duplicated in an object-letter, it loses its symbolic meaning and stands merely for one of a number indicating time, or, if incense, curds, or saffron be sent also, place. The message ran then – 'A widow – *dhak* flower and *bhusa*, – at eleven o'clock.' The pinch of *bhusa* enlightened Trejago. He saw – this kind of letter leaves much to instinctive knowledge – that the *bhusa* referred to the big heap of cattle-food over which he had fallen in Amir Nath's Gully, and that the message must come from the person behind the grating; she being a widow. So the message ran then – 'A widow, in the gully in which is the heap of *bhusa*, desires you to come at eleven o'clock.'

Trejago threw all the rubbish into the fireplace and laughed. He knew that men in the East do not make love under windows at eleven in the forenoon, nor do women fix appointments a week in advance. So he went, that very night at eleven, into Amir Nath's Gully, clad in a *boorka*, which cloaks a man as well as a woman. Directly the gongs of the city made the hour, the little voice behind the grating took up 'The Love Song of Har Dyal' at the verse where the Pathan girl calls upon Har Dyal to return. The song is really pretty in the vernacular. In English you miss the wail of it. It runs something like this:

> Alone upon the housetops, to the North
>   I turn and watch the lightning in the sky, –
> The glamour of thy footsteps in the North.
>   *Come back to me, Beloved, or I die!*
>
> Below my feet the still bazaar is laid –
>   Far, far, below the weary camels lie, –
> The camels and the captives of thy raid.
>   *Come back to me, Beloved, or I die!*
>
> My father's wife is old and harsh with years,
>   And drudge of all my father's house am I. –
> My bread is sorrow and my drink is tears,
>   *Come back to me, Beloved, or I die!*

As the song stopped, Trejago stepped up under the grating and whispered – 'I am here.'

Bisesa was good to look upon.

That night was the beginning of many strange things, and of a double life so wild that Trejago today sometimes wonders if it were not all a dream. Bisesa, or her old handmaiden who had thrown the object-letter, had detached the heavy grating from the brick-work of the wall; so that the window slid inside, leaving only a square of raw masonry into which an active man might climb.

In the daytime, Trejago drove through his routine of office-work, or put on his calling-clothes and called on the ladies of the Station, wondering how long they would know him if they knew of poor little Bisesa. At night, when all the city was still, came the walk under the evil-smelling *boorka*, the patrol through Jitha Megji's *bustee*, the quick turn into Amir Nath's Gully between the sleeping cattle and the dead walls, and then, last of all, Bisesa, and the deep, even breathing of the old woman who slept outside the door of the bare little room that Durga Charan allotted to his sister's daughter. Who or what Durga Charan was, Trejago never inquired; and why in the world he was not discovered and knifed never occurred to him till his madness was over, and Bisesa. . . . But this comes later.

Bisesa was an endless delight to Trejago. She was as ignorant as a bird; and her distorted versions of the rumours from the outside world, that had reached her in her room, amused Trejago almost as much as her lisping attempts to pronounce his name – 'Christopher'. The first syllable was always more than she could manage, and she made funny little gestures with her roseleaf hands, as one throwing the name away, and then, kneeling before Trejago, asked him, exactly as an Englishwoman would do, if he were sure he loved her. Trejago swore that he loved her more than anyone else in the world. Which was true.

After a month of this folly, the exigencies of his other life compelled Trejago to be especially attentive to a lady of his acquaintance. You may take it for a fact that anything of this kind is not only noticed and discussed by a man's own race, but by some hundred and fifty natives as well. Trejago had to walk with this lady and talk to her at the bandstand, and once or twice to drive with her; never for an instant dreaming that this would affect his dearer, out-of-the-way life. But the news flew, in the usual mysterious fashion, from mouth to mouth, till Bisesa's duenna heard of it and told Bisesa. The child was so troubled that she did the household work evilly, and was beaten by Durga Charan's wife in consequence.

A week later Bisesa taxed Trejago with the flirtation. She understood no gradations and spoke openly. Trejago laughed, and Bisesa stamped her little feet – little feet, light as marigold flowers, that could lie in the palm of a man's one hand.

Much that is written about Oriental passion and impulsiveness is exaggerated and compiled at second-hand, but a little of it is true; and when an Englishman finds that little, it is quite as startling as any passion in his own proper life. Bisesa raged and stormed, and finally threatened to kill herself if Trejago did not at once drop the alien Memsahib who had come between them. Trejago tried to explain, and to show her that she did not understand these things from a Western standpoint. Bisesa drew herself up, and said simply – 'I do not. I know only this – it is not good that I should have made you dearer than my own heart to me, Sahib. You are an Englishman. I am only a black girl' – she was fairer than bar-gold in the Mint – 'and the widow of a black man.'

Then she sobbed and said – 'But on my soul and my Mother's soul,

I love you. There shall no harm come to you, whatever happens to me.'

Trejago argued with the child, and tried to soothe her, but she seemed quite unreasonably disturbed. Nothing would satisfy her save that all relations between them should end. He was to go away at once. And he went. As he dropped out of the window she kissed his forehead twice, and he walked home wondering.

A week, and then three weeks, passed without a sign from Bisesa. Trejago, thinking that the rupture had lasted quite long enough, went down to Amir Nath's Gully for the fifth time in the three weeks, hoping that his rap at the sill of the shifting grating would be answered. He was not disappointed.

There was a young moon, and one stream of light fell down into Amir Nath's Gully, and struck the grating which was drawn away as he knocked. From the black dark Bisesa held out her arms into the moonlight. Both hands had been cut off at the wrists, and the stumps were nearly healed.

Then, as Bisesa bowed her head between her arms and sobbed, some one in the room grunted like a wild beast, and something sharp – knife, sword, or spear – thrust at Trejago in his *boorka*. The stroke missed his body, but cut into one of the muscles of the groin, and he limped slightly from the wound for the rest of his days.

The grating went into its place. There was no sign whatever from inside the house – nothing but the moonlight strip on the high wall, and the blackness of Amir Nath's Gully behind.

The next thing Trejago remembers, after raging and shouting like a madman between those pitiless walls, is that he found himself near the river as the dawn was breaking, threw away his *boorka* and went home bareheaded.

What was the tragedy – whether Bisesa had, in a fit of causeless despair, told everything, or the intrigue had been discovered and she tortured to tell; whether Durga Charan knew his name and what became of Bisesa - Trejago does not know to this day. Something horrible had happened, and the thought of what it must have been comes upon Trejago in the night now and again, and keeps him company till the morning. One special feature of the case is that he does not know where lies the front of Durga Charan's house. It may open on to a courtyard common to two or more houses, or it may lie behind any one of the gates of Jitha Megji's *bustee*. Trejago cannot tell. He cannot get Bisesa – poor little Bisesa – back again. He has lost her in the city where each man's house is as guarded and as unknowable as the grave; and the grating that opens into Amir Nath's Gully has been walled up.

But Trejago pays his calls regularly, and is reckoned a very decent sort of man.

There is nothing peculiar about him, except a slight stiffness, caused by a riding-strain, in the right leg.

The Gate of the Hundred Sorrows

If I can attain Heaven for a pice, why should you be envious?
Opium smoker's proverb

THIS is no work of mine. My friend, Gabral Misquitta, the half-caste, spoke it all, between moonset and morning, six weeks before he died; and I took it down from his mouth as he answered my questions. So –

It lies between the Coppersmith's Gully and the pipe-stem sellers' quarter, within a hundred yards, too, as the crow flies, of the Mosque of Wazir Khan. I don't mind telling anyone this much, but I defy him to find the Gate, however well he may think he knows the city. You might even go through the very gully it stands in a hundred times, and be none the wiser. We used to call the gully, 'The Gully of the Black Smoke,' but its native name is altogether different of course. A loaded donkey couldn't pass between the walls; and, at one point, just before you reach the Gate, a bulged house-front makes people go along all sideways.

It isn't really a gate though. It's a house. Old Fung-Tching had it first five years ago. He was a boot-maker in Calcutta. They say that he murdered his wife there when he was drunk. That was why he dropped bazaar-rum and took to the Black Smoke instead. Later on, he came up north and opened the Gate as a house where you could get your smoke in peace and quiet. Mind you, it was a *pukka*, respectable opium-house, and not one of those stifling, sweltering *chandoo-khanas* that you can find all over the city. No; the old man knew his business thoroughly, and he was most clean for a Chinaman. He was a one-eyed little chap, not much more than five feet high, and both his middle fingers were gone. All the same, he was the handiest man at rolling black pills I have ever seen. Never seemed to be touched by the Smoke, either; and what he took day and night, night and day, was a caution. I've been at it five years, and I can do my fair share of the Smoke with any one; but I was a child to Fung-Tching that way. All the same, the old man was keen on his money: very keen; and that's what I can't understand. I heard he saved a good deal before he died, but his nephew has got all that now; and the old man's gone back to China to be buried.

He kept the big upper room, where his best customers gathered, as neat as a new pin. In one corner used to stand Fung-Tching's Joss – almost as ugly as Fung-Tching – and there were always sticks burning under his nose; but you never smelt 'em when the pipes were going thick. Opposite the Joss was Fung-Tching's coffin. He had spent a good deal of his savings on that, and whenever a new man came to the Gate he was always introduced to it. It was lacquered black, with red and gold writings on it, and I've heard that Fung-Tching brought it out all the way from China. I don't know whether that's true or not, but I know that, if I came first in the evening, I used to spread my mat just at the foot of it. It was a quiet corner, you see, and a sort of breeze from the gully came in at the window now and then. Besides the mats, there was no other furniture in the room – only the coffin, and the old Joss all green and blue and purple with age and polish.

Fung-Tching never told us why he called the place 'The Gate of the Hundred Sorrows'. (He was the only Chinaman I know who used bad-sounding fancy names. Most of them are flowery. As you'll see in Calcutta.) We used to find that out for ourselves. Nothing grows on you so much, if you're white, as the Black Smoke. A yellow man is made different. Opium doesn't tell on him scarcely at all; but white and black suffer a good deal. Of course, there are some people that the Smoke doesn't touch any more than tobacco would at first. They just doze a bit, as one would fall asleep naturally, and next morning they are almost fit for work. Now, I was one of that sort when I began, but I've been at it for five years pretty steadily, and it's different now. There was an old aunt of mine, down Agra way, and she left me a little at her death. About sixty rupees a month secured. Sixty isn't much. I can recollect a time, seems hundreds and hundreds of years ago, that I was getting my three hundred a month, and pickings, when I was working on a big timber contract in Calcutta.

I didn't stick to that work for long. The Black Smoke does not allow of much other business; and even though I am very little affected by it, as men go I couldn't do a day's work now to save my life. After all, sixty rupees is what I want. When old Fung-Tching was alive he used to draw the money for me, give me about half of it to live on (I eat very little), and the rest he kept himself. I was free of the Gate at any time of the day and night, and could smoke and sleep there when I liked, so I didn't care. I know the old man made a good thing out of it; but that's no matter. Nothing matters much to me; and besides, the money always came fresh and fresh each month.

There was ten of us met at the Gate when the place was first opened. Me, and two Babus from a Government office somewhere in Anarkulli, but they got the sack and couldn't pay (no man who has to work in the daylight can do the Black Smoke for any length of time straight on); a Chinaman that was Fung-Tching's nephew; a bazaar-woman that had got a lot of money somehow; an English loafer – MacSomebody, I think, but I have forgotten – that smoked heaps, but never seemed to pay anything (they said he had saved Fung-Tching's life at some trial in Calcutta when he was a barrister); another Eurasian, like myself, from Madras; a half-caste woman, and a couple of men who said they had come from the North. I think they must have been Persians or Afghans or something. There are not more than five of us living now, but we come regular. I don't know what happened to the Babus; but the bazaar-woman she died after six months of the Gate, and I think Fung-Tching took her bangles and nose-ring for himself. But I'm not certain. The Englishman, he drank as well as smoked, and he dropped off. One of the Persians got killed in a row at night by the big well near the mosque a long time ago, and the police shut up the well, because they said it was full of foul air. They found him dead at the bottom of it. So, you see, there is only me, the Chinaman, the half-caste woman that we call the Memsahib (she used to live with Fung-Tching), the other Eurasian, and one of the Persians. The Memsahib looks very old now. I think she was a young woman when the Gate was opened; but we are all old for the matter of that. Hundreds and hundreds of years old. It is very hard to keep count of time in the Gate, and, besides, time doesn't matter to me. I draw my sixty rupees fresh and fresh every month. A very, very long while ago, when I used to be getting three hundred and fifty rupees a month, and pickings, on a big timber contract at Calcutta, I had a wife of sorts. But she's dead now. People said that I killed her by taking to the Black Smoke. Perhaps I did, but it's so long since that it doesn't matter. Sometimes when I first came to the Gate, I used to feel sorry for it; but that's all over and done with long ago, and I draw my sixty rupees fresh and fresh every month, and am quite happy. Not *drunk* happy, you know, but always quiet and soothed and contented.

How did I take to it? It began at Calcutta. I used to try it in my own house, just to see what it was like. I never went very far, but I think my wife must have died then. Anyhow, I found myself here, and got to know Fung-Tching. I don't remember rightly how that came about; but he told me of the Gate and I used to go there, and, somehow, I have never got away from it since. Mind you, though, the Gate was a respectable place in Fung-Tching's time, where you could be comfortable and not at all like the *chandoo-khanas* where the niggers go. No; it was clean, and quiet, and not crowded. Of course, there were others beside us ten and the man; but we always had a mat apiece, with a wadded woollen headpiece, all covered with black and red dragons and things, just like the coffin in the corner.

At the end of one's third pipe the dragons used to move about and fight. I've watched 'em many and many a night through. I used to regulate my Smoke that way, and now it takes a dozen pipes to make 'em stir. Besides, they are all torn and dirty, like the mats, and old Fung-Tching is dead. He died a couple of years ago, and gave me the pipe I always use now – a silver one, with queer beasts crawling up and down the receiver-bottle below the cup. Before that, I think, I used a big bamboo stem with a copper cup, a very small one, and a green jade mouthpiece. It was a little thicker than a walking-stick stem, and smoked sweet, very sweet. The bamboo seemed to suck up the smoke. Silver doesn't, and I've got to clean it out now and then, that's a great deal of trouble, but I smoke it for the old man's sake. He must have made a good thing out of me, but he always gave me clean mats and pillows, and the best stuff you could get anywhere.

When he died, his nephew Tsin-ling took up the Gate, and he called it the 'Temple of the Three Possessions'; but we old ones speak of it as the 'Hundred Sorrows', all the same. The nephew does things very shabbily, and I think the Memsahib must help him. She lives with him; same as she used to do with the old man. The two let in all sorts of low people, niggers and all, and the Black Smoke isn't as good as it used to be. I've found burnt bran in my pipe over and over again. The old man would have died if that had happened in his time. Besides, the room is never cleaned, and all the mats are torn and cut at the edges. The coffin is gone – gone to China again – with the old man and two ounces of Smoke inside it, in case he should want 'em on the way.

The Joss doesn't get so many sticks burnt under his nose as he used to; that's a sign of ill-luck, as sure as death. He's all brown, too, and no one ever attends to him. That's the Memsahib's work, I know; because, when Tsin-ling tried to burn gilt paper before him, she said it was a waste of money, and, if he kept a stick burning very slowly, the Joss wouldn't know the difference. So now we've got the sticks mixed with a lot of glue, and they take half an hour longer to burn, and smell stinky; let alone the smell of the room by itself. No business can get on if they try that sort of thing. The Joss doesn't like it. I can see that. Late at night, sometimes, he turns all sorts of queer colours – blue and green and red – just as he used to do when old Fung-Tching was alive; and he rolls his eyes and stamps his feet like a devil.

I don't know why I don't leave the place and smoke quietly in a little room of my own in the bazaar. Most like, Tsin-ling would kill me if I went away – he draws my sixty rupees now – and besides, it's so much trouble, and I've grown to be very fond of the Gate. It's not much to look at. Not what it was in the old man's time, but I couldn't leave it. I've seen so many come in and out. And I've seen so many die here on the mats that I should be afraid of dying in the open now. I've seen some things that people would call strange enough; but nothing is strange when you're on the Black Smoke, except the Black Smoke. And if it was, it wouldn't matter. Fung-Tching used to be very particular about his people, and never got in any one who'd give trouble by dying messy and such. But the nephew isn't half so careful. He tells everywhere that he keeps a 'first-chop' house. Never tries to get men in quietly, and make them comfortable like Fung-Tching did. That's why the Gate is getting a little bit more known than it used to be. Among the niggers of course. The nephew daren't get a white, or, for matter of that, a mixed skin into the place. He has to keep us three, of course – me and the Memsahib and the other Eurasian. We're fixtures. But he wouldn't give us credit for a pipeful – not for anything.

One of these days, I hope, I shall die in the Gate. The Persian and the Madras man are terribly shaky now. They've got a boy to light their pipes for them. I always do that myself. Most like, I shall see them carried out before me. I don't think I shall ever outlive the Memsahib or Tsin-ling. Women last longer than men at the Black Smoke, and Tsin-ling has a deal of the old man's blood in him, though he does smoke cheap stuff. The bazaar-woman knew when she was going two days before her time; and she died on a clean mat with a nicely wadded pillow, and the old man hung up her pipe just above the Joss. He was always fond of her, I fancy. But he took her bangles just the same.

I should like to die like the bazaar-woman – on a clean, cool mat with a pipe of good stuff between my lips. When I feel I'm going, I shall ask Tsin-ling for them, and he can draw my sixty rupees a month, fresh and fresh, as long as he pleases. Then I shall lie back, quiet and comfortable, and watch the black and red dragons have their last big fight together; and then . . .

Well, it doesn't matter. Nothing matters much to me – only I wish Tsin-ling wouldn't put bran into the Black Smoke.

The Story of Muhammad Din

Who is the happy man? He that sees in his own house at home, little children crowned with dust, leaping and falling and crying.

Munichandra, translated by Professor Peterson

THE polo-ball was an old one, scarred, chipped, and dented. It stood on the mantelpiece among the pipe-stems which Imam Din, *khitmatgar*, was cleaning for me.

'Does the Heaven-born want this ball?' said Imam Din deferentially.

The Heaven-born set no particular store by it; but of what use was a polo-ball to a *khitmatgar*?

'By Your Honour's favour, I have a little son. He has seen this ball, and desires it to play with. I do not want it for myself.'

No one would for an instant accuse portly old Imam Din of wanting to play with polo-balls. He carried out the battered thing into the veranda; and there followed a hurricane of joyful squeaks, a patter of small feet, and the *thud-thud-thud* of the ball rolling along the ground. Evidently the little son had been waiting outside the door to secure his treasure. But how had he managed to see that polo-ball?

Next day, coming back from office half an hour earlier than usual, I was aware of a small figure in the dining-room – a tiny, plump figure in a ridiculously inadequate shirt which came, perhaps, half-way down the tubby stomach. It wandered round the room, thumb in mouth, crooning to itself as it took stock of the pictures. Undoubtedly this was the 'little son'.

He had no business in my room, of course; but was so deeply absorbed in his discoveries that he never noticed me in the doorway. I stepped into the room and startled him nearly into a fit. He sat down on the ground with a gasp. His eyes opened, and his mouth followed suit. I knew what was coming, and fled, followed by a long, dry howl which reached the servants' quarters far more quickly than any command of mine had ever done. In ten seconds Imam Din was in the dining-room. Then despairing sobs arose, and I returned to find Imam Din admonishing the small sinner who was using most of his shirt as a handkerchief.

'This boy,' said Imam Din judicially, 'is a *budmash* - a big *budmash*. He will, without doubt, go to the *jail-khana* for his behaviour.' Renewed yells from the penitent, and an elaborate apology to myself from Imam Din.

'Tell the baby,' said I, 'that the *Sahib* is not angry, and take him away.' Imam Din conveyed my forgiveness to the offender, who had now gathered all his shirt round his neck, stringwise, and the yell subsided into a sob. The two set off for the door. 'His name,' said Imam Din, as though the name were part of the crime, 'is Muhammad Din, and he is a *budmash*.' Freed from present danger, Muhammad Din turned round in his father's arms, and said gravely, 'It is true that my name is Muhammad Din, *Tahib*, but I am not a *budmash*. I am a *man*!'

From that day dated my acquaintance with Muhammad Din. Never again did he come into my dining-room, but on the neutral ground of the garden we greeted each other with much state, though our conversation was confined to '*Talaam, Tahib*' from his side, and '*Salaam, Muhammad Din*' from mine. Daily on my return from office, the little white shirt and the fat little body used to rise from the shade of the creeper-covered trellis where they had been hid; and daily I checked my horse here, that my salutation might not be slurred over or given unseemly.

Muhammad Din never had any companions. He used to trot about the compound, in and out of the castor-oil bushes, on mysterious errands of his own. One day I stumbled upon some of his handiwork far down the grounds. He had half buried the polo-ball in dust, and stuck six shrivelled old marigold flowers in a circle round it. Outside that circle again was a rude square, traced out in bits of red brick alternating with fragments of broken china; the whole bounded by a little bank of dust. The water-man from the well-curb put in a plea for the small architect, saying that it was only the play of a baby and did not much disfigure my garden.

Heaven knows that I had no intention of touching the child's work then or later; but, that evening, a stroll through the garden brought me unawares full on it; so that I trampled, before I knew, marigold-heads, dust-bank, and fragments of broken soap-dish into confusion past all hope of mending. Next morning, I came upon Muhammad Din crying softly to himself over the ruin I had wrought. Some one had cruelly told him that the *Sahib* was very angry with him for spoiling the garden, and had scattered his rubbish, using bad language the while. Muhammad Din laboured for an hour at effacing every trace of the dust-bank and pottery fragments, and it was with a tearful and apologetic face that he said, *'Talaam Tahib,'* when I came home from office. A hasty inquiry resulted in Imam Din informing Muhammad Din that, by my singular favour, he was permitted to disport himself as he pleased. Whereat the child took heart and fell to tracing the ground-plan of an edifice which was to eclipse the marigold-polo-ball creation.

For some months the chubby little eccentricity revolved in his humble orbit among the castor-oil bushes and in the dust; always fashioning magnificent palaces from stale flowers thrown away by the bearer, smooth water-worn pebbles, bits of broken glass, and feathers pulled, I fancy, from my fowls – always alone, and always crooning to himself.

A gaily-spotted seashell was dropped one day close to the last of his little buildings; and I looked that Muhammad Din should build something more than ordinarily splendid on the strength of it. Nor was I disappointed. He meditated for the better part of an hour, and his crooning rose to a jubilant song. Then he began tracing in the dust. It would certainly be a wondrous palace, this one, for it was two yards long and a yard broad in ground-plan. But the palace was never completed.

Next day there was no Muhammad Din at the head of the carriage-drive, and no *'Talaam, Tahib'* to welcome my return. I had grown accustomed to the greeting, and its omission troubled me. Next day Imam Din told me that the child was suffering slightly from fever and needed quinine. He got the medicine, and an English doctor.

'They have no stamina, these brats,' said the doctor, as he left Imam Din's quarters.

A week later, though I would have given much to have avoided it, I met on the road to the Mussulman burying-ground Imam Din, accompanied by one other friend, carrying in his arms, wrapped in a white cloth, all that was left of little Muhammad Din.

The Man who would be King

Brother to a Prince and fellow to a beggar
if he be found worthy.

THE Law, as quoted, lays down a fair conduct of life, and one not easy to follow. I have been fellow to a beggar again and again under circumstances which prevented either of us finding out whether the other was worthy. I have still to be brother to a prince, though I once came near to kinship with what might have been a veritable King, and was promised the reversion of a Kingdom–army, law-courts, revenue, and policy all complete. But, today, I greatly fear that my King is dead, and if I want a crown I must go hunt it for myself.

The beginning of everything was in a railway train upon the road to Mhow from Ajmir. There had been a deficit in the budget, which necessitated travelling, not second-class, which is only half as dear as first-class, but by intermediate, which is very awful indeed. There are no cushions in the intermediate class, and the population are either intermediate, which is Eurasian, or native, which for a long night journey is nasty, or Loafer, which is amusing though intoxicated. Intermediates do not buy from refreshment-rooms. They carry their food in bundles and pots, and buy sweets from the native sweetmeat-sellers, and drink the roadside water. That is why in the hot weather intermediates are taken out of the carriages dead, and in all weathers are most properly looked down upon.

My particular intermediate happened to be empty till I reached Nasirabad, when a big black-browed gentleman in shirt-sleeves entered, and, following the custom of intermediates, passed the time of day. He was a wanderer and a vagabond like myself, but with an educated taste for whisky. He told tales of things he had seen and done, of out-of-the-way corners of the Empire into which he had penetrated, and of adventures in which he risked his life for a few days' food.

'If India was filled with men like you and me, not knowing more than the crows where they'd get their next day's rations, it isn't seventy millions of revenue the land would be paying – it's seven hundred millions,' said he; and as I looked at his mouth and chin I was disposed to agree with him.

We talked politics – the politics of Loaferdom, that sees things from the underside where the lath and plaster is not smoothed off – and we talked postal arrangements because my friend wanted to send a telegram back from the next station to Ajmir, the turning-off place from the Bombay to the Mhow line as you travel westward. My friend had no money beyond eight annas, which he wanted for dinner, and I had no money at all, owing to the hitch in the budget before mentioned. Further, I was going into a wilderness where, though I should resume touch with the Treasury, there were no telegraph offices. I was, therefore, unable to help him in any way.

'We might threaten a station-master, and make him send a wire on tick,' said my friend, 'but that'd mean inquiries for you and for me, and *I*'ve got my hands full these days. Did you say you are travelling back along this line within any days?'

'Within ten,' I said.

'Can't you make it eight?' said he. 'Mine is rather urgent business.'

'I can send your telegram within ten days if that will serve you,' I said.

'I couldn't trust the wire to fetch him now I think of it. It's this way. He leaves Delhi on the 23rd for Bombay. That means he'll be running through Ajmir about the night of the 23rd.'

'But I'm going into the Indian Desert,' I explained.

'Well *and* good,' said he. 'You'll be changing at Marwar Junction to get into Jodhpore territory – you must do that – and he'll be coming through Marwar Junction in the early morning of the 24th by the Bombay Mail. Can you be at Marwar Junction on that time? 'Twon't be inconveniencing you because I know that there's precious few pickings to be got out of these Central India States – even though you pretend to be correspondent of the *Backwoodsman*.'

'Have you ever tried that trick?' I asked.

'Again and again, but the residents find you out, and then you get escorted to the border before you've time to get your knife into them. But about my friend here. I *must* give him a word o' mouth to tell him what's come to me or else he won't know where to go. I would take it more than kind of you if you was to come out of Central India in time to catch him at Marwar Junction, and say to him: "He has gone South for the week." He'll know what that means. He's a big man with a red beard, and a great swell he is. You'll find him sleeping like a gentleman with all his luggage round him in a second-class compartment. But don't you be afraid. Slip down the window, and say: "He has gone South for the week," and he'll tumble. It's only cutting your time of stay in those parts by two days. I ask you as a stranger – going to the West,' he said with emphasis.

'Where have *you* come from?' said I.

'From the East,' said he, 'and I am hoping that you will give him the message on the Square – for the sake of my mother as well as your own.'

Englishmen are not usually softened by appeals to the memory of their mothers, but for certain reasons, which will be fully apparent, I saw fit to agree.

'It's more than a little matter,' said he, 'and that's why I asked you to do it – and now I know that I can depend on you doing it. A second-class carriage at Marwar Junction, and a red-haired man asleep in it. You'll be sure to remember. I get out at the next station, and I must hold on there till he comes or sends me what I want.'

'I'll give the message if I catch him,' I said, 'and for the sake of your mother as well as mine I'll give you a word of advice. Don't try to run the Central India States just now as the correspondent of the *Backwoodsman*. There's a real one knocking about here, and it might lead to trouble.'

'Thank you,' said he simply, 'and when will the swine be gone? I can't starve because he's ruining my work. I wanted to get hold of the Degumber Rajah down here about his father's widow, and give him a jump.'

'What did he do to his father's widow, then?'

'Filled her up with red pepper and slippered her to death as she hung from a beam. I found that out myself, and I'm the only man that would dare going into the State to get hush-money for it. They'll try to poison me, same as they did in Chortumna when I went on the loot there. But you'll give the man at Marwar Junction my message?'

He got out at a little roadside station, and I reflected. I had heard, more than once, of men personating correspondents of newspapers and bleeding small Native States with threats of exposure, but I had never met any of the caste before. They led a hard life, and generally die with great suddenness. The Native States have a wholesome horror of English newspapers which may throw light on their peculiar methods of government, and do their best to choke correspondents with champagne, or drive them out of their mind with four-in-hand barouches. They do not understand that nobody cares a straw for the internal administration of Native States so long as oppression and crime are kept within decent limits, and the ruler is not drugged, drunk, or diseased from one end of the year to the other. They are the dark places of the earth, full of unimaginable cruelty, touching the railway and the telegraph on one side, and, on the other, the days of Harun-al-Raschid. When I left the train I did business with divers Kings, and in eight days passed through many changes of life. Sometimes I wore dress-clothes and consorted with Princes and Politicals, drinking from crystal and eating from silver. Sometimes I lay out upon the ground and devoured what I could get, from a plate made of leaves, and drank the running water, and slept under the same rug as my servant. It was all in the day's work.

Then I headed for the Great Indian Desert upon the proper date, as I had promised, and the night Mail set me down at Marwar Junction, where a funny, little, happy-go-lucky, native-managed railway runs to Jodhpore. The Bombay Mail from Delhi makes a short halt at Marwar. She arrived as I got in, and I had just time to hurry to her platform and go down the carriages. There was only one second-class on the train. I slipped the window and looked down upon a flaming red beard, half covered by a railway rug. That was my man, fast asleep, and I dug him gently in the ribs. He woke with a grunt, and I saw his face in the light of the lamps. It was a great and shining face.

'Tickets again?' said he.

'No,' said I. 'I am to tell you that he is gone South for the week. He has gone South for the week!'

The train had begun to move out. The red man rubbed his eyes. 'He has gone South for the week,' he repeated. 'Now that's just like his impidence. Did he say that I was to give you anything? 'Cause I won't.'

'He didn't,' I said, and dropped away, and watched the red lights die out in the dark. It was horribly cold because the wind was blowing off the sands. I climbed into my own train – not an intermediate carriage this time – and went to sleep.

If the man with the beard had given me a rupee I should have kept it as a memento of a rather curious affair. But the consciousness of having done my duty was my only reward.

Later on I reflected that two gentlemen like my friends could not do any good if they forgathered and personated correspondents of newspapers, and might, if they blackmailed one of the little rat-trap states of Central India or Southern Rajputana, get themselves into serious difficulties. I therefore took some trouble to describe them as accurately as I could remember to people who would be interested in deporting them; and succeeded, so I was later informed, in having them headed back from the Degumber borders.

Then I became respectable, and returned to an office where there were no kings and no incidents outside the daily manufacture of a newspaper. A newspaper office seems to attract every conceivable sort of person, to the prejudice of discipline. Zenana-mission ladies arrive, and beg that the editor will instantly abandon all his duties to describe a Christian prize-giving in a back-slum of a perfectly inaccessible village; colonels who have been overpassed for command sit down and sketch the outline of a series of ten, twelve, or twenty-four leading articles on seniority *versus* selection; missionaries wish to know why they have not been permitted to escape from their regular vehicles of abuse and swear at a brother-missionary under special patronage of the editorial We; stranded theatrical companies troop up to explain that they cannot pay for their advertisements, but on their return from New Zealand or Tahiti will do so with interest; inventors of patent punkah-pulling machines, carriage couplings, and unbreakable swords and axle-trees, call with specifications in their pockets and hours at their disposal; tea-companies enter and elaborate their prospectuses with the office pens; secretaries of ball-committees clamour to have the glories of their last dance more fully described; strange ladies rustle in and say, 'I want a hundred lady's cards printed *at once*, please,' which is manifestly part of an editor's duty; and every dissolute ruffian that ever tramped the Grand Trunk Road makes it his business to ask for employment as a proof-reader. And, all the time, the telephone-bell is ringing madly, and kings are being killed on the Continent, and Empires are saying, 'You're another,' and Mister Gladstone is calling down brimstone upon the British Dominions, and the little black copy-boys are whining, *'kaa-pi chay-ha-yeh'* (copy wanted) like tired bees, and most of the paper is as blank as Modred's shield.

But that is the amusing part of the year. There are six other months when none ever comes to call, and the thermometer walks inch by inch up to the top of the glass, and the office is darkened to just above reading-light, and the press-machines are red-hot of touch, and nobody writes anything but accounts of amusements in the hill-stations or obituary notices. Then the telephone becomes a tinkling terror, because it tells you of the sudden deaths of men and women that you knew intimately, and the prickly-heat covers you with a garment, and you sit down and write: 'A slight increase of sickness is reported from the Khuda Janta Khan District. The outbreak is purely sporadic in its nature, and, thanks to the energetic efforts of the district authorities, is now almost at an end. It is, however, with deep regret we record the death, etc.'

Then the sickness really breaks out, and the less recording and reporting the better for the peace of the subscribers. But the Empires and the Kings continue to divert themselves as selfishly as before, and the foreman thinks that a daily paper really ought to come out once in twenty-four hours, and all the people at the hill-stations in the middle of their amusements say: 'Good gracious! Why can't the paper be sparkling? I'm sure there's plenty going on up here.'

That is the dark half of the moon, and, as the advertisements say, 'must be experienced to be appreciated'.

It was in that season, and a remarkably evil season, that the paper began running the last issue of the week on Saturday night, which is to say Sunday morning, after the custom of a London paper. This was a great convenience, for immediately after the paper was put to bed, the dawn would lower the thermometer from 96° to almost 84° for half an hour, and in that chill – you have no idea how cold is 84° on the grass until you begin to pray for it – a very tired man could get off to sleep ere the heat roused him.

One Saturday night it was my pleasant duty to put the paper to bed alone. A King or courtier or a courtesan or a Community was going to die or get a new Constitution, or do something that was important on the other side of the world, and the paper was to be held open till the latest possible minute in order to catch the telegram.

It was a pitchy black night, as stifling as a June night can be, and the *loo*, the red-hot wind from the westward, was booming among the tinder-dry trees and pretending that the rain was on its heels. Now and again a spot of almost boiling water would fall on the dust with the flop of a frog, but all our weary world knew that was only pretence. It was a shade cooler in the press-room than the office, so I sat there, while the type ticked and clicked, and the night-jars hooted at the windows, and the all but naked compositors wiped the sweat from their foreheads, and called for water. The thing that was keeping us back, whatever it was, would not come off, though the *loo* dropped and the last type was set, and the whole round earth stood still in the choking heat, with its finger on its lip, to wait the event. I drowsed, and wondered whether the telegraph was a blessing, and whether this dying man, or struggling people, might be aware of the inconvenience the delay was causing. There was no special reason beyond the heat and worry to make tension, but, as the clock-hands crept up to three o'clock, and the machines spun their fly-wheels two or three times to see that all was in order before I said the word that would set them off, I could have shrieked aloud.

Then the roar and rattle of the wheels shivered the quiet into little bits. I rose to go away, but two men in white clothes stood in front of me. The first one said: 'It's him!' The second said: 'So it is!' And they both laughed almost as loudly as the machinery roared, and mopped their foreheads. 'We seed there was a light burning across the road, and we were sleeping in that ditch there for coolness, and I said to my friend here, The office is open. Let's come along and speak to him as turned us back from the Degumber State,' said the smaller of the two. He was the man I had met in the Mhow train, and his fellow was the red-bearded man of Marwar Junction. There was no mistaking the eyebrows of the one or the beard of the other.

I was not pleased, because I wished to go to sleep, not to squabble with loafers. 'What do you want?' I asked.

'Half an hour's talk with you, cool and comfortable, in the office,' said the red-bearded man. 'We'd *like* some drink – the Contrack doesn't begin yet, Peachey, so you needn't look – but what we really want is advice. We don't want money. We ask you as a favour, because we found out you did us a bad turn about Degumber State.'

I led from the press-room to the stifling office with the maps on the walls, and the red-haired man rubbed his hands. 'That's something like,' said he. 'This was the proper shop to come to. Now, sir, let me introduce to you Brother Peachey Carnehan, that's him, and Brother Daniel Dravot, that is *me*, and the less said about our professions the better, for we have been most things in our time. Soldier, sailor, compositor, photographer, proof-reader, street-preacher, and correspondents of the *Backwoodsman* when we thought the paper wanted one. Carnehan is sober, and so am I. Look at us first, and see that's sure. It will save you cutting into my talk. We'll take one of your cigars apiece, and you shall see us light up.'

I watched the test. The men were absolutely sober, so I gave them each a tepid whisky and soda.

'Well *and* good,' said Carnehan of the eyebrows, wiping the froth from his moustache. 'Let me talk now, Dan. We have been all over India, mostly on foot. We have been boiler-fitters, engine-drivers, petty contractors, and all that, and we have decided that India isn't big enough for such as us.'

They certainly were too big for the office. Dravot's beard seemed to fill half the room and Carnehan's shoulders the other half, as they sat on the big table. Carnehan continued: 'The country isn't half worked out because they that governs it won't let you touch it. They spend all their blessed time in governing it, and you can't lift a spade, nor chip a rock, nor look for oil, nor anything like that, without all the government saying, "Leave it alone, and let us govern." Therefore, such *as* it is, we will let it alone, and go away to some other place where a man isn't crowded and can come to his own. We are not little men, and there is nothing that we are afraid of except drink, and we have signed a Contrack on that. *Therefore*, we are going away to be Kings.'

'Kings in our own right,' muttered Dravot.

'Yes, of course,' I said. 'You've been tramping in the sun, and it's a very warm night, and hadn't you better sleep over the notion? Come tomorrow.'

'Neither drunk nor sunstruck,' said Dravot. 'We have slept over the notion half a year, and require to see books and atlases, and we have decided that there is only one place now in the world that two strong men can Sar-a-*whack*. They call it Kafiristan. By my reckoning it's the top right-hand corner of Afghanistan, not more than three hundred miles from Peshawar. They have two-and-thirty heathen idols there, and we'll be the thirty-third and fourth. It's a mountainous country, and the women of those parts are very beautiful.'

'But that is provided against in the Contrack,' said Carnehan. 'Neither woman nor liquor, Daniel.'

'And that's all we know, except that no one has gone there, and they fight, and in any place where they fight a man who knows how to drill men can always be a king. We shall go to those parts and say to any king we find – "D'you want to vanquish your foes?" and we will show him how to drill men; for that we know better than anything else. Then we will subvert that king and seize his throne and establish a dy-nasty.'

'You'll be cut to pieces before you're fifty miles across the Border,' I said. 'You have to travel through Afghanistan to get to that country. It's one mass of mountains and peaks and glaciers, and no Englishman has been through it. The people are utter brutes, and even if you reached them you couldn't do anything.'

'That's more like,' said Carnehan. 'If you could think us a little more mad we would be more pleased. We have come to you to know about this country, to read a book about it, and to be shown maps. We want you to tell us that we are fools and to show us your books.' He turned to the bookcases.

'Are you at all in earnest?' I said.

'A little,' said Dravot sweetly. 'As big a map as you have got, even if it's all blank where Kafiristan is, and any books you've got. We can read, though we aren't very educated.'

I uncased the big thirty-two-miles-to-the-inch map of India, and two smaller Frontier maps, hauled down volume INF-KAN of the *Encyclopedia Britannica*, and the men consulted them.

'See here!' said Dravot, his thumb on the map. 'Up to Jagdallak, Peachey and me know the road. We was there with Roberts' Army. We'll have to turn off to the right at Jagdallak through Laghmann territory. Then we get among the hills – fourteen thousand feet – fifteen thousand – it will be cold work there, but it don't look very far on the map.'

I handed him Wood on the *Sources of the Oxus*. Carnehan was deep in the *Encyclopedia*.

'They're a mixed lot,' said Dravot reflectively; 'and it won't help us to know the names of their tribes. The more tribes the more they'll fight, and the better for us. From Jagdallak to Ashang. H'mm!'

'But all the information about the country is as sketchy and inaccurate as can be,' I protested. 'No one knows anything about it really. Here's the file of the *United Services' Institute*. Read what Bellew says.'

'Blow Bellew!' said Carnehan. 'Dan, they're a stinkin' lot of heathens, but this book here says they think they're related to us English.'

I smoked while the men pored over Raverty, Wood, the maps, and the *Encyclopedia*.

'There is no use your waiting,' said Dravot politely. 'It's about four o'clock now. We'll go before six o'clock if you want to sleep, and we won't steal any of the papers. Don't you sit up. We're two harmless lunatics, and if you come tomorrow evening down to the Serai we'll say goodbye to you.'

'You *are* two fools,' I answered. 'You'll be turned back at the Frontier or cut up the minute you set foot in Afghanistan. Do you want any money or a recommendation down-country? I can help you to the chance of work next week.'

'Next week we shall be hard at work ourselves, thank you,' said Dravot. 'It isn't so easy being a king as it looks. When we've got our kingdom in going order we'll let you know, and you can come up and help us to govern it.'

'Would two lunatics make a contrack like that?' said Carnehan, with subdued pride, showing me a greasy half-sheet of notepaper on which was written the following. I copied it, then and there, as a curiosity:

This Contract between me and you persuing witnesseth in the name of God – Amen and so forth.

(One) *That me and you will settle this matter together;* i.e. *to be Kings of Kafiristan.*

(Two) *That you and me will not, while this matter is being settled, look at any Liquor, nor any Woman black, white, or brown, so as to get mixed up with one or the other harmful.*

(Three) *That we conduct ourselves with Dignity and Discretion, and if one of us gets into trouble the other will stay by him.*

Signed by you and me this day.
Peachey Taliaferro Carnehan.
Daniel Dravot.
Both Gentlemen at Large.

'There was no need for the last article,' said Carnehan, blushing modestly; 'but it looks regular. Now you know the sort of men that loafers are – we *are* loafers, Dan, until we get out of India – and *do* you think that we would sign a Contrack like that unless we was in earnest? We have kept away from the two things that make life worth having.'

'You won't enjoy your lives much longer if you are going to try this idiotic adventure. Don't set the office on fire,' I said, 'and go away before nine o'clock.'

I left them still poring over the maps and making notes on the back of the 'Contrack'. 'Be sure to come down to the Serai tomorrow,' were their parting words.

The Kumharsen Serai is the great four-square sink of humanity where the strings of camels and horses from the North load and unload. All the nationalities of Central Asia may be found there, and most of the folk of India proper. Balkh and Bokhara there meet Bengal and Bombay, and try to draw eye-teeth. You can buy ponies, turquoises, Persian pussy-cats, saddle-bags, fat-tailed sheep and musk in the Kumharsen Serai, and get many strange things for nothing. In the afternoon I went down to see whether my friends intended to keep their word or were lying there drunk.

A priest attired in fragments of ribbons and rags stalked up to me, gravely twisting a child's paper whirligig. Behind him was his servant bending under the load of a crate of mud toys. The two were loading up two camels, and the inhabitants of the Serai watched them with shrieks of laughter.

'The priest is mad,' said a horse-dealer to me. 'He is going up to Kabul to sell toys to the Amir. He will either be raised to honour or have his head cut off. He came in here this morning and has been behaving madly ever since.'

'The witless are under the protection of God,' stammered a flat-cheeked Usbeg in broken Hindi. 'They foretell future events.'

'Would they could have foretold that my caravan would have been cut up by the Shinwaris almost within shadow of the Pass!' grunted the Eusufzai agent of a Rajputana trading-house whose goods had been diverted into the hands of other robbers just across the Border, and whose misfortunes were the laughing-stock of the bazaar. 'Ohé, priest, whence come you and whither do you go?'

'From Roum have I come,' shouted the priest, waving his whirligig; 'from Roum, blown by the breath of a hundred devils across the sea! O thieves, robbers, liars, the blessing of Pir Khan on pigs, dogs, and perjurers! Who will take the Protected of God to the North to sell charms that are never still to the Amir? The camels shall not gall, the sons shall not fall sick, and the wives shall remain faithful while they are away, of the men who give me place in their caravan. Who will assist me to slipper the King of the Roos with a golden slipper with a silver heel? The protection of Pir Khan be upon his labours!' He spread out the skirts of his gaberdine and pirouetted between the lines of tethered horses.

'There starts a caravan from Peshawar to Kabul in twenty days, *Huzrut*,' said the Eusufzai trader. 'My camels go therewith. Do thou also go and bring us good luck.'

'I will go even now!' shouted the priest. 'I will depart upon my winged camels, and be at Peshawar in a day! Ho! Hazar Mir Khan,' he yelled to his servant, 'drive out the camels, but let me first mount my own.'

He leaped on the back of his beast as it knelt, and, turning round to me, cried: 'Come thou also, Sahib, a little along the road, and I will sell thee a charm – an amulet that shall make thee King of Kafiristan.'

Then the light broke upon me, and I followed the two camels out of the Serai till we reached open road and the priest halted.

'What d'you think o' that?' said he in English. 'Carnehan can't talk their patter, so I've made him my servant. He makes a handsome servant. 'Tisn't for nothing that I've been knocking about the country for fourteen years. Didn't I do that talk neat? We'll hitch on to a caravan at Peshawar till we get to Jagdallak, and then we'll see if we can get donkeys for our camels, and strike into Kafiristan. Whirligigs for the Amir, O Lor! Put your hand under the camel-bags and tell me what you feel.'

I felt the butt of a Martini, and another and another.

'Twenty of 'em,' said Dravot placidly. 'Twenty of 'em and ammunition to correspond, under the whirligigs and the mud dolls.'

'Heaven help you if you are caught with those things!' I said. 'A Martini is worth her weight in silver among the Pathans.'

'Fifteen hundred rupees of capital – every rupee we could beg, borrow, or steal – are invested on these two camels,' said Dravot. 'We won't get caught. We're going through the Khyber with a regular caravan. Who'd touch a poor mad priest?'

'Have you got everything you want?' I asked, overcome with astonishment.

'Not yet, but we shall soon. Give us a memento of your kindness, *Brother*. You did me a service, yesterday, and that time in Marwar. Half my kingdom shall you have, as the saying is.' I slipped a small charm compass from my watch-chain and handed it up to the priest.

'Goodbye,' said Dravot, giving me hand cautiously. 'It's the last time we'll shake hands with an Englishman these many days. Shake hands with him, Carnehan,' he cried, as the second camel passed me.

Carnehan leaned down and shook hands. Then the camels passed away along the dusty road, and I was left alone to wonder. My eye could detect no failure in the disguises. The scene in the Serai proved that they were complete to the native mind. There was just the chance, therefore, that Carnehan and Dravot would be able to wander through Afghanistan without detection. But, beyond, they would find death – certain and awful death.

Ten days later a native correspondent giving me the news of the day from Peshawar, wound up his letter with: 'There has been much laughter here on account of a certain mad priest who is going in his estimation to sell petty gauds and insignificant trinkets which he ascribes as great charms to H.H. the Amir of Bokhara. He passed through Peshawar and associated himself to the Second Summer caravan that goes to Kabul. The merchants are pleased because through superstition they imagine that such mad fellows bring good fortune.'

The two, then, were beyond the Border. I would have prayed for them, but, that night, a real King died in Europe, and demanded an obituary notice.

The wheel of the world swings through the same phases again and again. Summer passed and winter thereafter, and came and passed again. The daily paper continued and I with it, and upon the third summer there fell a hot night, a night-issue, and a strained waiting for something to be telegraphed from the other side of the world, exactly as had happened before. A few great men had died in the past two years, the machines worked with more clatter, and some of the trees in the office garden were a few feet taller. But that was all the difference.

I passed over to the press-room, and went through just such a scene as I have already described. The nervous tension was stronger than it had been two years before, and I felt the heat more acutely. At three o'clock I cried, 'Print off', and turned to go, when there crept to my chair what was left of a man. He was bent into a circle, his head was sunk between his shoulders, and he moved his feet one over the other like a bear. I could hardly see whether he walked or crawled – this rag-wrapped, whining cripple who addressed me by name, crying that he was come back. 'Can you give me a drink?' he whimpered. 'For the Lord's sake give me a drink!'

I went back to the office, the man following with groans of pain, and I turned up the lamp.

'Don't you know me?' he gasped, dropping into a chair, and he turned his drawn face, surmounted by a shock of grey hair, to the light.

I looked at him intently. Once before had I seen eyebrows that met over the nose in an inch-broad black band, but for the life of me I could not tell where.

'I don't know you,' I said, handing him the whisky. 'What can I do for you?'

He took a gulp of the spirit raw, and shivered in spite of the suffocating heat.

'I've come back,' he repeated; 'and I was the King of Kafiristan – me and Dravot – crowned kings we was! In this office we settled it – you setting there and giving us the books. I am Peachey – Peachey Taliaferro Carnehan, and you've been setting here ever since – O Lord!'

I was more than a little astonished, and expressed my feelings accordingly.

'It's true,' said Carnehan, with a dry cackle, nursing his feet, which were wrapped in rags. 'True as gospel. Kings we were, with crowns upon our heads – me and Dravot – poor Dan – oh, poor, poor Dan, that would never take advice, not though I begged of him!'

'Take the whisky,' I said, 'and take your own time. Tell me all you can recollect of everything from beginning to end. You got across the Border on your camels, Dravot dressed as a mad priest and you his servant. Do you remember that?'

'I ain't mad – yet, but I shall be that way soon. Of course I remember. Keep looking at me, or maybe my words will go all to pieces. Keep looking at me in my eyes and don't say anything.'

I leaned forward and looked into his face as steadily as I could. He dropped one hand upon the table and I grasped it by the wrist. It was twisted like a bird's claw, and upon the back was a ragged red diamond-shaped scar.

'No, don't look there. Look at *me*,' said Carnehan. 'That comes afterwards, but for the Lord's sake don't distrack me. We left with that caravan, me and Dravot playing all sorts of antics to amuse the people we were with. Dravot used to make us laugh in the evenings when all the people was cooking their dinners – cooking their dinners, and . . . what did they do then? They lit little fires with sparks that went into Dravot's beard, and we all laughed – fit to die. Little red fires they was, going into Dravot's big red beard – so funny.' His eyes left mine and he smiled foolishly.

'You went as far as Jagdallak with that caravan,' I said at a venture, 'after you had lit those fires. To Jagdallak, where you turned off to try to get into Kafiristan.'

'No, we didn't neither. What are you talking about? We turned off before Jagdallak, because we heard the roads was good. But they wasn't good enough for our two camels – mine and Dravot's. When we left the caravan, Dravot took off all his clothes and mine too, and said we would be heathen, because the Kafirs didn't allow Mohammedans to talk to them. So we dressed betwixt and between, and such a sight as Daniel Dravot I never saw yet nor expect to see again. He burned half his beard, and slung a sheep-skin over his shoulder, and shaved his head into patterns. He shaved mine, too, and made me wear outrageous things to look like a heathen. That was in a most mountainous country, and our camels couldn't go along any more because of the mountains. They were tall and black, and coming home I saw them fight like wild goats – there are lots of goats in Kafiristan. And these mountains, they never keep still, no more than the goats. Always fighting they are, and don't let you sleep at night.'

'Take some more whisky,' I said very slowly. 'What did you and Daniel Dravot do when the camels could go no farther because of the rough roads that led into Kafiristan?'

'What did which do? There was a party called Peachey Taliaferro Carnehan that was with Dravot. Shall I tell you about him? He died out there in the cold. Slap from the bridge fell old Peachey, turning and twisting in the air like a penny whirligig that you can sell to the Amir – No; they was for three-ha'pence, those whirligigs, or I am much mistaken and woeful sore. . . . .And then these camels were no use, and Peachey said to Dravot – "For the Lord's sake let's get out of this before our heads are chopped off," and with that they killed the camels all among the mountains, not having anything in particular to eat, but first they took off the boxes with the guns and the ammunition, till two men came along driving four mules. Dravot up and dances in front of them, singing – "Sell me four mules." Says the first man – "If you are rich enough to buy, you are rich enough to rob"; but before ever he could put his hand to his knife, Dravot breaks his neck over his knee, and the other party runs away. So Carnehan loaded the mules with the rifles that was taken off the camels, and together we starts forward into those bitter cold mountainous parts, and never a road broader than the back of your hand.'

He paused for a moment, while I asked him if he could remember the nature of the country through which he had journeyed.

'I am telling you as straight as I can, but my head isn't as good as it might be. They drove nails through it to make me hear better how Dravot died. The country was mountainous and the mules were most contrary, and the inhabitants was dispersed and solitary. They went up and up, and down and down, and that other party, Carnehan, was imploring of Dravot not to sing and whistle so loud, for fear of bringing down the tremenjus avalanches. But Dravot says that if a King couldn't sing it wasn't worth being King, and whacked the mules over the rump, and never took no heed for ten cold days. We came to a big level valley all among the mountains, and the mules were near dead, so we killed them, not having anything special for them or us to eat. We sat upon the boxes, and played odd and even with the cartridges that was jolted out.

'Then ten men with bows and arrows ran down that valley, chasing twenty men with bows and arrows, and the row was tremenjus. They was fair men – fairer than you or me – with yellow hair and remarkable well built. Says Dravot, unpacking the guns – "This is the beginning of the business. We'll fight for the ten men," and with that he fires two rifles at the twenty men, and drops one of them at two hundred yards from the rock where he was sitting. The other men began to run, but Carnehan and Dravot sits on the boxes picking them off at all ranges, up and down the valley. Then we goes up to the ten men that had run across the snow too, and they fires a footy little arrow at us. Dravot he shoots above their heads and they all falls down flat. Then he walks over them and kicks them, and then he lifts them up and shakes hands all round to make them friendly like. He calls them and gives them the boxes to carry, and waves his hand for all the world as though he was King already. They takes the boxes and him across the valley and up the hill into a pine wood on the top, where there was half a dozen big stone idols. Dravot he goes to the biggest – a fellow they call Imbra – and lays a rifle and a cartridge at his feet, rubbing his nose respectful with his own nose, patting him on the head, and saluting in front of it. He turns round to the men and nods his head, and says – "That's all right. I'm in the know, too, and all these old jim-jams are my friends." Then he opens his mouth and points down it, and when the first man brings him food, he says – "No"; and when the second man brings him food he says – "No"; but when one of the old priests and the boss of the village brings him food, he says – "Yes", very haughty, and eats it slow. That was how we came to our first village, without any trouble, just as though we had tumbled from the skies. But we tumbled from one of those damned rope-bridges, you see, and – you couldn't expect a man to laugh much after that?'

'Take some more whisky and go on,' I said. 'That was the first village you came into. How did you get to be King?'

'I wasn't King,' said Carnehan. 'Dravot he was the King, and a handsome man he looked with the gold crown on his head and all. Him and the other party stayed in that village, and every morning Dravot sat by the side of old Imbra, and the people came and worshipped. That was Dravot's order. Then a lot of men came into the valley, and Carnehan and Dravot picks them off with the rifles before they knew where they was, and runs down into the valley and up again the other side and finds another village, same as the first one, and Dravot says – "Now what is the trouble between you two villages?" and the people points to a woman, as fair as you or me, that was carried off, and Dravot takes her back to the first village and counts up the dead – eight there was. For each dead man Dravot pours a little milk on the ground and waves his arms like a whirligig, and "That's all right," says he. Then he and Carnehan takes the big boss of each village by the arm and walks them down into the valley, and shows them how to scratch a line with a spear right down the valley, and gives each a sod of turf from both sides of the line. Then all the people comes down and shouts like the devil and all, and Dravot says – "Go and dig the land, and be fruitful and multiply," which they did, though they didn't understand. Then we asks the names of things in their lingo – bread and water and fire and idols and such, and Dravot leads the priest of each village up to the idol, and says he must sit there and judge the people, and if anything goes wrong he is to be shot.

'Next week they was all turning up the land in the valley as quiet as bees and much prettier, and the priests heard all the complaints and told Dravot in dumb show what it was about. "That's just the beginning," says Dravot. "They think we're Gods." He and Carnehan picks out twenty good men and shows them how to click off a rifle, and form fours, and advance in line, and they was very pleased to do so, and clever to see the hang of it. Then he takes out his pipe and his baccy-pouch and leaves one at one village, and one at the other, and off we two goes to see what was to be done in the next valley. That was all rock, and there was a little village there, and Carnehan says – "Send 'em to the old valley to plant", and takes 'em there, and gives 'em some land that wasn't took before. They were a poor lot, and we blooded 'em with a kid before letting 'em into the new kingdom. That was to impress the people, and then they settled down quiet, and Carnehan went back to Dravot who had got into another valley, all snow and ice and most mountainous. There was no people there and the Army got afraid, so Dravot shoots one of them, and goes on till he finds some people in a village, and the Army explains that unless the people wants to be killed they had better not shoot their little matchlocks; for they had matchlocks. We makes friends with the priest, and I stays there alone with two of the Army, teaching the men how to drill, and a thundering big Chief comes across the snow with kettle-drums and horns twanging, because he heard there was a new God kicking about. Carnehan sights for the brown of the men half a mile across the snow and wings one of them. Then he sends a message to the Chief that, unless he wished to be killed, he must come and shake hands with me and leave his arms behind. The Chief comes alone first, and Carnehan shakes hands with him and whirls his arms about, same as Dravot used, and very much surprised that Chief was, and strokes my eyebrows. Then Carnehan goes alone to the Chief, and asks him in dumb show if he had an enemy he hated. "I have," says the Chief. So Carnehan weeds out the pick of his men, and sets the two of the Army to show them drill, and at the end of two weeks the men can manoeuvre about as well as Volunteers. So he marches with the Chief to a great big plain on the top of a mountain, and the Chief's men rushes into a village and takes it; we three Martinis firing into the brown of the enemy. So we took that village too, and I gives the Chief a rag from my coat and says "Occupy till I come"; which was scriptural. By way of a reminder, when me and the Army was eighteen hundred yards away, I drops a bullet near him standing on the snow, and all the people falls flat on their faces. Then I sends a letter to Dravot wherever he be by land or by sea.'

At the risk of throwing the creature out of train I interrupted – 'How could you write a letter up yonder?'

'The letter? – Oh! – The letter! Keep looking at me between the eyes, please. It was a string-talk letter, that we'd learned the way of it from a blind beggar in the Punjab.'

I remember that there had once come to the office a blind man with a knotted twig and a piece of string which he wound round the twig according to some cipher of his own. He could, after the lapse of days or hours, repeat the sentence which he had reeled up. He had reduced the alphabet to eleven primitive sounds, and tried to teach me his method, but I could not understand.

'I sent that letter to Dravot,' said Carnehan; 'and told him to come back because this kingdom was growing too big for me to handle, and then I struck for the first valley, to see how the priests were working. They called the village we took along with the Chief, Bashkai, and the first village we took, Er-Heb. The priests at Er-Heb was doing all right, but they had a lot of pending cases about land to show me, and some men from another village had been firing arrows at night. I went out and looked for that village, and fired four rounds at it from a thousand yards. That used all the cartridges I cared to spend, and I waited for Dravot, who had been away two or three months, and I kept my people quiet.

'One morning I heard the devil's own noise of drums and horns, and Dan Dravot marches down the hill with his Army and a tail of hundreds of men, and, which was the most amazing, a great gold crown on his head. "My Gord, Carnehan," says Daniel, "this is a tremenjus business, and we've got the whole country as far as it's worth having. I am the son of Alexander by Queen Semiramis, and you're my younger brother and a God too! It's the biggest thing we've ever seen. I've been marching and fighting for six weeks with the Army, and every footy little village for fifty miles has come in rejoiceful; and more than that, I've got the key of the whole show, as you'll see, and I've got a crown for you! I told 'em to make two of 'em at a place called Shu, where the gold lies in the rock like suet in mutton. Gold I've seen, and turquoise I've kicked out of the cliffs, and there's garnets in the sands of the river, and here's a chunk of amber that a man brought me. Call up all the priests and, here, take your crown."

'One of the men opens a black hair bag, and I slips the crown on. It was too small and too heavy, but I wore it for the glory. Hammered gold it was – five pound weight, like a hoop of a barrel.

'"Peachey," says Dravot, "we don't want to fight no more. The Craft's the trick, so help me!" and he brings forward that same Chief that I left at Bashkai – Billy Fish we called him afterwards, because he was so like Billy Fish that drove the big tank-engine at Mach on the Bolan in the old days. "Shake hands with him," says Dravot, and I shook hands and nearly dropped, for Billy Fish gave me the Grip. I said nothing, but tried him with the Fellow Craft Grip. He answers all right, and I tried the Master's Grip, but that was a slip. "A Fellow Craft he is!" I says to Dan. "Does he know the word?" – "He does," says Dan, "and all the priests know. It's a miracle! The Chiefs and the priests can work a Fellow Craft Lodge in a way that's very like ours, and they've cut the marks on the rocks, but they don't know the Third Degree, and they've come to find out. It's Gord's Truth. I've known these long years that the Afghans knew up to the Fellow Craft Degree, but this is a miracle. A God and a Grand-Master of the Craft am I, and a Lodge in the Third Degree I will open, and we'll raise the head priests and the chiefs of the villages."

'"It's against all the law," I says, "holding a Lodge without warrant from any one; and you know we never held office in any Lodge."

'"It's a master-stroke o' policy," says Dravot. "It means running the country as easy as a four-wheeled bogie on a down grade. We can't stop to inquire now, or they'll turn against us. I've forty chiefs at my heel, and passed and raised according to their merit they shall be. Billet these men on the villages, and see that we run up a Lodge of some kind. The temple of Imbra will do for the Lodge-room. The women must make aprons as you show them. I'll hold a levee of Chiefs tonight and Lodge tomorrow."

'I was fair run off my legs, but I wasn't such a fool as not to see what a pull this Craft business gave us. I showed the priests' families how to make aprons of the degrees, but for Dravot's apron the blue border and marks was made of turquoise lumps on white hide, not cloth. We took a great square stone in the temple for the Master's chair, and little stones for the officers' chairs, and painted the black pavement with white squares, and did what we could to make things regular.

'At the levee which was held that night on the hillside with big bonfires, Dravot gives out that him and me were Gods and sons of Alexander, and Past Grand-Masters in the Craft, and was come to make Kafiristan a country where every man should eat in peace and drink in quiet, and specially obey us. Then the chiefs come round to shake hands, and they were so hairy and white and fair it was just shaking hands with old friends. We gave them names according as they was like men we had known in India – Billy Fish, Holly Dilworth, Pikky Kergan, that was Bazaar-master when I was at Mhow, and so on, and so on.

'*The* most amazing miracles was at Lodge next night. One of the old priests was watching us continuous, and I felt uneasy, for I knew we'd have to fudge the Ritual, and I didn't know what the men knew. The old priest was a stranger come in from beyond the village of Bashkai. The minute Dravot puts on the Master's apron that the girls had made for him, the priest fetches a whoop and a howl, and tries to overturn the stone that Dravot was sitting on. "It's all up now," I says. "That comes of meddling with the Craft without warrant!" Dravot never winked an eye, not when ten priests took and tilted over the Grand-Master's chair – which was to say the stone of Imbra. The priest begins rubbing the bottom end of it to clear away the black dirt, and presently he shows all the other priests the Master's Mark, same as was on Dravot's apron, cut into the stone. Not even the priests of the temple of Imbra knew it was there. The old chap falls flat on his face at Dravot's feet and kisses 'em. "Luck again," says Dravot, across the Lodge to me; "they say it's the missing Mark that no one could understand the why of. We're more than safe now." Then he bangs the butt of his gun for a gavel and says: "By virtue of the authority vested in me by my own right hand and the help of Peachey, I declare myself Grand-Master of all Freemasonry in Kafiristan in this the Mother Lodge o' the country, and King of Kafiristan equally with Peachey!" At that he puts on his crown and I puts on mine – I was doing Senior Warden – and we opens the Lodge in most ample form. It was a amazing miracle! The priests moved in Lodge through the first two degrees almost without telling, as if the memory was coming back to them. After that, Peachey and Dravot raised such as was worthy – high priests and chiefs of far-off villages. Billy Fish was the first, and I can tell you we scared the soul out of him. It was not in any way according to Ritual, but it served our turn. We didn't raise more than ten of the biggest men, because we didn't want to make the Degree common. And they was clamouring to be raised.

'"In another six months," says Dravot, "we'll hold another Communication, and see how you are working." Then he asks them about their villages, and learns that they was fighting one against the other, and were sick and tired of it. And when they wasn't doing that they was fighting with the Mohammedans. "You can fight those when they come into our country," says Dravot. "Tell off every tenth man of your tribes for a Frontier guard, and send two hundred at a time to this valley to be drilled. Nobody is going to be shot or speared any more so long as he does well, and I know that you won't cheat me, because you're white people – sons of Alexander – and not like common, black Mohammedans. You are *my* people, and by God," says he, running off into English at the end – "I'll make a damned fine nation of you, or I'll die in the making!"

'I can't tell all we did for the next six months, because Dravot did a lot I couldn't see the hang of, and he learned their lingo in a way I never could. My work was to help the people plough, and now and again go out with some of the Army and see what the other villages were doing, and make 'em throw rope-bridges across the ravines which cut up the country horrid. Dravot was very kind to me, but when he walked up and down in the pine wood pulling that bloody red beard of his with both fists I knew he was thinking plans I could not advise about, and I just waited for orders.

'But Dravot never showed me disrespect before the people. They were afraid of me and the Army, but they loved Dan. He was the best of friends with the priests and the chiefs; but anyone could come across the hills with a complaint, and Dravot would hear him out fair, and call four priests together and say what was to be done. He used to call in Billy Fish from Bashkai, and Pikky Kergan from Shu, and an old chief we called Kafuzelum – it was like enough to his real name – and hold councils with 'em when there was any fighting to be done in small villages. That was his Council of War, and the four priests of Bashkai, Shu, Khawak, and Madora was his Privy Council. Between the lot of 'em they sent me, with forty men and twenty rifles and sixty men carrying turquoises, into the Ghorband country to buy those hand-made Martini rifles, that come out of the Amir's workshops at Kabul, from one of the Amir's Herati regiments that would have sold the very teeth out of their mouths for turquoises.

'I stayed in Ghorband a month, and gave the Governor there the pick of my baskets for hush-money, and bribed the Colonel of the regiment some more, and, between the two and the tribes-people, we got more than a hundred hand-made Martinis, a hundred good Kohat Jezails that'll throw to six hundred yards, and forty man-loads of very bad ammunition for the rifles. I came back with what I had, and distributed 'em among the men that the chiefs sent in to me to drill. Dravot was too busy to attend to those things, but the old Army that we first made helped me, and we turned out five hundred men that could drill, and two hundred that knew how to hold arms pretty straight. Even those cork-screwed, hand-made guns was a miracle to them. Dravot talked big about powder-shops and factories, walking up and down in the pine wood when the winter was coming on.

'"I won't make a nation," says he. "I'll make an empire! These men aren't niggers; they're English! Look at their eyes – look at their mouths. Look at the way they stand up. They sit on chairs in their own houses. They're the Lost Tribes, or something like it, and they've grown to be English. I'll take a census in the spring if the priests don't get frightened. There must be a fair two million of 'em in these hills. The villages are full o' little children. Two million people – two hundred and fifty thousand fighting men – and all English! They only want the rifles and a little drilling. Two hundred and fifty thousand men, ready to cut in on Russia's right flank when she tries for India! Peachey, man," he says, chewing his beard in great hunks, "we shall be Emperors–Emperors of the Earth! Rajah Brooke will be a suckling to us. I'll treat with the Viceroy on equal terms. I'll ask him to send me twelve picked English – twelve that I know of – to help us govern a bit. There's Mackray, Sergeant-pensioner at Segowli – many's the good dinner he's given me, and his wife a pair of trousers. There's Donkin, the Warder of Tounghoo Jail; there's hundreds that I could lay my hand on if I was in India. The Viceroy shall do it for me. I'll send a man through in the spring for those men, and I'll write for a dispensation from the Grand Lodge for what I've done as Grand-Master. That – and all the Sniders that'll be thrown out when the native troops in India take up the Martini. They'll be worn smooth, but they'll do for fighting in these hills. Twelve English, a hundred thousand Sniders run through the Amir's country in driblets – I'd be content with twenty thousand in one year – and we'd be an empire. When everything was shipshape, I'd hand over the crown – this crown I'm wearing now – to Queen Victoria on my knees, and she'd say: 'Rise up, Sir Daniel Dravot.' Oh, it's big! It's big, I tell you! But there's so much to be done in every place – Bashkai, Khawak, Shu, and everywhere else."

'"What is it?" I says. "There are no more men coming in to be drilled this autumn. Look at those fat, black clouds. They're bringing the snow."

'"It isn't that," says Daniel, putting his hand very hard on my shoulder; "and I don't wish to say anything that's against you, for no other living man would have followed me and made me what I am as you have done. You're a first-class Commander-in-Chief, and the people know you; but – it's a big country, and somehow you can't help me, Peachey, in the way I want to be helped."

'"Go to your blasted priests, then!" I said, and I was sorry when I made that remark, but it did hurt me sore to find Daniel talking so superior when I'd drilled all the men, and done all he told me.

'"Don't let's quarrel, Peachey," says Daniel without cursing. "You're a King too, and the half of this Kingdom is yours; but can't you see, Peachey, we want cleverer men than us now – three or four of 'em, that we can scatter about for our Deputies. It's a hugeous great state, and I can't always tell the right thing to do, and I haven't time for all I want to do, and here's the winter coming on and all." He put half his beard into his mouth, all red like the gold of his crown.

'"I'm sorry, Daniel," says I. "I've done all I could. I've drilled the men and shown the people how to stack their oats better; and I've brought in those tinware rifles from Ghorband – but I know what you're driving at. I take it Kings always feel oppressed that way."

'"There's another thing too," says Dravot, walking up and down. "The winter's coming and these people won't be giving much trouble, and if they do we can't move about. I want a wife."

'"For Gord's sake leave the women alone!" I says. "We've both got all the work we can, though I *am* a fool. Remember the Contrack, and keep clear o' women."

'"The Contrack only lasted till such time as we was Kings; and Kings we have been these months past," says Dravot, weighing his crown in his hand. "You go get a wife too, Peachey – a nice, strappin', plump girl that'll keep you warm in the winter. They're prettier than English girls, and we can take the pick of 'em. Boil 'em once or twice in hot water and they'll come out like chicken and ham."

'"Don't tempt me!" I says. "I will not have any dealings with a woman not till we are a dam' side more settled than we are now. I've been doing the work o' two men, and you've been doing the work o' three. Let's lie off a bit, and see if we can get some better tobacco from Afghan country and run in some good liquor; but no women."

'"Who's talking o' *women*?" says Dravot. "I said *wife* – a Queen to breed a King's son for the King. A Queen out of the strongest tribe, that'll make them your blood-brothers, and that'll lie by your side and tell you all the people thinks about you and their own affairs. That's what I want."

'"Do you remember that Bengali woman I kept at Mogul Serai when I was a plate-layer?" says I. "A fat lot o' good she was to me. She taught me the lingo and one or two other things; but what happened? She ran away with the station-master's servant and half my month's pay. Then she turned up at Dadur Junction in tow of a half-caste, and had the impidence to say I was her husband – all among the drivers in the running-shed too!"

'"We've done with that," says Dravot; "these women are whiter than you or me, and a Queen I will have for the winter months."

'" For the last time o' asking, Dan, do *not*," I says. "It'll only bring us harm. The Bible says that Kings ain't to waste their strength on women, 'specially when they've got a new raw Kingdom to work over."

'"For the last time of answering I will," said Dravot, and he went away through the pine trees looking like a big red devil, the sun being on his crown and beard and all.

'But getting a wife was not as easy as Dan thought. He put it before the Council, and there was no answer till Billy Fish said that he'd better ask the girls. Dravot damned them all round. "What's wrong with me?" he shouts, standing by the idol Imbra. "Am I a dog or am I not enough of a man for your wenches? Haven't I put the shadow of my hand over this country? Who stopped the last Afghan raid?" It was me really, but Dravot was too angry to remember. "Who bought your guns? Who repaired the bridges? Who's the Grand-Master of the sign cut in the stone?" says he, and he thumped his hand on the block that he used to sit on in Lodge, and at Council, which opened like Lodge always. Billy Fish said nothing and no more did the others. "Keep your hair on, Dan," said I; "and ask the girls. That's how it's done at home, and these people are quite English."

'"The marriage of the King is a matter of State," says Dan, in a white-hot rage, for he could feel, I hope, that he was going against his better mind. He walked out of the Council-room, and the others sat still, looking at the ground.

'"Billy Fish," says I to the Chief of Bashkai, "what's the difficulty here? A straight answer to a true friend."

'"You know," says Billy Fish. "How should a man tell you who knows everything? How can daughters of men marry Gods or Devils? It's not proper."

'I remembered something like that in the Bible; but if, after seeing us as long as they had, they still believed we were Gods, it wasn't for me to undeceive them.

'"A God can do anything," says I. "If the King is fond of a girl he'll not let her die." – "She'll have to," said Billy Fish. "There are all sorts of Gods and Devils in these mountains, and now and again a girl marries one of them and isn't seen any more. Besides, you two know the Mark cut in the stone. Only the Gods know that. We thought you were men till you showed the sign of the Master."

'I wished then that we had explained about the loss of the genuine secrets of a Master-Mason at the first go-off; but I said nothing. All that night there was a blowing of horns in a little dark temple half-way down the hill, and I heard a girl crying fit to die. One of the priests told us that she was being prepared to marry the King.

'"I'll have no nonsense of that kind," says Dan. "I don't want to interfere with your customs, but I'll take my own wife." – "The girl's a little bit afraid," says the priest. "She thinks she's going to die, and they are a-heartening of her up down in the temple."

'"Hearten her very tender, then," says Dravot, "or I'll hearten you with the butt of a gun so you'll never want to be heartened again." He licked his lips, did Dan, and stayed up walking about more than half the night, thinking of the wife that he was going to get in the morning. I wasn't any means comfortable, for I knew that dealings with a woman in foreign parts, though you was a crowned King twenty times over, could not but be risky. I got up very early in the morning while Dravot was asleep, and I saw the priests talking together in whispers, and the Chiefs talking together too, and they looked at me out of the corners of their eyes.

'"What is up, Fish?" I say to the Bashkai man, who was wrapped up in his furs and looking splendid to behold.

'"I can't rightly say," says he; "but if you can make the King drop all this nonsense about marriage, you'll be doing him and me and yourself a great service."

'"That I do believe," says I. "But sure, you know, Billy, as well as me, having fought against and for us, that the King and me are nothing more than two of the finest men that God Almighty ever made. Nothing more, I do assure you."

'"That may be," says Billy Fish, "and yet I should be sorry if it was." He sinks his head upon his great fur cloak for a minute and thinks. "King," says he, "be you man or God or Devil, I'll stick by you today. I have twenty of my men with me, and they will follow me. We'll go to Bashkai until the storm blows over."

'A little snow had fallen in the night, and everything was white except the greasy fat clouds that blew down and down from the north. Dravot came out with his crown on his head, swinging his arms and stamping his feet, and looking more pleased than Punch.

'"For the last time, drop it, Dan," says I in a whisper, "Billy Fish here says that there will be a row."

'"A row among my people!" says Dravot. "Not much. Peachey, you're a fool not to get a wife too. Where's the girl?" says he with a voice as loud as the braying of a jackass. "Call up all the Chiefs and priests, and let the Emperor see if his wife suits him."

'There was no need to call any one. They were all there leaning on their guns and spears round the clearing in the centre of the pine wood. A lot of priests went down to the little temple to bring up the girl, and the horns blew fit to wake the dead. Billy Fish saunters round and gets as close to Daniel as he could, and behind him stood his twenty men with matchlocks. Not a man of them under six feet. I was next to Dravot, and behind me was twenty men of the regular Army. Up comes the girl, and a strapping wench she was, covered with silver and turquoises, but white as death, and looking back every minute at the priests.

'"She'll do," said Dan, looking her over. "What's to be afraid of, lass? Come and kiss me." He puts his arm round her. She shuts her eyes, gives a bit of a squeak, and down goes her face in the side of Dan's flaming red beard.

'"The slut's bitten me!" says he, clapping his hand to his neck, and, sure enough, his hand was red with blood. Billy Fish and two of his matchlock-men catches hold of Dan by the shoulders and drags him into the Bashkai lot, while the priests howls in their lingo – "Neither God nor Devil but a man!" I was all taken aback, for a priest cut at me in front, and the Army behind began firing into the Bashkai men.

'"God A'mighty!" says Dan. "What is the meaning o' this?"

'"Come back! Come away!" says Billy Fish. "Ruin and mutiny is the matter. We'll break for Bashkai if we can."

'I tried to give some sort of orders to my men – the men o' the regular Army – but it was no use, so I fired into the brown of 'em with an English Martini and drilled three beggars in a line. The valley was full of shouting, howling creatures, and every soul was shrieking, "Not a God nor a Devil but only a man!" The Bashkai troops stuck to Billy Fish all they were worth, but their matchlocks wasn't half as good as the Kabul breech-loaders, and four of them dropped. Dan was bellowing like a bull, for he was very wrathy; and Billy Fish had a hard job to prevent him running out at the crowd.

'"We can't stand," says Billy Fish. "Make a run for it down the valley! The whole place is against us." The matchlock-men ran, and we went down the valley in spite of Dravot. He was swearing horrible and crying out he was a King. The priests rolled great stones on us, and the regular Army fired hard, and there wasn't more than six men, not counting Dan, Billy Fish, and me, that came down to the bottom of the valley alive.

'Then they stopped firing and the horns in the temple blew again. "Come away – for God's sake come away!" says Billy Fish. "They'll send runners out to all the villages before ever we get to Bashkai. I can protect you there, but I can't do anything now."

'My own notion is that Dan began to go mad in his head from that hour. He stared up and down like a stuck pig. Then he was all for walking back alone and killing the priests with his bare hands; which he could have done. "An Emperor am I," says Daniel, "and next year I shall be a Knight of the Queen."

'"All right, Dan," says I; "but come along now while there's time."

'"It's your fault," says he, "for not looking after your Army better. There was mutiny in the midst, and you didn't know – you damned engine-driving, plate-laying, missionary's-pass-hunting hound!" He sat upon a rock and called me every foul name he could lay tongue to. I was too heart-sick to care, though it was all his foolishness that brought the smash.

'"I'm sorry, Dan," says I, "but there's no accounting for natives. This business is our Fifty-Seven. Maybe we'll make something out of it yet, when we've got to Bashkai."

'"Let's get to Bashkai, then," says Dan, "and, by God, when I come back here again I'll sweep the valley so there isn't a bug in a blanket left!"

'We walked all that day, and all that night Dan was stumping up and down on the snow, chewing his beard and muttering to himself.

'"There's no hope o' getting clear," said Billy Fish. "The priests will have sent runners to the villages to say that you are only men. Why didn't you stick on as Gods till things was more settled? I'm a dead man," says Billy Fish, and he throws himself down on the snow and begins to pray to his Gods.

'Next morning we was in a cruel bad country – all up and down, no level ground at all, and no food either. The six Bashkai men looked at Billy Fish hungry-way as if they wanted to ask something, but they said never a word. At noon we came to the top of a flat mountain all covered with snow, and when we climbed up into it, behold, there was an Army in position waiting in the middle!

'"The runners have been very quick," says Billy Fish, with a little bit of a laugh. "They are waiting for us."

'Three or four men began to fire from the enemy's side, and a chance shot took Daniel in the calf of the leg. That brought him to his senses. He looks across the snow at the Army, and sees the rifles that we had brought into the country.

'"We're done for," says he. "They are Englishmen, these people – and it's my blasted nonsense that has brought you to this. Get back, Billy Fish, and take your men away; you've done what you could, and now cut for it. Carnehan," says he, "shake hands with me and go along with Billy. Maybe they won't kill you. I'll go and meet 'em alone. It's me that did it. Me, the King!"

'"Go!" says I. "Go to Hell, Dan! I'm with you here. Billy Fish, you clear out, and we two will meet those folk."

'"I'm a Chief," says Billy Fish, quite quiet. "I stay with you. My men can go."

'The Bashkai fellows didn't wait for a second word, but ran off, and Dan and me and Billy Fish walked across to where the drums were drumming and the horns were horning. It was cold – awful cold. I've got that cold in the back of my head now. There's a lump of it there.'

The punkah-coolies had gone to sleep. Two kerosene lamps were blazing in the office, and the perspiration poured down my face and splashed on the blotter as I leaned forward. Carnehan was shivering, and I feared that his mind might go. I wiped my face, took a fresh grip of the piteously mangled hands, and said: 'What happened after that?'

The momentary shift of my eyes had broken the clear current.

'What was you pleased to say?' whined Carnehan. 'They took them without any sound. Not a little whisper all along the snow, not though the King knocked down the first man that set hand on him – not though old Peachey fired his last cartridge into the brown of 'em. Not a single solitary sound did those swines make. They just closed up tight, and I tell you their furs stunk. There was a man called Billy Fish, a good friend of us all, and they cut his throat, sir, then and there, like a pig; and the King kicks up the bloody snow and says: "We've had a dashed fine run for our money. What's coming next?" But Peachey, Peachey Taliaferro, I tell you, sir, in confidence as betwixt two friends, he lost his head, sir. No, he didn't neither. The King lost his head, so he did, all along o' one of those cunning rope-bridges. Kindly let me have the paper-cutter, sir. It tilted this way. They marched him a mile across that snow to a rope-bridge over a ravine with a river at the bottom. You may have seen such. They prodded him behind like an ox. "Damn your eyes!" says the King. "D'you suppose I can't die like a gentleman?" He turns to Peachey – Peachey that was crying like a child. "I've brought you to this, Peachey," says he. "Brought you out of your happy life to be killed in Kafiristan, where you was late Commander-in-Chief of the Emperor's forces. Say you forgive me, Peachey." – "I do," says Peachey. "Fully and freely do I forgive you, Dan." – "Shake hands, Peachey," says he. "I'm going now." Out he goes, looking neither right nor left, and when he was plumb in the middle of those dizzy dancing ropes — "Cut, you beggars," he shouts; and they cut, and old Dan fell, turning round and round and round, twenty thousand miles, for he took half an hour to fall till he struck the water, and I could see his body caught on a rock with the gold crown close beside.

'But do you know what they did to Peachey between two pine trees? They crucified him, sir, as Peachey's hand will show. They used wooden pegs for his hands and his feet; and he didn't die. He hung there and screamed, and they took him down next day, and said it was a miracle that he wasn't dead. They took him down – poor old Peachey that hadn't done them any harm – that hadn't done them any —'

He rocked to and fro and wept bitterly, wiping his eyes with the back of his scarred hands and moaning like a child for some ten minutes.

'They was cruel enough to feed him up in the temple, because they said he was more of a God than old Daniel that was a man. Then they turned him out on the snow, and told him to go home, and Peachey came home in about a year, begging along the roads quite safe; for Daniel Dravot he walked before and said: "Come along, Peachey. It's a big thing we're doing." The mountains they danced at night, and the mountains they tried to fall on Peachey's head, but Dan he held up his hand, and Peachey came along bent double. He never let go of Dan's hand and he never let go of Dan's head. They gave it to him as a present in the temple, to remind him not to come again, and though the crown was pure gold, and Peachey was starving, never would Peachey sell the same. You knew Dravot, sir! You knew Right Worshipful Brother Dravot! Look at him now!'

He fumbled in the mass of rags round his bent waist; brought out a black horsehair bag embroidered with silver thread, and shook therefrom on to my table – the dried, withered head of Daniel Dravot! The morning sun that had long been paling the lamps struck the red beard and blind sunken eyes; struck, too, a heavy circlet of gold studded with raw turquoises, that Carnehan placed tenderly on the battered temples.

'You be'old now,' said Carnehan, 'the Emperor in his 'abit as he lived – the King of Kafiristan with his crown upon his head. Poor old Daniel that was a monarch once!'

I shuddered, for in spite of defacements manifold, I recognized the head of the man of Marwar Junction. Carnehan rose to go. I attempted to stop him. He was not fit to walk abroad. 'Let me take away the whisky, and give me a little money,' he gasped. 'I was a

King once. I'll go to the Deputy Commissioner and ask to set in the poorhouse till I get my health. No, thank you, I can't wait till you get a carriage for me. I've urgent private affairs – in the south – at Marwar.'

He shambled out of the office and departed in the direction of the Deputy Commissioner's house. That day at noon I had occasion to go down the blinding hot Mall, and I saw a crooked man crawling along the white dust of the roadside, his hat in his hand, quavering dolorously after the fashion of the street-singers at home. There was not a soul in sight, and he was out of all possible earshot of the houses. And he sang through his nose, turning his head from right to left:

'The Son of Man goes forth to war,
  A golden crown to gain;
His blood-red banner streams afar –
  Who follows in his train?'

I waited to hear no more, but put the poor wretch into my carriage and drove him off to the nearest missionary for eventual transfer to the asylum. He repeated the hymn twice while he was with me whom he did not in the least recognize, and I left him singing it to the missionary.

Two days later I inquired after his welfare of the Superintendent of the asylum.

'He was admitted suffering from sunstroke. He died early yesterday morning,' said the Superintendent. 'Is it true that he was half an hour bare-headed in the sun at midday?'

'Yes,' said I, 'but do you happen to know if he had anything upon him by any chance when he died?'

'Not to my knowledge,' said the Superintendent.

And there the matter rests.

Baa Baa, Black Sheep

Baa Baa, Black Sheep,
Have you any wool?
Yes, Sir, yes, Sir, three bags full.
One for the Master, one for the Dame–
None for the Little Boy that cries down the lane.

Nursery Rhyme

THE FIRST BAG

When I was in my father's house, I was in a better place.

THEY were putting Punch to bed – the *ayah* and the *hamal* and Meeta, the big *Surti* boy, with the red and gold turban. Judy, already tucked inside her mosquito-curtains, was nearly asleep. Punch had been allowed to stay up for dinner. Many privileges had been accorded to Punch within the last ten days, and a greater kindness from the people of his world had encompassed his ways and works, which were mostly obstreperous. He sat on the edge of his bed and swung his bare legs defiantly.

'Punch-*baba* going to bye-lo?' said the *ayah* suggestively.

'No,' said Punch. 'Punch-*baba* wants the story about the Ranee that was turned into a tiger. Meeta must tell it, and the *hamal* shall hide behind the door and make tiger-noises at the proper time.'

'But Judy-*baba* will wake up,' said the *ayah*.

'Judy-*baba* is waked,' piped a small voice from the mosquito-curtains. 'There was a Ranee that lived at Delhi. Go on, Meeta,' and she fell fast asleep again while Meeta began the story.

Never had Punch secured the telling of that tale with so little opposition. He reflected for a long time. The *hamal* made the tiger-noises in twenty different keys.

''Top!' said Punch authoritatively. 'Why doesn't Papa come in and say he is going to give me *put-put*?'

'Punch-*baba* is going away,' said the *ayah*. 'In another week there will be no Punch-*baba* to pull my hair any more.' She sighed softly, for the boy of the household was very dear to her heart.

'Up the Ghauts in a train?' said Punch, standing on his bed. 'All the way to Nassick where the Ranee-Tiger lives?'

'Not to Nassick this year, little Sahib,' said Meeta, lifting him on his shoulder. 'Down to the sea where the coconuts are thrown, and across the sea in a big ship. Will you take Meeta with you to *Belait?*'

'You shall all come,' said Punch, from the height of Meeta's strong arms. 'Meeta and the *ayah* and the *hamal* and Bhini-in-the-Garden, and the salaam-Captain-Sahib-snake-man.'

There was no mockery in Meeta's voice when he replied – 'Great is the Sahib's favour,' and laid the little man down in the bed, while the *ayah*, sitting in the moonlight at the doorway, lulled him to sleep with an interminable canticle such as they sing in the Roman Catholic Church at Parel. Punch curled himself into a ball and slept.

Next morning Judy shouted that there was a rat in the nursery, and thus he forgot to tell her the wonderful news. It did not much matter, for Judy was only three and she would not have understood. But Punch was five; and he knew that going to England would be much nicer than a trip to Nassick.

Papa and Mamma sold the brougham and the piano, and stripped the house, and curtailed the allowance of crockery for the daily meals, and took long counsel together over a bundle of letters bearing the Rocklington postmark.

'The worst of it is that one can't be certain of anything,' said Papa, pulling his moustache. 'The letters in themselves are excellent, and the terms are moderate enough.'

'The worst of it is that the children will grow up away from me,' thought Mamma; but she did not say it aloud.

'We are only one case among hundreds,' said Papa bitterly. 'You shall go home again in five years, dear.'

'Punch will be ten then – and Judy eight. Oh, how long and long and long the time will be! And we have to leave them among strangers.'

'Punch is a cheery little chap. He's sure to make friends wherever he goes.'

'And who could help loving my Ju?'

They were standing over the cots in the nursery late at night, and I think that Mamma was crying softly. After Papa had gone away, she knelt down by the side of Judy's cot. The *ayah* saw her and put up a prayer that the Memsahib might never find the love of her children taken away from her and given to a stranger.

Mamma's own prayer was a slightly illogical one. Summarized it ran: 'Let strangers love my children and be as good to them as I should be, but let *me* preserve their love and their confidence for ever and ever. Amen.' Punch scratched himself in his sleep, and Judy moaned a little.

Next day they all went down to the sea, and there was a scene at the Apollo Bunder when Punch discovered that Meeta could not come too, and Judy learned that the *ayah* must be left behind. But Punch found a thousand fascinating things in the rope, block, and steam-pipe line on the big P. and O. steamer long before Meeta and the *ayah* had dried their tears.

'Come back, Punch-*baba*,' said the *ayah*.

'Come back,' said Meeta, 'and be a *Burra Sahib*' (a big man).

'Yes,' said Punch, lifted up in his father's arms to wave goodbye. 'Yes, I will come back, and I will be a *Burra Sahib Bahadur*!' (a very big man indeed).

At the end of the first day Punch demanded to be set down in England, which he was certain must be close at hand. Next day there was a merry breeze, and Punch was very sick. 'When I come back to Bombay,' said Punch on his recovery, 'I will come by the road – in a broom-*gharri*. This is a very naughty ship.'

The Swedish boatswain consoled him, and he modified his opinions as the voyage went on. There was so much to see and to handle and ask questions about that Punch nearly forgot the *ayah* and Meeta and the *hamal*, and with difficulty remembered a few words of the Hindustani once his second-speech.

But Judy was much worse. The day before the steamer reached Southampton, Mamma asked her if she would not like to see the *ayah* again. Judy's blue eyes turned to the stretch of sea that had swallowed all her tiny past, and she said: '*Ayah!* What *ayah*?'

Mamma cried over her and Punch marvelled. It was then that he heard for the first time Mamma's passionate appeal to him never to let Judy forget Mamma. Seeing that Judy was young, ridiculously young, and that Mamma, every evening for four weeks past, had come into the cabin to sing her and Punch to sleep with a mysterious rune that he called 'Sonny, my soul,' Punch could not understand what Mamma meant. But he strove to do his duty; for, the moment Mamma left the cabin, he said to Judy: 'Ju, you bemember Mamma?'

''Torse I do,' said Judy.

'Then *always* bemember Mamma, 'r else I won't give you the paper ducks that the red-haired Captain Sahib cut out for me.'

So Judy promised always to 'bemember Mamma'.

Many and many a time was Mamma's command laid upon Punch, and Papa would say the same thing with an insistence that awed the child.

'You must make haste and learn to write, Punch,' said Papa, 'and then you'll be able to write letters to us in Bombay.'

'I'll come into your room,' said Punch, and Papa choked.

Papa and Mamma were always choking in those days. If Punch took Judy to task for not 'bemembering', they choked. If Punch sprawled on the sofa in the Southampton lodging-house and sketched his future in purple and gold, they choked; and so they did if Judy put up her mouth for a kiss.

Through many days all four were vagabonds on the face of the earth – Punch with no one to give orders to, Judy too young for anything, and Papa and Mamma grave, distracted, and choking.

'Where,' demanded Punch, wearied of a loathsome contrivance on four wheels with a mound of luggage atop – '*where* is our broom-*gharri*? This thing talks so much that *I* can't talk. Where is our *own* broom-*gharri*? When I was at Bandstand before we comed away, I asked Inverarity Sahib why he was sitting in it, and he said it was his own. And I said, "I will *give* it you" – I like Inverarity Sahib – and I said, "Can you put your legs through the pully-wag loops by the windows?" And Inverarity Sahib said No, and laughed. *I* can put my legs through the pully-wag loops. I can put my legs through *these* pully-wag loops. Look! Oh, Mamma's crying again! I didn't know I wasn't not to do *so*.'

Punch drew his legs out of the loops of the four-wheeler: the door opened and he slid to the earth, in a cascade of parcels, at the door of an austere little villa whose gates bore the legend 'Downe Lodge'. Punch gathered himself together and eyed the house with disfavour. It stood on a sandy road, and a cold wind tickled his knicker-bockered legs.

'Let us go away,' said Punch. 'This is not a pretty place.'

But Mamma and Papa and Judy had left the cab, and all the luggage was being taken into the house. At the doorstep stood a woman in black, and she smiled largely, with dry chapped lips. Behind her was a man, big, bony, grey, and lame as to one leg – behind him a boy of twelve, black-haired and oily in appearance. Punch surveyed the trio, and advanced without fear, as he had been accustomed to do in Bombay when callers came and he happened to be playing in the veranda.

'How do you do?' said he. 'I am Punch.' But they were all looking at the luggage – all except the grey man, who shook hands with Punch, and said he was a 'smart little fellow'. There was much running about and banging of boxes, and Punch curled himself up on the sofa in the dining-room and considered things.

'I don't like these people,' said Punch. 'But never mind. We'll go away soon. We have always went away soon from everywhere. I wish we was gone back to Bombay *soon*.'

The wish bore no fruit. For six days Mamma wept at intervals, and showed the woman in black all Punch's clothes – a liberty which Punch resented. 'But p'raps she's a new white *ayah*,' he thought. 'I'm to call her Antirosa, but she doesn't call *me* Sahib. She says just Punch,' he confided to Judy. 'What is Antirosa?'

Judy didn't know. Neither she nor Punch had heard anything of an animal called an aunt. Their world had been Papa and Mamma, who knew everything, permitted everything, and loved everybody – even Punch when he used to go into the garden at Bombay and fill his nails with mould after the weekly nail-cutting, because, as he explained between two strokes of the slipper to his sorely-tried Father, his fingers 'felt so new at the ends'.

In an undefined way Punch judged it advisable to keep both parents between himself and the woman in black and the boy in black hair. He did not approve of them. He liked the grey man, who had expressed a wish to be called 'Uncleharri'. They nodded at each other when they met, and the grey man showed him a little ship with rigging that took up and down.

'She's a model of the *Brisk* – the little *Brisk* that was sore exposed that day at Navarino.' The grey man hummed the last words and fell into a reverie. 'I'll tell you about Navarino, Punch, when we go for walks together; and you mustn't touch the ship, because she's the *Brisk*.'

Long before that walk, the first of many, was taken, they roused Punch and Judy in the chill dawn of a February morning to say Goodbye; and of all people in the wide earth to Papa and Mamma – both crying this time. Punch was very sleepy and Judy was cross.

'Don't forget us,' pleaded Mamma. 'Oh, my little son, don't forget us, and see that Judy remembers too.'

'I've told Judy to bemember,' said Punch, wriggling, for his father's beard tickled his neck, 'I've told Judy – ten – forty – 'leven thousand times. But Ju's so young – quite a baby – isn't she?'

'Yes,' said Papa, 'quite a baby, and you must be good to Judy, and make haste to learn to write and – and – and —'

Punch was back in his bed again. Judy was fast asleep, and there was the rattle of a cab below. Papa and Mamma had gone away. Not to Nassick; that was across the sea. To some place much nearer, of course, and equally of course they would return. They came back after dinner-parties, and Papa had come back after he had been to a place called 'The Snows', and Mamma with him, to Punch and Judy at Mrs Inverarity's house in Marine Lines. Assuredly they would come back again. So Punch fell asleep till the true morning, when the black-haired boy met him with the information that Papa and Mamma had gone to Bombay, and that he and Judy were to stay at Downe Lodge 'for ever'. Antirosa, tearfully appealed to for a contradiction, said that Harry had spoken the truth, and that it behoved Punch to fold up his clothes neatly on going to bed. Punch went out and wept bitterly with Judy, into whose fair head he had driven some ideas of the meaning of separation.

When a matured man discovers that he has been deserted by Providence, deprived of his God, and cast without help, comfort, or sympathy, upon a world which is new and strange to him, his despair, which may find expression in evil-living, the writing of his experiences, or the more satisfactory diversion of suicide, is generally supposed to be impressive. A child, under exactly similar circumstances as far as its knowledge goes, cannot very well curse God and die. It howls till its nose is red, its eyes are sore, and its head aches. Punch and Judy, through no fault of their own, had lost all their world. They sat in the hall and cried; the black-haired boy looking on from afar.

The model of the ship availed nothing, though the grey man assured Punch that he might pull the rigging up and down as much as he pleased; and Judy was promised free entry into the kitchen. They wanted Papa and Mamma gone to Bombay beyond the seas, and their grief while it lasted was without remedy.

When the tears ceased the house was very still. Antirosa had decided that it was better to let the children 'have their cry out', and the boy had gone to school. Punch raised his head from the floor and sniffed mournfully. Judy was nearly asleep. Three short years had not taught her how to bear sorrow with full knowledge. There was a distant, dull boom in the air – a repeated heavy thud. Punch knew that sound in Bombay in the Monsoon. It was the sea – the sea that must be traversed before anyone could get to Bombay.

'Quick, Ju!' he cried, 'we're close to the sea. I can hear it! Listen! That's where they've went. P'raps we can catch them if we was in time. They didn't mean to go without us. They've only forgot.'

'Iss,' said Judy. 'They've only forgotted. Less go to the sea.'

The hall-door was open and so was the garden-gate.

'It's very, very big, this place,' he said, looking cautiously down the road, 'and we will get lost; but *I* will find a man and order him to take me back to my house – like I did in Bombay.'

He took Judy by the hand, and the two ran hatless in the direction of the sound of the sea. Downe Villa was almost the last of a range of newly-built houses running out, through a field of brick-mounds, to a heath where gypsies occasionally camped and where the Garrison Artillery of Rocklington practised. There were few people to be seen, and the children might have been taken for those of the soldiery who ranged far. Half an hour the wearied little legs tramped across heath, potato-patch, and sand-dune.

'I'se so tired,' said Judy, 'and Mamma will be angry.'

'Mamma's *never* angry. I suppose she is waiting at the sea now while Papa gets tickets. We'll find them and go along with them. Ju, you mustn't sit down. Only a little more and we'll come to the sea. Ju, if you sit down I'll *thmack* you!' said Punch.

They climbed another dune, and came upon the great grey sea at low tide. Hundreds of crabs were scuttling about the beach, but there was no trace of Papa and Mamma, not even of a ship upon the waters – nothing but sand and mud for miles and miles.

And 'Uncleharri' found them by chance – very muddy and very forlorn – Punch dissolved in tears, but trying to divert Judy with an 'ickle trab', and Judy wailing to the pitiless horizon for 'Mamma, Mamma!' – and again 'Mamma!'

THE SECOND BAG

Ah, well-a-day, for we are souls bereaved!
Of all the creatures under Heaven's wide scope
We are most hopeless, who had once most hope,
And most beliefless, who had most believed.
The City of Dreadful Night

All this time not a word about Black Sheep. He came later, and Harry the black-haired boy was mainly responsible for his coming.

Judy – who could help loving little Judy? – passed, by special permit, into the kitchen and thence straight to Aunty Rosa's heart. Harry was Aunty Rosa's one child, and Punch was the extra boy about the house. There was no special place for him or his little affairs, and he was forbidden to sprawl on sofas and explain his ideas about the manufacture of this world and his hopes for his future. Sprawling was lazy and wore out sofas, and little boys were not expected to talk. They were talked to, and the talking to was intended for the benefit of their morals. As the unquestioned despot of the house at Bombay, Punch could not quite understand how he came to be of no account in this his new life.

Harry might reach across the table and take what he wanted; Judy might point and get what she wanted. Punch was forbidden to do either. The grey man was his great hope and stand-by for many months after Mamma and Papa left, and he had forgotten to tell Judy to 'bemember Mamma'.

This lapse was excusable, because in the interval he had been introduced by Aunty Rosa to two very impressive things – an abstraction called God, the intimate friend and ally of Aunty Rosa, generally believed to live behind the kitchen-range because it was hot there – and a dirty brown book filled with unintelligible dots and marks. Punch was always anxious to oblige everyone. He therefore welded the story of the Creation on to what he could recollect of his Indian fairy tales, and scandalized Aunty Rosa by repeating the result to Judy. It was a sin, a grievous sin, and Punch was talked to for a quarter of an hour. He could not understand where the iniquity came in, but was careful not to repeat the offence, because Aunty Rosa told him that God had heard every word he had said and was very angry. If this were true why didn't God come and say so, thought Punch, and dismissed the matter from his mind. Afterwards he learned to know the Lord as the only thing in the world more awful than Aunty Rosa – as a creature that stood in the background and counted the strokes of the cane.

But the reading was, just then, a much more serious matter than any creed. Aunty Rosa sat him upon a table and told him that A B meant ab.

'Why?' said Punch. 'A is a and B is bee. *Why* does A B mean ab?'

'Because I tell you it does,' said Aunty Rosa, 'and you've got to say it.'

Punch said it accordingly, and for a month, hugely against his will, stumbled through the brown book, not in the least comprehending what it meant. But Uncle Harry, who walked much and generally alone, was wont to come into the nursery and suggest to Aunty Rosa that Punch should walk with him. He seldom spoke, but he showed Punch all Rocklington, from the mudbanks and the sand of the back-bay to the great harbours where ships lay at anchor, and the dockyards where the hammers were never still, and the marine-store shops, and the shiny brass counters in the offices where Uncle Harry went once every three months with a slip of blue paper and received sovereigns in exchange; for he held a wound-pension. Punch heard, too, from his lips the story of the battle of Navarino, where the sailors of the Fleet, for three days afterwards, were deaf as posts and could only sign to each other. 'That was because of the noise of the guns,' said Uncle Harry, 'and I have got the wadding of a bullet somewhere inside me now.'

Punch regarded him with curiosity. He had not the least idea what wadding was, and his notion of a bullet was a dockyard cannonball bigger than his own head. How could Uncle Harry keep a cannonball inside him? He was ashamed to ask, for fear Uncle Harry might be angry.

Punch had never known what anger – real anger – meant until one terrible day when Harry had taken his paint-box to paint a boat with, and Punch had protested. Then Uncle Harry had appeared on the scene and, muttering something about 'strangers' children', had with a stick smitten the black-haired boy across the shoulders till he wept and yelled, and Aunty Rosa came in and abused Uncle Harry for cruelty to his own flesh and blood, and Punch shuddered to the tips of his shoes. 'It wasn't my fault,' he explained to the boy, but both Harry and Aunty Rosa said that it was, and that Punch had told tales, and for a week there were no more walks with Uncle Harry.

But that week brought a great joy to Punch.

He had repeated till he was thrice weary the statement that 'the Cat lay on the Mat and the Rat came in'.

'Now I can truly read,' said Punch, 'and now I will never read anything in the world.'

He put the brown book in the cupboard where his schoolbooks lived and accidentally tumbled out a venerable volume, without covers, labelled *Sharpe's Magazine*. There was the most portentous picture of a griffin on the first page, with verses below. The griffin carried off one sheep a day from a German village, till a man came with a 'falchion' and split the griffin open. Goodness only knew what a falchion was, but there was the griffin, and his history was an improvement upon the eternal cat.

'This,' said Punch, 'means things, and now I will know all about everything in all the world.' He read till the light failed, not understanding a tithe of the meaning, but tantalized by glimpses of new worlds hereafter to be revealed.

'What is a "falchion"? What is a "e-wee lamb"? What is a "base *uss*urper"? What is a "verdant me-ad"?' he demanded with flushed cheeks, at bedtime, of the astonished Aunty Rosa.

'Say your prayers and go to sleep,' she replied, and that was all the help Punch then or afterwards found at her hands in the new and delightful exercise of reading.

'Aunty Rosa only knows about God and things like that,' argued Punch. 'Uncle Harry will tell me.'

The next walk proved that Uncle Harry could not help either; but he allowed Punch to talk, and even sat down on a bench to hear about the griffin. Other walks brought other stories as Punch ranged farther afield, for the house held large store of old books that no one ever opened – from *Frank Fairlegh* in serial numbers, and the earlier poems of Tennyson, contributed anonymously to *Sharpe's Magazine*, to '62 Exhibition Catalogues, gay with colours and delightfully incomprehensible, and odd leaves of *Gulliver's Travels.*

As soon as Punch could string a few pot-hooks together he wrote to Bombay, demanding by return of post 'all the books in all the world'. Papa could not comply with this modest indent, but sent *Grimm's Fairy Tales* and a Hans Andersen. That was enough. If he were only left alone Punch could pass, at any hour he chose, into a land of his own, beyond reach of Aunty Rosa and her God, Harry and his teasements, and Judy's claims to be played with.

'Don't disturve me, I'm reading. Go and play in the kitchen,' grunted Punch. 'Aunty Rosa lets *you* go there.' Judy was cutting her second teeth and was fretful. She appealed to Aunty Rosa, who descended on Punch.

'I was reading,' he explained, 'reading a book I *want* to read.'

'You're only doing that to show off,' said Aunty Rosa. 'But we'll see. Play with Judy now, and don't open a book for a week.'

Judy did not pass a very enjoyable playtime with Punch, who was consumed with indignation. There was a pettiness at the bottom of the prohibition which puzzled him.

'It's what I like to do,' he said, 'and she's found out that and stopped me. Don't cry, Ju – it wasn't your fault – *please* don't cry, or she'll say I made you.'

Ju loyally mopped up her tears, and the two played in their nursery, a room in the basement and half underground, to which they were regularly sent after the midday dinner while Aunty Rosa slept. She drank wine – that is to say, something from a bottle in the cellaret – for her stomach's sake, but if she did not fall asleep she would sometimes come into the nursery to see that the children were really playing. Now bricks, wooden hoops, ninepins, and chinaware cannot amuse for ever, especially when all Fairyland is to be won by the mere opening of a book, and, as often as not, Punch would be discovered reading to Judy or telling her interminable tales. That was an offence in the eyes of the law, and Judy would be whisked off by Aunty Rosa, while Punch was left to play alone, 'and be sure that I hear you doing it'.

It was not a cheering employ, for he had to make a playful noise. At last, with infinite craft, he devised an arrangement whereby a table could be supported as to three legs on toy bricks, leaving the fourth to bring down on the floor. He could work the table with one hand clear and hold a book with the other. This he did till an evil day when Aunty Rosa pounced upon him unawares and told him that he was 'acting a lie'.

'If you're old enough to do that,' she said – her temper was always worst after dinner – 'you're old enough to be beaten.'

'But – I'm – I'm not a animal!' said Punch aghast. He remembered Uncle Harry and the stick, and turned white. Aunty Rosa had hidden a light cane behind her, and Punch was beaten then and there over the shoulders. It was a revelation to him. The room door was shut, and he was left to weep himself into repentance and work out his own gospel of life.

Aunty Rosa, he argued, had the power to beat him with many stripes. It was unjust and cruel, and Mamma and Papa would never have allowed it. Unless perhaps, as Aunty Rosa seemed to imply, they had sent secret orders. In which case he was abandoned indeed. It would be discreet in the future to propitiate Aunty Rosa, but, then, again, even in matters in which he was innocent, he had been accused of wishing to 'show off'. He had 'shown off' before visitors when he had attacked a strange gentleman – Harry's uncle, not his own – with requests for information about the griffin and the falchion, and the precise nature of the Tilbury in which Frank Fairlegh rode – all points of paramount interest which he was bursting to understand. Clearly it would not do to pretend to care for Aunty Rosa.

At this point Harry entered and stood afar off, eyeing Punch, a dishevelled heap in the corner of the room, with disgust.

'You're a liar – a young liar,' said Harry, with great unction, 'and you're to have tea down here because you're not fit to speak to us. And you're not to speak to Judy again till Mother gives you leave. You'll corrupt her. You're only fit to associate with the servant. Mother says so.'

Having reduced Punch to a second agony of tears, Harry departed upstairs with the news that Punch was still rebellious.

Uncle Harry sat uneasily in the dining-room. 'Damn it all, Rosa,' said he at last, 'can't you leave the child alone? He's a good enough little chap when I meet him.'

'He puts on his best manners with you, Henry,' said Aunty Rosa, 'but I'm afraid, I'm very much afraid, that he is the Black Sheep of the family.'

Harry heard and stored up the name for future use. Judy cried till she was bidden to stop, her brother not being worth tears; and the evening concluded with the return of Punch to the upper regions and a private sitting at which all the blinding horrors of Hell were revealed to Punch with such store of imagery as Aunty Rosa's narrow mind possessed.

Most grievous of all was Judy's round-eyed reproach, and Punch went to bed in the depths of the Valley of Humiliation. He shared his room with Harry and knew the torture in store. For an hour and a half he had to answer that young gentleman's questions as to his motives for telling a lie, and a grievous lie, the precise quantity of punishment inflicted by Aunty Rosa, and had also to profess his deep gratitude for such religious instruction as Harry thought fit to impart.

From that day began the downfall of Punch, now Black Sheep.

'Untrustworthy in one thing, untrustworthy in all,' said Aunty Rosa, and Harry felt that Black Sheep was delivered into his hands. He would wake him up in the night to ask him why he was such a liar.

'I don't know,' Punch would reply.

'Then don't you think you ought to get up and pray to God for a new heart?'

'Y-yess.'

'Get out and pray, then!' And Punch would get out of bed with raging hate in his heart against all the world, seen and unseen. He was always tumbling into trouble. Harry had a knack of cross-examining him as to his day's doings, which seldom failed to lead him, sleepy and savage, into half a dozen contradictions – all duly reported to Aunty Rosa next morning.

'But it *wasn't* a lie,' Punch would begin, charging into a laboured explanation that landed him more hopelessly in the mire. 'I said that I didn't say my prayers *twice* over in the day, and *that* was on Tuesday. *Once* I did. I *know* I did, but Harry said I didn't,' and so forth, till the tension brought tears, and he was dismissed from the table in disgrace.

'You usen't to be as bad as this,' said Judy, awe-stricken at the catalogue of Black Sheep's crimes. 'Why are you so bad now?'

'I don't know,' Black Sheep would reply. 'I'm not, if I only wasn't bothered upside down. I knew what I *did*, and I want to say so; but Harry always makes it out different somehow, and Aunty Rosa doesn't believe a word I say. Oh, Ju! don't *you* say I'm bad too.'

'Aunty Rosa says you are,' said Judy. 'She told the Vicar so when he came yesterday.'

'Why does she tell all the people outside the house about me? It isn't fair,' said Black Sheep. 'When I was in Bombay, and was bad –

doing bad, not made-up bad like this – Mamma told Papa, and Papa told me he knew, and that was all. *Outside* people didn't know too – even Meeta didn't know.'

'I don't remember,' said Judy wistfully. 'I was all little then. Mamma was just as fond of you as she was of me, wasn't she?'

''Course she was. So was Papa. So was everybody.'

'Aunty Rosa likes me more than she does you. She says that you are a Trial and a Black Sheep, and I'm not to speak to you more than I can help.'

'Always? Not outside of the times when you mustn't speak to me at all?'

Judy nodded her head mournfully. Black Sheep turned away in despair, but Judy's arms were round his neck.

'Never mind, Punch,' she whispered. 'I *will* speak to you just the same as ever and ever. You're my own own brother though you are – though Aunty Rosa says you're bad and Harry says you are a little coward. He says that if I pulled your hair hard, you'd cry.'

'Pull, then,' said Punch.

Judy pulled gingerly.

'Pull harder – as hard as you can! There! I don't mind how much you pull it *now*. If you'll speak to me same as ever I'll let you pull it as much as you like – pull it out if you like. But I know if Harry came and stood by and made you do it I'd cry.'

So the two children sealed the compact with a kiss, and Black Sheep's heart was cheered within him, and by extreme caution and careful avoidance of Harry he acquired virtue, and was allowed to read undisturbed for a week. Uncle Harry took him for walks, and consoled him with rough tenderness, never calling him Black Sheep. 'It's good for you, I suppose, Punch,' he used to say. 'Let us sit down. I'm getting tired.' His steps led him now not to the beach, but to the cemetery of Rocklington, amid the potato-fields. For hours the grey man would sit on a tombstone, while Black Sheep would read epitaphs, and then with a sigh would stump home again.

'I shall lie there soon,' said he to Black Sheep, one winter evening, when his face showed white as a worn silver coin under the light of the lych-gate. 'You needn't tell Aunty Rosa.'

A month later he turned sharp round, ere half a morning walk was completed, and stumped back to the house. 'Put me to bed, Rosa,' he muttered. 'I've walked my last. The wadding has found me out.'

They put him to bed, and for a fortnight the shadow of his sickness lay upon the house, and Black Sheep went to and fro unobserved. Papa had sent him some new books, and he was told to keep quiet.

He retired into his own world, and was perfectly happy. Even at night his felicity was unbroken. He could lie in bed and string himself tales of travel and adventure while Harry was downstairs.

'Uncle Harry's going to die,' said Judy, who now lived almost entirely with Aunty Rosa.

'I'm very sorry,' said Black Sheep soberly. 'He told me that a long time ago.'

Aunty Rosa heard the conversation. 'Will nothing check your wicked tongue?' she said angrily. There were blue circles round her eyes.

Black Sheep retreated to the nursery and read *Cometh up as a Flower* with deep and uncomprehending interest. He had been forbidden to open it on account of its 'sinfulness', but the bonds of the Universe were crumbling and Aunty Rosa was in great grief.

'I'm glad,' said Black Sheep. 'She's unhappy now. It wasn't a lie, though. *I* knew. He told me not to tell.'

That night Black Sheep woke with a start. Harry was not in the room, and there was a sound of sobbing on the next floor. Then the voice of Uncle Harry, singing the song of the Battle of Navarino, came through the darkness:

'Our vanship was the *Asia* –
The *Albion* and *Genoa*!'

'He's getting well,' thought Black Sheep, who knew the song through all its seventeen verses. But the blood froze at his little heart as he thought. The voice leapt an octave, and rang shrill as a boatswain's pipe:

'And next came on the lovely *Rose*,
The *Philomel*, her fire-ship, closed,
And the little *Brisk* was sore exposed
That day at Navarino.'

'That day at Navarino, Uncle Harry!' shouted Black Sheep, half wild with excitement and fear of he knew not what.

A door opened, and Aunty Rosa screamed up the staircase: 'Hush! For God's sake hush, you little devil. Uncle Harry is *dead*!'

THE THIRD BAG

Journeys end in lovers' meeting,
Every wise man's son doth know.

'I wonder what will happen to me now,' thought Black Sheep, when semi-pagan rites peculiar to the burial of the dead in middle-class houses had been accomplished, and Aunty Rosa, awful in black crêpe, had returned to this life. 'I don't think I've done anything bad that she knows of. I suppose I will soon. She will be very cross after Uncle Harry's dying, and Harry will be cross too. I'll keep in the nursery.'

Unfortunately for Punch's plans, it was decided that he should be sent to a day-school which Harry attended. This meant a morning walk with Harry, and perhaps an evening one; but the prospect of freedom in the interval was refreshing. 'Harry'll tell everything I do, but I won't do anything,' said Black Sheep. Fortified with this virtuous resolution, he went to school only to find that Harry's version of his character had preceded him, and that life was a burden in consequence. He took stock of his associates. Some of them were unclean, some of them talked in dialect, many dropped their h's, and there were two Jews and a Negro, or someone quite as dark, in the assembly. 'That's a *hubshi*,' said Black Sheep to himself. 'Even Meeta used to laugh at a *hubshi*. I don't think this is a proper place.' He was indignant for at least an hour, till he reflected that any expostulation on his part would be by Aunty Rosa construed into 'showing off', and that Harry would tell the boys.

'How do you like school?' said Aunty Rosa at the end of the day.

'I think it is a very nice place,' said Punch quietly.

'I suppose you warned the boys of Black Sheep's character?' said Aunty Rosa to Harry.

'Oh yes,' said the censor of Black Sheep's morals. 'They know all about him.'

'If I was with my father,' said Black Sheep, stung to the quick, 'I shouldn't *speak* to those boys. He wouldn't let me. They live in shops. I saw them go into shops – where their fathers live and sell things.'

'You're too good for that school, are you?' said Aunty Rosa, with a bitter smile. 'You ought to be grateful, Black Sheep, that those boys speak to you at all. It isn't every school that takes little liars.'

Harry did not fail to make much capital out of Black Sheep's ill-considered remark; with the result that several boys, including the *hubshi*, demonstrated to Black Sheep the eternal equality of the human race by smacking his head, and his consolation from Aunty Rosa was that it 'served him right for being vain'. He learned, however, to keep his opinions to himself, and by propitiating Harry in carrying books and the like to get a little peace. His existence was not too joyful. From nine till twelve he was at school, and from two to four, except on Saturdays. In the evenings he was sent down into the nursery to prepare his lessons for the next day, and every night came the dreaded cross-questionings at Harry's hand. Of Judy he saw but little. She was deeply religious – at six years of age religion is easy to come by – and sorely divided between her natural love for Black Sheep and her love for Aunty Rosa, who could do no wrong.

The lean woman returned that love with interest, and Judy, when she dared, took advantage of this for the remission of Black Sheep's penalties. Failures in lessons at school were punished at home by a week without reading other than schoolbooks, and Harry brought the news of such failure with glee. Further, Black Sheep was then bound to repeat his lessons at bedtime to Harry, who generally succeeded in making him break down, and consoled him by gloomiest forebodings for the morrow. Harry was at once spy, practical joker, inquisitor, and Aunty Rosa's deputy executioner. He filled his many posts to admiration. From his actions, now that Uncle Harry was dead, there was no appeal. Black Sheep had not been permitted to keep any self-respect at school: at home he was, of course, utterly discredited, and grateful for any pity that the servant girls – they changed frequently at Downe Lodge because they, too, were liars – might show. 'You're just fit to row in the same boat with Black Sheep,' was a sentiment that each new Jane or Eliza might expect to hear, before a month was over, from Aunty Rosa's lips; and Black Sheep was used to ask new girls whether they had yet been compared to him. Harry was 'Master Harry' in their mouths; Judy was officially 'Miss Judy'; but Black Sheep was never anything more than Black Sheep *tout court*.

As time went on and the memory of Papa and Mamma became wholly overlaid by the unpleasant task of writing them letters, under Aunty Rosa's eye, each Sunday, Black Sheep forgot what manner of life he had led in the beginning of things. Even Judy's appeals to 'try and remember about Bombay' failed to quicken him.

'I can't remember,' he said. 'I know I used to give orders and Mamma kissed me.'

'Aunty Rosa will kiss you if you are good,' pleaded Judy.

'Ugh! I don't want to be kissed by Aunty Rosa. She'd say I was doing it to get something more to eat.'

The weeks lengthened into months, and the holidays came; but just before the holidays Black Sheep fell into deadly sin.

Among the many boys whom Harry had incited to 'punch Black Sheep's head because he daren't hit back', was one more aggravating than the rest, who, in an unlucky moment, fell upon Black Sheep when Harry was not near. The blows stung, and Black Sheep struck back at random with all the power at his command. The boy dropped and whimpered. Black Sheep was astounded at his own act, but, feeling the unresisting body under him, shook it with both his hands in blind fury and then began to throttle his enemy; meaning honestly to slay him. There was a scuffle, and Black Sheep was torn off the body by Harry and some colleagues, and cuffed home tingling but exultant. Aunty Rosa was out: pending her arrival, Harry set himself to lecture Black Sheep on the sin of murder – which he described as the offence of Cain.

'Why didn't you fight him fair? What did you hit him when he was down for, you little cur?'

Black Sheep looked up at Harry's throat and then at a knife on the dinner-table.

'I don't understand,' he said wearily. 'You always set him on me and told me I was a coward when I blubbed. Will you leave me alone until Aunty Rosa comes in? She'll beat me if you tell her I ought to be beaten; so it's all right.'

'It's all wrong,' said Harry magisterially. 'You nearly killed him, and I shouldn't wonder if he dies.'

'Will he die?' said Black Sheep.

'I daresay,' said Harry, 'and then you'll be hanged, and go to Hell.'

'All right,' said Black Sheep, picking up the table-knife. 'Then I'll kill *you* now. You say things and do things and – and *I* don't know how things happen, and you never leave me alone – and I don't care *what* happens!'

He ran at the boy with the knife, and Harry fled upstairs to his room, promising Black Sheep the finest thrashing in the world when Aunty Rosa returned. Black Sheep sat at the bottom of the stairs, the table-knife in his hand, and wept for that he had not killed Harry. The servant-girl came up from the kitchen, took the knife away, and consoled him. But Black Sheep was beyond consolation. He would be badly beaten by Aunty Rosa; then there would be another beating at Harry's hands; then Judy would not be allowed to speak to him; then the tale would be told at school, and then —

There was no one to help and no one to care, and the best way out of the business was by death. A knife would hurt, but Aunty Rosa had told him, a year ago, that if he sucked paint he would die. He went into the nursery, unearthed the now disused Noah's Ark, and sucked the paint off as many animals as remained. It tasted abominable, but he had licked Noah's Dove clean by the time Aunty Rosa and Judy returned. He went upstairs and greeted them with: 'Please, Aunty Rose, I believe I've nearly killed a boy at school, and I've tried to kill Harry, and when you've done all about God and Hell, will you beat me and get it over?'

The tale of the assault as told by Harry could only be explained on the ground of possession by the Devil. Wherefore Black Sheep was not only most excellently beaten, once by Aunty Rosa and once, when thoroughly cowed down, by Harry, but he was further prayed for at family prayers, together with Jane who had stolen a cold rissole from the pantry, and snuffled audibly as her sin was brought before the Throne of Grace. Black Sheep was sore and stiff but triumphant. He would die that very night and be rid of them all. No, he would ask for no forgiveness from Harry, and at bedtime would stand no questioning at Harry's hands, even though addressed as 'Young Cain'.

'I've been beaten,' said he, 'and I've done other things. I don't care what I do. If you speak to me tonight, Harry, I'll get out and try to kill you. Now you can kill me if you like.'

Harry took his bed into the spare room, and Black Sheep lay down to die.

It may be that the makers of Noah's Arks know that their animals are likely to find their way into young mouths, and paint them accordingly. Certain it is that the common, weary next morning broke through the windows and found Black Sheep quite well and a good deal ashamed of himself, but richer by the knowledge that he could, in extremity, secure himself against Harry for the future.

When he descended to breakfast on the first day of the holidays, he was greeted with the news that Harry, Aunty Rosa, and Judy were going away to Brighton, while Black Sheep was to stay in the house with the servant. His latest outbreak suited Aunty Rosa's plans admirably. It gave her good excuse for leaving the extra boy behind. Papa in Bombay, who really seemed to know a young sinner's wants to the hour, sent, that week, a package of new books. And with these, and the society of Jane on board-wages, Black Sheep was left alone for a month.

The books lasted for ten days. They were eaten too quickly in long gulps of twelve hours at a time. Then came days of doing absolutely nothing, of dreaming dreams and marching imaginary armies up and downstairs, of counting the number of banisters, and of measuring the length and breadth of every room in handspans – fifty down the side, thirty across and fifty back again. Jane made many friends, and, after receiving Black Sheep's assurance that he would not tell of her absences, went out daily for long hours. Black Sheep would follow the rays of the sinking sun from the kitchen to the dining-room and thence upward to his own bedroom until all was grey dark, and he ran down to the kitchen fire and read by its light. He was happy in that he was left alone and could read as much as he pleased. But, later, he grew afraid of the shadows of window-curtains and the flapping of doors and the creaking of shutters. He went out into the garden, and the rustling of the laurel-bushes frightened him.

He was glad when they all returned – Aunty Rosa, Harry, and Judy – full of news, and Judy laden with gifts. Who could help loving loyal little Judy? In return for all her merry babblement, Black Sheep confided to her that the distance from the hall-door to the top of the first landing was exactly one hundred and eighty-four handspans. He had found it out himself.

Then the old life recommenced; but with a difference, and a new sin. To his other iniquities Black Sheep had now added a phenomenal clumsiness – was as unfit to trust in action as he was in word. He himself could not account for spilling everything he touched, upsetting glasses as he put his hand out, and bumping his head against doors that were manifestly shut. There was a grey haze upon all his world, and it narrowed month by month, until at last it left Black Sheep almost alone with the flapping curtains that were so like ghosts, and the nameless terrors of broad daylight that were only coats on pegs after all.

Holidays came and holidays went, and Black Sheep was taken to see many people whose faces were all exactly alike; was beaten when occasion demanded, and tortured by Harry on all possible occasions; but defended by Judy through good and evil report, though she hereby drew upon herself the wrath of Aunty Rosa.

The weeks were interminable, and Papa and Mamma were clean forgotten. Harry had left school and was a clerk in a banking-office. Freed from his presence, Black Sheep resolved that he should no longer be deprived of his allowance of pleasure-reading. Consequently when he failed at school he reported that all was well, and conceived a large contempt for Aunty Rosa as he saw how easy it was to deceive her. 'She says I'm a little liar when I don't tell lies, and now I do, she doesn't know,' thought Black Sheep. Aunty Rosa had credited him in the past with petty cunning and stratagem that had never entered into his head. By the light of the sordid knowledge that she had revealed to him he paid her back full tale. In a household where the most innocent of his motives, his natural yearning for a little affection, had been interpreted into a desire for more bread and jam, or to ingratiate himself with strangers and so put Harry into the background, his work was easy. Aunty Rosa could penetrate certain kinds of hypocrisy, but not all. He set his child's wits against hers and was no more beaten. It grew monthly more and more of a trouble to read the schoolbooks, and even the pages of the open-print story-books danced and were dim. So Black Sheep brooded in the shadows that fell about him and cut him off from the world; inventing horrible punishments for 'dear Harry', or plotting another line of the tangled web of deception that he wrapped round Aunty Rosa.

Then the crash came and the cobwebs were broken. It was impossible to foresee everything. Aunty Rosa made personal inquiries as to Black Sheep's progress and received information that startled her. Step by step, with a delight as keen as when she convicted an underfed housemaid of the theft of cold meats, she followed the trail of Black Sheep's delinquencies. For weeks and weeks, in order to escape banishment from the bookshelves, he had made a fool of Aunty Rosa, of Harry, of God, of all the world! Horrible, most horrible, and evidence of an utterly depraved mind.

Black Sheep counted the cost. 'It will only be one big beating and then she'll put a card with "Liar" on my back, same as she did before. Harry will whack me and pray for me, and she will pray for me at prayers and tell me I'm a Child of the Devil and give me hymns to learn. But I've done all my reading and she never knew. She'll say she knew all along. She's an old liar too,' said he.

For three days Black Sheep was shut in his own bedroom – to prepare his heart. 'That means two beatings. One at school and one here. *That* one will hurt most.' And it fell even as he thought. He was thrashed at school before the Jews and the *hubshi* for the heinous crime of carrying home false reports of progress. He was thrashed at home by Aunty Rosa on the same count, and then the placard was produced. Aunty Rosa stitched it between his shoulders and bade him go for a walk with it upon him.

'If you make me do that,' said Black Sheep very quietly, 'I shall burn this house down, and perhaps I'll kill you. I don't know whether I *can* kill you – you're so bony – but I'll try.'

No punishment followed this blasphemy, though Black Sheep held himself ready to work his way to Aunty Rosa's withered throat, and grip there till he was beaten off. Perhaps Aunty Rosa was afraid, for Black Sheep, having reached the Nadir of Sin, bore himself with a new recklessness.

In the midst of all the trouble there came a visitor from over the seas to Downe Lodge, who knew Papa and Mamma, and was commissioned to see Punch and Judy. Black Sheep was sent to the drawing-room and charged into a solid tea-table laden with china.

'Gently, gently, little man,' said the visitor, turning Black Sheep's face to the light slowly. 'What's that big bird on the palings?'

'What bird?' asked Black Sheep.

The visitor looked deep down into Black Sheep's eyes for half a minute, and then said suddenly: 'Good God, the little chap's nearly blind!'

It was a most businesslike visitor. He gave orders, on his own responsibility, that Black Sheep was not to go to school or open a book until Mamma came home. 'She'll be here in three weeks, as you know of course,' said he, 'and I'm Inverarity Sahib. I ushered you into this wicked world, young man, and a nice use you seem to have made of your time. You must do nothing whatever. Can you do that?'

'Yes,' said Punch in a dazed way. He had known that Mamma was coming. There was a chance, then, of another beating. Thank Heaven, Papa wasn't coming too. Aunty Rosa had said of late that he ought to be beaten by a man.

For the next three weeks Black Sheep was strictly allowed to do nothing. He spent his time in the old nursery looking at the broken toys, for all of which account must be rendered to Mamma. Aunty Rosa hit him over the hands if even a wooden boat were broken. But that sin was of small importance compared to the other revelations, so darkly hinted at by Aunty Rosa. 'When your mother comes, and hears what I have to tell her, she may appreciate you properly,' she said grimly, and mounted guard over Judy lest that small maiden should attempt to comfort her brother, to the peril of her soul.

And Mamma came – in a four-wheeler – fluttered with tender excitement. Such a Mamma! She was young, frivolously young, and beautiful, with delicately-flushed cheeks, eyes that shone like stars, and a voice that needed no appeal of outstretched arms to draw little ones to her heart. Judy ran straight to her, but Black Sheep hesitated. Could this wonder be 'showing off'? She would not put out her arms when she knew of his crimes. Meantime was it possible that by fondling she wanted to get anything out of Black Sheep? Only all his love and all his confidence; but that Black Sheep did not know. Aunty Rosa withdrew and left Mamma, kneeling between her children, half-laughing, half-crying, in the very hall where Punch and Judy had wept five years before.

'Well, chicks, do you remember me?'

'No,' said Judy frankly, 'but I said, "God bless Papa and Mamma" ev'vy night.'

'A little,' said Black Sheep. 'Remember I wrote to you every week, anyhow. That isn't to show off, but 'cause of what comes afterwards.'

'What comes after? What should come after, my darling boy?' And she drew him to her again. He came awkwardly, with many angles. 'Not used to petting,' said the quick Mother-soul. 'The girl is.'

'She's too little to hurt anyone,' thought Black Sheep, 'and if I said I'd kill her, she'd be afraid. I wonder what Aunty Rosa will tell.'

There was a constrained late dinner, at the end of which Mamma picked up Judy and put her to bed with endearments manifold. Faithless little Judy had shown her defection from Aunty Rosa already. And that lady resented it bitterly. Black Sheep rose to leave the room.

'Come and say goodnight,' said Aunty Rosa, offering a withered cheek.

'Huh!' said Black Sheep. 'I never kiss you, and I'm not going to show off. Tell that woman what I've done, and see what she says.'

Black Sheep climbed into bed feeling that he had lost Heaven after a glimpse through the gates. In half an hour 'that woman' was bending over him. Black Sheep flung up his right arm. It wasn't fair to come and hit him in the dark. Even Aunty Rosa never tried that. But no blow followed.

'Are you showing off? I won't tell you anything more than Aunty Rosa has, and *she* doesn't know everything,' said Black Sheep as clearly as he could for the arms round his neck.

'Oh, my son – my little, little son! It was my fault – *my* fault, darling – and yet how could we help it? Forgive me, Punch.' The voice died out in a broken whisper, and two hot tears fell on Black Sheep's forehead.

'Has she been making you cry too?' he asked. 'You should see Jane cry. But you're nice, and Jane is a Born Liar – Aunty Rosa says so.'

'Hush, Punch, hush! My boy, don't talk like that. Try to love me a little bit – a little bit. You don't know how I want it. Punch-*baba*, come back to me! I am your mother – your own mother – and never mind the rest. I know – yes, I know, dear. It doesn't matter now. Punch, won't you care for me a little?'

It is astonishing how much petting a big boy of ten can endure when he is quite sure that there is no one to laugh at him. Black Sheep had never been made much of before, and here was this beautiful woman treating him – Black Sheep, the Child of the Devil and the inheritor of undying flame – as though he were a small God.

'I care for you a great deal, Mother dear,' he whispered at last, 'and I'm glad you've come back; but are you sure Aunty Rosa told you everything?'

'Everything. What *does* it matter? but —' the voice broke with a sob that was also laughter – 'Punch, my poor, dear, half-blind darling, don't you think it was a little foolish of you?'

'*No*. It saved a lickin'.'

Mamma shuddered and slipped away in the darkness to write a long letter to Papa. Here is an extract:

> . . . Judy is a dear, plump little prig who adores the woman, and wears with as much gravity as her religious opinions – only eight, Jack! – a venerable horse-hair atrocity which she calls her Bustle! I have just burnt it, and the child is asleep in my bed as I write. She will come to me at once. Punch I cannot quite understand. He is well nourished, but seems to have been worried into a system of small deceptions which the woman magnifies into deadly sins. Don't you recollect our own upbringing, dear, when the Fear of the Lord was so often the beginning of falsehood? I shall win Punch to me before long. I am taking the children away into the country to get them to know me, and, on the whole, I am content, or shall be when you come home, dear boy, and then, thank God, we shall be all under one roof again at last!

Three months later, Punch, no longer Black Sheep, has discovered that he is the veritable owner of a real, live, lovely Mamma, who is also a sister, comforter, and friend, and that he must protect her till the Father comes home. Deception does not suit the part of a protector, and, when one can do anything without question, where is the use of deception?

'Mother would be awfully cross if you walked through that ditch,' says Judy, continuing a conversation.

'Mother's never angry,' says Punch. 'She'd just say, "You're a little *pagal*;" and that's not nice, but I'll show.'

Punch walks through the ditch and mires himself to the knees. 'Mother, dear,' he shouts, 'I'm just as dirty as I can pos-*sib*-ly be!'

'Then change your clothes as quickly as you pos-*sib*-ly can!' Mother's clear voice rings out from the house. 'And don't be a little *pagal*!'

'There! Told you so,' says Punch. 'It's all different now, and we are just as much Mother's as if she had never gone.'

Not altogether, O Punch, for when young lips have drunk deep of the bitter waters of Hate, Suspicion, and Despair, all the Love in the world will not wholly take away that knowledge; though it may turn darkened eyes for a while to the light, and teach Faith where no Faith was.

Dray Wara Yow Dee

For jealousy is the rage of a man: therefore he will not spare in the day of vengeance.

Proverbs vi. 34

ALMONDS and raisins, Sahib? Grapes from Kabul? Or a pony of the rarest if the Sahib will only come with me. He is thirteen-three, Sahib, plays polo, goes in a cart, carries a lady and – Holy Kurshed and the Blessed Imams, it is the Sahib himself! My heart is made fat and my eye glad. May you never be tired! As is cold water in the Tirah, so is the sight of a friend in a far place. And what do *you* in this accursed land? South of Delhi, Sahib, you know the saying – 'Rats are the men and trulls the women.' It was an order? Ahoo! An order is an order till one is strong enough to disobey. O my brother, O my friend, we have met in an auspicious hour! Is all well in the heart and body and the house? In a lucky day have we two come together again.

I am to go with you? Your favour is great. Will there be picket-room in the compound? I have three horses and the bundles and the horse-boy. Moreover, remember that the police here hold me a horse-thief. What do these Lowland bastards know of horse-thieves? Do you remember that time in Peshawar when Kamal hammered on the gates of Jumrud – mountebank that he was – and lifted the Colonel's horse all in one night? Kamal is dead now, but his nephew has taken up the matter, and there will be more horses a-missing if the Khyber Levies do not look to it.

The Peace of God and the favour of His Prophet be upon this house and all that is in it! Shafiz Ullah, rope the mottled mare under the tree and draw water. The horses can stand in the sun, but double the felts over the loins. Nay, my friend, do not trouble to look them over. They are to sell to the officer-fools who know so many things of the horse. The mare is heavy in foal; the grey is a devil unlicked; and the dun – but you know the trick of the peg. When they are sold I go back to Pubbi, or, it may be, the Valley of Peshawar.

O friend of my heart, it is good to see you again. I have been bowing and lying all day to the Officer-Sahibs in respect to those horses; and my mouth is dry for straight talk. *Auggrh!* Before a meal tobacco is good. Do not join me, for we are not in our own country.

Sit in the veranda and I will spread my cloth here. But first I will drink. *In the name of God returning thanks, thrice!* This is sweet water, indeed – sweet as the water of Sheoran when it comes from the snows.

They are all well and pleased in the North – Khoda Baksh and the others. Yar Khan has come down with the horses from Kurdistan – six-and-thirty head only, and a full half pack-ponies – and has said openly in the Kashmir Serai that you English should send guns and blow the Amir into Hell. There are *fifteen* tolls now on the Kabul road; and at Dakka, when he thought he was clear, Yar Khan was stripped of all his Balkh stallions by the Governor! This is a great injustice, and Yar Khan is hot with rage. And of the others: Mahbub Ali is still at Pubbi, writing God knows what. Tugluq Khan is in jail for the business of the Kohat Police Post. Faiz Beg came down from Ismail-ki-Dhera with a Bokhariot belt for thee, my brother, at the closing of the year, but none knew whither thou hadst gone: there was no news left behind. The Cousins have taken a new run near Pakpattan to breed mules for the Government carts, and there is a story in the bazaar of a priest. Oho! Such a salt tale! Listen—

Sahib, why do you ask that? My clothes are fouled because of the dust on the road. My eyes are sad because of the glare of the sun. My feet are swollen because I have washed them in bitter water, and my cheeks are hollow because the food here is bad. Fire burn your money! What do I want with it? I am rich. I thought you were my friend. But you are like the others – a Sahib. Is a man sad? Give him money, say the Sahibs. Is he dishonoured? Give him money, say the Sahibs. Hath he a wrong upon his head? Give him money, say the Sahibs. Such are the Sahibs, and such art thou – even thou.

Nay, do not look at the feet of the dun. Pity it is that I ever taught you to know the legs of a horse. Footsore? Be it so. What of that? The roads are hard. And the mare footsore? She bears a double burden, Sahib.

And now, I pray you, give me permission to depart. Great favour and honour has the Sahib done me, and graciously has he shown his belief that the horses are stolen. Will it please him to send me to the Thana? To call a sweeper and have me led away by one of these lizard-men? I am the Sahib's friend. I have drunk water in the shadow of his house, and he has blackened my face. Remains there anything more to do? Will the Sahib give me eight annas to make smooth the injury and – complete the insult —?

Forgive me, my brother. I knew not – I know not now – what I say. Yes, I lied to you! I will put dust on my head – and I am an Afridi! The horses have been marched footsore from the Valley to this place, and my eyes are dim, and my body aches for the want of sleep, and my heart is dried up with sorrow and shame. But as it was my shame, so by God the Dispenser of Justice – by Allah-al-Mumît – it shall be my own revenge!

We have spoken together with naked hearts before this, and our hands have dipped into the same dish, and thou hast been to me as a brother! Therefore I pay thee back with lies and ingratitude – as a Pathan. Listen now! When the grief of the soul is too heavy for endurance it may be a little eased by speech; and, moreover, the mind of a true man is as a well, and the pebble of confession dropped therein sinks and is no more seen. From the Valley have I come on foot, league by league, with a fire in my chest like the fire of the Pit. And why? Hast thou, then, so quickly forgotten our customs, among this folk who sell their wives and their daughters for silver? Come back with me to the North and be among men once more. Come back, when this matter is accomplished and I call for thee! The bloom of the peach-orchards is upon all the Valley, and *here* is only dust and a great stink. There is a pleasant wind among the mulberry trees, and the streams are bright with snow-water, and the caravans go up and the caravans go down, and a hundred fires sparkle in the gut of the Pass, and tent-peg answers hammer-nose, and pack-horse squeals to pack-horse across the drift-smoke of the evening. It is good in the North now. Come back with me. Let us return to our own people! Come!

Whence is my sorrow? Does a man tear out his heart and make fritters thereof over a slow fire for aught other than a woman? Do not laugh, friend of mine, for your time will also be. A woman of the Abazai was she, and I took her to wife to staunch the feud between our village and the men of Ghor. I am no longer young? The lime has touched my beard? True. I had no need of the wedding? Nay, but I loved her. What saith Rahman? 'Into whose heart Love enters, there is Folly *and naught else*. By a glance of the eye she hath blinded thee; and by the eyelids and the fringe of the eyelids taken thee into the captivity without ransom, *and naught else*.' Dost thou remember that song at the sheep-roasting in the Pindi camp among the Uzbegs of the Amir?

The Abazai are dogs and their women the servants of sin. There was a lover of her own people, but of that her father told me naught. My friend, curse for me in your prayers, as I curse at each praying from the Fakr to the Isha, the name of Daoud Shah, Abazai, whose head is still upon his neck, whose hands are still upon his wrists, who has done me dishonour, who has made my name a laughing-stock among the women of Little Malikand.

I went into Hindustan at the end of two months – to Cherat. I was gone twelve days only; but I had said that I would be fifteen days absent. This I did to try her, for it is written: 'Trust not the incapable.' Coming up the gorge alone in the falling of the light, I heard the voice of a man singing at the door of my house; and it was the voice of Daoud Shah, and the song that he sang was '*Dray wara yow dee*' – 'All three are one.' It was as though a heel-rope had been slipped round my heart and all the devils were drawing it tight past endurance. I crept silently up the hill-road, but the fuse of my matchlock was wetted with the rain, and I could not slay Daoud Shah from afar. Moreover, it was in my mind to kill the woman also. Thus he sang, sitting outside my house, and, anon, the woman opened the door, and I came nearer, crawling on my belly among the rocks. I had only my knife to my hand. But a stone slipped under my foot, and the two looked down the hillside, and he, leaving his matchlock, fled from my anger, because he was afraid for the life that was in him. But the woman moved not till I stood in front of her, crying: 'O woman, what is this that thou hast done?' And she, void of fear, though she knew my thought, laughed, saying: 'It is a little thing. I loved him, and *thou* art a dog and cattle-thief coming by night. Strike!' And I, being still blinded by her beauty, for, O my friend, the women of the Abazai are very fair, said: 'Hast thou no fear?' And she answered: 'None – but only the fear that I do not die.' Then said I: 'Have no fear.' And she bowed her head, and I smote it off at the neck-bone so that it leaped between my feet. Thereafter the rage of our people came upon me, and I hacked off the breasts, that the men of Little Malikand might know the crime, and cast the body into the watercourse that flows to the Kabul River. *Dray wara yow dee! Dray wara yow dee!* The body without the head, the soul without light, and my own darkling heart – all three are one – all three are one!

That night, making no halt, I went to Ghor and demanded news of Daoud Shah. Men said: 'He is gone to Pubbi for horses. What wouldst thou of him? There is peace between the villages.' I made answer: 'Ay! The peace of treachery and the love that the Devil Atala bore to Gurel.' So I fired thrice into the tower-gate and laughed and went my way.

In those hours, brother and friend of my heart's heart, the moon and stars were as blood above me, and in my mouth was the taste of dry earth. Also, I broke no bread, and my drink was the rain of the valley of Ghor upon my face.

At Pubbi I found Mahbub Ali, the writer, sitting upon his charpoy, and gave up my arms according to your Law. But I was not grieved, for it was in my heart that I should kill Daoud Shah with my bare hands thus – as a man strips a bunch of raisins. Mahbub Ali said: 'Daoud Shah had even now gone hot-foot to Peshawar, and he will pick up his horses upon the road to Delhi, for it is said that the Bombay Tramway Company are buying horses there by the truckload; eight horses to the truck.' And that was a true saying.

Then I saw that the hunting would be no little thing, for the man was gone into your borders to save himself against my wrath. And shall he save himself so? Am I not alive? Though he run northward to the Dora and the snow, or southerly to the Black Water, I will follow him, as a lover follows the footsteps of his mistress, and coming upon him I will take him tenderly – Aho! so tenderly! – in my arms, saying: 'Well hast thou done and well shalt thou be repaid.' And out of that embrace Daoud Shah shall not go forth with the breath in his nostils. *Auggrh!* Where is the pitcher? I am as thirsty as a mother mare in the first month.

Your Law! What is your Law to me? When the horses fight on the runs do they regard the boundary pillars; or do the kites of Ali Musjid forbear because the carrion lies under the shadow of the Ghor Kuttri? The matter began across the Border. It shall finish where God pleases. Here; in my own country; or in Hell. All three are one.

Listen now, sharer of the sorrow of my heart, and I will tell of the hunting. I followed to Peshawar from Pubbi, and I went to and fro about the streets of Peshawar like a houseless dog, seeking for my enemy. Once I thought that I saw him washing his mouth in the conduit in the big square, but when I came up he was gone. It may be that it was he, and, seeing my face, he had fled.

A girl of the bazaar said that he would go to Nowshera. I said: 'O heart's heart, does Daoud Shah visit thee?' And she said: 'Even so.' I said: 'I would fain see him, for we be friends parted for two years. Hide me, I pray, here in the shadow of the window-shutter, and I will wait for his coming.' And the girl said: 'O Pathan, look into my eyes!' And I turned, leaning upon her breast, and looked into her eyes, swearing that I spoke the very Truth of God. But she answered: 'Never friend waited friend with such eyes. Lie to God and the Prophet, but to a woman ye cannot lie. Get hence! There shall no harm befall Daoud Shah by cause of me.'

I would have strangled that girl but for the fear of your police; and thus the hunting would have come to naught. Therefore I only laughed and departed, and she leaned over the window-bar in the night and mocked me down the street. Her name is Jamun. When I have made my account with the man I will return to Peshawar and – her lovers shall desire her no more for her beauty's sake. She shall not be *Jamun*, but *Ak*, the cripple among trees. Ho! ho! *Ak* shall she be!

At Peshawar I bought the horses and grapes, and the almonds and dried fruits, that the reason of my wanderings might be open to the Government, and that there might be no hindrance upon the road. But when I came to Nowshera he was gone; and I knew not where to go. I stayed one day at Nowshera, and in the night a Voice spoke in my ears as I slept among the horses. All night it flew round my head and would not cease from whispering. I was upon my belly, sleeping as the devils sleep, and it may have been that the Voice was the voice of a devil. It said: 'Go south, and thou shalt come upon Daoud Shah.' Listen, my brother and chiefest among friends - listen! Is the tale a long one? Think how it was long to me. I have trodden every league of the road from Pubbi to this place; and from Nowshera my guide was only the Voice and the lust of vengeance.

To the Uttock I went, but that was no hindrance to me. Ho! ho! A man may turn the word twice, even in his trouble. The Uttock was no *uttock* [obstacle] to me; and I heard the Voice above the noise of the waters beating on the big rock, saying: 'Go to the right.' So I went to Pindigheb, and in those days my sleep was taken from me utterly, and the head of the woman of the Abazai was before me night and day, even as it had fallen between my feet. *Dray wara yow dee! Dray wara yow dee!* Fire, ashes, and my couch, all three are one – all three are one!

Now I was far from the winter path of the dealers who had gone to Sialkot, and so south by the rail and the Big Road to the line of cantonments; but there was a Sahib in camp at Pindigheb who bought from me a white mare at a good price, and told me that one Daoud Shah had passed to Shahpur with horses. Then I saw that the warning of the Voice was true, and made swift to come to the Salt Hills. The Jhelum was in flood, but I could not wait, and, in the crossing, a bay stallion was washed down and drowned. Herein was God hard to me – not in respect of the beast, of that I had no care – but in this snatching. While I was upon the right bank urging the horses into the water, Daoud Shah was upon the left; for – *Alghias! Alghias!* - the hoofs of my mare scattered the hot ashes of his fires when we came up the hither bank in the light of morning. But he had fled. His feet were made swift by the terror of death. And I went south from

Shahpur as the kite flies. I dared not turn aside lest I should miss my vengeance – which is my right. From Shahpur I skirted the Jhelum, for I thought that he would avoid the Desert of the Rechna. But, presently, at Sahiwal, I turned away upon the road to Jhang, Samundri, and Gugera, till, upon a night, the mottled mare breasted the fence of the rail that runs to Montgomery. And that place was Okara, and the head of the woman of the Abazai lay upon the sand between my feet.

Thence I went to Fazilka, and they said that I was mad to bring starved horses there. The Voice was with me, and I was *not* mad, but only wearied, because I could not find Daoud Shah. It was written that I should not find him at Rania nor Bahadurgarh, and I came into Delhi from the west, and there also I found him not. My friend, I have seen many strange things in my wanderings. I have seen the devils rioting across the Rechna as the stallions riot in spring. I have heard the *Djinns* calling to each other from holes in the sand, and I have seen them pass before my face. There are no devils, say the Sahibs? They are very wise, but they do not know all things about devils or – horses. Ho! ho! I say to you who are laughing at my misery, that I have seen the devils at high noon whooping and leaping on the shoals of the Chenab. And was I afraid? My brother, when the desire of a man is set upon one thing alone, he fears neither God nor Man nor Devil. If my vengeance failed, I would splinter the Gates of Paradise with the butt of my gun, or I would cut my way into Hell with my knife, and I would call upon Those who govern there for the body of Daoud Shah. What love so deep as hate?

Do not speak. I know the thought in your heart. Is the white of this eye clouded? How does the blood beat at the wrist? There is no madness in my flesh, but only the vehemence of the desire that has eaten me up. Listen!

South of Delhi I knew not the country at all. Therefore I cannot say where I went, but I passed through many cities. I knew only that it was laid upon me to go south. When the horses could march no more, I threw myself upon the earth and waited till the day. There was no sleep with me in that journeying; and that was a heavy burden. Dost thou know, brother of mine, the evil of wakefulness that cannot break – when the bones are sore for lack of sleep, and the skin of the temples twitches with weariness, and yet – there is no sleep – there is no sleep? *Dray wara yow dee! Dray wara yow dee!* The eye of the Sun, the eye of the Moon, and my own unrestful eyes – all three are one – all three are one!

There was a city the name whereof I have forgotten, and there the

Voice called all night. That was ten days ago. It has cheated me afresh.

I have come hither from a place called Hamirpur, and, behold, it is my fate that I should meet with thee to my comfort, and the increase of friendship. This is a good omen. By the joy of looking upon thy face the weariness has gone from my feet, and the sorrow of my so long travel is forgotten. Also my heart is peaceful; for I know that the end is near.

It may be that I shall find Daoud Shah in this city going northwards, since a Hillman will ever head back to his hills when the spring warns. And shall he see those hills of our country? Surely I shall overtake him! Surely my vengeance is safe! Surely God hath him in the hollow of His hand against my claiming! There shall no harm befall Daoud Shah till I come; for I would fain kill him quick and whole with the life sticking firm in his body. A pomegranate is sweetest when the cloves break away unwilling from the rind. Let it be in the daytime, that I may see his face, and my delight may be crowned.

And when I have accomplished the matter and my Honour is made clean, I shall return thanks unto God, the Holder of the Scales of the Law, and I shall sleep. From the night, through the day, and into the night again I shall sleep; and no dream shall trouble me.

And now, O my brother, the tale is all told. *Ahi! Ahi! Alghias! Ahi!*

On Greenhow Hill

To Love's low voice she lent a careless ear;
Her hand within his rosy fingers lay,
A chilling weight. She would not turn or hear;
But with averted face went on her way.
But when pale Death, all featureless and grim,
Lifted his bony hand, and beckoning
Held out his cypress-wreath, she followed him,
And Love was left forlorn and wondering,
That she who for his bidding would not stay,
At Death's first whisper rose and went away.

Rivals

'OHÉ, *Ahmed Din! Shafiz Ullah ahoo!* Bahadur Khan, where are you? Come out of the tents, as I have done, and fight against the English. Don't kill your own kin! Come out to me!'

The deserter from a native corps was crawling round the outskirts of the camp, firing at intervals, and shouting invitations to his old comrades. Misled by the rain and the darkness, he came to the English wing of the camp, and with his yelping and rifle-practice disturbed the men. They had been making roads all day, and were tired.

Ortheris was sleeping at Learoyd's feet. 'Wot's all that?' he said thickly. Learoyd snored, and a Snider bullet ripped its way through the tent wall. The men swore. 'It's that bloomin' deserter from the Aurangabadis,' said Ortheris. 'Git up, someone, an' tell 'im 'e's come to the wrong shop.'

'Go to sleep, little man,' said Mulvaney, who was steaming nearest the door. 'I can't arise an' expaytiate with him. 'Tis rainin' entrenchin' tools outside.'

''Taint because you bloomin' can't. It's 'cause you bloomin' won't, ye long, limp, lousy, lazy beggar, you. 'Ark to 'im 'owlin'!'

'Wot's the good of argifying? Put a bullet into the swine! 'E's keepin' us awake!' said another voice.

A subaltern shouted angrily, and a dripping sentry whined from the darkness –

''Tain't no good, sir. I can't see 'im. 'E's 'idin' somewhere down 'ill.'

Ortheris tumbled out of his blanket. 'Shall I try to get 'im, sir?' said he.

'No,' was the answer. 'Lie down. I won't have the whole camp shooting all round the clock. Tell him to go and pot his friends.'

Ortheris considered for a moment. Then, putting his head under the tent wall, he called, as a bus conductor calls in a block, ''Igher up, there! 'Igher up!'

The men laughed, and the laughter was carried down wind to the deserter, who, hearing that he had made a mistake, went off to worry his own regiment half a mile away. He was received with shots; the Aurangabadis were very angry with him for disgracing their colours.

'An' that's all right,' said Ortheris, withdrawing his head as he heard the hiccough of the Sniders in the distance. 'S'elp me Gawd, tho', that man's not fit to live – messin' with my beauty-sleep this way.'

'Go out and shoot him in the morning, then,' said the subaltern incautiously. 'Silence in the tents now. Get your rest, men.'

Ortheris lay down with a happy little sigh, and in two minutes there was no sound except the rain on the canvas and the all-embracing and elemental snoring of Learoyd.

The camp lay on a bare ridge of the Himalayas, and for a week had been waiting for a flying column to make connection. The nightly rounds of the deserter and his friends had become a nuisance.

In the morning the men dried themselves in hot sunshine and cleaned their grimy accoutrements. The native regiment was to take its turn of road-making that day while the Old Regiment loafed.

'I'm goin' to lay for a shot at that man,' said Ortheris, when he had finished washing out his rifle. ''E comes up the watercourse every evenin' about five o'clock. If we go and lie out on the north 'ill a bit this afternoon we'll get 'im.'

'You're a bloodthirsty little mosquito,' said Mulvaney, blowing blue clouds into the air. 'But I suppose I will have to come wid you. Fwhere's Jock?'

'Gone out with the Mixed Pickles, 'cause 'e thinks 'isself a bloomin' marksman,' said Ortheris with scorn.

The 'Mixed Pickles' were a detachment of picked shots, generally employed in clearing spurs of hills when the enemy were too impertinent. This taught the young officers how to handle men, and did not do the enemy much harm. Mulvaney and Ortheris strolled out of the camp, and passed the Aurangabadis going to their road-making.

'You've got to sweat today,' said Ortheris genially. 'We're going to get your man. You didn't knock 'im out last night by any chance, any of you?'

'No. The pig went away mocking us. I had one shot at him,' said a private. 'He's my cousin and *I* ought to have cleared our dishonour. But good luck to you.'

They went cautiously to the north hill, Ortheris leading, because, as he explained, 'this is a long-range show, an' I've got to do it.' His was an almost passionate devotion to his rifle, which, by barrack-room report, he was supposed to kiss every night before turning in. Charges and scuffles he held in contempt, and, when they were inevitable, slipped between Mulvaney and Learoyd, bidding them to fight for his skin as well as their own. They never failed him. He trotted along, questing like a hound on a broken trail, through the wood of the north hill. At last he was satisfied, and threw himself down on the soft pine-needled slope that commanded a clear view of the watercourse and a brown, bare hillside beyond it. The trees made a scented darkness in which an army corps could have hidden from the sun-glare without.

''Ere's the tail o' the wood,' said Ortheris. ''E's got to come up the watercourse, 'cause it gives 'im cover. We'll lay 'ere. 'Tain't not arf so bloomin' dusty neither.'

He buried his nose in a clump of scentless white violets. No one had come to tell the flowers that the season of their strength was long past, and they had bloomed merrily in the twilight of the pines.

'This is something like,' he said luxuriously. 'Wot a 'evinly clear drop for a bullet acrost. How much d'you make it, Mulvaney?'

'Seven hunder. Maybe a trifle less, bekaze the air's so thin.'

Wop! Wop! Wop! went a volley of musketry on the rear face of the north hill.

'Curse them Mixed Pickles firin' at nothin'! They'll scare arf the country.'

'Thry a sightin' shot in the middle of the row,' said Mulvaney, the man of many wiles. 'There's a red rock yonder he'll be sure to pass. Quick!'

Ortheris ran his sight up to six hundred yards and fired. The bullet threw up a feather of dust by a clump of gentians at the base of the rock.

'Good enough!' said Ortheris, snapping the scale down. 'You snick your sights to mine or a little lower. You're always firin' high. But remember, first shot to me. O Lordy! but it's a lovely afternoon.'

The noise of the firing grew louder, and there was a tramping of men in the wood. The two lay very quiet, for they knew that the British soldier is desperately prone to fire at anything that moves or calls. Then Learoyd appeared, his tunic ripped across the breast by a bullet, looking ashamed of himself. He flung down on the pine-needles, breathing in snorts.

'One o' them damned gardeners o' th' Pickles,' said he, fingering the rent. 'Firin' to th' right flank, when he knowed I was there. If I knew who he was I'd 'a' rippen the hide offan him. Look at ma tunic!'

'That's the spishil trustability av a marksman. Train him to hit a fly wid a stiddy rest at seven hunder, an' he'll loose on anythin' he sees or hears up to th' mile. You're well out av that fancy-firin' gang, Jock. Stay here.'

'Bin firin' at the bloomin' wind in the bloomin' treetops,' said Ortheris with a chuckle. 'I'll show you some firin' later on.'

They wallowed in the pine-needles, and the sun warmed them where they lay. The Mixed Pickles ceased firing, and returned to camp, and left the wood to a few scared apes. The watercourse lifted up its voice in the silence, and talked foolishly to the rocks. Now and again the dull thump of a blasting charge three miles away told that the Aurangabadis were in difficulties with their road-making. The men smiled as they listened and lay still, soaking in the warm leisure. Presently Learoyd, between the whiffs of his pipe –

'Seems queer – about 'im yonder – desertin' at all.'

''E'll be a bloomin' side queerer when I've done with 'im,' said Ortheris. They were talking in whispers, for the stillness of the wood and the desire of slaughter lay heavy upon them.

'I make no doubt he had his reasons for desertin'; but, my faith! I make less doubt ivry man has good reason for killin' him,' said Mulvaney.

'Happen there was a lass tewed up wi' it. Men do more than more for th' sake of a lass.'

'They make most av us 'list. They've no manner av right to make us desert.'

'Ah; they make us 'list, or their fathers do,' said Learoyd softly, his helmet over his eyes.

Ortheris's brows contracted savagely. He was watching the valley. 'If it's a girl I'll shoot the beggar twice over, an' second time for bein' a fool. You're blasted sentimental all of a sudden. Thinkin' o' your last near shave?'

'Nay, lad; ah was but thinkin' o' what has happened.'

'An' fwhat has happened, ye lumberin' child av calamity, that you're lowing like a cow-calf at the back av the pasture, an' suggestin' invidious excuses for the man Stanley's goin' to kill. Ye'll have to wait another hour yet, little man. Spit it out, Jock, an' bellow melojus to the moon. It takes an earthquake or a bullet graze to fetch aught out av you. Discourse, Don Juan! The a-moors av Lotharius Learoyd! Stanley, kape a rowlin' rig'mental eye on the valley.'

'It's along o' yon hill there,' said Learoyd, watching the bare sub-Himalayan spur that reminded him of his Yorkshire moors. He was speaking more to himself than his fellows. 'Ay,' said he, 'Rumbolds Moor stands up ower Skipton town, an' Greenhow Hill stands up ower Pately Brig. I reckon you've never heeard tell o' Greenhow Hill, but yon bit o' bare stuff if there was nobbut a white road windin' is like ut; strangely like. Moors an' moors an' moors, wi' never a tree for shelter, an' grey houses wi' flagstone rooves, and pewits cryin', an' a windhover goin' to and fro just like these kites. And cold! A wind that cuts you like a knife. You could tell Greenhow Hill folk by the red-apple colour o' their cheeks an' nose tips, and their blue eyes, driven into pin-points by the wind. Miners mostly, burrowin' for lead i' th' hillsides, followin' the trail of th' ore vein same as a field-rat. It was the roughest minin' I ever seen. Yo'd come on a bit o' creakin' wood windlass like a well-head, an' you was let down i' th' bight of a rope, fendin' yoursen off the side wi' one hand, carryin' a candle stuck in a lump o' clay with t'other, an' clickin' hold of a rope with t'other hand.'

'An' that's three of them,' said Mulvaney. 'Must be a good climate in those parts.'

Learoyd took no heed.

'An' then yo' came to a level, where you crept on your hands and knees through a mile o' windin' drift, an' you come out into a cave-place as big as Leeds Townhall, with a engine pumpin' water from workin's 'at went deeper still. It's a queer country, let alone minin', for the hill is full of those natural caves, an' the rivers an' the becks drops into what they call pot-holes, an' come out again miles away.'

'Wot was you doin' there?' said Ortheris.

'I was a young chap then, an' mostly went wi' 'osses, leadin' coal and lead ore; but at th' time I'm tellin' on I was drivin' the waggon-team i' the' big sumph. I didn't belong to that country-side by rights. I went there because of a little difference at home, an' at fust I took up wi' a rough lot. One night we'd been drinkin', an' I must ha' hed more than I could stand, or happen th'ale was none so good. Though i' them days, By for God, I never seed bad ale.' He flung his arms over his head, and gripped a vast handful of white violets. 'Nah,' said he, 'I never seed the ale I could not drink, the bacca I could not smoke, nor the lass I could not kiss. Well, we mun have a race home, the lot on us. I lost all th'others, an' when I was climbin' ower one of them walls built o' loose stones, I comes down into the ditch, stones and all, an' broke my arm. Not as I knawed much about it, for I fell on th' back of my head, an' was knocked stupid like. An' when I come to mysen it were mornin', an' I were lyin' on the settle i' Jesse Roantree's house-place, an' 'Liza Roantree was settin' sewin'. I ached all ovver, and my mouth were like a lime-kiln. She gave me a drink out of a china mug wi' gold letters – "A Present from Leeds" – as I looked at many and many a time at after. "Yo're to lie still while Dr Warbottom comes, because your arm's broken, and father has sent a lad to fetch him. He found yo' when he was goin' to work, an' carried you here on his back," sez she. "Oa!" sez I; an' I shet my eyes, for I felt ashamed o' mysen. "Father's gone to his work these three hours, an' he said he'd tell 'em to get somebody to drive the tram." The clock ticked, an' a bee comed in the house, an' they rung i' my head like mill-wheels. An' she give me another drink an' settled the pillow. "Eh, but yo're young to be getten drunk an' such like, but yo' won't do it again, will yo'?" – "Noa," sez I, "I wouldn't if she'd nobbut stop they mill-wheels clatterin'."'

'Faith, it's a good thing to be nursed by a woman when you're sick!' said Mulvaney. 'Dir' cheap at the price av twenty broken heads.'

Ortheris turned to frown across the valley. He had not been nursed by many women in his life.

'An' then Dr Warbottom comes ridin' up, an' Jesse Roantree along with 'im. He was a high-larned doctor, but he talked wi' poor folk same as theirsens. "What's ta bin agaate on naa?" he sings out. "Brekkin' tha thick head?" An' he felt me all ovver. "That's none broken. Tha's nobbut knocked a bit sillier than ordinary, an' that's daaft eneaf." An' soa he went on, callin' me all the names he could think on, but settin' my arm, wi' Jesse's help, as careful as could be. "Yo' mun let the big oaf bide here a bit, Jesse," he says, when he hed strapped me up an' given me a dose o' physic; "an' you an' 'Liza will tend him, though he's scarcelins worth the trouble. An' tha'll lose tha work," sez he, "an' tha'll be upon th' Sick Club for a couple o' months an' more. Doesn't tha think tha's a fool?"'

'But whin was a young man, high or low, the other av a fool, I'd like to know?' said Mulvaney. 'Sure, folly's the only safe way to wisdom, for I've thried it.'

'Wisdom!' grinned Ortheris, scanning his comrades with uplifted chin. 'You're bloomin' Solomons, you two, ain't you?'

Learoyd went calmly on, with a steady eye like an ox chewing the cud.

'And that was how I comed to know 'Liza Roantree. There's some tunes as she used to sing – aw, she were always singin' – that fetches Greenhow Hill before my eyes as fair as yon brow across there. And she would learn me to sing bass, an' I was to go to th' chapel wi' 'em, where Jesse and she led the singin', the old man playin' the fiddle. He was a strange chap, old Jesse, fair mad wi' music, an' he made me promise to learn the big fiddle when my arm was better. It belonged to him, and it stood up in a big case alongside o' th' eight-day clock, but Willie Satherthwaite, as played it in the chapel, had getten deaf as a door-post, and it vexed Jesse, as he had to rap him ower his head wi' th' fiddlestick to make him give ower sawin' at th' right time.

'But there was a black drop in it all, an' it was a man in a black coat that brought it. When th' Primitive Methodist preacher came to Greenhow, he would always stop wi' Jesse Roantree, an' he laid hold of me from th' beginning. It seemed I wor a soul to be saved, and he meaned to do it. At th' same time I jealoused 'at he were keen o' savin' 'Liza Roantree's soul as well, and I could ha' killed him many a time. An' this went on till one day I broke out, an' borrowed th' brass for a drink from 'Liza. After fower days I come back, wi' my tail between my legs, just to see 'Liza again. But Jesse were at home an' th' preacher – th' Reverend Amos Barraclough. 'Liza said naught, but a bit o' red come into her face as were white of a regular thing. Says Jesse, tryin' his best to be civil, "Nay, lad, it's like this. You've getten to choose which way it's goin' to be. I'll ha' nobody across ma doorstep as goes a-drinkin', an' borrows my lass's money to spend i' their drink. Ho'd tha tongue, 'Liza," sez he, when she wanted to put in a word 'at I were welcome to th' brass, and she were none afraid that I wouldn't pay it back. Then the Reverend cuts in, seein' as Jesse were losin' his temper, an' they fair beat me among them. But it were 'Liza, as looked an' said naught, as did more than either o' their tongues, an' soa I concluded to get converted.'

'Fwhat!' shouted Mulvaney. Then, checking himself, he said softly, 'Let be! Let be! Sure the Blessed Virgin is the mother of all religion an' most women; an' there's a dale av piety in a girl if the men would only let ut stay there. I'd ha' been converted myself under the circumstances.'

'Nay, but,' pursued Learoyd with a blush, 'I meaned it.'

Ortheris laughed as loudly as he dared, having regard to his business at the time.

'Ay, Ortheris, you may laugh, but you didn't know yon preacher

Barraclough – a little white-faced chap, wi' a voice as 'ud wile a bird offan a bush, and a way o' layin' hold of folks as made them think they'd never had a live man for a friend before. You never saw him, an' – an' – you never seed 'Liza Roantree – never seed 'Liza Roantree. . . . Happen it was as much 'Liza as th' preacher and her father, but anyways they all meaned it, an' I was fair shamed o' mysen, an' so I become what they called a changed character. And when I think on, it's hard to believe as yon chap going to prayer-meetin's, chapel, and class-meetin's were me. But I never had naught to say for mysen, though there was a deal o' shoutin', and old Sammy Strother, as were almost clemmed to death and doubled up with the rheumatics, would sing out, "Joyful! Joyful!" and 'at it were better to go up to Heaven in a coal-basket than down to Hell i' a coach an' six. And he would put his poor old claw on my shoulder, sayin', "Doesn't tha feel it, tha great lump? Doesn't tha feel it?" An' sometimes I thought I did, and then again I thought I didn't, an' how was that?'

'The iverlastin' nature av mankind,' said Mulvaney. 'An', furthermore, I misdoubt you were built for the Primitive Methodians. They're a new corps anyways. I hold by the Ould Church, for she's the mother of them all – ay, an' the father, too. I like her bekaze she's most remarkable regimental in her fittings. I may die in Honolulu, Nova Zambra, or Cape Cayenne, but wherever I die, me bein' fwhat I am, an' a priest handy, I go under the same orders an' the same words an' the same unction as tho' the Pope himself come down from the roof av St Peter's to see me off. There's neither high nor low, nor broad nor deep, nor betwixt nor between wid her, an' that's what I like. But mark you, she's no manner av Church for a wake man, bekaze she takes the body and the soul av him, onless he has his proper work to do. I remember when my father died that was three months comin' to his grave; begad he'd ha' sold the shebeen above our heads for ten minutes quittance of purgathory. An' he did all he could. That's why I say ut takes a strong man to deal with the Ould Church, an' for that reason you'll find so many women go there. An' that sames a conundrum.'

'Wot's the use o' worrittin' 'bout these things?' said Ortheris. 'You're bound to find all out quicker nor you want to, any'ow.' He jerked the cartridge out of the breech-block into the palm of his hand. ''Ere's my chaplain,' he said, and made the venomous black-headed bullet bow like a marionette. ''E's goin' to teach a man all about which is which, an' wot's true, after all, before sundown. But wot 'appened after that, Jock?'

'There was one thing they boggled at, and almost shut th' gate i' my face for, and that were my dog, Blast, th' only one saved out o' a litter o' pups as was blowed up when a keg o' minin' powder loosed off in th' store-keeper's hut. They liked his name no better than his business, which were fightin' every dog he comed across; a rare good dog, wi' spots o' black and pink on his face, one ear gone, and lame o' one side wi' being driven in a basket through an iron roof, a matter of half a mile.

'They said I mun give him up 'cause he were worldly and low; and would I let mysen be shut out of Heaven for the sake on a dog? "Nay," says I, "if th' door isn't wide enough for th' pair on us, we'll stop outside, for we'll none be parted." And th' preacher spoke up for Blast, as had a likin' for him from th' first – I reckon that was why I come to like th' preacher – and wouldn't hear o' changin' his name to Bless, as some o' them wanted. So th' pair on us became reg'lar chapel-members. But it's hard for a young chap o' my build to cut traces from the world, th' flesh, an' the devil all uv a heap. Yet I stuck to it for a long time, while th' lads as used to stand about th' town-end an' lean ower th' bridge, spittin' into th' beck o' a Sunday, would call after me, "Sitha, Learoyd, when's ta bean to preach, 'cause we're comin' to hear tha." – "Ho'd tha jaw. He hasn't getten th' white choaker on ta morn," another lad would say, and I had to double my fists hard i' th' bottom of my Sunday coat, and say to mysen, "If 'twere Monday and I warn't a member o' the Primitive Methodists, I'd leather all th' lot of yond'." That was th' hardest of all – to know that I could fight and I mustn't fight.'

Sympathetic grunts from Mulvaney.

'So what wi' singin', practisin', and class-meetin's, and th' big fiddle, as he made me take between my knees, I spent a deal o' time i' Jesse Roantree's house-place. But often as I was there, th' preacher fared to me to go oftener, and both th' old man an' th' young woman were pleased to have him. He lived i' Pately Brig, as were a goodish step off, but he come. He come all the same. I liked him as well or better as any man I'd ever seen i' one way, and yet I hated him wi' all my heart i' t'other, and we watched each other like cat and mouse, but civil as you please, for I was on my best behaviour, and he was that fair and open that I was bound to be fair with him. Rare good company he was, if I hadn't wanted to wring his cliver little neck half of the time. Often and often when he was goin' from Jesse's I'd set him a bit on the road.'

'See 'im 'ome, you mean?' said Ortheris.

'Ay!' It's a way we have i' Yorkshire o' seein' friends off. Yon was a friend as I didn't want to come back, and he didn't want me to come back neither, and so we'd walk together towards Pately, and then he'd set me back again, and there we'd be wal two o'clock i' the mornin' settin' each other to an' fro like a blasted pair o' pendulums twixt hill and valley, long after th' light had gone out i' 'Liza's window, as both on us had been looking at, pretending to watch the moon.'

'Ah!' broke in Mulvaney, 'ye'd no chanst against the maraudin' psalm-singer. They'll take the airs an' the graces instid av the man nine times out av ten, an' they only find the blunder later – the wimmen.'

'That's just where yo're wrong,' said Learoyd, reddening under the freckled tan of his cheeks. 'I was th' first wi 'Liza, an' you'd think that were enough. But th' parson were a steady-gaited sort o' chap, and Jesse were strong o' his side, and all th' women i' the congregation dinned it to 'Liza 'at she were fair fond to take up wi' a wastrel ne'er-do-weel like me, as was scarcelins respectable an' a fighting dog at his heels. It was all very well for her to be doing me good and saving my soul, but she must mind as she didn't do herself harm. They talk o' rich folk bein' stuck up an' genteel, but for cast-iron pride o' respectability there's naught like poor chapel folk. It's as cold as th' wind o' Greenhow Hill – ay, and colder, for 'twill never change. And now I come to think on it, one at strangest things I know is 'at they couldn't abide th' thought o' soldiering. There's a vast o' fightin' i' th' Bible, and there's a deal of Methodists i' th' Army; but to hear chapel folk talk yo'd think that soldierin' were next door, an' t'other side, to hangin'. I' their meetin's all their talk is o' fightin'. When Sammy Strother were stuck for summat to say in his prayers, he'd sing out, "Th' sword o' th' Lord and o' Gideon." They were allus at it about puttin' on th' whole armour o' righteousness, an' fightin' the good fight o' faith. And then, atop o' 't all, they held a prayer-meetin' ower a young chap as wanted to 'list, and nearly deafened him, till he picked up his hat and fair ran away. And they'd tell tales in th' Sunday-school o' bad lads as had been thumped and brayed for bird-nesting o' Sundays and playin' truant o' weekdays, and how they took to wrestlin', dog-fightin', rabbit-runnin', and drinkin, till at last, as if 'twere a hepitaph on a gravestone, they damned him across th'moors wi', "an' then he went and 'listed for a soldier," an they'd all fetch a deep breath, and throw up their eyes like a hen drinkin'.'

'Fwhy is ut?' said Mulvaney, bringing down his hand on his thigh with a crack. 'In the name av God, fwhy is ut? I've seen ut, tu. They cheat an' they swindle an' they lie an' they slander, an' fifty things fifty times worse; but the last an' the worst by their reckonin' is to serve the Widdy honest. It's like the talk av childer – seein' things all round.'

'Plucky lot of fightin' good fights of whatsername they'd do if we didn't see they had a quiet place to fight in. And such fightin' as theirs is! Cats on the tiles. T'other callin' to which to come on. I'd give a month's pay to get some o' them broad-backed beggars in London sweatin' through a day's road-makin' an' a night's rain. They'd carry on a deal afterwards – same as we're supposed to carry on. I've bin turned out of a measly arf-licence pub down Lambeth way, full o' greasy kebmen, 'fore now,' said Ortheris with an oath.

'Maybe you were dhrunk,' said Mulvaney soothingly.

'Worse nor that. The Forders were drunk. *I* was wearin' the Queen's uniform.'

'I'd no particular thought to be a soldier i' them days,' said Learoyd, still keeping his eye on the bare hill opposite, 'but this sort o' talk put it i' my head. They was so good, th' chapel folk, that they tumbled ower t'other side. But I stuck to it for 'Liza's sake, specially as she was learning me to sing the bass part in a horotorio as Jesse were gettin' up. She sung like a throstle hersen, and we had practisin's night after night for a matter of three months.'

'I know what a horotorio is,' said Ortheris pertly. 'It's a sort of chaplain's sing-song – words all out of the Bible, and hullabaloojah choruses.'

'Most Greenhow Hill folks played some instrument or t'other, an' they all sung so you might have heard them miles away, and they were so pleased wi' the noise they made they didn't fare to want anybody to listen. The preacher sung high seconds when he wasn't playin' the flute, an' they set me, as hadn't got far with big fiddle, again Willie Satterthwaite, to jog his elbow when he had to get agate playin'. Old Jesse was happy if ever a man was, for he were th' conductor an' th' first fiddle an' th' leadin' singer, beatin' time wi' his fiddlestick, till at times he'd rap with it on the table, and cry out, "Now, you mun all stop; it's my turn." And he'd face round to his front, fair sweating wi' pride, to sing th' tenor solos. But he were grandest i' th' choruses, waggin' his head, flinging his arms round like a windmill, and singin' hisself black in the face. A rare singer were Jesse.

'Yo' see, I was not o' much account wi' 'em all exceptin' to 'Liza Roantree, and I had a deal o' time settin' quiet at meetings and horotorio practices to hearken their talk, and if it were strange to me at beginnin', it got stranger still at after, when I was shut on it, and could study what it meaned.

'Just after th' horotorios came off, 'Liza, as had allus been weakly like, was took very bad. I walked Dr Warbottom's horse up and down a deal of times while he were inside, where they wouldn't let me go, though I fair ached to see her.

'"She'll be better i' noo, lad – better i' noo," he used to say. "Tha mun ha' patience." Then they said if I was quiet I might go in, and th' Reverend Amos Barraclough used to read to her lyin' propped up among th' pillows. Then she began to mend a bit, and they let me carry her on to th' settle, and when it got warm again she went about same as afore. Th' preacher and me and Blast was a deal together i' them days, and i' one way we was rare good comrades. But I could ha' stretched him time and again with a good will. I mind one day he said he would like to go down into th' bowels o' th' earth, and see how th' Lord had builded th' framework o' th' everlastin' hills. He were one of them chaps as had a gift o' sayin' things. They rolled off the tip of his clever tongue, same as Mulvaney here, as would ha' made a rare good preacher if he had nobbut given his mind to it. I lent him a suit o' miner's kit as almost buried th' little man, and his white face down i' th' coat-collar and hat-flap looked like the face of a boggart, and he cowered down i' th' bottom o' the waggon. I was drivin' a tram as led up a bit of an incline up to th' cave where the engine was pumpin', and where th' ore was brought up and put into th' waggons as went down o' themselves, me puttin' th' brake on and th' horses a-trottin' after. Long as it was daylight we were good friends, but when we got fair into th' dark, and could nobbut see th' day shinin' at the hole like a lamp at a street-end, I feeled downright wicked. Ma religion dropped all away from me when I looked back at him as were always comin' between me and 'Liza. The talk was 'at they were to be wed when she got better, an' I couldn't get her to say yes or nay to it. He began to sing a hymn in his thin voice, and I came out wi' a chorus that was all cussin' an' swearin' at my horses, an' I began to know how I hated him. He were such a little chap, too. I could drop him wi' one hand down Garstang's Copper-hole – a place where th' beck slithered ower th' edge on a rock, and fell wi' a bit of a whisper into a pit as no rope i' Greenhow could plump.'

Again Learoyd rooted up the innocent violets. 'Ay, he should see th' bowels o' th' earth an' never naught else. I could take him a mile or two along th' drift, and leave him wi' his candle doused to cry hallelujah, wi' none to hear him and say amen. I was to lead him down th' ladder-way to th' drift where Jesse Roantree was workin', and why shouldn't he slip on th' ladder, wi' my feet on his fingers till they loosed grip, and I put him down wi' my heel? If I went fust down th' ladder I could click hold on him and chuck him over my head, so as he should go squshin' down the shaft, breakin' his bones at ev'ry timberin' as Bill Appleton did when he was fresh, and hadn't a bone left when he wrought to th' bottom. Niver a blasted leg to walk from Pately. Niver an arm to put round 'Liza Roantree's waist. Niver no more – niver no more.'

The thick lips curled back over the yellow teeth, and that flushed face was not pretty to look upon. Mulvaney nodded sympathy, and Ortheris, moved by his comrade's passion, brought up the rifle to his shoulder, and searched the hillside for his quarry, muttering ribaldry about a sparrow, a spout, and a thunderstorm. The voice of the watercourse supplied the necessary small talk till Learoyd picked up his story.

'But it's none so easy to kill a man like yon. When I'd given up my horses to th' lad as took my place and I was showin' th' preacher th' workin's, shoutin' into his ear across th' clang o' th' pumpin' engines, I saw he were afraid o' naught; and when the lamplight showed his black eyes, I could feel as he was masterin' me again. I were no better nor Blast chained up short and growlin' i' the depths of him while a strange dog went safe past.

'"Th'art a coward and a fool," I said to mysen; an' I wrestled i' my mind again' him till, when we come to Garstang's Copper-hole, I laid hold o' the preacher and liften him up over my head and held him into the darkest on it. "Now, lad," I says, "it's to be one or t'other on us – thee or me – for 'Liza Roantree. Why, isn't thee afraid for thysen?" I says, for he were still i' my arms as a sack. "Nay; I'm but afraid for thee, my poor lad, as knows naught," says he. I set him down on th' edge, an' th' beck run stiller, an' there was no more buzzin' in my head like when th' bee come through th' window o' Jesse's house. "What dost tha mean?" says I.

'"I've often thought as thou ought to know," says he, "but 'twas hard to tell thee. 'Liza Roantree's for neither on us, nor for nobody o' this earth. Dr Warbottom says – and he knows her, and her mother before her – that she is in a decline, and she cannot live six months longer. He's known it for many a day. Steady, John! Steady!" says he. And that weak little man pulled me further back and set me again' him, and talked it all over quiet and still, me turnin' a bunch o' candles in my hand, and counting them ower and ower again as I listened. A deal on it were th' regular preachin' talk, but there were a vast lot as made me begin to think as he were more of a man than I'd ever given him credit for, till I were cut as deep for him as I were for mysen.

'Six candles we had, and we crawled and climbed all that day while they lasted, and I said to mysen, "'Liza Roantree hasn't six months to live." And when we came into th' daylight again we were like dead men to look at, an' Blast come behind us without so much as waggin' his tail. When I saw 'Liza again she looked at me a minute and says, "Who's telled tha? For I see tha knows." And she tried to smile as she kissed me, and I fair broke down.

'Yo'see, I was a young chap i' them days, and had seen naught o' life, let alone death, as is allus a-waitin'. She telled me as Dr Warbottom said as Greenhow air was too keen, and they were goin' to Bradford, to Jesse's brother David, as worked i' a mill, and I mun hold up like a man and a Christian, and she'd pray for me. Well, and they went away, and the preacher that same back end o' th' year were appointed to another circuit, as they call it, and I were left alone on Greenhow Hill.

'I tried, and I tried hard, to stick to th' chapel, but 'tweren't th' same thing at after. I hadn't 'Liza's voice to follow i' th' singin', nor her eyes a'shinin' acrost their heads. And i' th' class-meetings they said as I mun have some experiences to tell, and I hadn't a word to say for mysen.

'Blast and me moped a good deal, and happen we didn't behave ourselves over well, for they dropped us and wondered however they'd come to take us up. I can't tell how we got through th' time, while i' th' winter I gave up my job and went to Bradford. Old Jesse were at th' door o' th' house, in a long street o' little houses. He'd been sendin' th' children 'way as were clatterin' their clogs in th' causeway, for she were asleep.

'"Is it thee?" he says; "but you're not to see her. I'll none have her wakened for a nowt like thee. She's goin' fast, and she mun go in peace. Thou'lt never be good for naught i' th' world, and as long as thou lives thou'll never play the big fiddle. Get away, lad, get away!" So he shut the door softly i' my face.

'Nobody never made Jesse my master, but it seemed to me he was about right, and I went away into the town and knocked up against a recruiting sergeant. The old tales o' th' chapel folk came buzzin' into my head. I was to get away, and this were th' regular road for the likes o' me. I 'listed there and then, took th' Widow's shillin', and had a bunch o' ribbons pinned i' my hat.

'But next day I found my way to David Roantree's door, and Jesse came to open it. Says he, "Thou's come back again wi' th' devil's colours flyin' – thy true colours, as I always telled thee."

'But I begged and prayed of him to let me see her nobbut to say goodbye, till a woman calls down th' stairway,"She says John Learoyd's to come up." Th' old man shifts aside in a flash, and lays his hand on my arm, quite gentle like. "But thou'lt be quiet, John," says he, "for she's rare and weak. Thou was allus a good lad."

'Her eyes were all alive wi' light, and her hair was thick on the pillow round her, but her cheeks were thin – thin to frighten a man that's strong. "Nay, father, yo' mayn't say th' devil's colours. Them ribbons is pretty." An' she held out her hands for th' hat, an' she put all straight as a woman will wi' ribbons. "Nay, but what they're pretty," she says. "Eh, but I'd ha' liked to see thee i' thy red coat, John, for thou was allus my own lad – my very own lad, and none else."

'She lifted up her arms, and they come round my neck i' a gentle grip, and they slacked away, and she seemed fainting. "Now yo' mun get away, lad," says Jesse, and I picked up my hat and I came downstairs.

'Th' recruiting sergeant were waitin' for me at th' corner public-house. "Yo've seen your sweetheart?" says he. "Yes, I've seen her," says I. "Well, we'll have a quart now, and you'll do your best to forget her," says he, bein' one o' them smart, bustlin' chaps. "Ay, sergeant," says I. "Forget her." And I've been forgettin' her ever since.'

He threw away the wilted clump of white violets as he spoke. Ortheris suddenly rose to his knees, his rifle at his shoulder, and peered across the valley in the clear afternoon light. His chin cuddled the stock, and there was a twitching of the muscles of the right cheek as he sighted; Private Stanley Ortheris was engaged on his business. A speck of white crawled up the watercourse.

'See that beggar? . . . Got 'im.'

Seven hundred yards away, and a full two hundred down the hillside, the deserter of the Aurangabadis pitched forward, rolled down a red rock, and lay very still, with his face in a clump of blue gentians, while a big raven flapped out of the pine wood to make investigation.

'That's a clean shot, little man,' said Mulvaney.

Learoyd thoughtfully watched the smoke clear away. 'Happen there was a lass tewed up wi' him, too,' said he.

Ortheris did not reply. He was staring across the valley, with the smile of the artist who looks on the completed work.

The Dream of Duncan Parrenness

LIKE Mr Bunyan of old, I, Duncan Parrenness, Writer to the Most Honourable the East India Company, in this God-forgotten city of Calcutta, have dreamed a dream, and never since that Kitty my mare fell lame have I been so troubled. Therefore, lest I should forget my dream, I have made shift to set it down here. Though Heaven knows how unhandy the pen is to me who was always readier with sword than ink-horn when I left London two long years since.

When the Governor-General's great dance (that he gives yearly at the latter end of November) was finisht, I had gone to mine own room which looks over that sullen, un-English stream, the Hoogly, scarce so sober as I might have been. Now, roaring drunk in the West is but fuddled in the East, and I was drunk Nor'-Nor' Easterly as Mr Shakespeare might have said. Yet, in spite of my liquor, the cool night winds (though I have heard that they breed chills and fluxes innumerable) sobered me somewhat; and I remembered that I had been but a little wrung and wasted by all the sicknesses of the past four months, whereas those young bloods that came eastward with me in the same ship had been all, a month back, planted to Eternity in the foul soil north of Writers' Buildings. So then, I thanked God mistily (though, to my shame, I never kneeled down to do so) for licence to live, at least till March should be upon us again. Indeed, we that were alive (and our number was less by far than those who had gone to their last account in the hot weather late past) had made very merry that evening, by the ramparts of the Fort, over this kindness of Providence; though our jests were neither witty nor such as I should have liked my mother to hear.

When I had lain down (or rather thrown me on my bed) and the fumes of my drink had a little cleared away, I found that I could get no sleep for thinking of a thousand things that were better left alone. First, and it was a long time since I had thought of her, the sweet face of Kitty Somerset drifted, as it might have been drawn in a picture, across the foot of my bed, so plainly, that I almost thought she had been present in the body. Then I remembered how she drove me to this accursed country to get rich, that I might the more quickly marry her, our parents on both sides giving their consent; and then how she thought better (or worse maybe) of her troth, and wed Tom Sanderson but a short three months after I had sailed. From Kitty I fell a-musing on Mrs Vansuythen, a tall pale woman with violet eyes that had come to Calcutta from the Dutch Factory at Chinsura, and had set all our young men, and not a few of the factors, by the ears. Some of our ladies, it is true, said that she had never a husband or marriage-lines at all; but women, and specially those who have led only indifferent good lives themselves, are cruel hard one on another. Besides, Mrs Vansuythen was far prettier than them all. She had been most gracious to me at the Governor-General's rout, and indeed I was looked upon by all as her *preux chevalier* – which is French for a much worse word. Now, whether I cared so much as the scratch of a pin for this same Mrs Vansuythen (albeit I had vowed eternal love three days after we met) I knew not then nor did till later on; but mine own pride, and a skill in the small sword that no man in Calcutta could equal, kept me in her affections. So that I believed I worshipt her.

When I had dismist her violet eyes from my thoughts, my reason reproacht me for ever having followed her at all; and I saw how the one year that I had lived in this land had so burnt and seared my mind with the flames of a thousand bad passions and desires, that I had aged ten months for each one in the Devil's school. Whereat I thought of my mother for a while, and was very penitent: making in my sinful tipsy mood a thousand vows of reformation – all since broken, I fear me, again and again. Tomorrow, says I to myself, I will live cleanly for ever. And I smiled dizzily (the liquor being still strong in me) to think of the dangers I had escaped; and built all manner of fine castles in Spain, whereof a shadowy Kitty Somerset that had the violet eyes and the sweet slow speech of Mrs Vansuythen, was always Queen.

Lastly, a very fine and magnificent courage (that doubtless had its birth in Mr Hastings' Madeira) grew upon me, till it seemed that I could become Governor-General, Nawab, Prince, ay, even the Great Mogul himself, by the mere wishing of it. Wherefore, taking my first steps, random and unstable enough, towards my new kingdom, I kickt my servants sleeping without till they howled and ran from me, and called Heaven and Earth to witness that I, Duncan Parrenness, was a writer in the service of the Company and afraid of no man. Then, seeing that neither the Moon nor the Great Bear were minded to accept my challenge, I lay down again and must have fallen asleep.

I was waked presently by my last words repeated two or three times, and I saw that there had come into the room a drunken man, as I thought, from Mr Hastings' rout. He sate down at the foot of my bed for all the world as it belonged to him, and I took note, as a well as I could, that his face was somewhat like mine own grown older, save when it changed to the face of the Governor-General or my father, dead these six months. But this seemed to me only natural, and the due result of too much wine; and I was so angered at his entry all unannounced, that I told him, not over civilly, to go. To all my words he made no answer whatever, only saying slowly, as though it were some sweet morsel: 'Writer in the Company's service and afraid of no man.' Then he stops short, and turning round sharp upon me, says that one of my kidney need fear neither man nor devil; that I was a brave young man, and like enough, should I live so long, to be Governor-General. But for all these things (and I supposed that he meant thereby the changes and chances of our shifty life in these parts) I must pay my price. By this time I had sobered somewhat, and being well waked out of my first sleep, was disposed to look upon the matter as a tipsy man's jest. So, says I merrily: 'And what price shall I pay for this palace of mine, which is but twelve feet square, and my five poor pagodas a month? The devil take you and your jesting: I have paid my price twice over in sickness.' At that moment my man turns full toward me: so that by the moonlight I could see every line and wrinkle of his face. Then my drunken mirth died out of me, as I have seen the waters of our great rivers die away in one night; and I, Duncan Parrenness, who was afraid of no man, was taken with a more deadly terror than I hold it has ever been the lot of mortal man to know. For I saw that his face was my very own, but marked and lined and scarred with the furrows of disease and much evil living – as I once, when I was (Lord help me) very drunk indeed, have seen mine own face, all white and drawn and grown old, in a mirror. I take it that any man would have been even more greatly feared than I; for I am in no way wanting in courage.

After I had laid still for a little, sweating in my agony, and waiting until I should awake from this terrible dream (for dream I knew it to be), he says again that I must pay my price; and a little after, as though it were to be given in pagodas and sicca rupees: 'What price will you pay?' Says I, very softly: 'For God's sake let me be, whoever you are, and I will mend my ways from tonight.' Says he, laughing a little at my words, but otherwise making no motion of having heard them: 'Nay, I would only rid so brave a young ruffler as yourself of much that will be a great hindrance to you on your way through life in the Indies; for believe me,' and here he looks full on me once more, 'there is no return.' At all this rigmarole, which I could not then understand, I was a good deal put aback and waited for what should come next. Says he very calmly: 'Give me your trust in man.' At that I saw how heavy would be my price, for I never doubted but that he could take from me all that he asked, and my head was, through terror and wakefulness, altogether cleared of the wine I had drunk. So I takes him up very short, crying that I was not so wholly bad as he would make believe, and that I trusted my fellows to the full as much as they were worthy of it. 'It was none of my fault,' says I, 'if one-half of them were liars and the other half deserved to be burnt in the hand, and I would once more ask him to have done with his questions.' Then I stopped, a little afraid, it is true, to have let my tongue so run away with me, but he took no notice of this, and only laid his hand lightly on my left breast and I felt very cold there for a while. Then he says, laughing more: 'Give me your faith in women.' At that I started in my bed as though I had been stung, for I thought of my sweet mother in England, and for a while fancied that my faith in God's best creatures could neither be shaken nor stolen from me. But later, myself's hard eyes being upon me, I fell to thinking, for the second time that night, of Kitty (she that jilted me and married Tom Sanderson) and of Mistress Vansuythen, whom only my devilish pride made me follow, and how she was even worse than Kitty, and I worst of them all – seeing that with my life's work to be done, I must needs go dancing down the Devil's swept and garnished causeway, because, forsooth, there was a light woman's smile at the end of it. And I thought that all women in the world were either like Kitty or Mistress Vansuythen (as indeed they have ever since been to me), and this put me to such an extremity of rage and sorrow, that I was beyond word glad when myself's hand fell again on my left breast, and I was no more troubled by these follies.

After this he was silent for a little, and I made sure that he must go or I awake ere long; but presently he speaks again (and very softly) that I was a fool to care for such follies as those he had taken from me, and that ere he went he would only ask me for a few other trifles such as no man, or for matter of that boy either, would keep about him in this country. And so it happened that he took from out of my very heart as it were, looking all the time into my face with my own eyes, as much as remained to me of my boy's soul and conscience. This was to me a far more terrible loss than the two that I had suffered before. For though, Lord help me, I had travelled far enough from all paths of decent or godly living, yet there was in me, though I myself write it, a certain goodness of heart which, when I was sober (or sick) made me very sorry of all that I had done before the fit came on me. And this I lost wholly: having in place thereof another deadly coldness at the heart. I am not, as I have before said, ready with my pen, so I fear that what I have just written may not be readily understood. Yet there be certain times in a young man's life, when, through great sorrow or sin, all the boy in him is burnt and seared away so that he passes at one step to the more sorrowful state of manhood: as our staring Indian day changes into night with never so much as the grey of twilight to temper the two extremes. This shall perhaps make my state more clear, if it be remembered that my torment was ten times as great as comes in the natural course of nature to any man. At that time I dared not think of the change that had come over me, and all in one night: though I have often thought of it since. 'I have paid the price,' says I, my teeth chattering, for I was deadly cold, 'and what is my return?' At this time it was nearly dawn, and myself had begun to grow pale and thin against the white light in the east, as my mother used to tell me is the custom of ghosts and devils and the like. He made as if he would go, but my words stopt him and he laughed – as I remember that I laughed when I ran Angus Macalister through the sword-arm last August, because he said that Mrs Vansuythen was no better than she should be. 'What return?' – says he, catching up my last words – 'Why, strength to live as long as God or the Devil pleases, and so long as you live, my young master, my gift.' With that he puts something into my hand, though it was still too dark to see what it was, and when next I lookt up he was gone.

When the light came I made shift to behold his gift, and saw that it was a little piece of dry bread.

The Disturber of Traffic

From the wheel and the drift of Things
  Deliver us, good Lord;
And we will meet the wrath of kings,
  The faggot, and the sword.

Lay not Thy toil before our eyes,
  Nor vex us with Thy wars,
Lest we should feel the straining skies
  O'ertrod by trampling stars.

A veil 'twixt us and Thee, dread Lord,
  A veil 'twixt us and Thee:
Lest we should hear too clear, too clear,
  And unto madness see!

Miriam Cohen

THE Brothers of the Trinity order that none unconnected with their service shall be found in or on one of their Lights during the hours of darkness; but their servants can be made to think otherwise. If you are fair-spoken and take an interest in their duties, they will allow you to sit with them through the long night and help to scare the ships into mid-channel.

Of the English south-coast Lights, that of St Cecilia-under-the-Cliff is the most powerful, for it guards a very foggy coast. When the sea-mist veils all, St Cecilia turns a hooded head to the sea and sings a song of two words once every minute. From the land that song resembles the bellowing of a brazen bull; but offshore they understand, and the steamers grunt gratefully in answer.

Fenwick, who was on duty one night, lent me a pair of black glass spectacles, without which no man can look at the Light unblinded, and busied himself in last touches to the lenses before twilight fell. The width of the English Channel beneath us lay as smooth and as many-coloured as the inside of an oyster shell. A little Sunderland cargo-boat had made her signal to Lloyd's Agency, half a mile up the coast, and was lumbering down to the sunset, her wake lying white behind her. One star came out over the cliffs, the waters turned to lead colour, and St Cecilia's Light shot out across the sea in eight long pencils that wheeled slowly from right to left, melted into one beam of solid light laid down directly in front of the tower, dissolved again into eight, and passed away. The light-frame of the thousand lenses circled on its rollers, and the compressed-air engine that drove it hummed like a bluebottle under a glass. The hand of the indicator on the wall pulsed from mark to mark. Eight pulse-beats timed one half-revolution of the Light; neither more nor less.

Fenwick checked the first few revolutions carefully; he opened the engine's feed-pipe a trifle, looked at the racing governor, and again at the indicator, and said: 'She'll do for the next few hours. We've just sent our regular engine to London, and this spare one's not by any manner so accurate.'

'And what would happen if the compressed air gave out?' I asked.

'We'd have to turn the flash by hand, keeping an eye on the indicator. There's a regular crank for that. But it hasn't happened yet. We'll need all our compressed air tonight.'

'Why?' said I. I had been watching him for not more than a minute.

'Look,' he answered, and I saw that the dead sea-mist had risen out of the lifeless sea and wrapped us while my back had been turned. The pencils of the Light marched staggeringly across tilted floors of white cloud. From the balcony round the light-room the white walls of the lighthouse ran down into swirling, smoking space. The noise of the tide coming in very lazily over the rocks was choked down to a thick drawl.

'That's the way our sea-fogs come,' said Fenwick, with an air of ownership. 'Hark, now, to that little fool calling out 'fore he's hurt.'

Something in the mist was bleating like an indignant calf; it might have been half a mile or half a hundred miles away.

'Does he suppose we've gone to bed?' continued Fenwick. 'You'll hear us talk to him in a minute. He knows puffickly where he is, and he's carrying on to be told like if he was insured.'

'Who is "he"?'

'That Sunderland boat, o' course. Ah!'

I could hear a steam-engine hiss down below in the mist where the dynamos that fed the Light were clacking together. Then there came a roar that split the fog and shook the lighthouse.

'GIT-*toot*!' blared the fog-horn of St Cecilia. The bleating ceased.

'Little fool!' Fenwick repeated. Then, listening: 'Blest if that aren't another of them! Well, well, they always say that a fog do draw the ships of the sea together. They'll be calling all night, and so'll the siren. We're expecting some tea-ships up-Channel . . . If you put my coat on that chair, you'll feel more so-fash, sir.'

It is no pleasant thing to thrust your company upon a man for the night. I looked at Fenwick, and Fenwick looked at me; each gauging the other's capacities for boring and being bored. Fenwick was an old, clean-shaven, grey-haired man who had followed the sea for thirty years, and knew nothing of the land except the lighthouse in which he served. He fenced cautiously to find out the little that I knew, and talked down to my level till it came out that I had met a captain in the merchant service who had once commanded a ship in which Fenwick's son had served; and further, that I had seen some places that Fenwick had touched at. He began with a dissertation on pilotage in the Hugli. I had been privileged to know a Hugli pilot intimately. Fenwick had only seen the imposing and masterful breed from a ship's chains, and his intercourse had been cut down to 'Quarter less five', and remarks of a strictly business-like nature. Hereupon he ceased to talk down to me, and became so amazingly technical that I was forced to beg him to explain every other sentence. This set him fully at his ease; and then we spoke as men together, each too interested to think of anything except the subject in hand. And that subject was wrecks, and voyages, and old-time trading, and ships cast away in desolate seas, steamers we both had known, their merits and demerits, lading, Lloyd's, and, above all, Lights. The talk always came back to Lights; Lights of the Channel; Lights on forgotten islands, and men forgotten on them; Light-ships – two months' duty and one month's leave – tossing on kinked cables in ever-troubled tideways; and Lights that men had seen where never lighthouse was marked on the charts.

Omitting all those stories, and omitting also the wonderful ways by which he arrived at them, I tell here, from Fenwick's mouth, one that was not the least amazing. It was delivered in pieces between the roller-skate rattle of the revolving lenses, the bellowing of the fog-horn below, the answering calls from the sea, and the sharp tap of reckless night-birds that flung themselves at the glasses. It concerned a man called Dowse, once an intimate friend of Fenwick, now a waterman at Portsmouth, believing that the guilt of blood is on his head, and finding no rest either at Portsmouth or Gosport Hard.

. . . 'And if anybody was to come to you and say, "I know the Javva currents", don't you listen to him; for those currents is never yet known to mortal man. Sometimes they're here, sometimes they're there, but they never runs less than five knots an hour through and among those islands of the Eastern Archipelagus. There's reverse currents in the Gulf of Boni – and that's up north in Celebes – that no man can explain; and through all those Javva passages from the Bali Narrows, Dutch Gut, and Ombay, which I take it is the safest, they chop and they change, and they banks the tides fust on one shore and then on another, till your ship's tore in two. I've come through the Bali Narrows, stern first, in the heart o' the south-east monsoon, with a sou'-sou'-west wind blowing atop of the northerly flood, and our skipper said he wouldn't do it again, not for all Jamrach's. You've heard o' Jamrach's, sir?'

'Yes; and was Dowse stationed in the Bali Narrows?' I said.

'No; he was not at Bali, but much more east o' them passages, and that's Flores Strait, at the east end o' Flores. It's all on the way south to Australia when you're running through that Eastern Archipelagus. Sometimes you go through Bali Narrows if you're full-powered, and sometimes through Flores Strait, so as to stand south at once, and fetch round Timor, keeping well clear o' the Sahul Bank. Elseways, if you aren't full-powered, why it stands to reason you go round by the Ombay Passage, keeping careful to the north side. You understand that, sir?'

I was not full-powered, and judged it safer to keep to the north side – of Silence.

'And on Flores Strait, in the fairway between Adonare Island and the mainland, they put Dowse in charge of a screw-pile Light called the Wurlee Light. It's less than a mile across the head of Flores Strait. Then it opens out to ten or twelve mile for Solor Strait, and then it narrows again to a three-mile gut, with a topplin' flamin' volcano by it. That's old Loby Toby by Loby Toby Strait, and if you keep his light and the Wurlee Light in a line you won't take much harm, not on the darkest night. That's what Dowse told me, and I can well believe him, knowing these seas myself; but you must ever be mindful of the currents. And there they put Dowse, since he was the only man that that Dutch government which owns Flores could find that would go to Wurlee and tend a fixed Light. Mostly they uses Dutch and Italians; Englishmen being said to drink when alone. I never could rightly find out what made Dowse accept that position, but accept he did, and used to sit for to watch the tigers come out of the forests to hunt for crabs and such like round about the lighthouse at low tide. The water was always warm in those parts, as I know well, and uncommon sticky, and it ran with the tides as thick and smooth as hogwash in a trough. There was another man along with Dowse in the light, but he wasn't rightly a man. He was a Kling. No, nor yet a Kling he wasn't, but his skin was in little flakes and cracks all over, from living so much in the salt water as was his usual custom. His hands was all webby-foot, too. He was called, I remember Dowse saying now, an Orange-Lord, on account of his habits. You've heard of an Orange-Lord, sir?'

'Orang-Laut?' I suggested.

'That's the name,' said Fenwick, smacking his knee. 'An Orang-Laut, of course, and his name was Challong; what they call a sea-gypsy. Dowse told me that that man, long hair and all, would go swimming up and down the straits just for something to do; running down on one tide and back again with the other, swimming side-stroke, and the tides going tremenjus strong. Elseways he'd be skipping about the beach along with the tigers at low tide, for he was most part a beast; or he'd sit in a little boat praying to old Loby Toby of an evening when the volcano was spitting red at the south end of the strait. Dowse told me that he wasn't a companionable man, like you and me might have been to Dowse.

'Now I can never rightly come at what it was that began to ail Dowse after he had been there a year or something less. He was saving of all his pay and tending to his Light, and now and again he'd have a fight with Challong and tip him off the Light into the sea. Then, he told me, his head began to feel streaky from looking at the tide so long. He said there was long streaks of white running inside it; like wallpaper that hadn't been properly pasted up, he said. The streaks, they would run with the tides, north and south, twice a day, accordin' to them currents, and he'd lie down on the planking – it was a screw-pile Light – with his eye to a crack and watch the water streaking through the piles just so quiet as hogwash. He said the only comfort he got was at slack water. Then the streaks in his head went round and round like a sampan in a tide-rip; but that was heaven, he said, to the other kind of streaks – the straight ones that looked like arrows on a wind-chart, but much more regular, and that was the trouble of it. No more he couldn't ever keep his eyes off the tides that ran up and down so strong, but as soon as ever he looked at the high hills standing all along Flores Strait for rest and comfort his eyes would be pulled down like to the nesty streaky water; and when they once got there he couldn't pull them away again till the tide changed. He told me all this himself, speaking just as though he was talking of somebody else.'

'Where did you meet him?' I asked.

'In Portsmouth harbour, a-cleaning the brasses of a Ryde boat, but I'd known him off and on through following the sea for many years. Yes, he spoke about himself very curious, and all as if he was in the next room laying there dead. Those streaks, they preyed upon his intellecks, he said; and he made up his mind, every time that the Dutch gunboat that attends to the lights in those parts come along, that he'd ask to be took off. But as soon as she did come something went click in his throat, and he was so took up with watching her masts, because they ran longways, in the contrary direction to his streaks, that he could never say a word until she was gone away and her masts was under sea again. Then, he said, he'd cry by the hour; and Challong swum round and round the light, laughin' at him and splashin' water with his webby-foot hands. At last he took it into his pore sick head that the ships, and particularly the steamers that came by – there wasn't many of them – made the streaks, instead of the tides as was natural. He used to sit, he told me, cursing every boat that come along – sometimes a junk, sometimes a Dutch brig, and now and again a steamer rounding Flores Head and poking about in the mouth of the strait. Or there'd come a boat from Australia running north past old Loby Toby hunting for a fair current, but never throwing out any papers that Challong might pick up for Dowse to read. Generally speaking, the steamers kept more westerly, but now and again they came looking for Timor and the west coast of Australia. Dowse used to shout to them to go round by the Ombay Passage, and not to come streaking past him, making the water all streaky, but it wasn't likely they'd hear. He says to himself after a month, "I'll give them one more chance," he says. "If the next boat don't attend to my just representation" – he says he remembers using those very words to Challong – "I'll stop the fairway."

'The next boat was a Two-streak cargo-boat very anxious to make her northing. She waddled through under old Loby Toby at the south end of the strait, and she passed within a quarter of a mile of the Wurlee Light at the north end, in seventeen fathom o' water, the tide against her. Dowse took the trouble to come out with Challong in a little prow that they had – all bamboos and leakage – and he lay in the fairway waving a palm branch, and, so he told me, wondering why and what for he was making this fool of himself. Up come the Two-streak boat, and Dowse shouts: "Don't you come this way again, making my head all streaky! Go round by Ombay, and leave me alone." Someone looks over the port bulwarks and shies a banana at Dowse, and that's all. Dowse sits down in the bottom of the boat and cries fit to break his heart. Then he says, "Challong, what am I a-crying for?" and they fetches up by the Wurlee Light on the half-flood.

'"Challong," he says, "there's too much traffic here, and that's why the water's so streaky as it is. It's the junks and the brigs and the steamers that do it," he says; and all the time he was speaking he was thinking, "Lord, Lord, what a crazy fool I am!" Challong said nothing, because he couldn't speak a word of English except say "dam", and he said that where you or me would say "yes". Dowse lay down on the planking of the Light with his eye to the crack, and he saw the muddy water streaking below, and he never said a word till slack water, because the streaks kept him tongue-tied at such times. At slack water he says, "Challong, we must buoy this fairway for wrecks," and he holds up his hands several times, showing that dozens of wrecks had come about in the fairway; and Challong says, "Dam".

'That very afternoon he and Challong rows to Wurlee, the village in the woods that the Light was named after, and buys canes – stacks and stacks of canes, and coir rope thick and fine, all sorts – and they sets to work making square floats by lashing of the canes together. Dowse said he took longer over those floats than might have been needed, because he rejoiced in the corners, they being square, and the streaks in his head all running longways. He lashed the canes together, criss-cross and thwartways – any way but longways – and they made up twelve-foot square floats, like rafts. Then he stepped a twelve-foot bamboo or a bundle of canes in the centre, and to the head of that he lashed a big six-foot W letter, all made of canes, and painted the float dark green and the W white, as a wreck-buoy should be painted. Between them two they makes a round dozen of these new kind of wreck-buoys, and it was a two months' job. There was no big traffic, owing to it being on the turn of the monsoon, but what there was Dowse cursed at, and the streaks in his head, they ran with the tides, as usual.

'Day after day, so soon as a buoy was ready, Challong would take it out, with a big rock that half sunk the prow and a bamboo grapnel, and drop it dead in the fairway. He did this day and night, and Dowse would see him of a clear night, when the sea brimed, climbing about the buoys with the sea-fire dripping off him. They was all put into place, twelve of them in seventeen-fathom water; not in a straight line, on account of a well-known shoal there, but slantways, and two, one behind the other, mostly in the centre of the fairway. You must keep the centre of those Javva currents, for currents at the side is different, and in narrow water, before you can turn a spoke, you get your nose took round and rubbed upon the rocks and the woods. Dowse knew that just as well as any skipper. Likeways he knew that no skipper daren't run through uncharted wrecks in a six-knot current. He told me he used to lie outside the

Light watching his buoys ducking and dipping so friendly with the tide; and the motion was comforting to him on account of its being different from the run of the streaks in his head.

'Three weeks after he'd done his business up comes a steamer through Loby Toby Straits, thinking she'd run into Flores Sea before night. He saw her slow down; then she backed. Then one man and another come up on the bridge, and he could see there was a regular powwow, and the flood was driving her right on to Dowse's wreck-buoys. After that she spun round and went back south, and Dowse nearly killed himself with laughing. But a few weeks after that a couple of junks came shouldering through from the north, arm in arm, like junks go. It takes a good deal to make a Chinaman understand danger. They junks set well in the current, and went down the fairway, right among the buoys, ten knots an hour, blowing horns and banging tin pots all the time. That made Dowse very angry; he having taken so much trouble to stop the fairway. No boats run Flores Straits by night, but it seemed to Dowse that if junks'd do that in the day, the Lord knew but what a steamer might trip over his buoys at night; and he sent Challong to run a coir rope between three of the buoys in the middle of the fairway, and he fixed naked lights of coir steeped in oil to that rope. The tides was the only things that moved in those seas, for the airs was dead still till they began to blow, and *then* they would blow your hair off. Challong tended those lights every night after the junks had been so impident – four lights in about a quarter of a mile hung up in iron skillets on the rope; and when they was alight – and coir burns well, very like a lamp wick – the fairway seemed more madder than anything else in the world. First there was the Wurlee Light, then these four queer lights, that couldn't be riding-lights, almost flush with the water, and behind them, twenty mile off, but the biggest light of all, there was the red top of old Loby Toby volcano. Dowse told me that he used to go out in the prow and look at his handiwork, and it made him scared, being like no lights that ever was fixed.

'By and by some more steamers came along, snorting and snifting at the buoys, but never going through, and Dowse says to himself: "Thank goodness I've taught them not to come streaking through my water. Ombay Passage is good enough for them and the like of them." But he didn't remember how quick that sort of news spreads among the shipping. Every steamer that fetched up by those buoys told another steamer and all the port officers concerned in those seas that there was something wrong with Flores Straits that hadn't been charted yet. It was block-buoyed for wrecks in the fairway, they said, and no sort of passage to use. Well, the Dutch, of course they didn't know anything about it. They thought our Admiralty Survey had been there, and they thought it very queer but neighbourly. You understand us English are always looking up marks and lighting sea-ways all the world over, never asking with your leave or by your leave, seeing that the sea concerns us more than any one else. So the news went to and back from Flores to Bali, and Bali to Probolingo, where the railway is that runs to Batavia. All through the Javva seas everybody got the word to keep clear o' Flores Straits, and Dowse, he was left alone except for such steamers and small craft as didn't know. They'd come up and look at the straits like a bull over a gate, but those nodding wreck-buoys scared them away. By and by the Admiralty Survey ship – the *Britomarte* I think she was – lay in Macassar Roads off Fort Rotterdam, alongside of the *Amboina*, a dirty little Dutch gunboat that used to clean there; and the Dutch captain says to our captain, "What's wrong with Flores Straits?" he says.

'"Blowed if I know," says our captain, who'd just come up from the Angelica Shoal.

'"Then why did you go and buoy it?" says the Dutchman.

'"Blowed if I have," says our captain. "That's your lookout."

'"Buoyed it is," says the Dutch captain, "according to what they tell me; and a whole fleet of wreck-buoys, too."

'"Gummy!" says our captain. "It's a dorg's life at sea, any way. I must have a look at this. You come along after me as soon as you can;" and down he skimmed that very night, round the heel of Celebes, three days' steam to Flores Head, and he met a Two-streak liner, very angry, backing out of the head of the strait; and the merchant captain gave our survey ship something of his mind for leaving wrecks uncharted in those narrow waters and wasting his company's coal.

'"It's no fault o' mine," says our captain.

'"I don't care whose fault it is," says the merchant captain, who had come aboard to speak to him just at dusk. "The fairway's choked with wreck enough to knock a hole through a dock-gate. I saw their big ugly masts sticking up just under my forefoot. Lord ha' mercy on us!" he says, spinning round. "The place is like Regent Street of a hot summer night."

'And so it was. They two looked at Flores Straits, and they saw lights one after the other stringing across the fairway. Dowse, he had seen the steamers hanging there before dark, and he said to Challong: "We'll give 'em something to remember. Get all the skillets and iron pots you can and hang them up alongside o' the regular four lights. We must teach 'em to go round by the Ombay Passage, or they'll be streaking up our water again!" Challong took a header off the lighthouse, got aboard the little leaking prow, with his coir soaked in oil and all the skillets he could muster, and he began to show his lights, four regulation ones and half a dozen new lights hung on that rope which was a little above the water. Then he went to all the spare buoys with all his spare coir, and hung a skillet-flare on every pole that he could get at – about seven poles. So you see, taking one with another, there was the Wurlee Light, four lights on the rope between the three centre fairway wreck-buoys that was hung out as a usual custom, six or eight extry ones that Challong had hung up on the same rope, and seven dancing flares that belonged to seven wreck-buoys – eighteen or twenty lights in all crowded into a mile of seventeen-fathom water, where no tide'd ever let a wreck rest for three weeks, let alone ten or twelve wrecks, as the flares showed.

'The Admiralty captain, he saw the lights come out one after another, same as the merchant skipper did who was standing at his side, and he said:

'"There's been an international cata-strophe here or elseways," and then he whistled. "I'm going to stand on and off all night till the Dutchman comes," he says.

'"I'm off," says the merchant skipper. "My owners don't wish for me to watch illuminations. That strait's choked with wreck, and I shouldn't wonder if a typhoon hadn't driven half the junks o' China there." With that he went away; but the survey ship, she stayed all night at the head o' Flores Strait, and the men admired of the lights till the lights was burning out, and then they admired more than ever.

'A little bit before morning the Dutch gunboat come flustering up, and the two ships stood together watching the lights burn out and out, till there was nothing left 'cept Flores Straits, all green and wet, and a dozen wreck-buoys, and Wurlee Light.

'Dowse had slept very quiet that night, and got rid of his streaks by means of thinking of the angry steamers outside. Challong was busy, and didn't come back to his bunk till late. In the grey early morning Dowse looked out to sea, being, as he said, in torment, and saw all the navies of the world riding outside Flores Strait fairway in a half-moon, seven miles from wing to wing, most wonderful to behold. Those were the words he used to me time and again in telling the tale.

'Then, he says, he heard a gun fired with a most tremenjus explosion, and all them great navies crumbled to little pieces of clouds, and there was only two ships remaining, and a man-o'-war's boat rowing to the light, with the oars going sideways instead o' longways as the morning tides, ebb or flow, would continually run.

'"What the devil's wrong with this strait?" says a man in the boat as soon as they was in hailing distance. "Has the whole English Navy sunk here, or what?"

'"There's nothing wrong," says Dowse, sitting on the platform outside the Light, and keeping one eye very watchful on the streakiness of the tide, which he always hated, 'specially in the mornings. "You leave me alone and I'll leave you alone. Go round by the Ombay Passage, and don't cut up my water. You're making it streaky." All the time he was saying that he kept on thinking to himself, "Now that's foolishness – now that's nothing but foolishness"; and all the time he was holding tight to the edge of the platform in case the streakiness of the tide should carry him away.

'Somebody answers from the boat, very soft and quiet, "We're going round by Ombay in a minute, if you'll just come and speak to our captain and give him his bearings."

'Dowse, he felt very highly flattered, and he slipped into the boat, not paying any attention to Challong. But Challong swum along to the ship after the boat. When Dowse was in the boat, he found, so he says, he couldn't speak to the sailors 'cept to call them "white mice with chains about their neck", and Lord knows he hadn't seen or thought o' white mice since he was a little bit of a boy with them in his handkerchief. So he kept himself quiet, and so they come to the survey ship; and the man in the boat hails the quarter-deck with something that Dowse could not rightly understand, but there was one word he spelt out again and again – m-a-d, mad – and he heard someone behind him saying of it backwards. So he had two words – m-a-d, mad, d-a-m, dam; and he put they two words together as he come on the quarter-deck, and he says to the captain very slowly, "I be damned if I am mad," but all the time his eye was held like by the coils of rope on the belaying pins, and he followed those ropes up and up with his eye till he was quite lost and comfortable among the rigging, which ran criss-cross, and slopeways, and up and down, and any way but straight along under his feet north and south. The deck-seams, they ran *that* way, and Dowse daresn't look at them. They was the same as the streaks of the water under the planking of the lighthouse.

'Then he heard the captain talking to him very kind, and for the life of him he couldn't tell why; and what he wanted to tell the captain was that Flores Strait was too streaky, like bacon, and the steamers only made it worse; but all he could do was to keep his eye very careful on the rigging and sing:

"I saw a ship a-sailing,
A-sailing on the sea;
And oh, it was all lading
With pretty things for me!"

'Then he remembered that was foolishness, and he started off to say about the Ombay Passage, but all he said was: "The captain was a duck – meaning no offence to you, sir – but there was something on his back that I've forgotten.

"And when the ship began to move
The captain says, 'Quack-quack!'"

'He notices the captain turns very red and angry, and he says to himself, "My foolish tongue's run away with me again. I'll go forward;" and he went forward, and catched the reflection of himself in the binnacle brasses; and he saw that he was standing there and talking mother-naked in front of all them sailors, and he ran into the fo'c's'le howling most grievous. He must ha' gone naked for weeks on the Light, and Challong o' course never noticed it. Challong was swimmin' round and round the ship, sayin' "dam" for to please the men and to be took aboard, because he didn't know any better.

'Dowse didn't tell what happened after this, but seemingly our survey ship lowered two boats and went over to Dowse's buoys. They took one sounding, and then finding it was all correct they cut the buoys that Dowse and Challong had made, and let the tide carry 'em out through the Loby Toby end of the strait; and the Dutch gunboat, she sent two men ashore to take care o' the Wurlee Light, and the *Britomarte*, she went away with Dowse, leaving Challong to try to follow them, a-calling "dam – dam" all among the wake of the screw, and half heaving himself out of water and joining his webby-foot hands together. He dropped astern in five minutes, and I suppose he went back to the Wurlee Light. You can't drown an Orange-Lord, not even in Flores Strait on flood-tide.

'Dowse come across me when he came to England with the survey ship, after being more than six months in her, and cured of his streaks by working hard and not looking over the side more than he could help. He told me what I've told you, sir, and he was very much ashamed of himself; but the trouble on his mind was to know whether he hadn't sent something or other to the bottom with his buoyings and his lightings and such like. He put it to me many times, and each time more and more sure he was that something had happened in the straits because of him. I think that distructed him, because I found him up at Fratton one day, in a red jersey, a-praying before the Salvation Army, which had produced him in their papers as a Reformed Pirate. They knew from his mouth that he had committed evil on the deep waters – that was what he told them – and piracy, which no one does now except Chineses, was all they knew of. I says to him: "Dowse, don't be a fool. Take off that jersey and come along with me." He says: "Fenwick, I'm a-saving of my soul; for I do believe that I have killed more men in Flores Strait than Trafalgar". I says: "A man that thought he'd seen all the navies of the earth standing round in a ring to watch his foolish false wreck-buoys" (those was my very words I used) "ain't fit to have a soul, and if he did he couldn't kill a louse with it. John Dowse, you was mad then, but you are a damn sight madder now. Take off that there jersey!"

'He took it off and come along with me, but he never got rid o' that suspicion that he'd sunk some ships a-cause of his foolishness at Flores Straits; and now he's a wherryman from Portsmouth to Gosport, where the tides run crossways and you can't row straight for ten strokes together . . So late as all this! Look!'

Fenwick left his chair, passed to the Light, touched something that clicked, and the glare ceased with a suddenness that was pain. Day had come, and the Channel needed St Cecilia no longer. The sea-fog rolled back from the cliffs in trailed wreaths and dragged patches, as the sun rose and made the dead sea alive and splendid. The stillness of the morning held us both silent as we stepped on the balcony. A lark went up from the cliffs behind St Cecilia, and we smelt a smell of cows in the lighthouse pastures below.

Then we were both at liberty to thank the Lord for another day of clean and wholesome life.

'The Finest Story in the World'

Or ever the knightly years were gone
  With the old world to the grave,
I was a king in Babylon
  And you were a Christian slave.

W.E. Henley

HIS name was Charlie Mears; he was the only son of his mother who was a widow, and he lived in the north of London, coming into the City every day to work in a bank. He was twenty years old and was full of aspirations. I met him in a public billiard-saloon where the marker called him by his first name, and he called the marker 'Bullseye'. Charlie explained, a little nervously, that he had only come to the place to look on, and since looking on at games of skill is not a cheap amusement for the young, I suggested that Charlie should go back to his mother.

That was our first step towards better acquaintance. He would call on me sometimes in the evenings instead of running about London with his fellow-clerks; and before long, speaking of himself as a young man must, he told me of his aspirations, which were all literary. He desired to make himself an undying name chiefly through verse, though he was not above sending stories of love and death to the penny-in-the-slot journals. It was my fate to sit still while Charlie read me poems of many hundred lines, and bulky fragments of plays that would surely shake the world. My reward was his unreserved confidence, and the self-revelations and troubles of a young man are almost as holy as those of a maiden. Charlie had never fallen in love, but was anxious to do so on the first opportunity; he believed in all things good and all things honourable, but at the same time, was curiously careful to let me see that he knew his way about the world as befitted a bank-clerk on twenty-five shillings a week. He rhymed 'dove' with 'love' and 'moon' with 'June', and devoutly believed that they had never so been rhymed before. The long lame gaps in his plays he filled up with hasty words of apology and description and swept on, seeing all that he intended to do so clearly that he esteemed it already done, and turned to me for applause.

I fancy that his mother did not encourage his aspirations; and I know that his writing-table at home was the edge of his washstand. This he told me almost at the outset of our acquaintance – when he was ravaging my bookshelves, and a little before I was implored to speak the truth as to his chances of 'writing something really great, you know'. Maybe I encouraged him too much, for, one night, he called on me, his eyes flaming with excitement, and said breathlessly:

'Do you mind – can you let me stay here and write all this evening? I won't interrupt you, I won't really. There's no place for me to write at my mother's.'

'What's the trouble?' I said, knowing well what that trouble was.

'I've a notion in my head that would make the most splendid story that was ever written. Do let me write it out here. It's *such* a notion!'

There was no resisting the appeal. I set him a table; he hardly thanked me, but plunged into his work at once. For half an hour the pen scratched without stopping. Then Charlie sighed and tugged his hair. The scratching grew slower, there were more erasures, and at last ceased. The finest story in the world would not come forth.

'It looks such awful rot now,' he said mournfully. 'And yet it seemed so good when I was thinking about it. What's wrong?'

I could not dishearten him by saying the truth. So I answered: 'Perhaps you don't feel in the mood for writing.'

'Yes I do – except when I look at this stuff. Ugh!'

'Read me what you've done,' I said.

He read, and it was wondrous bad, and he paused at all the specially turgid sentences, expecting a little approval; for he was proud of those sentences, as I knew he would be.

'It needs compression,' I suggested cautiously.

'I hate cutting my things down. I don't think you could alter a word here without spoiling the sense. It reads better aloud than when I was writing it.'

'Charlie, you're suffering from an alarming disease afflicting a numerous class. Put the thing by, and tackle it again in a week.'

'I want to do it at once. What do you think of it?'

'How can I judge from a half-written tale? Tell me the story as it lies in your head.'

Charlie told, and in the telling there was everything that his ignorance had so carefully prevented from escaping into the written word. I looked at him, wondering whether it were possible that he did not know the originality, the power of the notion that had come in his way? It was distinctly a Notion among notions. Men had been puffed up with pride by ideas not a tithe as excellent and practicable.

But Charlie babbled on serenely, interrupting the current of pure fancy with samples of horrible sentences that he purposed to use. I heard him out to the end. It would be folly to allow his thought to remain in his own inept hands, when I could do so much with it. Not all that could be done indeed; but, oh so much!

'What do you think?' he said at last. 'I fancy I shall call it "The Story of a Ship".'

'I think the idea's pretty good; but you won't be able to handle it for ever so long. Now I—'

'Would it be of any use to you? Would you care to take it? I should be proud,' said Charlie promptly.

There are few things sweeter in this world than the guileless, hot-headed, intemperate, open admiration of a junior. Even a woman in her blindest devotion does not fall into the gait of the man she adores, tilt her bonnet to the angle at which he wears his hat, or interlard her speech with his pet oaths. And Charlie did all these things. Still it was necessary to salve my conscience before I possessed myself of Charlie's thoughts.

'Let's make a bargain. I'll give you a fiver for the notion,' I said.

Charlie became a bank-clerk at once.

'Oh, that's impossible. Between two pals, you know, if I may call you so, and speaking as a man of the world, I couldn't. Take the notion if it's any use to you. I've heaps more.'

He had – none knew this better than I – but they were the notions of other men.

'Look at it as a matter of business – between men of the world,' I returned. 'Five pounds will buy you any number of poetry-books. Business is business, and you may be sure I shouldn't give that price unless—'

'Oh, if you put it *that* way,' said Charlie, visibly moved by the thought of the books. The bargain was clinched with an agreement that he should at unstated intervals come to me with all the notions that he possessed, should have a table of his own to write at, and unquestioned right to inflict upon me all his poems and fragments of poems. Then I said, 'Now tell me how you came by this idea.'

'It came by itself.' Charlie's eyes opened a little.

'Yes, but you told me a great deal about the hero that you must have read before somewhere.'

'I haven't any time for reading, except when you let me sit here, and on Sundays I'm on my bicycle or down the river all day. There's nothing wrong about the hero, is there?'

'Tell me again and I shall understand clearly. You say that your hero went pirating. How did he live?'

'He was on the lower deck of this ship-thing that I was telling you about.'

'What sort of ship?'

'It was the kind rowed with oars, and the sea spurts through the oar-holes and the men row sitting up to their knees in water. Then there's a bench running down between the two lines of oars and an overseer with a whip walks up and down the bench to make the men work.'

'How do you know that?'

'It's in the tale. There's a rope running overhead, looped to the upper deck, for the overseer to catch hold of when the ship rolls. When the overseer misses the rope once and falls among the rowers, remember the hero laughs at him and gets licked for it. He's chained to his oar of course – the hero.'

'How is he chained?'

'With an iron band round his waist fixed to the bench he sits on, and a sort of handcuff on his left wrist chaining him to the oar. He's on the lower deck where the worst men are sent, and the only light comes from the hatchways and through the oar-holes. Can't you imagine the sunlight just squeezing through between the handle and the hole and wobbling about as the ship moves?'

'I can, but I can't imagine your imagining it.'

'How could it be any other way? Now you listen to me. The long oars on the upper deck are managed by four men to each bench, the lower ones by three, and the lowest of all by two. Remember it's quite dark on the lowest deck and all the men there go mad. When a man dies at his oar on that deck he isn't thrown overboard, but cut up in his chains and stuffed through the oar-hole in little pieces.'

'Why?' I demanded amazed, not so much at the information as the tone of command in which it was flung out.

'To save trouble and to frighten the others. It needs two overseers to drag a man's body up to the top deck; and if the men at the lower deck oars were left alone, of course they'd stop rowing and try to pull up the benches by all standing up together in their chains.'

'You've a most provident imagination. Where have you been reading about galleys and galley-slaves?'

'Nowhere that I remember. I row a little when I get the chance. But, perhaps, if you say so, I may have read something.'

He went away shortly afterwards to deal with booksellers, and I wondered how a bank-clerk aged twenty could put into my hands with a profligate abundance of detail, all given with absolute assurance, the story of extravagant and bloodthirsty adventure, riot, piracy, and death in unnamed seas. He had led his hero a desperate dance through revolt against the overseers, to command of a ship of his own, and at last to the establishment of a kingdom on an island 'somewhere in the sea, you know'; and, delighted with my paltry five pounds, had gone out to buy the notions of other men, that these might teach him how to write. I had the consolation of knowing that this notion was mine by right of purchase, and I thought that I could make something of it.

When next he came to me he was drunk – royally drunk on many poets for the first time revealed to him. His pupils were dilated, his words tumbled over each other, and he wrapped himself in quotations – as a beggar would enfold himself in the purple of emperors. Most of all was he drunk with Longfellow.

'Isn't it splendid? Isn't it superb?' he cried, after hasty greetings. 'Listen to this –

'"Wouldst thou," – so the helmsman answered,
"Know the secret of the sea?
Only those who brave its dangers
Comprehend its mystery."

By gum!

'"Only those who brave its dangers
Comprehend its mystery,"'

he repeated twenty times, walking up and down the room and forgetting me. 'But *I* can understand it too,' he said to himself. 'I don't know how to thank you for that fiver. And this; listen –

'"I remember the black wharves and the slips
And the sea-tides tossing free;
And the Spanish sailors with bearded lips,
And the beauty and mystery of the ships,
And the magic of the sea."

I haven't braved any dangers, but I feel as if I know all about it.'

'You certainly seem to have a grip of the sea. Have you ever seen it?'

'When I was a little chap I went to Brighton once; we used to live in Coventry, though, before we came to London. I never saw it,

'"When descends on the Atlantic
The gigantic
Storm-wind of the Equinox."'

He shook me by the shoulder to make me understand the passion that was shaking himself.

'When that storm comes,' he continued, 'I think that all the oars in the ship that I was talking about get broken, and the rowers have their chests smashed in by the oar-heads bucking. By the way, have you done anything with that notion of mine yet?'

'No. I was waiting to hear more of it from you. Tell me how in the world you're so certain about the fittings of the ship. You know nothing of ships.'

'I don't know. It's as real as anything to me until I try to write it down. I was thinking about it only last night in bed, after you had lent me *Treasure Island*; and I made up a whole lot of new things to go into the story.'

'What sort of things?'

'About the food the men ate; rotten figs and black beans and wine in a skin bag, passed from bench to bench.'

'Was the ship built so long ago as *that*?'

'As what? I don't know whether it was long ago or not. It's only a notion, but sometimes it seems just as real as if it was true. Do I bother you with talking about it?'

'Not in the least. Did you make up anything else?'

'Yes, but it's nonsense.' Charlie flushed a little.

'Never mind; let's hear about it.'

'Well, I was thinking over the story, and after awhile I got out of bed and wrote down on a piece of paper the sort of stuff the men might be supposed to scratch on their oars with the edges of their handcuffs. It seemed to make the thing more life-like. It *is* so real to me, y'know.'

'Have you the paper on you?'

'Ye–es, but what's the use of showing it? It's only a lot of scratches. All the same, we might have 'em reproduced in the book on the front page.'

'I'll attend to those details. Show me what your men wrote.'

He pulled out of his pocket a sheet of notepaper, with a single line of scratches upon it, and I put this carefully away.

'What is it supposed to mean in English?' I said.

'Oh, I don't know. I mean it to mean "I'm beastly tired". It's great nonsense,' he repeated, 'but all those men in the ship seem as real as real people to me. Do do something to the notion soon; I should like to see it written and printed.'

'But all you've told me would make a long book.'

'Make it then. You've only to sit down and write it out.'

'Give me a little time. Have you any more notions?'

'Not just now. I'm reading all the books I've bought. They're splendid.'

When he had left I looked at the sheet of notepaper with the inscription upon it. Then I took my head tenderly between both hands, to make certain that it was not coming off or turning round. Then . . . but there seemed to be no interval between quitting my rooms and finding myself arguing with a policeman outside a door marked *Private* in a corridor of the British Museum. All I demanded, as politely as possible, was 'the Greek antiquity man'. The policeman knew nothing except the rules of the Museum, and it became necessary to forage through all the houses and offices inside the gates. An elderly gentleman called away from his lunch put an end to my search by holding the notepaper between finger and thumb and sniffing at it scornfully.

'What does this mean? H'mm,' said he. 'So far as I can ascertain it is an attempt to write extremely corrupt Greek on the part' – here he glared at me with intention – 'of an extremely illiterate – ah – person.' He read slowly from the paper, '*Pollock, Erckmann, Tauchnitz, Henniker*' – four names familiar to me.

'Can you tell me what the corruption is supposed to mean – the gist of the thing?' I asked.

'I have been – many times – overcome with weariness in this particular employment. This is the meaning.' He returned me the paper, and I fled without a word of thanks, explanation, or apology.

I might have been excused for forgetting much. To me of all men had been given the chance to write the most marvellous tale in the world, nothing less than the story of a Greek galley-slave, as told by himself. Small wonder that his dreaming had seemed real to Charlie. The Fates that are so careful to shut the doors of each successive life behind us had, in this case, been neglectful, and Charlie was looking, though that he did not know, where never man had been permitted to look with full knowledge since Time began. Above all, he was absolutely ignorant of the knowledge sold to me for five pounds; and he would retain that ignorance, for bank-clerks do not understand metempsychosis, and a sound commercial education does not include Greek. He would supply me – here I capered among the dumb gods of Egypt and laughed in their battered faces – with material to make my tale sure – so sure that the world would hail it as an impudent and vamped fiction. And I – I alone would know that it was absolutely and literally true. I – I alone held this jewel to my hand for the cutting and polishing! Therefore I danced again among the gods of the Egyptian court till a policeman saw me and took steps in my direction.

It remained now only to encourage Charlie to talk, and here there was no difficulty. But I had forgotten those accursed books of poetry. He came to me time after time, as useless as a surcharged phonograph – drunk on Byron, Shelley, or Keats. Knowing now what the boy had been in his past lives, and desperately anxious not to lose one word of his babble, I could not hide from him my respect and interest. He misconstrued both into respect for the present soul of Charlie Mears, to whom life was as new as it was to Adam, and interest in his readings; and stretched my patience to breaking point by reciting poetry – not his own now, but that of others. I wished every English poet blotted out of the memory of mankind. I blasphemed the mightiest names of song because they had drawn Charlie from the path of direct narrative, and would, later, spur him to imitate them; but I choked down my impatience until the first flood of enthusiasm should have spent itself and the boy returned to his dreams.

'What's the use of my telling you what *I* think, when these chaps wrote things for the angels to read?' he growled, one evening. 'Why don't you write something like theirs?'

'I don't think you're treating me quite fairly,' I said, speaking under strong restraint.

'I've given you the story,' he said shortly, re-plunging into 'Lara'.

'But I want the details.'

'The things I make up about that damned ship that you call a galley? They're quite easy. You can just make 'em up for yourself. Turn up the gas a little, I want to go on reading.'

I could have broken the gas globe over his head for his amazing stupidity. I could indeed make up things for myself did I only know what Charlie did not know that he knew. But since the doors were shut behind me I could only wait his youthful pleasure and strive to keep him in good temper. One minute's want of guard might spoil a priceless revelation: now and again he would toss his books aside – he kept them in my rooms, for his mother would have been shocked at the waste of good money had she seen them – and launched into his sea-dreams. Again I cursed all the poets of England. The plastic mind of the bank-clerk had been overlaid, coloured, and distorted by that which he had read, and the result as delivered was a confused tangle of other voices most like the mutter and hum through a City telephone in the busiest part of the day.

He talked of the galley – his own galley had he but known it – with illustrations borrowed from the 'Bride of Abydos'. He pointed the experiences of his hero with quotations from 'The Corsair', and threw in deep and desperate moral reflections from 'Cain' and 'Manfred', expecting me to use them all. Only when the talk turned on Longfellow were the jarring cross-currents dumb, and I knew that Charlie was speaking the truth as he remembered it.

'What do you think of this?' I said one evening, as soon as I understood the medium in which his memory worked best, and, before he could expostulate, read him nearly the whole of 'The Saga of King Olaf!'

He listened open-mouthed, flushed, his hands drumming on the back of the sofa where he lay, till I came to the Song of Einar Tamberskelver and the verse:

> 'Einar then, the arrow taking
>   From the loosened string,
> Answered, "That was Norway breaking
>   'Neath thy hand, O King."'

He gasped with pure delight of sound.

'That's better than Byron, a little?' I ventured.

'Better! Why it's *true*! How could he have known?'

I went back and repeated:

> '"What was that?" said Olaf, standing
>   On the quarter-deck
> "Something heard I like the stranding
>   Of a shattered wreck."'

'How could he have known how the ships crash and the oars rip out and go *z-zzp* all along the line? Why only the other night ... But go back please and read "The Skerry of Shrieks" again.'

'No, I'm tired. Let's talk. What happened the other night?'

'I had an awful dream about that galley of ours. I dreamed I was drowned in a fight. You see we ran alongside another ship in harbour. The water was dead still except where our oars whipped it up. You know where I always sit in the galley?' He spoke haltingly at first, under a fine English fear of being laughed at.

'No. That's news to me,' I answered meekly, my heart beginning to beat.

'On the fourth oar from the bow on the right side on the upper deck. There were four of us at that oar, all chained. I remember watching the water and trying to get my handcuffs off before the row began. Then we closed up on the other ship, and all their fighting men jumped over our bulwarks, and my bench broke and I was pinned down with the three other fellows on top of me, and the big oar jammed across our backs.'

'Well?' Charlie's eyes were alive and alight. He was looking at the wall behind my chair.

'I don't know how we fought. The men were trampling all over my back, and I lay low. Then our rowers on the left side – tied to their oars, you know – began to yell and back water. I could hear the water sizzle, and we spun round like a cockchafer and I knew, lying where I was, that there was a galley coming up bow-on, to ram us on the left side. I could just lift up my head and see her sail over the bulwarks. We wanted to meet her bow to bow, but it was too late. We could only turn a little bit because the galley on our right had hooked herself on to us and stopped our moving. Then, by gum! there was a crash! Our left oars began to break as the other galley, the moving one y'know, stuck her nose into them. Then the lower-deck oars shot up through the deck planking, butt first, and one of them jumped clear up into the air and came down again close at my head.'

'How was that managed?'

'The moving galley's bow was plunking them back through their own oar-holes, and I could hear no end of a shindy in the decks below. Then her nose caught us nearly in the middle, and we tilted sideways, and the fellows in the right-hand galley unhitched their hooks and ropes, and threw things on to our upper deck – arrows, and hot pitch or something that stung, and we went up and up and up on the left side, and the right side dipped, and I twisted my head round and saw the water stand still as it topped the right bulwarks, and then it curled over and crashed down on the whole lot of us on the right side, and I felt it hit my back, and I woke.'

'One minute, Charlie. When the sea topped the bulwarks, what did it look like?' I had my reasons for asking. A man of my acquaintance had once gone down with a leaking ship in a still sea, and had seen the water-level pause for an instant ere it fell on the deck.

'It looked just like a banjo-string drawn tight, and it seemed to stay there for years,' said Charlie.

Exactly! The other man had said: 'It looked like a silver wire laid down along the bulwarks, and I thought it was never going to break.'

He had paid everything except the bare life for this little valueless piece of knowledge, and I had travelled ten thousand weary miles to meet him and take his knowledge at second hand. But Charlie, the bank-clerk on twenty-five shillings a week, who had never been out of sight of a made road, knew it all. It was no consolation to me that once in his lives he had been forced to die for his gains. I also must have died scores of times, but behind me, because I could have used my knowledge, the doors were shut.

'And then?' I said, trying to put away the devil of envy.

'The funny thing was, though, in all the row I didn't feel a bit astonished or frightened. It seemed as if I'd been in a good many fights, because I told my next man so when the row began. But that cad of an overseer on my deck wouldn't unloose our chains and give us a chance. He always said that we'd all be set free after a battle, but we never were; we never were.' Charlie shook his head mournfully.

'What a scoundrel!'

'I should say he was. He never gave us enough to eat, and sometimes we were so thirsty that we used to drink salt-water. I can taste that salt-water still.'

'Now tell me something about the harbour where the fight was fought.'

'I didn't dream about that. I know it was a harbour, though; because we were tied up to a ring on a white wall and all the face of the stone under water was covered with wood to prevent our ram getting chipped when the tide made us rock.'

'That's curious. Our hero commanded the galley, didn't he?'

'Didn't he just! He stood by the bows and shouted like a good 'un. He was the man who killed the overseer.'

'But you were all drowned together, Charlie, weren't you?'

'I can't make that fit quite,' he said, with a puzzled look. 'The galley must have gone down with all hands, and yet I fancy that the hero went on living afterwards. Perhaps he climbed into the attacking ship. I wouldn't see that, of course. I was dead, you know.'

He shivered slightly and protested that he could remember no more.

I did not press him further, but to satisfy myself that he lay in ignorance of the workings of his own mind, deliberately introduced him to Mortimer Collins's *Transmigration*, and gave him a sketch of the plot before he opened the pages.

'What rot it all is!' he said frankly, at the end of an hour. 'I don't understand his nonsense about the Red Planet Mars and the King, and the rest of it. Chuck me the Longfellow again.'

I handed him the book and wrote out as much as I could remember of his description of the sea-fight, appealing to him from time to time for confirmation of fact or detail. He would answer without raising his eyes from the book, as assuredly as though all his knowledge lay before him on the printed page. I spoke under the normal key of my voice that the current might not be broken, and I knew that he was not aware of what he was saying, for his thoughts were out on the sea with Longfellow.

'Charlie,' I asked, 'when the rowers on the galleys mutinied how did they kill their overseers?'

'Tore up the benches and brained 'em. That happened when a heavy sea was running. An overseer on the lower deck slipped from the centre plank and fell among the rowers. They choked him to death against the side of the ship with their chained hands quite quietly, and it was too dark for the other overseer to see what had happened. When he asked, he was pulled down too and choked, and the lower deck fought their way up deck by deck, with the pieces of the broken benches banging behind 'em. How they howled!'

'And what happened after that?'

'I don't know. The hero went away – red hair and red beard and all. That was after he had captured our galley, I think.'

The sound of my voice irritated him, and he motioned slightly with his left hand as a man does when interruption jars.

'You never told me he was red-headed before, or that he captured your galley,' I said, after a discreet interval.

Charlie did not raise his eyes.

'He was as red as a red bear,' said he abstractedly. 'He came from the north; they said so in the galley when he looked for rowers – not slaves, but free men. Afterwards – years and years afterwards – news came from another ship, or else he came back—'

His lips moved in silence. He was rapturously retasting some poem before him.

'Where had he been, then?' I was almost whispering that the sentence might come gently to whichever section of Charlie's brain was working on my behalf.

'To the Beaches – the Long and Wonderful Beaches!' was the reply after a minute of silence.

'To Furdurstrandi?' I asked, tingling from head to foot.

'Yes, to Furdurstrandi,' he pronounced the word in a new fashion. 'And I too saw—' The voice failed.

'Do you know what you have said?' I shouted incautiously.

He lifted his eyes, fully roused now. 'No!' he snapped. 'I wish you'd let a chap go on reading. Hark to this:

'"But Othere, the old sea captain,
He neither paused nor stirred
  Till the king listened, and then
  Once more took up his pen
And wrote down every word.

'"And to the King of the Saxons
In witness of the truth,
  Raising his noble head,
  He stretched his brown hand and said,
'Behold this walrus tooth.'"

By Jove, what chaps those must have been, to go sailing all over the shop never knowing where they'd fetch the land! Hah!'

'Charlie,' I pleaded, 'if you'll only be sensible for a minute or two I'll make our hero in our tale every inch as good as Othere.'

'Umph! Longfellow wrote that poem. I don't care about writing things any more. I want to read.' He was thoroughly out of tune now, and raging over my own ill-luck, I left him.

Conceive yourself at the door of the world's treasure-house guarded by a child – an idle irresponsible child playing knuckle-bones – on whose favour depends the gift of the key, and you will imagine one-half of my torment. Till that evening Charlie had spoken nothing that might not lie within the experiences of a Greek galley-slave. But now, or there was no virtue in books, he had talked of some desperate adventure of the Vikings, of Thorfin Karlesfne's sailing to Wineland, which is America, in the ninth or tenth century. The battle in the harbour he had seen; and his own death he had described. But this was a much more startling plunge into the past. Was it possible that he had skipped half a dozen lives and was then dimly remembering some episode of a thousand years later? It was a maddening jumble, and the worst of it was that Charlie Mears in his normal condition was the last person in the world to clear it up. I could only wait and watch, but I went to bed that night full of the wildest imaginings. There was nothing that was not possible if Charlie's detestable memory only held good.

I might rewrite the Saga of Thorfin Karlsefne as it had never been written before, might tell the story of the first discovery of America, myself the discoverer. But I was entirely at Charlie's mercy, and so long as there was a three-and-sixpenny Bohn volume within his reach Charlie would not tell. I dared not curse him openly; I hardly dared jog his memory, for I was dealing with the experiences of a thousand years ago, told through the mouth of a boy of today; and a boy of today is affected by every change of tone and gust of opinion, so that he must lie even when he most desires to speak the truth.

I saw no more of Charlie for nearly a week. When next I met him it was in Gracechurch Street with a bill-book chained to his waist. Business took him over London Bridge, and I accompanied him. He was very full of the importance of that book and magnified it. As we passed over the Thames we paused to look at a steamer unloading great slabs of white and brown marble. A barge drifted under the steamer's stern and a lonely ship's cow in that barge bellowed. Charlie's face changed from the face of the bank-clerk to that of an unknown and – though he would not have believed this – a much shrewder man. He flung out his arm across the parapet of the bridge and laughing very loudly, said:

'When they heard *our* bulls bellow the Skroelings ran away!'

I waited only for an instant, but the barge and the cow had disappeared under the bows of the steamer before I answered.

'Charlie, what do you suppose are Skroelings?'

'Never heard of 'em before. They sound like a new kind of seagull. What a chap you are for asking questions!' he replied. 'I have to go to the cashier of the Omnibus Company yonder. Will you wait for me and we can lunch somewhere together? I've a notion for a poem.'

'No, thanks. I'm off. You're sure you know nothing about Skroelings?'

'Not unless he's been entered for the Liverpool Handicap.' He nodded and disappeared into the crowd.

Now it is written in the Saga of Eric the Red or that of Thorfin Karlsefne, that nine hundred years ago when Karlsefne's galleys came to Lief's booths, which Leif had erected in the unknown land called Markland, which may or may not have been Rhode Island, the Skroelings – and the Lord He knows who these may or may not have been – came to trade with the Vikings, and ran away because they were frightened at the bellowing of the cattle which Thorfin had brought with him in the ships. But what in the world could a Greek slave know of that affair? I wandered up and down among the streets trying to unravel the mystery, and the more I considered it, the more baffling it grew. One thing only seemed certain, and that certainty took away my breath for a moment. If I came to full knowledge of anything at all, it would not be one life of the soul in Charlie Mears's body, but half a dozen – half a dozen several and separate existences spent on blue water in the morning of the world!

Then I reviewed the situation.

Obviously if I used my knowledge I should stand alone and unapproachable until all men were as wise as myself. That would be something, but manlike I was ungrateful. It seemed bitterly unfair that Charlie's memory should fail me when I needed it most. Great Powers Above – I looked up at them through the fog-smoke – did the Lords of Life and Death know what this meant to me? Nothing less than eternal fame of the best kind, that comes from One, and is shared by one alone. I would be content – remembering Clive, I stood astounded at my own moderation – with the mere right to tell one story, to work out one little contribution to the light literature of the day. If Charlie were permitted full recollection for one hour – for sixty short minutes – of existences that had extended over a thousand years – I would forgo all profit and honour from all that I should make of his speech. I would take no share in the commotion that would follow throughout the particular corner of the Earth that calls itself 'the world'. The thing should be put forth anonymously. Nay, I would make other men believe that they had written it. They would hire bull-hided self-advertising Englishmen to bellow it abroad. Preachers would found a fresh conduct of life upon it, swearing that it was new and that they had lifted the fear of death from all mankind. Every Orientalist in Europe would patronize it discursively with Sanskrit and Pali texts. Terrible women would invent unclean variants of the men's belief for the elevation of their sisters. Churches and religions would war over it. Between the hailing and re-starting of an omnibus I foresaw the scuffles that would arise among half a dozen denominations all professing 'the doctrine of the True Metempsychosis as applied to the world and the New Era'; and saw, too, the respectable English newspapers shying, like frightened kine, over the beautiful simplicity of the tale. The mind leaped forward a hundred – two hundred – a thousand years. I saw with sorrow that men would mutilate and garble the story ; that rival creeds would turn it upside down till, at last, the western world which clings to the dread of death more closely than the hope of life, would set it aside as an interesting superstition and stampede after some faith so long forgotten that it seemed altogether new. Upon this I changed the terms of the bargain that I would make with the Lords of Life and Death. Only let me know, let me write the story with sure knowledge that I wrote the truth, and I would burn the manuscript as a solemn sacrifice. Five minutes after the last line was written I would destroy it all. But I must be allowed to write it with absolute certainty.

There was no answer. The flaming colours of an aquarium poster caught my eye, and I wondered whether it would be wise or prudent to lure Charlie into the hands of the professional mesmerist then, and whether, if he were under his power, he would speak of his past lives. If he did, and if people believed him . . . but Charlie would be frightened and flustered, or made conceited by the interviews. In either case he would begin to lie, through fear or vanity. He was safest in my own hands.

'They are very funny fools, your English,' said a voice at my elbow, and turning round I recognized a casual acquaintance, a young Bengali law student, called Grish Chunder, whose father had sent him to England to become civilized. The old man was a retired native official, and on an income of five pounds a month contrived to allow his son two hundred pounds a year, and the run of his teeth in a city where he could pretend to be the cadet of a royal house, and tell stories of the brutal Indian bureaucrats who ground the faces of the poor.

Grish Chunder was a young, fat, full-bodied Bengali, dressed with scrupulous care in frock coat, tall hat, light trousers, and tan gloves. But I had known him in the days when the brutal Indian Government paid for his university education, and he contributed cheap sedition to the *Sachi Durpan*, and intrigued with the wives of his fourteen-year-old schoolmates.

'That is very funny and very foolish,' he said, nodding at the poster. 'I am going down to the Northbrook Club. Will you come too?'

I walked with him for some time. 'You are not well,' he said. 'What is there on your mind? You do not talk.'

'Grish Chunder, you've been too well educated to believe in a God, haven't you?'

'Oah, yes, *here*! But when I go home I must conciliate popular superstition, and make ceremonies of purification, and my women will anoint idols.'

'And hang up *tulsi* and feast the *purohit*, and take you back into caste again and make a good *khuttri* of you again, you advanced Freethinker. And you'll eat *desi* food, and like it all, from the smell in the courtyard to the mustard oil over you.'

'I shall very much like it,' said Grish Chunder unguardedly. 'Once a Hindu – always a Hindu. But I like to know what the English think they know.'

'I'll tell you something that one Englishman knows. It's an old tale to you.'

I began to tell the story of Charlie in English, but Grish Chunder put a question in the vernacular, and the history went forward naturally in the tongue best suited for its telling. After all, it could never have been told in English. Grish Chunder heard me, nodding from time to time, and then came up to my rooms, where I finished the tale.

'Beshak,' he said philosophically. *'Lekin darwaza band hai.* (Without doubt; but the door is shut.) I have heard of this remembering of previous existences among my people. It is of course an old tale with us, but, to happen to an Englishman – a cow-fed *Mlechh* - an outcast. By Jove, that is *most* peculiar!'

'Outcast yourself, Grish Chunder! You eat cow-beef every day. Let's think the thing over. The boy remembers his incarnations.'

'Does he know that?' said Grish Chunder quietly, swinging his legs as he sat on my table. He was speaking in his English now.

'He does not know anything. Would I speak to you if he did? Go on!'

'There is no going on at all. If you tell that to your friends they will say you are mad and put it in the papers. Suppose, now, you prosecute for libel.'

'Let's leave that out of the question entirely. Is there any chance of his being made to speak?'

'There is a chance. Oah, yess! But *if* he spoke it would mean that all this world would end now – *instanto* – fall down on your head. These things are not allowed, you know. As I said, the door is shut.'

'Not a ghost of a chance?'

'How can there be? You are a Christi-an, and it is forbidden to eat, in your books, of the Tree of Life, or else you would never die. How shall you all fear death if you all know what your friend does not know that he knows? I am afraid to be kicked, but I am not afraid to die, because I know what I know. You are not afraid to be kicked, but you are afraid to die. If you were not, by God! you English would be all over the shop in an hour, upsetting the balances of power, and making commotions. It would not be good. But no fear. He will remember a little and a little less, and he will call it dreams. Then he will forget altogether. When I passed my First Arts Examination in Calcutta that was all in the cram-book on Wordsworth. "Trailing clouds of glory", you know.'

'This seems to be an exception to the rule.'

'There are no exceptions to rules. Some are not so hard-looking as others, but they are all the same when you touch. If this friend of yours said so-and-so and so-and-so, indicating that he remembered all his lost lives, or one piece of a lost life, he would not be in the bank another hour. He would be what you called sack because he was mad, and they would send him to an asylum for lunatics. You can see that, my friend.'

'Of course I can, but I wasn't thinking of him. His name need never appear in the story.'

'Ah! I see. That story will never be written. You can try.'

'I am going to.'

'For your own credit and for the sake of money, *of* course?'

'No. For the sake of writing the story. On my honour that will be all.'

'Even then there is no chance. You cannot play with the gods. It is a very pretty story now. As they say, Let it go on that – I mean at that. Be quick; he will not last long.'

'How do you mean?'

'What I say. He has never, so far, thought about a woman.'

'Hasn't he, though!' I remembered some of Charlie's confidences.

'I mean no woman has thought about him. When that comes; *bus – hogya* – all up! I know. There are millions of women here. Housemaids, for instance. They kiss you behind doors.'

I winced at the thought of my story being ruined by a housemaid. And yet nothing was more probable.

Grish Chunder grinned.

'Yes – also pretty girls – cousins of his house, and perhaps *not* of his house. One kiss that he gives back again and remembers will cure all this nonsense, or else—'

'Or else what? Remember he does not know that he knows.'

'I know that. Or else, if nothing happens he will become immersed in the trade and the financial speculation like the rest. It must be so. You can see that it must be so. But the woman will come first, *I* think.'

There was a rap at the door, and Charlie charged in impetuously. He had been released from office, and by the look in his eyes I could see that he had come over for a long talk; most probably with poems in his pockets. Charlie's poems were very wearying, but sometimes they led him to speak about the galley.

Grish Chunder looked at him keenly for a minute.

'I beg your pardon,' Charlie said uneasily; 'I didn't know you had any one with you.'

'I am going,' said Grish Chunder.

He drew me into the lobby as he departed.

'That is your man,' he said quickly. 'I tell you he will never speak all you wish. That is rot – bosh. But he would be most good to make to see things. Suppose now we pretend that it was only play' – I had never seen Grish Chunder so excited – 'and pour the ink-pool into his hand. Eh, what do you think? I tell you that he could see *anything* that a man could see. Let me get the ink and the camphor. He is a seer and he will tell us very many things.'

'He may be all you say, but I'm not going to trust him to your gods and devils.'

'It will not hurt him. He will only feel a little stupid and dull when he wakes up. You have seen boys look into the ink-pool before.'

'That is the reason why I am not going to see it any more. You'd better go, Grish Chunder.'

He went, insisting far down the staircase that it was throwing away my only chance of looking into the future.

This left me unmoved, for I was concerned for the past, and no peering of hypnotized boys into mirrors and ink-pools would help me to that. But I recognized Grish Chunder's point of view and sympathized with it.

'What a big black brute that was!' said Charlie, when I returned to him. 'Well, look here, I've just done a poem; did it instead of playing dominoes after lunch. May I read it?'

'Let me read it to myself.'

'Then you miss the proper expression. Besides, you always make my things sound as if the rhymes were all wrong.'

'Read it aloud, then. You're like the rest of 'em.'

Charlie mouthed me his poem, and it was not much worse than the average of his verses. He had been reading his books faithfully, but he was not pleased when I told him that I preferred my Longfellow undiluted with Charlie.

Then we began to go through the MS line by line; Charlie parrying every objection and correction with:

'Yes, that may be better, but you don't catch what I'm driving at.'

Charlie was, in one way at least, very like one kind of poet.

There was a pencil scrawl at the back of the paper and 'What's that?' I said.

'Oh that's not poetry at all. It's some rot I wrote last night before I went to bed, and it was too much bother to hunt for rhymes; so I made it a sort of blank verse instead.'

Here is Charlie's 'blank verse.'

'We pulled for you when the wind was against us and the sails were low.
Will you never let us go?

We ate bread and onions when you took towns, or ran aboard quickly when you were beaten back by the foe,

The captains walked up and down the deck in fair weather singing songs, but we were below,

We fainted with our chins on the oars and you did not see that we were idle for we still swung to and fro.

Will you never let us go?

The salt made the oar-handles like shark-skin; our knees were cut to the bone with salt cracks; our hair was stuck to our foreheads; and our lips were cut to our gums and you whipped us because we could not row.

Will you never let us go?

But in a little time we shall run out of the portholes as the water runs along the oar-blade, and though you tell the others to row after us you will never catch us till you catch the oar-thresh and tie up the winds in the belly of the sail. Aho!

Will you never let us go?

'H'm. What's oar-thresh, Charlie?'

'The water washed up by the oars. That's the sort of song they might sing in the galley y' know. Aren't you ever going to finish that story and give me some of the profits?'

'It depends on yourself. If you had only told me more about your hero in the first instance it might have been finished by now. You're so hazy in your notions.'

'I only want to give you the general notion of it – the knocking about from place to place and the fighting and all that. Can't you fill in the rest yourself? Make the hero save a girl on a pirate-galley and marry her or do something.'

'You're a really helpful collaborator. I suppose the hero went through some few adventures before he married.'

'Well then, make him a very artful card – a low sort of man – a sort of political man who went about making treaties and breaking them–a black-haired chap who hid behind the mast when the fighting began.'

'But you said the other day that he was red-haired.'

'I couldn't have. Make him black-haired of course. You've no imagination.'

Seeing that I had just discovered the entire principles upon which the half-memory falsely called imagination is based, I felt entitled to laugh, but forbore, for the sake of the tale.

'You're right. *You're* the man with imagination. A black-haired chap in a decked ship,' I said.

'No, an open ship – like a big boat.'

This was maddening.

'Your ship has been built and designed, closed and decked in; you said so yourself,' I protested.

'No, no, not that ship. That was open or half-decked because— By Jove, you're right. You made me think of the hero as a red-haired chap. Of course if he were red, the ship would be an open one with painted sails.'

Surely, I thought, he would remember now that he had served in two galleys at least – in a three-decked Greek one under the black-haired 'political man', and again in a Viking's open sea-serpent under the man 'red as a red bear' who went to Markland. The devil prompted me to speak.

'Why, "of course", Charlie?' said I.

'I don't know. Are you making fun of me?'

The current was broken for the time being. I took up a notebook and pretended to make many entries in it.

'It's a pleasure to work with an imaginative chap like yourself,' I said, after a pause. 'The way that you've brought out the character of the hero is simply wonderful.'

'Do you think so?' he answered, with a pleased flush. 'I often tell myself that there's more in me than my mo— than people think.'

'There's an enormous amount in you.'

'Then, won't you let me send an essay on The Ways of Bank-Clerks to *Tit-Bits*, and get the guinea prize?'

'That wasn't exactly what I meant, old fellow: perhaps it would be better to wait a little and go ahead with the galley-story.'

'Ah, but I shan't get the credit of that. *Tit-Bits* would publish my name and address if I win. What are you grinning at? They *would*.'

'I know it. Suppose you go for a walk. I want to look through my notes about our story.'

Now this reprehensible youth who left me, a little hurt and put back, might for aught he or I knew have been one of the crew of the *Argo* – had been certainly slave or comrade to Thorfin Karlsefne. Therefore he was deeply interested in guinea competitions. Remembering what Grish Chunder had said I laughed aloud. The Lords of Life and Death would never allow Charlie Mears to speak with full knowledge of his pasts, and I must even piece out what he had told me with my own poor inventions while Charlie wrote of the ways of bank-clerks.

I got together and placed on one file all my notes; and the net result was not cheering. I read them a second time. There was nothing that might not have been compiled at second-hand from other people's books – except, perhaps, the story of the fight in the harbour. The adventures of a Viking had been written many times before; the history of a Greek galley-slave was no new thing, and though I wrote both, who could challenge or confirm the accuracy of my details? I might as well tell a tale of two thousand years hence. The Lords of Life and Death were as cunning as Grish Chunder had hinted. They would allow nothing to escape that might trouble or make easy the minds of men. Though I was convinced of this, yet I could not leave the tale alone. Exaltation followed reaction, not once, but twenty times in the next few weeks. My mood varied with the March sunlight and flying clouds. By night or in the beauty of a spring morning I perceived that I could write that tale and shift continents thereby. In the wet windy afternoons, I saw that the tale might indeed be written, but would be nothing more than a faked, false-varnished, sham-rusted piece of Wardour Street work in the end. Then I blessed Charlie in many ways – though it was no fault of his. He seemed to be busy with prize competitions, and I saw less and less of him as the weeks went by and the earth cracked and grew ripe to spring, and the buds swelled in their sheaths. He did not care to read or talk of what he had read, and there was a new ring of self-assertion in his voice. I hardly cared to remind him of the galley when we met; but Charlie alluded to it on every occasion, always as a story from which money was to be made.

'I think I deserve twenty-five per cent, don't I, at least?' he said, with beautiful frankness. 'I supplied all the ideas, didn't I?'

This greediness for silver was a new side in his nature. I assumed that it had been developed in the City, where Charlie was picking up the curious nasal drawl of the underbred City man.

'When the thing's done we'll talk about it. I can't make anything of it at present. Red-haired or black-haired hero are equally difficult.'

He was sitting by the fire staring at the red coals. '*I* can't understand what you find so difficult. It's all as clear as mud to me,' he replied. A jet of gas puffed out between the bars, took light, and whistled softly. 'Suppose we take the red-haired hero's adventures first, from the time that he came south to my galley and captured it and sailed to the Beaches.'

I knew better now than to interrupt Charlie. I was out of reach of pen and paper, and dared not move to get them lest I should break the current. The gas-jet puffed and whinnied, Charlie's voice dropped almost to a whisper, and he told a tale of the sailing of an open galley to Furdurstrandi, of sunsets on the open sea, seen under the curve of the one sail evening after evening when the galley's beak was notched into the centre of the sinking disc, and 'we sailed by that for we had no other guide,' quoth Charlie. He spoke of a landing on an island and explorations in its woods, where the crew killed three men whom they found asleep under the pines. Their ghosts, Charlie said, followed the galley, swimming and choking in the water, and the crew cast lots and threw one of their number overboard as a sacrifice to the strange gods whom they had offended. Then they ate seaweed when their provisions failed, and their legs swelled, and their leader, the red-haired man, killed two rowers who mutinied, and after a year spent among the woods they set sail for their own country, and a wind that never failed carried them back so safely that they all slept at night. This, and much more Charlie told. Sometimes the voice fell so low that I could not catch the words, though every nerve was on the strain. He spoke of their leader, the red-haired man, as a pagan speaks of his god; for it was he who cheered them and slew them impartially as he thought best for their needs; and it was he who steered them for three days among floating ice, each floe crowded with strange beasts that 'tried to sail with us', said Charlie, 'and we beat them back with the handles of the oars.'

The gas-jet went out, a burnt coal gave way, and the fire settled with a tiny crash to the bottom of the grate. Charlie ceased speaking, and I said no word.

'By Jove!' he said at last, shaking his head. 'I've been staring at the fire till I'm dizzy. What was I going to say?'

'Something about the galley-book.'

'I remember now. It's twenty-five per cent of the profits, isn't it?'

'It's anything you like when I've done the tale.'

'I wanted to be sure of that. I must go now. I've – I've an appointment.' And he left me.

Had not my eyes been held I might have known that that broken muttering over the fire was the swan-song of Charlie Mears. But I thought it the prelude to fuller revelation. At last and at last I should cheat the Lords of Life and Death!

When next Charlie came to me I received him with rapture. He was nervous and embarrassed, but his eyes were very full of light, and his lips a little parted.

'I've done a poem,' he said; and then, quickly: 'It's the best I've ever done. Read it.' He thrust it into my hand and retreated to the window.

I groaned inwardly. It would be the work of half an hour to

criticize – that is to say, praise – the poem sufficiently to please Charlie. Then I had good reason to groan, for Charlie, discarding his favourite centipede metres, had launched into shorter and choppier verse, and verse with a motive at the back of it. This is what I read:

'The day is most fair, the cheery wind
  Halloos behind the hill,
Where he bends the wood as seemeth good,
  And the sapling to his will!
Riot, O wind; there is that in my blood
  That would not have thee still!

'She gave me herself, O Earth, O Sky;
  Grey sea, she is mine alone!
Let the sullen boulders hear my cry,
  And rejoice tho' they be but stone!

'Mine! I have won her, O good brown earth,
  Make merry! 'Tis hard on Spring;
Make merry; my love is doubly worth
  All worship your fields can bring!
Let the hind that tills you feel my mirth
  At the early harrowing!'

'Yes, it's the early harrowing, past a doubt,' I said, with a dread at my heart. Charlie smiled, but did not answer.

'Red cloud of the sunset, tell it abroad;
  I am victor. Greet me, O Sun,
Dominant master and absolute lord
  Over the soul of one!'

'Well?' said Charlie, looking over my shoulder.

I thought it far from well, and very evil indeed, when he silently laid a photograph on the paper – the photograph of a girl with a curly head, and a foolish slack mouth.

'Isn't it – isn't it wonderful?' he whispered, pink to the tips of his ears, wrapped in the rosy mystery of first love. 'I didn't know; I didn't think – it came like a thunderclap.'

'Yes. It comes like a thunderclap. Are you very happy, Charlie?'

'My God – she – she loves me!' He sat down repeating the last words to himself. I looked at the hairless face, the narrow shoulders already bowed by desk-work, and wondered when, where, and how he had loved in his past lives.

'What will your mother say?' I asked cheerfully.

'I don't care a damn what she says!'

At twenty the things for which one does not care a damn should, properly, be many, but one must not include mothers in the list. I told him this gently; and he described Her, even as Adam must have described to the newly-named beasts the glory and tenderness and beauty of Eve. Incidentally I learned that She was a tobacconist's assistant with a weakness for pretty dress, and had told him four or five times already that She had never been kissed by a man before.

Charlie spoke on and on, and on; while I, separated from him by thousands of years, was considering the beginnings of things. Now I understood why the Lords of Life and Death shut the doors so carefully behind us. It is that we may not remember our first and most beautiful wooings. Were this not so, our world would be without inhabitants in a hundred years.

'Now, about that galley-story,' I said still more cheerfully, in a pause in the rush of the speech.

Charlie looked up as though he had been hit. 'The galley – what galley? Good heavens, don't joke, man! This is serious! You don't know how serious it is!'

Grish Chunder was right. Charlie had tasted the love of woman that kills remembrance, and the finest story in the world would never be written.

'Love-o'-Women'

'A lamentable tale of things
Done long ago, and ill done.'

THE horror, the confusion, and the separation of the murderer from his comrades were all over before I came. There remained only on the barrack-square the blood of man calling from the ground. The hot sun had dried it to a dusky goldbeater-skin film, cracked lozenge-wise by the heat; and as the wind rose, each lozenge, rising a little, curled up at the edges as if it were a dumb tongue. Then a heavier gust blew all away down wind in grains of dark coloured dust. It was too hot to stand in the sunshine before breakfast. The men were in barracks talking the matter over. A knot of soldiers' wives stood by one of the entrances to the married quarters, while inside a woman shrieked and raved with wicked filthy words.

A quiet and well-conducted sergeant had shot down, in broad daylight just after early parade, one of his own corporals, had then returned to barracks and sat on a cot till the guard came to him. He would, therefore, in due time be handed over to the High Court for trial. Further, but this he could hardly have considered in his scheme of revenge, he would horribly upset my work; for the reporting of that trial would fall on me without a relief. What that trial would be like I knew even to weariness. There would be the rifle carefully uncleaned, with the fouling marks about breech and muzzle, to be sworn to by half a dozen superfluous privates; there would be heat, reeking heat, till the wet pencil slipped sideways between your fingers; and the punkah would swish and the pleaders would jabber in the verandas, and his commanding officer would put in certificates to the prisoner's moral character, while the jury would pant and the summer uniforms of the witnesses would smell of dye and soaps; and some abject barrack-sweeper would lose his head in cross-examination, and the young barrister who always defended soldiers' cases for the credit that they never brought him, would say and do wonderful things, and would then quarrel with me because I had not reported him correctly. At the last, for he surely would not be hanged, I might meet the prisoner again, ruling blank account-forms in the Central Jail, and cheer him with the hope of his being made a warder in the Andamans.

The Indian Penal Code and its interpreters do not treat murder, under any provocation whatever, in a spirit of jest. Sergeant Raines would be very lucky indeed if he got off with seven years, I thought. He had slept the night upon his wrongs, and killed his man at twenty yards before any talk was possible. That much I knew. Unless, therefore, the case was doctored a little, seven years would be his least; and I fancied it was exceedingly well for Sergeant Raines that he had been liked by his company.

That same evening – no day is so long as the day of a murder – I met Ortheris with the dogs, and he plunged defiantly into the middle of the matter. 'I'll be one o' the witnesses,' said he. 'I was in the veranda when Mackie come along. 'E come from Mrs Raines's quarters. Quigley, Parsons, an' Trot, they was in the inside veranda, so *they* couldn't 'ave 'eard nothing. Sergeant Raines was in the veranda talkin' to me, an' Mackie 'e come along acrost the square an' 'e sez, "Well," sez 'e, "'ave they pushed your 'elmet off yet, Sergeant?" 'e sez. An' at that Raines 'e catches 'is breath an' 'e sez, "My Gawd, I can't stand this!" sez 'e, an' 'e picks up my rifle and shoots Mackie. See?'

'But what were you doing with your rifle in the outer veranda an hour after parade?'

'Cleanin' 'er,' said Ortheris, with the sullen brassy stare that always went with his choicer lies.

He might as well have said that he was dancing naked, for at no time did his rifle need hand or rag on her twenty minutes after parade. Still, the High Court would not know his routine.

'Are you going to stick to that – on the Book?' I asked.

'Yes. Like a bloomin' leech.'

'All right, I don't want to know any more. Only remember that Quigley, Parsons, and Trot couldn't have been where you say they were without hearing something; and there's nearly certain to be a barrack-sweeper who was knocking about the square at the time. There always is.'

''Twasn't the sweeper. It was the beastie. 'E's all right.'

Then I knew that there was going to be some spirited doctoring, and I felt sorry for the government advocate who would conduct the prosecution.

When the trial came on I pitied him more, for he was always quick to lose his temper and made a personal matter of each lost cause. Raines's young barrister had for once put aside his unslaked and welling passion for alibis and insanity, had forsworn gymnastics and fireworks, and worked soberly for his client. Mercifully the hot weather was yet young, and there had been no flagrant cases of barrack-shootings up to the time; and the jury was a good one, even for an Indian jury, where nine men out of every twelve are accustomed to weighing evidence. Ortheris stood firm and was not shaken by any cross-examination. The one weak point in his tale – the presence of his rifle in the outer veranda – went unchallenged by civilian wisdom, though some of the witnesses could not help smiling. The government advocate called for the rope, contending throughout that the murder had been a deliberate one. Time had passed, he argued, for that reflection which comes so naturally to a man whose honour is lost. There was also the Law, ever ready and anxious to right the wrongs of the common soldier if, indeed, wrong had been done. But he doubted much whether there had been any sufficient wrong. Causeless suspicion over-long brooded upon had led, by his theory, to deliberate crime. But his attempts to minimize the motive failed. The most disconnected witnesses knew – had known for weeks – the causes of offence; and the prisoner, who naturally was the last of all to know, groaned in the dock while he listened. The one question that the trial circled round was whether Raines had fired under sudden and blinding provocation given that very morning; and in the summing-up it was clear that Ortheris's evidence told. He had contrived most artistically to suggest that he personally hated the sergeant, who had come into the veranda to give him a talking to for insubordination. In a weak moment the government advocate asked one question too many. 'Beggin' *your* pardon, sir,' Ortheris replied, ''e was callin' me a dam' impudent little lawyer.' The court shook. The jury brought it in a killing, but with every provocation and extenuation known to God or man, and the judge put his hand to his brow before giving sentence, and the Adam's apple in the prisoner's throat went up and down like mercury pumping before a cyclone.

In consideration of all considerations, from his commanding officer's certificate of good conduct to the sure loss of pension, service, and honour, the prisoner would get two years, to be served in India, and – there need be no demonstration in court. The government advocate scowled and picked up his papers; the guard wheeled with a clash, and the prisoner was relaxed to the Secular Arm, and driven to the jail in a broken-down *ticca-gharri*.

His guard and some ten or twelve military witnesses, being less important, were ordered to wait till what was officially called the cool of the evening before marching back to cantonments. They gathered together in one of the deep red brick verandas of a disused lock-up and congratulated Ortheris, who bore his honours modestly. I sent my work into the office and joined them. Ortheris watched the government advocate driving off to lunch.

'That's a nasty little bald-'eaded little butcher, that is,' he said. ''E don't please me. 'E's got a colley dog wot do, though. I'm goin' up to Murree in a week. That dawg'll bring fifteen rupees anywheres.'

'You had better spend ut in Masses,' said Terence, unbuckling his belt; for he had been on the prisoner's guard, standing helmeted and bolt upright for three long hours.

'Not me,' said Ortheris cheerfully. 'Gawd'll put it down to B Comp'ny's barrick-damages one o' these days. You look strapped, Terence.'

'Faith, I'm not so young as I was. That guard-mountin' wears on the sole av the fut, and this' – he sniffed contemptuously at the brick veranda – 'is as hard setting as standin'!'

'Wait a minute. I'll get the cushions out of my cart,' I said.

''Strewth – sofies. We're going it gay,' said Ortheris, as Terence dropped himself section by section on the leather cushions, saying prettily, 'May ye niver want a soft place wheriver you go, an' power to share ut wid a frind. Another for yourself? That's good. It lets me sit longways. Stanley, pass me a pipe. Augrrh! An' that's another man gone all to pieces bekaze av a woman. I must ha' been on forty or fifty prisoners' gyards, first an' last; an' I hate ut new ivry time.'

'Let's see. You were on Losson's, Lancey's, Dugard's, and Stebbins's, that I can remember,' I said.

'Ay, an' before that an' before that – scores av thim,' he answered with a worn smile. ''Tis better to die than to live for them, though. Whin Raines comes out – he'll be changin' his kit at the jail now – he'll think that too. He shud ha' shot hemself an' the woman by rights an' made a clean bill av all. Now he's left the woman – she tuk tay wid Dinah Sunday gone last – an' he's left himself. Mackie's the lucky man.'

'He's probably getting it hot where he is,' I ventured, for I knew something of the dead corporal's record.

'Be sure av that,' said Terence, spitting over the edge of the veranda. 'But fwhat he'll get there is light marchin'-ordher to fwhat he'd ha' got here if he'd lived.'

'Surely not. He'd have gone on and forgotten – like the others.'

'Did you know Mackie well, sorr?' said Terence.

'He was on the Pattiala guard of honour last winter, and I went out shooting with him in an *ekka* for the day, and I found him rather an amusing man.'

'Well, he'll ha' got shut av amusemints, excipt turnin' from wan side to the other, these few years to come. I knew Mackie, an' I've seen too many to be mistuk in the muster av wan man. He might ha' gone an' forgot as you say, sorr, but he was a man wid an educashin, an' he used ut for his schames; an' the same educashin, an' talkin', an' all that made him able to do fwhat he had a mind to wid a woman, that same wud turn back again in the long-run an' tear him alive. I can't say fwhat that I mane to say bekaze I don't know how, but Mackie was the spit an' livin' image of a man that I saw march the same march *all but*; an' 'twas worse for him that he did not come by Mackie's ind. Wait while I remember now. 'Twas whin I was in the Black Tyrone, an' he was drafted us from Portsmouth; an' fwhat was his misbegotten name? Larry – Larry Tighe ut was; an' wan of the draft said he was a gentleman-ranker, an' Larry tuk an' three-parts killed him for saying so. An' he was a big man, an' a strong man, an' a handsome man, an' that tells heavy in practice wid some women, but, takin' 'em by an' large, not wid all. Yet 'twas wid all that Larry dealt – *all* – for he cud put the comether on any woman that trod the green earth av God, an' he knew ut. Like Mackie that's roastin' now, he knew ut, an' niver did he put the comether on any woman save an' excipt for the black shame. 'Tis not me that shud be talkin', dear knows, dear knows, but the most av my mis – misallinces was for pure devilry, an' mighty sorry I have been whin harm came; an' time an' time again wid a girl, ay, an' a woman too, for the matter av that, whin I have seen by the eyes av her that I was makin' more throuble than I talked, I have hild off an' let be for the sake av the mother that bore me. But Larry, I'm thinkin', he was suckled by a she-divil, for he never let wan go that came nigh to listen to him. 'Twas his business, as if it might ha' ben sinthry-go. He was a good soldier too. Now there was the Colonel's governess – an' he a privit too! – that was never known in barricks; an' wan av the Major's maids, and she was promised to a man; an' some more outside; an' fwhat ut was amongst *us* we'll never know till Judgment Day. 'Twas the nature av the baste to put the comether on the best av thim – not the prettiest by any manner av manes – but the like av such women as you cud lay your hand on the Book an' swear there was niver thought av foolishness in. An' for that very reason, mark you, he was niver caught. He came close to ut wanst or twice, but caught he niver was, an' that cost him more at the ind than the beginnin'. He talked to me more than most, bekaze he tould me, barrin' the accident av my educashin, I'd av been the same kind av divil as he was. "An' is ut like," he wud say, houldin' his head high –

"is ut like that I'd iver be thrapped? For fwhat am I when all's said an' done?' he sez. "A damned privit," sez he. "An' is ut like, think you, that thim I know wud be connect wid a privit like me? Number tin thousand four hundred an' sivin," he sez grinnin'. I knew by the turn av his spache when he was not takin' care to talk rough-shod that he was a gentleman-ranker.

'"I do not undherstan' ut at all," I sez; "but I know," sez I, "that the divil looks out av your eyes, an' I'll have no share wid you. A little fun by way av amusemint where 'twill do no harm, Larry, is right and fair, but I am mistook if 'tis any amusemint to you," I sez.

'"You are much mistook," he sez. "An' I counsel you not to judge your betters."

'"My betthers!" I sez. "God help you, Larry. There's no betther in this; 'tis all bad, as ye will find for yoursilf."

'"You're not like me," he says, tossin' his head.

'"Praise the Saints, I am not," I sez. "Fwhat I have done I have done an' been crool sorry for. Fwhin your time comes," sez I, "ye'll remimber fwhat I say."

'"An' whin that time comes," sez he, "I'll come to you for ghostly consolation, Father Terence," an' at that he wint off afther some more divil's business – for to get expayrience, he tould me. He was wicked – rank wicked – wicked as all Hell! I'm not construct by nature to go in fear av any man, but, begad, I was afraid av Larry. He'd come in to barricks wid his cap on three hairs, an' lie on his cot and stare at the ceilin', and now an' again he'd fetch a little laugh, the like av a splash in the bottom av a well, an' by that I knew he was schamin' new wickedness, an' I'd be afraid. All this was long an' long ago, but ut hild me straight – for a while.

'I tould you, did I not, sorr, that I was caressed an' pershuaded to lave the Tyrone on account av a throuble?'

'Something to do with a belt and a man's head wasn't it?' Terence had never given the tale in full.

'It was. Faith, ivry time I go on prisoner's gyard in coort I wondher fwhy I was not where the pris'ner is. But the man I struk tuk it in fair fight an' he had the good sinse not to die. Considher now, fwhat wud ha' come to the Arrmy if he had! I was enthreated to exchange, an' my commandin' orf'cer pled wid me. I wint, not to be disobligin', and Larry tould me he was powerful sorry to lose me, though fwhat I'd done to make him sorry I do not know. So to the Ould Reg'mint I came, lavin' Larry to go to the divil his own way, an' niver expectin' to see him again excipt as a shootin'-case in barracks . . . Who's that quittin' the compound?' Terence's quick eye had caught sight of a white uniform skulking behind the hedge.

'The Sergeant's gone visiting,' said a voice.

'Thin I command here, an' I will have no sneakin' away to the bazaar, an' huntin' for you wid a pathrol at midnight. Nalson, for I know ut's you, come back to the veranda.'

Nalson, detected, slunk back to his fellows. There was a grumble that died away in a minute or two, and Terence turning on the other side went on:

'That was the last I saw av Larry for a while. Exchange is the same as death for not thinkin' an' by token I married Dinah, an' that kept me from remimberin' ould times. Thin we went up to the Front, an' ut tore my heart in tu to lave Dinah at the Depôt in Pindi. Consequint, whin I was at the Front I fought circumspectuous till I warrmed up, an' thin I fought double tides. You remember fwhat I tould you in the gyard-gate av the fight at Silver's Theatre?'

'Wot's that about Silver's Theayter?' said Ortheris quickly, over his shoulder.

'Nothin', little man. A tale that ye know. As I was sayin', afther that fight, us av the Ould Rig'mint an' the Tyrone was all mixed together takin' shtock av the dead, an' av coorse I wint about to find if there was any man that remembered me. The second man I came acrost – an' how I'd missed him in the fight I do not know – was Larry, an' a fine man he looked, but oulder, by reason that he had fair call to be. "Larry," sez I, "how is ut wid you?"

'"Ye're callin' the wrong man," he sez, wid his gentleman's smile, "Larry has been dead these three years. They call him 'Love-o'-Women' now," he sez. By that I knew the ould divil was in him yet, but the ind av a fight is no time for the beginnin' av confession, so we sat down an' talked av times.

'"They tell me you're a married man," he sez, puffin' slow at his poipe. "Are ye happy?"

'"I will be whin I get back to Depôt," I sez. "'Tis a reconnaissance-honeymoon now."

'"I'm married too," he sez, puffin' slow an' more slow, an' stopperin' wid his forefinger.

'"Send you happiness," I sez. "That's the best hearin' for a long time."

'"Are ye av that opinion?" he sez; an' thin he began talkin' av the campaign. The sweat av Silver's Theatre was not dhry upon him an' he was prayin' for more work. I was well contint to lie and listen to the cook-pot lids.

'Whin he got up off the ground he shtaggered a little, an' laned over all twisted.

'"Ye've got more than ye bargained for," I sez. "Take an inventory, Larry. 'Tis like you're hurt."

'He turned round stiff as a ramrod an' damned the eyes av me up an' down for an impartinent Irish-faced ape. If that had been in barracks, I'd ha' stretched him an' no more said; but 'twas at the Front, an' afther such a fight as Silver's Theatre I knew there was no callin' a man to account for his tempers. He might as well ha' kissed me. Aftherwards I was well pleased I kept my fists home. Thin our Captain Crook – Cruik-na-bulleen – came up. He'd been talkin' to the little orf'cer bhoy av the Tyrone. "We're all cut to windystraws," he sez, "but the Tyrone are damned short for noncoms. Go you over there, Mulvaney, an' be deputy-sergeant, corp'ral, lance, an' everything else ye can lay hands on till I bid you stop."

'I wint over an' tuk hould. There was wan sergeant left standin', an' they'd pay no heed to him. The remnint was me, an' 'twas full time I came. Some I talked to, an' some I did not, but before night the bhoys av the Tyrone stud to attention, by gad, if I sucked on my poipe above a whishper. Betune you an' me an' Bobbs I was commandin' the company, an' that was what Crook had thransferred me for; an' the little orf'cer bhoy knew ut, and I knew ut, but the comp'ny did not. And *there*, mark you, is the vartue that no money an' no dhrill can buy – the vartue av the ould soldier that knows his orf'cer's work an' does ut for him at the salute!

'Thin the Tyrone, wid the Ould Rig'mint in touch, was sint maraudin' an' prowlin' acrost the hills promishcuous an' on-satisfactory. 'Tis my privit opinion that a gin'ral does not know half his time fwhat to do with three-quarthers his command. So he shquats on his hunkers an' bids them run round an' round forninst him while he considhers on it. Whin by the process av nature, they get sejuced into a big fight that was none av their seekin', he sez: "Obsarve my shuperior janius. I meant ut to come so." We ran round an' about, an' all we got was shootin' into the camp at night, an' rushin' empty *sungars* wid the long bradawl, an' bein' hit from behind rocks till we was wore out – all excipt Love-o'-Women. That puppy-dog business was mate an' dhrink to him. Begad he cud niver get enough av ut. Me well knowin' that it is just this desultorial campaignin' that kills the best men, an' suspicionin' that if I was cut, the little orf'cer bhoy wud expind all his men in thryin' to get out, I would lie most powerful doggo whin I heard a shot, an' curl my long legs behind a bowlder, an' run like blazes whin the ground was clear. Faith, if I led the Tyrone in rethreat wanst I led thim forty times! Love-o'-Women wud stay pottin' an' pottin' from behind a rock, and wait till the fire was heaviest, an' thin stand up an' fire man-height clear. He wud lie out in camp too at night, snipin' at the shadows, for he never tuk a mouthful av slape. My commandin' orf'cer – save his little soul! – cud not see the beauty av my strategims, an' whin the Ould Rig'mint crossed us, an' that was wanst a week, he'd throt off to Crook, wid his big blue eyes as round as saucers, an' lay an information against me. I heard thim wanst talkin' through the tent-wall, an' I nearly laughed.

'"He runs – runs like a hare," sez the little orf'cer bhoy. "'Tis demoralizin' my men."

'"Ye damned little fool," sez Crook laughin'. "He's larnin' you your business. Have ye been rushed at night yet?"

'"No," sez that child; wishful he had been.

'"Have you any wounded?" sez Crook.

'"No," he sez. "There was no chanst for that. They follow Mulvaney too quick," he sez.

'"Fwhat more do you want, thin?" sez Crook. "Terence is bloodin' you neat an' handy," he sez. "He knows fwhat you do not, an' that's that there's a time for ivrything. He'll not lead you wrong," he sez, "but I'd give a month's pay to larn fwhat he thinks av you."

'That kept the babe quiet, but Love-o'-Women was pokin' at me for ivrything I did, an' specially my manoeuvres.

'"Mr Mulvaney," he sez wan evenin', very contempshus, "you're growin' very *jeldy* on your feet. Among gentlemen," he sez, "among gentlemen that's called no pretty name."

'"Among privits 'tis different," I sez. "Get back to your tent. I'm sergeant here," I sez.

'There was just enough in the voice av me to tell him he was playin' wid his life betune his teeth. He wint off, an' I noticed that this man that was contempshus set off from the halt wid a shunt as tho' he was bein' kicked behind. That same night there was a Paythan picnic in the hills about, an' firin' into our tents fit to wake the livin' dead. "Lie down all," I sez. "Lie down an' kape still. They'll no more than waste ammunition."

'I heard a man's feet on the ground, an' thin a 'Tini joinin' in the chorus. I'd been lyin' warm, thinkin' av Dinah an' all, but I crup out wid the bugle for to look round in case there was a rush; an' the 'Tini was flashin' at the fore-ind av the camp, an' the hill near by was fair flickerin' wid long-range fire. Undher the starlight I behild Love-o'-Women settin' on a rock wid his belt and helmet off. He shouted wanst or twice, an' thin I heard him say: "They shud ha' got the range long ago. Maybe they'll fire at the flash." Thin he fired again, an' that dhrew a fresh volley, and the long slugs that they chew in their teeth came floppin' among the rocks like tree-toads av a hot night. "That's better," sez Love-o'-Women. "Oh Lord, how long, how long!" he sez, an' at that he lit a match an' held ut above his head.

'"Mad," thinks I, "mad as a coot," an' I tuk wan stip forward, an' the nixt I knew was the sole av my boot flappin' like a cavalry gydon an' the funny-bone av my toes tinglin'. 'Twas a clane-cut shot – a slug - that niver touched sock or hide, but set me bare-fut on the rocks. At that I tuk Love-o'-Women by the scruff an' threw him under a bowlder, an' whin I sat down I heard the bullets patterin' on that same good stone.

'"Ye may dhraw your own wicked fire," I sez, shakin' him, "but I'm not goin' to be kilt too."

'"Ye've come too soon," he sez. "Ye've come too soon. In another minute they cudn't ha' missed me. Mother av' God," he sez, "fwhy did ye not lave me be? Now 'tis all to do again," an' he hides his face in his hands.

'"So that's it," I sez, shakin' him again. "That's the manin' av your disobeyin' ordhers."

'"I dare not kill meself," he sez, rockin' to and fro. "My own hand wud not let me die, and there's not a bullet this month past wud touch me. I'm to die slow," he sez. "I'm to die slow. But I'm in Hell now," he sez, shriekin' like a woman. "I'm in Hell now!"

'"God be good to us all," I sez, for I saw his face. "Will ye tell a man the throuble? If 'tis not murder, maybe we'll mend it yet."

'At that he laughed. "D'you remember fwhat I said in the Tyrone barricks about comin' to you for ghostly consolation. I have not forgot," he sez. "That came back, and the rest av my time is on me now, Terence. I've fought ut off for months an' months, but the liquor will not bite any more. Terence," he sez, "I can't get dhrunk!"

'Thin I knew he spoke the truth about bein' in Hell, for whin liquor does not take hould the sowl av a man is rotten in him. But me bein' such as I was, fwhat could I say to him?

'"Di'monds an' pearls," he begins again. "Di'monds an' pearls I have thrown away wid both hands – an' fwhat have I left?"

'He was shakin' an' thremblin' up against my shouldher, an' the slugs were singin' overhead, an' I was wonderin' whether my little bhoy wud have sinse enough to kape his men quiet through all this firin'.

'"So long as I did not think," sez Love-o'-Women, "so long I did not see – I wud not see, but I can now, what I've lost. The time an' the place," he sez, "an' the very words I said whin ut pleased me to go off alone to Hell. But thin, even thin," he sez, wrigglin' tremenjous, "I wud not ha' been happy. There was too much behind av me. How cud I ha' believed her sworn oath – me that have bruk mine again an' again for the sport av seein' thim cry? An' there are the others," he sez. "Oh, what will I do – what will I do?" He rocked back an' forward again, an' I think he was cryin' like wan av the women he talked av.

'The full half of fwhat he said was Brigade Ordhers to me, but from the rest an' the remnint I suspicioned somethin' av his throuble. 'Twas the judgmint av God had grup the heel av him, as I tould him 'twould in the Tyrone barricks. The slugs was singin' over our rock more an' more, an' I sez for to divart him: "Let bad alone," I sez. "They'll be tryin' to rush the camp in a minut'."

'I had no more than said that whin a Paythan man crep' up on his belly wid a knife betune his teeth, not twinty yards from us. Love-'o-Women jumped up an' fetched a yell, an' the man saw him an' ran at him (he'd left his rifle under the rock) wid the knife. Love-o'-Women niver turned a hair, but by the Living Power, for I saw ut, a stone twisted under the Paythan man's feet an' he came down full sprawl, an' his knife wint tinkling acrost the rocks! "I tould you I was Cain," sez Love-o'-Women. "Fwhat's the use av killin' him? He's an honust man – by compare."

'I was not dishputin' about the morils av Paythans that tide, so I dhropped Love-o'-Women's butt acrost the man's face, an' "Hurry into camp," I sez, "for this may be the first av a rush."

'There was no rush after all, though we waited undher arms to give them a chanst. The Paythan man must ha' come alone for the mischief, an' afther a while Love-o'-Women wint back to his tint wid that quare lurchin' sind-off in his walk that I cud niver understand. Begad, I pitied him, an' the more bekaze he made me think for the rest av the night av the day whin I was confirmed corp'ril, not actin' lef'tinant, an' my thoughts was not good to me.'

'Ye can ondersthand that afther that night we came to talkin' a dale together, an' bit by bit ut came out fwhat I'd suspicioned. The whole av his carr'in's on an' divilments had come back on him hard, as liquor comes back whin you've been on the dhrink for a wake. All he'd said an' all he'd done, an' only he cud tell how much that was, come back, and there was niver a minut's peace in his sowl. 'Twas the Horrors widout any cause to see, an' yet, an' yet – fwhat am I talkin' av? He'd ha' taken the Horrors wid thankfulness. Beyon' the repentince av the man, an' that was beyon' the nature av man – awful, awful, to behould! – there was more that was worst than any repentince. Av the scores an' scores that he called over in his mind (an' they were drivin' him mad), there was, mark you, wan woman av all an' she was not his wife, that cut him to the quick av his marrow. 'Twas there he said that he'd thrown away di'monds an' pearls past count, an' thin he'd begin again like a blind *byle* in an oil-mill, walkin' round and round, to considher (him that was beyond all touch av bein' happy this side Hell!) how happy he wud ha' been wid *her*. The more he considhered, the more he'd consate himself that he'd lost mighty happiness, an' thin he wud work ut all backwards, an' cry that he niver cud ha' been happy anyway.

'Time an' time an' again in camp, on p'rade, ay, an' in action, I've seen that man shut his eyes an' duck his head as ye wud duck to the flicker av a baynit. For 'twas thin, he tould me, that the thought av all he'd missed came an' stud forninst him like red-hot irons. For what he'd done wid the others he was sorry, but he did not care; but this wan woman that I've tould of, by the Hilts av God, she made him pay for all the others twice over! Niver did I know that a man cud enjure such tormint widout his heart crackin' in his ribs, an' I have been' – Terence turned the pipe-stem slowly between his teeth - 'I have been in some black cells. All I iver suffered tho' was not to be talked of alongside av *him* . . an' what could I do? Paternosters was no more than peas on plates for his sorrows.

'Evenshually we finished our prom'nade acrost the hills, and, thanks to me for the same, there was no casualties an' no glory. The campaign was comin' to an ind, an' all the rig'mints was being drawn together for to be sint back home. Love-o'-Women was mighty sorry bekaze he had no work to do, an' all his time to think in. I've heard that man talkin' to his belt-plate an' his side-arms while he was soldierin' thim, all to prevent himself from thinkin', an' ivry time he got up afther he had been settin' down or wint on from the halt, he'd start wid that kick an' traverse that I tould you of – his legs sprawlin' all ways to wanst. He wud niver go see the docthor, tho' I tould him to be wise. He'd curse me up an' down for my advice; but I knew he was no more a man to be reckoned wid than the little bhoy was a commanding orf'cer, so I let his tongue run if it aised him.

'Wan day – 'twas on the way back – I was walkin' round camp wid him, an' he stopped an' struck ground wid his right fut three or four times doubtful. "Fwhat is ut?" I sez. "Is that ground?" sez he; an' while I was thinkin' his mind was goin', up comes the docthor, who'd been anatomizin' a dead bullock. Love-o'-Women starts to go on quick, an' lands me a kick on the knee while his legs was gettin' into marchin' ordher.

'"Hould on there," sez the doctor; an' Love-o'-Women's face, that was lined like a gridiron, turns red as brick.

'"'Tention," says the doctor; an' Love-o'-Women stud so. "Now shut your eyes," sez the docthor. "No, ye must not hould by your comrade."

'"'Tis all up," sez Love-o'-Women, thrying to smile. "I'd fall, docthor, an' you know ut."

"Fall?" I sez. "Fall at attention wid your eyes shut! Fwhat do you mane?"

'"The doctor knows," he sez. "I've hild up as long as I can, but begad I'm glad 'tis all done. But I will die slow," he sez, "I will die very slow."

'I cud see by the docthor's face that he was mortial sorry for the man, an' he ordered him to hospital. We wint back together, an' I was dumb-struck. Love-o'-Women was cripplin' and crumblin' at ivry step. He walked wid a hand on my shoulder all slued sideways, an' his right leg swingin' like a lame camel. Me not knowin' more than the dead fwhat ailed him, 'twas just as though the docthor's word had done ut all – as if Love-o'-Women had but been waitin' for the word to let go.

'In hospital he sez somethin' to the docthor that I could not catch.

'"Holy Shmoke!" sez the docthor, "an' who are you, to be givin' names to your diseases? 'Tis agin all the reg'lations."

'"I'll not be a privit much longer," sez Love-o'-Women in his gentleman's voice, an' the docthor jumped.

"Thrate me as a study, Doctor Lowndes," he sez; an' that was the first time I'd iver heard a docthor called his name.

'"Goodbye, Terence," sez Love-o'-Women. "'Tis a dead man I am widout the pleasure av dyin'. You'll come an' set wid me sometimes for the peace av my soul."

'Now I had been minded for to ask Crook to take me back to the Ould Rig'mint; the fightin' was over, an' I was wore out wid the ways av the bhoys in the Tyrone; but I shifted my will, an' hild on, and wint to set wid Love-o'-Women in the hospital. As I have said, sorr, the man bruk all to little pieces under my hand. How long he had hild up an' forced himself fit to march I cannot tell, but in hospital but two days later he was such as I hardly knew. I shuk hands wid him, an' his grip was fair strong, but his hands wint all ways to wanst, an' he cud not button his tunic.

'"I'll take long an' long to die yet," he sez, "for the wages av sin they're like interest in the rig'mintal savin's-bank – sure, but a damned long time bein' paid."

'The docthor sez to me, quiet one day, "Has Tighe there anythin' on his mind?" he sez. "He's burnin' himself out."

'"How shud I know, sorr?" I sez, as innocint as putty.

'"They call him Love-o'-Women in the Tyrone, do they not?" he sez. "I was a fool to ask. Be wid him all you can. He's houldin' on to your strength."

'"But fwhat ails him, docthor?" I sez.

'"They call ut Locomotus Attacks us," he sez, "bekaze," sez he, "ut attacks us like a locomotive, if ye know fwhat that manes. An' ut comes," sez he, lookin' at me, "ut comes from bein' called Love-o'-Women."

'"You're jokin', docthor," I sez.

'"Jokin'!" sez he. "If iver you feel that you've got a felt sole in your boot instid av a government bull's-wool, come to me," he sez, "an' I'll show you whether 'tis a joke."

'You would not belave ut, sorr, but that, an' seein' Love-o'-Women overtuk widout warning', put the cowld fear av Attacks us on me so strong that for a week an' more I was kickin' my toes against shoes an' stumps for the pleasure av feelin' thim hurt.

'An Love-o'-Women lay in the cot (he might have gone down wid the wounded before an' before, but he asked to stay wid me), and fwhat there was in his mind had full swing at him night an' day an' ivry hour av the day an' the night, and he shrivelled like beef-rations in a hot sun, an' his eyes was like owls' eyes, an' his hands was mut'nous.

'They was gettin' the rig'mints away wan by wan, the campaign bein' inded, but as ushuil they was behavin' as if niver a rig'mint had been moved before in the mem'ry av man. Now, fwhy is that, sorr? There's fightin', in an' out, nine months av the twelve somewhere in the Army. There has been – for years an' years an' years; an' I wud ha' thought they'd begin to get the hang av providin' for throops. But no! Ivry time 'tis like a girls' school meetin' a big red bull whin they're goin' to church; an' "Mother av God," sez the commissariat an' the railways an' the barrick-masters, "fwhat will we do now?" The ordhers came to us av the Tyrone an' the Ould Rig'mint an' half a dozen more to go down, an' there the ordhers stopped dumb. We wint down, by the special grace av God – down the Khaiber anyways. There was sick wid us, an' I've thinkin' that some av thim was jolted to death in the doolies, but they was anxious to be kilt so if they cud get to Peshawar alive the sooner. I walked by Love-o'-Women – there was no marchin', an' Love-o'-Women was not in a stew to get on. "If I'd only ha' died up there," sez he through the dooli-curtains, an' thin he'd twist up his eyes an' duck his head for the thoughts that come an' raked him.

'Dinah was in Depôt at Pindi, but I wint circumspectuous, for well I knew 'tis just at the rump-ind av all things that his luck turns on a man. By token I had seen a dhriver of a batthery goin' by at a trot singin' "Home, swate home" at the top av his shout, and takin' no heed to his bridle-hand – I had seen that man dhrop under the gun in the middle of a word, and come out by the limber like – like a frog on a pavestone. No. I wud *not* hurry, though, God knows, my heart was all in Pindi. Love-o'-Women saw fwhat was in my mind, an' "Go on, Terence," he sez, "I know fwhat's waitin' for you." "I will not," I sez. "'Twill kape a little yet."

'Ye know the turn of the pass fornist Jumrood and the nine-mile road on the flat to Peshawar? All Peshawar was along that road day and night waitin' for frinds – men, women, childer, and bands. Some av the throops was camped round Jumrood, an' some wint on to Peshawar to get away down to their cantonmints. We came through in the early mornin', havin' been awake the night through, and we dhruv sheer into the middle av the mess. Mother av Glory, will I iver forget that comin' back? The light was not fair lifted, and the first we heard was "For 'tis my delight av a shiny night", frum a band that thought we was the second four comp'nies av the Lincolnshire. At that we was forced to sind them a yell to say who we was, an' thin up wint "The wearin' av the Green". It made me crawl all up my backbone, not havin' taken my brequist. Then right smash into our rear came fwhat was left av the Jock Elliott's - wid four pipers an' not half a kilt among thim, playing for the dear life, an' swingin' their rumps like buck-rabbits, an' a native rig'mint shriekin' blue murther. Ye niver heard the like! There was men cryin' like women that did – an' faith I do not blame them! Fwhat bruk me down was the Lancers' Band – shinin' an' spick like angils, wid the ould dhrum-horse at the head an' the silver kettle-dhrums an' all an' all, waitin' for their men that was behind us. They shtruck up the Cavalry Canter; an' begad those poor ghosts that had not a sound fut in a throop they answered to ut; the men rockin' in their saddles. We thried to cheer them as they wint by, but ut came out like a big gruntin' cough, so there must have been many that was feelin' like me. Oh, but I'm forgettin'! The Fly-by-Nights was waitin' for their second battalion, an' whin ut came out, there was the

Colonel's horse led at the head – saddle-empty. The men fair worshipped him, an' he'd died at Ali Musjid on the road down. They waited till the remnint av the battalion was up, and thin – clane against ordhers, for who wanted *that* chune that day? – they wint back to Peshawar slow-time an' tearin' the bowils out av ivry man that heard, wid "The Dead March". Right acrost our line they wint, an' ye know their uniforms are as black as the Sweeps, crawlin' past like the dead, an' the other bands damnin' them to let be.

'Little they cared. The carpse was wid them, an' they'd ha' taken ut so through a coronation. Our ordhers was to go into Peshawar, an' we wint hot-fut past the Fly-by-Nights, not singin', to lave that chune behind us. That was how we tuk the road of the other corps.

''Twas ringin' in my ears still whin I felt in the bones of me that Dinah was comin', an' I heard a shout, an' thin I saw a horse an' a tattoo latherin' down the road, hell-to-shplit, under women. I knew – I knew! Wan was the Tyrone Colonel's wife – ould Beeker's lady – her grey hair flyin' an' her fat round carkiss rowlin' in the saddle, an' the other was Dinah, that shud ha' been at Pindi. The Colonel's lady she charged the head av our column like a stone wall, an' she all but knocked Beeker off his horse, throwin' her arms round his neck an' blubberin', "Me bhoy! me bhoy!" an' Dinah wheeled left an' came down our flank, an' I let a yell that had suffered inside av me for months and – Dinah came! Will I iver forget that while I live! She'd come on pass from Pindi, an' the Colonel's lady had lint her the tattoo. They'd been huggin' an' cryin' in each other's arms all the long night.

'So she walked along wid her hand in mine, asking forty questions to wanst, an' beggin' me on the Virgin to make oath that there was not a bullet consaled in me, unbeknownst somewhere, an' thin I remembered Love-o'-Women. He was watchin' us, an' his face was like the face av a divil that has been cooked too long. I did not wish Dinah to see ut, for whin a woman's runnin' over with happiness she's like to be touched, for harm afterwards, by the laste little thing in life. So I dhrew the curtain, an' Love-o'-Women lay back and groaned.

'Whin we marched into Peshawar Dinah wint to barracks to wait for me, an', me feelin' so rich that tide, I wint on to take Love-o'-Women to hospital. It was the last I cud do, an' to save him the dust an' the smother I turned the dooli-men down a road well clear av the rest av the throops, an' we wint along, me talkin' through the curtains. Av a sudden I heard him say:

'"Let me look. For the mercy av Hiven, let me look." I had been so tuk up wid gettin' him out av the dust an' thinkin' av Dinah that I had not kept my eyes about me. There was a woman ridin' a little behind av us; an' talkin' ut over wid Dinah afterwards, that same woman must ha' rid out far on the Jumrood road. Dinah said that she had been hoverin' like a kite on the left flank av the columns.

'I halted the dooli to set the curtains, an' she rode by, walkin' pace, an' Love-o'-Women's eyes wint afther her as if he wud fair haul her down from the saddle.

'"Follow there," was all he sez, but I niver heard a man speak in that voice before or since; an' I knew by those two wan words an' the look in his face that she was Di'monds-an'-Pearls that he'd talked av in his disthresses.

'We followed till she turned into the gate av a little house that stud near the Edwardes' Gate. There was two girls in the veranda, an' they ran in whin they saw us. Faith, at long eye-range it did not take me a wink to see fwhat kind av house ut was. The throops bein' there an' all, there was three or four such; but aftherwards the polis bade thim go. At the veranda Love-o'-Women sez, catchin' his breath, "Stop here," an' thin, an' thin, wid a grunt that must ha' tore the heart up from his stomick, he swung himself out av the dooli, an' my troth he stud up on his feet wid the sweat pourin' down his face! If Mackie was to walk in here now I'd be less tuk back that I was thin. Where he'd dhrawn his power from, God knows – or the Divil – but 'twas a dead man walkin' in the sun, wid the face av a dead man and the breath av a dead man, hild up by the Power, an' the legs an' the arms av the carpse obeyin' ordhers.

'The woman stud in the veranda. She'd been a beauty too, though her eyes was sunk in her head, an' she looked Love-o'-Women up an' down terrible. "An'," she sez, kicking back the tail av her habit – "An'," she sez, "fwhat are you doin' *here*, married man?"

'Love-o'-Women said nothin', but a little froth came to his lips, an' he wiped ut off wid his hand an' looked at her an' the paint on her, an' looked, an' looked, an' looked.

'"An' yet," she sez, wid a laugh. (Did you hear Raines' wife laugh whin Mackie died? Ye did not? Well for you.) "An' yet," she sez, "who but you have betther right," sez she. "You taught me the road. You showed me the way," she sez. "Ay, look," she sez, "for 'tis your work; you that tould me – d'you remimber it? – that a woman who was false to wan man cud be false to two. I have been that," she sez, "that an' more, for you always said I was a quick learner, Ellis. Look well," she sez, "for it is me that you called your wife in the sight av God long since." An' she laughed.

'Love-o'-Women stud still in the sun widout answerin'. Thin he groaned an coughed to wanst, an' I thought 'twas the death-rattle, but he niver tuk his eyes off her face, not for a blink. Ye cud ha' put her eyelashes through the flies av an E.P. tent, they were so long.

'"Fwhat do you do here?" she sez, word by word, "that have taken away my joy in my man this five years gone – that have broken my rest an' killed my body an' damned my soul for the sake av seein' how 'twas done. Did your expayrience aftherwards bring you acrost any woman that give you more than I did? Wud I not ha' died for you, an' wid you, Ellis? Ye know that, man! If iver your lyin' sowl saw truth in uts life ye know that."

'An' Love-o'-Women lifted up his head and said, "I knew," an' that was all. While she was spakin' the Power hild him up parade-set in the sun, an' the sweat dhripped undher his helmet. 'Twas more an' more throuble for him to talk, an' his mouth was running twistways.

"Fwhat do you do *here*?" she sez, an' her voice wint up. 'Twas like bells tollin' before. "Time was whin you were quick enough wid your words – you that talked me down to Hell. Are ye dumb now?" An' Love-o'-Women got his tongue, an' sez simple, like a little child, "May I come in?" he sez.

'"The house is open day an' night," she sez, wid a laugh; an' Love-o'-Women ducked his head an' hild up his hand as tho' he was gyardin'. The Power was on him still – it hild him up still, for, by my sowl, as I'll never save ut, he walked up the veranda steps that had been a livin' carpse in hospital for a month!

'"An' now?" she sez, lookin' at him; an' the red paint stud lone on the white av her face like a bull's-eye on a target.

'He lifted up his eyes, slow an' very slow, an' he looked at her long an' very long , an' he tuk his spache betune his teeth wid a wrench that shuk him.

'"I'm dying, Aigypt – dyin'," he sez. Ay, those were his words, for I remimber the name he called her. He was turnin' the death-colour, but his eyes niver rowled. They were set – set on her. Widout word or warnin' she opened her arms full stretch, an' "Here!" she sez. (Oh, fwhat a golden mericle av a voice ut was!) "Die here!" she sez, an' Love-o'-Women dhropped forward, an' she hild him up, for she was a fine big woman.

'I had no time to turn, bekaze that minut I heard the sowl quit him – tore out in the death-rattle – an' she laid him back in a long chair, an' she sez to me, "Misther soldier," she sez, "will ye not wait an' talk to wan av the girls? This sun's too much for him."

'Well I knew there was no sun he'd iver see, but I cud not spake, so I wint away wid the empty dooli to find the docthor. He'd been breakfastin' an' lunchin' iver since we'd come in, an' he was full as a tick.

'"Faith, ye've got dhrunk mighty soon," he sez, whin I'd tould him, "to see that man walk. Barrin' a puff or two av life, he was a carpse before we left Jumrood. I've a great mind," he sez, "to confine you."

'"There's a dale of liquor runnin' about, docthor," I sez, solemn as a hard-boiled egg. "Maybe 'tis so; but will ye not come an' see the carpse at the house?"

'"'Tis dishgraceful," he sez, "that I would be expected to go to a place like that. Was she a pretty woman?" he sez, an' at that he set off double-quick.

'I cud see that the two was in the veranda where I'd left them, an' I knew by the hang ar her head an' the noise av the crows fwhat had happened. 'Twas the first and the last time that I'd iver known woman to use the pistol. They fear the shot as a rule, but Di'monds-an'-Pearls she did not – she did not.

'The docthor touched the long black hair av her head ('twas all loose upon Love-o'-Women's tunic), an' that cleared the liquor out av him. He stud considherin' a long time, his hands in his pockets, an' at last he sez to me, "Here's a double death from naturil causes, most naturil causes; an' in the present state av affairs the rig'mint will be thankful for wan grave the less to dig. *Issiwasti*," he sez. "*Issiwasti*, Privit Mulvaney, these two will be buried together in the Civil Cemet'ry at my expinse; an' may the good God," he sez, "make it so much for me whin my time comes. Go you to your wife," he sez. "Go an' be happy. I'll see to this all."

'I left him still considherin'. They was buried in the Civil Cemet'ry together, wid a Church av England service. There was too many buryin's thin to ask questions, an' the docthor – he ran away wid Major – Major Van Dyce's lady that year – he saw to ut all. Fwhat the right an' the wrong av Love-o'-Women an' Di'monds-an'-Pearls was I niver knew, an' I will niver know; but I've tould ut as I came acrost ut – here an' there in little pieces. *So*, being fwhat I am, an' knowin' fwhat I knew, that's fwhy I say in this shootin'-case here, Mackie that's dead an' in Hell is the lucky man. There are times, sorr, whin 'tis better for the man to die than to live, an' by consequince forty million times betther for the woman.

'H'up there!' said Ortheris. 'It's time to go.'

The witnesses and guard formed up in the thick white dust of the parched twilight and swung off, marching easy and whistling. Down the road to the green by the church I could hear Ortheris, the black Book-lie still uncleansed on his lips, setting, with a fine sense of the fitness of things, the shrill quickstep that runs –

'Oh, do not despise the advice of the wise,
  Learn wisdom from those that are older,
And don't try for things that are out of your reach –
  An' that's what the Girl told the Soldier!
      Soldier! soldier!
  Oh, that's what the Girl told the Soldier!'

The Elephant's Child

IN the High and Far-Off Times the Elephant, O Best Beloved, had no trunk. He had only a blackish, bulgy nose, as big as a boot, that he could wriggle about from side to side; but he couldn't pick up things with it. But there was one Elephant–a new Elephant–an Elephant's Child–who was full of 'satiable curtiosity, and that means he asked ever so many questions. And he lived in Africa, and he filled all Africa with his 'satiable curtiosities. He asked his tall aunt, the Ostrich, why her tail feathers grew just so, and his tall aunt, the Ostrich, spanked him with her hard, hard claw. He asked his tall uncle, the Giraffe, what made his skin spotty, and his tall uncle, the Giraffe, spanked him with his hard, hard hoof. And still he was full of 'satiable curtiosity! He asked his broad aunt, the Hippopotamus, why her eyes were red, and his broad aunt, the Hippopotamus, spanked him with her broad, broad hoof; and he asked his hairy uncle, the Baboon, why melons tasted just so, and his hairy uncle, the Baboon, spanked him with his hairy, hairy paw. And *still* he was full of 'satiable curtiosity! He asked questions about everything that he saw, or heard, or felt, or smelt, or touched, and all his uncles and aunts spanked him. And still he was full of 'satiable curtiosity!

One fine morning in the middle of the Precession of the Equinoxes this 'satiable Elephant's Child asked a new fine question that he had never asked before. He asked, 'What does the Crocodile have for dinner?' Then everybody said, 'Hush!' in a loud and dretful tone, and they spanked him immediately and directly, without stopping for a long time.

By and by, when that was finished, he came upon Kolokolo Bird sitting in the middle of a wait-a-bit thorn-bush, and he said, 'My father has spanked me, and my mother has spanked me; all my aunts and uncles have spanked me for my 'satiable curtiosity; and *still* I want to know what the Crocodile has for dinner!'

Then Kolokolo Bird said, with a mournful cry, 'Go to the banks of the great grey-green, greasy Limpopo River, all set about with fever-trees, and find out.'

That very next morning, when there was nothing left of the Equinoxes, because the Precession has preceded according to precedent, this 'satiable Elephant's Child took a hundred pounds of bananas (the little short red kind), and a hundred pounds of sugar-cane (the long purple kind), and seventeen melons (the greeny-crackly kind), and said to all his dear families, 'Goodbye. I am going to the great grey-green, greasy Limpopo River, all set about with fever-trees, to find out what the Crocodile has for dinner.' And they all spanked him once more for luck, though he asked them most politely to stop.

Then he went away, a little warm, but not at all astonished, eating melons, and throwing the rind about, because he could not pick it up.

He went from Graham's Town to Kimberley, and from Kimberley to Khama's Country, and from Khama's Country he went east by north, eating melons all the time, till at last he came to the banks of the great grey-green, greasy Limpopo River, all set about with fever-trees, precisely as Kolokolo Bird had said.

Now you must know and understand, O Best Beloved, that till that very week, and day, and hour, and minute, this 'satiable Elephant's Child had never seen a Crocodile, and did not know what one was like. It was all his 'satiable curtiosity.

The first thing that he found was a Bi-Coloured-Python-Rock-Snake curled round a rock.

''Scuse me,' said the Elephant's Child most politely, 'but have you seen such a thing as a Crocodile in these promiscuous parts?'

'*Have* I seen a Crocodile?' said the Bi-Coloured-Python-Rock-Snake, in a voice of dretful scorn. 'What will you ask me next?'

''Scuse me,' said the Elephant's Child, 'but could you kindly tell me what he has for dinner?'

Then the Bi-Coloured-Python-Rock-Snake uncoiled himself very quickly from the rock, and spanked the Elephant's Child with his scalesome, flailsome tail.

'That is odd,' said the Elephant's Child, 'because my father and my mother, and my uncle and my aunt, not to mention my other aunt, the Hippopotamus, and my other uncle, the Baboon, have all spanked me for my 'satiable curtiosity–and I suppose this is the same thing.'

So he said goodbye very politely to the Bi-Coloured-Python-Rock-Snake, and helped to coil him up on the rock again, and went on, a little warm, but not at all astonished, eating melons, and throwing the rind about, because he could not pick it up, till he trod on what he thought was a log of wood at the very edge of the great grey-green, greasy Limpopo River, all set about with fever-trees.

But it was really the Crocodile, O Best Beloved, and the Crocodile winked one eye – like this!

''Scuse me,' said the Elephant's Child most politely, 'but do you happen to have seen a Crocodile in these promiscuous parts?'

Then the Crocodile winked the other eye, and lifted half his tail out of the mud; and the Elephant's Child stepped back most politely, because he did not wish to be spanked again.

'Come hither, Little One,' said the Crocodile. 'Why do you ask such things?'

''Scuse me,' said the Elephant's Child most politely, 'but my father has spanked me, my mother has spanked me, not to mention my tall aunt, the Ostrich, and my tall uncle, the Giraffe, who can kick ever so hard, as well as my broad aunt, the Hippopotamus, and my hairy uncle, the Baboon, *and* including the Bi-Coloured-Python-Rock-Snake, with the scalesome, flailsome tail, just up the bank, who spanks harder than any of them; and *so*, if it's quite all the same to you, I don't want to be spanked any more.'

'Come hither, Little One,' said the Crocodile, 'for I am the Crocodile,' and he wept crocodile-tears to show it was quite true.

Then the Elephant's Child grew all breathless, and panted, and kneeled down on the bank and said, 'You are the very person I have been looking for all these long days. Will you please tell me what you have for dinner?'

'Come hither, Little One,' said the Crocodile, 'and I'll whisper.'

Then the Elephant's Child put his head down close to the Crocodile's musky, tusky mouth, and the Crocodile caught him by his little nose, which up to that very week, day, hour, and minute, had been no bigger than a boot, though much more useful.

'I think,' said the Crocodile – and he said it between his teeth, like this – 'I think today I will begin with Elephant's Child!'

At this, O Best Beloved, the Elephant's Child was much annoyed, and he said, speaking through his nose, like this, 'Led go! You are hurtig be!'

Then the Bi-Coloured-Python-Rock-Snake scuffled down from the bank and said, 'My young friend, if you do not now, immediately and instantly, pull as hard as ever you can, it is my opinion that your acquaintance in the large-pattern leather ulster' (and by this he meant the Crocodile) 'will jerk you into yonder limpid stream before you can say Jack Robinson.'

This is the way Bi-Coloured-Python-Rock-Snakes always talk.

Then the Elephant's Child sat back on his little haunches, and pulled, and pulled, and pulled, and his nose began to stretch. And the Crocodile floundered into the water, making it all creamy with great sweeps of his tail, and *he* pulled, and pulled, and pulled.

And the Elephant's Child's nose kept on stretching; and the Elephant's Child spread all his little four legs and pulled, and pulled, and pulled, and his nose kept on stretching; and the Crocodile threshed his tail like an oar, and *he* pulled, and pulled, and pulled, and at each pull the Elephant's Child's nose grew longer and longer – and it hurt him hijjus!

Then the Elephant's Child felt his legs slipping, and he said through his nose, which was now nearly five feet long, 'This is too butch for be!'

Then the Bi-Coloured-Python-Rock-Snake came down from the bank, and knotted himself in a double-clove-hitch round the Elephant's Child's hind-legs, and said, 'Rash and inexperienced traveller, we will now seriously devote ourselves to a little high tension, because if we do not, it is my impression that yonder self-propelling man-of-war with the armour-plated upper deck (and by this, O Best Beloved, he meant the Crocodile) 'will permanently vitiate your future career.'

That is the way all Bi-Coloured-Python-Rock-Snakes always talk.

So he pulled, and the Elephant's Child pulled, and the Crocodile pulled; but the Elephant's Child and the Bi-Coloured-Python-Rock-Snake pulled hardest; and at last the Crocodile let go of the Elephant's Child's nose with a plop that you could hear all up and down the Limpopo.

Then the Elephant's Child sat down most hard and sudden; but first he was careful to say 'Thank you' to the Bi-Coloured-Python-Rock-Snake; and next he was kind to his poor pulled nose, and wrapped it all up in cool banana leaves, and hung it in the great grey-green, greasy Limpopo to cool.

'What are you doing that for?' said the Bi-Coloured-Python-Rock-Snake.

''Scuse me,' said the Elephant's Child, 'but my nose is badly out of shape, and I am waiting for it to shrink.'

'Then you will have to wait a long time,' said the Bi-Coloured-Python-Rock-Snake. 'Some people do not know what is good for them.'

The Elephant's Child sat there for three days waiting for his nose to shrink. But it never grew any shorter, and, besides, it made him squint. For, O Best Beloved, you will see and understand that the Crocodile had pulled it out into a really truly trunk same as all Elephants have today.

At the end of the third day a fly came and stung him on the shoulder, and before he knew what he was doing he lifted up his trunk and hit that fly dead with the end of it.

''Vantage number one!' said the Bi-Coloured-Python-Rock-Snake. 'You couldn't have done that with a mere-smear nose. Try and eat a little now.'

Before he thought what he was doing the Elephant's Child put out his trunk and plucked a large bundle of grass, dusted it clean against his fore-legs, and stuffed it into his own mouth.

''Vantage number two!' said the Bi-Coloured-Python-Rock-Snake. 'You couldn't have done that with a mere-smear nose. Don't you think the sun is very hot here?'

'It is,' said the Elephant's Child, and before he thought what he was doing he schlooped up a schloop of mud from the banks of the great grey-green, greasy Limpopo, and slapped it on his head, where it made a cool, schloopy-slosh mud-cap all trickly behind his ears.

''Vantage number three!' said the Bi-Coloured-Python-Rock-Snake. 'You couldn't have done that with a mere-smear nose. Now how do you feel about being spanked again?'

''Scuse me,' said the Elephant's Child, 'but I should not like it at all.'

'How would you like to spank somebody?' said the Bi-Coloured-Python-Rock-Snake.

'I should like it very much indeed,' said the Elephant's Child.

'Well,' said the Bi-Coloured-Python-Rock-Snake, 'you will find that new nose of yours very useful to spank people with.'

'Thank you,' said the Elephant's Child, 'I'll remember that; and now I think I'll go home to all my dear families and try.'

So the Elephant's Child went home across Africa frisking and whisking his trunk. When he wanted fruit to eat he pulled fruit down from a tree, instead of waiting for it to fall as he used to do. When he wanted grass he plucked grass up from the ground, instead of going on his knees as he used to do. When the flies bit him he broke off the branch of a tree and used it as a fly-whisk; and he made himself a new, cool, slushy-squshy mud-cap whenever the sun was hot. When he felt lonely walking through Africa he sang to himself down his trunk, and the noise was louder than several brass bands. He went especially out of his way to find a broad Hippopotamus (she was no relation of his), and he spanked her very hard, to make sure that the Bi-Coloured-Python-Rock-Snake had spoken the truth about his new trunk. The rest of the time he picked up the melon rinds that he had dropped on his way to the Limpopo – for he was a Tidy Pachyderm.

One dark evening he came back to all his dear families, and he coiled up his trunk and said, 'How do you do?' They were very glad to see him, and immediately said, 'Come here and be spanked for your 'satiable curtiosity.'

'Pooh,' said the Elephant's Child, 'I don't think you peoples know anything about spanking; but *I* do, and I'll show you.'

Then he uncurled his trunk and knocked two of his dear brothers head over heels.

'O Bananas!' said they, 'where did you learn that trick, and what have you done to your nose?'

'I got a new one from the Crocodile on the banks of the great grey-green, greasy Limpopo River,' said the Elephant's Child. 'I asked him what he had for dinner, and he gave me this to keep.'

'It looks very ugly,' said his hairy uncle, the Baboon.

'It does,' said the Elephant's Child. 'But it's very useful,' and he picked up his hairy uncle, the Baboon, by one hairy leg, and hove him into a hornet's nest.

Then that bad Elephant's Child spanked all his dear families for a long time, till they were very warm and greatly astonished. He pulled out his tall Ostrich aunt's tail-feathers; and he caught his tall uncle, the Giraffe, by the hind-leg, and dragged him through a thorn-bush; and he shouted at his broad aunt, the Hippopotamus, and blew bubbles into her ear when she was sleeping in the water after meals; but he never let any one touch Kolokolo Bird.

At last things grew so exciting that his dear families went off one by one in a hurry to the banks of the great grey-green, greasy Limpopo River, all set about with fever-trees, to borrow new noses from the Crocodile. When they came back nobody spanked anybody any more; and ever since that day, O Best Beloved, all the Elephants you will ever see, besides all those that you won't, have trunks precisely like the trunk of the 'satiable Elephant's Child.

'I KEEP SIX HONEST SERVING-MEN'

I keep six honest serving-men
  (They taught me all I knew);
Their names are What and Why and When
  And How and Where and Who.
I send them over land and sea,
  I send them east and west;
But after they have worked for me,
  I give them all a rest.

I let them rest from nine till five,
  For I am busy then,
As well as breakfast, lunch, and tea,
  For they are hungry men:
But different folk have different views;
  I know a person small –
She keeps ten million serving-men,
  Who get no rest at all!
She sends 'em abroad on her own affairs,
  From the second she opens her eyes –
One million Hows, two million Wheres,
  And seven million Whys!

THE RUNNERS

News!

What is the word that they tell now – now – now!
The little drums beating in the bazaars?
They beat (among the buyers and the sellers)
'Nimrud – ah, Nimrud!
God sends a gnat against Nimrud!'
Watchers, O Watchers a thousand!

News!

At the edge of the crops – now – now – where the well-wheels are halted,
One prepares to loose the bullocks and one scrapes his hoe,
They beat (among the sowers and the reapers)
'Nimrud - ah, Nimrud!
God prepares an ill day for Nimrud!'
Watchers, O Watchers ten thousand.

News!

By the fires of the camps – now – now – where the travellers meet,
Where the camels come in and the horses: their men conferring,
They beat (among the packmen and the drivers)
'Nimrud - ah, Nimrud!
Thus it befell last noon to Nimrud!'
Watchers, O Watchers an hundred thousand!

News!

Under the shadow of the border-peels – now – now – now!
In the rocks of the passes where the expectant shoe their horses,
They beat (among the rifles and the riders)
'Nimrud – ah, Nimrud!
Shall we go up against Nimrud?'
Watchers, O Watchers a thousand thousand!

News!

Bring out the heaps of grain – open the account-books again!
Drive forward the well-bullocks against the taxable harvest!
Eat and lie under the trees – pitch the police-guarded fair-grounds,
O dancers!
Hide away the rifles and let down the ladders from the watch-
towers!

They beat (among all the peoples)
'Now – now – now!
God has reserved the Sword for Nimrud!
God has given Victory to Nimrud!
Let us abide under Nimrud!'
O Well-disposed and Heedful, an hundred thousand thousand!

A Sahibs' War

PASS? Pass? Pass? I have one pass already, allowing me to go by the *rêl* from Kroonstadt to Eshtellenbosch, where the horses are, where I am to be paid off, and whence I return to India. I am a – trooper of the Gurgaon Rissala (cavalry regiment), the One Hundred and Forty-first Punjab Cavalry. Do not herd me with these black Kaffirs. I am a Sikh – a trooper of the State. The Lieutenant-Sahib does not understand my talk? Is there *any* Sahib on this train who will interpret for a trooper of the Gurgaon Rissala going about his business in this devil's devising of a country, where there is no flour, no oil, no spice, no red pepper, and no respect paid to a Sikh? Is there no help? . . . God be thanked, here is such a Sahib! Protector of the Poor! Heaven-born! Tell the young Lieutenant-Sahib that my name is Umr Singh: I am – I was – servant to Kurban Sahib, now dead; and I have a pass to go to Eshtellenbosch, where the horses are. Do not let him herd me with these black Kaffirs! . . . Yes, I will sit by this truck till the Heaven-born has explained the matter to the young Lieutenant-Sahib who does not understand our tongue.

What orders? The young Lieutenant-Sahib will not detain me? Good! I go down to Eshtellenbosch by the next *terain*? Good! I go with the Heaven-born? Good! Then for this day I am the Heaven-born's servant. Will the Heaven-born bring the honour of his presence to a seat? Here is an empty truck; I will spread my blanket over one corner thus – for the sun is hot, though not so hot as our Punjab in May. I will prop it up thus, and I will arrange this hay thus, so the Presence can sit at ease till God sends us a *terain* for Eshtellenbosch . . .

The Presence knows the Punjab? Lahore? Amritzar? Attaree, belike? My village is north over the fields three miles from Attaree, near the big white house which was copied from a certain place of the Great Queen's by – by – I have forgotten the name. Can the Presence recall it? Sirdar Dyal Singh Attareewalla! Yes, that is the very man; but how does the Presence know? Born and bred in Hind, was he? O-o-oh! This is quite a different matter. The Sahib's nurse was a Surtee woman from the Bombay side? That was a pity. She should have been an up-country wench; for those make stout nurses. There is no land like the Punjab. There are no people like the Sikhs. Umr Singh is my name, yes. An old man? Yes. A trooper only after all these years? Ye-es. Look at my uniform, if the Sahib doubts. Nay – nay; the Sahib looks too closely. All marks of rank were picked off it long ago, but – but it is true – mine is not a common cloth such as troopers use for their coats, and – the Sahib has sharp eyes – that black mark is such a mark as a silver chain leaves when long worn on the breast. The Sahib says that troopers do not wear silver chains? No-o. Troopers do not wear the Arder of Beritish India? No. The Sahib should have been in the Police of the Punjab. I am not a trooper, but I have been a Sahib's servant for nearly a year – bearer, butler, sweeper, any and all three. The Sahib says that Sikhs do not take menial service? True; but it was for Kurban Sahib – my Kurban Sahib – dead these three months!

Young – of a reddish face – with blue eyes, and he lilted a little on his feet when he was pleased, and cracked his finger-joints. So did his father before him, who was Deputy-Commissioner of Jullundur in my father's time when I rode with the Gurgaon Rissala. *My* father? Jwala Singh. A Sikh of Sikhs – he fought against the English at Sobraon and carried the mark to his death. So we were knit as it were by a blood-tie, I and my Kurban Sahib. Yes, I was a trooper first – nay, I had risen to a Lance-Duffadar, I remember – and my father gave me a dun stallion of his own breeding on that day; and *he* was a little baba, sitting upon a wall by the parade-ground with his ayah – all in white, Sahib – laughing at the end of our drill. And his father and mine talked together, and mine beckoned to me, and I dismounted, and the baba put his hand into mine – eighteen – twenty-five – twenty-seven years gone now – Kurban Sahib – my Kurban Sahib! Oh, we were great friends after that! He cut his teeth on my sword-hilt, as the saying is. He called me Big Umr Singh – Buwwa Umwa Singh, for he could not speak plain. He stood only this high, Sahib, from the bottom of this truck, but he knew all our troopers by name – every one . . . And he went to England, and he became a young man, and back he came, lilting a little in his walk, and cracking his finger-joints – back to his own regiment and to me. He had not forgotten either our speech or our customs. He was a Sikh at heart, Sahib. He was rich, open-handed, just, a friend of poor troopers, keen-eyed, jestful, and careless. *I* could tell tales about him in his first years. There was very little he hid from *me*. I was his Umr Singh, and when we were alone he called me Father, and I called him

Son. Yes, that was how we spoke. We spoke freely together on everything – about war, and women, and money, and advancement, and such all.

We spoke about this war, too, long before it came. There were many box-wallahs, pedlars, with Pathans a few, in this country, notably at the city of Yunasbagh (Johannesburg), and they sent news in every week how the Sahibs lay without weapons under the heel of the Boer-log; and how big guns were hauled up and down the streets to keep Sahibs in order; and how a Sahib called Eger Sahib (Edgar?) was killed for a jest by the Boer-log. The Sahib knows how we of Hind hear all that passes over the Earth? There was not a gun cocked in Yunasbagh that the echo did not come into Hind in a month. The Sahibs are very clever, but they forget their own cleverness has created the *dak* (the post), and that for an anna or two all things become known. We of Hind listened and heard and wondered; and when it was a sure thing, as reported by the pedlars and the vegetable-sellers, that the Sahibs of Yunasbagh lay in bondage to the Boer-log, certain among us asked questions and waited for signs. Others of us mistook the meaning of those signs. *Wherefore, Sahib, came the long war in the Tirah!* This Kurban Sahib knew, and we talked together. He said, 'There is no haste. Presently we shall fight, and we shall fight for all Hind in that country round Yunasbagh.' Here he spoke truth. Does the Sahib not agree? Quite so. It is for Hind that the Sahibs are fighting this war. Ye cannot in one place rule and in another bear service. Either ye must everywhere rule or everywhere obey. God does not make the nations ringstraked. True – true – true!

So did matters ripen – a step at a time. It was nothing to me, except I think – and the Sahib sees this, too? – that it is foolish to make an army and break their hearts in idleness. Why have they not sent for the men of the Tochi – the men of the Tirah – the men of Buner? Folly, a thousand times. *We* could have done it all so gently – so gently.

Then, upon a day, Kurban Sahib sent for me and said, 'Ho, Dada, I am sick, and the doctor gives me a certificate for many months.' And he winked, and I said, 'I will get leave and nurse thee, Child. Shall I bring my uniform?' He said, 'Yes, and a sword for a sick man to lean on. We go to Bombay, and thence by sea to the country of the Hubshis (niggers).' Mark his cleverness! He was first of all our men among the native regiments to get leave for sickness and to come here. Now they will not let our officers go away, sick or well, except they sign a bond not to take part in this war-game upon the road. But *he* was clever. There was no whisper of war when he took his sick-leave. I came also? Assuredly. I went to my Colonel, and sitting in the chair (I am – I was – of rank for which a chair is placed when we speak with the Colonel) I said, 'My child goes sick. Give me leave, for I am old and sick also.'

And the Colonel, making the word double between English and our tongue, said 'Yes, thou art truly *Sikh*'; and he called me an old devil – jestingly, as one soldier may jest with another; and he said my Kurban Sahib was a liar as to his health (that was true, too), and at long last he stood up and shook my hand, and bade me go and bring my Sahib safe again. My Sahib back again – aie me!

So I went to Bombay with Kurban Sahib, but there, at sight of the Black Water, Wajib Ali, his bearer, checked, and said that his mother was dead. Then I said to Kurban Sahib, 'What is one Mussulman pig more or less? Give me the keys of the trunks, and I will lay out the white shirts for dinner.' Then I beat Wajib Ali at the back of Watson's Hotel, and that night I prepared Kurban Sahib's razors. I say, Sahib, that I; a Sikh of the Khalsa, an unshorn man, prepared the razors. But I did not put on my uniform while I did it. On the other hand, Kurban Sahib took for me, upon the steamer, a room in all respects like to his own, and would have given me a servant. We spoke of many things on the way to this country; and Kurban Sahib told me what he perceived would be the conduct of the war. He said, 'They have taken men afoot to fight men ahorse, and they will foolishly show mercy to these Boer-log because it is believed that they are white.' He said, 'There is but one fault in this war, and that is that the Government have not employed *us*, but have made it altogether a Sahibs' war. Very many men will thus be killed, and no vengeance will be taken.' True talk – true talk! It fell as Kurban Sahib foretold.

And we came to this country, even to Cape Town over yonder, and Kurban Sahib said, 'Bear the baggage to the big dak-bungalow. and I will look for employment fit for a sick man.' I put on the uniform of my rank and went to the big dak-bungalow, called Maun Nihâl Seyn,* and I caused the heavy baggage to be bestowed in that dark lower place – is it known to the Sahib? – which was already full of the swords and baggage of officers. It is fuller now – dead men's kit all! I was careful to secure a receipt for all three pieces. I have it in my belt. They must go back to the Punjab.

Anon came Kurban Sahib, lilting a little in his step, which sign I knew, and he said, 'We are born in a fortunate hour. We go to

*Mount Nelson?

Eshtellenbosch to oversee the despatch of horses.' Remember, Kurban Sahib was squadron-leader of the Gurgaon Rissala, and *I* was Umr Singh. So I said, speaking as we do – we did – when none was near, 'Thou art a groom and I am a grass-cutter, but is this any promotion, Child?' At this he laughed, saying, 'It is the way to better things. Have patience, Father.' (Aye, he called me father when none were by.) 'This war ends not tomorrow nor the next day. I have seen the new Sahibs,' he said, 'and they are fathers of owls – all – all – all!'

So we went to Eshtellenbosch, where the horses are; Kurban Sahib doing the service of servants in that business. And the whole business was managed without forethought by new Sahibs from God knows where, who had never seen a tent pitched or a peg driven. They were full of zeal, but empty of all knowledge. Then came, little by little from Hind, those Pathans – they are just like those vultures up there, Sahib – they always follow slaughter. And there came to Eshtellenbosch some Sikhs – Muzbees, though – and some Madras monkey-men. They came with horses. Puttiala sent horses. Jhind and Nabha sent horses. All the nations of the Khalsa sent horses. All the ends of the earth sent horses. God knows what the army did with them, unless they ate them raw. They used horses as a courtesan uses oil: with both hands. These horses needed many men. Kurban Sahib appointed me to the command (what a command for me!) of certain woolly ones – *Hubshis* – whose touch and shadow are pollution. They were enormous eaters; sleeping on their bellies; laughing without cause; wholly like animals. Some were called Fingoes, and some, I think, Red Kaffirs, but they were all Kaffirs – filth unspeakable. I taught them to water and feed, and sweep and rub down. Yes, I oversaw the work of sweepers – a *jemadar* of *mehtars* (headman of a refuse-gang) was I, and Kurban Sahib little better, for five months. Evil months! The war went as Kurban Sahib had said. Our new men were slain and no vengeance was taken. It was a war of fools armed with the weapons of magicians. Guns that slew at half a day's march, and men who, being new, walked blind into high grass and were driven off like cattle by the Boer-log! As to the city of Eshtellenbosch, I am not a Sahib – only a Sikh. I would have quartered one troop only of the Gurgaon Rissala in that city – one little troop – and I would have schooled that city till its men learned to kiss the shadow of a government horse upon the ground. There are many *mullahs* (priests) in Eshtellenbosch. They preached the Jehad against us. This is true – all the camp knew it. And most of the houses were thatched! A war of fools indeed!

At the end of five months my Kurban Sahib, who had grown lean, said, 'The reward has come. We go up towards the front with horses tomorrow, and, once away, I shall be too sick to return. Make ready the baggage.' Thus we got away, with some Kaffirs in charge of new horses for a certain new regiment that had come in a ship. The second day by *terain*, when we were watering at a desolate place without any sort of a bazaar to it, slipped out from the horse-boxes one Sikandar Khan, that had been a *jemandar* of *saises* (head-groom) at Eshtellenbosch, and was by service a trooper in a Border regiment. Kurban Sahib gave him big abuse for his desertion; but the Pathan put up his hands as excusing himself, and Kurban Sahib relented and added him to our service. So there were three of us – Kurban Sahib, I, and Sikandar Khan – Sahib, Sikh, and *Sag* (dog). But the man said truly, 'We be far from our homes and both servants of the Raj. Make truce till we see the Indus again.' I have eaten from the same dish as Sikandar Khan – beef, too, for aught I know! He said, on the night he stole some swine's flesh in a tin from a mess-tent, that in his Book, the Koran, it is written that whoso engages in a holy war is freed from ceremonial obligations. Wah! He had no more religion than the sword-point picks up of sugar and water at baptism. He stole himself a horse at a place where there lay a new and very raw regiment. I also procured myself a grey gelding there. They let their horses stray too much, those new regiments.

Some shameless regiments would indeed have made away with *our* horses on the road! They exhibited indents and requisitions for horses, and once or twice would have uncoupled the trucks ; but Kurban Sahib was wise, and I am not altogether a fool. There is not much honesty at the front. Notably, there was one congregation of hard-bitten horse-thieves; tall, light Sahibs, who spoke through their noses for the most part, and upon all occasions they said, 'Oah Hell!' which, in our tongue, signifies *Jehannum ko jao*. They bore each man a vine-leaf upon their uniforms, and they rode like Rajputs. Nay, they rode like Sikhs. They rode like the Ustrelyahs! The Ustrelyahs, whom we met later, also spoke through their noses not little, and they were tall, dark men, with grey, clear eyes, heavily eyelashed like camel's eyes – very proper men – a new brand of Sahib to me. They said on all occasions, 'No fee-ah,' which in our tongue means *Durro mut* ('Do not be afraid'), so we called them the *Durro Muts*. Dark, tall men, most excellent horsemen, hot and angry, waging war *as* war, and drinking tea as a sandhill drinks water. Thieves? A little, Sahib. Sikandar Khan swore to me – and he comes of a horse-stealing clan for ten generations – he swore a Pathan was a babe beside a *Durro Mut* in regard to horse-lifting. The *Durro Muts* cannot walk on their feet at all. They are like hens on the high road. Therefore they must have horses. Very proper men, with a just lust for the war. Aah – 'No fee-ah,' say the *Durro Muts. They* saw the worth of Kurban Sahib. *They* did not ask him to sweep stables. They would by no means let him go. He did substitute for one of their troop-leaders who had a fever, one long day in a country full of little hills – like the mouth of the Khaibar; and when they returned in the evening, the *Durro Muts* said, 'Wallah! This is a man. Steal him!' So they stole my Kurban Sahib as they would have stolen anything else that they needed, and they sent a sick officer back to Eshtellenbosch in his place. Thus Kurban Sahib came to his own again, and I was his bearer, and Sikandar Khan was his cook. The law was strict that this was a Sahibs' war, but there was no order that a bearer and a cook should not ride with their Sahib – and we had naught to wear but our uniforms. We rode up and down this accursed country, where there is no bazaar, no pulse, no flour, no oil, no spice, no red pepper, no firewood; nothing but raw corn and a little cattle. There were no great battles as I saw it, but a plenty of gun-firing. When we were many, the Boer-log came out with coffee to greet us, and to show us *purwanas* (permits) from foolish English generals who had gone that way before, certifying they were peaceful and well-disposed. When we were few, they hid behind stones and shot us. Now the order was that they were Sahibs, and this was a Sahibs' war. Good! But, as I understand it, when a Sahib goes to war, he puts on the cloth of war, and only those who wear that cloth may take part in the war. Good! That also I understand. But these people were as they were in Burma, or as the Afridis are. They shot at their pleasure, and when pressed hid the gun and exhibited *purwanas*, or lay in a house and said they were farmers. Even such farmers as cut up the Madras troops at Hlinedatalone in Burma! Even such farmers as slew Cavagnari Sahib and the Guides at Kabul! We schooled *those* men, to be sure – fifteen, aye, twenty of a morning pushed off the veranda in front of the Bala Hissar. I looked that the Jung-i-lat-Sahib (the Commander-in-Chief) would have remembered the old days; but – no. All the people shot at us everywhere, and he issued proclamations saying that he did not fight the people, but a certain army, which army, in truth, was all the Boer-log, who, between them, did not wear enough of uniform to make a loin-cloth. A fools' war from first to last; for it is manifest that he who fights should be hung if he fights with a gun in one hand and a *purwana* in the other, as did all these people. Yet we, when they had had their bellyful for the time, received them with honour, and gave them permits, and refreshed them and fed their wives and their babes, and severely punished our soldiers who took their fowls. So the work was to be done not once with a few dead, but thrice and four times over. I talked much with Kurban Sahib on this, and he said, 'It is a Sahibs' war. That is the order'; and one night, when Sikandar Khan would have lain out beyond the pickets with his knife and shown them how it is worked on the Border, he hit Sikandar Khan between the eyes and came near to breaking in his head. Then Sikandar Khan, a bandage over his eyes, so that he looked like a sick camel, talked to him half one march, and he was more bewildered than I, and vowed he would return to Eshtellenbosch. But privately to me Kurban Sahib said we should have loosed the Sikhs and the Gurkhas on these people till they came in with their foreheads in the dust. For the war was not of that sort which they comprehended.

They shot us? Assuredly they shot us from houses adorned with a white flag; but when they came to know our custom their widows sent word by Kaffir runners, and presently there was not quite so much firing. *No fee-ah!* All the Boer-log with whom we dealt had *purwanas* signed by mad generals attesting that they were well disposed to the State. They had also rifles not a few, and cartridges, which they hid in the roof. The women wept very greatly when we burned such houses, but they did not approach too near after the flames had taken good hold of the thatch, for fear of the bursting cartridges. The women of the Boer-log are very clever. They are more clever than the men. The Boer-log are clever? Never, never, no! It is the Sahibs who are fools. For their own honour's sake the Sahibs must say that the Boer-logs are clever; but it is the Sahibs' wonderful folly that has made the Boer-log. The Sahibs should have sent *us* into the game.

But the *Durro Muts* did well. They dealt faithfully with all that country thereabouts – not in any way as we of Hind should have dealt, but they were not altogether fools. One night when we lay on the top of a ridge in the cold, I saw far away a light in a house that appeared for the sixth part of an hour and was obscured. Anon it appeared again thrice for the twelfth part of an hour. I showed this to Kurban Sahib, for it was a house that had been spared – the people having many permits and swearing fidelity at our stirrup-leathers. I said to Kurban Sahib, 'Send half a troop, Child, and finish that house. They signal to their brethren.' And he laughed where he lay and said, 'If I listened to my bearer Umr Singh, there would not be left ten houses in all this land.' I said, 'What need to leave one? This is as it was in Burma. They are farmers today and fighters tomorrow.

Let us deal justly with them.' He laughed and curled himself up in his blanket, and I watched the far light in the house till day. I have been on the Border in eight wars, not counting Burma. The first Afghan War; the second Afghan War; two Mahsud Waziri wars (that is four); two Black Mountain wars, if I remember right; the Malakand and Tirah. I do not count Burma, or some small things. *I* know when house signals to house!

I pushed Sikandar Khan with my foot, and he saw it too. He said, 'One of the Boer-log who brought pumpkins for the mess, which I fried last night, lives in yonder house.' I said, 'How dost thou know?' He said, 'Because he rode out of the camp another way, but I marked how his horse fought with him at the turn of the road; and before the light fell I stole out of the camp for evening prayer with Kurban Sahib's glasses, and from a little hill I saw the pied horse of that pumpkin-seller hurrying to that house.' I said naught, but took Kurban Sahib's glasses from his greasy hands and cleaned them with a silk handkerchief and returned them to their case. Sikandar Khan told me that he had been the first man in the Zenab valley to use glasses – whereby he had finished two blood-feuds cleanly in the course of three months' leave. But he was otherwise a liar.

That day Kurban Sahib, with some ten troopers, was sent on to spy the land for our camp. The *Durro Muts* moved slowly at that time. They were weighted with grain and forage and carts, and they greatly wished to leave these all in some town and go on light to other business which pressed. So Kurban Sahib sought a short cut for them, a little off the line of march. We were twelve miles before the main body, and we came to a house under a high bushed hill, with a nullah, which they call a donga, behind it, and an old sangar of piled stones, which they call a kraal, before it. Two thorn bushes grew on either side of the door, like babul bushes, covered with a golden-coloured bloom, and the roof was all of thatch. Before the house was a valley of stones that rose to another bush-covered hill. There was an old man in the veranda – an old man with a white beard and a wart upon the left side of his neck; and a fat woman with the eyes of a swine and the jowl of a swine; and a tall young man deprived of understanding. His head was hairless, no larger than an orange, and the pits of his nostrils were eaten away by a disease. He laughed and slavered and he sported sportively before Kurban Sahib. The man brought coffee and the woman showed us *purwanas* from three General-Sahibs, certifying that they were people of peace and goodwill. Here are the *purwanas*, Sahib. Does the Sahib know the generals who signed them?

They swore the land was empty of Boer-log. They held up their hands and swore it. That was about the time of the evening meal. I stood near the veranda with Sikandar Khan, who was nosing like a jackal on a lost scent. At last he took my arm and said, 'See yonder! There is the sun on the window of the house that signalled last night. This house can see that house from here,' and he looked at the hill behind him all hairy with bushes, and sucked in his breath. Then the idiot with the shrivelled head danced by me and threw back that head, and regarded the roof and laughed like a hyena, and the fat woman talked loudly, as it were, to cover some noise. After this I passed to the back of the house on pretence to get water for tea, and I saw fresh horse-dung on the ground, and that the ground was cut with the new marks of hoofs; and there had dropped in the dirt one cartridge. Then Kurban Sahib called to me in our tongue, saying, 'Is this a good place to make tea?' and I replied, knowing what he meant, 'There are over many cooks in the cook-house. Mount and go, Child.' Then I returned, and he said, smiling to the woman, 'Prepare food, and when we have loosened our girths we will come in and eat;' but to his men he said in a whisper, 'Ride away!' No. He did not cover the old man or the fat woman with his rifle. That was not his custom. Some fool of the *Durro Muts*, being hungry, raised his voice to dispute the order to flee, and before we were in our saddles many shots came from the roof – from rifles thrust through the thatch. Upon this we rode across the valley of stones, and men fired at us from the nullah behind the house, and from the hill behind the nullah, as well as from the roof of the house – so many shots that it sounded like a drumming in the hills. Then Sikandar Khan, riding low, said, 'This play is not for us alone, but for the rest of the *Durro Muts*,' and I said, 'Be quiet. Keep place!' for his place was behind me, and I rode behind Kurban Sahib. But these new bullets will pass through five men a-row! We were not hit – not one of us – and we reached the hill of rocks and scattered among the stones, and Kurban Sahib turned in his saddle and said, 'Look at the old man!' He stood in the veranda firing swiftly with a gun, the woman beside him and the idiot also – both with guns. Kurban Sahib laughed, and I caught him by the wrist, but – his fate was written at that hour. The bullet passed under my arm-pit and struck him in the liver, and I pulled him backward between two great rocks a-tilt – Kurban Sahib, my Kurban Sahib! From the nullah behind the house and from the hills came our Boer-log in number more than a hundred, and Sikandar Khan said, '*Now* we see the meaning of last night's signal. Give me the rifle.' He took Kurban Sahib's rifle – in this war of fools only the doctors carry swords – and lay belly-flat to the work, but Kurban Sahib turned where he lay and said, 'Be still. It is a Sahibs' war,' and Kurban Sahib put up his hand – thus; and then his eyes rolled on me, and I gave him water that he might pass the more quickly. And at the drinking his Spirit received permission . . .

Thus went our fight, Sahib. We *Durro Muts* were on a ridge working from the north to the south, where lay our main body, and the Boer-log lay in a valley working from east to west. There were more than a hundred, and our men were ten, but they held the Boer-log in the valley while they swiftly passed along the ridge to the south. I saw three Boers drop in the open. Then they all hid again and fired heavily at the rocks that hid our men; but our men were clever and did not show, but moved away and away, always south; and the noise of the battle withdrew itself southward, where we could hear the sound of big guns. So it fell stark dark, and Sikandar Khan found a deep old jackal's earth amid rocks, into which we slid the body of Kurban Sahib upright. Sikandar Khan took his glasses, and I took his handkerchief and some letters and a certain thing which I knew hung round his neck, and Sikandar Khan is witness that I wrapped them in the handkerchief. Then we took an oath together, and lay still and mourned for Kurban Sahib. Sikandar Khan wept till daybreak – even he, a Pathan, a Mohammedan! All that night we heard firing to the southward, and when the dawn broke the valley was full of Boer-log in carts and on horses. They gathered by the house, as we could see through Kurban Sahib's glasses, and the old man, who, I take it, was a priest, blessed them, and preached the holy war, waving his arm; and the fat woman brought coffee, and the idiot capered among them and kissed their horses. Presently they went away in haste; they went over the hills and were not; and a black slave came out and washed the door-sills with bright water. Sikandar Khan saw through the glasses that the stain was blood, and he laughed, saying, 'Wounded men lie there. We shall yet get vengeance.'

About noon we saw a thin, high smoke to the southward, such a smoke as a burning house will make in sunshine, and Sikandar Khan, who knows how to take a bearing across a hill, said, 'At last we have burned the house of the pumpkin-seller whence they signalled.' And I said, 'What need now that they have slain my child? Let me mourn.' It was a high smoke, and the old man, as I saw, came out into the veranda to behold it, and shook his clenched hands at it. So we lay till the twilight, foodless and without water, for we had vowed a vow neither to eat nor to drink till we had accomplished the matter. I had a little opium left, of which I gave Sikandar Khan the half, because he loved Kurban Sahib. When it was full dark we sharpened our sabres upon a certain softish rock which, mixed with water, sharpens steel well, and we took off our boots and we went down to the house and looked through the windows very softly. The old man sat reading in a book, and the woman sat by the hearth; and the idiot lay on the floor with his head against her knee, and he counted his fingers and laughed, and she laughed again. So I knew they were mother and son, and I laughed, too, for I had suspected this when I claimed her life and her body from Sikandar Khan, in our discussion of the spoil. Then we entered with bare swords . . Indeed, these Boer-log do not understand the steel, for the old man ran towards a rifle in the corner; but Sikandar Khan prevented him with a blow of the flat across the hands, and he sat down and held up his hands, and I put my fingers on my lips to signify they should be silent. But the woman cried, and one stirred in an inner room, and a door opened, and a man, bound about the head with rags, stood stupidly fumbling with a gun. His whole head fell inside the door, and none followed him. It was a very pretty stroke – for a Pathan. Then they were silent, staring at the head upon the floor, and I said to Sikandar Khan, 'Fetch ropes! Not even for Kurban Sahib's sake will I defile my sword.' So he went to seek and returned with three long leather ones, and said, 'Four wounded lie within and doubtless each has a permit from a general,' and he stretched the ropes and laughed. Then I bound the old man's hands behind his back, and unwillingly – for he laughed in my face, and would have fingered my beard – the idiot's. At this the woman with the swine's eyes and the jowl of a swine ran forward, and Sikandar Khan said, 'Shall I strike or bind? She was thy property on the division.' And I said, 'Refrain! I have made a chain to hold her. Open the door.' I pushed out the two across the veranda into the darker shade of the thorn trees, and she followed upon her knees and lay along the ground, and pawed at my boots and howled. Then Sikandar Khan bore out the lamp, saying that he was a butler and would light the table, and I looked for a branch that would bear fruit. But the woman hindered me not a little with her screechings and plungings, and spoke fast in her tongue, and I replied in my tongue, 'I am childless tonight because of thy perfidy, and *my* child was praised among men and loved among women. He would have begotten men – not animals. Thou hast more years to live than I, but my grief is the greater.'

I stooped to make sure the noose upon the idiot's neck, and flung the end over the branch, and Sikandar Khan held up the lamp that she might well see. Then appeared suddenly, a little beyond the light of the lamp, the spirit of Kurban Sahib. One hand he held to his side, even where the bullet had struck him, and the other he put forward thus, and said, 'No. It is a Sahibs' war.' And I said, 'Wait a while, Child, and thou shalt sleep.' But he came nearer, riding, as it were, upon my eyes, and said, 'No. It is a Sahibs' war.' And Sikandar Khan said, 'Is it too heavy?' and set down the lamp and came to me; and as he turned to tally on the rope, the spirit of Kurban Sahib stood up within arm's reach of us, and his face was very angry, and a third time he said, 'No. It is a Sahibs' war.' And a little wind blew out the lamp, and I heard Sikandar Khan's teeth chatter in his head.

So we stayed side by side, the ropes in our hand, a very long while, for we could not shape any words. Then I heard Sikandar Khan open his water-bottle and drink; and when his mouth was slaked he passed to me and said, 'We are absolved from our vow.' So I drank, and together we waited for the dawn in that place where we stood – the ropes in our hand. A little after third cockcrow we heard the feet of horses and gun-wheels very far off, and so soon as the light came a shell burst on the threshold of the house, and the roof of the veranda that was thatched fell in and blazed before the windows. And I said, 'What of the wounded Boer-log within?' And Sikandar Khan said, 'We have heard the order. It is a Sahibs' war. Stand still.' Then came a second shell – good line, but short – and scattered dust upon us where we stood; and then came ten of the little quick shells from the gun that speaks like a stammerer – yes, pompom the Sahibs call it – and the face of the house folded down like the nose and the chin of an old man mumbling, and the forefront of the house lay down. Then Sikandar Khan said, 'If it be the fate of the wounded to die in the fire, *I* shall not prevent it.' And he passed to the back of the house and presently came back, and four wounded Boer-log came after him, of whom two could not walk upright. And I said, 'What has thou done?' And he said, 'I have neither spoken to them nor laid hand on them. They follow in hope of mercy.' And I said, 'It is a Sahibs' war. Let them wait the Sahibs' mercy.' So they lay still, the four men and the idiot, and the fat woman under the thorn tree, and the house burned furiously. Then began the known sound of cartouches in the roof – one or two at first; then a trill, and last of all one loud noise and the thatch blew here and there, and the captives would have crawled aside on acount of the heat that was withering the thorn-trees, and on account of wood and bricks flying at random. But I said, 'Abide! Abide! Ye be Sahibs, and this is a Sahibs' war, O

Sahibs. There is no order that ye should depart from this war.' They did not understand my words. Yet they abode and they lived.

Presently rode down five troopers of Kurban Sahib's command, and one I knew spoke my tongue, having sailed to Calcutta often with horses. So I told him all my tale, using bazaar-talk, such as his kidney of Sahib would understand; and at the end I said, 'An order has reached us here from the dead that this is a Sahibs' war. I take the soul of my Kurban Sahib to witness that I give over to the justice of the Sahibs these Sahibs who have made me childless.' Then I gave him the ropes and fell down senseless, my heart being very full, but my belly was empty, except for the little opium.

They put me into a cart with one of their wounded, and after a while I understood that they had fought against the Boer-log for two days and two nights. It was all one big trap, Sahib, of which we, with Kurban Sahib, saw no more than the outer edge. They were very angry, the *Durro Muts* – very angry indeed. I have never seen Sahibs so angry. They buried my Kurban Sahib with the rites of his faith upon the top of the ridge overlooking the house, and I said the proper prayers of the faith, and Sikandar Khan prayed in his fashion and stole five signalling-candles, which have each three wicks, and lighted the grave as if it had been the grave of a saint on a Friday. He wept very bitterly all that night, and I wept with him, and he took hold of my feet and besought me to give him a remembrance from Kurban Sahib. So I divided equally with him one of Kurban Sahib's handkerchiefs – not the silk ones, for those were given him by a certain woman; and I also gave him a button from a coat, and a little steel ring of no value that Kurban Sahib used for his keys, and he kissed them and put them into his bosom. The rest I have here in that little bundle, and I must get the baggage from the hotel in Cape Town – some four shirts we sent to be washed, for which we could not wait when we went up-country – and I must give them all to my Colonel-Sahib at Sialkote in the Punjab. For my child is dead – my baba is dead! . . .

I would have come away before; there was no need to stay, the child being dead; but we were far from the rail, and the *Durro Muts* were as brothers to me, and I had come to look upon Sikandar Khan as in some sort a friend, and he got me a horse and I rode up and down with them; but the life had departed. God knows what they called me – orderly, *chaprassi* (messenger), cook, sweeper, I did not know nor care. But once I had pleasure. We came back in a month after wide circles to that very valley. I knew it every stone, and I went up to the grave, and a clever Sahib of the *Durro Muts* (we left a troop there for a week to school those people with *purwanas*) had cut an inscription upon a great rock; and they interpreted it to me, and it was a jest such as Kurban Sahib himself would have loved. Oh! I have the inscription well copied here. Read it aloud, Sahib, and I will explain the jests. There are two very good ones. Begin, Sahib:

In Memory of
WALTER DECIES CORBYN
Late Captain 141st Punjab Cavalry

The Gurgaon Rissala, that is. Go on, Sahib.

Treacherously shot near this place by
The connivance of the late
HENDRIK DIRK UYS
A Minister of God
Who thrice took the oath of neutrality
And Piet his son,
This little work

Aha! This is the first jest. The Sahib should see this little work!

Was accomplished in partial
And inadequate recognition of their loss
By some men who loved him

—

Si monumentum requiris circumspice

That is the second jest. It signifies that those who would desire to behold a proper memorial to Kurban Sahib must look out at the house. And, Sahib, the house is not there, nor the well, nor the big tank which they call dams, nor the little fruit trees, nor the cattle. There is nothing at all, Sahib, except the two trees withered by the fire. The rest is like the desert here – or my hand – or my heart. Empty, Sahib – all empty!

KASPAR'S SONG IN 'VARDA'

(From the Swedish of Stagnelius)

Eyes aloft, over dangerous places,
  The children follow where Psyche flies,
And, in the sweat of their upturned faces,
  Slash with a net at the empty skies.

So it goes they fall amid brambles,
  And sting their toes on the nettle-tops,
Till after a thousand scratches and scrambles
  They wipe their brows, and the hunting stops.

Then to quiet them comes their father
  And stills the riot of pain and grief,
Saying, 'Little ones, go and gather
  Out of my garden a cabbage leaf.

'You will find on it whorls and clots of
  Dull grey eggs that, properly fed,
Turn, by way of the worm, to lots of
  Radiant Psyches raised from the dead.'

. . .

'Heaven is beautiful, Earth is ugly,'
  The three-dimensioned preacher saith.
So we must not look where the snail and the slug lie
  For Psyche's birth . . . And that is our death!

'Wireless'

'IT'S a funny thing, this Marconi business, isn't it?' said Mr Shaynor, coughing heavily. 'Nothing seems to make any difference, by what they tell me – storms, hills, or anything; but if that's true we shall know before morning.'

'Of course it's true,' I answered, stepping behind the counter. 'Where's old Mr Cashell?'

'He's had to go to bed on account of his influenza. He said you'd very likely drop in.'

'Where's his nephew?'

'Inside, getting the things ready. He told me that the last time they experimented they put the pole on the roof of one of the big hotels here, and the batteries electrified all the water-supply, and' – he giggled – 'the ladies got shocks when they took their baths.'

'I never heard of that.'

'The hotel wouldn't exactly advertise it, would it? Just now, by what Mr Cashell tells me, they're trying to signal from here to Poole, and they're using stronger batteries than ever. But, you see, he being the guvnor's nephew and all that (and it will be in the papers too), it doesn't matter how they electrify things in this house. Are you going to watch?'

'Very much. I've never seen this game. Aren't you going to bed?'

'We don't close till ten on Saturdays. There's a good deal of influenza in town, too, and there'll be a dozen prescriptions coming in before morning. I generally sleep in the chair here. It's warmer than jumping out of bed every time. Bitter cold, isn't it?'

'Freezing hard. I'm sorry your cough's worse.'

'Thank you. I don't mind the cold so much. It's this wind that fair cuts me to pieces.' He coughed again hard and hackingly, as an old lady came in for ammoniated quinine. 'We've just run out of it in bottles, madam,' said Mr Shaynor, returning to the professional tone, 'but if you will wait two minutes, I'll make it up for you, madam.'

I had used the shop for some time, and my acquaintance with the proprietor had ripened into friendship. It was Mr Cashell who revealed to me the purpose and power of Apothecaries' Hall what time a fellow-chemist had made an error in a prescription of mine, had lied to cover his sloth, and when error and lie were brought home to him had written vain letters.

'A disgrace to our profession,' said the thin, mild-eyed man, hotly, after studying the evidence. 'You couldn't do a better service to the profession than report him to Apothecaries' Hall.'

I did so, not knowing what djinns I should evoke; and the result was such an apology as one might make who had spent a night on the rack. I conceived a great respect for Apothecaries' Hall and esteem for Mr Cashell, a zealous craftsman who magnified his calling. Until Mr Shaynor came down from the North his assistants had by no means agreed with Mr Cashell. 'They forget,' said he, 'that, first and foremost, the compounder is a medicine-man. On him depends the physician's reputation. He holds it literally in the hollow of his hand, sir.'

Mr Shaynor's manners had not, perhaps, the polish of the grocery and Italian warehouse next door, but he knew and loved his dispensary work in every detail. For relaxation he seemed to go no farther afield that the romance of drugs – their discovery, preparation, packing, and export – but it led him to the ends of the earth, and on this subject, and the Pharmaceutical Formulary, and Nicholas Culpepper, most confident of physicians, we met.

Little by little I grew to know something of his beginnings and his hopes – of his mother, who had been a school-teacher in one of the northern counties, and of his red-headed father, a small job-master at Kirby Moors, who died when he was a child; of the examinations he had passed and of their exceeding and increasing difficulty; of his dreams of a shop in London; of his hate for the price-cutting Co-operative stores; and, most interesting, of his mental attitude towards his customers.

'There's a way you get into,' he told me, 'of serving them carefully, and I hope, politely, without stopping your own thinking. I've been reading Christy's *New Commercial Plants* all this autumn, and that needs keeping your mind on it, I can tell you. So long as it isn't a prescription, of course, I can carry as much as half a page of Christy in my head, and at the same time I could sell out all that window twice over, and not a penny wrong at the end. As to prescriptions, I think I could make up the general run of 'em in my sleep, almost.'

For reasons of my own, I was deeply interested in Marconi experiments at their outset in England; and it was of a piece with Mr Cashell's unvarying thoughtfulness that, when his nephew the electrician appropriated the house for a long-range installation, he should, as I have said, invite me to see the result.

The old lady went away with her medicine, and Mr Shaynor and I stamped on the tiled floor behind the counter to keep ourselves warm. The shop, by the light of the many electrics, looked like a Paris-diamond mine, for Mr Cashell believed in all the ritual of his craft. Three superb glass jars – red, green, and blue – of the sort that led Rosamond to parting with her shoes – blazed in the broad plate-glass windows, and there was a confused smell of orris, Kodak films, vulcanite, tooth-powder, sachets, and almond-cream in the air. Mr Shaynor fed the dispensary stove, and we sucked cayenne-pepper jujubes and menthol lozenges. The brutal east wind had cleared the streets, and the few passers-by were muffled to their puckered eyes. In the Italian warehouse next door some gay feathered birds and game, hung upon hooks, sagged to the wind across the left edge of our window-frame.

'They ought to take these poultry in – all knocked about like that,' said Mr Shaynor. 'Doesn't it make you feel perishing? See that old hare! The wind's nearly blowing the fur off him.'

I saw the belly-fur of the dead beast blown apart in ridges and streaks as the wind caught it, showing bluish skin underneath. 'Bitter cold,' said Mr Shaynor, shuddering. 'Fancy going out on a night like this! Oh, here's young Mr Cashell.'

The door of the inner office behind the dispensary opened, and an energetic, spade-bearded man stepped forth, rubbing his hands.

'I want a bit of tin-foil, Shaynor,' he said. 'Good evening. My uncle told me you might be coming.' This to me, as I began the first of a hundred questions.

'I've everything in order,' he replied. 'We're only waiting until Poole calls us up. Excuse me a minute. You can come in whenever you like – but I'd better be with the instruments. Give me that tin-foil. Thanks.'

While we were talking, a girl – evidently no customer – had come into the shop, and the face and bearing of Mr Shaynor changed. She leaned confidently across the counter.

'But I can't,' I heard him whisper uneasily – the flush on his cheek was dull red, and his eyes shone like a drugged moth's. 'I can't. I tell you I'm alone in the place.'

'No, you aren't. Who's *that*? Let him look after it for half an hour. A brisk walk will do you good. Ah, come now, John.'

'But he isn't —'

'I don't care. I want you to; we'll only go round by St Agnes'. If you don't —'

He crossed to where I stood in the shadow of the dispensary counter, and began some sort of broken apology about a lady-friend.

'Yes,' she interrupted. 'You take the shop for half an hour – to oblige *me*, won't you?'

She had a singularly rich and promising voice that well matched her outline.

'All right,' I said. 'I'll do it – but you'd better wrap yourself up, Mr Shaynor.'

'Oh, a brisk walk ought to help me. We're only going round by the church.' I heard him cough grievously as they went out together.

I refilled the stove, and, after reckless expenditure of Mr Cashell's coal, drove some warmth into the shop. I explored many of the glass-knobbed drawers that lined the walls, tasted some disconcerting drugs, and, by the aid of a few cardamoms, ground ginger, chloric-ether, and dilute alcohol, manufactured a new and wildish drink, of which I bore a glassful to young Mr Cashell, busy in the back office. He laughed shortly when I told him that Mr Shaynor had stepped out – but a frail coil of wire held all his attention, and he had no word for me bewildered among the batteries and rods. The noise of the sea on the beach began to make itself heard as the traffic in the street ceased. Then briefly, but very lucidly, he gave me the names and uses of the mechanism that crowded the tables and the floor.

'When do you expect to get the message from Poole?' I demanded, sipping my liquor out of a graduated glass.

'About midnight, if everything is in order. We've got our installation-pole fixed to the roof of the house. I shouldn't advise you to turn on a tap or anything tonight. We've connected up with the plumbing, and all the water will be electrified.' He repeated to me the history of the agitated ladies at the hotel at the time of the first installation.

'But what *is* it?' I asked. 'Electricity is out of my beat altogether.'

'Ah, if you knew *that* you'd know something nobody knows. It's just It – what we call electricity, but the magic – the manifestations – the Hertzian waves – are all revealed by *this*. The coherer, we call it.'

He picked up a glass tube not much thicker than a thermometer, in which, almost touching, were two tiny silver plugs, and between them an infinitesimal pinch of metallic dust. 'That's all,' he said, proudly, as though himself responsible for the wonder. 'That is the thing that will reveal to us the Powers – whatever the Powers may be – at work – through space – a long distance away.'

Just then Mr Shaynor returned alone and stood coughing his heart out on the mat.

'Serves you right for being such a fool,' said young Mr Cashell, as annoyed as myself at the interruption. 'Never mind – we've all the night before us to see wonders.'

Shaynor clutched the counter, his handkerchief to his lips. When he brought it away I saw two bright red stains.

'I've – I've got a bit of a rasped throat from smoking cigarettes,' he panted. 'I think I'll try a cubeb.'

'Better take some of this. I've been compounding while you've been away.' I handed him the brew.

''Twon't make me drunk, will it? I'm almost a teetotaller. My word! That's grateful and comforting.'

He set down the empty glass to cough afresh.

'Brr! But it was cold out there! I shouldn't care to be lying in my grave a night like this. Don't *you* ever have a sore throat from smoking?' He pocketed the handkerchief after a furtive peep.

'Oh, yes, sometimes,' I replied, wondering, while I spoke, into what agonies of terror I should fall if ever I saw those bright-red danger-signals under my nose. Young Mr Cashell among the batteries coughed slightly to show that he was quite ready to continue his scientific explanations, but I was thinking still of the girl with the rich voice and the significantly cut mouth, at whose command I had taken charge of the shop. It flashed across me that she distantly resembled the seductive shape on a gold-framed toilet-water advertisement whose charms were unholily heightened by the glare from the red bottle in the window. Turning to make sure, I saw Mr Shaynor's eyes bent in the same direction, and by instinct recognized that the flamboyant thing was to him a shrine. 'What do you take for your – cough?' I asked.

'Well, I'm on the wrong side of the counter to believe much in patent medicines. But there are asthma cigarettes and there are pastilles. To tell you the truth, if you don't object to the smell, which is very like incense, I believe, though I'm not a Roman Catholic, Blaudett's Cathedral Pastilles relieve me as much as anything.'

'Let's try.' I had never raided a chemist's shop before, so I was thorough. We unearthed the pastilles – brown, gummy cones of benzoin – and set them alight under the toilet-water advertisement, where they fumed in thin blue spirals.

'Of course,' said Mr Shaynor, to my question, 'what one uses in the shop for one's self comes out of one's pocket. Why, stock-taking in our business is nearly the same as with jewellers – and I can't say more than that. But one gets them' – he pointed to the pastille-box - 'at trade prices.' Evidently the censing of the gay, seven-tinted wench with the teeth was an established ritual which cost something.

'And when do we shut up shop?'

'We stay like this all night. The guv – old Mr Cashell, doesn't believe in locks and shutters as compared with electric light. Besides, it brings trade. I'll just sit here in the chair by the stove and write a letter, if you don't mind. Electricity isn't my prescription.'

The energetic young Mr Cashell snorted within, and Shaynor settled himself up in his chair over which he had thrown a staring red, black, and yellow Austrian jute blanket, rather like a table-cover. I cast about, amid patent-medicine pamphlets, for something to read, but finding little, returned to the manufacture of the new drink. The Italian warehouse took down its game and went to bed. Across the street blank shutters flung back the gaslight in cold smears; the dried pavement seemed to rough up in gooseflesh under the scouring of the savage wind, and we could hear, long ere he passed, the policeman flapping his arms to keep himself warm. Within, the flavours of cardamoms and chloric-ether disputed those of the pastilles and a score of drugs and perfume and soap scents. Our electric lights, set low down in the windows before the tun-bellied Rosamond jars, flung inward three monstrous daubs of red, blue, and green, that broke into kaleidoscopic lights on the faceted knobs of the drug-drawers, the cut-glass scent flagons, and the bulbs of the sparklet bottles. They flushed the white-tiled floor in gorgeous patches; splashed along the nickel-silver counter-rails, and turned the polished mahogany counter-panels to the likeness of intricate grained marbles – slabs of porphyry and malachite. Mr Shaynor unlocked a drawer, and ere he began to write, took out a meagre bundle of letters. From my place by the stove, I could see the scalloped edges of the paper with a flaring monogram in the corner and could even smell the reek of chypre. At each page he turned toward the toilet-water lady of the advertisement and devoured her with over-luminous eyes. He had drawn the Austrian blanket over his shoulders, and among those warring lights he looked more than ever the incarnation of a drugged moth – a tiger-moth as I thought.

He put his letter into an envelope, stamped it with stiff mechanical movements, and dropped it in the drawer. Then I became aware of the silence of a great city asleep - the silence that underlay the even voice of the breakers along the sea-front - a thick, tingling quiet of warm life stilled down for its appointed time, and unconsciously I moved about the glittering shop as one moves in a sick-room. Young Mr Cashell was adjusting some wire that crackled from time to time with the tense, knuckle-stretching sound of the electric spark. Upstairs, where a door shut and opened swiftly, I could hear his uncle coughing abed.

'Here,' I said, when the drink was properly warmed, 'take some of this, Mr Shaynor.'

He jerked in his chair with a start and a wrench, and held out his hand for the glass. The mixture, of a rich port-wine colour, frothed at the top.

'It looks,' he said, suddenly, 'it looks – those bubbles – like a string of pearls winking at you – rather like the pearls round that young lady's neck.' He turned again to the advertisement where the female in the dove-coloured corset had seen fit to put on all her pearls before she cleaned her teeth.

'Not bad, is it?' I said.

'Eh?'

He rolled his eyes heavily full on me, and, as I stared, I beheld all meaning and consciousness die out of the swiftly dilating pupils. His figure lost its stark rigidity, softened into the chair, and, chin on chest, hands dropped before him, he rested open-eyed, absolutely still.

'I'm afraid I've rather cooked Shaynor's goose,' I said, bearing the fresh drink to young Mr Cashell. 'Perhaps it was the chloric-ether.'

'Oh, he's all right.' The spade-bearded man glanced at him pityingly. 'Consumptives go off in those sort of dozes very often. It's exhaustion ... I don't wonder. I daresay the liquor will do him good. It's grand stuff.' He finished his share appreciatively. 'Well, as I was saying – before he interrupted – about this little coherer. The pinch of dust, you see, is nickel-filings. The Hertzian waves, you see, come out of space from the station that despatches 'em, and all these little particles are attracted together – cohere, we call it – for just so long as the current passes through them. Now, it's important to remember that the current is an induced current. There are a good many kinds of induction —'

'Yes, but what *is* induction?'

'That's rather hard to explain untechnically. But the long and the short of it is that when a current of electricity passes through a wire there's a lot of magnetism present round that wire; and if you put another wire parallel to, and within what we call its magnetic field – why, then the second wire will also become charged with electricity.'

'On its own account?'

'On its own account.'

'Then let's see if I've got it correctly. Miles off, at Poole, or wherever it is —'

'It will be anywhere in ten years.'

'You've got a charged wire —'

'Charged with Hertzian waves which vibrate, say, two hundred and thirty million times a second.' Mr Cashell snaked his forefinger rapidly through the air.

'All right – a charged wire at Poole, giving out these waves into space. Then this wire of yours sticking out into space – on the roof of the house – in some mysterious way gets charged with those waves from Poole —'

'Or anywhere – it only happens to be Poole tonight.'

'And those waves set the coherer at work, just like an ordinary telegraph-office ticker?'

'No! That's where so many people make the mistake. The Hertzian waves wouldn't be strong enough to work a great heavy Morse instrument like ours. They can only just make that dust cohere, and while it coheres (a little while for a dot and a longer while for a dash) the current from this battery – the home battery' – he laid his hand on the thing – 'can get through to the Morse printing-machine to record the dot or dash. Let me make it clearer. Do you know anything about steam?'

'Very little. But go on.'

'Well, the coherer is like a steam-valve. Any child can open a valve and start a steamer's engines, because a turn of the hand lets in the main steam, doesn't it? Now, this home battery here ready to print is the main steam. The coherer is the valve, always ready to be turned on. The Hertzian wave is the child's hand that turns it.'

'I see. That's marvellous.'

'Marvellous, isn't it? And, remember, we're only at the beginning. There's nothing we shan't be able to do in ten years. I want to live – my God, how I want to live, and see it develop!' He looked through the door at Shaynor breathing lightly in his chair. 'Poor beast! And he wants to keep company with Fanny Brand.'

'Fanny *who*?' I said, for the name struck an obscurely familiar chord in my brain – something connected with a stained handkerchief, and the word 'arterial.'

'Fanny Brand – the girl you kept shop for.' He laughed. 'That's all I know about her, and for the life of me I can't see what Shaynor sees in her, or she in him.'

'*Can't* you see what he sees in her?' I insisted.

'Oh, yes, if *that's* what you mean. She's a great, big, fat lump of a girl, and so on. I suppose that's why he's so crazy after her. She isn't his sort. Well, it doesn't matter. My uncle says he's bound to die before the year's out. Your drink's given him a good sleep, at any rate.' Young Mr Cashell could not catch Mr Shaynor's face, which was half turned to the advertisement.

I stoked the stove anew, for the room was growing cold, and lighted another pastille. Mr Shaynor in his chair, never moving, looked through and over me with eyes as wide and lustreless as those of a dead hare.

'Poole's late,' said young Mr Cashell, when I stepped back. 'I'll just send them a call.'

He pressed a key in the semi-darkness, and with a rending crackle there leaped between two brass knobs a spark, streams of sparks, and sparks again.

'Grand, isn't it? *That's* the Power – our unknown Power – kicking and fighting to be let loose,' said young Mr Cashell. 'There she goes – kick – kick – kick into space. I never get over the strangeness of it when I work a sending-machine, waves going into space you know. T.R. is our call. Poole ought to answer with L.L.L.'

We waited two, three, five minutes. In that silence, of which the boom of the tide was an orderly part, I caught the clear '*kiss – kiss – kiss*' of the halliards on the roof, as they were blown against the installation-pole.

'Poole is not ready. I'll stay here and call you when he is.'

I returned to the shop, and set down my glass on a marble slab with a careless clink. As I did so, Shaynor rose to his feet, his eyes fixed once more on the advertisement, where the young woman bathed in the light from the red jar simpered pinkly over her pearls. His lips moved without cessation. I stepped nearer to listen.

'And threw – and threw – and threw,' he repeated, his face all sharp with some inexplicable agony.

I moved forward astonished. But it was then he found words – delivered roundly and clearly. These:

And threw warm gules on Madeleine's young breast.

The trouble passed off his countenance, and he returned lightly to his place, rubbing his hands.

It had never occurred to me, though we had many times discussed reading and prize-competitions as a diversion, that Mr Shaynor ever read Keats, or could quote him at all appositely. There was, after all, a certain stained-glass effect of light on the high bosom of the highly-polished picture which might, by stretch of fancy, suggest, as a vile chromo recalls some incomparable canvas, the line he had spoken. Night, my drink, and solitude were evidently turning Mr Shaynor into a poet. He sat down again and wrote swiftly on his villainous note-paper, his lips quivering.

I shut the door into the inner office and moved up behind him. He made no sign that he saw or heard. I looked over his shoulder, and read, amid half-formed words, sentences, and wild scratches;

— Very cold it was. Very cold
The hare – the hare – the hare –
The birds —

He raised his head sharply, and frowned towards the blank shutters of the poulterer's shop where they jutted out against our window. Then one clear line came:

The hare, in spite of fur, was very cold.

The head, moving machine-like, turned right to the advertisement where the Blaudett's Cathedral pastille reeked abominably. He grunted, and went on:

Incense in a censer –
Before her darling picture framed in gold –
Maiden's picture – angel's portrait –

'Hsh!' said Mr Cashell guardedly from the inner office, as though in the presence of spirits. 'There's something coming through from somewhere; but it isn't Poole.' I heard the crackle of sparks as he depressed the keys of the transmitter. In my own brain, too, something crackled, or it might have been the hair on my head. Then I heard my own voice, in a harsh whisper: 'Mr Cashell, there is something coming through here, too. Leave me alone till I tell you.'

'But I thought you'd come to see this wonderful thing – Sir,' indignantly at the end.

'Leave me alone till I tell you. Be quiet.'

I watched – I waited. Under the blue-veined hand – the dry hand of the consumptive – came away clear, without erasure:

And my weak spirit fails
To think how the dead must freeze –

he shivered as he wrote –

Beneath the churchyard mould.

Then he stopped, laid the pen down, and leaned back.

For an instant, that was half an eternity, the shop spun before me in a rainbow-tinted whirl, in and through which my own soul most dispassionately considered my own soul as that fought with an over-mastering fear. Then I smelt the strong smell of cigarettes from Mr Shaynor's clothing, and heard, as though it had been the rending of trumpets, the rattle of his breathing. I was still in my place of observation, much as one would watch a rifle-shot at the butts, half-bent, hands on my knees, and head within a few inches of the black, red, and yellow blanket of his shoulder. I was whispering encouragement, evidently to my other self, sounding sentences, such as men pronounce in dreams.

'If he has read Keats, it proves nothing. If he hasn't – like causes *must* beget like effects. There is no escape from this law. *You* ought to be grateful that you know "St Agnes' Eve" without the book; because, given the circumstances, such as Fanny Brand, who is the key of the enigma, and approximately represents the latitude and longitude of Fanny Brawne; allowing also for the bright red colour of the arterial blood upon the handkerchief, which was just what you were puzzling over in the shop just now; and counting the effect of the professional environment, here almost perfectly duplicated – the result is logical and inevitable. As inevitable as induction.'

Still, the other half of my soul refused to be comforted. It was cowering in some minute and inadequate corner – at an immense distance.

Hereafter, I found myself one person again, my hands still gripping my knees, and my eyes glued on the page before Mr Shaynor. As dreamers accept and explain the upheaval of landscapes and the resurrection of the dead, with excerpts from the evening hymn or the multiplication-table, so I had accepted the facts, whatever they might be, that I should witness, and had devised a theory, sane and plausible to my mind, that explained them all. Nay, I was even in advance of my facts, walking hurriedly before them, assured that they would fit my theory. And all that I now recall of that epoch-making theory are the lofty words: 'If he has read Keats it's the chloric-ether. If he hasn't, it's the identical bacillus, or Hertzian wave of tuberculosis, *plus* Fanny Brand and the professional status which, in conjunction with the main-stream of subconscious thought common to all mankind, has thrown up temporarily an induced Keats.'

Mr Shaynor returned to his work, erasing and rewriting as before with swiftness. Two or three blank pages he tossed aside. Then he wrote, muttering;

The little smoke of a candle that goes out.

'No,' he muttered. 'Little smoke – little smoke – little smoke. What else?' He thrust his chin forward toward the advertisement, whereunder the last of the Blaudett's Cathedral pastilles fumed in its holder. 'Ah!' Then with relief:

The little smoke that dies in moonlight cold.

Evidently he was snared by the rhymes of his first verse, for he wrote and rewrote 'gold – cold – mould' many times. Again he sought inspiration from the advertisement, and set down, without erasure, the line I had overheard;

And threw warm gules on Madeleine's young breast.

As I remembered the original it is 'fair' – a trite word – instead of 'young', and I found myself nodding approval, though I admitted that the attempt to reproduce 'Its little smoke in pallid moonlight died' was a failure.

Followed without a break ten or fifteen lines of bald prose – the naked soul's confession of its physical yearning for its beloved – unclean as we count uncleanliness; unwholesome, but human exceedingly; the raw material, so it seemed to me in that hour and in that place, whence Keats wove the twenty-sixth, seventh, and eighth stanzas of his poem. Shame I had none in overseeing this revelation; and my fear had gone with the smoke of the pastille.

'That's it,' I murmured. 'That's how it's blocked out. Go on! Ink it in, man. Ink it in!'

Mr Shaynor returned to broken verse wherein 'loveliness' was made to rhyme with a desire to look upon 'her empty dress'. He picked up a fold of the gay, soft blanket, spread it over one hand, caressed it with infinite tenderness, thought, muttered, traced some snatches which I could not decipher, shut his eyes drowsily, shook his head, and dropped the stuff. Here I found myself at fault, for I could not then see (as I do now) in what manner a red, black, and yellow Austrian blanket coloured his dreams.

In a few minutes he laid aside his pen, and, chin on hand, considered the shop with thoughtful and intelligent eyes. He threw down the blanket, rose, passed along a line of drug-drawers, and read the names on the labels aloud. Returning, he took from his desk Christy's *New Commercial Plants* and the old Culpeper that I had given him, opened and laid them side by side with a clerky air, all trace of passion gone from his face, read first in one and then in the other, and paused with pen behind his ear.

'What wonder of Heaven's coming now?' I thought.

'Manna – manna – manna,' he said at last, under wrinkled brows. 'That's what I wanted. Good! Now then! Now then! Good! Good! Oh, by God, that's good!' His voice rose and he spoke rightly and fully without a falter:

Candied apple, quince and plum and gourd,
With jellies smoother than the creamy curd,
And lucent syrops tinct with cinnamon;
Manna and dates in argosy transferred
From Fez, and spicèd dainties, every one
From silken Samarcand to cedared Lebanon.

He repeated it once more, using 'blander' for 'smoother' in the second line; then wrote it down without erasure, but this time (my set eyes missed no stroke of any word) he substituted 'soother' for his atrocious second thought, so that it came away under his hand as it is written in the book – as it is written in the book.

A wind went shouting down the street, and on the heels of the wind followed a spurt and rattle of rain.

After a smiling pause – and good right had he to smile – he began anew, always tossing the last sheet over his shoulder:

The sharp rain falling on the window-pane,
Rattling sleet – the wind-blown sleet.

Then prose: 'It is very cold of mornings when the wind brings rain and sleet with it. I heard the sleet on the window-pane outside, and thought of you, my darling. I am always thinking of you. I wish we could both run away like two lovers into the storm and get that little cottage by the sea which we are always thinking about, my own dear darling. We could sit and watch the sea beneath our windows. It would be a fairyland all of our own – a fairy sea – a fairy sea . . .'

He stopped, raised his head, and listened. The steady drone of the Channel along the sea-front that had borne us company so long leaped up a note to the sudden fuller surge that signals the change from ebb to flood. It beat in like the change of step throughout an army – this renewed pulse of the sea – and filled our ears till they, accepting it, marked it no longer.

A fairyland for you and me
Across the foam – beyond . . .
A magic foam, a perilous sea.

He grunted again with effort and bit his underlip. My throat dried, but I dared not gulp to moisten it lest I should break the spell that was drawing him nearer and nearer to the highwater mark but two of the sons of Adam have reached. Remember that in all the millions permitted there are no more than five – five little lines – of which one can say: 'These are the pure Magic. These are the clear Vision. The rest is only poetry.' And Mr Shaynor was playing hot and cold with two of them!

I vowed no unconscious thought of mine should influence the blindfold soul, and pinned myself desperately to the other three, repeating and re-repeating:

> A savage place! as holy and enchanted
> As e'er beneath a waning moon was haunted
> By woman wailing for her demon-lover.

But though I believed my brain thus occupied, my every sense hung upon the writing under the dry, bony hand, all brown-fingered with chemicals and cigarette-smoke.

> Our windows fronting on the dangerous foam,

(he wrote, after long, irresolute snatches), and then –

> Our open casements facing desolate seas
> Forlorn – forlorn –

Here again his face grew peaked and anxious with that sense of loss I had first seen when the Power snatched him. But this time the agony was tenfold keener. As I watched it mounted like mercury in the tube. It lighted his face from within till I thought the visibly scourged soul must leap forth naked between his jaws, unable to endure. A drop of sweat trickled from my forehead down my nose and splashed on the back of my hand.

> Our windows facing on the desolate seas
> And pearly foam of magic fairyland –

'Not yet – not yet,' he muttered, 'wait a minute. *Please* wait a minute. I shall get it then –

> Our magic windows fronting on the sea,
> The dangerous foam of desolate seas . . .
> For aye.

Ouh, my God!'

From head to heel he shook – shook from the marrow of his bones outwards – then leaped to his feet with raised arms, and slid the chair screeching across the tiled floor where it struck the drawers behind and fell with a jar. Mechanically, I stooped to recover it.

As I rose, Mr Shaynor was stretching and yawning at leisure.

'I've had a bit of a doze,' he said. 'How did I come to knock the chair over? You look rather —'

'The chair startled me,' I answered. 'It was so sudden in this quiet.'

Young Mr Cashell behind his shut door was offendedly silent.

'I suppose I must have been dreaming,' said Mr Shaynor.

'I suppose you must,' I said. 'Talking of dreams – I – I noticed you writing – before —'

He flushed consciously.

'I meant to ask you if you've ever read anything written by a man called Keats.'

'Oh! I haven't much time to read poetry, and I can't say that I remember the name exactly. Is he a popular writer?'

'Middling. I thought you might know him because he's the only poet who was ever a druggist. And he's rather what's called the lover's poet.'

'Indeed. I must dip into him. What did he write about?'

'A lot of things. Here's a sample that may interest you.'

Then and there, carefully, I repeated the verse he had twice spoken and once written not ten minutes ago.

'Ah! Anybody could see he was a druggist from that line about the tinctures and syrups. It's a fine tribute to our profession.'

'I don't know,' said young Mr Cashell, with icy politeness, opening the door one half-inch, 'if you still happen to be interested in our trifling experiments. But, should such be the case —'

I drew him aside, whispering, 'Shaynor seemed going off into some sort of fit when I spoke to you just now. I thought, even at the risk of being rude, it wouldn't do to take you off your instruments just as the call was coming through. Don't you see?'

'Granted – granted as soon as asked,' he said, unbending. 'I *did* think it a shade odd at the time. So that was why he knocked the chair down?'

'I hope I haven't missed anything,' I said.

'I'm afraid I can't say that, but you're just in time for the end of a rather curious performance. You can come in too, Mr Shaynor. Listen, while I read it off.'

The Morse instrument was ticking furiously. Mr Cashell interpreted: '"*K.K.V. Can make nothing of your signals.*"' A pause. '"*M.M.V. M.M.V. Signals unintelligible. Purpose anchor Sandown Bay.*

Examine instruments tomorrow." Do you know what that means? It's a couple of men-o'-war working Marconi signals off the Isle of Wight. They are trying to talk to each other. Neither can read the other's messages, but all their messages are being taken in by our receiver here. They've been going on for ever so long. I wish you could have heard it.'

'How wonderful!' I said. 'Do you mean we're overhearing Portsmouth ships trying to talk to each other – that we're eavesdropping across half South England?'

'Just that. Their transmitters are all right, but their receivers are out of order, so they only get a dot here and a dash there. Nothing clear.'

'Why is that?'

'God knows – and science will know tomorrow. Perhaps the induction is faulty; perhaps the receivers aren't tuned to receive just the number of vibrations per second that the transmitter sends. Only a word here and there. Just enough to tantalize.'

Again the Morse sprang to life.

'That's one of 'em complaining now. Listen: "*Disheartening – most disheartening*." It's quite pathetic. Have you ever seen a spiritualistic séance? It reminds me of that sometimes – odds and ends of messages coming out of nowhere – a word here and there – no good at all.'

'But mediums are all imposters,' said Mr Shaynor, in the doorway, lighting an asthma-cigarette. 'They only do it for the money they can make. I've seen 'em.'

'Here's Poole, at last – clear as a bell. L.L.L. *Now* we shan't be long.' Mr Cashell rattled the keys merrily. 'Anything you'd like to tell 'em?'

'No, I don't think so,' I said. 'I'll go home and get to bed. I'm feeling a little tired.'

THE RETURN OF THE CHILDREN

Neither the harps nor the crowns amused, nor the cherubs' dove-winged races –
Holding hands forlornly the Children wandered beneath the Dome;
Plucking the radiant robes of the passers-by, and with pitiful faces
Begging what Princes and Powers refused: 'Ah, please will you let us go home?'

Over the jewelled floor, nigh weeping, ran to them Mary the Mother,
Kneeled and caressed and made promise with kisses, and drew them along to the gateway –
Yea, the all-iron unbribeable Door which Peter must guard and none other.
Straightway She took the Keys from his keeping, and opened and freed them straightway.

Then to Her Son, Who had seen and smiled, She said: 'On the night that I bore Thee
What didst Thou care for a love beyond mine or a heaven that was not my arm?
Didst Thou push from the nipple, O Child, to hear the angels adore Thee?
When we two lay in the breath of the kine?' And He said: – 'Thou hast done no harm.'

So through the Void the Children ran homeward merrily hand in hand,
Looking neither to left nor right where the breathless Heavens stood still;
And the Guards of the Void resheathed their swords, for they heard the Command:
'Shall I that have suffered the children to come to me hold them against their will?'

'They'

ONE view called me to another; one hilltop to its fellow, half across the county, and since I could answer at no more trouble than the snapping forward of a lever, I let the county flow under my wheels. The orchid-studded flats of the East gave way to the thyme, ilex, and grey grass of the Downs; these again to the rich cornland and fig-trees of the lower coast, where you carry the beat of the tide on your left hand for fifteen level miles; and when at last I turned inland through a huddle of rounded hills and woods I had run myself clean out of my known marks. Beyond that precise hamlet which stands godmother to the capital of the United States, I found hidden villages where bees, the only things awake, boomed in eighty-foot lindens that overhung grey Norman churches; miraculous brooks diving under stone bridges built for heavier traffic than would ever vex them again; tithe-barns larger than their churches, and an old smithy that cried out aloud how it had once been a hall of the Knights of the Temple. Gypsies I found on a common where the gorse, bracken, and heath fought it out together up a mile of Roman road; and a little farther on I disturbed a red fox rolling dog-fashion in the naked sunlight.

As the wooded hills closed about me I stood up in the car to take the bearings of that great Down whose ringed head is a landmark for fifty miles across the low countries. I judged that the lie of the country would bring me across some westward-running road that went to his feet, but I did not allow for the confusing veils of the woods. A quick turn plunged me first into a green cutting brim-full of liquid sunshine, next into a gloomy tunnel where last year's dead leaves whispered and scuffled about my tyres. The strong hazel stuff meeting overhead had not been cut for a couple of generations at least, nor had any axe helped the moss-cankered oak and beech to spring above them. Here the road changed frankly into a carpeted ride on whose brown velvet spent primrose-clumps showed like jade, and a few sickly, white-stalked bluebells nodded together. As the slope favoured I shut off the power and slid over the whirled leaves, expecting every moment to meet a keeper; but I only heard a jay, far off, arguing against the silence under the twilight of the trees.

Still the track descended. I was on the point of reversing and working my way back on the second speed ere I ended in some swamp, when I saw sunshine through the tangle ahead and lifted the brake.

It was down again at once. As the light beat across my face my fore-wheels took the turf of a great still lawn from which sprang horsemen ten feet high with levelled lances, monstrous peacocks, and sleek round-headed maids of honour – blue, black, and glistening – all of clipped yew. Across the lawn – the marshalled woods besieged it on three sides – stood an ancient house of lichened and weather-worn stone, with mullioned windows and roofs of rose-red tile. It was flanked by semi-circular walls, also rose-red, that closed the lawn on the fourth side, and at their feet a box hedge grew man-high. There were doves on the roof about the slim brick chimneys, and I caught a glimpse of an octagonal dove-house behind the screening wall.

Here, then, I stayed: a horseman's green spear laid at my breast; held by the exceeding beauty of that jewel in that setting.

'If I am not packed off for a trespasser, or if this knight does not ride a wallop at me,' thought I, 'Shakespeare and Queen Elizabeth at least must come out of that half-open garden door and ask me to tea.'

A child appeared at an upper window, and I thought the little thing waved a friendly hand. But it was to call a companion, for presently another bright head showed. Then I heard a laugh among the yew-peacocks, and turning to make sure (till then I had been watching the house only) I saw the silver of a fountain behind a hedge thrown up against the sun. The doves on the roof cooed to the cooing water; but between the two notes I caught the utterly happy chuckle of a child absorbed in some light mischief.

The garden door – heavy oak sunk deep in the thickness of the wall – opened further: a woman in a big garden hat set her foot slowly on the time-hallowed stone step and as slowly walked across the turf. I was forming some apology when she lifted up her head, and I saw that she was blind.

'I heard you,' she said. 'Isn't that a motor car?'

'I'm afraid I've made a mistake in my road. I should have turned off up above – I never dreamed —' I began.

'But I'm very glad. Fancy a motor car coming into the garden! It will be such a treat —' She turned and made as though looking about her. 'You – you haven't seen any one, have you – perhaps?'

'No one to speak to, but the children seemed interested at a distance.'

'Which?'

'I saw a couple up at the window just now, and I think I heard a little chap in the grounds.'

'Oh, lucky you!' she cried, and her face brightened. 'I hear them, of course, but that's all. You've seen them and heard them?'

'Yes,' I answered. 'And if I know anything of children, one of them's having a beautiful time by the fountain yonder. Escaped, I should imagine.'

'You're fond of children?'

I gave her one or two reasons why I did not altogether hate them.

'Of course, of course,' she said. 'Then you understand. Then you won't think it foolish if I ask you to take your car though the gardens, once or twice – quite slowly. I'm sure they'd like to see it. They see so little, poor things. One tries to make their lives pleasant, but —' she threw out her hands towards the woods. 'We're so out of the world here.'

'That will be splendid,' I said. 'But I can't cut up your grass.'

She faced to the right. 'Wait a minute,' she said. 'We're at the South gate, aren't we? Behind those peacocks there's a flagged path. We call it the Peacocks' Walk. You can't see it from here, they tell me, but if you squeeze along by the edge of the wood you can turn at the first peacock and get on to the flags.'

It was sacrilege to wake that dreaming house-front with the clatter of machinery, but I swung the car to clear the turf, brushed along the edge of the wood and turned in on the broad stone path where the fountain-basin lay like one star-sapphire.

'May I come too?' she cried. 'No, please don't help me. They'll like it better if they see me.'

She felt her way lightly to the front of the car, and with one foot on the step she called: 'Children, oh, children! Look and see what's going to happen!'

The voice would have drawn lost souls from the Pit, for the yearning that underlay its sweetness, and I was not surprised to hear an answering shout behind the yews. It must have been the child by the fountain, but he fled at our approach, leaving a little toy boat in the water. I saw the glint of his blue blouse among the still horsemen.

Very disposedly we paraded the length of the walk and at her request backed again. This time the child had got the better of his panic, but stood far off and doubting.

'The little fellow's watching us,' I said. 'I wonder if he'd like a ride.'

'They're very shy still. Very shy. But, oh, lucky you to be able to see them! Let's listen.'

I stopped the machine at once, and the humid stillness, heavy with the scent of box, cloaked us deep. Shears I could hear where some gardener was clipping; a mumble of bees and broken voices that might have been the doves.

'Oh, unkind!' she said weariedly.

'Perhaps they're only shy of the motor. The little maid at the window looks tremendously interested.'

'Yes?' She raised her head. 'It was wrong of me to say that. They are really fond of me. It's the only thing that makes life worth living – when they're fond of you, isn't it? I daren't think what the place would be without them. By the way, is it beautiful?'

'I think it is the most beautiful place I have ever seen.'

'So they all tell me. I can feel it, of course, but that isn't quite the same thing.'

'Then have you never —?' I began, but stopped abashed.

'Not since I can remember. It happened when I was only a few months old, they tell me. And yet I must remember something, else how could I dream about colours. I see light in my dreams, and colours, but I never see *them*. I only hear them just as I do when I'm awake.'

'It's difficult to see faces in dreams. Some people can, but most of us haven't the gift,' I went on, looking up at the window where the child stood all but hidden.

'I've heard that too,' she said. 'And they tell me that one never sees a dead person's face in a dream. Is that true?'

'I believe it is – now I come to think of it.'

'But how is it with yourself – yourself?' The blind eyes turned towards me.

'I have never seen the faces of my dead in any dream,' I answered.

'Then it must be as bad as being blind.'

The sun had dipped behind the woods and the long shades were possessing the insolent horsemen one by one. I saw the light die from off the top of a glossy-leafed lance and all the brave hard green turn to soft black. The house, accepting another day at its end, as it had accepted an hundred thousand gone, seemed to settle deeper into its rest among the shadows.

'Have you ever wanted to?' she said after the silence.

'Very much sometimes,' I replied. The child had left the window as the shadows closed upon it.

'Ah! So've I, but I don't suppose it's allowed . . . Where d'you live?'

'Quite the other side of the county – sixty miles and more, and I must be going back. I've come without my big lamps.'

'But it's not dark yet. I can feel it.'

'I'm afraid it will be by the time I get home. Could you lend me someone to set me on my road at first? I've utterly lost myself.'

'I'll send Madden with you to the crossroads. We are so out of the world, I don't wonder you were lost! I'll guide you round to the front of the house; but you will go slowly, won't you, till you're out of the grounds? It isn't foolish, do you think?'

'I promise you I'll go like this,' I said, and let the car start herself down the flagged path.

We skirted the left wing of the house, whose elaborately cast lead guttering alone was worth a day's journey; passed under a great rose-grown gate in the red wall, and so round to the high front of the house, which in beauty and stateliness as much excelled the back as that all others I had seen.

'Is it so very beautiful?' she said wistfully when she heard my raptures. 'And you like the lead figures too? There's the old azalea garden behind. They say that this place must have been made for children. Will you help me out, please? I should like to come with you as far as the crossroads, but I mustn't leave them. Is that you, Madden? I want you to show this gentleman the way to the crossroads. He has lost his way, but – he has seen them.'

A butler appeared noiselessly at the miracle of old oak that must be called the front door, and slipped aside to put on his hat. She stood looking at me with open blue eyes in which no sight lay, and I saw for the first time that she was beautiful.

'Remember,' she said quietly, 'if you are fond of them you will come again,' and disappeared within the house.

The butler in the car said nothing till we were nearly at the lodge gates, where catching a glimpse of a blue blouse in the shrubbery I swerved amply lest the devil that leads little boys to play should drag me into child-murder.

'Excuse me,' he asked of a sudden, 'but why did you do that, sir?'

'The child yonder.'

'Our young gentleman in blue?'

'Of course.'

'He runs about a good deal. Did you see him by the fountain, sir?'

'Oh, yes, several times. Do we turn here?

'Yes, sir. And did you 'appen to see them upstairs too?'

'At the upper window? Yes.'

'Was that before the mistress come out to speak to you, sir?'

'A little before that. Why d'you want to know?'

He paused a little. 'Only to make sure that – that they had seen the car, sir, because with children running about, though I'm sure you're driving particularly careful, there might be an accident. That was all, sir. Here are the crossroads. You can't miss your way from now on. Thank you, sir, but that isn't *our* custom, not with —'

'I beg your pardon,' I said, and thrust away the British silver.

'Oh, it's quite right with the rest of 'em as a rule. Goodbye, sir.'

He retired into the armour-plated conning-tower of his caste and walked away. Evidently a butler solicitous for the honour of his house, and interested, probably through a maid, in the nursery.

Once beyond the signposts at the crossroads I looked back, but the crumpled hills interlaced so jealously that I could not see where the house had lain. When I asked its name at a cottage along the road, the fat woman who sold sweetmeats there gave me to understand that people with motor cars had small right to live – much less to 'go about talking like carriage folk'. They were not a pleasant-mannered community.

When I retraced my route on the map that evening I was little wiser. Hawkin's Old Farm appeared to be the Survey title of the place, and the old County Gazetteer, generally so ample, did not allude to it. The big house of those parts was Hodnington Hall, Georgian with early Victorian embellishments, as an atrocious steel engraving attested. I carried my difficulty to a neighbour – a deep-rooted tree of that soil – and he gave me a name of a family which conveyed no meaning.

A month or so later – I went again, or it may have been that my car took the road of her own volition. She over-ran the fruitless Downs, threaded every turn of the maze of lanes below the hills, drew through the high-walled woods, impenetrable in their full leaf, came out at the crossroads where the butler had left me, and a little farther on developed an internal trouble which forced me to turn her in on a grass way-waste that cut into a summer-silent hazel wood. So far as I could make sure by the sun and a six-inch Ordnance map, this should be the road flank of that wood which I had first explored from the heights above. I made a mighty serious business of my repairs and a glittering shop of my repair kit, spanners, pump, and the like, which I spread out orderly upon a rug. It was a trap to catch all childhood, for on such a day, I argued, the children would not be far off. When I paused in my work I listened, but the wood was so full of the noises of summer (though the birds had mated) that I could not at first distinguish these from the tread of small cautious feet stealing across the dead leaves. I rang my bell in an alluring manner, but the feet fled, and I repented, for to a child a sudden noise is very real terror. I must have been at work half an hour when I heard in the wood the voice of the blind woman crying: 'Children, oh, children! Where are you?' and the stillness made slow to close on the perfection of that cry. She came towards me, half feeling her way between the tree boles, and though a child, it seemed, clung to her skirt, it swerved into the leafage like a rabbit as she drew nearer.

'Is that you?' she said, 'from the other side of the county?'

'Yes, it's me from the other side of the county.'

'Then why didn't you come through the upper woods? They were there just now.'

'They were here a few minutes ago. I expect they knew my car had broken down, and came to see the fun.'

'Nothing serious, I hope? How do cars break down?'

'In fifty different ways. Only mine has chosen the fifty-first.'

She laughed merrily at the tiny joke, cooed with delicious laughter, and pushed her hat back.

'Let me hear,' she said.

'Wait a moment,' I cried, 'and I'll get you a cushion.'

She set her foot on the rug all covered with spare parts, and stooped above it eagerly. 'What delightful things!' The hands through which she saw glanced in the chequered sunlight. 'A box here – another box! Why, you've arranged them like playing shop!'

'I confess now that I put it out to attract them. I don't need half those things really.'

'How nice of you! I heard your bell in the upper wood. You say they were here before that?'

'I'm sure of it. Why are they so shy? That little fellow in blue who was with you just now ought to have got over his fright. He's been watching me like a Red Indian.'

'It must have been your bell,' she said. 'I heard one of them go past me in trouble when I was coming down. They're shy – so shy even with me.' She turned her face over her shoulder and cried again: 'Children, oh, children! Look and see!'

'They must have gone off together on their own affairs,' I suggested, for there was a murmur behind us of lowered voices broken by the sudden squeaking giggles of childhood. I returned to my tinkerings and she leaned forward, her chin on her hand, listening interestedly.

'How many are they?' I said at last. The work was finished, but I saw no reason to go.

Her forehead puckered a little in thought. 'I don't quite know,' she said simply. 'Sometimes more – sometimes less. They come and stay with me because I love them, you see.'

'That must be very jolly,' I said, replacing a drawer, and as I spoke I heard the inanity of my answer.

'You – you aren't laughting at me?' she cried. 'I – I haven't any of my own. I never married. People laugh at me sometimes about them because – because –'

'Because they're savages,' I returned. 'It's nothing to fret for. That sort laugh at everything that isn't in their own fat lives.'

'I don't know. How should I? I only don't like being laughed at about *them*. It hurts; and when one can't see ... I don't want to seem silly,' her chin quivered like a child's as she spoke, 'but we blindies have only one skin, I think. Everything outside hits straight at our souls. It's different with you. You've such good defences in your eyes – looking out – before anyone can really pain you in your soul. People forget that with us.'

I was silent, reviewing that inexhaustible matter – the more than inherited (since it is also carefully taught) brutality of the Christian peoples, beside which the mere heathendom of the West Coast nigger is clean and restrained. It led me a long distance into myself.

'Don't do that!' she said of a sudden, putting her hand before her eyes.

'What?'

She made a gesture with her hand.

'That! It's – it's all purple and black. Don't! That colour hurts.'

'But how in the world do you know about colours?' I exclaimed, for here was a revelation indeed.

'Colours as colours?' she asked.

'No. *Those* Colours which you saw just now.'

'You know as well as I do,' she laughed, 'else you wouldn't have asked that question. They aren't in the world at all. They're in *you* – when you went so angry.'

'D'you mean a dull purplish patch, like port wine mixed with ink?' I said.

'I've never seen ink or port wine, but the colours aren't mixed. They are separate – all separate.'

'Do you mean black streaks and jags across the purple?'

She nodded. 'Yes – if they are like this,' and zig-zagged her finger again, 'but it's more red than purple – that bad colour.'

'And what are the colours at the top of the – whatever you see?'

Slowly she leaned forward and traced on the rug the figure of the Egg itself.

'I see them so,' she said, pointing with a grass stem, 'white, green, yellow, red, purple, and when people are angry or bad, black across the red – as you were just now.'

'Who told you anything about it – in the beginning?' I demanded.

'About the colours? No one. I used to ask what colours were when I was little – in table-covers and curtains and carpets, you see – because some colours hurt me and some made me happy. People told me; and when I got older that was how I saw people.' Again she traced the outline of the Egg which it is given to very few of us to see.

'All by yourself?' I repeated.

'All by myself. There wasn't anyone else. I only found out afterwards that other people did not see the Colours.'

She leaned against the tree bole plaiting and unplaiting chance-plucked grass stems. The children in the wood had drawn nearer. I could see them with the tail of my eye frolicking like squirrels.

'Now I am sure you will never laugh at me,' she went on after a long silence. 'Nor at *them*.'

'Goodness! No!' I cried, jolted out of my train of thought. 'A man who laughs at a child – unless the child is laughing too – is a heathen!'

'I didn't mean that, of course. You'd never laugh *at* children, but I thought – I used to think – that perhaps you might laugh at *them*. So now I beg your pardon . . . What are you going to laugh at?'

I had made no sound, but she knew.

'At the notion of your begging my pardon. If you had done your duty as a pillar of the State and a landed proprietress you ought to have summoned me for trespass when I barged through your woods the other day. It was disgraceful of me – inexcusable.'

She looked at me, her head against the tree-trunk – long and steadily – this woman who could see the naked soul.

'How curious,' she half whispered. 'How very curious.'

'Why, what have I done?'

'You don't understand . . . and yet you understood about the Colours. Don't you understand?'

She spoke with a passion that nothing had justified, and I faced her bewilderedly as she rose. The children had gathered themselves in a roundel behind a bramble bush. One sleek head bent over something smaller, and the set of the little shoulders told me that fingers were on lips. They, too, had some child's tremendous secret. I alone was hopelessly astray there in the broad sunlight.

'No,' I said, and shook my head as though the dead eyes could note. 'Whatever it is, I don't understand yet. Perhaps I shall later – if you'll let me come again.'

'You will come again,' she answered. 'You will surely come again and walk in the wood.'

'Perhaps the children will know me well enough by that time to let me play with them – as a favour. You know what children are like.'

'It isn't a matter of favour but of right,' she replied, and while I wondered what she meant, a dishevelled woman plunged round the bend of the road, loose-haired, purple, almost lowing with agony as she ran. It was my rude, fat friend of the sweetmeat shop. The blind woman heard and stepped forward. 'What is it, Mrs Madehurst?' she asked.

The woman flung her apron over her head and literally grovelled in the dust, crying that her grandchild was sick to death, that the local doctor was away fishing, that Jenny the mother was at her wits' end, and so forth, with repetitions and bellowings.

'Where's the next nearest doctor?' I asked between paroxysms.

'Madden will tell you. Go round to the house and take him with you. I'll attend to this. Be quick!' She half-supported the fat woman into the shade. In two minutes I was blowing all the horns of Jericho under the front of the House Beautiful, and Madden, in the pantry, rose to the crisis like a butler and a man.

A quarter of an hour at illegal speeds caught us a doctor five miles away. Within the half-hour we had decanted him, much interested in motors, at the door of the sweetmeat shop, and drew up the road to await the verdict.

'Useful things cars,' said Madden, all man and no butler. 'If I'd had one when mine took sick she wouldn't have died.'

'How was it?' I asked.

'Croup. Mrs Madden was away. No one knew what to do. I drove eight miles in a tax-cart for the doctor. She was choked when we came back. This car 'd ha' saved her. She'd have been close on ten now.'

'I'm sorry,' I said. 'I thought you were rather fond of children from what you told me going to the crossroads the other day.'

'Have you seen 'em again, sir – this mornin'?'

'Yes, but they're well broke to cars. I couldn't get any of them within twenty yards of it.'

He looked at me carefully as a scout considers a stranger – not as a menial should lift his eyes to his divinely appointed superior.

'I wonder why,' he said just above the breath that he drew.

We waited on. A light wind from the sea wandered up and down the long lines of the woods, and the wayside grasses, whitened already with summer dust, rose and bowed in sallow waves.

A woman, wiping the suds off her arms, came out of the cottage next the sweetmeat shop.

'I've be'n listenin' in de back-yard,' she said cheerily. 'He says Arthur's unaccountable bad. Did ye hear him shruck just now? Unaccountable bad. I reckon 'twill come Jenny's turn to walk in de wood nex' week along, Mr Madden.'

'Excuse me, sir, but your lap-robe is slipping,' said Madden deferentially. The woman started, dropped a curtsey, and hurried away.

'What does she mean by "walking in the wood"?' I asked.

'It must be some saying they use hereabouts. I'm from Norfolk myself,' said Madden. 'They're an independent lot in this county. She took you for a chauffeur, sir.'

I saw the doctor come out of the cottage followed by a draggle-tailed wench who clung to his arm as though he could make treaty for her with Death. 'Dat sort,' she wailed – 'dey're just as much to us dat has 'em as if dey was lawful born. Just as much – just as much! An' God he'd be just as pleased if you saved 'un, Doctor. Don't take it from me. Miss Florence will tell ye de very same. Don't leave 'im, Doctor!'

'I know, I know,' said the man; 'but he'll be quiet for a while now. We'll get the nurse and the medicine as fast as we can.' He signalled me to come forward with the car, and I strove not to be privy to what followed; but I saw the girl's face, blotched and frozen with grief, and I felt the hand without a ring clutching at my knees when we moved away.

The doctor was a man of some humour, for I remember he claimed my car under the Oath of Æsculapius, and used it and me without mercy. First we convoyed Mrs Madehurst and the blind woman to wait by the sick-bed till the nurse should come. Next we invaded a neat county town for prescriptions (the doctor said the trouble was cerebro-spinal meningitis), and when the County Institute, banked and flanked with scared market cattle, reported itself out of nurses for the moment we literally flung ourselves loose upon the county. We conferred with the owners of great houses – magnates at the ends of overarching avenues whose big-boned womenfolk strode away from their tea-tables to listen to the imperious doctor. At last a white-haired lady sitting under a cedar of Lebanon and surrounded by a court of magnificent Borzois – all hostile to motors – gave the doctor, who received them as from a princess, written orders which we bore many miles at top speed, through a park, to a French nunnery, where we took over in exchange a pallid-faced and trembling sister. She knelt at the bottom of the tonneau telling her beads without pause till, by short cuts of the doctor's invention, we had her to the sweetmeat shop once more. It was a long afternoon crowded with mad episodes that rose and dissolved like the dust of our wheels; cross-sections of remote and incomprehensible lives through which we raced at right angles; and I went home in the dusk, wearied out, to dream of the clashing horns of cattle; round-eyed nuns walking in a garden of graves; pleasant tea-parties beneath shady trees; the carbolic-scented, grey-painted corridors of the County Institute; the steps of shy children in the wood, and the hands that clung to my knees as the motor began to move.

I had intended to return in a day or two, but it pleased Fate to hold me from that side of the county, on many pretexts, till the elder and the wild rose had fruited. There came at last a brilliant day, swept clear from the south-west, that brought the hills within hand's reach – a day of unstable airs and high filmy clouds. Through no merit of my own I was free, and set the car for the third time on that known road. As I reached the crest of the Downs I felt the soft air change, saw it glaze under the sun; and, looking down at the sea, in that instant beheld the blue of the Channel turn through polished silver and dulled steel to dingy pewter. A laden collier hugging the coast steered outward for deeper water, and, across copper-coloured haze, I saw sails rise one by one on the anchored fishing-fleet. In a deep dene behind me an eddy of sudden wind drummed through sheltered oaks, and spun aloft the first dry sample of autumn leaves. When I reached the beach road the sea-fog fumed over the brickfields, and the tide was telling all the groynes of the gale beyond Ushant. In less than an hour summer England vanished in chill grey. We were again the shut island of the North, all the ships of the world bellowing at our perilous gates; and between their outcries ran the piping of bewildered gulls. My cap dripped moisture, the folds of the rug held it in pools or sluiced it away in runnels, and the salt-rime stuck to my lips.

Inland the smell of autumn loaded the thickened fog among the trees, and the drip became a continuous shower. Yet the late flowers – mallow of the wayside, scabious of the field, and dahlia of the garden – showed gay in the mist, and beyond the sea's breath there was little sign of decay in the leaf. Yet in the villages the house doors were all open, and bare-legged, bare-headed children sat at ease on the damp doorsteps to shout 'pip-pip' at the stranger.

I made bold to call at the sweetmeat shop, where Mrs Madehurst met me with a fat woman's hospitable tears. Jenny's child, she said, had died two days after the nun had come. It was, she felt, best out of the way, even though the insurance offices, for reasons which she did not pretend to follow, would not willingly insure such stray lives. 'Not but what Jenny didn't tend to Arthur as though he'd come all proper at de end of de first year – like Jenny herself.' Thanks to Miss Florence, the child had been buried with a pomp which, in Mrs Madehurst's opinion, more than covered the small irregularity of its birth. She described the coffin, within and without, the glass hearse, and the evergreen lining of the grave.

'But how's the mother?' I asked.

'Jenny? Oh, she'll get over it. I've felt dat way with one or two o' my own. She'll get over. She's walkin' in de wood now.'

'In this weather?'

Mrs Madehurst looked at me with narrowed eyes across the counter.

'I dunno but it opens de 'eart like. Yes, it opens de 'eart. Dat's where losin' and bearin' comes so alike in de long run, we do say.'

Now the wisdom of the old wives is greater than that of all the Fathers, and this last oracle sent me thinking so extendedly as I went up the road, that I nearly ran over a woman and a child at the wooded corner by the lodge gates of the House Beautiful.

'Awful weather!' I cried, as I slowed dead for the turn.

'Not so bad,' she answered placidly out of the fog. 'Mine's used to 'un. You'll find yours indoors, I reckon.'

Indoors, Madden received me with professional courtesy, and kind enquiries for the health of the motor, which he would put under cover.

I waited in a still, nut-brown hall, pleasant with late flowers, and warmed with a delicious wood fire – a place of good influence and great peace. (Men and women may sometimes, after great effort, achieve a creditable lie; but the house, which is their temple, cannot say anything save the truth of those who have lived in it.) A child's cart and a doll lay on the black-and-white floor, where a rug had been kicked back. I felt that the children had only just hurried away – to hide themselves, most like – in the many turns of the great adzed staircase that climbed statelily out of the hall, or to crouch at gaze behind the lions and roses of the carven gallery above me. Then I heard her voice above me, singing as the blind sing – from the soul:

In the pleasant orchard-closes.

And all my early summer came back at the call.

In the pleasant orchard-closes,
God bless all our gains say we –
But may God bless all our losses,
Better suits with our degree.

She dropped the marring fifth line, and repeated –

Better suits with our degree!

I saw her lean over the gallery, her linked hands white as pearl against the oak.

'Is that you – from the other side of the county?' she called.

'Yes, me – from the other side of the county,' I answered, laughing.

'What a long time before you had to come here again.' She ran down the stairs, one hand lightly touching the broad rail. 'It's two months and four days. Summer's gone!'

'I meant to come before, but Fate prevented.'

'I knew it. Please do something to that fire. They won't let me play with it, but I can feel it's behaving badly. Hit it!'

I looked on either side of the deep fireplace, and found but a half-charred hedge-stake with which I punched a black log into flame.

'It never goes out, day or night,' she said, as though explaining. 'In case any one comes in with cold toes, you see.'

'It's even lovelier inside than it was out,' I murmured. The red light poured itself along the age-polished dusky panels till the Tudor roses and lions of the gallery took colour and motion. An old eagle-topped convex mirror gathered the picture into its mysterious heart, distorting afresh the distorted shadows, and curving the gallery lines into the curves of a ship. The day was shutting down in half a gale as the fog turned to stringy scud. Through the uncurtained mullions of the broad window I could see the valiant horsemen of the lawn rear and recover against the wind that taunted them with legions of dead leaves.

'Yes, it must be beautiful,' she said. 'Would you like to go over it? There's still light enough upstairs.'

I followed her up the unflinching, waggon-wide staircase to the gallery whence opened the thin fluted Elizabethan doors.

'Feel how they put the latch low down for the sake of the children.' She swung a light door inward.

'By the way, where are they?' I asked. 'I haven't even heard them today.'

She did not answer at once. Then, 'I can only hear them,' she replied softly. 'This is one of their rooms – everything ready, you see.'

She pointed into a heavily-timbered room. There were little low gate tables and children's chairs. A doll's house, its hooked front half open, faced a great dappled rocking-horse, from whose padded saddle it was but a child's scramble to the broad window-seat overlooking the lawn. A toy gun lay in a corner beside a gilt wooden cannon.

'Surely they've only just gone,' I whispered. In the failing light a door creaked cautiously. I heard the rustle of a frock and the patter of feet – quick feet through a room beyond.

'I heard that,' she cried triumphantly. 'Did you? Children, oh, children! Where are you?'

The voice filled the walls that held it lovingly to the last perfect note, but there came no answering shout such as I had heard in the garden. We hurried on from room to oak-floored room; up a step here, down three steps there; among a maze of passages; always mocked by our quarry. One might as well have tried to work an unstopped warren with a single ferret. There were bolt-holes innumerable – recesses in walls, embrasures of deep-slitten windows now darkened, whence they could start up behind us; and abandoned fireplaces, six feet deep in the masonry, as well as the tangle of communicating doors. Above all, they had the twilight for their helper in our game. I had caught one or two joyous chuckles of evasion, and once or twice had seen the silhouette of a child's frock against some darkening window at the end of a passage; but we returned empty-handed to the gallery, just as a middle-aged woman was setting a lamp in its niche.

'No, I haven't seen her either this evening, Miss Florence,' I heard her say, 'but that Turpin he says he wants to see you about his shed.'

'Oh, Mr Turpin must want to see me very badly. Tell him to come to the hall, Mrs Madden.'

I looked down into the hall whose only light was the dulled fire, and deep in the shadow I saw them at last. They must have slipped down while we were in the passages, and now thought themselves perfectly hidden behind an old gilt leather screen. By child's law, my fruitless chase was as good as an introduction, but since I had taken so much trouble I resolved to force them to come forward later by the simple trick, which children detest, of pretending not to notice them. They lay close, in a little huddle, no more than shadows except when a quick flame betrayed an outline.

'And now we'll have some tea,' she said. 'I believe I ought to have offered it you at first, but one doesn't arrive at manners somehow when one lives alone and is considered – h'm – peculiar.' Then with very pretty scorn, 'Would you like a lamp to see to eat by?'

'The firelight's much pleasanter, I think.' We descended into that delicious gloom and Madden brought tea.

I took my chair in the direction of the screen ready to surprise or be surprised as the game should go, and at her permission, since a hearth is always sacred, bent forward to play with the fire.

'Where do you get these beautiful short faggots from?' I asked idly. 'Why, they are tallies!'

'Of course,' she said. 'As I can't read or write I'm driven back on the early English tally for my accounts. Give me one and I'll tell you what it meant.'

I passed her an unburned hazel-tally, about a foot long, and she ran her thumb down the nicks.

'This is the milk-record for the home farm for the month of April last year, in gallons,' said she. 'I don't know what I should have done without tallies. An old forester of mine taught me the system. It's out of date now for everyone else; but my tenants respect it. One of them's coming now to see me. Oh, it doesn't matter. He has no business here out of office hours. He's a greedy, ignorant man – very greedy, or – he wouldn't come here after dark.'

'Have you much land then?'

'Only a couple of hundred acres in hand, thank goodness. The other six hundred are nearly all let to folk who knew my folk before me, but this Turpin is quite a new man – and a highway robber.'

'But are you sure I shan't be —'

'Certainly not. You have the right. He hasn't any children.'

'Ah, the children!' I said, and slid my low chair back till it nearly touched the screen that hid them. 'I wonder whether they'll come out for me.'

There was a murmur of voices – Madden's and a deeper note – at the low, dark side door, and a ginger-headed, canvas-gaitered giant of the unmistakable tenant-farmer type stumbled or was pushed in.

'Come to the fire, Mr Turpin,' said she.

'If – if you please, Miss, I'll be quite as well by the door.' He clung to the latch as he spoke like a frightened child. Of a sudden I realized that he was in the grip of some almost overpowering fear.

'Well?'

'About that new shed for the young stock – that was all. These first autumn storms settin' in . . . but I'll come again, Miss.' His teeth did not chatter much more than the door-latch.

'I think not,' she answered levelly. 'The new shed – m'm. What did my agent write you on the fifteenth?'

'I – fancied p'raps that if I came to see you – ma – man to man like, Miss. But —'

His eyes rolled into every corner of the room wide with horror. He half opened the door through which he had entered, but I noticed it shut again – from without and firmly.

'He wrote what I told him,' she went on. 'You are overstocked already. Dunnett's Farm never carried more than fifty bullocks – even in Mr Wright's time. And *he* used cake. You've sixty-seven and you don't cake. You've broken the lease in that respect. You're dragging the heart out of the farm.'

'I'm – I'm getting some minerals – superphosphates – next week. I've as good as ordered a truck-load already. I'll go down to the station tomorrow about 'em. Then I can come and see you man to man like, Miss, in the daylight . . . That gentleman's not going away, is he?' He almost shrieked.

I had only slid the chair a little farther back, reaching behind me to tap on the leather of the screen, but he jumped like a rat.

'No. Please attend to me, Mr Turpin.' She turned in her chair and faced him with his back to the door. It was an old and sordid little piece of scheming that she forced from him – his plea for the new cow-shed at his landlady's expense; that he might with the covered manure pay his next year's rent out of the valuation after, as she made clear, he had bled the enriched pastures to the bone. I could not but admire the intensity of his greed, when I saw him outfacing for its sake whatever terror it was that ran wet on his forehead.

I ceased to tap the leather – was, indeed, calculating the cost of the shed – when I felt my relaxed hand taken and turned softly between the soft hands of a child. So at last I had triumphed. In a moment I would turn and acquaint myself with those quick-footed wanderers . . .

The little brushing kiss fell in the centre of my palm – as a gift on which the fingers were, once, expected to close: as the all-faithful half-reproachful signal of a waiting child not used to neglect even when grown-ups were busiest – a fragment of the mute code devised very long ago.

Then I knew. And it was as though I had known from the first day when I looked across the lawn at the high window.

I heard the door shut. The woman turned to me in silence, and I felt that she knew.

What time passed after this I cannot say. I was roused by the fall of a log, and mechanically rose to put it back. Then I returned to my place in the chair very close to the screen.

'Now you understand,' she whispered, across the packed shadows.

'Yes, I understand – now. Thank you.'

'I – I only hear them.' She bowed her head in her hands. 'I have no right, you know – no other right. I have neither borne nor lost – neither borne nor lost!'

'Be very glad then,' said I, for my soul was torn open within me.

'Forgive me!'

She was still, and I went back to my sorrow and my joy.

'It was because I loved them so,' she said at last, brokenly. '*That* was why it was, even from the first – even before I knew that they – they were all I should ever have. And I loved them so!'

She stretched out her arms to the shadows and the shadows within the shadow.

'They came because I loved them – because I needed them. I – I must have made them come. Was that wrong, think you?'

'No – no.'

'I – I grant you that the toys and – and all that sort of thing were nonsense, but – but I used to so hate empty rooms myself when I was little.' She pointed to the gallery. 'And the passages all empty . . . And how could I ever bear the garden door shut? Suppose —'

'Don't! For pity's sake, don't!' I cried. The twilight had brought a cold rain with gusty squalls that plucked at the leaded windows.

'And the same thing with keeping the fire in all night. *I* don't think it so foolish – do you?'

I looked at the broad brick hearth, saw, through tears, I believe, that there was no unpassable iron on or near it, and bowed my head.

'I did all that and lots of other things – just to make believe. Then they came. I heard them, but I didn't know that they were not mine by right till Mrs Madden told me —'

'The butler's wife? What?'

'One of them – I heard – she saw. And knew. Hers! *Not* for me. I didn't know at first. Perhaps I was jealous. Afterwards, I began to understand that it was only because I loved them, not because — Oh, you *must* bear or lose,' she said piteously. 'There is no other way – and yet they love me. They must! Don't they?'

There was no sound in the room except the lapping voices of the fire, but we two listened intently, and she at least took comfort from what she heard. She recovered herself and half rose. I sat still in my chair by the screen.

'Don't think me a wretch to whine about myself like this, but – but I'm all in the dark, you know, and *you* can see.'

In truth I could see, and my vision confirmed me in my resolve, though that was like the very parting of spirit and flesh. Yet a little longer I would stay since it was the last time.

'You think it is wrong, then?' she cried sharply, though I had said nothing.

'Not for you. A thousand times no. For you it is right . . . I am grateful to you beyond words. For me it would be wrong. For me only . . .'

'Why?' she said, but passed her hand before her face as she had done at our second meeting in the wood. 'Oh, I see,' she went on simply as a child. 'For you it would be wrong.' Then with a little indrawn laugh, 'And, d'you remember, I called you lucky – once – at first. You who must never come here again!'

She left me to sit a little longer by the screen, and I heard the sound of her feet die out along the gallery above.

FROM LYDEN'S *IRENIUS*

ACT III. SCENE 2

GOW: Had it been your Prince instead of a groom caught in this noose there's not an astrologer of the city –

PRINCE: Sacked! Sacked! We were a city yesterday.

GOW: So be it, but I was not governor. Not an astrologer, but would ha' sworn he'd foreseen it at the last versary of Venus, when Vulcan caught her with Mars in the house of stinking Capricorn. But since 'tis Jack of the Straw that hangs, the forgetful stars had it not on their tablets.

PRINCE: Another life! Were there any left to die? How did the poor fool come by it?

GOW: *Simpliciter* thus. She that damned him to death knew not that she did it, or would have died ere she had done it. For she loved him. He that hangs him does so in obedience to the Duke, and asks no more than 'Where is the rope?' The Duke, very exactly he hath told us, works God's will, in which holy employ he's not to be questioned. We have then left upon this finger, only Jack whose soul now plucks the left sleeve of Destiny in Hell to overtake why she clapped him up like a fly on a sunny wall. Whuff! Soh!

PRINCE: Your cloak, Ferdinand. I'll sleep now.

FERDINAND: Sleep, then . . . He, too, loved his life?

GOW: He was born of woman . . . but at the end threw life from him, like your Prince, for a little sleep . . . 'Have I any look of a King?' said he, clanking his chain – 'to be so baited on all sides by Fortune, that I must e'en die now to live with myself one day longer.' I left him railing at Fortune and woman's love.

FERDINAND: Ah, woman's love!

(*Aside*) Who knows not Fortune, glutted on easy thrones,
Stealing from feasts as rare to coneycatch
Privily in the hedgerows for a clown
With that same cruel-lustful hand and eye,
Those nails and wedges, that one hammer and lead,
And the very gerb of long-stored lightnings loosed
Yesterday 'gainst some King.

Mrs Bathurst

THE day that I chose to visit HMS *Peridot* in Simon's Bay was the day that the Admiral had chosen to send her up the coast. She was just steaming out to sea as my train came in, and since the rest of the Fleet were either coaling or busy at the rifle-ranges a thousand feet up the hill, I found myself stranded, lunchless, on the sea-front with no hope of return to Cape Town before 5 p.m. At this crisis I had the luck to come across my friend Inspector Hooper, Cape Government Railways, in command of an engine and a brake-van chalked for repair.

'If you get something to eat,' he said, 'I'll run you down to Glengariff siding till the goods comes along. It's cooler there than here, you see.'

I got food and drink from the Greeks who sell all things at a price, and the engine trotted us a couple of miles up the line to a bay of drifted sand and a plank-platform half buried in sand not a hundred yards from the edge of the surf. Moulded dunes, whiter than any snow, rolled far inland up a brown and purple valley of splintered rocks and dry scrub. A crowd of Malays hauled at a net beside two blue and green boats on the beach; a picnic party danced and shouted barefoot where a tiny river trickled across the flat, and a circle of dry hills, whose feet were set in sands of silver, locked us in against a seven-coloured sea. At either horn of the bay the railway line, cut just above high water mark, ran round a shoulder of piled rocks, and disappeared.

'You see, there's always a breeze here,' said Hooper, opening the door as the engine left us in the siding on the sand, and the strong south-easter buffeting under Elsie's Peak dusted sand into our tickey beer. Presently he sat down to a file full of spiked documents. He had returned from a long trip up-country, where he had been reporting on damaged rolling-stock, as far away as Rhodesia. The weight of the bland wind on my eyelids; the song of it under the car-roof, and high up among the rocks; the drift of fine grains chasing each other musically ashore; the tramp of the surf; the voices of the picnickers; the rustle of Hooper's file, and the presence of the assured sun, joined with the beer to cast me into magical slumber.

The hills of False Bay were just dissolving into those of fairyland when I heard footsteps on the sand outside, and the clink of our couplings.

'Stop that!' snapped Hooper, without raising his head from his work. 'It's those dirty little Malay boys, you see: they're always playing with the trucks . . . '

'Don't be hard on 'em. The railway's a general refuge in Africa,' I replied.

''Tis – up-country at any rate. That reminds me,' he felt in his waistcoat-pocket. 'I've got a curiosity for you from Wankies – beyond Bulawayo. It's more of a souvenir perhaps than —'

'The old hotel's inhabited,' cried a voice. 'White men, from the language. Marines to the front! Come on, Pritch. Here's your Belmont. Wha – i – i!'

The last word dragged like a rope as Mr Pyecroft ran round to the open door, and stood looking up into my face. Behind him an enormous sergeant of marines trailed a stalk of dried seaweed, and dusted the sand nervously from his fingers.

'What are you doing here?' I asked. 'I thought the *Hierophant* was down the coast?'

'We came in last Tuesday – from Tristan d'Acunha – for overhaul and we shall be in dockyard 'ands for two months, with boiler-seatings.'

'Come and sit down.' Hooper put away the file.

'This is Mr Hooper of the Railway,' I explained, as Pyecroft turned to haul up the black-moustached sergeant.

'This is Sergeant Pritchard, of the *Agaric*, an old shipmate,' said he. 'We were strollin' on the beach.' The monster blushed and nodded. He filled up one side of the van when he sat down.

'And this is my friend, Mr Pyecroft,' I added to Hooper, already busy with the extra beer which my prophetic soul had bought from the Greeks.

'*Moi aussi*,' quoth Pyecroft, and drew out beneath his coat a labelled quart bottle.

'Why, it's Bass!' cried Hooper.

'It was Pritchard,' said Pyecroft. 'They can't resist him.'

'That's not so,' said Pritchard mildly.

'Not *verbatim* per'aps, but the look in the eye came to the same thing.'

'Where was it?' I demanded.

'Just on beyond here – at Kalk Bay. She was slappin' a rug in a back veranda. Pritch 'adn't more than brought his batteries to bear, before she stepped indoors an' sent it flyin' over the wall.'

Pyecroft patted the warm bottle.

'It was all a mistake,' said Pritchard. 'I shouldn't wonder if she mistook me for Maclean. We're about of a size.'

I had heard householders of Muizenberg, St James, and Kalk Bay complain of the difficulty of keeping beer or good servants at the seaside, and I began to see the reason. None the less, it was excellent Bass, and I too drank to the health of that large-minded maid.

'It's the uniform that fetches 'em, an' they fetch it,' said Pyecroft. 'My simple navy blue is respectable, but not fascinatin'. Now Pritch in 'is Number One rig is always "purr Mary, on the terrace" – *ex officio* as you might say.'

'She took me for Maclean, I tell you,' Pritchard insisted. 'Why – why – to listen to him you wouldn't think that only yesterday —'

'Pritch,' said Pyecroft, 'be warned in time. If we begin tellin' what we know about each other we'll be turned out of the pub. Not to mention aggravated desertion on several occasions —'

'Never anything more than absence without leaf - I defy you to prove it,' said the sergeant hotly. 'An' if it comes to that, how about Vancouver in '87?'

'How about it? Who pulled bow in the gig going ashore? Who told Boy Niven . . . ?'

'Surely you were court-martialled for that?' I said. The story of Boy Niven who lured seven or eight able-bodied seamen and marines into the woods of British Columbia used to be a legend of the Fleet.

'Yes, we were court-martialled to rights,' said Pritchard, 'but we should have been tried for murder if Boy Niven 'adn't been unusually tough. He told us he had an uncle 'oo'd give us land to farm. 'E said he was born at the back o' Vancouver Island, and *all* the time the beggar was a barmy Barnado orphan!'

'*But* we believed him,' said Pyecroft. 'I did – you did – Paterson did – an' 'oo was the marine that married the cocoanut-woman afterwards – him with the mouth?'

'Oh, Jones, Spit-Kid Jones. I 'aven't thought of 'im in years,' said Pritchard. 'Yes, Spit-Kid believed it, an' George Anstey and Moon. We were very young an' very curious.'

'*But* lovin' an' trustful to a degree,' said Pyecroft.

'Remember when 'e told us to walk in single file for fear o' bears? Remember, Pye, when 'e 'opped about in that bog full o' ferns an' sniffed an' said 'e could smell the smoke of 'is uncle's farm? An' *all* the time it was a dirty little outlyin' uninhabited island. We walked round it in a day, an' come back to our boat lyin' on the beach. A whole day Boy Niven kept us walkin' in circles lookin' for 'is uncle's farm! He said his uncle was compelled by the law of the land to give us a farm!'

'Don't get hot, Pritch. We believed,' said Pyecroft.

'He'd been readin' books. He only did it to get a run ashore an' have himself talked of. A day an' a night – eight of us – followin' Boy Niven round an uninhabited island in the Vancouver archipelago! Then the picket came for us an' a nice pack o' idiots we looked!'

'What did you get for it?' Hooper asked.

'Heavy thunder with continuous lightning for two hours. Thereafter sleet-squalls, a confused sea, and cold, unfriendly weather till conclusion o' cruise,' said Pyecroft. 'It was only what we expected, but what we felt – an' I assure you, Mr Hooper, even a sailor-man has a heart to break – was bein' told that we able seamen an' promisin' marines 'ad misled Boy Niven. Yes, we poor back-to-the-landers was supposed to 'ave misled him! He rounded on us, o' course, an' got off easy.'

'Excep' for what we gave him in the steerin'-flat when we came out o' cells. 'Eard anything of 'im lately, Pye?'

'Signal boatswain in the Channel Fleet, I believe – Mr L.L. Niven is.'

'An' Anstey died o' fever in Benin,' Pritchard mused. 'What come to Moon? Spit-Kid we know about.'

'Moon – Moon! Now where did I last . . . ? Oh yes, when I was in the *Palladium*. I met Quigley at Buncrana Station. He told me Moon 'ad run when the *Astrild* sloop was cruising among the South Seas three years back. He always showed signs o' bein' a Mormonastic beggar. Yes, he slipped off quietly an' they 'adn't time to chase 'im round the islands even if the navigatin' officer 'ad been equal to the job.'

'Wasn't he?' said Hooper.

'Not so. Accordin' to Quigley the *Astrild* spent half her commission rompin' up the beach like a she-turtle, an' the other half hatching turtles' eggs on the top o' numerous reefs. When she was docked at Sydney her copper looked like Aunt Maria's washing on the line – an' her 'midship frames was sprung. The commander swore the dockyard 'ad done it haulin' the pore thing on to the slips. They *do* do strange things at sea, Mr Hooper.'

'Ah! I'm not a taxpayer,' said Hooper, and opened a fresh bottle. The sergeant seemed to be one who had a difficulty in dropping subjects.

'How it all comes back, don't it?' he said. 'Why, Moon must 'ave 'ad sixteen years' service before he ran.'

'It takes 'em at all ages. Look at – you know,' said Pyecroft.

'Who?' I asked.

'A service man within eighteen months of his pension is the party you're thinkin' of,' said Pritchard. 'A warrant 'oo's name begins with a V, isn't it?'

'But, in a way o' puttin' it, we can't say that he actually did desert,' Pyecroft suggested.

'Oh no,' said Pritchard. 'It was only permanent absence up-country without leaf. That was all.'

'Up-country?' said Hooper. 'Did they circulate his description?'

'What for?' said Pritchard, most impolitely.

'Because deserters are like columns in the war. They don't move away from the line, you see. I've known a chap caught at Salisbury that way tryin' to get to Nyassa. They tell me, but o' course I don't know, that they don't ask questions on the Nyassa Lake Flotilla up there. I've heard of a P and O quartermaster in full command of an armed launch there.'

'Do you think Click 'ud ha' gone up that way?' Pritchard asked.

'There's no saying. He was sent up to Bloemfontein to take over some Navy ammunition left in the fort. We know he took it over and saw it into the trucks. Then there was no more Click – then or thereafter. Four months ago it transpired, and thus the *casus belli* stands at present,' said Pyecroft.

'What were his marks?' said Hooper again.

'Does the Railway get a reward for returnin' 'em, then?' said Pritchard.

'If I did d'you suppose I'd talk about it?' Hooper retorted angrily.

'You seemed so very interested,' said Pritchard with equal crispness.

'Why was he called Click?' I asked, to tide over an uneasy little break in the conversation. The two men were staring at each other very fixedly.

'Because of an ammunition hoist carryin' away,' said Pyecroft. 'And it carried away four of 'is teeth – on the lower port side, wasn't it, Pritch? The substitutes which he bought weren't screwed home, in a manner o' sayin'. When he talked fast they used to lift a little on the bedplate. 'Ence, "Click". They called 'im a superior man, which is what we'd call a long, black-'aired, genteelly speakin', 'alf-bred beggar on the lower deck.'

'Four false teeth in the lower left jaw,' said Hooper, his hand in his waistcoat-pocket. 'What tattoo marks?'

'Look here,' began Pritchard, half-rising. 'I'm sure we're very grateful to you as a gentleman for your 'orspitality, but per'aps we may 'ave made an error in —'

I looked at Pyecroft for aid – Hooper was crimsoning rapidly.

'If the fat marine now occupying the foc'sle will kindly bring 'is *status quo* to an anchor yet once more, we may be able to talk like gentlemen – not to say friends,' said Pyecroft. 'He regards you, Mr Hooper, as a emissary of the law.'

'I only wish to observe that when a gentleman exhibits such a peculiar, or I should rather say, such a *bloomin'* curiosity in identification marks as our friend here —'

'Mr Pritchard,' I interposed, 'I'll take all the responsibility for Mr Hooper.'

'An' *you*'ll apologize all round,' said Pyecroft. 'You're a rude little man, Pritch.'

'But how was I —' he began, wavering.

'I don't know an' I don't care. Apologize!'

The giant looked round bewildered and took our little hands into his vast grip, one by one.

'I was wrong,' he said meekly as a sheep. 'My suspicions were unfounded. Mr Hooper, I apologize.'

'You did quite right to look out for your own end o' the line,' said Hooper. 'I'd ha' done the same with a gentleman I didn't know, you see. If you don't mind I'd like to hear a little more o' your Mr Vickery. It's safe with me, you see.'

'Why did Vickery run?' I began, but Pyecroft's smile made me turn my question to 'Who was she?'

'She kep' a little hotel at Hauraki – near Auckland,' said Pyecroft.

'By Gawd!' roared Pritchard, slapping his hand on his leg. 'Not Mrs Bathurst!'

Pyecroft nodded slowly, and the sergeant called all the powers of darkness to witness his bewilderment.

'So far as I could get at it, Mrs B was the lady in question.'

'But Click was married,' cried Pritchard.

'An' 'ad a fifteen-year-old daughter. 'E's shown me her photograph. Settin' that aside, so to say, 'ave you ever found these little things make much difference? Because I haven't.'

'Good Lord Alive an' Watchin'! . . . Mrs Bathurst . . .' Then with another roar: 'You can say what you please, Pye, but you don't make me believe it was any of 'er fault. She wasn't *that*!'

'If I was going to say what I please, I'd begin by callin' you a silly ox an' work up to the higher pressures at leisure. I'm trying to say solely what transpired. M'rover, for once you're right. It wasn't her fault.'

'You couldn't 'aven't made me believe it if it 'ad been,' was the answer.

Such faith in a sergeant of marines interested me greatly. 'Never mind about that,' I cried. 'Tell me what she was like.'

'She was a widow,' said Pyecroft. 'Left so very young and never re-spliced. She kep' a little hotel for warrants and non-coms close to Auckland, an' she always wore black silk, and 'er neck —'

'You ask what she was like,' Pritchard broke in. 'Let me give you an instance. I was at Auckland first in '97, at the end o' the *Marroquin*'s commission, an' as I'd been promoted I went up with the others. She used to look after us all, an' she never lost by it – not a penny! "Pay me now," she'd say, "or settle later. I know you won't let me suffer. Send the money from home if you like." Why, gentlemen all, I tell you I've seen that lady take her own gold watch an' chain off her neck in the bar an' pass it to a bosun 'oo'd come ashore without 'is ticker an' 'ad to catch the last boat. "I don't know your name," she said, "but when you've done with it, you'll find plenty that know me on the front. Send it back by one o' them" And it was worth thirty pounds if it was worth 'arf-a-crown. The little gold watch, Pye, with the blue monogram at the back. But, as I was sayin', in those days she kep' a beer that agreed with me – Slits it was called. One way an' another I must 'ave punished a good few bottles of it while we was in the bay – comin' ashore every night or so. Chaffin' across the bar like, once when we were alone, "Mrs B," I said, "when next I call I want you to remember that this is my particular – just as you're my particular." (She'd let you go *that* far!) "Just as you're my particular," I said. "Oh, thank you, Sergeant Pritchard," she says, an' put 'er hand up to the curl be'ind 'er ear. Remember that way she had, Pye?'

'I think so,' said the sailor.

'Yes. "Thank you, Sergeant Pritchard," she says. "The least I can do is to mark it for you in case you change your mind. There's no great demand for it in the Fleet," she says, "but to make sure I'll put it at the back o' the shelf," an' she snipped off a piece of her hair ribbon with that old dolphin cigar-cutter on the bar – remember it, Pye? – an' she tied a bow round what was left – just four bottles. That was '97 – no, '96. In '98 I was in the *Resilient* – China station – full commission. In Nineteen One, mark you, I was in the *Carthusian*, back in Auckland Bay again. Of course I went up to Mrs B's with the rest of us to see how things were goin'. They were the same as ever. (Remember the big tree on the pavement by the side-bar, Pye?) I never said anythin' in special (there was too many of us talkin' to her), but she saw me at once.'

'That wasn't difficult?' I ventured.

'Ah, but wait. I was comin' up to the bar, when, "Ada," she says to her niece, "get me Sergeant Pritchard's particular," and, gentlemen all, I tell you before I could shake 'ands with the lady, there were those four bottles o' Slits, with 'er 'air-ribbon in a bow round each o' their necks, set down in front o' me, an' as she drew the cork she looked at me under her eyebrows in that blindish way she had o' lookin', an', "Sergeant Pritchard," she says, "I do 'ope you 'aven't changed your mind about your particulars." That's the kind o' woman she was – after five years!'

'I don't *see* her yet somehow,' said Hooper, but with sympathy.

'She – she never scrupled to feed a lame duck or set 'er foot on a scorpion at any time of 'er life,' Pritchard added valiantly.

'That don't help me either. My mother's like that for one.'

The giant heaved inside his uniform and rolled his eyes at the car-roof. Said Pyecroft suddenly:

'How many women have you been intimate with all over the world, Pritch?'

Pritchard blushed plum-colour to the short hairs of his seventeen-inch neck.

''Undreds,' said Pyecroft. 'So've I. How many of 'em can you remember in your own mind, settin' aside the first – an' per'aps the last – *and one more*?'

'Few, wonderful few, now I tax myself,' said Sergeant Pritchard relievedly.

'An' how many times might you 'ave been at Auckland?'

'One – two,' he began – 'why, I can't make it more than three times in ten years. But I can remember every time that I ever saw Mrs B.'

'So can I – an' I've only been to Auckland twice – how she stood an' what she was sayin' an' what she looked like. That's the secret. 'Tisn't beauty, so to speak, nor good talk necessarily. It's just It. Some women'll stay in a man's memory if they once walk down a street, but most of 'em you can live with a month on end, an' next commission you'd be put to it to certify whether they talked in their sleep or not, as one might say.'

'Ah!' said Hooper. 'That's more the idea. I've known just two women of that nature.'

'An' it was no fault o' theirs?' asked Pritchard.

'None whatever. I know *that*!'

'An' if a man gets struck with that kind o' woman, Mr Hooper?' Pritchard went on.

'He goes crazy – or just saves himself,' was the slow answer.

'You've hit it,' said the sergeant. 'You've seen an' known somethin' in the course o' your life, Mr Hooper. I'm lookin' at you!' He set down his bottle.

'And how often had Vickery seen her?' I asked.

'That's the dark an' bloody mystery,' Pyecroft answered. 'I'd never come across him till I come out in the *Hierophant* just now, an' there wasn't any one in the ship who knew much about him. You see, he was what you call a superior man. 'E spoke to me once or twice about Auckland and Mrs B on the voyage out. I called that to mind subsequently. There must 'ave been a good deal between 'em, to my way o' thinkin'. Mind you, I'm only giving you my *résumé* of it all, because all I know is second-hand so to speak, or rather I should say more than second-'and.'

'How?' said Hooper peremptorily. 'You must have seen it or heard it.'

'Ye-es,' said Pyecroft. 'I used to think seein' and hearin' was the only regulation aids to ascertainin' facts, but as we get older we get more accommodatin'. The cylinders work easier, I suppose . . . Were you in Cape Town last December when Phyllis's Circus came?'

'No – up-country,' said Hooper, a little nettled at the change of venue.

'I ask because they had a new turn of a scientific nature called "Home and Friends for a Tickey".'

'Oh, you mean the cinematograph – the pictures of prize-fights and steamers. I've seen 'em up-country.'

'Biograph or cinematograph was what I was alludin' to. London Bridge with the omnibuses – a troopship goin' to the war – marines on parade at Portsmouth, an' the Plymouth Express arrivin' at Paddin'ton.'

'Seen 'em all. Seen 'em all,' said Hooper impatiently.

'We *Hierophants* came in just before Christmas week an' leaf was easy.'

'I think a man gets fed up with Cape Town quicker than anywhere else on the station. Why, even Durban's more like Nature. We was there for Christmas,' Pritchard put in.

'Not bein' a devotee of Indian *peeris*, as our doctor said to the Pusser, I can't exactly say. Phyllis's was good enough after musketry practice at Mozambique. I couldn't get off the first two or three nights on account of what you might call an imbroglio with our torpedo lieutenant in the submerged flat, where some pride of the West Country had sugared up a gyroscope; but I remember Vickery went ashore with our Carpenter Rigdon – old Crocus we called him.

As a general rule Crocus never left 'is ship unless an' until he was 'oisted out with a winch, but *when* 'e went 'e would return noddin' like a lily gemmed with dew. We smothered him down below that night, but the things 'e said about Vickery as a fittin' playmate for a warrant officer of 'is cubic capacity, before we got him quiet, was what I should call pointed.'

'I've been with Crocus – in the *Redoubtable*,' said the sergeant. 'He's a character if there is one.'

'Next night I went into Cape Town with Dawson and Pratt; but just at the door of the Circus I came across Vickery. "Oh!" he says, "you're the man I'm looking for. Come and sit next me. This way to the shillin' places!" I went astern at once, protestin' because tickey seats better suited my so-called finances. "Come on," says Vickery, "I'm payin'." Naturally I abandoned Pratt and Dawson in anticipation o' drinks to match the seats. "No," he says, when this was 'inted – "not now. Not now. As many as you please afterwards, but I want you sober for the occasion." I caught 'is face under a lamp just then, an' the appearance of it quite cured me of my thirst. Don't mistake. It didn't frighten me. It made me anxious. I can't tell you what it was like, but that was the effect which it 'ad on me. If you want to know, it reminded me of those things in bottles in those herbalistic shops at Plymouth – preserved in spirits of wine. White an' crumply things – previous to birth as you might say.'

'You 'ave a beastial mind, Pye,' said the sergeant, relighting his pipe.

'Perhaps. We were in the front row, an' "Home an' Friends" came on early. Vickery touched me on the knee when the number went up. "If you see anything that strikes you," he says, "drop me a hint"; then he went on clicking. We saw London Bridge an' so forth an' so on, an' it was most interestin'. I'd never seen it before. You 'eard a little dynamo like buzzin', but the pictures were the real thing – alive an' movin'.'

'I've seen 'em,' said Hooper. 'Of course they are taken from the very thing itself – you see.'

'Then the Western Mail came in to Paddin'ton on the big magic-lantern sheet. First we saw the platform empty an' the porters standin' by. Then the engine come in, head on, an' the women in the front row jumped: she headed so straight. Then the doors opened and the passengers came out and the porters got the luggage – just like life. Only – only when any one came down too far towards us that was watchin', they walked right out o' the picture, so to speak. I was 'ighly interested, I can tell you. So were all of us. I watched an old man with a rug 'oo'd dropped a book an' was tryin' to pick it up, when quite slowly, from be'ind two porters – carryin' a little reticule an' lookin' from side to side – comes out Mrs Bathurst. There was no mistakin' the walk in a hundred thousand. She come forward – right forward – she looked out straight at us with that blindish look which Pritch alluded to. She walked on and on till she melted out of the picture – like – like a shadow jumpin' over a candle, an' as she went I 'eard Dawson in the tickey seats be'ind sing out: "Christ! there's Mrs B!"'

Hooper swallowed his spittle and leaned forward intently.

'Vickery touched me on the knee again. He was clickin' his four false teeth with his jaw down like an enteric at the last kick. "Are you sure?" says he. "Sure," I says, "didn't you 'ear Dawson give tongue? Why, it's the woman herself." "I was sure before," he says, "but I brought you to make sure. Will you come again with me tomorrow?"

'"Willingly," I says, "it's like meetin' old friends."

'"Yes," he says, openin' his watch, "very like. It will be four-and-twenty hours less four minutes before I see her again. Come and have a drink," he says. "It may amuse you, but it's no sort of earthly use to me." He went out shaking his head an' stumblin' over people's feet as if he was drunk already. I anticipated a swift drink an' a speedy return, because I wanted to see the performin' elephants. Instead o' which Vickery began to navigate the town at the rate o' knots, lookin' in at a bar every three minutes approximate Greenwich time. I'm not a drinkin' man, though there are those present' – he cocked his unforgettable eye at me – 'who may have seen me more or less imbued with the fragrant spirit. None the less when I drink I like to do it at anchor an' not at an average speed of eighteen knots on the measured mile. There's a tank as you might say at the back o' that big hotel up the hill – what do they call it?'

'The Molteno Reservoir,' I suggested, and Hooper nodded.

'That was his limit o' drift. We walked there an' we come down through the Gardens – there was a south-easter blowin' – an' we finished up by the docks. Then we bore up the road to Salt River, and wherever there was a pub Vickery put in sweatin'. He didn't look at what he drunk – he didn't look at the change. He walked an' he drunk an' he perspired in rivers. I understood why old Crocus 'ad come back in the condition 'e did, because Vickery an' I 'ad two an' a half hours o' this gypsy manoeuvre, an' when we got back to the station there wasn't a dry atom on or in me.'

'Did he say anything?' Pritchard asked.

'The sum total of 'is conversation from 7.45 p.m. till 11.15 p.m. was

"Let's have another." Thus the mornin' an' the evenin' were the first day, as Scripture says . . . To abbreviate a lengthy narrative, I went into Cape Town for five consecutive nights with Master Vickery, and in that time I must 'ave logged about fifty knots over the ground an' taken in two gallon o' all the worst spirits south the Equator. The evolution never varied. Two shilling seats for us two; five minutes o' the pictures, an' perhaps forty-five seconds o' Mrs B walking down towards us with that blindish look in her eyes an' the reticule in her hand. Then out-walk – and drink till train time.'

'What did you think?' said Hooper, his hand fingering his waistcoat-pocket.

'Several things,' said Pyecroft. 'To tell you the truth, I aren't quite done thinkin' about it yet. Mad? The man was a dumb lunatic – must 'ave been for months – years p'raps. I know somethin' o' maniacs, as every man in the Service must. I've been shipmates with a mad skipper – an' a lunatic number one, but never both together, I thank 'Eaven. I could give you the names o' three captains now 'oo ought to be in an asylum, but you don't find me interferin' with the mentally afflicted till they begin to lay about 'em with rammers an' winch-handles. Only once I crept up a little into the wind towards Master Vickery. "I wonder what she's doin' in England," I says. "Don't it seem to you she's lookin' for somebody?" That was in the Gardens again, with the south-easter blowin' as we were makin' our desperate round. "She's lookin' for me," he says, stoppin' dead under a lamp an' clickin'. When he wasn't drinkin', in which case all 'is teeth clicked on the glass, 'e was clickin' 'is four false teeth like a Marconi ticker. "Yes! lookin' for me," he said, an' he went on very softly an' as you might say affectionately. "*But*," he went on, "in future, Mr Pyecroft, I should take it kindly if you'd confine your remarks to the drinks set before you. Otherwise," he says, "with the best will in the world towards you, I may find myself guilty of murder! Do you understand?" he says. "Perfectly," I says, "but would it at all soothe you to know that in such a case the chances o' your being killed are precisely equivalent o' me being outed." "Why, no," he says, "I'm almost afraid that 'ud be a temptation." Then I said – we was right under the lamp by that arch at the end o' the Gardens where the trams come round – "Assumin' murder was done – or attempted murder – I put it to you that you would still be left so badly crippled, as one might say, that your subsequent capture by the police – to 'oom you would 'ave to explain – would be largely inevitable." "That's better," 'e says, passin' 'is hands over his forehead. "That's much better, because," he says, "do you know, as I am now, Pye, I'm not so sure if I could explain anything much." Those were the only particular words I had with 'im in our walks as I remember.'

'What walks!' said Hooper, 'Oh my soul, what walks!'

'They were chronic,' said Pyecroft gravely, 'but I didn't anticipate any danger till the Circus left. Then I anticipated that, bein' deprived of 'is stimulant, he might react on me, so to say, with a hatchet. Consequently, after the final performance an' the ensuin' wet walk, I kep' myself aloof from my superior officer on board in the execution of 'is duty, as you might put it. Consequently, I was interested when the sentry informs me while I was passin' on my lawful occasions that Click had asked to see the captain. As a general rule warrant officers don't dissipate much of the owner's time, but Click put in an hour and more be'ind that door. My duties kep' me within eyeshot of it. Vickery came out first, an' 'e actually nodded at me an' smiled. This knocked me out o' the boat, because, havin' seen 'is face for five consecutive nights, I didn't anticipate any change there more than a condenser in hell, so to speak. The owner emerged later. His face didn't read off at all, so I fell back on his cox, 'oo'd been eight years with him and knew him better than boat signals. Lamson – that was the cox's name – crossed 'is bows once or twice at low speeds an' dropped down to me visibly concerned. "He's shipped 'is court-martial face," says Lamson. "Some one's goin' to be 'ung. I've never seen that look but once before, when they chucked the gun-sights overboard in the *Fantastic*." Throwin' gun-sights overboard, Mr Hooper, is the equivalent for mutiny in these degenerate days. It's done to attract the notice of the authorities an' the *Western Mornin' News* – generally by a stoker. Naturally, word went round the lower deck an' we had a private over'aul of our little consciences. But, barrin' a shirt which a second-class stoker said 'ad walked into 'is bag from the marines' flat by itself, nothin' vital transpired. The owner went about flyin' the signal for "attend public execution", so to say, but there was no corpse at the yard-arm. 'E lunched on the beach an' 'e returned with 'is regulation harbour-routine face about 3 p.m. Thus Lamson lost prestige for raising false alarms. The only person 'oo might 'ave connected the epicycloidal gears correctly was one Pyecroft, when he was told that Mr Vickery would go up-country the same evening to take over certain naval ammunition left after the war in Bloemfontein Fort. No details was ordered to accompany Master Vickery. He was told off first person singular – as a unit – by himself.'

The marine whistled penetratingly.

'That's what I thought,' said Pyecroft. 'I went ashore with him in the cutter an' 'e asked me to walk through the station. He was clickin' audibly, but otherwise seemed happy-ish.

'"You might like to know," he says, stoppin' just opposite the admiral's front gate, "that Phyllis's Circus will be performin' at Worcester tomorrow night. So I shall see 'er yet once again. You've been very patient with me," he says.

'"Look here, Vickery," I said, "this thing's come to be just as much as I can stand. Consume your own smoke. I don't want to know any more."

'"You!" he said. "What have you got to complain of? – you've only 'ad to watch. I'm *it*," he says, "but that's neither here nor there," he says. "I've one thing to say before shakin' 'ands. Remember," 'e says – we were just by the admiral's garden-gate then – "remember that I am *not* a murderer, because my lawful wife died in childbed six weeks after I came out. That much at least I am clear of," 'e says.

'"Then what have you done that signifies?" I said. "What's the rest of it?"

'"The rest," 'e says, "is silence," an' he shook 'ands and went clickin' into Simonstown station.'

'Did he stop to see Mrs Bathurst at Worcester?' I asked.

'It's not known. He reported at Bloemfontein, saw the ammunition into the trucks, and then 'e disappeared. Went out – deserted, if you care to put it so – within eighteen months of his pension, an' if what 'e said about 'is wife was true he was a free man as 'e then stood. How do you read it off?'

'Poor devil!' said Hooper. 'To see her that way every night! I wonder what it was.'

'I've made my 'ead ache in that direction many a long night.'

'But I'll swear Mrs B 'ad no 'and in it,' said the sergeant, unshaken.

'No. Whatever the wrong or deceit was, he did it, I'm sure o' that. I 'ad to look at 'is face for five consecutive nights. I'm not so fond o' navigatin' about Cape Town with a South-Easter blowin' these days. I can hear those teeth click, so to say.'

'Ah, those teeth,' said Hooper, and his hand went to his waistcoat-pocket once more. 'Permanent things false teeth are. You read about 'em in all the murder trials.'

'What d'you suppose the captain knew – or did?' I asked.

'I've never turned my searchlight that way,' Pyecroft answered unblushingly.

We all reflected together, and drummed on empty beer bottles as the picnic-party, sunburned, wet, and sandy, passed our door singing 'The Honeysuckle and the Bee'.

'Pretty girl under that kapje,' said Pyecroft.

'They never circulated his description?' said Pritchard.

'I was askin' you before these gentlemen came,' said Hooper to me, 'whether you knew Wankies – on the way to the Zambesi – beyond Bulawayo?'

'Would he pass there – tryin' to get to that Lake what's 'is name?' said Pritchard.

Hooper shook his head and went on: 'There's a curious bit o' line there, you see. It runs through solid teak forest – a sort o' mahogany really – seventy-two miles without a curve. I've had a train derailed there twenty-three times in forty miles. I was up there a month ago relievin' a sick inspector, you see. He told me to look out for a couple of tramps in the teak.'

'Two?' Pyecroft said. 'I don't envy that other man if —'

'We get heaps of tramps up there since the war. The inspector told me I'd find 'em at M'Bindwe siding waiting to go North. He'd given 'em some grub and quinine, you see. I went up on a construction train. I looked out for 'em. I saw them miles ahead along the straight, waiting in the teak. One of 'em was standin' up by the dead-end of the siding an' the other was squattin' down lookin' up at 'im, you see.'

'What did you do for 'em?' said Pritchard.

'There wasn't much I could do, except bury 'em. There'd been a bit of a thunderstorm in the teak, you see, and they were both stone dead and black as charcoal. That's what they really were, you see – charcoal. They fell to bits when we tried to shift 'em. The man who was standin' up had the false teeth. I saw 'em shinin' against the black. Fell to bits he did too, like his mate squatting down an' watching him, both of 'em wet in the rain. Both burned to charcoal, you see. And – that's what made me ask about marks just now – the false-toother was tattooed on the arms and chest – a crown and foul anchor with M.V. above.'

'I've seen that,' said Pyecroft quickly. 'It was so.'

'But if he was all charcoal-like?' said Pritchard, shuddering.

'You know how writing shows up white on a burned letter? Well, it was like that, you see. We buried 'em in the teak and I kept . . . But he was a friend of you two gentlemen, you see.'

Mr Hooper brought his hand away from his waistcoat-pocket – empty.

Pritchard covered his face with his hands for a moment, like a child shutting out an ugliness.

'And to think of her at Hauraki!' he murmured – 'with 'er

'air-ribbon on my beer. "Ada," she said to her niece . . . Oh my Gawd!' . . .

'On a summer afternoon, when the honeysuckle blooms,
And all Nature seems at rest,
Underneath the bower, 'mid the perfume of the flower,
Sat a maiden with the one she loves the best —'

sang the picnic-party waiting for their train at Glengariff.

'Well, I don't know how you feel about it,' said Pyecroft, 'but 'avin' seen 'is face for five consecutive nights on end, I'm inclined to finish what's left of the beer an' thank Gawd he's dead!'

THE BEE BOY'S SONG

Bees! Bees! Hark to your bees!
'Hide from your neighbours as much as you please,
But all that has happened, to *us* you must tell.
Or else we will give you no honey to sell!'

A maiden in her glory,
Upon her wedding-day,
Must tell her Bees the story,
Or else they'll fly away.
Fly away – die away –
Dwindle down and leave you!
But if you don't deceive your Bees,
Your Bees will not deceive you.

Marriage, birth or buryin',
News across the seas,
All you're sad or merry in,
You must tell the Bees.
Tell 'em coming in an' out,
Where the Fanners fan,
'Cause the Bees are justabout
As curious as a man!

Don't you wait where trees are,
When the lightnings play;
Nor don't you hate where Bees are,
Or else they'll pine away.
Pine away – dwine away –
Anything to leave you!
But if you never grieve your Bees,
Your Bees'll never grieve you.

'Dymchurch Flit'

JUST at dusk, a soft September rain began to fall on the hop-pickers. The mothers wheeled the bouncing perambulators out of the gardens; bins were put away, and tally-books made up. The young couples strolled home, two to each umbrella, and the single men walked behind them laughing. Dan and Una, who had been picking after their lessons, marched off to roast potatoes at the oast-house, where old Hobden, with Blue-eyed Bess, his lurcher dog, lived all the month through, drying the hops.

They settled themselves, as usual, on the sack-strewn cot in front of the fires, and, when Hobden drew up the shutter, stared, as usual, at the flameless bed of coals spouting its heat up the dark well of the old-fashioned roundel. Slowly he cracked off a few fresh pieces of coal, packed them, with fingers that never flinched, exactly where they would do most good; slowly he reached behind him till Dan tilted the potatoes into his iron scoop of a hand; carefully he arranged them round the fire, and then stood for a moment, black against the glare. As he closed the shutter, the oast-house seemed dark before the day's end, and he lit the candle in the lanthorn. The children liked all these things because they knew them so well.

The Bee Boy, Hobden's son, who is not quite right in his head, though he can do anything with bees, slipped in like a shadow. They only guessed it when Bess's stump-tail wagged against them.

A big voice began singing outside in the drizzle:

'Old Mother Laidinwool had nigh twelve months been dead,
She heard the hops were doing well, and then popped up her head.'

'There can't be two people made to holler like that!' cried old Hobden, wheeling round.

'For, says she, "The boys I've picked with when I was young and fair,
They're bound to be at hoppin', and I'm —"'

A man showed at the doorway.

'Well, well! They do say hoppin'll draw the very deadest, and now I belieft 'em. You, Tom? Tom Shoesmith!' Hobden lowered his lanthorn.

'You're a hem of a time makin' your mind to it, Ralph!' The stranger strode in – three full inches taller than Hobden, a grey-whiskered, brown-faced giant with clear blue eyes. They shook hands, and the children could hear the hard palms rasp together.

'You ain't lost none o' your grip,' said Hobden. 'Was it thirty or forty year back you broke my head at Peasmarsh Fair?'

'Only thirty an' no odds 'tween us regardin' heads, neither. You had it back at me with a hop-pole. How did we get home that night? Swimmin'?'

'Same way the pheasant come into Gubbs's pocket – by a little luck an' a deal o' conjurin'.' Old Hobden laughed in his deep chest.

'I see you've not forgotten your way about the woods. D'ye do any o' *this* still?' The stranger pretended to look along a gun.

Hobden answered with a quick movement of the hand as though he were pegging down a rabbit-wire.

'No. *That's* all that's left me now. Age she must as Age she can. An' what's your news since all these years?'

'Oh, I've bin to Plymouth, I've bin to Dover –
I've bin ramblin', boys, the wide world over,'

the man answered cheerily. 'I reckon I know as much of Old England as most.' He turned towards the children and winked boldly.

'I lay they told you a sight o' lies, then. I've been into England fur as Wiltsheer once. I was cheated proper over a pair of hedging-gloves,' said Hobden.

'There's fancy-talkin' everywhere. *You*'ve cleaved to your own parts pretty middlin' close, Ralph.'

'Can't shift an old tree 'thout it dyin',' Hobden chuckled. 'An' I be no more anxious to die than you look to be to help me with my hops tonight.'

The great man leaned against the brickwork of the roundel, and swung his arms abroad. 'Hire me!' was all he said, and they stumped upstairs laughing.

The children heard their shovels rasp on the cloth where the yellow hops lie drying above the fires, and all the oast-house filled with the sweet, sleepy smell as they were turned.

'Who is it?' Una whispered to the Bee Boy.

'Dunno, no more'n you – if *you* dunno,' said he, and smiled.

The voices on the drying-floor talked and chuckled together, and the heavy footsteps moved back and forth. Presently a hop-pocket dropped through the press-hole overhead, and stiffened and flattened as they shovelled it full. 'Clank!' went the press, and rammed the loose stuff into tight cake.

'Gently!' they heard Hobden cry. 'You'll bust her crop if you lay on so. You be as careless as Gleason's bull, Tom. Come an' sit by the fires. She'll do now.'

They came down, and as Hobden opened the shutter to see if the potatoes were done Tom Shoesmith said to the children, 'Put a plenty salt on 'em. That'll show you the sort o' man *I* be.' Again he winked, and again the Bee Boy laughed and Una stared at Dan.

'*I* know what sort o' man you be,' old Hobden grunted, groping for the potatoes round the fire.

'Do ye?' Tom went on behind his back. 'Some of us can't abide Horseshoes, or Church Bells, or Running Water; an', talkin' o' runnin' water' – he turned to Hobden, who was backing out of the roundel – 'd'you mind the great floods at Robertsbridge, when the miller's man was drowned in the street?'

'Middlin' well.' Old Hobden let himself down on the coals by the fire door. 'I was courtin' my woman on the Marsh that year. Carter to Mus' Plum I was, gettin' ten shillin's week. Mine was a Marsh woman.'

'Won'erful odd-gates place – Romney Marsh,' said Tom Shoesmith. 'I've heard say the world's divided like into Europe, Ashy, Afriky, Ameriky, Australy, an' Romney Marsh.'

'The Marsh folk think so,' said Hobden. 'I had a hem o' trouble to get my woman to leave it.'

'Where did she come out of? I've forgot, Ralph.'

'Dymchurch under the Wall,' Hobden answered, a potato in his hand.

'Then she'd be a Pett – or a Whitgift, would she?'

'Whitgift.' Hobden broke open the potato and ate it with the curious neatness of men who make most of their meals in the blowy open. 'She growed to be quite reasonable-like after livin' in the Weald awhile, but our first twenty year or two she was odd-fashioned, no bounds. And she was a won'erful hand with bees.' He cut away a little piece of potato and threw it out to the door.

'Ah! I've heard say the Whitgifts could see further through a millstone than most,' said Shoesmith. 'Did she, now?'

'She was honest-innocent of any nigromancin',' said Hobden. 'Only she'd read signs and sinnifications out o' birds flyin', stars fallin', bees hivin', and such. An' she'd lie awake – listenin' for calls, she said.'

'That don't prove naught,' said Tom. 'All Marsh folk has been smugglers since time everlastin'. 'Twould be in her blood to listen out o' nights.'

'Nature-ally,' old Hobden replied, smiling. 'I mind when there was smugglin' a sight nearer us than the Marsh be. But that wasn't my woman's trouble. 'Twas a passel o' no-sense talk,' he dropped his voice, 'about Pharisees.'

'Yes. I've heard Marsh men belieft in 'em.' Tom looked straight at the wide-eyed children beside Bess.

'Pharisees,' cried Una. 'Fairies? Oh, *I* see!'

'People o' the Hills,' said the Bee Boy, throwing half of his potato towards the door.

'There you be!' said Hobden, pointing at him. 'My boy, he has her eyes and her out-gate senses. That's what *she* called 'em!'

'And what did you think of it all?'

'Um – um,' Hobden rumbled. 'A man that uses fields an' shaws after dark as much as I've done, he don't go out of his road excep' for keepers.'

'But settin' that aside?' said Tom, coaxingly. 'I saw ye throw the Good Piece out-at-doors just now. Do ye believe or – *do* ye?'

'There was a great black eye to that tater,' said Hobden, indignantly.

'My liddle eye didn't see un, then. It looked as if you meant it for – for Any One that might need it. But settin' that aside. D'ye believe or – *do* ye?'

'I ain't sayin' nothin', because I've heard naught, an' I've seen naught. But if you was to say there was more things after dark in the shaws than men, or fur, or feather, or fin, I dunno as I'd go far about to call you a liar. Now turnagain, Tom. What's your say?'

'I'm like you. I say nothin'. But I'll tell you a tale, an' you can fit it *as* how you please.'

'Passel o' no-sense stuff,' growled Hobden, but he filled his pipe.

'The Marsh men they call it Dymchurch Flit,' Tom went on slowly. 'Hap you have heard it?'

'My woman she've told it me scores o' times. Dunno as I didn't end by belieftin' it – sometimes.'

Hobden crossed over as he spoke, and sucked with his pipe at the yellow lanthorn flame. Tom rested one great elbow on one great knee, where he sat among the coal.

'Have you ever bin in the Marsh?' he said to Dan.

'Only as far as Rye, once,' Dan answered.

'Ah, that's but the edge. Back behind of her there's steeples settin' beside churches, an' wise women settin' beside their doors, an' the sea settin' above the land, an' ducks herdin' wild in the diks' (he meant ditches). 'The Marsh is justabout riddled with diks an' sluices, an' tide-gates an' water-lets. You can hear 'em bubblin' an' grummelin' when the tide works in 'em, an' then you hear the sea rangin' left and right-handed all up along the Wall. You've seen how flat she is – the Marsh? You'd think nothin' easier than to walk eend-on acrost her? Ah, but the diks an' the water-lets, they twists the roads about as ravelly as witch-yarn on the spindles. So ye get all turned round in broad daylight.'

'That's because they've dreened the waters into the diks,' said Hobden. 'When I courted my woman the rushes was green – Eh me! the rushes was green – an' the Bailiff o' the Marshes, he rode up and down as free as the fog.'

'Who was he?' said Dan.

'Why, the Marsh fever an' ague. He've clapped me on the shoulder once or twice till I shook proper. But now the dreenin' off of the waters have done away with the fevers; so they make a joke, like, that the Bailiff o' the Marshes broke his neck in a dik. A won'erful place for bees an' ducks 'tis too.'

'An' old,' Tom went on. 'Flesh an' Blood have been there since Time Everlastin' Beyond. Well, now, speakin' among themselves, the Marshmen say that from Time Everlastin' Beyond, the Pharisees favoured the Marsh above the rest of Old England. I lay the Marshmen ought to know. They've been out after dark, father an' son, smugglin' some one thing or t'other, since ever wool grew to sheep's backs. They say there was always a middlin' few Pharisees to be seen on the Marsh. Impident as rabbits, they was. They'd dance on the nakid roads in the nakid daytime; they'd flash their liddle green lights along the diks, comin' an' goin', like honest smugglers. Yes, an' times they'd lock the church doors against the parson an' clerk of Sundays.'

'That 'ud be smugglers layin' in the lace or the brandy till they could run it out o' the Marsh. I've told my woman so,' said Hobden.

'I'll lay she didn't belieft it, then – not if she was a Whitgift. A won'erful choice place for Pharisees, the Marsh, by all accounts, till Queen Bess's father he come in with his Reformatories.'

'Would that be a Act o' Parliament like?' Hobden asked.

'Sure-ly. Can't do nothing in Old England without Act, Warrant, an' Summons. He got his Act allowed him, an', they say, Queen

Bess's father he used the parish churches something shameful. Justabout tore the gizzards out of I dunnamany. Some folk in England they held with 'en; but some they saw it different, an' it eended in 'em takin' sides an' burnin' each other no bounds, accordin' which side was top, time bein'. That tarrified the Pharisees: for Good-will among Flesh an' Blood is meat an' drink to 'em, an' ill-will is poison.'

'Same as bees,' said the Bee Boy. 'Bees won't stay by a house where there's hating.'

'True,' said Tom. 'This Reformations tarrified the Pharisees same as the reaper goin' round a last stand o' wheat tarrifies rabbits. They packed into the Marsh from all parts, and they says, "Fair or foul, we must flit out o' this, for Merry England's done with, an' we're reckoned among the Images."'

'Did they *all* see it that way?' said Hobden.

'All but one that was called Robin – if you've heard of him. What are you laughing at?' Tom turned to Dan. 'The Pharisees's trouble didn't tech Robin, because he'd cleaved middlin' close to people like. No more he never meant to go out of Old England – not he; so he was sent messagin' for help among Flesh an' Blood. But Flesh an' Blood must always think of their own concerns, an' Robin couldn't get *through* at 'em, ye see. They thought it was tide-echoes off the Marsh.'

'What did you – what did the fai – Pharisees want?' Una asked.

'A boat, to be sure. Their liddle wings could no more cross Channel than so many tired butterflies. A boat an' a crew they desired to sail 'em over to France, where yet awhile folks hadn't tore down the Images. They couldn't abide cruel Canterbury Bells ringin' to Bulverhithe for more pore men an' women to be burnded, nor the King's proud messenger ridin' through the land givin' orders to tear down the Images. They couldn't abide it no shape. Nor yet they couldn't get their boat an' crew to flit by without Leave an' Good-will from Flesh an' Blood; an' Flesh an' Blood came an' went about its own business the while the Marsh was swarvin' up, and swarvin' up with Pharisees from all England over, striving all means to get *through* at Flesh an' Blood to tell 'em their sore need . . . I don't know as you've ever heard say Pharisees are like chickens?'

'My woman used to say that too,' said Hobden, folding his brown arms.

'They be. You run too many chickens together, an' the ground sickens like, an' you get a squat, an' your chickens die. 'Same way, you crowd Pharisees, all in one place – *they* don't die, but Flesh an'

Blood walkin' among 'em is apt to sick up an' pine off. *They* don't mean it, an' Flesh an' Blood don't know it, but that's the truth – as I've heard. The Pharisees through bein' all stenched up an' frighted, an' tryin' to come *through* with their supplications, they nature-ally changed the thin airs and humours in Flesh an' Blood. It lay on the Marsh like thunder. Men saw their churches ablaze with the wildfire in the windows after dark; they saw their cattle scatterin' and no man scarin'; their sheep flockin' and no man drivin'; their horses latherin' an' no man leadin'; they saw the liddle low green lights more than ever in the dik-sides; they heard the liddle feet patterin' more than ever round the houses; an' night an' day, day an' night, 'twas all as though they were bein' creeped up on, and hinted at by Some One or other that couldn't rightly shape their trouble. Oh, I lay they sweated! Man an' maid, woman an' child, their Nature done 'em no service all the weeks while the Marsh was swarvin' up with Pharisees. But they was Flesh an' Blood, an' Marshmen before all. They reckoned the signs sinnified trouble for the Marsh. Or that the sea 'ud rear up against Dymchurch Wall an' they'd be drownded like Old Winchelsea; or that the Plague was comin'. So they looked for the meanin' in the sea or in the clouds – far an' high up. They never thought to look near an' knee-high, where they could see naught.

'Now there was a poor widow at Dymchurch under the Wall, which, lacking man or property, she had the more time for feeling: and she come to feel there was a Trouble outside her doorstep bigger an' heavier than aught she'd ever carried over it. She had two sons – one born blind, and t'other struck dumb through fallin' off the Wall when he was liddle. They was men grown, but not wage-earnin', an' she worked for 'em, keepin' bees and answerin' Questions.'

'What sort of questions?' said Dan.

'Like where lost things might be found, an' what to put about a crooked baby's neck, an' how to join parted sweethearts. She felt the Trouble on the Marsh same as eels feel thunder. She was a wise woman.'

'My woman was won'erful weather-tender, too,' said Hobden. 'I've seen her brish sparks like off an anvil out of her hair in thunderstorms. But she never laid out to answer Questions.'

'This woman was a Seeker like, an' Seekers they sometimes find. One night, while she lay abed, hot an' aching, there come a Dream an' tapped at her window, and "Widow Whitgift," it said, "Widow Whitgift!"

'First, by the wings an' the whistling, she thought it was peewits, but last she arose an' dressed herself, an' opened her door to the

Marsh, an' she felt the Trouble an' the Groaning all about her, strong as fever an' ague, an' she calls: "What is it? Oh, what is it?"

'Then 'twas all like the frogs in the diks peeping: then 'twas all like the reeds in the diks clip-clapping; an' then the great Tide-wave rummelled along the Wall, an' she couldn't hear proper.

'Three times she called, an' three times the Tide-wave did her down. But she catched the quiet between, an' she cries out, "What is the Trouble on the Marsh that's been lying down with my heart an' arising with my body this month gone?" She felt a liddle hand lay hold on her gown-hem, an' she stooped to the pull o' that liddle hand.'

Tom Shoesmith spread his huge fist before the fire and smiled at it.

'"Will the sea drown the Marsh?" she says. She was a Marsh-woman first an' foremost.

'"No," says the liddle voice. "Sleep sound for all o' that."

'"Is the Plague comin' to the Marsh?" she says. Them was all the ills she knowed.

'"No. Sleep sound for all o' that," says Robin.

'She turned about, half-mindful to go in, but the liddle voices grieved that shrill an' sorrowful she turns back, an' she cries: "If it is not a Trouble of Flesh an' Blood, what can I do?"

'The Pharisees cried out upon her from all round to fetch them a boat to sail to France, an' come back no more.

'"There's a boat on the Wall," she says, "but I can't push it down to the sea, nor sail it when 'tis there."

'"Lend us your sons," says all the Pharisees. "Give 'em Leave an' Good-will to sail it for us, Mother – O Mother!"

'"One's dumb, an' t'other's blind," she says. "But all the dearer me for that; and you'll lose them in the big sea." The voices just about pierced through her; an' there was childern's voices too. She stood out all she could, but she couldn't rightly stand against *that*. So she says: "If you can draw my sons for your job, I'll not hinder 'em. You can't ask no more of a Mother."

'She saw them liddle green lights dance an' cross till she was dizzy; she heard them liddle feet patterin' by the thousand; she heard cruel Canterbury Bells ringing to Bulverhithe, an' she heard the great Tide-wave ranging along the Wall. That was while the Pharisees was workin' a Dream to wake her two sons asleep: an' while she bit on her fingers she saw them two she'd bore come out an' pass her with never a word. She followed 'em, cryin' pitiful, to the old boat on the Wall, an' that they took an' runned down to the Sea.

'When they'd stepped mast an' sail the blind son speaks: "Mother, we're waitin' your Leave an' Good-will to take Them over."'

Tom Shoesmith threw back his head and half shut his eyes.

'Eh, me!' he said. 'She was a fine, valiant woman, the Widow Whitgift. She stood twistin' the eends of her long hair over her fingers, an' she shook like a poplar, makin' up her mind. The Pharisees all about they hushed their children from cryin' an' they waited dumb-still. She was all their dependence. 'Thout her Leave an' Good-will they could not pass; for she was the Mother. So she shook like a aps-tree makin' up her mind. 'Last she drives the word past her teeth, an' "Go!" she says. "Go with my Leave an' Good-will."

'Then I saw – then, they say, she had to brace back same as if she was wadin' in tide-water; for the Pharisees just about flowed past her – down the beach to the boat, *I* dunnamany of 'em – with their wives an' children an' valooables, all escapin' out of cruel Old England. Silver you could hear clinkin', an' liddle bundles hove down dunt on the bottom-boards, an' passels o' liddle swords an' shields raklin', an' liddle fingers an' toes scratchin' on the boatside to board her when the two sons pushed her off. That boat she sunk lower an' lower, but all the Widow could see in it was her boys movin' hampered-like to get at the tackle. Up sail they did, an' away they went, deep as a Rye barge, away into the offshore mistes, an' the Widow Whitgift she sat down and eased her grief till mornin' light.'

'I never heard she was *all* alone,' said Hobden.

'I remember now. The one called Robin he stayed with her, they tell. She was all too grievious to listen to his promises.'

'Ah! She should ha' made her bargain before-hand. I allus told my woman so!' Hobden cried.

'No. She loaned her sons for a pure love-loan, bein' as she sensed the Trouble on the Marshes, an' was simple good-willing to ease it.' Tom laughed softly. 'She done that. Yes, she done that! From Hithe to Bulverhithe, fretty man an' petty maid, ailin' woman an' wailin' child, they took the advantage of the change in the thin airs just about *as* soon as the Pharisees flitted. Folks come out fresh an' shining all over the Marsh like snails after wet. An' that while the Widow Whitgift sat grievin' on the Wall. She might have belieft us – she might have trusted her sons would be sent back! She fussed, no bounds, when their boat come in after three days.'

'And, of course, the sons were both quite cured?' said Una.

'No-o. That would have been out o' Nature. She got 'em back *as* she sent 'em. The blind man he hadn't seen naught of anything, an' the dumb man nature-ally, he couldn't say aught of what he'd seen. I reckon that was why the Pharisees pitched on 'em for the ferrying job.'

'But what did you – what did Robin promise the Widow?' said Dan.

'What *did* he promise, now?' Tom pretended to think. 'Wasn't your woman a Whitgift, Ralph? Didn't she ever say?'

'She told me a passel o' no-sense stuff when he was born.' Hobden pointed at his son. 'There was always to be one of 'em could see further into a millstone than most.'

'Me! That's me!' said the Bee Boy so suddenly that they all laughed.

'I've got it now!' cried Tom, slapping his knee. 'So long as Whitgift blood lasted, Robin promised there would allers be one o' her stock that – that no Trouble 'ud lie on, no Maid 'ud sigh on, no Night could frighten, no Fright could harm, no Harm could make sin, an' no Woman could make a fool of.'

'Well, ain't that just me?' said the Bee Boy, where he sat in the silver square of the great September moon that was staring into the oast-house door.

'They was the exact words she told me when we first found he wasn't like others. But it beats me how you known 'em,' said Hobden.

'Aha! There's more under my hat besides hair!' Tom laughed and stretched himself. 'When I've seen these two young folk home, we'll make a night of old days, Ralph, with passin' old tales – eh? An' where might you live?' he said, gravely, to Dan. 'An' do you think your Pa 'ud give me a drink for takin' you there, Missy?'

They giggled so at this that they had to run out. Tom picked them both up, set one on each broad shoulder, and tramped across the ferny pasture where the cows puffed milky puffs at them in the moonlight.

'Oh, Puck! Puck! I guessed you right from when you talked about the salt. How could you ever do it?' Una cried, swinging along delighted.

'Do what?' he said, and climbed the stile by the pollard oak.

'Pretend to be Tom Shoesmith,' said Dan, and they ducked to avoid the two little ashes that grow by the bridge over the brook. Tom was almost running.

'Yes. That's my name, Mus' Dan,' he said, hurrying over the silent shining lawn, where a rabbit sat by the big white-thorn near the croquet ground. 'Here you be.' He strode into the old kitchen yard, and slid them down as Ellen came to ask questions.

'I'm helping in Mus' Spray's oast-house,' he said to her. 'No, I'm no foreigner. I knowed this country 'fore your Mother was born; an' – yes, it's dry work oasting, Miss. Thank you.'

Ellen went to get a jug, and the children went in – magicked once more by Oak, Ash, and Thorn!

A THREE-PART SONG

I'm just in love with all these three,
The Weald and the Marsh and the Down countrie;
Nor I don't know which I love the most,
The Weald or the Marsh or the white chalk coast!

I've buried my heart in a ferny hill,
Twix' a liddle low shaw an' a great high gill.
Oh hop-bine yaller and woodsmoke blue,
I reckon you'll keep her middling true!

I've loosed my mind for to out and run,
On a Marsh that was old when Kings begun:
Oh Romney level and Brenzett reeds,
I reckon you know what my mind needs!

I've given my soul to the Southdown grass,
And sheep-bells tinkled where you pass.
Oh Firle an' Ditchling an' sails at sea,
I reckon you keep my soul for me!

Friendly Brook

(March 1914)

THE valley was so choked with fog that one could scarcely see a cow's length across a field. Every blade, twig, bracken-frond, and hoof-print carried water, and the air was filled with the noise of rushing ditches and field-drains, all delivering to the brook below. A week's November rain on water-logged land had gorged her to full flood, and she proclaimed it aloud.

Two men in sackcloth aprons were considering an untrimmed hedge that ran down the hillside and disappeared into mist beside those roarings. They stood back and took stock of the neglected growth, tapped an elbow of hedge-oak here, a mossed beech-stub there, swayed a stooled ash back and forth, and looked at each other.

'I reckon she's about two rod thick,' said Jabez the younger, 'an she hasn't felt iron since – when has she, Jesse?'

'Call it twenty-five year, Jabez, an' you won't be far out.'

'Umm!' Jabez rubbed his wet handbill on his wetter coat-sleeve. 'She ain't a hedge. She's all manner o' trees. We'll just about have to —' He paused, as professional etiquette required.

'Just about have to side her up an' see what she'll bear. But hadn't we best —?' Jesse paused in his turn, both men being artists and equals.

'Get some kind o' line to go by.' Jabez ranged up and down till he found a thinner place, and with clean snicks of the handbill revealed the original face of the fence. Jesse took over the dripping stuff as it fell forward, and, with a grasp and a kick, made it to lie orderly on the bank till it should be faggoted.

By noon a length of unclean jungle had turned itself into a cattle-proof barrier, tufted here and there with little plumes of the sacred holly which no woodman touches without orders.

'Now we've a witness-board to go by!' said Jesse at last.

'She won't be as easy as this all along,' Jabez answered. 'She'll need plenty stakes and binders when we come to the brook.'

'Well, ain't we plenty?' Jesse pointed to the ragged perspective ahead of them that plunged downhill into the fog. 'I lay there's a cord an' a half o' firewood, let alone faggots, 'fore we get anywheres anigh the brook.'

'The brook's got up a piece since morning,' said Jabez. 'Sounds like's if she was over Wickenden's door-stones.'

Jesse listened, too. There was a growl in the brook's roar as though she worried something hard.

'Yes. She's over Wickenden's door-stones,' he replied. 'Now she'll flood acrost Alder Bay an' that'll ease her.'

'She won't ease Jim Wickenden's hay none if she do,' Jabez grunted. 'I told Jim he'd set that liddle hay-stack o' his too low down in the medder. I *told* him so when he was drawin' the bottom for it.'

'I told him so, too,' said Jesse. 'I told him 'fore ever you did. I told him when the County Council tarred the roads up along.' He pointed up-hill, where unseen automobiles and road-engines droned past continually. 'A tarred road, she shoots every drop o' water into the valley same's a slate roof. 'Tisn't as 'twas in the old days, when the waters soaked in and soaked out in the way o' nature. It rooshes off they tarred roads all of a lump, and naturally every drop is bound to descend into the valley. And there's tar roads both two sides this valley for ten mile. That's what I told Jim Wickenden when they tarred the roads last year. But he's a valley-man. He don't hardly ever journey up-hill.'

'What did he say when you told him that?' Jabez demanded, with a little change of voice.

'Why? What did he say to you when *you* told him?' was the answer.

'What he said to you, I reckon, Jesse.'

'Then you don't need me to say it over again, Jabez.'

'Well, let be how 'twill, what was he gettin' *after* when he said what he said to me?' Jabez insisted.

'*I* dunno; unless you tell me what manner o' words he said to *you*.'

Jabez drew back from the hedge – all hedges are nests of treachery and eavesdropping – and moved to an open cattle-lodge in the centre of the field.

'No need to go ferretin' around,' said Jesse. 'None can't see us here 'fore we see them.'

'What was Jim Wickenden gettin' at when I said he'd set his stack too near anigh the brook?' Jabez dropped his voice. 'He was in his mind.'

'He ain't never been out of it yet to my knowledge,' Jesse drawled, and uncorked his tea-bottle.

'But then Jim says: "I ain't goin' to shift my stack a yard," he says. "The brook's been good friends to me, and if she be minded," he says, "to take a snatch at my hay, *I* ain't settin' out to withstand her."

That's what Jim Wickenden says to me last – last June-end 'twas,' said Jabez.

'Nor he hasn't shifted his stack, neither,' Jesse replied. 'An' if there's more rain, the brook she'll shift it for him.'

'No need tell *me*! But I want to know what Jim was gettin' *at*?'

Jabez opened his clasp-knife very deliberately; Jesse as carefully opened his. They unfolded the newspapers that wrapped their dinners, coiled away and pocketed the string that bound the packages, and sat down on the edge of the lodge manger. The rain began to fall again through the fog, and the brook's voice rose.

'But I always allowed Mary was his lawful child, like,' said Jabez, after Jesse had spoken for a while.

''Tain't so . . . Jim Wickenden's woman she never made nothing. She come out o' Lewes with her stockin's round her heels, an' she never made nor mended aught till she died. *He* had to light fire an' get breakfast every mornin' except Sundays, while she sowed it abed. Then she took an' died, sixteen, seventeen, year back; but she never had no children.'

'They was valley-folk,' said Jabez apologetically. 'I'd no call to go in among 'em, but I always allowed Mary —'

'No. Mary come out o' one o' those Lunnon Childern Societies. After his woman died, Jim got his mother back from his sister over to Peasmarsh, which she'd gone to house with when Jim married. His mother kept house for Jim after his woman died. They do say 'twas his mother led him on toward adoptin' of Mary – to furnish out the house with a child, like, and to keep him off of gettin' a noo woman. He mostly done what his mother contrived. 'Cardenly, twixt 'em, they asked for a child from one o' those Lunnon societies – same as it might ha' been these Barnardo children – an' Mary was sent down to 'em, in a candle-box, I've heard.'

'Then Mary is chance-born. I never knowed that,' said Jabez. 'Yet I must ha' heard it some time or other . . . '

'No. She ain't. 'Twould ha' been better for some folk if she had been. She come to Jim in a candle-box with all the proper papers – lawful child o' some couple in Lunnon somewheres – mother dead, father drinkin'. *And* there was that Lunnon society's five shillin's a week for her. Jim's mother she wouldn't despise weekend money, but I never heard Jim was much of a muck-grubber. Let be how 'twill, they two mothered up Mary no bounds, till it looked at last like they'd forgot she wasn't their own flesh an' blood. Yes, I reckon they forgot Mary wasn't their'n by rights.'

'That's no new thing,' said Jabez. 'There's more'n one or two in this parish wouldn't surrender back their Bernarders. You ask Mark Copley an' his woman an' that Bernarder cripple-babe o' theirs.'

'Maybe they need the five shillin',' Jesse suggested.

'It's handy,' said Jesse. 'But the child's more. "Dada" he says, an' "Mumma" he says, with his great rollin' head-piece all hurdled up in that iron collar. *He* won't live long – his backbone's rotten, like. But they Copleys do just about set store by him – five bob or no five bob.'

'Same way with Jim an' his mother,' Jesse went on. 'There was talk betwixt 'em after a few years o' not takin' any more weekend money for Mary; but let alone *she* never passed a farden in the mire 'thout longin's, Jim didn't care, like, to push himself forward into the Society's remembrance. So naun came of it. The weekend money would ha' made no odds to Jim – not after his uncle willed him they four cottages at Eastbourne *an'* money in the bank.'

'That was true, too, then? I heard something in a scadderin' word-o'-mouth way,' said Jabez.

'I'll answer for the house property, because Jim he reequested my signed name at the foot o' some papers concernin' it. Regardin' the money in the bank, he nature-ally wouldn't like such things talked about all round the parish, so he took strangers for witnesses.'

'Then 'twill make Mary worth seekin' after?'

'She'll need it. Her Maker ain't done much for her outside nor yet in.'

'That ain't no odds.' Jabez shook his head till the water showered off his hat-brim. 'If Mary has money, she'll be wed before any likely pore maid. She's cause to be grateful to Jim.'

'She hides it middlin' close, then,' said Jesse. 'It don't sometimes look to me as if Mary has her natural rightful feelin's. She don't put on an apron o' Mondays 'thout being druv to it – in the kitchen *or* the hen-house. She's studyin' to be a school-teacher. She'll make a beauty! I never knowed her show any sort o' kindness to nobody – not even when Jim's mother was took dumb. No! 'Twadn't no stroke. It stifled the old lady in the throat here. First she couldn't shape her words no shape; then she clucked, like, an' lastly she couldn't more than suck down spoon-meat an' hold her peace. Jim took her to Doctor Harding, an' Harding he bundled her off to Brighton Hospital on a ticket, but they couldn't make no stay to her afflictions there; and she was bundled off to Lunnon, an' they lit a great old lamp inside her, and Jim told me they couldn't make out nothing in no sort there; and, along o' one thing an' another, an' all their spyin's and pryin's, she come back a hem sight worse than when she started. Jim said he'd have no more hospitalizin', so he give her a slate, which she tied to her waist-string, and what she was minded to say she writ on it.'

'Now, I never knowed that! But they're valley-folk,' Jabez repeated.

''Twadn't particular noticeable, for she wasn't a talkin' woman any time o' her days. Mary had all three's tongue . . . Well, then, two years this summer, come what I'm tellin' you. Mary's Lunnon father, which they'd put clean out o' their minds, arrived down from Lunnon with the law on his side, sayin' he'd take his daughter back to Lunnon, after all. I was working for Mus' Dockett at Pounds Farm that summer, but I was obligin' Jim that evenin' muckin' out his pig-pen. I seed a stranger come traipsin' over the bridge agin' Wickenden's door-stones. 'Twadn't the new County Council bridge with the handrail. They hadn't given it in for a public right o' way then. 'Twas just a bit o' lathy old plank which Jim had throwed acrost the brook for his own conveniences. The man wasn't drunk - only a little concerned in liquor, like – an' his back was a mask where he'd slipped in the muck comin' along. He went up the bricks past Jim's mother, which was feedin' the ducks, an' set himself down at the table inside – Jim was just changin' his socks – an' the man let Jim know all his rights and aims regardin' Mary. Then there just about *was* a hurly-bulloo? Jim's fust mind was to pitch him forth, but he'd done that once in his young days, and got six months up to Lewes jail along o' the man fallin' on his head. So he swallowed his spittle an' let him talk. The law about Mary *was* on the man's side from fust to last, for he showed us all the papers. Then Mary come downstairs – she'd been studyin' for an examination –an' the man tells her who he was, an' she says he had ought to have took proper care of his own flesh and blood while he had it by him, an' not to think he could ree-claim it when it suited. He says somethin' or other, but she looks him up an' down, front an' backwent, an' she just tongues him scadderin' out o' doors, and he went away stuffin' all the papers back into his hat, talkin' most abusefully. Then she come back an' freed her mind against Jim an' his mother for not havin' warned her of her upbringin's, which it come out she hadn't ever been told. They didn't say naun to her. They never did. *I*'d ha' packed her off with any man that would ha' took her – an' God's pity on him!'

'Umm!' said Jabez, and sucked his pipe.

'So then, that was the beginnin'. The man come back again next week or so, an' he catched Jim alone, 'thout his mother this time, an' he fair beazled him with his papers an' his talk – for the law *was* on his side – till Jim went down into his money-purse an' give him ten shillings hush-money – he told me – to withdraw away for a bit an' leave Mary with 'em.'

'But that's no way to get rid o' man or woman,' Jabez said.

'No more 'tis. I told Jim so. "What can I do?" Jim says. "The law's *with* the man. I walk about daytimes thinkin' o' it till I sweats my underclothes wringin', an' I lie abed nights thinkin' o' it till I sweats my sheets all of a sop. 'Tisn't as if I was a young man," he says, "nor yet as if I was a pore man. Maybe he'll drink hisself to death." I e'en a'most told him outright what foolishness he was enterin' into, but he knowed it – he knowed it – because he said next time the man come 'twould be fifteen shillin's. An' next time 'twas. Just fifteen shillin's!'

'An' *was* the man her father?' asked Jabez.

'He had the proofs an' the papers. Jim showed me what that Lunnon Childern's Society had answered when Mary writ up to 'em an' taxed 'em with it. I lay she hadn't been proper polite in her letters to 'em, for they answered middlin' short. They said the matter was out o' their hands, but – let's see if I remember – oh, yes – they ree-gretted there had been an oversight. I reckon they had sent Mary out in the candle-box as a orphan instead o' havin' a father. Terrible awkward! Then, when he'd drinked up the money, the man come again – in his usuals – an' he kept hammerin' on and hammerin' on about his duty to his pore dear wife, an' what he'd do for his dear daughter in Lunnon, till the tears runned down his two dirty cheeks an' he come away with more money. Jim used to slip it into his hand behind the door, but his mother she heard the chink. She didn't hold with hush-money. She'd write out all her feelin's on the slate, an' Jim 'ud be settin' up half the night answerin' back an showing that the man had the law with him.'

'Hadn't that man no trade nor business, then?'

'He told me he was a printer. I reckon, though, he lived on the rates like the rest of 'em up there in Lunnon.'

'An' how did Mary take it?'

'She said she'd sooner go into service than go with the man. I reckon a mistress 'ud be middlin' put to it for a maid 'fore she put Mary into cap an' gown. She was studyin' to be a schoo-ool-teacher. A beauty she'll make! . . . Well, that was how things went that fall. Mary's Lunnon father kep' comin' an' comin' 'carden as he' drinked out the money Jim gave him; an' each time he'd put up his price for not takin' Mary away. Jim's mother, she didn't like partin' with no money, an' bein' obliged to write her feelin's on the slate instead o' givin' 'em vent by mouth, she was just about mad. Just about she *was* mad!

'Come November, I lodged with Jim in the outside room over 'gainst his hen-house. I paid *her* my rent. I was workin' for Dockett at Pounds – gettin' chestnut-bats out o' Perry Shaw. Just such weather as this be – rain atop o' rain after a wet October. (An' I remember it ended in dry frostes right away up to Christmas.) Dockett he'd sent up to Perry Shaw for me – no, he comes puffin' up to me himself – because a big corner-piece o' the bank had slipped into the brook where she makes that elber at the bottom o' the Seventeen Acre, an' all the rubbishy alders an' sallies which he ought to have cut out when he took the farm, they'd slipped with the slip, an' the brook was comin' rooshin' down atop of 'em, an' they'd just about back an' spill the waters over his winter wheat. The water was lyin' in the flats already. "Gor a-mighty, Jesse!" he bellers out at me, "Get that rubbish away all manners you can. Don't stop for no fagottin', but give the brook play or my wheat's past salvation. I can't lend you no help," he says, "but work an' I'll pay ye."'

'You had him there,' Jabez chuckled.

'Yes. I reckon I had ought to have drove my bargain, but the brook was backin' up on good bread-corn. So 'cardenly, I laid into the mess of it, workin' off the bank where the trees was drownin' themselves head-down in the roosh - just such weather as this - 'an the brook creepin' up on me all the time. 'Long toward noon, Jim comes mowchin' along with his toppin' axe over his shoulder.

'"Be you minded for an extra hand at your job?" he says.

'"Be you minded to turn to?" I ses, an' – no more talk to it – Jim laid in alongside o' me. He's no bunger with a toppin' axe.'

'Maybe, but I've seed him at a job o' throwin' in the woods, an' he didn't seem to make out no shape,' said Jabez. 'He haven't got the shoulders nor yet the judgment – *my* opinion – when he's dealin' with full-girt timber. He don't rightly make up his mind where he's goin' to throw her.'

'We wasn't throwin' nothin'. We was cuttin' out they soft alders, an' haulin' 'em up the bank 'fore they could back the waters on the wheat. Jim didn't say much, 'less it was that he'd had a postcard from Mary's Lunnon father, night before, sayin' he was comin' down that mornin'. Jim, he'd sweated all night, an' he didn't reckon hisself equal to the talkin' an' the swearin' an' the cryin', an' his mother blamin' him afterwards on the slate. "It spiled my day to think of it," he ses, when we was eatin' our pieces. "So I've fair cried dunghill an' run. Mother'll have to tackle him by herself. I lay *she* won't give him no hush-money," he ses. "I lay he'll be surprised by the time he's done with *her*," he ses. An' that was e'en a'most all the talk we had concernin' it. But he's no bunger with the toppin' axe.

'The brook she'd crep' up an' up on us, an' she kep' creepin' upon us till we was workin' knee-deep in the shallers, cuttin' an' pookin' an' pullin' what we could get to o' the rubbish. There was a middlin' lot comin' downstream, too – cattle-bars an' hop-poles and odds-ends bats, all poltin' down together; but they rooshed round the elber good shape by the time we'd backed out they drowned trees. Come four o'clock we reckoned we'd done a proper day's work, an' she'd take no harm if we left her. We couldn't puddle about there in the dark an' wet to no more advantage. Jim he was pourin' the water out of his boots – no, I was doin' that. Jim was kneelin' to unlace his'n. "Damn it all, Jesse," he ses, standin' up; "the flood must be over my doorsteps at home, for here comes my old white-top bee-skep!"'

'Yes. I allus heard he paints his bee-skeps,' Jabez put in. 'I dunno paint don't tarrify bees more'n it keeps 'em dry.'

'"I'll have a pook at it," he ses, an' he pooks at it as it comes round the elber. The roosh nigh jerked the pooker out of his hand-grips, an' he calls to me, an' I come runnin' barefoot. Then we pulled on the pooker, an' it reared up on eend in the roosh, an' we guessed what 'twas. 'Cardenly we pulled it in into a shaller, an' it rolled a piece, an' a great old stiff man's arm nigh hit me in the face. Then we was sure. "'Tis a man," ses Jim. But the face was all a mask. "I reckon it's Mary's Lunnon father," he ses presently. "Lend me a match and I'll make sure." He never used baccy. We lit three matches one by another, well's we could in the rain, an' he cleaned off some o' the slob with a tussick o' grass. "Yes," he ses. "It's Mary's Lunnon father. He won't tarrify us no more. D'you want him, Jesse?" he ses.

'"No," I ses. "If this was Eastbourne beach like, he'd be half-a-crown apiece to us 'fore the coroner; but now we'd only lose a day havin' to 'tend the inquest. I lay he fell into the brook."

'"I lay he did," ses Jim. "I wonder if he saw mother." He turns him over, an' opens his coat and puts his fingers in the waistcoat pocket an' start laughin'. "He's seen mother, right enough," he ses. "An' he's got the best of her, too. *She* won't be able to crow no more over *me* 'bout givin' him money. *I* never give him more than a sovereign. She's give him two!" an' he trousers 'em, laughin' all the time. "An' now we'll pook him back again, for I've done with him," he ses.

'So we pooked him back into the middle of the brook, an' we saw he went round the elber 'thout balkin', an' we walked quite a piece beside of him to set him on his ways. When we couldn't see no more, we went home by the high road, because we knowed the brook 'u'd be out acrost the medders, an' we wasn't goin' to hunt for Jim's little rotten old bridge in that dark – an' rainin' Heavens' hard, too. I was middlin' pleased to see light an' vittles again when we got home. Jim he pressed me to come insides for a drink. He don't drink in a generality, but he was rid of all his troubles that evenin', d'ye see? "Mother," he ses so soon as the door ope'd, "have you seen him?" She whips out her slate an' writes down – "No." "Oh, no," ses Jim. "You don't get out of it that way, Mother. I lay you *have* seen him, an' I lay he's bested you for all your talk, same as he bested me. Make a clean breast of it, Mother," he ses. "He got round you too." She was goin' for the slate again, but he stops her. "It's all right, Mother," he ses. "I've seen him sense you have, an' he won't trouble us no more." The old lady looks up quick as a robin, an' she writes, "Did he say so?" "No," ses Jim, laughin'. "He didn't say so. That's how I know. But he bested *you*, Mother. You can't have it in at *me* for bein' soft-hearted. You're twice as tender-hearted as what I be. Look!" he ses, an' he shows her the two sovereigns. "Put 'em away where they belong," he ses. "He won't never come for no more; an' now we'll have our drink," he ses, "for we've earned it."

'Nature-ally they weren't goin' to let me see where they kep' their monies. She went upstairs with it – for the whisky.'

'I never knowed Jim was a drinkin' man – in his own house, like,' said Jabez.

'No more he isn't: but what he takes he likes good. He won't tech no publican's hogwash acrost the bar. Four shillin's he paid for that bottle o' whisky. I know, because when the old lady brought it down there wasn't more'n jest a liddle few dreenin's an' dregs in it. Nothin' to set before neighbours, I do assure you.

'"Why, 'twas half-full last week, Mother," he ses. "You don't mean," he ses, "you've given him all that as well? It's two shillin's worth," he ses. (That's how I knowed he paid four.) "Well, well, Mother, you be too tender-'earted to live. But I don't grudge it to him,' he ses. "I don't grudge him nothin' he can keep." So, 'cardenly, we drinked up what little sup was left.'

'An' what come to Mary's Lunnon father?' said Jabez, after a full minute's silence.

'I be too tired to go readin' papers of evenin's; but Dockett he told me, that very week, I think, that they'd inquested on a man down at Robertsbridge which had polted and polted up agin' so many bridges an' banks, like, they couldn't make naun out of him.'

'An' what did Mary say to all these doin's?'

'The old lady bundled her off to the village 'fore her Lunnon father come, to buy weekend stuff (an' she forgot the half o' it). When we come in she was upstairs studyin' to be a school-teacher. None told her naun about it. 'Twadn't girls' affairs.'

"Reckon *she* knowed?' Jabez went on.

'She? She must have guessed it middlin' close when she saw her money come back. But she never mentioned it in writing so far's I know. She were more worritted that night on account of two-three her chickens bein' drowned, for the flood had skewed their old hen-house round on her postes. I cobbled her up next mornin' when the Brook shrinked.'

'An' where did you find the bridge? Some fur downstream, didn't ye?'

'Just where she allus was. She hadn't shifted but very little. The Brook had gulled out the bank a piece under one eend o' the plank, so's she was liable to tilt ye sideways if you wasn't careful. But I pooked three-four bricks under her, an' she was all plumb again.'

'Well, I dunno how it *looks* like, but let be how 'twill,' said Jabez, 'he hadn't no business to come down from Lunnon tarrifyin' people, an' threatenin' to take away children which they'd hobbed up for their lawful own – even if 'twas Mary Wickenden.'

'He had the business right enough, an' he had the law with him – no gettin' over that,' said Jesse. 'But he had the drink with him, too, an' that was where he failed, like.'

'Well, well! Let be how 'twill, the Brook was a good friend to Jim. I see it now. I allus *did* wonder what he was gettin' at when he said that, when I talked to him about shiftin' the stack. "You dunno everythin'," he ses. "The Brook's been a good friend to me," he ses, "an' if she's minded to have a snatch at my hay, *I* ain't settin' out to withstand her."'

'I reckon she's about shifted it, too, by now,' Jesse chuckled. 'Hark! That ain't any slip off the bank which she's got hold of.'

The Brook had changed her note again. It sounded as though she were mumbling something soft.

THE LAND

When Julius Fabricius, Sub-Prefect of the Weald,
In the days of Diocletian owned our Lower River-field,
He called to him Hobdenius – a Briton of the Clay,
Saying: 'What about that River-piece for layin' in to hay?'

And the aged Hobden answered: 'I remember as a lad
My father told your father that she wanted dreenin' bad.
An' the more that you neeglect her the less you'll get her clean.
Have it jest *as* you've a mind to, but, if I was you, I'd dreen.'

So they drained it long and crossways in the lavish Roman style.
Still we find among the river-drift their flakes of ancient tile,
And in drouthy middle August, when the bones of meadows show,
We can trace the lines they followed sixteen hundred years ago.

Then Julius Fabricius died as even Prefects do,
And after certain centuries, Imperial Rome died too.
Then did robbers enter Britain from across the Northern main
And our Lower River-field was won by Ogier the Dane.

Well could Ogier work his war-boat – well could Ogier
  wield his brand –
Much he knew of foaming waters – not so much of farming land.
So he called to him a Hobden of the old unaltered blood,
Saying: 'What about that River-bit, she doesn't look no good?'

And that aged Hobden answered: ''Tain't for *me* to interfere,
But I've known that bit o' meadow now for five and fifty year.
Have it *jest* as you've a mind to, but I've proved it time on time,
If you want to change her nature you have *got* to give her lime!'

Ogier sent his wains to Lewes, twenty hours' solemn walk,
And drew back great abundance of the cool, grey, healing chalk.
And old Hobden spread it broadcast, never heeding what was in't;
Which is why in cleaning ditches, now and then we find a flint.

Ogier died. His sons grew English. Anglo-Saxon was their name,
Till out of blossomed Normandy another pirate came;
For Duke William conquered England and divided with his men,
And our Lower River-field he gave to William of Warenne.

But the Brook (you know her habit) rose one rainy Autumn night
And tore down sodden flitches of the bank to left and right.
So, said William to his Bailiff as they rode their dripping rounds:
'Hob, what about that River-bit – the Brook's got up no bounds?'

And that aged Hobden answered: ''Tain't my business to advise,
But ye might ha' known 'twould happen from the way the valley lies.
When ye can't hold back the water you must try and save the sile.
Hev it jest as you've a *mind* to, but, if I was you, I'd spile!'

They spiled along the water-course with trunks of willow-trees
And planks of elms behind 'em and immortal oaken knees.
And when the spates of Autumn whirl the gravel-beds away
You can see their faithful fragments iron-hard in iron clay.

. . .

Georgii Quinti Anno Sexto, I, who own the River-field,
Am fortified with title-deeds, attested, signed and sealed,
Guaranteeing me, my assigns, my executors and heirs
All sorts of powers and profits which – are neither mine nor theirs.

I have rights of chase and warren, as my dignity requires.
I can fish – but Hobden tickles. I can shoot – but Hobden wires.
I repair, but he reopens certain gaps which, men allege,
Have been used by every Hobden since a Hobden swapped a hedge.

Shall I dog his morning progress o'er the track-betraying dew?
Demand his dinner-basket into which my pheasant flew?
Confiscate his evening faggot into which the conies ran,
And summons him to judgment? I would sooner summons Pan.

His dead are in the churchyard – thirty generations laid.
Their names went down in Domesday Book when Domesday Book
  was made.
And the passion and the piety and prowess of his line
Have seeded, rooted, fruited in some land the Law calls mine.

Not for any beast that burrows, not for any bird that flies,
Would I lose his large sound council, miss his keen amending eyes.
He is bailiff, woodman, wheelwright, field-surveyor, engineer,
And if flagrantly a poacher - 'tain't for me to interfere.

'Hob, what about that River-bit?' I turn to him again
With Fabricius and Ogier and William of Warenne.
'Hev it jest as you've a mind to, *but*' – and so he takes command.
For whoever pays the taxes old Mus' Hobden owns the land.

Mary Postgate

(1915)

OF Miss Mary Postgate, Lady McCausland wrote that she was 'thoroughly conscientious, tidy, companionable, and ladylike. I am very sorry to part with her, and shall always be interested in her welfare.'

Miss Fowler engaged her on this recommendation, and to her surprise, for she had had experience of companions, found that it was true. Miss Fowler was nearer sixty than fifty at the time, but though she needed care she did not exhaust her attendant's vitality. On the contrary, she gave out, stimulatingly and with reminiscences. Her father had been a minor Court official in the days when the Great Exhibition of 1851 had just set its seal on Civilization made perfect. Some of Miss Fowler's tales, none the less, were not always for the young. Mary was not young, and though her speech was as colourless as her eyes or her hair, she was never shocked. She listened unflinchingly to every one; said at the end, 'How interesting!' or 'How shocking!' as the case might be, and never again referred to it, for she prided herself on a trained mind, which 'did not dwell on these things'. She was, too, a treasure at domestic accounts, for which the village tradesmen, with their weekly books, loved her not. Otherwise she had no enemies; provoked no jealousy even among the plainest; neither gossip nor slander had ever been traced to her; she supplied the odd place at the rector's or the doctor's table at half an hour's notice; she was a sort of public aunt to very many small children of the village street, whose parents, while accepting everything, would have been swift to resent what they called 'patronage'; she served on the Village Nursing Committee as Miss Fowler's nominee when Miss Fowler was crippled by rheumatoid arthritis, and came out of six months' fortnightly meetings equally respected by all the cliques.

And when Fate threw Miss Fowler's nephew, an unlovely orphan of eleven, on Miss Fowler's hands, Mary Postgate stood to her share of the business of education as practised in private and public schools. She checked printed clothes-lists, and unitemized bills of extras; wrote to head and house masters, matrons, nurses and doctors, and grieved or rejoiced over half-term reports. Young

Wyndham Fowler repaid her in his holidays by calling her 'Gatepost', 'Postey' or 'Packthread', by thumping her between her narrow shoulders, or by chasing her bleating, round the garden, her large mouth open, her large nose high in air, at a stiff-necked shamble very like a camel's. Later on he filled the house with clamour, argument, and harangues as to his personal needs, likes and dislikes, and the limitations of 'you women', reducing Mary to tears of physical fatigue, or, when he chose to be humorous, of helpless laughter. At crises, which multiplied as he grew older, she was his ambassadress and his interpretress to Miss Fowler, who had no large sympathy with the young; a vote in his interest at the councils on his future; his sewing-woman, strictly accountable for mislaid boots and garments; always his butt and his slave.

And when he decided to become a solicitor, and had entered an office in London; when his greeting had changed from 'Hullo, Postey, you old beast', to 'Mornin', Packthread', there came a war which, unlike all wars that Mary could remember, did not stay decently outside England and in the newspapers, but intruded on the lives of people whom she knew. As she said to Miss Fowler, it was 'most vexatious'. It took the rector's son who was going into business with his elder brother; it took the colonel's nephew on the eve of fruit-farming in Canada; it took Mrs Grant's son who, his mother said, was devoted to the ministry; and, very early indeed, it took Wynn Fowler, who announced on a postcard that he had joined the Flying Corps and wanted a cardigan waistcoat.

'He must go, and he must have the waistcoat,' said Miss Fowler. So Mary got the proper-sized needles and wool, while Miss Fowler told the men of her establishment – two gardeners and an odd man, aged sixty – that those who could join the Army had better do so. The gardeners left. Cheape, the odd man, stayed on, and was promoted to the gardener's cottage. The cook scorning to be limited in luxuries, also left, after a spirited scene with Miss Fowler, and took the housemaid with her. Miss Fowler gazetted Nellie, Cheape's seventeen-year-old daughter, to the vacant post; Mrs Cheape to the rank of cook, with occasional cleaning bouts; and the reduced establishment moved forward smoothly.

Wynn demanded an increase in his allowance. Miss Fowler, who always looked facts in the face, said, 'He must have it. The chances are he won't live long to draw it, and if three hundred makes him happy —'

Wynn was grateful, and came over, in his tight-buttoned uniform, to say so. His training centre was not thirty miles away, and his talk was so technical that it had to be explained by charts of the various types of machines. He gave Mary such a chart.

'And you'd better study it, Postey,' he said. 'You'll be seeing a lot of 'em soon.' So Mary studied the chart, but when Wynn next arrived to swell and exalt himself before his womenfolk, she failed badly in cross-examination, and he rated her as in the old days.

'You *look* more or less like a human being,' he said in his new Service voice. 'You *must* have had a brain at some time in your past. What have you done with it? Where d'you keep it? A sheep would know more than you do, Postey. You're lamentable. You are less use than an empty tin can, you dowey old cassowary.'

'I suppose that's how your superior officer talks to *you*?' said Miss Fowler from her chair.

'But Postey doesn't mind,' Wynn replied. 'Do you, Packthread?'

'Why? Was Wynn saying anything? I shall get this right next time you come,' she muttered, and knitted her pale brows again over the diagrams of Taubes, Farmans and Zeppelins.

In a few weeks the mere land and sea battles which she read to Miss Fowler after breakfast passed her like idle breath. Her heart and her interest were high in the air with Wynn, who had finished 'rolling' (whatever that might be) and had gone on from a 'taxi' to a machine more or less his own. One morning it circled over their very chimneys, alighted on Vegg's Heath, almost outside the garden gate, and Wynn came in, blue with cold, shouting for food. He and she drew Miss Fowler's bath-chair, as they had often done, along the Heath footpath to look at the biplane. Mary observed that 'it smelt very badly.'

'Postey, I believe you think with your nose,' said Wynn. 'I know you don't with your mind. Now, what type's that?'

'I'll go and get the chart,' said Mary.

'You're hopeless! You haven't the mental capacity of a white mouse,' he cried, and explained the dials and the sockets for bomb-dropping till it was time to mount and ride the wet clouds once more.

'Ah!' said Mary, as the stinking thing flared upward. 'Wait till our Flying Corps gets to work! Wynn says it's much safer than in the trenches.'

'I wonder,' said Miss Fowler. 'Tell Cheape to come and tow me home again.'

'It's all downhill. I can do it,' said Mary, 'if you put the brake on.' She laid her lean self against the pushing-bar and home they trundled.

'Now, be careful you aren't heated and catch a chill,' said overdressed Miss Fowler.

'Nothing makes me perspire,' said Mary. As she bumped the chair under the porch she straightened her long back. The exertion had given her a colour, and the wind had loosened a wisp of hair across her forehead. Miss Fowler glanced at her.

'What do you ever think of, Mary?' she demanded suddenly.

'Oh, Wynn says he wants another three pairs of stockings – as thick as we can make them.'

'Yes. But I mean the things that women think about. Here you are, more than forty —'

'Forty-four,' said truthful Mary.

'Well?'

'Well?' Mary offered Miss Fowler her shoulder as usual.

'And you've been with me ten years now.'

'Let's see,' said Mary. 'Wynn was eleven when he came. He's twenty now, and I came two years before that. It must be eleven.'

'Eleven! And you've never told me anything that matters in all that while. Looking back, it seems to me that *I*'ve done all the talking.'

'I'm afraid I'm not much of a conversationalist. As Wynn says, I haven't the mind. Let me take your hat.'

Miss Fowler, moving stiffly from the hip, stamped her rubber-tipped stick on the tiled hall floor. 'Mary, aren't you *anything* except a companion? Would you *ever* have been anything except a companion?'

Mary hung up the garden hat on its proper peg. 'No,' she said after consideration. 'I don't imagine I ever should. But I've no imagination, I'm afraid.'

She fetched Miss Fowler her eleven-o'clock glass of Contrexeville.

That was the wet December when it rained six inches to the month, and the women went abroad as little as might be. Wynn's flying chariot visited them several times, and for two mornings (he had warned her by postcard) Mary heard the thresh of his propellers at dawn. The second time she ran to the window, and stared at the whitening sky. A little blur passed overhead. She lifted her lean arms towards it.

That evening at six o'clock there came an announcement in an official envelope that Second Lieutenant W. Fowler had been killed during a trial flight. Death was instantaneous. She read it and carried it to Miss Fowler.

'I never expected anything else,' said Miss Fowler; 'but I'm sorry it happened before he had done anything.'

The room was whirling round Mary Postgate, but she found herself quite steady in the midst of it.

'Yes,' she said. 'It's a great pity he didn't die in action after he had killed somebody.'

'He was killed instantly. That's one comfort,' Miss Fowler went on.

'But Wynn says the shock of a fall kills a man at once – whatever happens to the tanks,' quoted Mary.

The room was coming to rest now. She heard Miss Fowler say impatiently, 'But why can't we cry, Mary?' and herself replying, 'There's nothing to cry for. He has done his duty as much as Mrs Grant's son did.'

'And when he died, *she* came and cried all the morning,' said Miss Fowler. 'This only makes me feel tired – terribly tired. Will you help me to bed, please, Mary? – And I think I'd like the hot-water bottle.'

So Mary helped her and sat beside, talking of Wynn in his riotous youth.

'I believe,' said Miss Fowler suddenly, 'that old people and young people slip from under a stroke like this. The middle-aged feel it most.'

'I expect that's true,' said Mary, rising. 'I'm going to put away the things in his room now. Shall we wear mourning?'

'Certainly not,' said Miss Fowler. 'Except, of course, at the funeral. I can't go. You will. I want you to arrange about his being buried here. What a blessing it didn't happen at Salisbury!'

Every one, from the authorities of the Flying Corps to the rector, was most kind and sympathetic. Mary found herself for the moment in a world where bodies were in the habit of being despatched by all sorts of conveyances to all sorts of places. And at the funeral two young men in buttoned-up uniforms stood beside the grave and spoke to her afterwards.

'You're Miss Postgate, aren't you?' said one. 'Fowler told me about you. He was a good chap – a first-class fellow – a great loss.'

'Great loss!' growled his companion. 'We're all awfully sorry.'

'How high did he fall from?' Mary whispered.

'Pretty nearly four thousand feet, I should think, didn't he? You were up that day, Monkey?'

'All of that,' the other child replied. 'My bar made three thousand, and I wasn't as high as him by a lot.'

'Then *that's* all right,' said Mary. 'Thank you very much.'

They moved away as Mrs Grant flung herself weeping on Mary's chest, under the lych-gate, and cried, '*I* know how it feels! *I* know how it feels!'

'But both his parents are dead,' Mary returned, as she fended her off. 'Perhaps they've all met by now,' she added vaguely as she escaped towards the coach.

'I've thought of that too,' wailed Mrs Grant; 'but then he'll be practically a stranger to them. Quite embarrassing!'

Mary faithfully reported every detail of the ceremony to Mrs Fowler, who, when she described Mrs Grant's outburst, laughed aloud.

'Oh, how Wynn would have enjoyed it! He was always utterly unreliable at funerals. D'you remember —' And they talked of him again, each piecing out the other's gaps. 'And now,' said Miss Fowler, 'we'll pull up the blinds and we'll have a general tidy. That always does us good. Have you seen to Wynn's things?'

'Everything – since he first came,' said Mary. 'He was never destructive – even with his toys.'

They faced that neat room.

'It can't be natural not to cry,' Mary said at last. 'I'm *so* afraid you'll have a reaction.'

'As I told you, we old people slip from under the stroke. It's you I'm afraid for. Have you cried yet?'

'I can't. It only makes me angry with the Germans.'

'That's sheer waste of vitality,' said Miss Fowler. 'We must live till the war's finished.' She opened a full wardrobe. 'Now, I've been thinking things over. This is my plan. All his civilian clothes can be given away – Belgian refugees, and so on.'

Mary nodded. 'Boots, collars, and gloves?'

'Yes. We don't need to keep anything except his cap and belt.'

'They came back yesterday with his Flying Corps clothes' – Mary pointed to a roll on the little iron bed.

'Ah, but keep his Service things. Some one may be glad of them later. Do you remember his sizes?'

'Five feet eight and a half; thirty-six inches round the chest. But he told me he's just put on an inch and a half. I'll mark it on a label and tie it on his sleeping-bag.'

'So that disposes of *that*,' said Miss Fowler, tapping the palm of one hand with the ringed third finger of the other. 'What waste it all is! We'll get his old school trunk tomorrow and pack his civilian clothes.'

'And the rest?' said Mary. 'His books and pictures and the games and the toys – and – and the rest?'

'My plan is to burn every single thing,' said Miss Fowler. 'Then we shall know where they are and no one can handle them afterwards. What do you think?'

'I think that would be much the best,' said Mary. 'But there's such a lot of them.'

'We'll burn them in the destructor,' said Miss Fowler.

This was an open-air furnace for the consumption of refuse; a little circular four-foot tower of pierced brick over an iron grating. Miss Fowler had noticed the design in a gardening journal years ago, and had had it built at the bottom of the garden. It suited her tidy soul, for it saved unsightly rubbish-heaps, and the ashes lightened the stiff clay soil.

Mary considered for a moment, saw her way clear, and nodded again. They spent the evening putting away well-remembered civilian suits, underclothes that Mary had marked, and the regiments of very gaudy socks and ties. A second trunk was needed, and, after that, a little packing-case, and it was late next day when Cheape and the local carrier lifted them to the cart. The rector luckily knew of a friend's son, about five feet eight and a half inches high, to whom a complete Flying Corps outfit would be most acceptable, and sent his gardener's son down with a barrow to take delivery of it. The cap was hung up in Miss Fowler's bedroom, the belt in Miss Postgate's; for, as Miss Fowler said, they had no desire to make tea-party talk of them.

'That disposes of *that*,' said Miss Fowler. 'I'll leave the rest to you, Mary. I can't run up and down the garden. You'd better take the big clothes-basket and get Nellie to help you.'

'I shall take the wheelbarrow and do it myself,' said Mary, and for once in her life closed her mouth.

Miss Fowler, in moments of irritation, had called Mary deadly methodical. She put on her oldest waterproof and gardening-hat and her ever-slipping galoshes, for the weather was on the edge of more rain. She gathered fire-lighters from the kitchen, a half-scuttle of coals, and a faggot of brushwood. These she wheeled in the barrow down the mossed paths to the dank little laurel shrubbery where the destructor stood under the drip of three oaks. She climbed the wire fence into the rector's glebe just behind, and from his tenant's rick pulled two large armfuls of good hay, which she spread neatly on the fire-bars. Next, journey by journey, passing Miss Fowler's white face at the morning-room window each time, she brought down in the towel-covered clothes-basket, on the wheelbarrow, thumbed and used Hentys, Marryats, Levers, Stevensons, Baroness Orczys, Garvices, schoolbooks, and atlases, unrelated piles of the *Motor Cyclist*; the *Light Car*, and catalogues of Olympia Exhibitions; the remnants of a fleet of sailing-ships from ninepenny cutters to a three-guinea yacht; a prep-school dressing-gown; bats from three-and-sixpence to twenty-four shillings; cricket and tennis balls; disintegrated steam and clockwork locomotives with their twisted rails; a grey and red tin model of a submarine; a dumb gramophone and cracked records; golf-clubs that had to be broken across the knee, like his walking-sticks, and an assegai; photographs of private and public school cricket and football elevens, and his OTC on the line of march, Kodaks, and film-rolls; some pewters, and one real silver cup, for boxing competitions and Junior Hurdles; sheaves of school photographs; Miss Fowler's photograph; her own which he had borne off in fun and (good care she took not to ask!) had never returned; a playbox with a secret drawer; a load of flannels, belts and jerseys, and a pair of spiked shoes unearthed in the attic; a packet of all the letters that Miss Fowler and she had ever written to him, kept for some absurd reason through all these years; a five-day attempt at a diary; framed pictures of racing motors in full Brooklands career, and load upon load of undistinguishable wreckage of tool-boxes, rabbit-hutches, electric batteries, tin soldiers, fret-saw outfits, and jigsaw puzzles.

Miss Fowler at the window watched her come and go, and said to herself, 'Mary's an old woman. I never realized it before.'

After lunch she recommended her to rest.

'I'm not in the least tired,' said Mary. 'I've got it all arranged. I'm going to the village at two o'clock for some paraffin. Nellie hasn't enough, and the walk will do me good.'

She made one last quest round the house before she started, and found that she had overlooked nothing. It began to mist as soon as she had skirted Vegg's Heath, where Wynn used to descend – it seemed to her that she could almost hear the beat of his propellers overhead, but there was nothing to see. She hoisted her umbrella and lunged into the blind wet till she had reached the shelter of the empty village. As she came out of Mr Kidd's shop with a bottle full of paraffin in her string shopping-bag, she met Nurse Eden, the village nurse, and fell into talk with her, as usual, about the village children. They were just parting opposite the Royal Oak, when a gun, they fancied, was fired immediately behind the house. It was followed by a child's shriek dying into a wail.

'Accident!' said Nurse Eden promptly, and dashed through the empty bar, followed by Mary. They found Mrs Gerritt, the publican's wife, who could only gasp and point to the yard, where a little cart-lodge was sliding sideways amid a clatter of tiles. Nurse Eden snatched up a sheet drying before the fire, ran out, lifted something from the ground, and flung the sheet round it. The sheet turned scarlet and half her uniform too, as she bore the load into the kitchen. It was little Edna Gerritt, aged nine, whom Mary had known since her perambulator days.

'Am I hurted bad?' Edna asked, and died between Nurse Eden's dripping hands. The sheet fell aside and for an instant, before she could shut her eyes, Mary saw the ripped and shredded body.

'It's a wonder she spoke at all,' said Nurse Eden. 'What in God's name was it?'

'A bomb,' said Mary.

'One o' the Zeppelins?'

'No. An aeroplane. I thought I heard it on the Heath, but I fancied it was one of ours. It must have shut off its engines as it came down. That's why we didn't notice it.'

'The filthy pigs!' said Nurse Eden, all white and shaken. 'See the pickle I'm in! Go and tell Dr Hennis, Miss Postgate.' Nurse looked at the mother, who had dropped face down on the floor. 'She's only in a fit. Turn her over.'

Mary heaved Mrs Gerritt right side up, and hurried off for the doctor. When she told her tale, he asked her to sit down in the surgery till he got her something.

'But I don't need it, I assure you,' said she. 'I don't think it would be wise to tell Miss Fowler about it, do you? Her heart is so irritable in this weather.'

Dr Hennis looked at her admiringly as he packed up his bag.

'No. Don't tell anybody till we're sure,' he said, and hastened to the Royal Oak, while Mary went on with the paraffin. The village behind her was as quiet as usual, for the news had not yet spread. She frowned a little to herself, her large nostrils expanded uglily, and from time to time she muttered a phrase which Wynn, who never restrained himself before his women-folk, had applied to the enemy. 'Bloody pagans! They *are* bloody pagans. But,' she continued, falling back on the teaching that had made her what she was, 'one mustn't let one's mind dwell on these things.'

Before she reached the house Dr Hennis, who was also a special constable, overtook her in his car.

'Oh, Miss Postgate,' he said, 'I wanted to tell you that that accident at the Royal Oak was due to Gerritt's stable tumbling down. It's been dangerous for a long time. It ought to have been condemned.'

'I thought I heard an explosion too,' said Mary.

'You might have been misled by the beams snapping. I've been looking at 'em. They were dry-rotted through and through. Of course, as they broke, they would make a noise just like a gun.'

'Yes?' said Mary politely.

'Poor little Edna was playing underneath it,' he went on, still holding her with his eyes, 'and that and the tiles cut her to pieces, you see?'

'I saw it,' said Mary, shaking her head. 'I heard it too.'

'Well, we cannot be sure.' Dr Hennis changed his tone completely. 'I know both you and Nurse Eden (I've been speaking to her) are perfectly trustworthy, and I can rely on you not to say anything – yet at least. It is no good to stir up people unless —'

'Oh, I never do – anyhow,' said Mary, and Dr Hennis went on to the county town.

After all, she told herself, it might, just possibly, have been the collapse of the old stable that had done all those things to poor little Edna. She was sorry she had even hinted at other things, but Nurse Eden was discretion itself. By the time she reached home the affair seemed increasingly remote by its very monstrosity. As she came in, Miss Fowler told her that a couple of aeroplanes had passed half an hour ago.

'I thought I heard them,' she replied, 'I'm going down to the garden now. I've got the paraffin.'

'Yes, but – what *have* you got on your boots? They're soaking wet. Change them at once.'

Not only did Mary obey but she wrapped the boots in a newspaper, and put them into the string bag with the bottle. So, armed with the longest kitchen poker, she left.

'It's raining again,' was Miss Fowler's last word, 'but – I know you won't be happy till that's disposed of.'

'It won't take long. I've got everything down there, and I've put the lid on the destructor to keep the wet out.'

The shrubbery was filling with twilight by the time she had completed her arrangements and sprinkled the sacrificial oil. As she lit the match that would burn her heart to ashes, she heard a groan or a grunt behind the dense Portugal laurels.

'Cheape?' she called impatiently, but Cheape with his ancient lumbago, in his comfortable cottage would be the last man to profane the sanctuary. 'Sheep,' she concluded, and threw in the fusee. The pyre went up in a roar, and the immediate flame hastened night around her.

'How Wynn would have loved this!' she thought, stepping back from the blaze.

By its light she saw, half hidden behind a laurel not five paces away, a bareheaded man sitting very stiffly at the foot of one of the oaks. A broken branch lay across his lap – one booted leg protruded from beneath it. His head moved ceaselessly from side to side, but his body was as still as the tree's trunk. He was dressed – she moved sideways to look more closely – in a uniform something like Wynn's, with a flap buttoning across the chest. For an instant, she had some idea that it might be one of the young men she had met at the funeral. But their heads were dark and glossy. This man's was as pale as a baby's, and so closely cropped that she could see the disgusting pinky skin beneath. His lips moved.

'What do you say?' Mary moved towards him and stopped.

'Laty! Laty! Laty!' he muttered, while his hands picked at the dead wet leaves. There was no doubt as to his nationality. It made her so angry that she strode back to the destructor, though it was still too hot to use the poker there. Wynn's books seemed to be catching well. She looked up at the oak behind the man; several of the light upper and two or three rotten lower branches had broken and scattered their rubbish on the shrubbery path. On the lowest fork a helmet with dependent strings, showed like a bird's nest in the light of a long-tongued flame. Evidently this person had fallen through the tree. Wynn had told her that it was quite possible for people to fall out of aeroplanes. Wynn told her, too, that trees were useful things to break an aviator's fall, but in this case the aviator must have been broken or he would have moved from his queer position. He seemed helpless except for his horrible rolling head. On the other hand, she could see a pistol case at his belt – and Mary loathed pistols. Months ago, after reading certain Belgian reports together, she and Miss Fowler had had dealings with one – a huge revolver with flat-nosed bullets, which latter, Wynn said, were forbidden by the rules of war to be used against civilized enemies. 'They're good enough for us,' Miss Fowler had replied. 'Show Mary how it works.' And Wynn, laughing at the mere possibility of any such need, had led the craven winking Mary into the rector's disused quarry, and had shown her how to fire the terrible machine. It lay now in the top-left-hand drawer of her toilet-table - a memento not included in the burning. Wynn would be pleased to see how she was not afraid.

She slipped up to the house to get it. When she came through the rain, the eyes in the head were alive with expectation. The mouth even tried to smile. But at sight of the revolver its corners went down just like Edna Gerritt's. A tear trickled from one eye, and the head rolled from shoulder to shoulder as though trying to point out something.

'Cassée. Toute cassée,' it whimpered.

'What do you say?' said Mary disgustedly, keeping well to one side, though only the head moved.

'Cassée,' it repeated. 'Che me rends. Le médicin! Toctor!'

'Nein!' said she, bringing all her small German to bear with the big pistol. 'Ich haben der todt Kinder gesehn.'

The head was still. Mary's hand dropped. She had been careful to keep her finger off the trigger for fear of accidents. After a few moments' waiting, she returned to the destructor, where the flames were falling, and churned up Wynn's charring books with the poker. Again the head groaned for the doctor.

'Stop that!' said Mary, and stamped her foot. 'Stop that, you bloody pagan!'

The words came quite smoothly and naturally. They were Wynn's own words, and Wynn was a gentleman who for no consideration on earth would have torn little Edna into those vividly coloured strips and strings. But this thing hunched under the oak tree had done that thing. It was no question of reading horrors out of newspapers to Miss Fowler. Mary had seen it with her own eyes on the Royal Oak kitchen table. She must not allow her mind to dwell upon it. Now Wynn was dead, and everything connected with him was lumping and rustling and tinkling under her busy poker into red black dust and grey leaves of ash. The thing beneath the oak would die too. Mary had seen death more than once. She came of a family that had a knack of dying under, as she told Miss Fowler, 'most distressing circumstances.' She would stay where she was till she was entirely satisfied that It was dead – dead as dear papa in the late 'eighties; aunt Mary in 'eighty-nine; mamma in 'ninety-one; cousin Dick in 'ninety-five; Lady McCausland's housemaid in 'ninety-nine; Lady McCausland's sister in nineteen hundred and one; Wynn buried five days ago; and Edna Gerritt still waiting for decent earth to hide her. As she thought – her underlip caught up by one faded canine, brows knit and nostrils wide – she wielded the poker with lunges that jarred the grating at the bottom, and careful scrapes round the brickwork above. She looked at her wristwatch. It was getting on to half-past four, and the rain was coming down in earnest. Tea would be at five. If It did not die before that time, she would be soaked and would have to change. Meantime, and this occupied her, Wynn's things were burning well in spite of the hissing wet, though now and again a book-back with a quite distinguishable title would be heaved up out of the mass. The exercise of stoking had given her a glow which seemed to reach to the marrow of her bones. She hummed – Mary never had a voice – to herself. She had never believed in all those advanced views – though Miss Fowler herself leaned a little that way – of woman's work in the world; but now she saw there was much to be said for them. This, for instance, was *her* work – work which no man, least of all Dr Hennis, would ever have done. A man, at such a crisis, would be what Wynn called a 'sportsman'; would leave everything to fetch help, and would certainly bring It into the house. Now a woman's business was to make a happy home for – for a husband and children. Failing these – it was not a thing one should allow one's mind to dwell upon – but —

'Stop it!' Mary cried once more across the shadows. 'Nein, I tell you! Ich haben der todt Kinder gesehn.'

But it was a fact. A woman who had missed these things could still be useful – more useful than a man in certain respects. She thumped like a pavior through the settling ashes at the secret thrill of it. The rain was damping the fire, but she could feel – it was to dark to see – that her work was done. There was a dull red glow at the bottom of the destructor, not enough to char the wooden lid if she slipped it half over against the driving wet. This arranged, she leaned on the poker and waited, while an increasing rapture laid hold on her. She ceased to think. She gave herself up to feel. Her long pleasure was broken by a sound that she had waited for in agony several times in her life. She leaned forward and listened, smiling. There could be no mistake. She closed her eyes and drank it in. Once it ceased abruptly.

'Go on,' she murmured, half aloud. 'That isn't the end.'

Then the end came very distinctly in a lull between two rain-gusts. Mary Postgate drew her breath short between her teeth and shivered from head to foot. '*That's* all right,' said she contentedly, and went up to the house, where she scandalized the whole routine by taking a luxurious hot bath before tea, and came down looking, as Miss Fowler said when she saw her lying all relaxed on the other sofa, 'quite handsome!'

THE BEGINNINGS

It was not part of their blood,
  It came to them very late
With long arrears to make good,
  When the English began to hate.

They were not easily moved,
  They were icy willing to wait
Till every count should be proved,
  Ere the English began to hate.

Their voices were even and low,
  Their eyes were level and straight.
There was neither sign nor show,
  When the English began to hate.

It was not preached to the crowd,
  It was not taught by the State.
No man spoke it aloud,
  When the English began to hate.

It was not suddenly bred,
  It will not swiftly abate,
Through the chill years ahead,
  When Time shall count from the date
  That the English began to hate.

'LATE CAME THE GOD'

Late came the God, having sent his forerunners who were not regarded –
  Late, but in wrath;
Saying: "The wrong shall be paid, the contempt be rewarded
  On all that she hath.'
He poisoned the blade and struck home, the full bosom receiving
The wound and the venom in one, past cure or relieving.

He made treaty with Time to stand still that the grief might be fresh –
Daily renewed and nightly pursued through her soul to her flesh –
Mornings of memory, noontides of agony, midnights unslaked for her,
Till the stones of the streets of her Hells and her Paradise ached for her.

So she lived while her body corrupted upon her.
  And she called on the Night for a sign, and a Sign was allowed,
And she builded an Altar and served by the light of her Vision –
Alone, without hope of regard or reward, but uncowed,
Resolute, selfless, divine.
  These things she did in Love's honour . . .
What is a God beside Woman? Dust and derision!

The Wish House

THE new Church Visitor had just left after a twenty minutes' call. During that time, Mrs Ashcroft had used such English as an elderly, experienced, and pensioned cook should, who had seen life in London. She was the readier, therefore, to slip back into easy, ancient Sussex ('t's softening to 'd's as one warmed) when the bus brought Mrs Fettley from thirty miles away for a visit, that pleasant March Saturday. The two had been friends since childhood; but, of late, destiny had separated their meetings by long intervals.

Much was to be said, and many ends, loose since last time, to be ravelled up on both sides, before Mrs Fettley, with her bag of quilt-patches, took the couch beneath the window commanding the garden, and the football ground in the valley below.

'Most folk got out at Bush Tye for the match there,' she explained, 'so there weren't no one for me to cushion agin, the last five mile. An' she *do* just about bounce ye.'

'You've took no hurt,' said her hostess. 'You don't brittle by agein', Liz.'

Mrs Fettley chuckled and made to match a couple of patches to her liking. 'No, or I'd ha' broke twenty year back. You can't ever mind when I was so's to be called round, can ye?'

Mrs Ashcroft shook her head slowly – she never hurried – and went on stitching a sack-cloth lining into a list-bound rush tool-basket. Mrs Fettley laid out more patches in the spring light through the geraniums on the window-sill, and they were silent awhile.

'What like's this new visitor o' yourn?' Mrs Fettley inquired, with a nod towards the door. Being very short-sighted, she had, on her entrance, almost bumped into the lady.

Mrs Ashcroft suspended the big packing-needle judicially on high, ere she stabbed home. 'Settin' aside she don't bring much news with her yet, I dunno as I've anythin' special agin her.'

'Ourn, at Keyneslade,' said Mrs Fettley, 'she's full o' words an' pity, but she don't stay for answers. Ye can get on with your thoughts while she clacks.'

'This 'un don't clack. She's aimin' to be one o' those High Church nuns, like.'

'Ourn's married, but, by what they say, she've made no great gains of it . . . ' Mrs Fettley threw up her sharp chin. 'Lord! How they dam' cherubim do shake the very bones o' the place!'

The tile-sided cottage trembled at the passage of two specially chartered forty-seat charabancs on their way to the Bush Tye match; a regular Saturday 'shopping' bus, for the county's capital, fumed behind them; while, from one of the crowded inns, a fourth car backed out to join the procession, and held up the stream of through pleasure-traffic.

'You're as free-tongued as ever, Liz,' Mrs Ashcroft observed.

'Only when I'm with you. Otherwhiles, I'm Granny – three times over. I lay that basket's for one o' your gran'chiller – ain't it?'

''Tis for Arthur - my Jane's eldest.'

'But he ain't workin' nowheres, is he?'

'No. 'Tis a picnic-basket.'

'You're let off light. My Willie, he's allus at me for money for them aireated wash-poles folk puts up in their gardens to draw the music from Lunnon, like. An' I give it 'im – pore fool me!'

'An' he forgets to give you the promise-kiss after, don't he?' Mrs Ashcroft's heavy smile seemed to strike inwards.

'He do. No odds 'twixt boys now an' forty years back. Take all an' give naught – an' we to put up with it! Pore fool we! Three shillin' at a time Willie'll ask me for!'

'They don't make nothin' o' money these days,' Mrs Ashcroft said.

'An' on'y last week,' the other went on, 'me daughter, she ordered a quarter pound suet at the butcher's; an' she sent it back to 'im to be chopped. She said she couldn't bother with choppin' it.'

'I lay he charged her, then.'

'I lay he did. She told me there was a whisk-drive that afternoon at the Institute, an' she couldn't bother to do the choppin'.'

'Tck!'

Mrs Ashcroft put the last firm touches to the basket-lining. She had scarcely finished when her sixteen-year-old grandson, a maiden of the moment in attendance, hurried up the garden path shouting to know if the thing were ready, snatched it, and made off without acknowledgement. Mrs Fettley peered at him closely.

'They're goin' picnickin' somewheres,' Mrs Ashcroft explained.

'Ah,' said the other, with narrowed eyes. 'I lay *he* won't show much mercy to any he comes across, either. Now 'oo the dooce do he remind me of, all of a sudden?'

'They must look arter theirselves – same as we did.' Mrs Ashcroft began to set out the tea.

'No denyin' *you* could, Gracie,' said Mrs Fettley.

'What's in your head now?'

'Dunno . . . But it come over me, sudden-like – about dat woman from Rye – I've slipped the name – Barnsley, wadn't it?'

'Batten – Polly Batten, you're thinkin' of.'

'That's it – Polly Batten. That day she had it in for you with a hay-fork – time we was all hayin' at Smalldene – for stealin' her man.'

'But you heered me tell her she had my leave to keep him?' Mrs Ashcroft's voice and smile were smoother than ever.

'I did – an' we was all looking that she'd prod the fork spang through your breastes when you said it.'

'No-oo. She'd never go beyond bounds – Polly. She shruck too much for reel doin's.'

'Allus seems to *me*,' Mrs Fettley said after a pause, 'that a man 'twixt two fightin' women is the foolishest thing on earth. Like a dog bein' called two ways.'

'Mebbe. But what set ye off on those times, Liz?'

'That boy's fashion o' carryin' his head an' arms. I haven't rightly looked at him since he's growed. Your Jane never showed it, but – *him*! Why, 'tis Jim Batten and his tricks come to life again! . . . Eh?'

'Mebbe. There's some that would ha' made it out so – bein' barren-like, themselves.'

'Oho! Ah well! Dearie, dearie me, now! . . . An' Jim Batten's been dead this —'

'Seven and twenty year,' Mrs Ashcroft answered briefly. 'Won't ye draw up, Liz?'

Mrs Fettley drew up to buttered toast, currant bread, stewed tea, bitter as leather, some home-preserved pears, and a cold boiled pig's tail to help down the muffins. She paid all the proper compliments.

'Yes. I dunno as I've ever owed me belly much,' said Mrs Ashcroft thoughtfully. 'We only go through this world once.'

'But don't it lay heavy on ye, sometimes?' her guest suggested.

'Nurse says I'm a sight liker to die o' me indigestion than me leg.' For Mrs Ashcroft had a long-standing ulcer on her shin, which needed regular care from the village nurse, who boasted (or others did, for her) that she had dressed it one hundred and three times already during her term of office.

'An' you that *was* so able, too! It's all come on ye before your full time, like. *I've* watched ye goin'.' Mrs Fettley spoke with real affection.

'Somethin's bound to find ye sometime. I've me 'eart left me still,' Mrs Ashcroft returned.

'You was always big-hearted enough for three. That's somethin' to look back on at the day's eend.'

'I reckon you've *your* back-lookin's, too,' was Mrs Ashcroft's answer.

'You know it. But I don't think much regardin' such matters excep' when I'm along with you, Gra'. Takes two sticks to make a fire.'

Mrs Fettley stared, with jaw half-dropped, at the grocer's bright calendar on the wall. The cottage shook again to the roar of the motor traffic, and the crowded football ground below the garden roared almost as loudly; for the village was well set to its Saturday leisure.

Mrs Fettley had spoken very precisely for some time without interruption, before she wiped her eyes. 'And,' she concluded, 'they read 'is death-notice to me, out o' the paper last month. O' course it wadn't any o' *my* becomin' concerns – let be I 'adn't set eyes on him for so long. O' course *I* couldn't say nor show nothin'. Nor I've no rightful call to go to Eastbourne to see 'is grave, either. I've been schemin' to slip over there by the bus some day; but they'd ask questions at 'ome past endurance. So I aven't even *that* to stay me.'

'But you've 'ad your satisfactions?'

'Godd! Yess! Those four years 'e was workin' on the rail near us. An' the other drivers they gave him a brave funeral, too.'

'Then you've naught to cast-up about. 'Nother cup o' tea?'

The light and air had changed a little with the sun's descent, and the two elderly ladies closed the kitchen door against chill. A couple of jays squealed and skirmished through the undraped apple-trees in the garden. This time, the word was with Mrs Ashcroft, her elbows on the tea-table, and her sick leg propped on a stool . . .

'Well I never! But what did your 'usband say to that?' Mrs Fettley asked, when the deep-toned recital halted.'

''E said I might go where I pleased for all of 'im. But seein' 'e was bedrid, I said I'd 'tend 'im out. 'E knowed I wouldn't take no advantage of 'im in that state. 'E lasted eight or nine week. Then he was took with a seizure-like; an' laid stone-still for days. Then 'e propped 'imself up abed an' says: "You pray no man'll ever deal with you like you've dealed with some." "An' you?" I says, for *you* know, Liz, what a rover 'e was. "It cuts both ways," says 'e, "but *I'm* death-wise, an' I can see what's comin' to you." He died a-Sunday an' was buried a-Thursday . . . An' yet I'd set a heap by him – one time or – did I ever?'

'You never told me that before,' Mrs Fettley ventured.

'I'm payin' ye for what ye told me just now. Him bein' dead, I wrote up, sayin' I was free for good, to that Mrs Marshall in Lunnon – which gave me my first place as kitchen-maid – Lord, how long ago! She was well pleased, for they two was both gettin' on, an' I knowed their ways. You remember, Liz, I used to go to 'em in service between whiles, for years – when we wanted money, or – or my 'usband was away – on occasion.'

''E *did* get that six months at Chichester, didn't 'e?' Mrs Fettley whispered. 'We never rightly won to the bottom of it.'

''E'd ha' got more, but the man didn't die.'

'None o' your doin's, was it, Gra'?'

'No! 'Twas the woman's husband this time. An' so, my man bein' dead, I went back to them Marshall's, as cook, to get me legs under a gentleman's table again, and be called with a handle to me name. That was the year you shifted to Portsmouth.'

'Cosham,' Mrs Fettley corrected. 'There was a middlin' lot o' new buildin' bein' done there. My man went first, an' got the room, an' I follered.'

'Well, then, I was a year-abouts in Lunnon, all at a breath, like, four meals a day an' livin' easy. Then, 'long towards autumn, they two went travellin', like, to France; keepin' me on, for they couldn't do without me. I put the house to rights for the caretaker, an' then I slipped down 'ere to me sister Bessie – me wages in me pockets, an' all 'ands glad to be'old of me.'

'That would be when I was at Cosham,' said Mrs Fettley.

'*You* know, Liz, there wasn't no cheap-dog pride to folk, those days, no more than there was cinemas, nor whisk-drives. Man or woman 'ud lay hold o' any job that promised a shillin' to the backside of it, didn't they? I was all peaked up after Lunnon, an' I thought the fresh airs 'ud serve me. So I took on at Smalldene, obligin' with a hand at the early potato-liftin', stubbin' hens, an' such-like. They'd ha' mocked me sore in my kitchen in Lunnon, to see me in men's boots, an' me petticoats all shorted.'

'Did it bring ye any good?' Mrs Fettley asked.

''Twadn't for that I went. You know, 's well's me, that na'un happens to ye till it *'as* 'appened. Your mind don't warn ye before'and of the road ye've took, till you're at the far eend of it. We've only a backwent view of our proceedin's.'

''Oo was it?'

''Arry Mockler.' Mrs Ashcroft's face puckered to the pain of her sick leg.

Mrs Fettley gasped. ''Arry? Bert Mockler's son! An' *I'd* never guessed!'

Mrs Ashcroft nodded. 'An' I told myself – *an'* I beleft it – that I wanted field-work.'

'What did ye get out of it?'

'The usuals. Everythin' at first – worse than naught after. I had signs an' warnings a-plenty, but I took no heed of 'em. For we was burnin' rubbish one day, just when we'd come to know how 'twas with – with both of us. 'Twas early in the year for burnin', an' I said so. "No!" says he. "The sooner dat old stuff's off an' done with," 'e says, "the better." 'Is face was harder 'n rocks when he spoke. Then it come over me that I'd found me master, which I 'adn't ever before. I'd allus owned 'em, like.'

'Yes! Yes! They're yourn or you're theirn,' the other sighed. 'I like the right way best.'

'I didn't. But 'Arry did . . . 'Long then, it come time for me to go back to Lunnon. I couldn't. I clean couldn't! So, I took an' tipped a dollop o' scaldin' water out o' the copper one Monday mornin' over me left 'and and arm. Dat stayed me where I was for another fortnight.'

'Was it worth it?' said Mrs Fettley, looking at the silvery scar on the wrinkled fore-arm.

Mrs Ashcroft nodded. 'An' after that, we two made it up 'twixt us so's 'e could come to Lunnon for a job in a liv'ry stable not far from me. 'E got it. *I* 'tended to that. There wadn't no talk nowhere. His own mother never suspicioned how 'twas. He just slipped up to Lunnon, an' there we abode that winter, not 'alf a mile 'tother from each.'

'Ye paid 'is fare an' all, though'; Mrs Fettley spoke convincedly.

Again Mrs Ashcroft nodded. 'Dere wadn't much I didn't do for him. 'E was me master, an' – O God, help us! – we'd laugh over it walkin' together after dark in them paved streets, an' me corns fair wrenchin' in me boots! I'd never been like that before. Ner he! Ner he!'

Mrs Fettley clucked sympathetically.

'An' when did ye come to the eend?' she asked.

'When 'e paid it all back again, every penny. Then I knowed, but I wouldn't *suffer* meself to know. "You've been mortal kind to me," he says. "Kind!" I said. "'Twixt *us*?" But 'e kep' all on tellin' me 'ow kind I'd been an' 'e'd never forget it all his days. I held it from off o' me for three evenin's, because I would *not* believe. Then 'e talked about not bein' satisfied with 'is job in the stables, an' the men there puttin' tricks on 'im, an' all they lies which a man tells when 'e's leavin' ye. I heard 'im out, neither 'elpin' nor 'inderin'. At the last, I took off a liddle brooch which he'd give me an' I says: "Dat'll do. *I* ain't askin' na'un." An' I turned me round an' walked off to me own sufferin's. 'E didn't make 'em worse. 'E didn't come nor write after that. 'E slipped off 'ere back 'ome to 'is mother again.'

'An' 'ow often did ye look for 'en to come back?' Mrs Fettley demanded mercilessly.

'More 'n once – more 'n once! Goin' over the streets we'd used, I thought de very pave-stones 'ud shruck out under me feet.'

'Yes,' said Mrs Fettley. 'I dunno but dat don't 'urt as much as aught else. An' dat was all ye got?'

'No. 'Twadn't. That's the curious part, if you'll believe it, Liz.'

'I do. I lay you're further off lyin' now than in all your life, Gra'.'

'I am . . . An' I suffered, like I'd not wish my most arrantest enemies to. God's Own Name! I went through the hoop that spring! One part of it was 'eddicks which I'd never known all me days before. Think o' *me* with an 'eddick! But I come to be grateful for 'em. They kep' me from thinkin' . . .'

''Tis like a tooth,' Mrs Fettley commented. 'It must rage an' rugg till it tortures itself quiet on ye: an' then – then there's na'un left.'

'*I* got enough lef' to last me all *my* days on earth. It come about through our charwoman's liddle girl – Sophy Ellis was 'er name – all eyes an' elbers an' hunger. I used to give 'er vittles. Otherwhiles, I took no special notice of 'er, an' a sight less, o' course, when me trouble about 'Arry was on me. But – you know how liddle maids first feel it sometimes – she come to be crazy-fond o' me, pawin' an' cuddlin' all whiles; an' I 'adn't the 'eart to beat 'er off . . . One afternoon, early in spring 'twas, 'er mother 'ad sent 'er round to scutchel up what vittles she could off of us. I was settin' by the fire, me apern over me head, half-mad with the 'eddick, when she slips in. I reckon I was middlin' short with 'er. "Lor'!" she says. "Is *that* all? I'll take it off you in two-twos!" I told her not to lay a finger on me, for I thought she'd want to stroke my forehead; an' – I ain't that make. "*I* won't tech ye," she says, an' slips out again. She 'adn't been gone ten minutes 'fore me old 'eddick took off quick as bein' kicked. So I went about my work. Prasin'ly, Sophy comes back, an' creeps into my chair quiet as a mouse. 'Er eyes was deep in 'er 'ead an' er face all drawed. I asked 'er what 'ad 'appened. "Nothin'," she says. "On'y *I*'ve got it now." "Got what?" I says. "Your 'eddick," she says, all hoarse an' sticky-lipped. "I've took it on me." "Nonsense," I says, "it went of itself when you was out. Lay still an' I'll make ye a cup o' tea." "'Twon't do no good," she says, "till your time's up. 'Ow long do *your* 'eddicks last?" "Don't talk silly," I says, "or I'll send for the doctor." It looked to me like she might be hatchin' de measles. "Oh, Mrs Ashcroft," she says, stretchin' out 'er liddle thin arms. "I *do* love ye." There wasn't any holdin' agin that. I took 'er into my lap an' made much of 'er. "Is it truly gone?" she says. "Yes," I says, "an' if 'twas you took it away, I'm truly grateful." "'*Twas* me," she says, layin' 'er cheek to mine. "No one but me knows how." An' then she said she'd changed me 'eddick for me at a Wish 'Ouse.'

'Whatt?' Mrs Fettley spoke sharply.

'A Wish House. No! *I* 'adn't 'eard o' such things, either. I couldn't get it straight at first, but, puttin' all together, I made out that a Wish 'Ouse 'ad to be a house which 'ad stood unlet an' empty long enough for Some One, like, to come an' in'abit there. She said a liddle girl that she'd played with in the livery stables where 'Arry worked 'ad told 'er so. She said the girl 'ad belonged in a caravan that laid up, o' winters, in Lunnon. Gipsy, I judge.'

'Ooh! There's no sayin' what Gippos know, but *I*'ve never 'eard of a Wish 'Ouse, an' I know – some things,' said Mrs Fettley.

'Sophy said there was a Wish 'Ouse in Wadloes Road – just a few streets off, on the way to our greengrocer's. All you 'ad to do, she said, was to ring the bell an' wish your wish through the slit o' the letter-box. I asked 'er if the fairies give it 'er? "Don't ye know," she says, "there's no fairies in a Wish 'Ouse? There's on'y a Token."'

'Goo' Lord A'mighty! Where did she come by *that* word?' cried Mrs Fettley; for a Token is a wraith of the dead or, worse still, of the living.

'The caravan-girl 'ad told 'er, she said. Well, Liz, it troubled me to 'ear 'er, an' lyin' in me arms she must ha' felt it. "That's very kind o' you," I says, holdin' 'er tight, "to wish me 'eddick away. But why didn't ye ask somethin' nice for yourself?" "You can't do that," she says. "All you'll get at a Wish 'Ouse is leave to take someone else's trouble. I've took Ma's 'eddicks, when she's been kind to me; but this is the first time I've been able to do aught for you. Oh, Mrs Ashcroft, I *do* just about love you." An' she goes on all like that. Liz, I tell you my 'air e'en a'most stood on end to 'ear 'er. I asked 'er what like a Token was. "I dunno," she says, "but after you've ringed the bell, you'll 'ear it run up from the basement, to the front door. Then say your wish," she says, "an' go away." "The Token don't open de door to ye, then?" I says. "Oh no," she says. "You on'y 'ear gigglin', like, be'ind the front door. Then you say you'll take the trouble off of 'oo ever 'tis you've chose for your love; an' ye'll get it," she says. I didn't ask no more – she was too 'ot an' fevered. I made much of 'er till it come time to light de gas, an' a liddle after that, 'er 'eddick –

mine, I suppose – took off, an' she got down an' played with the cat.'

'Well, I never!' said Mrs Fettley. 'Did – did ye foller it up, anyways?'

'She askt me to, but I wouldn't 'ave no such dealin's with a child.'

'What *did* ye do, then?'

'Sat in me own room 'stid o' the kitchen when me 'eddicks come on. But it lay at de back o' me mind.'

''Twould. Did she tell ye more, ever?'

'No. Besides what the Gippo girl 'ad told 'er, she knew naught, 'cept that the charm worked. An', next after that – in May 'twas – I suffered the summer out in Lunnon. 'Twas hot an' windy for weeks, an' the streets stinkin' o' dried 'orse-dung blowin' from side to side an' lyin' level with the kerb. We don't get that nowadays. I 'ad my 'ol'day just before hoppin',* an' come down 'ere to stay with Bessie again. She noticed I'd lost flesh, an' was all poochy under the eyes.'

'Did ye see 'Arry?'

Mrs Ashcroft nodded. 'The fourth - no, the fifth day. Wednesday 'twas. I knowed 'e was workin' at Smalldene again. I asked 'is mother in the street, bold as brass. She 'adn't room to say much, for Bessie – you know 'er tongue – was talkin' full-clack. But that Wednesday, I was walkin' with one o' Bessie's chillern hangin' on me skirts, at de back o' Chanter's Tot. Prasin'ly, I felt 'e was be'ind me on the footpath, an' I knowed by 'is tread 'e'd changed 'is nature. I slowed, an' I heard 'im slow. Then I fussed a piece with the child, to force him past me, like. So 'e *'ad* to come past. 'E just says "Good evenin'", and goes on, tryin' to pull 'isself together.'

'Drunk, was he?' Mrs Fettley asked.

'Never! S'runk an' wizen; 'is clothes 'angin' on 'im like bags, an' the back of 'is neck whiter 'n chalk. 'Twas all I could do not to oppen my arms an' cry after him. But I swallered me spittle till I was back 'ome again an' the chillern abed. Then I says to Bessie, after supper, "What in de world's come to 'Arry Mockler?" Bessie told me 'e'd been a-hospital for two months, 'long o' cuttin' 'is foot wid a spade, muckin' out the old pond at Smalldene. There was poison in de dirt, an' it rooshed up 'is leg, like, an' come out all over him. 'E 'adn't been back to 'is job – carterin' at Smalldene ' more'n a fortnight. She told me the doctor said he'd go off, likely, with the November frostes; an' 'is mother 'ad told 'er that 'e didn't rightly eat nor sleep, an' sweated 'imself into pools, no odds 'ow chill 'e lay. An' spit terrible o' mornin's. "Dearie me," I says. "But, mebbe, hoppin' 'll set 'im right

* Hop-picking.

again," an' I licked me thread-point an' I fetched me needle's eye up to it an' I threads me needle under de lamp, steady as rocks. An' dat night (me bed was in de wash-house) I cried an' I cried. An' *you* know, Liz – for you've been with me in my throes – it takes summat to make me cry.'

'Yes; but chile-bearin' is on'y just pain,' said Mrs Fettley.

'I come round by cock-crow, an' dabbed cold tea on me eyes to take away the signs. Long towards nex' evenin' – I was settin' out to lay some flowers on me 'usband's grave, for the look o' the thing – I met 'Arry over against where the War Memorial is now. 'E was comin' back from 'is 'orses, so 'e couldn't *not* see me. I looked 'im all over, an' "'Arry," I says twix' me teeth, "come back an' rest-up in Lunnon." "I won't take it," he says, "for I can give ye naught." "I don't ask it," I says. "By God's Own Name, I don't ask na'un! On'y come up an' see a Lunnon doctor." 'E lifts 'is two 'eavy eyes at me: "'Tis past that, Gra'," 'e says. "I've but a few months left." "'Arry!" I says. "*My* man!" I says. I couldn't say no more. 'Twas all up in me throat. "Thank ye kindly, Gra'," 'e says (but 'e never says "my woman"), an' 'e went on up-street an' 'is mother – Oh, damn 'er! – she was watchin' for 'im, an' she shut de door be'ind 'im.'

Mrs Fettley stretched an arm across the table, and made to finger Mrs Ashcroft's sleeve at the wrist, but the other moved it out of reach.

'So I went on to the churchyard with my flowers, an' I remembered my 'usband's warnin' that night he spoke. 'E *was* death-wise, an' it '*ad* 'appened as 'e said. But as I was settin' down de jam-pot on the grave-mound, it come over me there was one thing I *could* do for 'Arry. Doctor or no doctor, I thought I'd make a trial of it. So I did. Nex' mornin', a bill came down from our Lunnon greengrocer. Mrs Marshall, she'd lef' me petty cash for suchlike – o' course – but I tole Bess 'twas for me to come an' open the 'ouse. So I went up, afternoon train.'

'An' – but I know you 'adn't – 'adn't you no fear?'

'What for? There was nothin' front o' me but my own shame an' God's croolty. I couldn't ever get 'Arry – 'ow *could* I? I knowed it must go on burnin' till it burned me out.'

'Aie!' said Mrs Fettley, reaching for the wrist again, and this time Mrs Ashcroft permitted it.

'Yit 'twas a comfort to know I could try *this* for 'im. So I went an' I paid the greengrocer's bill, an' put 'is receipt in me handbag, an' then I stepped round to Mrs Ellis – our char – an' got the 'ouse-keys an' opened the 'ouse. First, I made me bed to come back to (God's

Own Name! Me bed to lie upon!). Nex' I made me a cup o' tea an' sat down in the kitchen thinkin', till 'long towards dusk. Terrible close, 'twas. Then I dressed me an' went out with the receipt in me 'andbag, feignin' to study it for an address, like. Fourteen, Wadloes Road, was the place – a liddle basement-kitchen 'ouse, in a row of twenty-thirty such, an' tiddy strips o' walled garden in front – the paint off the front doors, an' na'un done to na'un since ever so long. There wasn't 'ardly no one in the streets 'cept the cats. *'Twas* 'ot, too! I turned into the gate bold as brass; up de steps I went an' I ringed the front-door bell. She pealed loud, like it do in an empty house. When she'd all ceased, I 'eard a cheer, like, pushed back on de floor o' the kitchen. Then I 'eard feet on de kitchen-stairs, like it might ha' been a heavy woman in slippers. They come up to de stair-head, acrost the hall – I 'eard the bare boards creak under 'em – an' at de front door dey stopped. I stooped me to the letter-box slit, an' I says: "Let me take everythin' bad that's in store for my man, 'Arry Mockler, for love's sake." Then, whatever it was 'tother side de door let its breath out, like, as if it 'ad been holdin' it for to 'ear better.'

'Nothin' was *said* to ye?' Mrs Fettley demanded.

'Na'un. She just breathed out – a sort of *A-ah*, like. Then the steps went back an' downstairs to the kitchen – all draggy – an' I heard the cheer drawed up again.'

'An' you abode on de doorstep, throughout all, Gra'?'

Mrs Ashcroft nodded.

'Then I went away, an' a man passin' says to me: "Didn't you know that house was empty?" "No," I says. "I must ha' been give the wrong number." An' I went back to our 'ouse an' I went to bed; for I was fair flogged out. 'Twas too 'ot to sleep more'n snatches, so I walked me about, lyin' down betweens, till crack o' dawn. Then I went to the kitchen to make me a cup o' tea, an' I hitted meself just above the ankle on an old roastin'-jack o' mine that Mrs Ellis had moved out from the corner, her last cleanin'. An' so – nex' after that – I waited till the Marshalls come back o' their holiday.'

'Alone there? I'd ha' thought you'd 'ad enough of empty houses,' said Mrs Fettley, horrified.

'Oh, Mrs Ellis an' Sophy was runnin' in an' out soon's I was back, an' 'twixt us we cleaned de house again top-to-bottom. There's allus a hand's turn more to do in every house. An' that's 'ow 'twas with me that autumn an' winter, in Lunnon.'

'Then na'un hap – overtook ye for your doin's?'

Mrs Ashcroft smiled. 'No. Not then. 'Long in November I sent Bessie ten shillin's.'

'You was allus free-'anded,' Mrs Fettley interrupted.

'An' I got what I paid for, with the rest o' the news. She said the hoppin' 'ad set 'im up wonderful. 'E'd 'ad six weeks of it, and now 'e was back again carterin' at Smalldene. No odds to me *'ow* it 'ad 'appened – 'slong's it *'ad*. But I dunno as my ten shillin's eased me much. 'Arry bein' *dead*, like, 'e'd ha' been mine, till Judgment. 'Arry bein' alive, 'e'd like as not pick up with some woman middlin' quick. I raged over that. Come spring, I 'ad something else to rage for. I'd growed a nasty little weepin' boil, like, on me shin, just above the boot-top, that wouldn't heal no shape. It made me sick to look at it, for I'm clean-fleshed by nature. Chop me all over with a spade, an' I'd heal like turf. Then Mrs Marshall she set 'er own doctor at me. 'E said I ought to ha' come to him at first go-off, 'stead o' drawin' all manner o' dyed stockin's over it for months. 'E said I'd stood up too much to me work, for it was settin' very close atop of a big swelled vein, like, behither the small o' me ankle. "Slow come, slow go," 'e says, "Lay your leg up on high an' rest it," he says, "an' 'twill ease off. Don't let it close up too soon. You've got a very fine leg, Mrs Ashcroft," 'e says. An' he put wet dressin's on it.'

''E done right.' Mrs Fettley spoke firmly. 'Wet dressin's to wet wounds. They draw de humours, same's a lamp-wick draws de oil.'

'That's true. An' Mrs Marshall was allus at me to make me set down more, an' dat nigh healed it up. An' then after a while they packed me off down to Bessie's to finish the cure; for I ain't the sort to sit down when I ought to stand up. You was back in the village then, Liz.'

'I was. I was, but – never did I guess!'

'I didn't desire ye to.' Mrs Ashcroft smiled. 'I saw 'Arry once or twice in de street, wonnerful fleshed up an' restored back. Then, one day I didn't see 'im, an' 'is mother told me one of 'is 'orses 'ad lashed out an' caught 'im on the 'ip. So 'e was abed an' middlin' painful. An' Bessie, she says to his mother, 'twas a pity 'Arry 'adn't a woman of 'is own to take the nursin' off 'er. And the old lady *was* mad! She told us that 'Arry 'ad never looked after any woman in 'is born days, an' as long as she was atop the mowlds, she'd contrive for 'im till 'er two 'ands dropped off. So I knowed she'd do watch-dog for me, 'thout askin' for bones.'

Mrs Fettley rocked with small laughter.

'That day,' Mrs Ashcroft went on, 'I'd stood on me feet nigh all the time, watchin' the doctor go in an' out; for they thought it might be 'is ribs, too. That made my boil break again, issuin' an' weepin'. But it turned out 'twadn't ribs at all, an' 'Arry 'ad a good night. When I heard that, nex' mornin', I says to meself, "I won't lay two an' two together *yit*. I'll keep me leg down a week, an' see what comes of it." It didn't hurt me that day, to speak of – seemed more to draw the strength out o' me like – an' 'Arry 'ad another good night. That made me persevere; but I didn't dare lay two an' two together till the weekend, an' then, 'Arry come forth e'en a'most 'imself again – na'un hurt outside ner in of him. I nigh fell on me knees in de wash-house when Bessie was up-street. "I've got ye now, my man," I says. "You'll take your good from me 'thout knowin' it till my life's end. O God, send me long to live for 'Arry's sake!" I says. An' I dunno that didn't still me ragin's.'

'For good?' Mrs Fettley asked.

'They come back, plenty times, but, let be how 'twould, I knowed I was doin' for 'im. I *knowed* it. I took an' worked me pains on an' off, like regulatin' my own range, till I learned to 'ave 'em at my commandments. An' that was funny, too. There was times, Liz, when my trouble 'ud all s'rink an' dry up, like. First, I used to try an' fetch it on again; bein' fearful to leave 'Arry alone too long for anythin' to lay 'old of. Prasin'ly I come to see that was a sign he'd do all right awhile, an' so I saved myself.'

''Ow long for?' Mrs Fettley asked, with deepest interest.

'I've gone de better part of a year onct or twice with na'un more to show than the liddle weepin' core of it, like. *All* s'rinked up an' dried off. Then he'd inflame up – for a warnin' – an' I'd suffer it. When I couldn't no more – an' I '*ad* to keep on goin' with my Lunnon work – I'd lay me leg high on a cheer till it eased. Not too quick. I knowed by the feel of it, those times, dat 'Arry was in need. Then I'd send another five shillin's to Bess, or somethin' for the chillern, to find out if, mebbe, 'e'd took any hurt through my neglects. 'Twas *so*! Year in, year out, I worked it dat way, Liz, an' 'e got 'is good from me 'thout knowin' – for years and years.'

'But what did *you* get out of it, Gra'?' Mrs Fettley almost wailed. 'Did ye see 'im reg'lar?'

'Times – when I was 'ere on me 'ol'days. An' more, now that I'm 'ere for good. But 'e's never looked at me, ner any other woman 'cept 'is mother. 'Ow I used to watch an' listen! So did she.'

'Years an' years!' Mrs Fettley repeated. 'An' where's 'e workin' at now?'

'Oh, 'e's give up carterin' quite a while. He's workin' for one o' them big tractorizin' firms – plowin' sometimes, an' sometimes off with lorries – fur as Wales, I've 'eard. He comes 'ome to 'is mother 'tween whiles; but I don't set eyes on him now, fer weeks on end. No odds! 'Is job keeps 'im from continuin' in one stay anywheres.'

'But – just for de sake o' sayin' somethin' – s'pose 'Arry *did* get married?' said Mrs Fettley.

Mrs Ashcroft drew her breath sharply between her still even and natural teeth. '*Dat* ain't been required of me,' she answered. 'I reckon my pains 'ull be counted agin that. Don't *you*, Liz?'

'It ought to be, dearie. It ought to be.'

'It *do* 'urt sometimes. You shall see it when nurse comes. She thinks I don't know it's turned.'

Mrs Fettley understood. Human nature seldom walks up to the word 'cancer'.

'Be ye certain sure, Gra'?' she asked.

'I was sure of it when old Mr Marshall 'ad me up to 'is study an' spoke a long piece about my faithful service. I've obliged 'em on an' off for a goodish time, but not enough for a pension. But they give me a weekly 'lowance for life. I knew what *that* sinnified – as long as three years ago.'

'Dat don't *prove* it, Gra'.'

'To give fifteen bob a week to a woman 'oo'd live twenty year in the course o' nature? It *do*!'

'You're mistook! You're mistook!' Mrs Fettley insisted.

'Liz, there's *no* mistakin' when the edges are all heaped up, like – same as a collar. You'll see it. An' I laid out Dora Wickwood, too. *She* 'ad it under the armpit, like.'

Mrs Fettley considered awhile, and bowed her head in finality.

''Ow long d'you reckon 'twill allow ye, countin' from now, dearie?'

'Slow come, slow go. But if I don't set eyes on ye 'fore next hoppin', this'll be goodbye, Liz.'

'Dunno as I'll be able to manage by then – not 'thout I have a liddle dog to lead me. For de chillern, dey won't be troubled, an' – O Gra'! – I'm blindin' up – I'm blindin' up!'

'Oh, *dat* was why you didn't more'n finger with your quilt-patches all this while! I was wonderin' . . . But the pain *do* count, don't ye think, Liz? The pain *do* count to keep 'Arry – where I want 'im. Say it can't be wasted, like.'

'I'm sure of it – sure of it, dearie. You'll 'ave your reward.'

'I don't want no more'n this – *if* de pain is taken into de reckonin'.'

''Twill be - 'twill be, Gra'.'

There was a knock on the door.

'That's nurse. She's before 'er time,' said Mrs Ashcroft. 'Open to 'er.'

The young lady entered briskly, all the bottles in her bag clicking. 'Evenin', Mrs Ashcroft,' she began. 'I've come raound a little earlier than usual because of the Institute dance to-na-ite. You won't ma-ind, will you?'

'Oh, no. Me dancin' days are over.' Mrs Ashcroft was the self-contained domestic at once. 'My old friend, Mrs Fettley 'ere, has been settin' talkin' with me a while.'

'I hope she 'asn't been fatiguing you?' said the nurse a little frostily.

'Quite the contrary. It 'as been a pleasure. Only – only – just at the end I felt a bit – a bit flogged out like.'

'Yes, yes.' The nurse was on her knees already, with the washes to hand. 'When old ladies get together they talk a deal too much, I've noticed.'

'Mebbe we do,' said Mrs Fettley, rising. 'So now I'll make myself scarce.'

'Look at it first, though,' said Mrs Ashcroft feebly. 'I'd like ye to look at it.'

Mrs Fettley looked, and shivered. Then she leaned over, and kissed Mrs Ashcroft once on the waxy yellow forehead, and again on the faded grey eyes.

'It *do* count, don't it – de pain?' The lips that still kept trace of their original moulding hardly more than breathed the words.

Mrs Fettley kissed them and moved towards the door.

RAHERE

Rahere, King Henry's Jester, feared by all the Norman Lords
For his eye that pierced their bosoms, for his tongue that shamed their swords;
Feed and flattered by the Churchmen – well they knew how deep he stood
In dark Henry's crooked counsels – fell upon an evil mood.

Suddenly, his days before him and behind him seemed to stand
Stripped and barren, fixed and fruitless, as those leagues of naked sand
When St Michael's ebb slinks outward to the bleak horizon-bound
And the trampling wide-mouthed waters are withdrawn from sight and sound.

Then a Horror of Great Darkness sunk his spirit and, anon,
(Who had seen him wince and whiten as he turned to walk alone)
Followed Gilbert the Physican, and muttered in his ear,
'Thou hast it, O my brother?' 'Yea, I have it,' said Rahere.

'So it comes,' said Gilbert smoothly, 'man's most immanent distress.
'Tis a humour of the Spirit which abhorreth all excess;
And, whatever breed the surfeit – Wealth, or Wit, or Power, or Fame –
(And thou hast each) the Spirit laboureth to expel the same.

'Hence the dulled eye's deep self-loathing – hence the loaded leaden brow;
Hence the burden of Wanhope that aches thy soul and body now.
Ay, the merriest fool must face it, and the wisest Doctor learn;
For it comes – it comes,' said Gilbert, 'as it passes – to return.'

But Rahere was in his torment, and he wandered, dumb and far,
Till he came to reeking Smithfield where the crowded gallows are,
(Followed Gilbert the Physician) and beneath the wry-necked dead,
Sat a leper and his woman, very merry, breaking bread.

He was cloaked from chin to ankle – faceless, fingerless, obscene –
Mere corruption swaddled man-wise, but the woman whole and clean;
And she waited on him crooning, and Rahere beheld the twain,
Each delighting in the other, and he checked and groaned again.

'So it comes – it comes,' said Gilbert, 'as it came when Life began.
'Tis a motion of the Spirit that revealeth God to man
In the shape of Love exceeding, which regards not taint or fall,
Since in perfect Love, saith Scripture, can be no excess at all.

'Hence the eye that sees no blemish – hence the hour that holds no shame.
Hence the Soul assured the Essence and the Substance are the same.
Nay, the meanest need not miss it, though the mightier pass it by;
For it comes – it comes,' said Gilbert, 'and, thou seest, it does not die!'

THE SURVIVAL

HORACE, Ode 22, Bk. V

Securely, after days
  Unnumbered, I behold
Kings mourn that promised praise
  Their cheating bards foretold.

Of earth-constricting wars,
  Of Princes passed in chains,
Of deeds out-shining stars,
  No word or voice remains.

Yet furthest times receive,
  And to fresh praise restore,
Mere flutes that breathe at eve,
  Mere seaweed on the shore;

A smoke of sacrifice;
  A chosen myrtle-wreath;
An harlot's altered eyes;
  A rage 'gainst love or death;

Glazed snow beneath the moon;
  The surge of storm-bowed trees –
The Caesars perished soon,
  And Rome Herself: But these

Endure while Empires fall
  And Gods for Gods make room . . .
Which greater God than all
  Imposed the amazing doom?

The Janeites

Jane lies in Winchester – blessed be her shade!
Praise the Lord for making her, and her for all she made!
And while the stones of Winchester, or Milsom Street, remain,
Glory, love, and honour unto England's Jane!

IN the Lodge of Instruction attached to 'Faith and Works No. 5837 E.C.,' which has already been described, Saturday afternoon was appointed for the weekly clean-up, when all visiting Brethren were welcome to help under the direction of the Lodge Officer of the day: their reward was light refreshment and the meeting of companions.

This particular afternoon – in the autumn of '20 – Brother Burges, P.M., was on duty and, finding a strong shift present, took advantage of it to strip and dust all hangings and curtains, to go over every inch of the Pavement – which was stone, not floorcloth – by hand; and to polish the Columns, Jewels, Working outfit and organ. I was given to clean some Officers' Jewels – beautiful bits of old Georgian silver-work humanized by generations of elbow-grease – and retired to the organ-loft; for the floor was like the quarterdeck of a battleship on the eve of a ball. Half a dozen brethren had already made the Pavement as glassy as the aisle of Greenwich Chapel; the brazen chapiters winked like pure gold at the flashing Marks on the Chairs; and a morose one-legged brother was attending to the Emblems of Mortality with, I think, rouge.

'They ought,' he volunteered to Brother Burges as we passed, 'to be betwixt the colour of ripe apricots an' a half-smoked meerschaum. That's how we kept 'em in my Mother-Lodge – a treat to look at.'

'I've never seen spit-and-polish to touch this,' I said.

'Wait till you see the organ,' Brother Burges replied. 'You could shave in it when they've done. Brother Anthony's in charge up there – the taxi-owner you met here last month. I don't think you've come across Brother Humberstall, have you?'

'I don't remember—' I began.

'You wouldn't have forgotten him if you had. He's a hairdresser now, somewhere at the back of Ebury Street. Was Garrison Artillery. Blown up twice.'

'Does he show it?' I asked at the foot of the organ-loft stairs.

'No-o. Not much more than Lazarus did, I expect.' Brother Burges fled off to set someone else to a job.

Brother Anthony, small, dark, and hump-backed, was hissing groom-fashion while he treated the rich acacia-wood panels of the Lodge organ with some sacred, secret composition of his own. Under his guidance Humberstall, an enormous, flat-faced man, carrying the shoulders, ribs, and loins of the old Mark '14 Royal Garrison Artillery, and the eyes of a bewildered retriever, rubbed the stuff in. I sat down to my task on the organ-bench, whose purple velvet cushion was being vacuum-cleaned on the floor below.

'Now,' said Anthony, after five minutes' vigorous work on the part of Humberstall. '*Now* we're gettin' somethin' worth lookin' at! Take it easy, an' go on with what you was tellin' me about that Macklin man.'

'I – I 'adn't anything against 'im,' said Humberstall, 'excep' he'd been a toff by birth; but that never showed till he was bosko absoluto. Mere bein' drunk on'y made a common 'ound of 'im. But when bosko, it all came out. Otherwise, he showed me my duties as mess-waiter very well on the 'ole.'

'Yes, yes. But what in 'ell made you go *back* to your Circus? The Board gave you down-an'-out fair enough, you said, after the dump went up at Eatables?'

'Board or no Board, *I* 'adn't the nerve to stay at 'ome – not with Mother chuckin' 'erself round all three rooms like a rabbit every time the Gothas tried to get Victoria; an' sister writin' me aunts four pages about it next day. Not for *me*, thank you! till the war was over. So I slid out with a draft – they wasn't particular in '17, so long as the tally was correct – and I joined up again with our Circus somewhere at the back of Lar Pug Noy, I think it was.' Humberstall paused for some seconds and his brow wrinkled. 'Then I – I went sick or somethin' or other, they told me; but I know *when* I reported for duty, our battery sergeant-major says that I wasn't expected back, an' – an', one thing leadin' to another – to cut a long story short – I went up before our major – Major – I shall forget my own name next – Major—'

'Never mind,' Anthony interrupted. 'Go on! It'll come back in talk!'

''Alf a mo'. 'Twas on the tip o' my tongue then.'

Humberstall dropped the polishing-cloth and knitted his brows again in most profound thought. Anthony turned to me and suddenly launched into a sprightly tale of his taxi's collision with a Marble Arch refuge on a greasy day after a three-yard skid.

'Much damage?' I asked.

'Oh no! Ev'ry bolt an' screw an' nut on the chassis strained; *but* nothing carried away, you understand me, an' not a scratch on the body. You'd never 'ave guessed a thing wrong till you took 'er in hand. It *was* a wop too: 'ead-on – like this!' And he slapped his tactful little forehead to show what a knock it had been.

'Did your major dish you up much?' he went on over his shoulder to Humberstall, who came out of his abstraction with a slow heave.

'We-ell! He told me I wasn't expected back either; an' he said 'e couldn't 'ang up the 'ole Circus till I'd rejoined; an' he said that my ten-inch Skoda which I'd been Number Three of, before the dump went up at Eatables, had 'er full crowd. But, 'e said, as soon as a casualty occurred he'd remember me. "Meantime," says he, "I particularly want you for actin' mess-waiter."

'"Beggin' your pardon, sir," I says perfectly respectful; "but I didn't exactly come back for *that*, sir."

'"Beggin' *your* pardon, 'Umberstall," says 'e, "but I 'appen to command the Circus! Now, you're a sharp-witted man," he says; "an' what we've suffered from fool-waiters in mess 'as been somethin' cruel. You'll take on, from now – under instruction to Macklin 'ere." So this man, Macklin, that I was tellin' you about, showed me my duties . . . 'Ammick! I've got it! 'Ammick was our major, an' Mosse was captain!' Humberstall celebrated his recapture of the name by labouring at the organ-panel on his knee.

'Look out! You'll smash it,' Anthony protested.

'Sorry! Mother's often told me I didn't know my strength. Now, here's a curious thing. This major of ours – it's all comin' back to me – was a high-up divorce-court lawyer; an' Mosse, our captain, was number one o' Mosse's Private Detective Agency. You've heard of it? Wives watched while you wait, an' so on. Well, these two 'ad been registerin' together, so to speak, in the Civil Line for years on end, but hadn't ever met till the war. Consequently, at mess their talk was mostly about famous cases they'd been mixed up in. 'Ammick told the law-courts' end o' the business, an' all what had been left out of the pleadin's; an' Mosse 'ad the actual facts concernin' the errin' parties – in hotels an' so on. I've heard better talk in our mess than ever before or since. It comes o' the Gunners bein' a scientific corps.'

'That be damned!' said Anthony. 'If anythin' 'appens to ' em they've got it all down in a book. There's no book when your lorry dies on you in the 'Oly Land. *That's* brains.'

'Well, *then*,' Humberstall continued, 'come on this secret society business that I started tellin' you about. When those two – 'Ammick an' Mosse – 'ad finished about their matrimonial relations – and, mind you, they weren't radishes – they seldom or ever repeated – they'd begin, as often as not, on this Secret Society woman I was tellin' you of – this Jane. She was the only woman I ever 'eard 'em say a good word for. 'Cordin' to them Jane was a nonesuch. *I* didn't know then she was a Society. Fact is, I only 'ung out 'arf an ear in their direction at first, on account of bein' under instruction for mess-duty to this Macklin man. What drew *my* attention to her was a new lieutenant joinin' up. We called 'im "Gander" on account of his profeel, which was the identical bird. 'E'd been a nactuary – workin' out 'ow long civilians 'ad to live. Neither 'Ammick nor Mosse wasted words on 'im at mess. They went on talking as usual, an' in due time, *as* usual, they got back to Jane. Gander cocks one of his big chilblainy ears an' cracks his cold finger-joints. "By God! Jane?" says 'e. "Yes, Jane," says 'Ammick pretty short an' senior. "Praise 'Eaven!" says Gander. "It was 'Bubbly' where I've come from down the line." (Some damn revue or other, I expect.) Well, neither 'Ammick nor Mosse was easy-mouthed, or for that matter mealy-mouthed; but no sooner 'ad Gander passed that remark than they both shook 'ands with the young squirt across the table an' called for the port back again. It *was* a password, all right! Then they went at it about Jane – all three, regardless of rank. That made me listen. Presently, I 'eard 'Ammick say—'

''Arf a mo',' Anthony cut in. 'But what was *you* doin' in mess?'

'Me an' Macklin was refixin' the sandbag screens to the dug-out passage in case o' gas. We never knew when we'd cop it in the 'Eavies, don't you see? But we knew we 'ad been looked for for some time, an' it might come any minute. But, as I was sayin', 'Ammick says what a pity 'twas Jane 'ad died barren. "I deny that," says Mosse. "I maintain she was fruitful in the 'ighest sense o' the word." An' Mosse knew about such things, too. "I'm inclined to agree with 'Ammick," says young Gander. "Any'ow, she's left no direct an' lawful prog'ny." I remember every word they said, on account o' what 'appened subsequently. I 'adn't noticed Macklin much, or I'd ha' seen he was bosko absoluto. Then *'e* cut in, leanin' over a packin'-case with a face on 'im like a dead mackerel in the dark. "Pa-hardon me, gents," Macklin says, "but this *is* a matter on which I *do* 'appen to be moderately well-informed. She *did* leave lawful issue in the shape o' one son; and 'is name was 'Enery James."

'"By what sire? Prove it," says Gander, before 'is senior officers could get in a word.

'"I will," says Macklin, surgin' on 'is two thumbs. *An'*, mark you, none of 'em spoke! I forget whom he said was the sire of this 'Enery James-man; but 'e delivered 'em a lecture on this Jane-woman for more than a quarter of an hour. I know the exact time, because my old Skoda was on duty at ten-minute intervals reachin' after some Jerry formin'-up area; and her blast always put out the dug-out candles. I relit 'em once, an' again at the end. In conclusion, this Macklin fell flat forward on 'is face, which was how 'e generally wound up 'is notion of a perfect day. Bosko absoluto!

'"Take 'im away," says 'Ammick to me. "'E's sufferin' from shell-shock."

'To cut a long story short, *that* was what first put the notion into my 'ead. Wouldn't it you? Even 'ad Macklin been a 'igh-up mason—'

'Wasn't 'e, then?' said Anthony, a little puzzled.

''E'd never gone beyond the Blue Degrees, 'e told me. Any'ow, 'e'd lectured 'is superior officers up an' down; 'e'd as good as called 'em fools most o' the time, in 'is toff's voice. I 'eard 'im an' I saw 'im. An' all he got was – me told off to put 'im to bed! And all on account o' Jane! Would *you* have let a thing like that get past you? Nor me, either! Next mornin', when his stummick was settled, I was at him full-cry to find out 'ow it was worked. Toff or no toff, 'e knew his end of a bargain. First, 'e wasn't takin' any. He said I wasn't fit to be initiated into the Society of the Janeites. That only meant five bob more – fifteen up to date.

'"Make it one Bradbury," 'e says. "It's dirt-cheap. You saw me 'old the Circus in the 'ollow of me 'and?"

'No denyin' it. I *'ad*. So, for one pound, he communicated me the Password of the First Degree, which was *Tilniz an' trap-doors*.

'"I know what a trap-door is," I says to 'im, "but what in 'ell's *Tilniz?"*

'"You obey orders," 'e says, "an' next time I ask you what you're thinkin' about you'll answer, *'Tilniz an' trap-doors,'* in a smart and soldierly manner. I'll spring that question at me own time. All you've got to do is to be distinck."

'We settled all this while we was skinnin' spuds for dinner at the back o' the rear-truck under our camouflage-screens. Gawd 'ow that glue-paint did stink! Otherwise, 'twasn't so bad, with the sun comin' through our pantomime-leaves, an' the wind marcelling the grasses in the cutting. Well, one thing leading to another, nothin' further 'appened in this direction till the afternoon. We 'ad a high standard o' livin' in mess – an' in the group, for that matter. I was takin' away Mosse's lunch – dinner 'e would never call it – an' Mosse was fillin' his cigarette-case previous to the afternoon's duty. Macklin, in the passage, comin' in as if 'e didn't know Mosse was there, slings 'is question at me, an' I give the countersign in a low but quite distinck voice, makin' as if I 'adn't seen Mosse. Mosse looked at me through and through, with his cigarette-case in his 'and. Then 'e jerks out 'arf a dozen – best Turkish – on the table an' exits. I pinched 'em an' divvied with Macklin.

'"You see 'ow it works," says Macklin. "Could you 'ave invested a Bradbury to better advantage?"

'"So far, no," I says. "Otherwise, though, if they start provin' an' tryin' me, I'm a dead bird. There must be a lot more to this Janeite game."

'"Eaps an' 'eaps," he says. "But to show you the sort of 'eart I 'ave, I'll communicate you all the 'Igher Degrees among the Janeites, includin' the Charges, for another Bradbury; but you'll 'ave to work, Dobbin."'

'Pretty free with your Bradburys, wasn't you?' Anthony grunted disapprovingly.

'What odds? *Ac*-tually, Gander told us, we couldn't expect to av'rage more than six weeks longer apiece, an', any'ow, *I* never regretted it. But make no mistake—the preparation was somethin' cruel. In the first place, I come under Macklin for direct instruction *re* Jane.'

'Oh! Jane *was* real, then?' Anthony glanced for an instant at me as he put the question. 'I couldn't quite make that out.'

'Real!' Humberstall's voice rose almost to a treble. 'Jane? Why, she was a little old maid 'oo'd written 'alf a dozen books about a hundred years ago. 'Twasn't as if there was anythin' *to* 'em, either. *I* know. I had to read 'em. They weren't adventurous, not smutty, nor what you'd call even interestin' – all about girls o' seventeen (they begun young then, I tell you), not certain 'oom they'd like to marry; an' their dances an' card-parties an' picnics, and their young blokes goin' off to London on 'orseback for 'air-cuts an' shaves. It took a full day in those days, if you went to a proper barber. They wore wigs, too, when they was chemists or clergymen. All that interested me on account o' me profession, an' cuttin' the men's 'air every fortnight. Macklin used to chip me about bein' an 'airdresser. 'E *could* pass remarks, too!'

Humberstall recited with relish a fragment of what must have been a superb commination-service, ending with, 'You lazy-minded, lousy-headed, long-trousered, perfumed perookier.'

'An' you took it?' Anthony's quick eyes ran over the man.

'Yes. I was after my money's worth; an' Macklin, havin' put 'is 'and to the plough, wasn't one to withdraw it. Otherwise, if I'd pushed 'im, I'd ha' slew 'im. Our battery sergeant-major nearly did. For Macklin had a wonderful way o' passing remarks on a man's civil life; an' he put it about that our BSM had run a dope an' dolly-shop with a Chinese woman, the wrong end o' Southwark Bridge. Nothin' you could lay 'old of, o' course; but—' Humberstall let us draw our own conclusions.

'That reminds me,' said Anthony, smacking his lips. 'I 'ad a bit of a fracas with a fare in the Fulham Road last month. He called me a paras-tit-ic Forder. I informed 'im I was owner-driver, an' 'e could see for 'imself the cab was quite clean. That didn't suit 'im. 'E said it was crawlin'.'

'What happened?' I asked.

'One o' them blue-bellied Bolshies of post-war police (neglectin' point-duty, as usual) asked us to flirt a little quieter. My joker chucked some Arabic at 'im. That was when we signed the Armistice. 'E'd been a Yeoman – a perishin' Gloucestershire Yeoman—that I'd helped gather in the orange crop with at Jaffa, in the 'Oly Land!'

'And after that?' I continued.

'It 'ud be 'ard to say. I know 'e lived at Hendon or Cricklewood. I drove 'im there. We must 'ave talked Zionism or somethin', because at seven next mornin' him an' me was tryin' to get petrol out of a milkshop at St Albans. They 'adn't any. In lots o' ways this war has been a public noosance, as one might say, but there's no denyin' it 'elps you slip through life easier. The dairyman's son 'ad done time on Jordan with camels. So he stood us rum an' milk.'

'Just like 'avin' the Password, eh?' was Humberstall's comment.

'That's right! Ours was *Imshee kelb*.* Not so 'ard to remember as your Jane stuff.'

'Jane wasn't so very 'ard – not the way Macklin used to put 'er,' Humberstall resumed. 'I 'ad only six books to remember. I learned the names by 'eart as Macklin placed 'em. There was one called *Persuasion*, first; an' the rest in a bunch, except another about some Abbey or other – last by three lengths. But, as I was sayin', what beat me was there was nothin' *to* 'em nor *in* 'em. Nothin' at all, believe me.'

'You seem good an' full of 'em, any'ow,' said Anthony.

'I mean that 'er characters was no *use!* They was only just like

* 'Get out, you dog.'

people you run across any day. One of 'em was a curate – the Reverend Collins – always on the make an' lookin' to marry money. Well, when I was a boy scout, 'im or 'is twin brother was our troop-leader. An' there was an upstandin' 'ard-mouthed duchess or a baronet's wife that didn't give a curse for any one 'oo wouldn't do what she told 'em to; the Lady – Lady Catherine (I'll get it in a minute) De Bugg. Before Ma bought the 'airdressin' business in London I used to know of an 'olesale grocer's wife near Leicester (I'm Leicestershire myself) that might 'ave been 'er duplicate. And – oh yes – there was a Miss Bates; just an old maid runnin' about like a hen with 'er 'ead cut off, an' her tongue loose at both ends. I've got an aunt like 'er. Good as gold – but, *you* know.'

'Lord, yes!' said Anthony, with feeling. 'An' did you find out what *Tilniz* meant? I'm always huntin' after the meanin' of things meself.'

'Yes, 'e was a swine of a major-general, retired, and on the make. They're all on the make, in a quiet way, in Jane. 'E was so much of a gentleman by 'is own estimation that 'e was always be'avin' like a hound. *You* know the sort. Turned a girl out of 'is own 'ouse because she 'adn't any money – *after,* mark you, encouragin' 'er to set 'er cap at his son, because 'e thought she had.'

'But that 'appens all the time,' said Anthony. 'Why, me own mother—'

'That's right. So would mine. But this Tilney was a man, an' some'ow Jane put it down all so naked it made you ashamed. I told Macklin that, an' he said I was shapin' to be a good Janeite. 'Twasn't *his* fault if I wasn't. 'Nother thing, too; 'avin' been at the Bath Mineral Waters 'Ospital in 'Sixteen, with trench-feet, was a great advantage to me, because I knew the names o' the streets where Jane 'ad lived. There was one of 'em – Laura, I think, or some other girl's name – which Macklin said was 'oly ground. "If you'd been initiated *then,*" he says, "you'd ha' felt your flat feet tingle every time you walked over those sacred pavin'-stones."

'"My feet tingled right enough," I said, "but not on account of Jane. Nothin' remarkable about that," I says.

'"'Eaven lend me patience!" he says, combin' 'is 'air with 'is little hands. "Every dam' thing about Jane is remarkable to a pukka Janeite! It was there," he says, "that Miss What's-her-Name" (he had the name; I've forgotten it) "made up 'er engagement again, after nine years, with Captain T'other Bloke." An' he dished me out a page an' a half of one of the books to learn by 'eart – *Persuasion,* I think it was.'

'You quick at gettin' things off by 'eart?' Anthony demanded.

'Not as a rule. I was then, though, or else Macklin knew 'ow to deliver the Charges properly. 'E said 'e'd been some sort o' schoolmaster once, and he'd make my mind resume work or break 'imself. That was just before the battery sergeant-major 'ad it in for him on account o' what he'd been sayin' about the Chinese wife an' the dolly-shop.'

'What did Macklin really say?' Anthony and I asked together. Humberstall gave us a fragment. It was hardly the stuff to let loose on a pious post-war world without revision.

'And what had your BSM been in civil life?' I asked at the end.

''Ead-embalmer to an 'olesale undertaker in the Midlands,' said Humberstall; 'but, o' course, *when* he thought 'e saw his chance he naturally took it. He came along one mornin' lickin' 'is lips. "You don't get past me this time," 'e says to Macklin. "You're for it, Professor."

'"'Ow so, me gallant Major," says Macklin; "an' what for?"

'"For writin' obese words on the breech o' the ten-inch," says the BSM. She was our old Skoda that I've been tellin' you about. We called 'er "Bloody Eliza". She 'ad a badly wore obturator an' blew through a fair treat. I knew by Macklin's face the BSM 'ad dropped it somewhere, but all he vow'saifed was, "Very good, Major. We will consider it in Common Room." The BSM couldn't ever stand Macklin's toff's way o' puttin' things; so he goes off rumblin' like 'ell's bells in an 'urricane, as the Marines say. Macklin put it to me at once, what had I been doin'? Some'ow he could read me like a book.

'Well, all *I'd* done – an' I told 'im *he* was responsible for it – was to chalk the guns. 'Ammick never minded what the men wrote up on 'em. 'E said it gave 'em an interest in their job. You'd see all sorts of remarks chalked up on the side-plates or the gear-casin's.'

'What sort of remarks?' said Anthony keenly.

'Oh! 'Ow Bloody Eliza, or Spittin' Jim – that was our old Mark Five Nine-point-two – felt that morning, an' such things. But it 'ad come over me – more to please Macklin than anythin' else – that it was time we Janeites 'ad a look in. So, as I was tellin' you, I'd taken an' rechristened all three of 'em, on my own, early that mornin'. Spittin' Jim I 'ad chalked "The Reverend Collins" – that curate I was tellin' you about; an' our cut-down Navy Twelve, "General Tilney", because it was worse wore in the groovin' than anything *I'd* ever seen. The Skoda (an' that was where *I* dropped it) I 'ad chalked up "The Lady Catherine De Bugg". I made a clean breast of it all to Macklin. He reached up an' patted me on the shoulder. "You done nobly," he says. "You're bringin' forth abundant fruit, like a good

Janeite. But I'm afraid your spellin' has misled our worthy BSM. *That's* what it is," 'e says, slappin' 'is little leg. "'Ow might you 'ave spelt De Bourgh for example?"

'I told 'im. 'Twasn't right; an' 'e nips off to the Skoda to make it so. When 'e comes back, 'e says that the Gander 'ad been before 'im an' corrected the error. But we two come up before the Major, just the same, that afternoon after lunch; 'Ammick in the chair, so to speak, Mosse in another, an' the BSM chargin' Macklin with writin' obese words on His Majesty's property, on active service. When it transpired that me an' not Macklin was the offendin' party, the BSM turned 'is hand in and sulked like a baby. 'E as good as told 'Ammick 'e couldn't hope to preserve discipline unless examples were made – meanin', 'o course, Macklin.'

'Yes, I've heard all that,' said Anthony, with a contemptuous grunt. 'The worst of it is, a lot of it's true.'

''Ammick took 'im up sharp about Military Law, which he said was even more fair than the civilian article.'

'My Gawd!' This came from Anthony's scornful midmost bosom.

'"Accordin' to the unwritten law of the 'Eavies," says 'Ammick, "there's no objection to the men chalkin' the guns, if decency is preserved. On the other 'and," says he, "we 'aven't yet settled the precise status of individuals entitled so to do. I 'old that the privilege is confined to combatants only."

'"With the permission of the court," says Mosse, who was another born lawyer, "I'd like to be allowed to join issue on that point. Prisoner's position is very delicate an' doubtful, an' he has no legal representative."

'"Very good," says 'Ammick. "Macklin bein' acquitted—"

'"With submission, me lud," says Mosse. "I hope to prove 'e was accessory before the fact."

'"*As* you please," says 'Ammick. "But in that case, 'oo the 'ell's goin' to get the port I'm tryin' to stand the court?"

'"I submit," says Mosse, "prisoner, bein' under direct observation o' the court, could be temporarily enlarged for that duty."

'So Macklin went an' got it, an' the BSM had 'is glass with the rest. Then they argued whether mess servants an' non-combatants was entitled to chalk the guns ('Ammick *versus* Mosse). After a bit, 'Ammick as CO give 'imself best, an' me an' Macklin was severely admonished for trespassin' on combatants' rights, an' the BSM was warned that if we repeated the offence 'e could deal with us summ'rily. He 'ad some glasses o' port an' went out quite 'appy. Then my turn come, while Macklin was gettin' them their tea; an' one thing leadin' to another, 'Ammick put me through all the Janeite Degrees, you might say. Never 'ad such a doin' in my life.'

'Yes, but what did you tell 'em?' said Anthony. 'I can't ever *think* my lies quick enough when I'm for it.'

'No need to lie. I told 'em that the backside view o' the Skoda, when she was run up, put Lady De Bugg into my 'ead. They gave me right there, but they said I was wrong about General Tilney. 'Cordin' to them, our Navy twelve-inch ought to 'ave been christened Miss Bates. I said the same idea 'ad crossed my mind, till I'd seen the general's groovin'. Then I felt it had to be the general or nothin'. But they give me full marks for the Reverend Collins – our Nine-point-two.'

'An you fed 'em *that* sort o' talk?' Anthony's fox-coloured eyebrows climbed almost into his hair.

'While I was assistin' Macklin to get tea – yes. Seein' it was an examination, I wanted to do 'im credit as a Janeite.'

'An' – an' what did they say?'

'They said it was 'ighly creditable to us both. I don't drink, so they give me about a hundred fags.'

'Gawd! What a Circus you must 'ave been,' was Anthony's gasping comment.

'It *was* a 'appy little group. I wouldn't 'a changed with any other.'

Humberstall sighed heavily as he helped Anthony slide back the organ-panel. We all admired it in silence, while Anthony repocketed his secret polishing mixture, which lived in a tin tobacco-box. I had neglected my work for listening to Humberstall. Anthony reached out quietly and took over a Secretary's Jewel and a rag. Humberstall studied his reflection in the glossy wood.

'Almost,' he said critically, holding his head to one side.

'Not with an Army. You could with a Safety, though,' said Anthony. And, indeed, as Brother Burges had foretold, one might have shaved in it with comfort.

'Did you ever run across any of 'em afterwards, any time?' Anthony asked presently.

'Not so many of 'em left to run after, now. With the 'Eavies it's mostly neck or nothin'. We copped it. In the neck. In due time.'

'Well, *you* come out of it all right.' Anthony spoke both stoutly and soothingly; but Humberstall would not be comforted.

'That's right; but I almost wish I 'adn't,' he sighed. 'I was 'appier there than ever before or since. Jerry's March push in 'Eighteen did us in; an' yet, 'ow could we 'ave expected it? 'Ow *could* we 'ave expected it? We'd been sent back for rest an' runnin'-repairs, back pretty near our base; an' our old loco' that used to shift us about o' nights, she'd gone down the line for repairs. But for 'Ammick we wouldn't even 'ave 'ad our camouflage-screens up. He told our brigadier that, whatever 'e might be in the gunnery line, as a leadin' divorce lawyer he never threw away a point in argument. So 'e 'ad us all screened in over in a cuttin' on a little spur-line near a wood; an' 'e saw to the screens 'imself. The leaves weren't more than comin' out then, an' the sun used to make our glue-paint stink. Just like actin' in a theatre, it was! But 'appy. *But* 'appy! I expect if we'd been caterpillars, like the new big six-inch hows, they'd ha' remembered us. But we was the old La Bassée '15 Mark o' Heavies that run on rails – not much more good than scrap-iron that late in the war. An', believe me, gents – or Brethren, as I should say – we copped it cruel. Look 'ere! It was in the afternoon, an' I was watchin' Gander instructin' a class in new sights at Lady Catherine. All of a sudden I 'eard our screens rip overhead, an' a runner on a motor-bike came sailin', sailin' through the air – like that bloke that used to bicycle off Brighton Pier – and landed one awful wop almost atop o' the class. "'Old 'ard," says Gander. "That's no way to report. What's the fuss?" "Your screens 'ave broke my back, for one thing," says the bloke on the ground; "an' for another, the 'ole front's gone." "Nonsense," says Gander. 'E 'adn't more than passed the remark when the man was vi'lently sick an' conked out. 'E 'ad plenty papers on 'im from brigadiers and CO's reporting 'emselves cut off an' askin' for orders. 'E was right both ways – his back an' our front. The 'ole Somme front washed out as clean as kiss-me-'and!' His huge hand smashed down open on his knee.

'We 'eard about it at the time in the 'Oly Land. Was it reelly as quick as all that?' said Anthony.

'Quicker! Look 'ere! The motorbike dropped in on us about four pip-emma. After that, we tried to get orders o' some kind or other, but nothin' came through excep' that all available transport was in use and not likely to be released. *That* didn't 'elp us any. About nine o'clock comes along a young brass 'at in brown gloves. We was quite a surprise to 'im. 'E said they were evacuating the area and we'd better shift. "Where to?" says 'Ammick, rather short.

'"Oh, somewhere Amiens way," he says. "Not that I'd guarantee Amiens for any length o' time; but Amiens might do to begin with." I'm giving you the very words. Then 'e goes off swingin' 'is brown gloves, and 'Ammick sends for Gander and orders 'im to march the men through Amiens to Dieppe; book thence to New'aven, take up positions be'ind Seaford, an' carry on the war. Gander said 'e'd see 'im damned first. 'Ammick says 'e'd see 'im court-martialled after. Gander says what 'e meant to say was that the men 'ud see all an' sundry damned before they went into Amiens with their gunsights wrapped up in their puttees. 'Ammick says 'e 'adn't said a word about puttees, an' carryin' off the gunsights was purely optional. "Well, anyhow," says Gander, "puttees *or* drawers, they ain't goin' to shift a step unless you lead the procession."

'"Mutinous 'ounds," says 'Ammick. "But we live in a democratic age. D'you suppose they'd object to kindly diggin' 'emselves in a bit?" "Not at all," says Gander. "The BSM's kept 'em at it like terriers for the last three hours." "That bein' so," says 'Ammick, "Macklin'll now fetch us small glasses o' port." Then Mosse comes in – he could smell port a mile off – an' he submits we'd only add to the congestion in Amiens if we took our crowd there, whereas, if we lay doggo where we was, Jerry might miss us, though he didn't seem to be missin' much that evenin'.

'The 'ole country was pretty noisy, an' our dumps we'd lit ourselves flarin' heavens-high as far as you could see. Lyin' doggo was our best chance. I believe we might ha' pulled it off, if we'd been left alone, but along towards midnight – there was some small stuff swishin' about, but nothin' particular – a nice little bald-headed old gentleman in uniform pushes into the dug-out wipin' his glasses an' sayin' 'e was thinkin' o' formin' a defensive flank on our left with 'is battalion which 'ad just come up. 'Ammick says 'e wouldn't form much if 'e was 'im. "Oh, don't say *that*," says the old gentleman, very shocked. "One must support the guns, mustn't one?" 'Ammick says we was refittin' an' about as effective, just then, as a public lav'tory. "Go into Amiens," he says, "an' defend 'em there." "Oh no," says the old gentleman, "me an' my laddies *must* make a defensive flank for you," an' he flips out of the dug-out like a performin' bullfinch, chirruppin' for his "laddies". Gawd in 'Eaven knows what sort o' push they was – little boys mostly – but they 'ung on to 'is coat-tails like a Sunday-school treat, an' we 'eard 'em muckin' about in the open for a bit. Then a pretty tight barrage was slapped down for ten minutes, an' 'Ammick thought the laddies had copped it already. "It'll be our turn next," says Mosse. "There's been a covey o' Gothas messin' about for the last 'alf-hour – lookin' for the Railway Shops, I expect. They're just as likely to take us." "Arisin' out o' that," says 'Ammick, "one of 'em sounds pretty low down now. We're for it, me learned colleagues!" "Jesus!" says Gander, "I believe you're right, sir." And that was the last word *I* 'eard on the matter.'

'Did they cop you then?' said Anthony.

'They did. I expect Mosse was right, an' they took us for the Railway Shops. When I come to, I was lyin' outside the cuttin', which was pretty well filled up. The Reverend Collins was all right; but Lady Catherine and the General was past prayin' for. I lay there, takin' it in, till I felt cold an' I looked at meself. Otherwise, I 'adn't much on excep' me boots. So I got up an' walked about to keep warm. Then I saw somethin' like a mushroom in the moonlight. It was the nice old gentleman's bald 'ead. I patted it. 'Im and 'is laddies 'ad copped it right enough. Some battalion run out in a 'urry from England, I suppose. They 'adn't even begun to dig in – pore little perishers! I dressed myself off 'em there, an' topped off with a British warm. Then I went back to the cuttin' an' some one says to me: "Dig, you ox, dig! Gander's under." So I 'elped shift things till I threw up blood an' bile mixed. Then I dropped, an' they brought Gander out – dead – an' laid 'im next me. 'Ammick 'ad gone too – fair tore in 'alf, the BSM said; but the funny thing was he talked quite a lot before 'e died, an' nothin' to 'im below 'is stummick, they told me. Mosse we never found. 'E'd been standing by Lady Catherine. She'd up-ended an' gone back on 'em, with 'alf the cuttin' atop of 'er, by the look of things.'

'And what come to Macklin?' said Anthony.

'Dunno . . . 'E was with 'Ammick. I expect I must ha' been blown clear of all by the first bomb; for I was the on'y Janeite left. We lost about half our crowd, either under, or after we'd got 'em out. The BSM went off 'is rocker when mornin' came, an' he ran about from one to another sayin': "That was a good push! That was a great crowd! Did ye ever know any push to touch 'em?" An' then 'e'd cry. So what was left of us made off for ourselves, an' I came across a lorry, pretty full, but they took me in.'

'Ah!' said Anthony with pride. '"They all take a taxi when it's rainin'." Ever 'eard that song?'

'They went a long way back. Then I walked a bit, an' there was a hospital-train fillin' up, an' one of the sisters – a grey-headed one – ran at me wavin' 'er red 'ands an' sayin' there wasn't room for a louse in it. I was past carin'. But she went on talkin' and talkin' about the war, an' her pa in Ladbroke Grove, an' 'ow strange for 'er at 'er time of life to be doin' this work with a lot o' men, an' next war, 'ow the nurses 'ud 'ave to wear khaki breeches on account o' the mud, like the Land Girls; an' that reminded 'er, she'd boil me an egg if she could lay 'ands on one, for she'd run a chicken-farm once. You never 'eard anythin' like it – outside o' Jane. It set me off laughin' again. Then a woman with a nose an' teeth on 'er, marched up. "What's all this?" she says. "What do you want?" "Nothing," I says, "only make Miss Bates, there, stop talkin' or I'll die." "Miss Bates?" she says. "What in 'Eaven's name makes you call 'er that?" "Because she is," I says. "D'you know what you're sayin'?" she says, an' slings her bony arm round me to get me off the ground. "Course I do," I says, "an' if you knew Jane you'd know too." "That's enough," says she. "You're comin' on this train if I have to kill a brigadier for you," an' she an' an ord'ly fair hove me into the train, on to a stretcher close to the cookers. That beef-tea went down well! Then she shook 'ands with me an' said I'd hit off Sister Molyneux in one, an' then she pinched me an extra blanket. It was 'er own 'ospital pretty much. I expect she was the Lady Catherine de Bourgh of the area. Well, an' so, to cut a long story short, nothing further transpired.'

''Adn't you 'ad enough by then?' asked Anthony.

'I expect so. Otherwise, if the old Circus 'ad been carryin' on, I might 'ave 'ad another turn with 'em before Armistice. Our BSM was right. There never was a 'appier push. 'Ammick an' Mosse an' Gander an' the BSM an' that pore little Macklin man makin' an' passin' an' raisin' me an' gettin' me on to the 'ospital train after 'e was dead, all for a couple of Bradburys. I lie awake nights still, reviewing matters. There never was a push to touch ours – never!'

Anthony handed me back the Secretary's Jewel resplendent.

'Ah,' said he. 'No denyin' that Jane business was more useful to you than the Roman Eagles or the Star an' Garter. Pity there wasn't any of you Janeites in the 'Oly Land. *I* never come across 'em.'

'Well, as pore Macklin said, it's a very select Society, an' you've got to be a Janeite in your 'eart, or you won't have any success. An' yet he made *me* a Janeite. I read all her six books now for pleasure 'tween times in the shop; an' it brings it all back – down to the smell of the glue-paint on the screens. You take it from me, Brethren, there's no one to touch Jane when you're in a tight place. Gawd bless 'er, whoever she was.'

Worshipful Brother Burges, from the floor of the Lodge, called us all from Labour to Refreshment. Humberstall hove himself up – so very a cart-horse of a man one almost expected to hear the harness creak on his back – and descended the steps.

He said he could not stay for tea because he had promised his mother to come home for it, and she would most probably be waiting for him now at the Lodge door.

'One or other of 'em always comes for 'im. He's apt to miss 'is gears sometimes,' Anthony explained to me, as we followed.

'Goes on a bust, d'you mean?'

''Im! He's no more touched liquor than 'e 'as women since 'e was born. No, 'e's liable to a sort o' quiet fits like. They came on after the dump blew up at Eatables. But for them, 'e'd ha' been battery sergeant-major.'

'Oh! I said. 'I couldn't make out why he took on as mess-waiter when he got back to his guns. That explains things a bit.'

''Is sister told me the dump goin' up knocked all 'is gunnery instruction clean out of 'im. The only thing 'e stuck to was to get back to 'is old crowd. Gawd knows 'ow 'e worked it, but 'e did. He fair deserted out of England to 'em, she says; an' when they saw the state 'e was in, they 'adn't the 'eart to send 'im back or into 'ospital. They kep' 'im for a mascot, as you might say. That's *all* dead true. 'Is sister told me so. But I can't guarantee that Janeite business, excep' 'e never told a lie since 'e was six. 'Is sister told me so. What do *you* think?'

'He isn't likely to have made it up out of his own head,' I replied.

'But people don't get so crazy-fond o' books as all that, do they? 'E's made 'is sister try to read 'em. She'd do anythin' to please him. But, as I keep tellin' 'er, so'd 'is mother. D'you 'appen to know anything about Jane?'

'I believe Jane was a bit of a matchmaker in a quiet way when she was alive, and I know all her books are full of match-making,' I said. '*You'd* better look out.'

'Oh, *that's* as good as settled,' Anthony replied, blushing.

JANE'S MARRIAGE

Jane went to Paradise:
  That was only fair.
Good Sir Walter followed her,
  And armed her up the stair.
Henry and Tobias,
  And Miguel of Spain
Stood with Shakespeare at the top
  To welcome Jane.

Then the Three Archangels
  Offered out of hand
Anything in Heaven's gift
  That she might command.
Azrael's eyes upon her,
  Raphael's wings above,
Michael's sword against her heart,
  Jane said: 'Love.'

Instantly the under-
  standing Seraphim
Laid their fingers on their lips
  And went to look for him.
Stole across the Zodiac,
  Harnessed Charles's Wain,
And whispered round the Nebulae:
  'Who loved Jane?'

In a private limbo
  Where none had thought to look,
Sat a Hampshire gentleman
  Reading of a book.
It was called *Persuasion*,
  And it told the plain
Story of the love between
  Him and Jane.

He heard the question
  Circle Heaven through –
Closed the book and answered:
  'I did – and do!'
Quietly and speedily
  (As Captain Wentworth moved)
Entered into Paradise
  The man Jane loved!

The Bull that Thought

WESTWARD from a town by the Mouths of the Rhône, runs a road so mathematically straight, so barometrically level, that it ranks among the world's measured miles and motorists use it for records.

I had attacked the distance several times, but always with a Mistral blowing, or the unchancy cattle of those parts on the move. But once, running from the East, into a high-piled, almost Egyptian sunset, there came a night which it would have been sin to have wasted. It was warm with the breath of summer in advance; moonlit till the shadow of every rounded pebble and pointed cypress windbreak lay solid on that vast flat-floored waste; and my Mr Leggatt, who had slipped out to make sure, reported that the road surface was unblemished.

'*Now,*' he suggested, 'we might see what she'll do under strict road conditions. She's been pullin' like the Blue de Luxe all day. Unless I'm all off, it's her night out.'

We arranged the trial for after dinner – thirty kilometres as near as might be; and twenty-two of them without even a level crossing.

There sat beside me at table d'hôte an elderly, bearded Frenchman wearing the rosette of by no means the lowest grade of the Legion of Honour, who had arrived in a talkative Citroën. I gathered that he had spent much of his life in the French Colonial Service in Annam and Tonquin. When the war came, his years barring him from the front line, he had supervised Chinese wood-cutters who, with axe and dynamite, deforested the centre of France for trench-props. He said my chauffeur had told him that I contemplated an experiment. He was interested in cars – had admired mine – would, in short, be greatly indebted to me if I permitted him to assist as an observer. One could not well refuse; and, knowing my Mr Leggatt, it occurred to me there might also be a bet in the background.

While he went to get his coat, I asked the proprietor his name. 'Voiron – Monsieur André Voiron,' was the reply. 'And his business?' 'Mon Dieu! He is Voiron! He is all those things, there!' The proprietor waved his hands at brilliant advertisements on the dining-room walls, which declared that Voiron Frères dealt in wines, agricultural implements, chemical manures, provisions and produce throughout that part of the globe.

He said little for the first five minutes of our trip, and nothing at all for the next ten – it being, as Leggatt had guessed, Esmeralda's night out. But, when her indicator climbed to a certain figure and held there for three blinding kilometres, he expressed himself satisfied, and proposed to me that we should celebrate the event at the hotel. 'I keep yonder,' said he, 'a wine on which I should value your opinion.'

On our return, he disappeared for a few minutes, and I heard him rumbling in a cellar. The proprietor presently invited me to the dining-room, where, beneath one frugal light, a table had been set with local dishes of renown. There was too, a bottle beyond most known sizes, marked black on red, with a date. Monsieur Voiron opened it, and we drank to the health of my car. The velvety, perfumed liquor, between fawn and topaz, neither too sweet nor too dry, creamed in its generous glass. But I knew no wine composed of the whispers of angels' wings, the breath of Eden and the foam and pulse of Youth renewed. So I asked what it might be.

'It is champagne,' he said gravely.

'Then what have I been drinking all my life?'

'If you were lucky, before the war, and paid thirty shillings a bottle, it is possible you may have drunk one of our better-class *tisanes.*'

'And where does one get this?'

'Here, I am happy to say. Elsewhere, perhaps, it is not so easy. We growers exchange these real wines among ourselves.'

I bowed my head in admiration, surrender, and joy. There stood the most ample bottle, and it was not yet eleven o'clock. Doors locked and shutters banged throughout the establishment. Some last servant yawned on his way to bed. Monsieur Voiron opened a window and the moonlight flooded in from a small pebbled court outside. One could almost hear the town of Chambres breathing in its first sleep. Presently, there was a thick noise in the air, the passing of feet and hoofs, lowings, and a stifled bark or two. Dust rose over the courtyard wall, followed by the strong smell of cattle.

'They are moving some beasts,' said Monsieur Voiron, cocking an ear. 'Mine, I think. Yes, I hear Christophe. Our beasts do not like automobiles – so we move at night. You do not know our country – the Crau, here, or the Camargue? I was – I am now, again – of it. All France is good; but this is the best.' He spoke, as only a Frenchman can, of his own loved part of his own lovely land.

'For myself, if I were not so involved in all these affairs' – he pointed to the advertisements – 'I would live on our farm with my cattle, and worship them like a Hindu. You know our cattle of the Camargue, Monsieur? No? It is not an acquaintance to rush upon lightly. There are no beasts like them. They have a mentality superior to that of others. They graze and they ruminate, by choice, facing our Mistral, which is more than some automobiles will do. Also they have in them the potentiality of thought – and when cattle think – I have seen what arrives.'

'Are they so clever as all that?' I asked idly.

'Monsieur, when your sportif chauffeur camouflaged your limousine so that she resembled one of your Army lorries, I would not believe her capacities. I bet him – ah – two to one – she would not touch ninety kilometres. It was proved that she could. I can give you no proof, but will you believe me if I tell you what a beast who thinks can achieve?'

'After the war,' said I spaciously, 'everything is credible.'

'That is true! Everything inconceivable has happened; but still we learn nothing and we believe nothing. When I was a child in my father's house – before I became a colonial administrator – my interest and my affection were among our cattle. We of the old rock live here – have you seen? – in big farms like castles. Indeed, some of them may have been Saracenic. The barns group round them – great white-walled barns, and yards solid as our houses. One gate shuts all. It is a world apart; an administration of all that concerns beasts. It was there I learned something about cattle. You see, they are our playthings in the Camargue and the Crau. The boy measures his strength against the calf that butts him in play among the manure-heaps. He moves in and out among the cows, who are – not so amiable. He rides with the herdsmen in the open to shift the herds. Sooner or later, he meets as bulls the little calves that knocked him over. So it was with me – till it became necessary that I should go to our colonies.' He laughed. 'Very necessary. That is a good time in youth, Monsieur, when one does these things which shock our parents. Why is it always Papa who is so shocked and has never heard of such things – and Mamma who supplies the excuses? . . . And when my brother – my elder who stayed and created the business – begged me to return and help him, I resigned my colonial career gladly enough. I returned to our own lands, and my well-loved, wicked white and yellow cattle of the Camargue and the Crau. My Faith, I could talk of them all night, for this stuff unlocks the heart, without making repentance in the morning . . . Yes! It was after the war that this happened. There was a calf, among Heaven knows how many of ours – a bull calf – an infant indistinguishable from his companions. He was sick, and he had been taken up with his mother into the big farmyard at home with us. Naturally the children of our herdsmen practised on him from the first. It is in their blood. The Spaniards make a cult of bull-fighting. Our little devils down here bait bulls as automatically as the English child kicks or throws balls. This calf would chase them with his eyes open, like a cow when she hunts a man. They would take refuge behind our tractors and wine-carts in the centre of the yard: he would chase them in and out as a dog hunts rats. More than that, he would study their psychology, his eyes in their eyes. Yes, he watched their faces to divine which way they would run. He himself, also, would pretend sometimes to charge directly at a boy. Then he would wheel right or left – one could never tell – and knock over some child pressed against a wall who thought himself safe. After this he would stand over him, knowing that his companions must come to his aid; and when they were all together, waving their jackets across his eyes and pulling his tail, he would scatter them – how he would scatter them! He could kick, too, sideways like a cow. He knew his ranges as well as our gunners, and he was as quick on his feet as our Carpentier. I observed him often. Christophe – the man who passed just now – our chief herdsman, who had taught me to ride with our beasts when I was ten – Christophe told me that he was descended from a yellow cow of those days that had chased us once into the marshes. "He kicks just like her," said Christophe. "He can side-kick as he jumps. Have you seen, too, that he is not deceived by the jacket when a boy waves it? He uses it to find the boy. They think they are feeling him. He is feeling them always. He thinks, that one." I had come to the same conclusion. Yes – the creature was a thinker along the lines necessary to his sport; and he was a humorist also, like so many natural murderers. One knows the type among beasts as well as among men. It possesses a curious truculent mirth—almost indecent but infallibly significant—'

Monsieur Voiron replenished our glasses with the great wine that went better at each descent.

'They kept him for some time in the yards to practise upon. Naturally he became a little brutal: so Christophe turned him out to learn manners among his equals in the grazing lands, where the Camargue joins the Crau. How old was he then? About eight or nine months, I think. We met again a few months later – he and I. I was riding one of our little half-wild horses, along a road of the Crau, when I found myself almost unseated. It was he! He had hidden himself behind a windbreak till we passed, and had then charged my horse from behind. Yes, he had deceived even my little horse! But I recognized him. I gave him the whip across the nose, and I said: "Apis, for this thou goest to Arles! It was unworthy of thee, between us two." But that creature had no shame. He went away laughing, like an Apache. If he had dismounted me, I do not think it is I who would have laughed – yearling as he was.'

'Why did you want to send him to Arles?' I asked.

'For the bullring. When your charming tourists leave us, we institute our little amusements there. Not a real bullfight, you understand, but young bulls with padded horns, and our boys from hereabouts and in the city go to play with them. Naturally, before we send them we try them in our yards at home. So we brought up Apis from his pastures. He knew at once that he was among friends of his youth – he almost shook hands with them – and he submitted like an angel to padding his horns. He investigated the carts and tractors in the yards, to choose his lines of defence and attack. And then – he attacked with an *élan* and he defended with a tenacity and forethought that delighted us. In truth, we were so pleased that I fear we trespassed upon his patience. We desired him to repeat himself, which no true artist will tolerate. But he gave us fair warning. He went out to the centre of the yard, where there was some dry earth; he kneeled down and – you have seen a calf whose horns fret him thrusting and rooting into a bank? He did just that, very deliberately, till he had rubbed the pads off his horns. Then he rose, dancing on those wonderful feet that twinkled, and he said: "Now my friends, the buttons are off the foils. Who begins?" We understood. We finished at once. He was turned out again on the pastures till it should be time to amuse them at our little metropolis. But, some time before he went to Arles – yes, I think I have it correctly – Christophe, who had been out on the Crau, informed me that Apis had assassinated a young bull who had given signs of developing into a rival. That happens, of course, and our herdsmen should prevent it. But Apis had killed in his own style – at dusk, from the ambush of a windbreak – by an oblique charge from behind which knocked the other over. He had then disembowelled him. All very possible, *but* – the murder accomplished – Apis went to the bank of a windbreak, knelt, and carefully, as he had in our yard, cleaned his horns in the earth. Christophe, who had never seen such a thing, at once borrowed (do you know, it is most efficacious when taken that way?) some Holy Water from our little chapel in those pastures, sprinkled Apis (whom it did not affect), and rode in to tell me. It was obvious that a thinker of that bull's type would also be meticulous in his toilette; so, when he was sent to Arles, I warned our consignees to exercise caution with him. Happily, the change of scene, the music, the general attention, and the meeting again with old friends – all our bad boys attended – agreeably distracted him. He became for the time a pure *farceur* again; but his wheelings, his rushes, his rat-huntings were more superb than ever. There was in them now, you understand, a breadth of technique that comes of reasoned art, and, above all, the passion that arrives after experience. Oh, he had learned out there, on the Crau. At the end of his little turn, he was, according to local rules, to be handled in all respects except for the sword, which was a stick, as a professional bull who must die. He was manoeuvred into, or he posed himself in, the proper attitude; made his rush; received the point on his shoulder and then – turned about and cantered towards the door by which he had entered the arena. He said to the world: "My friends, the representation is ended. I thank you for your applause. I go to repose myself." But our Arlesians, who are – not so clever as some, demanded an encore, and Apis was headed back again. We others from his country, we knew what would happen. He went to the centre of the ring, kneeled, and, slowly, with full parade, plunged his horns alternately in the dirt till the pads came off. Christophe shouts : "Leave him alone, you straight-nosed imbeciles! Leave him before you must." But they required emotion; for Rome has always debauched her loved Provincia with bread and circuses. It was given. Have you, Monsieur, ever seen a servant, with pan and broom, sweeping round the base-board of a room? In a half-minute Apis had them all swept out and over the barrier. Then he demands once more that the door shall be opened to him. It is opened and he retires as though – which, truly, is the case –loaded with laurels.'

Monsieur Voiron refilled the glasses, and allowed himself a cigarette, which he puffed for some time.

'And afterwards?' I said.

'I am arranging it in my mind. It is difficult to do it justice. Afterwards – yes, afterwards – Apis returned to his pastures and his mistresses and I to my business. I am no longer a scandalous old "sportif" in my shirt-sleeves howling encouragement to the yellow son of a cow. I revert to Voiron Frères – wines, chemical manures, etc. And next year, through some chicane which I have not the leisure to unravel, and also, thanks to our patriarchal system of paying our older men out of the increase of the herds, old Christophe possesses himself of Apis. Oh, yes, he proves it through descent from a certain cow that my father had given his father before the Republic. Beware, Monsieur, of the memory of the illiterate man! An ancestor of Christophe had been a soldier under our Soult against your Beresford, near Bayonne. He fell into the hands of Spanish guerrillas. Christophe and his wife used to tell me the details on certain Saint's Days when I was a child. Now, as compared with our recent war, Soult's campaign and retreat across the Bidassoa—'

'But did you allow Christophe just to annex the bull?' I demanded.

'You do not know Christophe. He had sold him to the Spaniards before he informed me. The Spaniards pay in coin – douros of very pure silver. Our peasants mistrust our paper. You know the saying: "A thousand francs paper; eight hundred metal, and the cow is yours." Yes, Christophe sold Apis, who was then two and a half years old, and to Christophe's knowledge thrice at least an assassin.'

'How was that?' I said.

'Oh, his own kind only; and always, Christophe told me, by the same oblique rush from behind, the same sideways overthrow, and the same swift disembowelment, followed by this levitical cleaning of the horns. In human life he would have kept a manicurist – this Minotaur. And so, Apis disappears from our country. That does not trouble me. I know in due time I shall be advised. Why? Because, in this land, Monsieur, not a hoof moves between Berre and the Saintes Maries without the knowledge of specialists such as Christophe. The beasts are the substance and the drama of their lives to them. So when Christophe tells me, a little before Easter Sunday, that Apis makes his début in the bullring of a small Catalan town on the road to Barcelona, it is only to pack my car and trundle there across the frontier with him. The place lacked importance and manufactures, but it had produced a matador of some reputation, who was condescending to show his art in his native town. They were even running one special train to the place. Now our French railway system is only execrable, but the Spanish—'

'You went down by road, didn't you?' said I.

'Naturally. It was not too good. Villamarti was the matador's name. He proposed to kill two bulls for the honour of his birthplace. Apis, Christophe told me, would be his second. It was an interesting trip, and that little city by the sea was ravishing. Their bullring dates from the middle of the seventeenth century. It is full of feeling. The ceremonial too – when the horsemen enter and ask the Mayor in his box to throw down the keys of the bullring – that was exquisitely conceived. You know, if the keys are caught in the horseman's hat, it is considered a good omen. They were perfectly caught. Our seats were in the front row beside the gates where the bulls enter, so we saw everything.

'Vilamarti's first bull was not too badly killed. The second matador, whose name escapes me, killed his without distinction – a foil to Villamarti. And the third, Chisto, a laborious, middle-aged professional who had never risen beyond a certain dull competence, was equally of the background. Oh, they are as jealous as the girls of the Comédie Française, these matadors! Villamarti's troupe stood ready for his second bull. The gates opened, and we saw Apis, beautifully balanced on his feet, peer coquettishly round the corner, as though he were at home. A picador – a mounted man with the long lance-goad – stood near the barrier on his right. He had not even troubled to turn his horse, for the capeadors – the men with the cloaks – were advancing to play Apis – to feel his psychology and intentions, according to the rules that are made for bulls who do not think . . . I did not realize the murder before it was accomplished! The wheel, the rush, the oblique charge from behind, the fall of horse and man were simultaneous. Apis leaped the horse, with whom he had no quarrel, and alighted, all four feet together (it was enough), between the man's shoulders, changed his beautiful feet on the carcass, and was away, pretending to fall nearly on his nose. Do you follow me? In that instant, by that stumble, he produced the impression that his adorable assassination was a mere bestial blunder. Then, Monsieur, I began to comprehend that it was an artist that we had to deal with. He did not stand over the body to draw the rest of the troupe. He chose to reserve that trick. He let the attendants bear out the dead, and went on to amuse himself among the capeadors. Now to Apis, trained among our children in the yards, the cloak was simply a guide to the boy behind it. He pursued, you understand, the person, not the propaganda – the proprietor, not the journal. If a third of our electors of France were as wise, my friend!. . . But it was done leisurely, with humour and a touch of truculence. He romped after one man's cloak as a clumsy dog might do, but I observed that he kept the man on his terrible left side. Christophe whispered to me: "Wait for his mother's kick. When he has made the fellow confident it will arrive." It arrived in the middle of a gambol. My God! He lashed out in the air as he frisked. The man dropped like a sack, lifted one hand a little towards his head, and – that was all. So you see, a body was again at his disposition; a second time the cloaks ran up to draw him off, but, a second time, Apis refused his grand scene. A second time he acted that his murder was accident and – he convinced his audience. It was as though he had knocked over a bridge-gate in the marshes by mistake. Unbelievable? I saw it.'

The memory sent Monsieur Voiron again to the champagne, and I accompanied him.

'But Apis was not the sole artist present. They say Villamarti comes of a family of actors. I saw him regard Apis with a new eye. He, too, began to understand. He took his cloak and moved out to play him before they should bring on another picador. He had his reputation. Perhaps Apis knew it. Perhaps Villamarti reminded him of some boy with whom he had practised at home. At any rate Apis permitted it – up to a certain point; but he did not allow Villamarti the stage. He cramped him throughout. He dived and plunged clumsily and slowly, but always with menace and always closing in. We could see that the man was conforming to the bull – not the bull to the man; for Apis was playing him towards the centre of the ring, and, in a little while – I watched his face – Villamarti knew it. But I could not fathom the creature's motive. "Wait," said old Christophe. "He wants that picador on the white horse yonder. When he reaches his proper distance he will get him. Villamarti is his cover. He used me once that way." And so it was, my friend! With the clang of one of our own Seventy-fives, Apis dismissed Villamarti with his chest – breasted him over – and had arrived at his objective near the barrier. The same oblique charge; the head carried low for the sweep of the horns; the immense sideways fall of the horse, broken-legged and half-paralysed; the senseless man on the ground, and – behold Apis between them, backed against the barrier – his right covered by the horse; his left by the body of the man at his feet. The simplicity of it! Lacking the carts and tractors of his early parade-grounds he, being a genius, had extemporised with the materials at hand, and dug himself in. The troupe closed up again, their left wing broken by the kicking horse, their right immobilized by the man's body which Apis bestrode with significance. Villamarti almost threw himself between the horns, but – it was more an appeal than an attack. Apis refused him. He held his base. A picador was sent at him – necessarily from the front, which alone was open. Apis charged – he who, till then, you realize, had not used the horn! The horse went over backwards, the man half beneath him. Apis halted, hooked him under the heart, and threw him to the barrier. We heard his head crack, but he was dead before he hit the wood. There was no demonstration from the audience. They also, had begun to realize this Foch among bulls! The arena occupied itself again with the dead. Two of the troupe irresolutely tried to play him – God knows in what hope! – but he moved out to the centre of the ring. "Look!" said Christophe. "Now he goes to clean himself. That always frightened me." He knelt down; he began to clean his horns. The earth was hard. He worried at it in an ecstasy of absorption. As he laid his head along and rattled his ears, it was as though he were interrogating the devils themselves upon their secrets, and always saying impatiently: "Yes, I know that – and *that* – and *that!* Tell me more – *more!'* In the silence that covered us, a woman cried: "He digs a grave! Oh, Saints, he digs a grave!" Some others echoed this – not loudly – as a wave echoes in a grotto of the sea.

And when his horns were cleaned, he rose up and studied poor Villamarti's troupe, eyes in eyes, one by one, with the gravity of an equal in intellect and the remote and merciless resolution of a master in his art. This was more terrifying than his toilette.'

'And they – Villamarti's men?' I asked.

'Like the audience, were dominated. They had ceased to posture, or stamp, or address insults to him. They conformed to him. The two other matadors stared. Only Chisto, the oldest, broke silence with some call or other, and Apis turned his head towards him. Otherwise he was isolated, immobile – sombre – meditating on those at his mercy. Ah!

'For some reason the trumpet sounded for the banderillas – those gay hooked darts that are planted in the shoulders of bulls who do not think, after their neck-muscles are tired by lifting horses. When such bulls feel the pain, they check for an instant, and, in that instant, the men step gracefully aside. Villamarti's banderillero answered the trumpet mechanically – like one condemned. He stood out, poised the darts and stammered the usual patter of invitation . . . And after? I do not assert that Apis shrugged his shoulders, but he reduced the episode to its lowest elements as could only a bull of Gaul. With his truculence was mingled always – owing to the shortness of his tail – a certain Rabelaisian abandon, especially when viewed from the rear. Christophe had often commented upon it. Now, Apis brought that quality into play. He circulated round that boy, forcing him to break up his beautiful poses. He studied him from various angles, like an incompetent photographer. He presented to him every portion of his anatomy except his shoulders. At intervals he feigned to run in upon him. My God, he was cruel! But his motive was obvious. He was playing for a laugh from the spectators which should synchronize with the fracture of the human morale. It was achieved. The boy turned and ran towards the barrier. Apis was on him before the laugh ceased;

passed him; headed him – what do I say? – herded him off to the left, his horns beside and a little in front of his chest: he did not intend him to escape into a refuge. Some of the troupe would have closed in, but Villamarti cried: "If he wants him he will take him. Stand!" They stood. Whether the boy slipped or Apis nosed him over I could not see. But he dropped, sobbing. Apis halted like a car with four brakes, struck a pose, smelt him very completely and turned away. It was dismissal more ignominious than degradation at the head of one's battalion. The representation was finished. Remained only for Apis to clear his stage of the subordinate characters.

'Ah! His gesture then! He gave a dramatic start – this Cyrano of the Camargue – as though he was aware of them for the first time. He moved. All their beautiful breeches twinkled for an instant along the top of the barrier. He held the stage alone! But Christophe and I, we trembled! For, observe, he had now involved himself in a stupendous drama of which he only could supply the third act. And, except for an audience on the razor-edge of emotion, he had exhausted his material. Molière himself – we have forgotten, my friend, to drink to the health of that great soul – might have been at a loss. And Tragedy is but a step behind Failure. We could see the four or five Civil Guards, who are sent always to keep order, fingering the breeches of their rifles. They were but waiting a word from the mayor to fire on him, as they do sometimes at a bull who leaps the barrier among the spectators. They would, of course, have killed or wounded several people – but that would not have saved Apis.

Monsieur Voiron drowned the thought at once, and wiped his beard.

'At that moment Fate – the Genius of France, if you will, – sent to assist in the incomparable finale, none other than Chisto, the eldest, and I should have said (but never again will I judge!) the least inspired of all; mediocrity itself, but at heart – and it is the heart that conquers always, my friend – at heart an artist. He descended stiffly into the arena, alone and assured. Apis regarded him, his eyes in his eyes. The man took stance, with his cloak, and called to the bull as to an equal: "Now, señor, we will show these honourable caballeros something together." He advanced thus against this thinker who at a plunge – a kick – a thrust – could, we all knew, have extinguished him. My dear friend, I wish I could convey to you something of the unaffected bonhomie, the humour, the delicacy, the consideration bordering on respect even, with which Apis, the supreme artist, responded to this invitation. It was the Master, wearied after a strenuous hour in the atelier, unbuttoned and at ease with some not inexpert but limited disciple. The telepathy was instantaneous between them. And for good reason! Christophe said to me: "All's well. That Chisto began among the bulls. I was sure of it when I heard him call just now. He has been a herdsman. He'll pull it off." There was a little feeling and adjustment, at first, for mutual distances and allowances.

'Oh, yes! And here occurred a gross impertinence of Villamarti. He had, after an interval, followed Chisto – to retrieve his reputation. My Faith! I can conceive the elder Dumas slamming his door on an intruder precisely as Apis did. He raced Villamarti into the nearest refuge at once. He stamped his feet outside it, and he snorted: "Go! I am engaged with an artist." Villamarti went – his reputation left behind for ever.

'Apis returned to Chisto saying: "Forgive the interruption. I am not always master of my time, but you were about to observe, my dear confrère . . . ?" Then the play began. Out of compliment to Chisto, Apis chose as his objective (every bull varies in this respect) the inner edge of the cloak – that nearest to the man's body. This allows but a few millimetres clearance in charging. But Apis trusted himself as Chisto trusted him, and, this time, he conformed to the man, with inimitable judgement and temper. He allowed himself to be played into the shadow or the sun, as the delighted audience demanded. He raged enormously; he feigned defeat; he despaired in statuesque abandon, and thence flashed into fresh paroxysms of wrath – but always with the detachment of the true artist who knows he is but the vessel of an emotion whence others, not he, must drink. And never once did he forget that honest Chisto's cloak was to him the gauge by which to spare even a hair on the skin. He inspired Chisto too. My God! His youth returned to that meritorious beef-sticker – the desire, the grace, and the beauty of his early dreams. One could almost see that girl of the past for whom he was rising, rising to these present heights of skill and daring. It was his hour too – a miraculous hour of dawn returned to gild the sunset. All he knew was at Apis' disposition. Apis acknowledged it with all that he had learned at home, at Arles and in his lonely murders on our grazing-grounds. He flowed round Chisto like a river of death – round his knees, leaping at his shoulders, kicking just clear of one side or the other of his head; behind his back, hissing as he shaved by; and once or twice – inimitable! – he reared wholly up before him while Chisto slipped back from beneath the avalanche of that instructed body. Those two, my dear friend, held five thousand people dumb with no sound but of their breathings – regular as pumps. It was unbearable. Beast and man realized together that we needed a change of note – a *détente*. They relaxed to pure buffoonery. Chisto fell back and talked to him outrageously. Apis pretended he had never heard such language. The audience howled with delight. Chisto slapped him; he took liberties with his short tail, to the end of which he clung while Apis pirouetted; he played about him in all postures; he had become the herdsman again – gross, careless, brutal, but comprehending. Yet Apis was always the more consummate clown. All that time (Christophe and I saw it) Apis drew off towards the gates of the toril where so many bulls enter but – have you ever heard of one that returned? *We* knew that Apis knew that as he had saved Chisto, so Chisto would save him. Life is sweet to us all; to the artist who lives many lives in one, sweetest. Chisto did not fail him. At the last, when none could laugh any longer, the man threw his cape across the bull's back, his arm round his neck. He flung up a hand at the gate, as Villamarti, young and commanding, but *not* a herdsman, might have raised it, and he cried: "Gentlemen, open to me and my honourable little donkey." They opened – I have misjudged Spaniards in my time! – those gates opened to the man and the bull together, and closed behind them. And then? From the mayor to the Guardia Civil they went mad for five minutes, till the trumpets blew and the fifth bull rushed out – an unthinking black Andalusian. I suppose someone killed him. My friend, my very dear friend, to whom I have opened my heart, I confess that I did not watch. Christophe and I, we were weeping together like children of the same Mother. Shall we drink to Her?'

ALNASCHAR AND THE OXEN

There's a pasture in a valley where the hanging woods divide,
  And a Herd lies down and ruminates in peace;
Where the pheasant rules the nooning, and the owl the twilight tide,
  And the war-cries of our world die out and cease.
Here I cast aside the burden that each weary week-day brings
  And, delivered from the shadows I pursue,
On peaceful, postless Sabbaths I consider Weighty Things –
  Such as Sussex Cattle feeding in the dew!

At the gate beside the river where the trouty shallows brawl,
  I know the pride that Lobengula felt,
When he bade the bars be lowered of the Royal Cattle Kraal,
  And fifteen mile of oxen took the veldt.
From the walls of Bulawayo in unbroken file they came
  To where the Mount of Council cuts the blue . . .
I have only six and twenty, but the principle's the same
  With my Sussex Cattle feeding in the dew!

To a luscious sound of tearing, where the clovered herbage rips,
  Level-backed and level-bellied watch 'em move –
See those shoulders, guess that heart-girth, praise those loins, admire those hips,
  And the tail set low for flesh to make above!
Count the broad unblemished muzzles, test the kindly mellow skin
  And, where yon heifer lifts her head at call,
Mark the bosom's just abundance 'neath the gay and clean-cut chin,
  And those eyes of Juno, overlooking all!

Here is colour, form and substance! I will put it to the proof
  And, next season, in my lodges shall be born
Some very Bull of Mithras, flawless from his agate hoof
  To his even-branching, ivory, dusk-tipped horn.
He shall mate with block-square virgins – kings shall seek his like in vain,
  While I multiply his stock a thousandfold,
Till an hungry world extol me, builder of a lofty strain
  That turns one standard ton at two years old!

There's a valley, under oakwood, where a man may dream his dream,
In the milky breath of cattle laid at ease,
Till the moon o'ertops the alders, and her image chills the stream,
And the river-mist runs silver round their knees!
Now the footpaths fade and vanish; now the ferny clumps deceive;
Now the hedgerow-folk possess their fields anew;
Now the Herd is lost in darkness, and I bless them as I leave,
My Sussex Cattle feeding in the dew!

GIPSY VANS

Unless you come of the gipsy stock
  That steals by night and day,
Lock your heart with a double lock
  And throw the key away.
Bury it under the blackest stone
  Beneath your father's hearth,
And keep your eyes on your lawful own
  And your feet to the proper path.
    Then you can stand at your door and mock
      When the gipsy-vans come through . . .
    For it isn't right that the Gorgio stock
      Should live as the Romany do.

Unless you come of the gipsy blood
  That takes and never spares
Bide content with your given good
  And follow your own affairs.
Plough and harrow and roll your land,
  And sow what ought to be sowed;
But never let loose your heart from your hand,
  Nor flitter it down the road!
    Then you can thrive on your boughten food
      As the gipsy-vans come through . . .
    For it isn't nature the Gorgio blood
      Should love as the Romany do.

Unless you carry the gipsy eyes
  That see but seldom weep,
Keep your head from the naked skies
  Or the stars'll trouble your sleep.
Watch your moon through your window-pane
  And take what weather she brews;
But don't run out in the midnight rain
  Nor home in the morning dews.

Then you can huddle and shut your eyes
As the gipsy-vans come through . . .
For it isn't fitting the Gorgio ryes
Should walk as the Romany do

Unless you come of the gipsy race
That counts all time the same,
Be you careful of Time and Place
And Judgment and Good Name:
Lose your life for to live your life
The way that you ought to do;
And when you are finished, your God and your wife
And the Gipsies 'll laugh at you!
Then you can rot in your burying-place
As the gipsy-vans come through . . .
For it isn't reason the Gorgio race
Should die as the Romany do.

A Madonna of the Trenches

'Whatever a man of the sons of men
  Shall say to his heart of the lords above,
They have shown man, verily, once and again,
  Marvellous mercies and infinite love.

'O sweet one love, O my life's delight,
  Dear, though the days have divided us,
Lost beyond hope, taken far out of sight,
  Not twice in the world shall the Gods do thus.'

Swinburne, *'Les Noyades'*

SEEING how many unstable ex-soldiers came to the Lodge of Instruction (attached to Faith and Works E.C. 5837) in the years after the war, the wonder is there was not more trouble from Brethren whom sudden meetings with old comrades jerked back into their still raw past. But our round, torpedo-bearded local doctor – Brother Keede, Senior Warden – always stood ready to deal with hysteria before it got out of hand; and when I examined Brethren unknown or imperfectly vouched for on the Masonic side, I passed on to him anything that seemed doubtful. He had had his experience as medical officer of a South London battalion, during the last two years of the war; and, naturally, often found friends and acquaintances among the visitors.

Brother C. Strangwick, a young, tallish, new-made Brother, hailed from some South London Lodge. His papers and his answers were above suspicion, but his red-rimmed eyes had a puzzled glare that might mean nerves. So I introduced him particularly to Keede, who discovered in him a headquarters orderly of his old battalion, congratulated him on his return to fitness – he had been discharged for some infirmity or other – and plunged at once into Somme memories.

'I hope I did right, Keede,' I said when we were robing before Lodge.

'Oh quite. He reminded me that I had him under my hands at Sampoux in 'Eighteen, when he went to bits. He was a runner.'

'Was it shock?' I asked

'Of sorts – but not what he wanted me to think it was. No, he wasn't shamming. He had Jumps to the limit – but he played up to mislead me about the reason of 'em. . . .Well, if we could stop patients from lying, medicine would be too easy, I suppose.'

I noticed that, after Lodge-working, Keede gave him a seat a couple of rows in front of us, that he might enjoy a lecture on the Orientation of King Solomon's Temple, which an earnest Brother thought would be a nice interlude between Labour and the high tea that we called our 'Banquet'. Even helped by tobacco it was a dreary performance. About half-way through, Strangwick, who had been fidgeting and twitching for some minutes, rose, drove back his chair grinding across the tesselated floor, and yelped: 'Oh, My Aunt! I can't stand this any longer.' Under cover of a general laugh of assent he brushed past us and stumbled towards the door.

'I thought so!' Keede whispered to me. 'Come along!' We overtook him in the passage, crowing hysterically and wringing his hands. Keede led him into the Tyler's Room, a small office where we stored odds and ends of regalia and furniture, and locked the door.

'I'm – I'm all right,' the boy began, piteously.

'Course you are.' Keede opened a small cupboard which I had seen called upon before, mixed sal volatile and water in a graduated glass, and, as Strangwick drank, pushed him gently on to an old sofa. 'There,' he went on. 'It's nothing to write home about. I've seen you ten times worse. I expect our talk has brought things back.'

He hooked up a chair behind him with one foot, held the patient's hands in his own, and sat down. The chair creaked.

'Don't!' Strangwick squealed. 'I can't stand it. There's nothing on earth creaks like they do! And – and when it thaws we – we've got to slap 'em back with a spa-ade! Remember those Frenchmen's little boots under the duckboards? . . .What'll I do? What'll I do about it?'

Some one knocked at the door, to know if all were well.

'Oh, quite, thanks!' said Keede over his shoulder. 'But I shall need this room awhile. Draw the curtains, please.'

We heard the rings of the hangings that drape the passage from Lodge to Banquet Room click along their poles, and what sound there had been, of feet and voices, was shut off.

Strangwick, retching impotently, complained of the frozen dead who creak in the frost.

'He's playing up still,' Keede whispered. '*That's* not his real trouble – any more than 'twas last time.'

'But surely,' I replied, 'men get those things on the brain pretty badly. 'Remember in October—'

'This chap hasn't though. I wonder what's really helling him.

What are you thinking of?' said Keede peremptorily.

'French End an' Butcher's Row,' Strangwick muttered.

'Yes, there were a few there. But suppose we face Bogey instead of giving him best every time.' Keede turned towards me with a hint in his eye that I was to play up to his leads.

'What was the trouble with French End?' I opened at a venture.

'It was a bit by Sampoux, that we had taken over from the French. They're tough, but you wouldn't call 'em tidy as a nation. They had faced both sides of it with dead to keep the mud back. All those trenches were like gruel in a thaw. Our people had to do the same sort of thing – elsewhere; but Butcher's Row in French End was the – er – showpiece. Luckily, we pinched a salient from Jerry just then, an' straightened things out – so we didn't need to use the Row after November. You remember, Strangwick?'

'My God, yes! When the duckboard-slats were missin' you'd tread on 'em, an' they'd creak.'

'They're bound to. Like leather,' said Keede. 'It gets on one's nerves a bit, but—'

'Nerves? It's real! It's real!' Strangwick gulped.

'But at your time of life, it'll all fall behind you in a year or so. I'll give you another sip of – paregoric, an' we'll face it quietly. Shall we?'

Keede opened his cupboard again and administered a carefully dropped dark dose of something that was not sal volatile. 'This'll settle you in a few minutes,' he explained. 'Lie still, an' don't talk unless you feel like it.'

He faced me, fingering his beard.

'Ye-es. Butcher's Row wasn't pretty,' he volunteered. 'Seeing Strangwick here, has brought it all back to me again. Funny thing! We had a platoon sergeant of Number Two – what the deuce was his name? – an elderly bird who must have lied like a patriot to get out to the front at his age; but he was a first-class non-com., and the last person, you'd think, to make mistakes. Well, he was due for a fortnight's home leave in January, 'Eighteen. You were at BHQ then, Strangwick, weren't you?'

'Yes. I was orderly. It was January twenty-first', Strangwick spoke with a thickish tongue, and his eyes burned. Whatever drug it was, had taken hold.

'About then,' Keede said. 'Well, this sergeant, instead of coming down from the trenches the regular way an' joinin' battalion details after dark, an' takin' that funny little train for Arras, thinks he'll warm himself first. So he gets into a dug-out, in Butcher's Row, that used to be an old French dressing-station, and fugs up between a couple of braziers of pure charcoal! As luck 'ud have it, that was the only dug-out with an inside door opening inwards – some French anti-gas fitting, I expect – and, by what we could make out, the door must have swung to while he was warming. Anyhow, he didn't turn up at the train. There was a search at once. We couldn't afford to waste platoon sergeants. We found him in the morning. He'd got his gas all right. A machine-gunner reported him, didn't he, Strangwick?'

'No, sir. Corporal Grant – o' the trench mortars.'

'So it was. Yes, Grant – the man with that little wen on his neck. Nothing wrong with your memory, at any rate. What was the sergeant's name?'

'Godsoe – John Godsoe,' Strangwick answered.

'Yes, that was it. I had to see him next mornin' – frozen stiff between the two braziers – and not a scrap of private papers on him. *That* was the only thing that made me think it mightn't have been – quite an accident.'

Strangwick's relaxing face set, and he threw back at once to the orderly room manner.

'I give my evidence – at the time – to you, sir. He passed – overtook me, I should say – comin' down from supports, after I'd warned him for leaf. I thought he was goin' through Parrot Trench as usual; but 'e must 'ave turned off into French End where the old bombed barricade was.'

'Yes. I remember now. You were the last man to see him alive. That was on the twenty-first of January, you say? Now, *when* was it that Dearlove and Billings brought you to me – clean out of your head?' . . . Keede dropped his hand, in the style of magazine detectives, on Strangwick's shoulder. The boy looked at him with cloudy wonder, and muttered: 'I was took to you on the evenin' of the twenty-fourth of January. But you don't think I did him in, do you?'

I could not help smiling at Keede's discomfiture; but he recovered himself. 'Then what the dickens *was* on your mind that evening – before I gave you the hypodermic?'

'The – the things in Butcher's Row. They kept on comin' over me. You've seen me like this before, sir.'

'But I knew that it was a lie. You'd no more got stiffs on the brain then than you have now. You've got something, but you're hiding it.'

''Ow do *you* know, doctor?' Strangwick whimpered.

'D'you remember what you said to me, when Dearlove and Billings were holding you down that evening?

'About the things in Butcher's Row?'

'Oh, no! You spun me a lot of stuff about corpses creaking; but you let yourself go in the middle of it – when you pushed that telegram at me. What did you mean, f'rinstance, by asking what advantage it was for you to fight beasts of officers if the dead didn't rise?'

'Did I say "Beasts of Officers"?'

'You did. It's out of the Burial Service.'

'I suppose, then, I must have heard it. As a matter of fact, I 'ave.' Strangwick shuddered extravagantly.

'Probably. And there's another thing – that hymn you were shouting till I put you under. It was something about Mercy and Love. Remember it?'

'I'll try,' said the boy obediently, and began to paraphrase, as nearly as possible thus: '"Whatever a man may say in his heart unto the Lord, yea, verily I say unto you – Gawd hath shown man, again and again, marvellous mercy an' – an' somethin' or other love."' He screwed up his eyes and shook.

'Now where did you get *that* from?' Keede insisted.

'From Godsoe – on the twenty-first Jan . . . 'Ow could *I* tell what 'e meant to do? ' he burst out in a high, unnatural key – 'Any more than I knew *she* was dead.'

'Who was dead?' said Keede.

'Me Auntie Armine.'

'The one the telegram came to you about, at Sampoux, that you wanted me to explain – the one that you were talking of in the passage out here just now when you began: "O Auntie," and changed it to "O Gawd," when I collared you?'

'That's her! I haven't a chance with you, Doctor. *I* didn't know there was anything wrong with those braziers. How could I? We're always usin' 'em. Honest to God, I thought at first go-off he might wish to warm himself before the leaf-train. I – I didn't know Uncle John meant to start – 'ouse-keepin'.' He laughed horribly, and then the dry tears came.

Keede waited for them to pass in sobs and hiccoughs before he continued: 'Why? Was Godsoe your uncle?'

'No,' said Strangwick, his head between his hands. 'Only we'd known him ever since we were born. Dad 'ad known him before that. He lived almost next street to us. Him an' Dad an' Ma an' – an' the rest had always been friends. So we called him Uncle – like children do.'

'What sort of man was he?'

'One o' *the* best, sir. Pensioned sergeant with a little money left him – quite independent – and very superior. They had a sittin'-room full o' Indian curios that him and his wife used to let sister an' me see when we'd been good.'

'Wasn't he rather old to join up?'

'That made no odds to him. He joined up as sergeant instructor at the first go-off, an' when the battalion was ready he got 'imself sent along. He wangled me into 'is platoon when I went out – early in 'Seventeen. Because Ma wanted it, I suppose.'

'I'd no notion you knew him that well,' was Keede's comment.

'Oh, it made no odds to him. He 'ad no pets in the platoon, but 'e'd write 'ome to Ma about me an' all the doin's. You see' – Strangwick stirred uneasily on the sofa – 'we'd known him all our lives – lived in the next street an' all . . .An' him well over fifty. Oh dear me! *Oh* dear me! What a bloody mix-up things are, when one's as young as me!' he wailed of a sudden.

But Keede held him to the point. 'He wrote to your mother about you?'

'Yes. Ma's eyes had gone bad followin' on air-raids. Blood-vessels broke behind 'em from sittin' in cellars an' bein' sick. She had to 'ave 'er letters read to her by Auntie. Now I think of it, that was the only thing that you might have called anything at all—'

'Was that the Aunt that died, and that you got the wire about?' Keede drove on.

'Yes – Auntie Armine – Ma's younger sister, an' she nearer fifty than forty. What a mix-up! An' if I'd been asked any time about it, I'd 'ave sworn there wasn't a single sol'tary item concernin' her that everybody didn't know an' hadn't known all along. No more conceal to her doin's than – than so much shop-front. She'd looked after sister an' me, when needful, – whoopin' cough an' measles – just the same as Ma. We was in an' out of her house like rabbits. You see, Uncle Armine is a cabinet-maker, an' second-'and furniture, an' we liked playin' with the things. She 'ad no children, and when the war came, she said she was glad of it. But she never talked much of her feelin's. She kept herself to herself, you understand.' He stared most earnestly at us to help out our understandings.

'What was she like?' Keede inquired.

'A biggish woman, an' had been 'andsome, I believe, but, bein' used to her, we two didn't notice much – except, per'aps, for one thing. Ma called her 'er proper name, which was Bella; but Sis an' me always called 'er Auntie Armine. See?'

'What for?'

'We thought it sounded more like her – like somethin' movin' slow, in armour.'

'Oh! And she read your letters to your mother, did she?'

'Every time the post came in she'd slip across the road from opposite an' read 'em. An' – an' I'll go bail for it that that was all there was to it for as far back as *I* remember. Was I to swing tomorrow, I'd go bail for *that!* 'Tisn't fair of 'em to 'ave unloaded it all on me, because – because – if the dead *do* rise, why, what in 'ell becomes of me an' all I've believed all me life?' I want to know *that!* I—'

But Keede would not be put off. 'Did the sergeant give you away at all in his letters?' he demanded, very quietly.

'There was nothin' to give away – we was too busy – but his letters about me were a great comfort to Ma. I'm no good at writin'. I saved it all up for my leafs. I got me fourteen days every six months an' one over . . . I was luckier than most, that way.'

'And when you came home, used you to bring 'em news about the sergeant?' said Keede.

'I expect I must have; but I didn't think much of it at the time. I was took up with me own affairs – naturally. Uncle John always wrote to me once each leaf, tellin' me what was doin' an' what I was li'ble to expect on return, an' Ma 'ud 'ave that read to her. Then o' course I had to slip over to his wife an' pass her the news. An' then there was the young lady that I'd thought of marryin' if I came through. We'd got as far as pricin' things in the windows together.'

'And you didn't marry her – after all?'

Another tremor shook the boy. '*No!*' he cried. ''Fore it ended, I knew what reel things reelly mean! I – I never dreamed such things could be! . . . An' she nearer fifty than forty an' me own Aunt! . . . - But there wasn't a sign nor a hint from first to last, so 'ow *could* I tell? Don't you *see* it? All she said to me after me Christmas leaf in 'Eighteen, when I come to say goodbye – all Auntie Armine said to me was: "You'll be seein' Mister Godsoe soon?" "Too soon for my likings," I says. "Well then, tell 'im from me," she says, "that I expect to be through with my little trouble by the twenty-first of next month, an' I'm dyin' to see him as soon as possible after that date."'

'What sort of trouble was it?' Keede turned professional at once.

'She'd 'ad a bit of a gatherin' in 'er breast, I believe. But she never talked of 'er body much to any one.'

'*I* see, said Keede. 'And she said to you?'

Strangwick repeated: '"Tell Uncle John I hope to be finished of my drawback by the twenty-first, an' I'm dying to see 'im as soon as 'e can after that date." An' then she says, laughin': "But you've a head like a sieve. I'll write it down, an' you can give it him when you see 'im." So she wrote it on a bit o' paper an' I kissed 'er goodbye – I was always her favourite, you see – an' I went back to Sampoux. The thing hardly stayed in my mind at all, d'you see. But the next time I was up in the front line – I was a runner, d'ye see – our platoon was in North Bay Trench an' I was up with a message to the trench mortar there that Corporal Grant was in charge of. Followin' on receipt of it, he borrowed a couple of men off the platoon, to slue 'er round or somethin'. I give Uncle John Auntie Armine's paper, an' I give Grant a fag, an' we warmed up a bit over a brazier. Then Grant says to me: "I don't like it"; an' he jerks 'is thumb at Uncle John in the bay studyin' Auntie's message. Well, *you* know, sir, you had to speak to Grant about 'is way of prophesyin' things – after Rankine shot himself with the Very light.'

'I did,' said Keede, and he explained to me: 'Grant had the Second Sight – confound him! It upset the men. I was glad when he got pipped. What happened after that, Strangwick?'

'Grant whispers to me: "Look, you damned Englishman. 'E's for it." Uncle John was leanin' up against the bay, 'an hummin' that hymn I was tryin' to tell you just now. He looked different all of a sudden – as if 'e'd got shaved. *I* don't know anything of these things, but I cautioned Grant as to his style of speakin', if an officer 'ad 'eard him, an' I went on. Passin' Uncle John in the bay, 'e nods an' smiles, which he didn't often, an' he says, pocketin' the paper: "This suits *me*. I'm for leaf on the twenty-first, too."'

'He said that to you, did he?' said Keede.

'*Pre*cisely the same as passin' the time o' day. O' course I returned the agreeable about hopin' he'd get it, an' in due course I returned to 'eadquarters. The thing 'ardly stayed in my mind a minute. That was the eleventh January – three days after I'd come back from leaf. You remember, sir, there wasn't anythin' doin' either side round Sampoux the first part o' the month. Jerry was gettin' ready for his March Push, an' as long as he kept quiet, we didn't want to poke 'im up.'

'I remember that,' said Keede. 'But what about the sergeant?'

'I must have met him, on an' off, I expect, goin' up an' down, through the ensuin' days, but it didn't stay in me mind. Why needed it? And on the twenty-first Jan., his name was on the leaf-paper when I went up to warn the leaf-men. I noticed *that,* o' course. Now that very afternoon Jerry 'ad been tryin' a new trench mortar, an' before our 'Eavies could out it, he'd got a stinker into a bay an' mopped up 'alf a dozen. They were bringin' 'em down when I went up to the supports, an' that blocked Little Parrot, same as it always did. *You* remember, sir?'

'Rather! And there was that big machine-gun behind the Half-House waiting for you if you got out,' said Keede.

'I remembered that too. But it was just on dark an' the fog was comin' off the Canal, so I hopped out of Little Parrot an' cut across the open to where those four dead Warwicks are heaped up. But the fog turned me round, an' the next thing I knew I was knee-over in that old 'alf-trench that runs west o' Little Parrot into French End. I dropped into it – almost atop o' the machine-gun platform by the side o' the old sugar boiler an' the two Zoo-ave skel'tons. That gave me my bearin's, an' so I went through French End, all up those missin' duckboards, into Butcher's Row where the *poy-looz* was laid in six deep each side, an' stuffed under the duckboards. It had froze tight, an' the drippin's had stopped, an' the creakin's had begun.'

'Did that really worry you at the time?' Keede asked.

'No,' said the boy with professional scorn. 'If a runner starts noticin' such things he'd better chuck. In the middle of the Row, just before the old dressin'-station you referred to, sir, it come over me that somethin' ahead on the duckboards was just like Auntie Armine, waitin' beside the door; an' I thought to meself 'ow truly comic it would be if she could be dumped where I was then. In 'alf a second I saw it was only the dark an' some rags o' gas-screen, 'angin' on a bit of board, 'ad played me the trick. So I went on up to the supports an' warned the leaf-men there, includin' Uncle John. Then I went up Rake Alley to warn 'em in the front line. I didn't hurry because I didn't want to get there till Jerry 'ad quieted down a bit. Well, then a company relief dropped in – an' the officer got the wind up over some lights on the flank, an' tied 'em into knots, an' I 'ad to hunt up me leaf-men all over the blinkin' shop. What with one thing an' another, it must 'ave been 'alf-past eight before I got back to the supports. There I run across Uncle John, scrapin' mud off himself, havin' shaved – quite the dandy. He asked about the Arras train, an' I said, if Jerry was quiet, it might be ten o'clock. "Good!" says 'e. "I'll come with you." So we started back down the old trench that used to run across Halnaker, back of the support dug-outs. *You* know, sir.'

Keede nodded.

'Then Uncle John says something to me about seein' Ma an' the rest of 'em in a few days, an' had I any messages for 'em? Gawd knows what made me do it, but I told 'im to tell Auntie Armine I never expected to see anything like *her* up in our part of the world. And while I told him I laughed. That's the last time I *'ave* laughed. "Oh – you've seen 'er, 'ave you?" says he, quite natural-like. Then I told 'im about the sand-bags an' rags in the dark, playin' the trick. "Very likely," says he, brushin' the mud off his putties. By this time, we'd got to the corner where the old barricade into French End was – before they bombed it down, sir. He turns right an' climbs across it. "No thanks," says I. "I've been there once this evenin'." But he wasn't attendin' to me. He felt behind the rubbish an' bones just inside the barricade, an' when he straightened up, he had a full brazier in each hand.

'"Come on, Clem," he says, an' he very rarely give me me own name. "You aren't afraid, are you?" he says. "It's just as short, an' if Jerry starts up again, he won't waste stuff here. He knows it's abandoned." "Who's afraid now?" I says. "Me for one," says he. "I don't want *my* leaf spoiled at the last minute." Then 'e wheels round an' speaks that bit you said come out o' ιe Burial Service.'

For some reason Keede repeated it in full, slowly: 'If after the manner of men I have fought with beasts at Ephesus, what advantageth it me, if the dead rise not?'

'That's it,' said Strangwick. 'So we went down French End together – everything froze up an' quiet, except for their creakin's. I remember thinkin'—' his eyes began to flicker.

'Don't think. Tell what happened,' Keede ordered.

'Oh! Beg y' pardon! He went on with his braziers, hummin' his hymn, down Butcher's Row. Just before we got to the old dressin'-station he stops and sets 'em down an' says: "Where did you say she was, Clem? Me eyes ain't as good as they used to be."

'"In 'er bed at 'ome," I says. "Come on down. It's perishin' cold, an *I'm* not due for leaf."

'"Well, I am," 'e says. "*I* am . . . " An' then – give you me word I didn't recognize the voice – he stretches out 'is neck a bit, in a way 'e 'ad, an' he says: "Why, Bella!" 'e says. "Oh, Bella!" 'e says. "Thank Gawd!" 'e says. Just like that! An' then I saw – I tell you I *saw* – Auntie Armine herself standin' by the old dressin'-station door where first I'd thought I'd seen her. He was lookin' at 'er an' she was lookin' at him. I saw it, an' me soul turned over inside me because – because it knocked out everything I'd believed in. I 'ad nothin' to lay 'old of, d'ye see? An' 'e was lookin' at 'er as though he could 'ave et 'er, an' she was lookin' at 'im the same way, out of 'er eyes. Then he says: "Why, Bella," 'e says, "this must be only the second time we've been alone together in all these years." An' I saw 'er half hold out her arms to 'im in that perishin' cold. An' she nearer fifty than forty an' me own aunt! You can shop me for a lunatic tomorrow, but I saw it – I *saw* 'er answerin' to his spoken word! . . . Then 'e made a snatch to unsling 'is rifle. Then 'e cuts 'is hand away saying: "No! Don't tempt me, Bella. We've all Eternity ahead of us. An hour or two won't make any odds." Then he picks up the braziers an' goes on to the dug-out door. He'd finished with me. He pours petrol on 'em, an' lights it with a match, an' carries 'em inside, flarin'. All that time Auntie Armine stood with 'er arms out – an' a look in 'er face! *I* didn't know such things was or could be! Then he comes out an' says: "Come in, my dear"; an' she stoops an' goes into the dug-out with that look on her face – that look on her face! An' then 'e shuts the door from inside an' starts wedgin' it up. So 'elp me Gawd, I saw an' 'eard all these things with my own eyes an' ears!'

He repeated his oath several times. After a long pause Keede asked him if he recalled what happened next.

'It was a bit of a mix-up, for me, from then on. I must have carried on – they told me I did, but – but I was – I felt a – a long way inside of meself, like – if you've ever had that feelin'. I wasn't rightly on the spot at all. They woke me up sometime next morning, because 'e 'adn't showed up at the train; an' some one had seen him with me. I wasn't 'alf cross-examined by all an' sundry till dinner-time.

'Then, I think, I volunteered for Dearlove, who 'ad a sore toe, for a front-line message. I had to keep movin', you see, because I hadn't anything to hold *on* to. Whilst up there, Grant informed me how he'd found Uncle John with the door wedged an' sand-bags stuffed in the cracks. I hadn't waited for that. The knockin' when 'e wedged up was enough for me. Like Dad's coffin.'

'No one told *me* the door had been wedged.' Keede spoke severely.

'No need to black a dead man's name, sir.'

'What made Grant go to Butcher's Row?'

'Because he'd noticed Uncle John had been pinchin' charcoal for a week past an' layin' it up behind the old barricade there. So when the 'unt began, he went that way straight as a string, an' when he saw the door shut, he knew. He told me he picked the sand-bags out of the cracks an' shoved 'is hand through and shifted the wedges before anyone come along. It looked all right. You said yourself, sir, the door must 'ave blown to.'

'Grant knew what Godsoe meant, then?' Keede snapped.

'Grant knew Godsoe was for it; an' nothin' earthly could 'elp or 'inder. He told me so.'

'And then what did you do?'

'I expect I must 'ave kept on carryin' on, till headquarters give me that wire from Ma – about Auntie Armine dyin'.'

'When had your aunt died?'

'On the mornin' of the twenty-first. The mornin' of the twenty-first! That tore it, d'ye see? As long as I could think, I had kep' tellin' myself it was like those things you lectured about at Arras when we was billeted in the cellars – the Angels of Mons, and so on. But that wire tore it.'

'Oh! Hallucinations! I remember. And that wire tore it?' said Keede.

'Yes! You see' – he half lifted himself off the sofa – 'there wasn't a single gor-dam thing left abidin' for me to take hold of, here or hereafter. If the dead *do* rise – and I saw 'em – why – why, *anything* can happen. Don't you understand?'

He was on his feet now, gesticulating stiffly.

'For I saw 'er,' he repeated. 'I saw 'im an' 'er – she dead since mornin' time, an' he killin' 'imself before my livin' eyes so's to carry on with 'er for all Eternity – an' she 'oldin' out 'er arms for it! I want to know where I'm *at!* Look 'ere, you two – why stand *we* in jeopardy every hour?'

'God knows,' said Keede to himself.

'Hadn't we better ring for some one?' I suggested. 'He'll go off the handle in a second.'

'No, he won't. It's the last kick-up before it takes hold. I know how the stuff works. Hul-lo!'

Strangwick, his hands behind his back and his eyes set, gave tongue in the strained, cracked voice of a boy reciting. 'Not twice in the world shall the gods do thus,' he cried again and again.

'And I'm damned if it's goin' to be even once for me!' he went on with sudden insane fury. '*I* don't care whether we *'ave* been pricin' things in the windows . . . *Let* 'er sue if she likes! She don't know what reel things mean. *I* do – I've 'ad occasion to notice 'em . . . *No,* I tell you! I'll 'ave 'em when I want 'em, an' be done with 'em; but not till I see that look on a face . . . that look . . . I'm not takin' any. The reel thing's life an' death. It *begins* at death, d'ye see. *She* can't understand . . . Oh, go on an' push off to Hell, you an' your lawyers. I'm fed up with it – fed up!'

He stopped as abruptly as he had started, and the drawn face broke back to its natural irresolute lines. Keede, holding both his hands, led him back to the sofa, where he dropped like a wet towel, took out some flamboyant robe from a press, and drew it neatly over him.

'Ye-es. *That's* the real thing at last,' said Keede. 'Now he's got it off his mind, he'll sleep. By the way, who introduced him?'

'Shall we go and find out?' I suggested.

'Yes; and you might ask him to come here. There's no need for us to stand to all night.'

So I went to the Banquet, which was in full swing, and was seized by an elderly, precise Brother from a South London Lodge, who followed me, concerned and apologetic. Keede soon put him at his ease.

'The boy's had trouble,' our visitor explained. 'I'm most mortified he should have performed his bad turn here. I thought he'd put it be'ind him.'

'I expect talking about old days with me brought it all back,' said Keede. 'It does sometimes.'

'Maybe! Maybe! But over and above that, Clem's had post-war trouble too.'

'Can't he get a job? He oughtn't to let that weigh on him, at his time of life,' said Keede cheerily.

'Tisn't that – he's provided for – but' – he coughed confidentially behind his dry hand – 'as a matter of fact, Worshipful Sir, he's – he's implicated for the present in a little breach of promise action.'

'Ah! That's a different thing,' said Keede.

'Yes. That's his reel trouble. No reason given, you understand. The young lady in every way suitable, an' she'd make him a good little wife too, if I'm any judge. But he says she ain't his ideel or something. No getting at what's in young people's minds these days, is there?'

'I'm afraid there isn't,' said Keede. 'But he's all right now. He'll sleep. You sit by him, and when he wakes, take him home quietly. . . . Oh, we're used to men getting a little upset here. You've nothing to thank us for, Brother – Brother—'

'Armine,' said the old gentleman. 'He's my nephew by marriage.'

'That's all that's wanted!' said Keede.

Brother Armine looked a little puzzled. Keede hastened to explain. 'As I was saying, all he wants now is to be kept quiet till he wakes.'

GOW'S WATCH

ACT V. SCENE 3

After the Battle. The PRINCESS *by the Standard on the Ravelin. Enter* Gow, *with the Crown of the Kingdom.*

GOW: Here's earnest of the Queen's submission.
  This by her last herald – and in haste.
PRINCESS: 'Twas ours already. Where is the woman?
GOW: Fled with her horse. They broke at dawn.
  Noon has not struck, and you're Queen questionless.
PRINCESS: By you – through you. How shall I honour *you*?
GOW: Me? But for what?
PRINCESS: For all – all – all –
  Since the realm sunk beneath us! Hear him!
    'For what?'
  Your body 'twixt my bosom and her knife,
  Your lips on the cup she proffered for my death;
  Your one cloak over me, that night in the snows
  We held the Pass at Bargi. Every hour
  New strengths, to this most unbelievable last.
  'Honour him?' I will honour–will honour you– . . .
  'Tis at your choice.
GOW: Child, mine was long ago.
  (*Enter* FERDINAND, *as from horse.*)
  But here's one worthy honour. Welcome, Fox!
FERDINAND: And to you, Watchdog. This day clenches all.
  We've made it and seen it.
GOW: Is the city held?
FERDINAND: Loyally. Oh, they're drunk with loyalty yonder.
  A virtuous mood. Your bombards helped 'em to it . . .
  But here's my word for you. The Lady Frances—
PRINCESS: I left her sick in the city. No harm, I pray.
FERDINAND: Nothing that she called harm.
  In truth, so little
  That (*To* GOW) I am bidden tell you, she'll be here
  Almost as soon as I.

GOW: She says it?
FERDINAND: Writes.
This. (*Gives him letter.*) Yester eve. 'Twas given me by the priest—
He with her in her hour.
GOW: So? (*Reads*) So it is.
She will be here. (*To* FERDINAND) And all is safe in the city?
FERDINAND: As thy long sword and my lean wits can make it.
You've naught to stay for. Is it the road again?
GOW: Ay. This time, not alone . . . She will be here.
PRINCESS: I am here. You have not looked at me awhile.
GOW: The rest is with you, Ferdinand . . . Then free.
PRINCESS: And at my service more than ever. I claim –
(Our wars have taught me) – being your Queen, now, claim
You wholly mine.
GOW: Then free . . . She will be here! A little while—
PRINCESS: (*To* FERDINAND). He looks beyond, not at me.
FERDINAND: Weariness.
We are not so young as once was. Two days' fight –
A worthy servitor – to be allowed
Some freedom.
PRINCESS: I have offered him all he would.
FERDINAND: He takes what he has taken.
(*The Spirit of the* LADY FRANCES *appears to* GOW.)
GOW: Frances!
PRINCESS: Distraught!
FERDINAND: An old head-blow, maybe. He has dealt in them.
GOW: (*To the* SPIRIT). What can the Grave have against us, O my Heart,
Comfort and light and reason in all things
Visible and invisible—my one God?
Thou that wast I these barren unyoked years
Of triflings now at an end! Frances!
PRINCESS: She's old.
FERDINAND: True. By most reckonings old. They must keep other count.
PRINCESS: He kisses his hand to the air!
FERDINAND: His ring, rather, he kisses. Yes – for sure – the ring.
GOW: Dear and most dear. And now, those very arms. (*Dies.*)
PRINCESS: Oh, look! He faints. Haste, you! Unhelm him! Help!
FERDINAND: Needless. No help
Avails against that poison. He is sped.

PRINCESS: By his own hand? *This* hour? When I had offered—
FERDINAND: He had made other choice – an old, old choice,
  Ne'er swerved from, and now patently sealed in death.
PRINCESS: He called on – the Lady Frances was it? Wherefore?
FERDINAND: Because she was his life. Forgive, my friend – (*Covers* GOW's *face*).
  God's uttermost beyond me in all faith,
  Service and passion – if I unveil at last
  The secret. (*To the* PRINCESS) Thought – dreamed you, it was for *you*
  He poured himself – for you resoldered the Crown?
  Struck here, held there, amended, broke, built up
  His multiplied imaginings for *you*?
PRINCESS: I thought – I thought he—
FERDINAND: Looked beyond. *Her* wish
  Was the sole Law he knew. *She* did not choose
  Your House should perish. Therefore he bade it stand.
  Enough for him when she had breathed a word:
  'Twas his to make it iron, stone, or fire,
  Driving our flesh and blood before his ways
  As the wind straws. Her one face unregarded
  Waiting you with your mantle or your glove –
  That is the God whom he is gone to worship.
  (*Trumpets without. Enter the Prince's* HERALDS.)
  And here's the work of Kingship begun again.
  These from the Prince of Bargi – to whose sword
  You owe such help as may, he thinks, be paid . . .
  He's equal in blood, in fortune more than peer,
  Young, most well favoured, with a heart to love—
  And two States in the balance. Do you meet him?
PRINCESS: God and my Misery! I have seen Love at last.
  What shall content me after?

UNTIMELY

Nothing in life has been made by man for man's using
But it was shown long since to man in ages
Lost as the name of the maker of it,

Who received oppression and scorn for his wages –
Hate, avoidance, and scorn in his daily dealings –
Until he perished, wholly confounded.

More to be pitied than he are the wise
Souls which foresaw the evil of loosing
Knowledge or Art before time, and aborted
Noble devices and deep-wrought healings,
Lest offence should arise.

Heaven delivers on earth the Hour that cannot be thwarted,
Neither advanced, at the price of a world or a soul, and its Prophet
Comes through the blood of the vanguards who dreamed – too soon –
 it had sounded.

The Eye of Allah

THE cantor of St Illod's being far too enthusiastic a musician to concern himself with its library, the sub-cantor, who idolized every detail of the work, was tidying up, after two hours' writing and dictation in the scriptorium. The copying-monks handed him in their sheets – it was a plain Four Gospels ordered by an abbot at Evesham – and filed out to vespers. John Otho, better known as John of Burgos, took no heed. He was burnishing a tiny boss of gold in his miniature of the Annunciation for his Gospel of St Luke, which it was hoped that Cardinal Falcodi, the papal legate, might later be pleased to accept.

'Break off, John,' said the sub-cantor in an undertone.

'Eh? Gone, have they? I never heard. Hold a minute, Clement.'

The sub-cantor waited patiently. He had known John more than a dozen years, coming and going at St Illod's, to which monastery John, when abroad, always said he belonged. The claim was gladly allowed, for, more even than other Fitz Othos, he seemed to carry all the arts under his hand, and most of their practical receipts under his hood.

The sub-cantor looked over his shoulder at the pinned-down sheet where the first words of the Magnificat were built up in gold washed with red-lac for a background to the Virgin's hardly yet fired halo. She was shown, hands joined in wonder, at a lattice of infinitely intricate arabesque, round the edges of which sprays of orange-bloom seemed to load the blue hot air that carried back over the minute parched landscape in the middle distance.

'You've made her all Jewess,' said the sub-cantor, studying the olive-flushed cheek and the eyes charged with foreknowledge.

'What else was Our Lady?' John slipped out the pins. 'Listen, Clement. If I do not come back, this goes into my Great Luke, whoever finishes it.' He slid the drawing between its guard-papers.

'Then you're for Burgos again – as I heard?'

'In two days. The new cathedral yonder – but they're slower than the Wrath of God, those masons – is good for the soul.'

'*Thy* soul?' The sub-cantor seemed doubtful.

'Even mine, by your permission. And down south – on the edge of the Conquered Countries – Granada way – there's some Moorish diaper-work that's wholesome. It allays vain thought and draws it toward the picture – as you felt, just now, in my Annunciation.'

'She–it was very beautiful. No wonder you go. But you'll not forget your absolution, John?'

'Surely.' This was a precaution John no more omitted on the eve of his travels than he did the recutting of the tonsure which he had provided himself with in his youth, somewhere near Ghent. The mark gave him privilege of clergy at a pinch, and a certain consideration on the road always.

'You'll not forget, either, what we need in the scriptorium. There's no more true ultramarine in this world now. They mix it with that German blue. And as for vermilion—'

'I'll do my best always.'

'And Brother Thomas' (this was the infirmarian in charge of the monastery hospital) 'he needs—'

'He'll do his own asking. I'll go over his side now, and get me re-tonsured.'

John went down the stairs to the lane that divides the hospital and cookhouse from the back-cloisters. While he was being barbered, Brother Thomas (St Illod's meek but deadly persistent infirmarian) gave him a list of drugs that he was to bring back from Spain by hook, crook, or lawful purchase. Here they were surprised by the lame, dark Abbot Stephen, in his fur-lined night-boots. Not that Stephen de Sautré was any spy; but as a young man he had shared an unlucky Crusade, which had ended, after a battle at Mansura, in two years' captivity among the Saracens at Cairo where men learn to walk softly. A fair huntsman and hawker, a reasonable disciplinarian, but a man of science above all, and a Doctor of Medicine under one Ranulphus, Canon of St Paul's, his heart was more in the monastery's hospital work than its religious. He checked their list interestedly, adding items of his own. After the infirmarian had withdrawn, he gave John generous absolution, to cover lapses by the way; for he did not hold with chance-bought indulgences.

'And what seek you *this* journey?' he demanded, sitting on the bench beside the mortar and scales in the little warm cell for stored drugs.

'Devils, mostly,' said John, grinning.

'In Spain? Are not Abana and Pharpar—?'

John, to whom men were but matter for drawings, and well-born to boot (since he was a de Sanford on his mother's side), looked the abbot full in the face and – 'Did *you* find it so?' said he.

'No. They were in Cairo too. But what's your special need of 'em?'

'For my Great Luke. He's the master-hand of all Four when it comes to devils.'

'No wonder. He was a physician. You're not.'

'Heaven forbid! But I'm weary of our Church-pattern devils. They're only apes and goats and poultry conjoined. Good enough for plain red-and-black Hells and Judgment Days – but not for me.'

'What makes you so choice in them?'

'Because it stands to reason and art that there are all musters of devils in Hell's dealings. Those Seven, for example, that were haled out of the Magdalene. They'd be she-devils – no kin at all to the beaked and horned and bearded devils-general.'

The abbot laughed.

'And see again! The devil that came out of the dumb man. What use is snout or bill to *him*? He'd be faceless as a leper. Above all – God send I live to do it! – the devils that entered the Gadarene swine. They'd be – they'd be – I know not yet what they'd be, but they'd be surpassing devils. I'd have 'em diverse as the Saints themselves. But now, they're all one pattern, for wall, window, or picture-work.'

'Go on, John. You're deeper in this mystery than I.'

'Heaven forbid! But I say there's respect due to devils, damned tho' they be.'

'Dangerous doctrine.'

'My meaning is that if the shape of anything be worth man's thought to picture to man, it's worth his best thought.'

'That's safer. But I'm glad I've given you absolution.'

'There's less risk for a craftsman who deals with the outside shapes of things – for Mother Church's glory.'

'Maybe so, but, John' – the Abbot's hand almost touched John's sleeve – 'tell me, now, is – is she Moorish or – or Hebrew?'

'She's mine,' John returned.

'Is that enough?'

'I have found it so.'

'Well – ah well! It's out of my jurisdiction, but – how do they look at it down yonder?'

'Oh, they drive nothing to a head in Spain – neither Church nor King, bless them! There's too many Moors and Jews to kill them all, and if they chased 'em away there'd be no trade nor farming. Trust me, in the Conquered Countries, from Seville to Granada, we live lovingly enough together – Spaniard, Moor, and Jew. Ye see, *we* ask no questions.'

'Yes – yes,' Stephen sighed. 'And always there's the hope she may be converted.'

'Oh yes, there's always hope.'

The abbot went on into the hospital. It was an easy age before Rome tightened the screw as to clerical connections. If the lady were not too forward, or the son too much of his father's beneficiary in ecclesiastical preferments and levies, a good deal was overlooked. But, as the Abbot had reason to recall, unions between Christian and Infidel led to sorrow. None the less, when John with mule, mails, and man, clattered off down the lane for Southampton and the sea, Stephen envied him.

He was back, twenty months later, in good hard case, and loaded down with fairings. A lump of richest lazuli, a bar of orange-hearted vermilion, and a small packet of dried beetles which make most glorious scarlet, for the sub-cantor. Besides that, a few cubes of milky marble, with yet a pink flush in them, which could be slaked and ground down to incomparable background-stuff. There were quite half the drugs that the abbot and Thomas had demanded, and there was a long deep-red cornelian necklace for the abbot's lady – Anne of Norton. She received it graciously, and asked where John had come by it.

'Near Granada,' he said.

'You left all well there?' Anne asked. (Maybe the abbot had told her something of John's confession.)

'I left all in the hands of God.'

'Ah me! How long since?'

'Four months less eleven days.'

'Were you – with her?'

'In my arms. Childbed.'

'And?'

'The boy too. There is nothing now.'

Anne of Norton caught her breath.

'I think you'll be glad of that,' she said after a while.

'Give me time, and maybe I'll compass it. But not now.'

'You have your handiwork and your art, and – John – remember there's no jealousy in the grave.'

'Ye-es! I have my art and Heaven knows I'm jealous of none.'

'Thank God for that at least,' said Anne of Norton, the always ailing woman who followed the abbot with her sunk eyes. 'And be sure I shall treasure this' – she touched the beads – 'as long as I shall live.'

'I brought – trusted – it to you for that,' he replied, and took leave. When she told the abbot how she had come by it, he said nothing, but as he and Thomas were storing the drugs that John handed over in the cell which backs on to the hospital kitchen-chimney, he observed, of a cake of dried poppy-juice: 'This has power to cut off all pain from a man's body.'

'I have seen it,' said John.

'But for pain of the soul there is, outside God's Grace, but one drug; and that is a man's craft, learning, or other helpful motion of his own mind.'

'That is coming to me, too,' was the answer.

John spent the next fair May day out in the woods with the monastery swineherd and all the porkers; and returned loaded with flowers and sprays of spring, to his own carefully kept place in the north bay of the scriptorium. There, with his travelling sketch-books under his left elbow, he sunk himself past all recollections in his Great Luke.

Brother Martin, senior copyist (who spoke about once a fortnight), ventured to ask, later, how the work was going.

'All here!' John tapped his forehead with his pencil. 'It has been only waiting these months to – ah God! – be born. Are ye free of your plain-copying, Martin?'

Brother Martin nodded. It was his pride that John of Burgos turned to him, in spite of his seventy years, for really good page-work.

'Then see!' John laid out a new vellum – thin but flawless. 'There's no better than this sheet from here to Paris. Yes! Smell it if you choose. Wherefore – give me the compasses and I'll set it out for you – if ye make one letter lighter or darker than its next, I'll stick ye like a pig.'

'Never, John!' The old man beamed happily.

'But I will! Now, follow! Here and here, as I prick, and in script of just this height to the hair's breadth, ye'll scribe the thirty-first and thirty-second verses of Eighth Luke.'

'Yes, the Gadarene Swine! "*And they besought him that he would not command them to go out into the abyss. And there was a herd of many swine*"'— Brother Martin naturally knew all the Gospels by heart.

'Just so! Down to "*and he suffered them*". Take your time to it. My Magdalene has to come off my heart first.'

Brother Martin achieved the work so perfectly that John stole some soft sweetmeats from the abbot's kitchen for his reward. The old man ate them; then repented; then confessed and insisted on penance. At which, the abbot, knowing there was but one way to reach the real sinner, set him a book called *De Virtutibus Herbarum* to fair-copy. St Illod's had borrowed it from the gloomy Cistercians, who do not hold with pretty things, and the crabbed text kept Martin busy just when John wanted him for some rather specially spaced letterings.

'See now,' said the sub-cantor improvingly. 'You should not do such things, John. Here's Brother Martin on penance for your sake—'

'No – for my Great Luke. But I've paid the abbot's cook. I've drawn him till his own scullions cannot keep straight-faced. *He*'ll not tell again.'

'Unkindly done! And you're out of favour with the abbot too. He's made no sign to you since you came back – never asked you to high table.'

'I've been busy. Having eyes in his head, Stephen knew it. Clement, there's no librarian from Durham to Torre fit to clean up after you.'

The sub-cantor stood on guard; he knew where John's compliments generally ended.

'But outside the scriptorium—'

'Where I never go.' The sub-cantor had been excused even digging in the garden, lest it should mar his wonderful book-binding hands.

'In all things outside the scriptorium you are the master-fool of Christendie. Take it from me, Clement. I've met many.'

'I take everything from you,' Clement smiled benignly. 'You use me worse than a singing-boy.'

They could hear one of that suffering breed in the cloister below, squalling as the cantor pulled his hair.

'God love you! So I do! But have you ever thought how I lie and steal daily on my travels – yes, and for aught you know, murder – to fetch you colours and earths?'

'True,' said just and conscience-stricken Clement. 'I have often thought that were I in the world – which God forbid! – I might be a strong thief in some matters.'

Even Brother Martin, bent above his loathed *De Virtutibus*, laughed.

But about mid-summer, Thomas the Infirmarian conveyed to John the abbot's invitation to supper in his house that night, with the request that he would bring with him anything that he had done for his Great Luke.

'What's toward?' said John, who had been wholly shut up in his work.

'Only one of his "wisdom" dinners. You've sat at a few since you were a man.'

'True: and mostly good. How would Stephen have us—?'

'Gown and hood over all. There will be a doctor from Salerno – one Roger, an Italian. Wise and famous with the knife on the body. He's been in the infirmary some ten days, helping me – even me!'

''Never heard the name. But our Stephen's *physicus* before *sacerdos*, always.'

'And his lady has a sickness of some time. Roger came hither in chief because of her.'

'Did he? Now I think of it, I have not seen the Lady Anne for a while.'

'Ye've seen nothing for a long while. She has been housed near a month – they have to carry her abroad now.'

'So bad as that, then?'

'Roger of Salerno will not yet say what he thinks. But—'

'God pity Stephen! . . . Who else at table, besides thee?'

'An Oxford friar. Roger is his name also. A learned and famous philosopher. And he holds his liquor too, valiantly.'

'Three doctors – counting Stephen. I've always found that means two atheists.'

Thomas looked uneasily down his nose. 'That's a wicked proverb,' he stammered. 'You should not use it.'

'Hoh! Never come you the monk over me, Thomas! You've been infirmarian at St Illod's eleven years – and a lay-brother still. Why have you never taken orders, all this while?'

'I – I am not worthy.'

'Ten times worthier than that new fat swine – Henry Who's-his-name – that takes the Infirmary Masses. He bullocks in with the viaticum, under your nose, when a sick man's only faint from being bled. So the man dies – of pure fear. Ye know it! I've watched your face at such times. Take orders, Didymus. You'll have a little more medicine and a little less mass with your sick then; and they'll live longer.'

'I am unworthy – unworthy,' Thomas repeated pitifully.

'Not you – but – to your own master you stand or fall. And now that my work releases me for awhile, I'll drink with any philosopher out of any school. And, Thomas,' he coaxed, 'a hot bath for me in the infirmary before vespers.'

When the abbot's perfectly cooked and served meal had ended, and the deep-fringed naperies were removed, and the prior had sent in the keys with word that all was fast in the monastery, and the keys had been duly returned with the word, 'Make it so till Prime,' the abbot and his guests went out to cool themselves in an upper cloister that took them, by way of the leads, to the south choir side of the triforium. The summer sun was still strong, for it was barely six o'clock, but the abbey church, of course, lay in her wonted darkness. Lights were being lit for choir-practice thirty feet below.

'Our cantor gives them no rest,' the abbot whispered. 'Stand by this pillar and we'll hear what he's driving them at now.'

'Remember, all!' the cantor's hard voice came up. 'This is the soul of Bernard himself, attacking our evil world. Take it quicker than yesterday, and throw all your words clean-bitten from you. In the loft there! Begin!'

The organ broke out for an instant, alone and raging. Then the voices crashed together into that first fierce line of the *'De Contemptu Mundi.'**

'Hora novissima – tempora pessima' – a dead pause till the assenting *sunt* broke, like a sob, out of the darkness, and one boy's voice, clearer than silver trumpets, returned the long-drawn *vigilemus.*

'Ecce minaciter, imminet Arbiter' (organ and voices were leashed together in terror and warning, breaking away liquidly to the *'ille supremus'*). Then the tone-colours shifted for the prelude to – *'Imminet, imminet, ut mala terminet—'*

'Stop! Again!' cried the cantor; and gave his reasons a little more roundly than was natural at choir-practice.

'Ah! Pity o' man's vanity! He's guessed we are here. Come away!' said the abbot. Anne of Norton, in her carried chair, had been listening too, further along the dark triforium, with Roger of Salerno. John heard her sob. On the way back, he asked Thomas how her health stood. Before Thomas could reply the sharp-featured Italian doctor pushed between them. 'Following on our talk together, I judged it best to tell her,' said he to Thomas.

'What?' John asked simply enough.

'What she knew already.' Roger of Salerno launched into a Greek quotation to the effect that every woman knows all about everything.

'I have no Greek,' said John stiffly. Roger of Salerno had been giving them a good deal of it, at dinner.

*Hymn No. 226, A. and M., 'The world is very evil.'

'Then I'll come to you in Latin. Ovid hath it neatly. "*Utque malum late solet immedicabile cancer–*" but doubtless you know the rest, worthy sir.'

'Alas! My school-Latin's but what I've gathered by the way from fools professing to heal sick women. "*Hocus-pocus—*" but doubtless you know the rest, worthy sir.'

Roger of Salerno was quite quiet till they regained the dining-room, where the fire had been comforted and the dates, raisins, ginger, figs, and cinnamon-scented sweetmeats set out, with the choicer wines, on the after-table. The abbot seated himself, drew off his ring, dropped it, that all might hear the tinkle, into an empty silver cup, stretched his feet towards the hearth, and looked at the great gilt and carved rose in the barrel-roof. The silence that keeps from Compline to Matins had closed on their world. The bull-necked friar watched a ray of sunlight split itself into colours on the rim of a crystal salt-cellar; Roger of Salerno had re-opened some discussion with Brother Thomas on a type of spotted fever that was baffling them both in England and abroad; John took note of the keen profile, and – it might serve as a note for the Great Luke – his hand moved to his bosom. The abbot saw, and nodded permission. John whipped out silver-point and sketch-book.

'Nay – modesty is good enough – but deliver your own opinion,' the Italian was urging the infirmarian. Out of courtesy to the foreigner nearly all the talk was in table-Latin; more formal and more copious than monk's patter. Thomas began with his meek stammer.

'I confess myself at a loss for the cause of the fever unless – as Varro saith in his *De Re Rustica* – certain small animals which the eye cannot follow enter the body by the nose and mouth, and set up grave diseases. On the other hand, this is not in Scripture.'

Roger of Salerno hunched head and shoulders like an angry cat. 'Always *that*!' he said, and John snatched down the twist of the thin lips.

'Never at rest, John.' The abbot smiled at the artist. 'You should break off every two hours for prayers, as we do. St Benedict was no fool. Two hours is all that a man can carry the edge of his eye or hand.'

'For copyists – yes. Brother Martin is not sure after one hour. But when a man's work takes him, he must go on till it lets him go.'

'Yes, that is the Demon of Socrates,' the friar from Oxford rumbled above his cup.

'The doctrine leans toward presumption,' said the abbot.

'Remember, "Shall mortal man be more just than his Maker?"'

'There is no danger of justice;' the friar spoke bitterly. 'But at least Man might be suffered to go forward in his art or his thought. Yet if Mother Church sees or hears him move anyward, what says she? "No!" Always "No."'

'But if the little animals of Varro be invisible' – this was Roger of Salerno to Thomas – 'how are we any nearer to a cure?'

'By experiment' – the friar wheeled round on them suddenly. 'By reason and experiment. The one is useless without the other. But Mother Church—'

'Ay!' Roger de Salerno dashed at the fresh bait like a pike. 'Listen, sirs. Her bishops – our princes – strew our roads in Italy with carcasses that they make for their pleasure or wrath. Beautiful corpses! Yet if I – if we doctors – so much as raise the skin of one of them to look at God's fabric beneath, what says Mother Church? "Sacrilege! Stick to your pigs and dogs, or you burn!"'

'And not Mother Church only!' the friar chimed in. '*Every* way we are barred – barred by the words of some man, dead a thousand years, which are held final. Who is any son of Adam that his one say-so should close a door towards truth? I would not except even Peter Peregrinus, my own great teacher.'

'Nor I Paul of Aegina,' Roger of Salerno cried. 'Listen, sirs! Here is a case to the very point. Apuleius affirmeth, if a man eat fasting of the juice of the cut-leaved buttercup – *sceleratus* we call it, which means "rascally"' – this with a condescending nod towards John – 'his soul will leave his body laughing. Now this is the lie more dangerous than truth, since truth of a sort is in it.'

'He's away!' whispered the abbot despairingly.

'For the juice of that herb, I know by experiment, burns, blisters, and wries the mouth. I know also the *rictus*, or pseudo-laughter, on the face of such as have perished by the strong poisons of herbs allied to this ranunculus. Certainly that spasm resembles laughter. It seems then, in my judgment, that Apuleius, having seen the body of one thus poisoned, went off at score and wrote that the man died laughing.'

'Neither staying to observe, nor to confirm observation by experiment,' added the friar, frowning.

Stephen the Abbot cocked an eyebrow toward John.

'How think *you*?' said he.

'I'm no doctor,' John returned, 'but I'd say Apuleius in all these years might have been betrayed by his copyists. They take short-cuts to save 'emselves trouble. Put case that Apuleius wrote the soul *seems to* leave the body laughing, after this poison. There's not three copyists in five (*my* judgment) would not leave out the "seems to". For who'd question Apuleius? If it seemed so to him, so it must be. Otherwise any child knows cut-leaved buttercup.'

'Have you knowledge of herbs?' Roger of Salerno asked curtly.

'Only that, when I was a boy in convent, I've made tetters round my mouth and on my neck with buttercup-juice, to save going to prayer o' cold nights.'

'Ah!' said Roger. 'I profess no knowledge of tricks.' He turned aside, stiffly.

'No matter! Now for your own tricks, John,' the tactful Abbot broke in. 'You shall show the doctors your Magdalene and your Gadarene Swine and the devils.'

'Devils? Devils? *I* have produced devils by means of drugs; and have abolished them by the same means. Whether devils be external to mankind or immanent, I have not yet pronounced.' Roger of Salerno was still angry.

'Ye dare not,' snapped the friar from Oxford. 'Mother Church makes Her own devils.'

'Not wholly! Our John has come back from Spain with brand-new ones.' Abbot Stephen took the vellum handed to him, and laid it tenderly on the table. They gathered to look. The Magdalene was drawn in palest, almost transparent, grisaille, against a raging, swaying background of woman-faced devils, each broke to and by her special sin, and each, one could see, frenziedly straining against the Power that compelled her.

'I've never seen the like of this grey shadow-work,' said the abbot. 'How came you by it?'

'*Non nobis!* It came to me,' said John, not knowing he was a generation or so ahead of his time in the use of that medium.

'Why is she so pale?' the friar demanded.

'Evil has all come out of her – she'd take any colour now.'

'Ay, like light through glass. *I* see.'

Roger of Salerno was looking in silence – his nose nearer and nearer the page. 'It is so,' he pronounced finally. 'Thus it is in epilepsy – mouth, eyes, and forehead – even to the droop of her wrist there. Every sign of it! She will need restoratives, that woman, and, afterwards, sleep natural. No poppy-juice, or she will vomit on her waking. And thereafter – but I am not in my schools.' He drew himself up. 'Sir,' said he, 'you should be of Our calling. For, by the Snakes of Aesculapius, you *see*!'

The two struck hands as equals.

'And how think you of the Seven Devils?' the abbot went on.

These melted into convoluted flower- or flame-like bodies, ranging in colour from phosphorescent green to the black purple of outworn iniquity, whose hearts could be traced beating through their substance. But, for sign of hope and the sane workings of life, to be regained, the deep border was of conventionalized spring flowers and birds, all crowned by a kingfisher in haste, atilt through a clump of yellow iris.

Roger of Salerno identified the herbs and spoke largely of their virtues.

'And now, the Gadarene Swine,' said Stephen. John laid the picture on the table.

Here were devils dishoused, in dread of being abolished to the Void, huddling and hurtling together to force lodgment by every opening into the brute bodies offered. Some of the swine fought the invasion, foaming and jerking; some were surrendering to it, sleepily, as to a luxurious back-scratching; others, wholly possessed, whirled off in bucking droves for the lake beneath. In one corner the freed man stretched out his limbs all restored to his control, and Our Lord, seated, looked at him as questioning what he would make of his deliverance.

'Devils indeed!' was the friar's comment. 'But wholly a new sort.'

Some devils were mere lumps, with lobes and protuberances – a hint of a fiend's face peering through jelly-like walls. And there was a family of impatient, globular devillings who had burst open the belly of their smirking parent, and were revolving desperately towards their prey. Others patterned themselves into rods, chains and ladders, single or conjoined, round the throat and jaws of a shrieking sow, from whose ear emerged the lashing, glassy tail of a devil that had made good his refuge. And there were granulated and conglomerate devils, mixed up with the foam and slaver where the attack was fiercest. Thence the eye carried on to the insanely active backs of the downward-racing swine, the swineherd's aghast face, and his dog's terror.

Said Roger of Salerno, 'I pronounce that these were begotten of drugs. They stand outside the rational mind.'

'Not these,' said Thomas the Infirmarian, who as a servant of the monastery should have asked his abbot's leave to speak. 'Not *these* – look! – in the bordure.'

The border to the picture was a diaper of irregular but balanced compartments or cellules, where sat, swam, or weltered, devils in blank, so to say – things as yet uninspired by Evil – indifferent, but lawlessly outside imagination. Their shapes resembled, again, ladders, chains, scourges, diamonds, aborted buds, or gravid phosphorescent globes – some well-nigh star-like.

Roger of Salerno compared them to the obsessions of a churchman's mind.

'Malignant?' the friar from Oxford questioned.

'"Count everything unknown for horrible,"' Roger quoted with scorn.

'Not I. But they are marvellous – marvellous. I think—'

The friar drew back. Thomas edged in to see better, and half opened his mouth.

'Speak,' said Stephen, who had been watching him. 'We are all in a sort doctors here.'

'I would say then' – Thomas rushed at it as one putting out his life's belief at the stake – 'that these lower shapes in the bordure may not be so much hellish and malignant as models and patterns upon which John has tricked out and embellished his proper devils among the swine above there!'

'And that would signify?' said Roger of Salerno sharply.

'In my poor judgment, that he may have seen such shapes – without help of drugs.'

'Now who – *who*,' said John of Burgos, after a round and unregarded oath, 'has made thee so wise of a sudden, my doubter?'

'I wise? God forbid! Only, John, remember – one winter six years ago – the snowflakes melting on your sleeve at the cookhouse-door. You showed me them through a little crystal, that made small things larger.'

'Yes. The Moors call such a glass the Eye of Allah,' John confirmed.

'You showed me them melting – six-sided. You called them, then, your patterns.'

'True. Snowflakes melt six-sided. I have used them for diaper-work often.'

'Melting snow-flakes as seen through a glass? By art optical?' the friar asked.

'Art optical? *I* have never heard!' Roger of Salerno cried.

'John,' said the Abbot of St Illod's commandingly, 'was it – is it so?'

'In some sort,' John replied, 'Thomas has the right of it. Those shapes in the bordure were my workshop-patterns for the devils above. In *my* craft, Salerno, we dare not drug. It kills hand and eye. My shapes are to be seen honestly, in nature.'

The abbot drew a bowl of rose-water towards him. 'When I was prisoner with – with the Saracens after Mansura,' he began, turning up the fold of his long sleeve, 'there were certain magicians – physicians – who could show –' he dipped his third finger delicately in the water – 'all the firmament of Hell, as it were, in –' he shook off one drop from his polished nail on to the polished table – 'even such a supernaculum as this.'

'But it must be foul water – not clean,' said John.

'Show us then – all – all,' said Stephen. 'I would make sure – once more.' The abbot's voice was official.

John drew from his bosom a stamped leather box, some six or eight inches long, wherein, bedded on faded velvet, lay what looked like silver-bound compasses of old box-wood, with a screw at the head which opened or closed the legs to minute fractions. The legs terminated, not in points, but spoon-shapedly, one spatula pierced with a metal-lined hole less than a quarter of an inch across, the other with a half-inch hole. Into this latter John, after carefully wiping with a silk rag, slipped a metal cylinder that carried glass or crystal, it seemed, at each end.

'Ah! Art optic!' said the friar. 'But what is that beneath it?'

It was a small swivelling sheet of polished silver no bigger than a florin, which caught the light and concentrated it on the lesser hole. John adjusted it without the friar's proffered help.

'And now to find a drop of water,' said he, picking up a small brush.

'Come to my upper cloister. The sun is on the leads still,' said the abbot, rising.

They followed him there. Half-way along, a drip from a gutter had made a greenish puddle in a worn stone. Very carefully, John dropped a drop of it into the smaller hole of the compass-leg, and, steadying the apparatus on a coping, worked the screw in the compass-joint, screwed the cylinder, and swung the swivel of the mirror till he was satisfied.

'Good!' He peered through the thing. 'My shapes are all here. Now look, Father! If they do not meet your eye at first, turn this nicked edge here, left- or right-handed.'

'I have not forgotten,' said the abbot, taking his place. 'Yes! They are here – as they were in my time – my time past. There is no end to them, I was told . . . There *is* no end!'

'The light will go. Oh, let me look! Suffer me to see, also!' the friar pleaded, almost shouldering Stephen from the eyepiece. The abbot gave way. His eyes were on time past. But the friar, instead of looking, turned the apparatus in his capable hands.

'Nay, nay,' John interrupted, for the man was already fiddling at the screws. 'Let the doctor see.'

Roger of Salerno looked, minute after minute. John saw his blue-veined cheek-bones turn white. He stepped back at last, as though stricken.

'It is a new world – a new world, and – Oh, God Unjust! – I am old!'

'And now Thomas,' Stephen ordered.

John manipulated the tube for the infirmarian, whose hands shook, and he too looked long. 'It is Life,' he said presently in a breaking voice. 'No Hell! Life created and rejoicing – the work of the Creator. They live, even as I have dreamed. Then it was no sin for me to dream. No sin – O God – no sin!'

He flung himself on his knees and began hysterically the *Benedicite omnia Opera*.

'And now I will see how it is actuated,' said the friar from Oxford, thrusting forward again.

'Bring it within. The place is all eyes and ears,' said Stephen.

They walked quietly back along the leads, three English counties laid out in evening sunshine around them; church upon church, monastery upon monastery, cell after cell, and the bulk of a vast cathedral moored on the edge of the banked shoals of sunset.

When they were at the after-table once more they sat down, all except the friar, who went to the window and huddled bat-like over the thing. 'I see! I see!' he was repeating to himself.

'He'll not hurt it,' said John. But the abbot, staring in front of him, like Roger of Salerno, did not hear. The infirmarian's head was on the table between his shaking arms.

John reached for a cup of wine.

'It was shown to me,' the abbot was speaking to himself, 'in Cairo, that man stands ever between two Infinities – of greatness and littleness. Therefore, there is no end – either to life – or—'

'And *I* stand on the edge of the grave,' snarled Roger of Salerno. 'Who pities *me*?'

'Hush!' said Thomas the Infirmarian. 'The little creatures shall be sanctified – sanctified to the service of His sick.'

'What need?' John of Burgos wiped his lips. 'It shows no more than the shapes of things. It gives good pictures. I had it at Granada. It was brought from the East, they told me.'

Roger of Salerno laughed with an old man's malice. 'What of Mother Church? Most Holy Mother Church? If it comes to Her ears that we have spied into Her Hell without Her leave, where do we stand?'

'At the stake,' said the Abbot of St Illod's, and, raising his voice a trifle, 'You hear that? Roger Bacon, heard you that?'

The friar turned from the window, clutching the compasses tighter.

'No, no!' he appealed. 'Not with Falcodi – not with our English-hearted Foulkes made Pope. He's wise – he's learned. He reads what I have put forth. Foulkes would never suffer it.'

'"Holy Pope is one thing, Holy Church another,"' Roger quoted.

'But I – *I* can bear witness it is no art magic,' the friar went on. 'Nothing is it, except art optical – wisdom after trial and experiment, mark you. I can prove it, and – my name weighs with men who dare think.'

'Find them!' croaked Roger of Salerno. 'Five or six in all the world. That makes less than fifty pounds by weight of ashes at the stake. I have watched such men – reduced.'

'I will not give this up!' The friar's voice cracked in passion and despair. 'It would be to sin against the Light.'

'No, no! Let us – let us sanctify the little animals of Varro,' said Thomas.

Stephen leaned forward, fished his ring out of the cup, and slipped it on his finger. 'My sons,' said he, 'we have seen what we have seen.'

'That it is no magic but simple art,' the friar persisted.

'Avails nothing. In the eyes of Mother Church we have seen more than is permitted to man.'

'But it was Life – created and rejoicing,' said Thomas.

'To look into Hell as we shall be judged – as we shall be proved – to have looked, is for priests only.'

'Or green-sick virgins on the road to sainthood who, for cause any midwife could give you—'

The abbot's half-lifted hand checked Roger of Salerno's outpouring.

'Nor may even priests see more in Hell than Church knows to be there. John, there is respect due to Church as well as to devils.'

'My trade's the outside of things,' said John quietly. 'I have my patterns.'

'But you may need to look again for more,' the friar said.

'In my craft, a thing done is done with. We go on to new shapes after that.'

'And if we trespass beyond bounds, even in thought, we lie open to the judgment of the Church,' the abbot continued.

'But thou knowest – *knowest*!' Roger of Salerno had returned to the attack. 'Here's all the world in darkness concerning the causes of things – from the fever across the lane to thy Lady's – thine own Lady's – eating malady. Think!'

'I have thought upon it, Salerno! I have thought indeed.'

Thomas the Infirmarian lifted his head again; and this time he did not stammer at all. 'As in the water, so in the blood must they rage and war with each other! I have dreamed these ten years – I thought it was a sin – but my dreams and Varro's are true! Think on it again! Here's the Light under our very hand!'

'Quench it! You'd no more stand to roasting than – any other. I'll give you the case as Church – as I myself – would frame it. Our John here returns from the Moors, and shows us a hell of devils contending in the compass of one drop of water. Magic past clearance! You can hear the faggots crackle.'

'But thou knowest! Thou hast seen it all before! For man's poor sake! For old friendship's sake – Stephen!' The friar was trying to stuff the compasses into his bosom as he appealed.

'What Stephen de Sautré knows, you his friends know also. I would have you, now, obey the Abbot of St Illod's. Give to me!' He held out his ringed hand.

'May I – may John here – not even make a drawing of one – one screw?' said the broken friar, in spite of himself.

'Nowise!' Stephen took it over. 'Your dagger, John. Sheathed will serve.'

He unscrewed the metal cylinder, laid it on the table, and with the dagger's hilt smashed some crystal to sparkling dust which he swept into a scooped hand and cast behind the hearth.

'It would seem,' said he, 'the choice lies between two sins. To deny the world a Light which is under our hand, or to enlighten the world before her time. What you have seen, I saw long since among the physicians at Cairo. And I know what doctrine they drew from it. Hast *thou* dreamed, Thomas? I also – with fuller knowledge. But this birth, my sons, is untimely. It will be but the mother of more death, more torture, more division, and greater darkness in this dark age. Therefore I, who know both my world and the Church, take this choice on my conscience. Go! It is finished.'

He thrust the wooden part of the compasses deep among the beech logs till all was burned.

THE LAST ODE

(*Nov*. 27. BC 8)

HORACE, Ode 31, Bk. V

As watchers couched beneath a Bantine oak,
    Hearing the dawn-wind stir,
Know that the present strength of night is broke
    Though no dawn threaten her
Till dawn's appointed hour – so Virgil died,
Aware of change at hand, and prophesied

Change upon all the Eternal Gods had made
    And on the Gods alike –
Fated as dawn but, as the dawn, delayed
    Till the just hour should strike –

A Star new-risen above the living and dead;
    And the lost shades that were our loves restored
As lovers, and for ever. So he said;
    Having received the word . . .

Maecenas waits me on the Esquiline:
    Thither tonight go I . . .
And shall this dawn restore us, Virgil mine,
    To dawn? Beneath what sky?

The Gardener

One grave to me was given,
   One watch till Judgment Day;
And God looked down from Heaven
   And rolled the stone away.

One day in all the years,
   One hour in that one day,
His Angel saw my tears,
   And rolled the stone away!

EVERYONE in the village knew that Helen Turrell did her duty by all her world, and by none more honourably than by her only brother's unfortunate child. The village knew, too, that George Turrell had tried his family severely since early youth, and were not surprised to be told that, after many fresh starts given and thrown away, he, an inspector of Indian Police, had entangled himself with the daughter of a retired non-commissioned officer, and had died of a fall from a horse a few weeks before his child was born. Mercifully, George's father and mother were both dead, and though Helen, thirty-five and independent, might well have washed her hands of the whole disgraceful affair, she most nobly took charge, though she was, at the time, under threat of lung trouble which had driven her to the South of France. She arranged for the passage of the child and a nurse from Bombay, met them at Marseilles, nursed the baby through an attack of infantile dysentery due to the carelessness of the nurse, whom she had had to dismiss, and at last, thin and worn but triumphant, brought the boy late in the autumn, wholly restored, to her Hampshire home.

All these details were public property, for Helen was as open as the day, and held that scandals are only increased by hushing them up. She admitted that George had always been rather a black sheep, but things might have been much worse if the mother had insisted on her right to keep the boy. Luckily, it seemed that people of that class would do almost anything for money, and, as George had always turned to her in his scrapes, she felt herself justified – her friends agreed with her – in cutting the whole non-commissioned officer connection, and giving the child every advantage. A christening, by the rector, under the name of Michael, was the first step. So far as she knew herself, she was not, she said, a child-lover, but, for all his faults, she had been very fond of George, and she pointed out that little Michael had his father's mouth to a line; which made something to build upon.

As a matter of fact, it was the Turrell forehead, broad, low, and well-shaped, with the widely spaced eyes beneath it, that Michael had most faithfully reproduced. His mouth was somewhat better cut than the family type. But Helen, who would concede nothing good to his mother's side, vowed he was a Turrell all over, and, there being no one to contradict, the likeness was established.

In a few years Michael took his place, as accepted as Helen had always been – fearless, philosophical, and fairly good-looking. At six, he wished to know why he could not call her 'Mummy', as other boys called their mothers. She explained that she was only his auntie, and that aunties were not quite the same as mummies, but that, if it gave him pleasure, he might call her 'Mummy' at bedtime, for a pet-name between themselves.

Michael kept his secret most loyally, but Helen, as usual, explained the fact to her friends; which when Michael heard, he raged.

'Why did you tell? *Why* did you tell?' came at the end of the storm.

'Because it's always best to tell the truth,' Helen answered, her arm round him as he shook in his cot.

'All right, but when the troof's ugly I don't think it's nice.'

'Don't you, dear?'

'No, I don't and' – she felt the small body stiffen – 'now you've told, I won't call you "Mummy" any more – not even at bedtimes.'

'But isn't that rather unkind?' said Helen softly.

'I don't care! I don't care! You've hurted me in my insides and I'll hurt you back. I'll hurt you as long as I live!'

'Don't, oh, don't talk like that, dear! You don't know what—'

'I will! And when I'm dead I'll hurt you worse!'

'Thank goodness, I shall be dead long before you, darling.'

'Huh! Emma says, "'Never know your luck."' (Michael had been talking to Helen's elderly, flat-faced maid.) 'Lots of little boys die quite soon. So'll I. *Then* you'll see!'

Helen caught her breath and moved towards the door, but the wail of 'Mummy! Mummy!' drew her back again, and the two wept together.

At ten years old, after two terms at a prep school, something or somebody gave him the idea that his civil status was not quite regular. He attacked Helen on the subject, breaking down her stammered defences with the family directness.

'Don't believe a word of it,' he said, cheerily, at the end. 'People wouldn't have talked like they did if my people had been married. But don't you bother, Auntie. I've found out all about my sort in English Hist'ry and the Shakespeare bits. There was William the Conqueror to begin with, and – oh, heaps more, and they all got on first-rate. 'Twon't make any difference to you, my being *that* – will it?'

'As if anything could—' she began.

'All right. We won't talk about it any more if it makes you cry.' He never mentioned the thing again of his own will, but when, two years later, he skilfully managed to have measles in the holidays, as his temperature went up to the appointed one hundred and four he muttered of nothing else, till Helen's voice, piercing at last his delirium, reached him with assurance that nothing on earth or beyond could make any difference between them.

The terms at his public school and the wonderful Christmas, Easter, and Summer holidays followed each other, variegated and glorious as jewels on a string; and as jewels Helen treasured them. In due time Michael developed his own interests, which ran their courses and gave way to others; but his interest in Helen was constant and increasing throughout. She repaid it with all that she had of affection or could command of counsel and money; and since Michael was no fool, the war took him just before what was like to have been a most promising career.

He was to have gone up to Oxford, with a scholarship, in October. At the end of August he was on the edge of joining the first holocaust of public-school boys who threw themselves into the Line; but the captain of his OTC, where he had been sergeant for nearly a year, headed him off and steered him directly to a commission in a battalion so new that half of it still wore the old Army red, and the other half was breeding meningitis through living overcrowdedly in damp tents. Helen had been shocked at the idea of direct enlistment.

'But it's in the family,' Michael laughed.

'You don't mean to tell me that you believed that old story all this time?' said Helen. (Emma, her maid, had been dead now several years.) 'I gave you my word of honour – and I give it again – that – that it's all right. It is indeed.'

'Oh, *that* doesn't worry me. It never did,' he replied valiantly. 'What I meant was, I should have got into the show earlier if I'd enlisted – like my grandfather.'

'Don't talk like that! Are you afraid of its ending so soon, then?'

'No such luck. You know what K. says.'

'Yes. But my banker told me last Monday it couldn't *possibly* last beyond Christmas – for financial reasons.'

'Hope he's right, but our colonel – and he's a Regular – says it's going to be a long job.'

Michael's battalion was fortunate in that, by some chance which meant several 'leaves', it was used for coast-defence among shallow trenches on the Norfolk coast; thence sent north to watch the mouth of a Scotch estuary, and, lastly, held for weeks on a baseless rumour of distant service. But, the very day that Michael was to have met Helen for four whole hours at a railway-junction up the line, it was hurled out, to help make good the wastage of Loos, and he had only just time to send her a wire of farewell.

In France luck again helped the battalion. It was put down near the Salient, where it led a meritorious and unexacting life, while the Somme was being manufactured; and enjoyed the peace of the Armentières and Laventie sectors when that battle began. Finding that it had sound views on protecting its own flanks and could dig, a prudent commander stole it out of its own division, under pretence of helping to lay telegraphs, and used it round Ypres at large.

A month later, and just after Michael had written Helen that there was nothing special doing and therefore no need to worry, a shell-splinter dropping out of a wet dawn killed him at once. The next shell uprooted and laid down over the body what had been the foundation of a barn wall, so neatly that none but an expert would have guessed that anything unpleasant had happened.

By this time the village was old in experience of war, and, English fashion, had evolved a ritual to meet it. When the postmistress handed her seven-year-old daughter the official telegram to take to Miss Turrell, she observed to the rector's gardener: 'It's Miss Helen's turn now.' He replied, thinking of his own son: 'Well, he's lasted longer than some.' The child herself came to the front door weeping aloud, because Master Michael had often given her sweets. Helen, presently, found herself pulling down the house-blinds one after one with great care, and saying earnestly to each: 'Missing *always* means dead.' Then she took her place in the dreary procession that was impelled to go through an inevitable series of unprofitable emotions. The rector, of course, preached hope and prophesied word, very soon, from a prison camp. Several friends, too, told her perfectly truthful tales, but always about other women, to whom, after months and months of silence, their missing had been miraculously restored. Other people urged her to communicate with infallible secretaries of organizations who could communicate with benevolent neutrals, who could extract accurate information from the most secretive of Hun prison commandants. Helen did and wrote and signed everything that was suggested or put before her.

Once, on one of Michael's leaves, he had taken her over a munition factory, where she saw the progress of a shell from blank-iron to the all but finished article. It struck her at the time that the wretched thing was never left alone for a single second; and 'I'm being manufactured into a bereaved next of kin,' she told herself, as she prepared her documents.

In due course, when all the organizations had deeply or sincerely regretted their inability to trace, etc., something gave way within her and all sensation – save of thankfulness for the release – came to an end in blessed passivity. Michael had died and her world had stood still and she had been one with the full shock of that arrest. Now she was standing still and the world was going forward, but it did not concern her – in now way or relation did it touch her. She knew this by the ease with which she could slip Michael's name into talk and incline her head to the proper angle, at the proper murmur of sympathy.

In the blessed realization of that relief, the Armistice with all its bells broke over her and passed unheeded. At the end of another year she had overcome her physical loathing of the living and returned young, so that she could take them by the hand and almost sincerely wish them well. She had no interest in any aftermath, national or personal, of the war, but, moving at an immense distance, she sat on various relief committees and held strong views – she heard herself delivering them – about the site of the proposed village War Memorial.

Then there came to her, as next of kin, an official intimation, backed by a page of a letter to her in indelible pencil, a silver identity-disc, and a watch, to the effect that the body of Lieutenant Michael Turrell had been found, identified, and re-interred in Hagenzeele Third Military Cemetery – the letter of the row and the grave's number in that row duly given.

So Helen found herself moved on to another process of the manufacture – to a world full of exultant or broken relatives, now strong in the certainty that there was an altar upon earth where they might lay their love. These soon told her, and by means of timetables made clear, how easy it was and how little it interfered with life's affairs to go and see one's grave.

'*So* different,' as the rector's wife said, 'if he'd been killed in Mesopotamia, or even Gallipoli.'

The agony of being waked up to some sort of second life drove Helen across the Channel, where, in a new world of abbreviated titles, she learnt that Hagenzeele Third could be comfortably reached by an afternoon train which fitted in with the morning boat, and that there was a comfortable little hotel not three kilometres from Hagenzeele itself, where one could spend quite a comfortable night and see one's grave next morning. All this she had from a Central Authority who lived in a board and tar-paper shed on the skirts of a razed city full of whirling lime-dust and blown papers.

'By the way,' said he, 'you know your grave, of course?'

'Yes, thank you,' said Helen, and showed its row and number typed on Michael's own little typewriter. The officer would have checked it, out of one of his many books; but a large Lancashire woman thrust between them and bade him tell her where she might find her son, who had been corporal in the ASC. His proper name, she sobbed, was Anderson, but, coming of respectable folk, he had of course enlisted under the name of Smith; and had been killed at Dickiebush, in early 'Fifteen. She had not his number nor did she know which of his two Christian names he might have used with his alias; but her Cook's tourist ticket expired at the end of Easter week, and if by then she could not find her child she should go mad. Whereupon she fell forward on Helen's breast; but the officer's wife came out quickly from a little bedroom behind the office, and the three of them lifted the woman on to the cot.

'They are often like this,' said the officer's wife, loosening the tight bonnet-strings. 'Yesterday she said he'd been killed at Hooge. Are you sure you know your grave? It makes such a difference.'

'Yes, thank you,' said Helen, and hurried out before the woman on the bed should begin to lament again.

Tea in a crowded mauve and blue striped wooden structure, with a false front, carried her still further into the nightmare. She paid her bill beside a stolid, plain-featured Englishwoman, who, hearing her inquire about the train to Hagenzeele, volunteered to come with her.

'I'm going to Hagenzeele myself,' she explained. 'Not to Hagenzeele Third; mine is Sugar Factory, but they call it La Rosière now. It's just south of Hagenzeele Three. Have you got your room at the hotel there?'

'Oh yes, thank you. I've wired.'

'That's better. Sometimes the place is quite full, and at others there's hardly a soul. But they've put bathrooms into the old Lion d'Or – that's the hotel on the west side of Sugar Factory – and it draws off a lot of people, luckily.'

'It's all new to me. This is the first time I've been over.'

'Indeed! This is my ninth time since the Armistice. Not on my own account. *I* haven't lost any one, thank God – but, like every one else, I've a lot of friends at home who have. Coming over as often as I do, I find it helps them to have some one just look at the – the place and tell them about it afterwards. And one can take photos for them, too. I get quite a list of commissions to execute.' She laughed nervously and tapped her slung Kodak. 'There are two or three to see at Sugar Factory this time, and plenty of others in the cemeteries all about. My system is to save them up, and arrange them, you know. And when I've got enough commissions for one area to make it worth while, I pop over and execute them. It *does* comfort people.'

'I suppose so,' Helen answered, shivering as they entered the little train.

'Of course it does. (Isn't it lucky we've got window-seats?) It must do or they wouldn't ask one to do it, would they? I've a list of quite twelve or fifteen commissions here' – she tapped the Kodak again – 'I must sort them out tonight. Oh, I forgot to ask you. What's yours?'

'My nephew,' said Helen. 'But I was very fond of him.'

'Ah, yes! I sometimes wonder whether *they* know after death? What do you think?'

'Oh, I don't – I haven't dared to think much about that sort of thing,' said Helen, almost lifting her hands to keep her off.

'Perhaps that's better,' the woman answered. 'The sense of loss must be enough, I expect. Well, I won't worry you any more.'

Helen was grateful, but when they reached the hotel Mrs Scarsworth (they had exchanged names) insisted on dining at the same table with her, and after the meal, in the little, hideous salon full of low-voiced relatives, took Helen through her 'commissions' with biographies of the dead, where she happened to know them, and sketches of their next of kin. Helen endured till nearly half-past nine, ere she fled to her room.

Almost at once there was a knock at her door and Mrs Scarsworth entered; her hands, holding the dreadful list, clasped before her.

'Yes – yes – *I* know,' she began. 'You're sick of me, but I want to tell you something. You – you aren't married, are you? Then perhaps you won't . . . But it doesn't matter. I've *got* to tell someone. I can't go on any longer like this.'

'But please—' Mrs Scarsworth had backed against the shut door, and her mouth worked dryly.

'In a minute,' she said. 'You – you know about these graves of mine I was telling you about downstairs, just now? They really *are* commissions. At least several of them are.' Her eye wandered round the room. 'What extraordinary wallpapers they have in Belgium, don't you think? . . . Yes. I swear they are commissions. But there's *one*, d'you see, and – and he was more to me than anything else in the world. Do you understand?'

Helen nodded.

'More than anyone else. And, of course, he oughtn't to have been. He ought to have been nothing to me. But he *was*. He *is*. That's why I do the commissions, you see. That's all.'

'But why do you tell me?' Helen asked desperately.

'Because I'm *so* tired of lying. Tired of lying – always lying – year in and year out. When I don't tell lies I've got to act 'em and I've got to think 'em, always. *You* don't know what that means. He was everything to me that he oughtn't to have been – the one real thing – the only thing that ever happened to me in all my life; and I've had to pretend he wasn't. I've had to watch every word I said, and think out what lie I'd tell next, for years and years!'

'How many years?' Helen asked.

'Six years and four months before, and two and three-quarters after. I've gone to him eight times, since. Tomorrow'll make the ninth, and – and I can't – I *can't* go to him again with nobody in the world knowing. I want to be honest with someone before I go. Do you understand? It doesn't matter about *me*. I was never truthful, even as a girl. But it isn't worthy of *him*. So – so I – I had to tell you. I can't keep it up any longer. Oh, I can't!'

She lifted her joined hands almost to the level of her mouth, and brought them down sharply, still joined, to full arms' length below her waist. Helen reached forward, caught them, bowed her head over them, and murmured: 'Oh, my dear! My dear!' Mrs Scarsworth stepped back, her face all mottled.

'My God!' said she. 'Is *that* how you take it?'

Helen could not speak, and the woman went out; but it was a long while before Helen was able to sleep.

Next morning Mrs Scarsworth left early on her round of commissions, and Helen walked alone to Hagenzeele Third. The place was still in the making, and stood some five or six feet above the metalled road, which it flanked for hundreds of yards. Culverts across a deep ditch served for entrances through the unfinished boundary wall. She climbed a few wooden-faced earthen steps and then met the entire crowded level of the thing in one held breath. She did not know that Hagenzeele Third counted twenty-one thousand dead already. All she saw was a merciless sea of black crosses, bearing little strips of stamped tin at all angles across their faces. She could distinguish no order or arrangement in their mass; nothing but a waist-high wilderness as of weeds stricken dead, rushing at her. She went forward, moved to the left and the right hopelessly, wondering by what guidance she should ever come to her own. A great distance away there was a line of whiteness. It proved to be a block of some two or three hundred graves whose headstones had already been set, whose flowers were planted out, and whose new-sown grass showed green. Here she could see clear-cut letters at the ends of the rows, and, referring to her slip, realized that it was not here she must look.

A man knelt behind a line of headstones – evidently a gardener, for he was firming a young plant in the soft earth. She went towards him, her paper in her hand. He rose at her approach and without prelude or salutation asked: 'Who are you looking for?'

'Lieutenant Michael Turrell – my nephew,' said Helen slowly and word for word, as she had many thousands of times in her life.

The man lifted his eyes and looked at her with infinite compassion before he turned from the fresh-sown grass toward the naked black crosses.

'Come with me,' he said, 'and I will show you where your son lies.'

When Helen left the cemetery she turned for a last look. In the distance she saw the man bending over his young plants; and she went away, supposing him to be the gardener.

THE BURDEN

One grief on me is laid
  Each day of every year,
Wherein no soul can aid,
  Whereof no soul can hear:
Whereto no end is seen
  Except to grieve again –
Ah, Mary Magdalene,
  Where is there greater pain?

To dream on dear disgrace
  Each hour of every day –
To bring no honest face
  To aught I do or say:
To lie from morn till e'en –
  To know my lies are vain –
Ah, Mary Magdalene,
  Where can be greater pain?

To watch my steadfast fear
  Attend my every way
Each day of every year –
  Each hour of every day:
To burn, and chill between –
  To quake and rage again –
Ah, Mary Magdalene,
  Where shall be greater pain?

One grave to me was given –
  To guard till Judgment Day –
But God looked down from Heaven
  And rolled the Stone away!
One day of all my years –
  One hour of that one day –
His Angel saw my tears
  And rolled the Stone away!

Dayspring Mishandled

C'est moi, c'est moi, c'est moi!
Je suis la Mandragore!
La fille des beaux jours qui s'éveille à l'aurore –
Et qui chante pour toi!

C. Nodier

IN the days beyond compare and before the Judgments, a genius called Graydon foresaw that the advance of education and the standard of living would submerge all mind-marks in one mudrush of standardized reading-matter, and so created the Fictional Supply Syndicate to meet the demand.

Since a few days' work for him brought them more money than a week's elsewhere, he drew many young men – some now eminent – into his employ. He bade them keep their eyes on the *Sixpenny Dream Book*, the Army and Navy Stores Catalogue (this for backgrounds and furniture as they changed), and *The Hearthstone Friend*, a weekly publication which specialized unrivalledly in the domestic emotions. Yet, even so, youth would not be denied, and some of the collaborated love-talk in 'Passion Hath Peril', and 'Ena's Lost Lovers', and the account of the murder of the earl in 'The Wickwire Tragedies' – to name but a few masterpieces now never mentioned for fear of blackmail – was as good as anything to which their authors signed their real names in more distinguished years.

Among the young ravens driven to roost awhile on Graydon's ark was James Andrew Manallace – a darkish, slow northerner of the type that does not ignite, but must be detonated. Given written or verbal outlines of a plot, he was useless; but, with a half-dozen pictures round which to write his tale, he could astonish.

And he adored that woman who afterwards became the mother of Vidal Benzaquen,* and who suffered and died because she loved one unworthy. There was, also, among the company a mannered, bellied person called Alured Castorley, who talked and wrote about 'Bohemia', but was always afraid of being 'compromised' by the weekly suppers at Neminaka's Café in Hestern Square, where the Syndicate work was apportioned, and where everyone looked out for himself. He, too, for a time, had loved Vidal's mother, in his own way.

*'The Village that voted the Earth was Flat.' *A Diversity of Creatures.*

Now, one Saturday at Neminaka's, Graydon, who had given Manallace a sheaf of prints – torn from an extinct children's book called *Philippa's Queen* – on which to improvise, asked for results. Manallace went down into his ulster-pocket, hesitated a moment, and said the stuff had turned into poetry on his hands.

'Bosh!'

'That's what it isn't,' the boy retorted. 'It's rather good.'

'Then it's no use to us.' Graydon laughed. 'Have you brought back the cuts?'

Manallace handed them over. There was a castle in the series; a knight or so in armour; an old lady in a horned head-dress; a young ditto; a very obvious Hebrew; a clerk, with pen and inkhorn, checking wine-barrels on a wharf; and a Crusader. On the back of one of the prints was a note, 'If he doesn't want to go, why can't he be captured and held to ransom?' Graydon asked what it all meant.

'I don't know yet. A comic opera, perhaps,' said Manallace.

Graydon, who seldom wasted time, passed the cuts on to someone else, and advanced Manallace a couple of sovereigns to carry on with, as usual; at which Castorley was angry and would have said something unpleasant but was suppressed. Half-way through supper, Castorley told the company that a relative had died and left him an independence; and that he now withdrew from 'hackwork' to follow 'Literature'. Generally, the Syndicate rejoiced in a comrade's good fortune, but Castorley had gifts of waking dislike. So the news was received with a vote of thanks, and he went out before the end, and, it was said, proposed to 'Dal Benzaquen's mother, who refused him. He did not come back. Manallace, who had arrived a little exalted, got so drunk before midnight that a man had to stay and see him home. But liquor never touched him above the belt, and when he had slept awhile, he recited to the gas-chandelier the poetry he had made out of the pictures; said that, on second thoughts, he would convert it into comic opera; deplored the Upas-tree influence of Gilbert and Sullivan: sang somewhat to illustrate his point; and – after words, by the way, with a negress in yellow satin – was steered to his rooms.

In the course of a few years, Graydon's foresight and genius were rewarded. The public began to read and reason upon higher planes, and the Syndicate grew rich. Later still, people demanded of their printed matter what they expected in their clothing and furniture. So, precisely as the three-guinea handbag is followed in three weeks by its thirteen and sevenpence ha'penny, indistinguishable sister, they enjoyed perfect synthetic substitutes for Plot, Sentiment, and

Emotion. Graydon died before the cinema-caption school came in, but he left his widow twenty-seven thousand pounds.

Manallace made a reputation, and, more important, money for Vidal's mother when her husband ran away and the first symptoms of her paralysis showed. His line was the jocundly-sentimental Wardour Street brand of adventure, told in a style that exactly met, but never exceeded, every expectation.

As he once said when urged to 'write a real book': 'I've got my label, and I'm not going to chew it off. If you save people thinking, you can do anything with 'em.' His output apart, he was genuinely a man of letters. He rented a small cottage in the country and economized on everything, except the care and charges of Vidal's mother.

Castorley flew higher. When his legacy freed him from 'hackwork', he became first a critic – in which calling he loyally scalped all his old associates as they came up – and then looked for some speciality. Having found it (Chaucer was the prey), he consolidated his position before he occupied it, by his careful speech, his cultivated bearing, and the whispered words of his friends whom he, too, had saved the trouble of thinking. It followed that, when he published his first serious articles on Chaucer, all the world which is interested in Chaucer said: 'This is an authority.' But he was no impostor. He learned and knew his poet and his age; and in a month-long dogfight in an austere literary weekly, met and mangled a recognized Chaucer expert of the day. He also, 'for old sake's sake', as he wrote to a friend, went out of his way to review one of Manallace's books with an intimacy of unclean deduction (this was before the days of Freud) which long stood as a record. Some member of the extinct Syndicate took occasion to ask him if he would – for old sake's sake – help Vidal's mother to a new treatment. He answered that he had 'known the lady very slightly and the calls on his purse were so heavy that', etc. The writer showed the letter to Manallace, who said he was glad Castorley hadn't interfered. Vidal's mother was then wholly paralysed. Only her eyes could move, and those always looked for the husband who had left her. She died thus in Manallace's arms in April of the first year of the war.

During the war he and Castorley worked as some sort of departmental dishwashers in the Office of Co-ordinated Supervisals. Here Manallace came to know Castorley again. Castorley, having a sweet tooth, cadged lumps of sugar for his tea from a typist, and when she took to giving them to a younger man, arranged that she should be reported for smoking in unauthorized apartments. Manallace possessed himself of every detail of the affair, as compensation for the review of his book. Then there came a night when, waiting for a big air-raid, the two men had talked humanly, and Manallace spoke of Vidal's mother. Castorley said something in reply, and from that hour – as was learned several years later – Manallace's real life-work and interests began.

The war over, Castorley set about to make himself Supreme Pontiff on Chaucer by methods not far removed from the employment of poison gas. The English Pope was silent, through private griefs, and influenza had carried off the learned Hun who claimed continental allegiance. Thus Castorley crowed unchallenged from Upsala to Seville, while Manallace went back to his cottage with the photo of Vidal's mother over the mantelpiece. She seemed to have emptied out his life, and left him only fleeting interests in trifles. His private diversions were experiments of uncertain outcome, which, he said, rested him after a day's gadzooking and vitalstapping. I found him, for instance, one weekend, in his toolshed-scullery, boiling a brew of slimy barks which were, if mixed with oak-galls, vitriol and wine, to become an ink-powder. We boiled it till the Monday, and it turned into an adhesive stronger than birdlime, and entangled us both.

At other times, he would carry me off, once in a few weeks, to sit at Castorley's feet, and hear him talk about Chaucer. Castorley's voice, bad enough in youth, when it could be shouted down, had, with culture and tact, grown almost insupportable. His mannerisms, too, had multiplied and set. He minced and mouthed, postured and chewed his words throughout those terrible evenings; and poisoned not only Chaucer, but every shred of English literature which he used to embellish him. He was shameless, too, as regarded self-advertisement and 'recognition' – weaving elaborate intrigues; forming petty friendships and confederacies, to be dissolved next week in favour of more promising alliances; fawning, snubbing, lecturing, organizing and lying as unrestingly as a politician, in chase of the knighthood due not to him (he always called on his Maker to forbid such a thought) but as tribute to Chaucer. Yet, sometimes, he could break from his obsession and prove how a man's work will try to save the soul of him. He would tell us charmingly of copyists of the fifteenth century in England and the Low Countries, who had multiplied the Chaucer MSS., of which there remained – he gave us the exact number – and how each scribe could by him (and, he implied, by him alone) be distinguished from every other by some peculiarity of letter-formation, spacing or like trick of pen-work; and how he could fix the dates of their work within five years. Sometimes he would give us an hour of really interesting stuff and then return to his overdue 'recognition'. The changes sickened me, but Manallace defended him, as a master in his own line who had revealed Chaucer to at least one grateful soul.

This, as far as I remembered, was the autumn when Manallace holidayed in the Shetlands or the Faroes, and came back with a stone 'quern' – a hand corn-grinder. He said it interested him from the ethnological standpoint. His whim lasted till next harvest, and was followed by a religious spasm which, naturally, translated itself into literature. He showed me a battered and mutilated Vulgate of 1485, patched up the back with bits of legal parchments, which he had bought for thirty-five shillings. Some monk's attempt to rubricate chapter-initials had caught, it seemed, his forlorn fancy, and he dabbled in shells of gold and silver paint for weeks.

That also faded out, and he went to the Continent to get local colour for a love-story, about Alva and the Dutch, and the next year I saw practically nothing of him. This released me from seeing much of Castorley, but, at intervals, I would go there to dine with him, when his wife – an unappetizing, ash-coloured woman – made no secret that his friends wearied her almost as much as he did. But at a later meeting, not long after Manallace had finished his Low Countries' novel, I found Castorley charged to bursting-point with triumph and high information hardly withheld. He confided to me that a time was at hand when great matters would be made plain, and 'recognition' would be inevitable. I assumed, naturally, that there was fresh scandal or heresy afoot in Chaucer circles, and kept my curiosity within bounds.

In time, New York cabled that a fragment of a hitherto unknown Canterbury Tale lay safe in the steel-walled vaults of the seven-million-dollar Sunnapia Collection. It was news on an international scale – the New World exultant – the Old deploring the 'burden of British taxation which drove such treasures, etc.', and the lighter-minded journals disporting themselves according to their publics; for 'our Dan', as one earnest Sunday editor observed, 'lies closer to the national heart than we wot of'. Common decency made me call on Castorley, who, to my surprise, had not yet descended into the arena. I found him, made young again by joy, deep in just-passed proofs.

Yes, he said, it was all true. He had, of course, been in it from the first. There had been found one hundred and seven new lines of Chaucer tacked on to an abridged end of *The Persone's Tale*, the whole the work of Abraham Mentzius, better known as Mentzel of Antwerp (1388–1438/9) – I might remember he had talked about him – whose distinguishing peculiarities were a certain Byzantine formation of his 'g's, the use of a 'sickle-slanted' reed-pen, which cut into the vellum at certain letters; and, above all, a tendency to spell English words on Dutch lines, whereof the manuscript carried one convincing proof. For instance (he wrote it out for me), a girl praying against an undesired marriage, says:

'Ah Jesu-Moder, pitie my oe peyne.
Daiespringe mishandeelt cometh nat agayne.'

Would I, please, note the spelling of 'mishandeelt'? Stark Dutch and Mentzel's besetting sin! But in *his* position one took nothing for granted. The page had been part of the stiffening of the side of an old Bible, bought in a parcel by Dredd, the big dealer, because it had some rubricated chapter-initials, and by Dredd shipped, with a consignment of similar odds and ends, to the Sunnapia Collection, where they were making a glass-cased exhibit of the whole history of illumination and did not care how many books they gutted for that purpose. There, someone who noticed a crack in the back of the volume had unearthed it. He went on: 'They didn't know what to make of the thing at first. But they knew about *me*! They kept quiet till I'd been consulted. You might have noticed I was out of England for three months.

'I was over there, of course. It was what is called a "spoil" – a page Mentzel had spoiled with his Dutch spelling – I expect he had had the English dictated to him – then had evidently used the vellum for trying out his reeds; and then, I suppose, had put it away. The "spoil" had been doubled, pasted together, and slipped in as stiffening to the old book-cover. I had it steamed open, and analysed the wash. It gave the flour-grains in the paste – coarse, because of the old millstone – and there were traces of the grit itself. What? Oh, possibly a handmill of Mentzel's own time. He may have doubled the spoilt page and used it for part of a pad to steady woodcuts on. It may have knocked about his workshop for years. That, indeed, is practically certain because a beginner from the Low Countries has tried his reed on a few lines of some monkish hymn – not a bad lilt tho' – which must have been common form. Oh yes, the page may have been used in other books before it was used for the Vulgate. That doesn't matter, but *this* does. Listen! I took a wash, for analysis, from a blot in one corner – that would be after Mentzel had given up trying to make a possible page of it, and had grown careless – and I got the actual *ink* of the period! It's a practically eternal stuff compounded on – I've forgotten his name for the minute – the scribe at Bury St Edmunds, of course – hawthorn bark and wine. Anyhow, on *his* formula. *That* wouldn't interest you either, but, taken with all the other testimony, it clinches the thing. (You'll see it all in my statement to the press on Monday.) Overwhelming, isn't it?'

'Overwhelming,' I said, with sincerity. 'Tell me what the tale was about, though. That's more in my line.'

'I know it; but *I* have to be equipped on all sides. The verses are relatively easy for one to pronounce on. The freshness, the fun, the humanity, the fragrance of it all, cries – no, shouts – itself as Dan's work. Why "Daiespringe mishandled" alone stamps it from Dan's mint. Plangent as doom, my dear boy – plangent as doom! It's all in my statement. Well, substantially, the fragment deals with a girl whose parents wish her to marry an elderly suitor. The mother isn't so keen on it, but the father, an old knight, is. The girl, of course, is in love with a younger and a poorer man. Common form? Granted. Then the father, who doesn't in the least want to, is ordered off to a Crusade and, by way of passing on the kick, as we used to say during the war, orders the girl to be kept in duresse till his return or her consent to the old suitor. Common form, again? Quite so. That's too much for her mother. She reminds the old knight of his age and infirmities, and the discomforts of crusading. Are you sure I'm not boring you?'

'Not at all,' I said, though time had begun to whirl backward through my brain to a red-velvet, pomatum-scented side-room at Neminaka's and Manallace's set face intoning to the gas.

'You'll read it all in my statement next week. The sum is that the old lady tells him of a certain knight-adventurer on the French coast, who, for a consideration, waylays knights who don't relish crusading and holds them to impossible ransoms till the trooping-season is over, or they are returned sick. He keeps a ship in the Channel to pick 'em up and transfers his birds to his castle ashore, where he has a reputation for doing 'em well. As the old lady points out:

'And if perchance thou fall into his honde
By God how canstow ride to Holilonde?'

'You see? Modern in essence as Gilbert and Sullivan, but handled as only Dan could! And she reminds him that "Honour and olde bones" parted company long ago. He makes one splendid appeal for the spirit of chivalry:

Lat all men change as Fortune may send,
But Knighthood beareth service to the end,

and *then*, of course, he gives in:

For what his woman willeth to be don
Her manne must or wauken Hell anon.

'Then she hints that the daughter's young lover, who is in the Bordeaux wine trade, could open negotiations for a kidnapping without compromising him. And *then* that careless brute Mentzel spoils his page and chucks it! But there's enough to show what's going to happen. You'll see it all in my statement. Was there ever anything in literary finds to hold a candle to it? . . . And they give grocers knighthoods for selling cheese!'

I went away before he could get into his stride on that course. I wanted to think, and to see Manallace. But I waited till Castorley's statement came out. He had left himself no loophole. And when, a little later, his (nominally the Sunnapia people's) 'scientific' account of their analyses and tests appeared, criticism ceased, and some journals began to demand 'public recognition'. Manallace wrote me on this subject, and I went down to his cottage, where he at once asked me to sign a memorial on Castorley's behalf. With luck, he said, we might get him a KBE in the next Honours List. Had I read the statement?

'I have,' I replied. 'But I want to ask you something first. Do you remember the night you got drunk at Neminaka's, and I stayed behind to look after you?'

'Oh, *that* time,' said he, pondering. 'Wait a minute! I remember Graydon advancing me two quid. He was a generous paymaster. And I remember – now, who the devil rolled me under the sofa – and what for?'

'We all did,' I replied. 'You wanted to read us what you'd written to those Chaucer cuts.'

'I don't remember that. No! I don't remember anything after the sofa-episode . . . *You* always said that you took me home – didn't you?'

'I did, and you told Kentucky Kate outside the old Empire that you had been faithful, Cynara, in your fashion.'

'Did I?' said he. 'My God! Well, I suppose I have.' He stared into the fire. 'What else?'

'Before we left Neminaka's you recited me what you had made out of the cuts – the whole tale! So – you see?'

'Ye-es.' He nodded. 'What are you going to do about it?'

'What are *you*?'

'I'm going to help him get his knighthood – first.'

'Why?'

'I'll tell you what he said about 'Dal's mother – the night there was that air-raid on the offices.'

He told it.

'That's why,' he said. 'Am I justified?'

He seemed to me entirely so.

'But after he gets his knighthood?' I went on.

'That depends. There are several things I can think of. It interests me.'

'Good Heavens! I've always imagined you a man without interests.'

'So I was. I owe my interests to Castorley. He gave me every one of 'em except the tale itself.'

'How did *that* come?'

'Something in those ghastly cuts touched off something in me – a sort of possession, I suppose. I was in love too. No wonder I got drunk that night. I'd *been* Chaucer for a week! Then I thought the notion might make a comic opera. But Gilbert and Sullivan were too strong.'

'So I remember you told me at the time.'

'I kept it by me, and it made me interested in Chaucer – philologically and so on. I worked on it on those lines for years. There wasn't a flaw in the wording even in 'Fourteen. I hardly had to touch it after that.'

'Did you ever tell it to anyone except me?'

'No, only 'Dal's mother – when she could listen to anything – to put her to sleep. But when Castorley said – what he did about her, I thought I might use it. 'Twasn't difficult. *He* taught me. D'you remember my birdlime experiments, and the stuff on our hands? I'd been trying to get that ink for more than a year. Castorley told me where I'd find the formula. And your falling over the quern, too?'

'That accounted for the stone-dust under the microscope?'

'Yes. I grew the wheat in the garden here, and ground it myself. Castorley gave me Mentzel complete. He put me on to an MS. in the British Museum which he said was the finest sample of his work. I copied his "Byzantine 'g's" for months.'

'And what's a "sickle-slanted" pen?' I asked.

'You nick one edge of your reed till it drags and scratches on the curves of the letters. Castorley told me about Mentzel's spacing and margining. I only had to get the hang of his script.'

'How long did that take you?'

'On and off – some years. I was too ambitious at first – I wanted to give the whole poem. That would have been risky. Then Castorley told me about spoiled pages and I took the hint. I spelt "Dayspring mishandeelt" Mentzel's way – to make sure of him. It's not a bad couplet in itself. Did you see how he admires the "plangency" of it?'

'Never mind him. Go on!' I said.

He did. Castorley had been his unfailing guide throughout, specifying in minutest detail every trap to be set later for his own feet. The actual vellum was an Antwerp find, and its introduction into the cover of the Vulgate was begun after a long course of amateur bookbinding. At last, he bedded it under pieces of an old deed, and a printed page (1686) of Horace's *Odes*, legitimately used for repairs by different owners in the seventeenth and eighteenth centuries; and at the last moment, to meet Castorley's theory that spoiled pages were used in workshops by beginners, he had written a few Latin words in fifteenth century script – the statement gave the exact date – across an open part of the fragment. The thing ran: '*Illa alma Mater ecca, secum afferens me acceptum. Nicolaus Atrib.*' The disposal of the thing was easiest of all. He had merely hung about Dredd's dark bookshop of fifteen rooms, where he was well known, occasionally buying but generally browsing, till, one day, Dredd Senior showed him a case of cheap black-letter stuff, English and Continental – being packed for the Sunnapia people – into which Manallace tucked his contribution, taking care to wrench the back enough to give a lead to an earnest seeker.

'And then?' I demanded.

'After six months or so Castorley sent for me. Sunnapia had found it, and as Dredd had missed it, and there was no money-motive sticking out, they were half-convinced it was genuine from the start. But they invited him over. He conferred with their experts, and suggested the scientific tests. *I* put that into his head, before he sailed. That's all. And now, will you sign our memorial?'

I signed. Before we had finished hawking it round there was a host of influential names to help us, as well as the impetus of all the literary discussion which arose over every detail of the glorious trove. The upshot was a KBE* for Castorley in the next Honours List; and Lady Castorley, her cards duly printed, called on friends that same afternoon.

*Officially it was on account of his good work in the Departmental of Co-ordinated Supervisals, but all true lovers of literature knew the real reason, and told the papers so.

Manallace invited me to come with him, a day or so later, to convey our pleasure and satisfaction to them both. We were rewarded by the sight of a man relaxed and ungirt – not to say wallowing naked – on the crest of success. He assured us that 'The Title' should not make any difference to our future relations, seeing it was in no sense personal, but, as he had often said, a tribute to Chaucer; 'and, after all,' he pointed out, with a glance at the mirror over the mantelpiece, 'Chaucer was the prototype of the "veray parfit gentil Knight" of the British Empire so far as that then existed.'

On the way back, Manallace told me he was considering either an unheralded revelation in the baser press which should bring Castorley's reputation about his own ears some breakfast-time, or a private conversation, when he would make clear to Castorley that he must now back the forgery as long as he lived, under threat of Manallace's betraying it if he flinched.

He favoured the second plan. 'If I pull the string of the shower-bath in the papers,' he said, 'Castorley might go off his veray parfit gentil nut. I want to keep his intellect.'

'What about your own position? The forgery doesn't matter so much. But if you tell this you'll kill him,' I said.

'I intend that. Oh – my position? I've been dead since – April Fourteen, it was. But there's no hurry. What was it *she* was saying to you just as we left?'

'She told me how much your sympathy and understanding had meant to him. She said she thought that even Sir Alured did not realize the full extent of his obligations to you.'

'She's right, but I don't like her putting it that way.'

'It's only common form – as Castorley's always saying.'

'Not with *her*. She can hear a man think.'

'She never struck me in that light.'

'*You* aren't playing against her.'

'Guilty conscience, Manallace?'

'H'm! I wonder. Mine or hers? I *wish* she hadn't said that. "More even than *he* realizes it." I won't call again for awhile.'

He kept away till we read that Sir Alured, owing to slight indisposition, had been unable to attend a dinner given in his honour.

Inquiries brought word that it was but natural reaction, after strain, which, for the moment, took the form of nervous dyspepsia, and he would be glad to see Manallace at any time. Manallace reported him as rather pulled and drawn, but full of his new life and position, and proud that his efforts should have martyred him so much. He was going to collect, collate, and expand all his pronouncements and inferences into one authoritative volume.

'I must make an effort of my own,' said Manallace. 'I've collected nearly all his stuff about the find that has appeared in the papers, and he's promised me everything that's missing. I'm going to help him. It will be a new interest.'

'How will you treat it?' I asked.

'I expect I shall quote his deductions on the evidence, and parallel 'em with my experiments – the ink and the paste and the rest of it. It ought to be rather interesting.'

'But even then there will only be your word. It's hard to catch up with an established lie,' I said. 'Especially when you've started it yourself.'

He laughed. 'I've arranged for *that* – in case anything happens to me. Do you remember the "Monkish Hymn"?'

'Oh yes! There's quite a literature about it already.'

'Well, you write those ten words above each other, and read down the first and second letters of 'em; and see what you get.* My bank has the formula.'

He wrapped himself lovingly and leisurely round his new task, and Castorley was as good as his word in giving him help. The two practically collaborated, for Manallace suggested that all Castorley's strictly scientific evidence should be in one place, with his deductions and dithyrambs as appendices. He assured him that the public would prefer this arrangement, and, after grave consideration, Castorley agreed.

'That's better,' said Manallace to me. 'Now I shan't have so many hiatuses in my extracts. Dots always give the reader the idea you aren't dealing fairly with your man. I shall merely quote him solid, and rip him up, proof for proof, and date for date, in parallel columns. His book's taking more out of him than I like, though. He's been doubled up twice with tummy attacks since I've worked with

**Illa*
alma
Mater
ecca
secùm
afferens
me
acceptum
Nicolaus
Atrib.

him. And he's just the sort of flatulent beast who may go down with appendicitis.'

We learned before long that the attacks were due to gall-stones, which would necessitate an operation. Castorley bore the blow very well. He had full confidence in his surgeon, an old friend of theirs; great faith in his own constitution; a strong conviction that nothing would happen to him till the book was finished, and, above all, the Will to Live.

He dwelt on these assets with a voice at times a little out of pitch and eyes brighter than usual beside a slightly-sharpening nose.

I had only met Gleeag, the surgeon, once or twice at Castorley's house, but had always heard him spoken of as a most capable man. He told Castorley that his trouble was the price exacted, in some shape or other, from all who had served their country; and that, measured in units of strain, Castorley had practically been at the front through those three years he had served in the Office of Co-ordinated Supervisals. However, the thing had been taken betimes, and in a few weeks he would worry no more about it.

'But suppose he dies?' I suggested to Manallace.

'He won't. I've been talking to Gleeag. He says he's all right.'

'Wouldn't Gleeag's talk be common form?'

'I *wish* you hadn't said that. But, surely, Gleeag wouldn't have the face to play with me – or her.'

'Why not? I expect it's been done before.'

But Manallace insisted that, in this case, it would be impossible.

The operation was a success and, some weeks later, Castorley began to recast the arrangement and most of the material of his book. 'Let me have my way,' he said, when Manallace protested. 'They are making too much of a baby of me. I really don't need Gleeag looking in every day now.' But Lady Castorley told us that he required careful watching. His heart had felt the strain, and fret or disappointment of any kind must be avoided. 'Even,' she turned to Manallace, 'though you know ever so much better how his book should be arranged than he does himself.'

'But really,' Manallace began. 'I'm very careful not to fuss—'

She shook her finger at him playfully. 'You don't think you do; but, remember, he tells me everything that you tell him, just the same as he told me everything that he used to tell *you*. Oh, I don't mean the things that men talk about. I mean about his Chaucer.'

'I didn't realize that,' said Manallace, weakly.

'I thought you didn't. He never spares me anything; but *I* don't mind,' she replied with a laugh, and went off to Gleeag, who was paying his daily visit. Gleeag said he had no objection to Manallace working with Castorley on the book for a given time – say, twice a week – but supported Lady Castorley's demand that he should not be over-taxed in what she called 'the sacred hours'. The man grew more and more difficult to work with, and the little check he had heretofore set on his self-praise went altogether.

'He says there has never been anything in the History of Letters to compare with it,' Manallace groaned. 'He wants now to inscribe – he never dedicates, you know – inscribe it to me, as his "most valued assistant". The devil of it is that *she* backs him up in getting it out soon. Why? How much do you think she knows?'

'Why should she know anything at all?'

'You heard her say he had told her everything that he had told me about Chaucer? (I *wish* she hadn't said that!) If she puts two and two together, she can't help seeing that every one of his notions and theories has been played up to. But then – but then . . . Why is she trying to hurry publication? She talks about me fretting him. *She's* at him, all the time, to be quick.'

Castorley must have over-worked, for, after a couple of months, he complained of a stitch in his right side, which Gleeag said was a slight sequel, a little incident of the operation. It threw him back awhile, but he returned to his work undefeated.

The book was due in the autumn. Summer was passing, and his publisher urgent, and – he said to me, when after a longish interval I called – Manallace had chosen this time, of all, to take holiday. He was not pleased with Manallace, once his indefatigable aide, but now dilatory, and full of time-wasting objections. Lady Castorley had noticed it, too.

Meantime, with Lady Castorley's help, he himself was doing the best he could to expedite the book: but Manallace had mislaid (did I think through jealousy?) some essential stuff which had been dictated to him. And Lady Castorley wrote Manallace, who had been delayed by a slight motor accident abroad, that the fret of waiting was prejudicial to her husband's health. Manallace, on his return from the Continent, showed me that letter.

'He has fretted a little, I believe,' I said.

Manallace shuddered. 'If I stay abroad, I'm helping to kill him. If I help him to hurry up the book, I'm expected to kill him. *She* knows,' he said.

'You're mad. You've got this thing on the brain.'

'I have not! Look here! You remember that Gleeag gave me from four to six, twice a week, to work with him. She called them the "sacred hours". You heard her? Well, they *are*! They are Gleeag's and hers. But she's so infernally plain, and I'm such a fool, it took me weeks to find it out.'

'That's their affair,' I answered. 'It doesn't prove she knows anything about the Chaucer.'

'She *does*! He told her everything that he had told me when I was pumping him, all those years. She put two and two together when the thing came out. She saw exactly how I had set my traps. I know it! She's been trying to make me admit it.'

'What did you do?'

'Didn't understand what she was driving at, of course. And then she asked Gleeag, before me, if he didn't think the delay over the book was fretting Sir Alured. He didn't think so. He said getting it out might deprive him of an interest. He had that much decency. *She's* the devil!'

'What do you suppose is her game, then?'

'If Castorley knows he's been had, it'll kill him. She's at me all the time, indirectly, to let it out. I've told you she wants to make it a sort of joke between us. Gleeag's willing to wait. He knows Castorley's a dead man. It slips out when they talk. They say "He was", not "He is". Both of 'em know it. But *she* wants him finished sooner.'

'I don't believe it. What are you going to do?'

'What can I? I'm not going to have him killed, though.'

Manlike, he invented compromises whereby Castorley might be lured up by-paths of interest, to delay publication. This was not a success. As autumn advanced Castorley fretted more, and suffered from returns of his distressing colics. At last, Gleeag told him that he thought they might be due to an overlooked gallstone working down. A second comparatively trivial operation would eliminate the bother once and for all. If Castorley cared for another opinion, Gleeag named a surgeon of eminence. 'And then,' said he, cheerily, 'the two of us can talk you over.' Castorley did not want to be talked over. He was oppressed by pains in his side, which, at first, had yielded to the liver-tonics Gleeag prescribed; but now they stayed – like a toothache – behind everything. He felt most at ease in his bedroom-study, with his proofs round him. If he had more pain than he could stand, he would consider the second operation. Meantime Manallace – 'the meticulous Manallace', he called him – agreed with him in thinking that the Mentzel page-facsimile, done by the Sunnapia Library, was not quite good enough for the great book, and the Sunnapia people were, very decently, having it re-processed. This would hold things back till early spring, which had its advantages, for he could run a fresh eye over all in the interval.

One gathered these news in the course of stray visits as the days shortened. He insisted on Manallace keeping to the 'sacred hours', and Manallace insisted on my accompanying him when possible. On these occasions he and Castorley would confer apart for half an hour or so, while I listened to an unendurable clock in the drawing-room. Then I would join them and help wear out the rest of the time, while Castorley rambled. His speech, now, was often clouded and uncertain – the result of the 'liver-tonics'; and his face came to look like old vellum.

It was a few days after Christmas – the operation had been postponed till the following Friday – that we called together. She met us with word that Sir Alured had picked up an irritating little winter cough, due to a cold wave, but we were not, therefore, to abridge our visit. We found him in steam perfumed with Friar's Balsam. He waved the old Sunnapia facsimile at us. We agreed that it ought to have been more worthy. He took a dose of his mixture, lay back and asked us to lock the door. There was, he whispered, something wrong somewhere. He could not lay his finger on it, but it was in the air. He felt he was being played with. He did not like it. There was something wrong all round him. Had we noticed it? Manallace and I severally and slowly denied that we had noticed anything of the sort.

With no longer break than a light fit of coughing, he fell into the hideous helpless panic of the sick – those worse than captives who lie at the judgment and mercy of the hale for every office and hope. He wanted to go away. Would we help him to pack his Gladstone? Or, if that would attract too much attention in certain quarters, help him to dress and go out? There was an urgent matter to be set right, and now that he had The Title and knew his own mind it would all end happily and he would be well again. *Please* would we let him go out, just to speak to – he named her; he named her by her 'little' name out of the old Neminaka days? Manallace quite agreed, and recommended a pull at the 'liver-tonic' to brace him after so long in the house. He took it, and Manallace suggested that it would be better if, after his walk, he came down to the cottage for a weekend and brought the revise with him. They could then re-touch the last chapter. He answered to that drug and to some praise of his work, and presently simpered drowsily. Yes, it *was* good – though he said it who should not. He praised himself awhile till, with a puzzled forehead and shut eyes, he told us that *she* had been saying lately that it was too good – the whole thing, if we understood, was *too* good. He wished us to get the exact shade of her meaning. She had suggested, or rather implied, this doubt. She had said – he would let us draw our own inferences – that the Chaucer find had 'anticipated the wants of humanity'. Johnson, of course. No need to tell *him* that. But what the hell was her implication? Oh God! Life had always been one long innuendo! *And* she had said that a man could do anything with anyone if he saved him the trouble of thinking. What did she mean by that? *He* had never shirked thought. He had thought sustainedly all his life. It *wasn't* too good, was it? Manallace didn't think it was too good – did he? But this pick-pick-picking at a man's brain and work was too bad, wasn't it? *What* did she mean? Why did she always bring in Manallace, who was only a friend – no scholar, but a lover of the game – Eh? – Manallace could confirm this if he were here, instead of loafing on the Continent just when he was most needed.

'I've come back,' Manallace interrupted, unsteadily. 'I can confirm every word you've said. You've nothing to worry about. It's *your* find – *your* credit – *your* glory and – all the rest of it.'

'Swear you'll tell her so then,' said Castorley. 'She doesn't believe a word I say. She told me she never has since before we were married. Promise!'

Manallace promised, and Castorley added that he had named him his literary executor, the proceeds of the book to go to his wife. 'All profits without deduction,' he gasped. 'Big sales if it's properly handled. *You* don't need money . . . Graydon'll trust *you* to any extent. It 'ud be a long . . .'

He coughed, and, as he caught breath, his pain broke through all the drugs, and the outcry filled the room. Manallace rose to fetch Gleeag, when a full, high, affected voice, unheard for a generation, accompanied, as it seemed, the clamour of a beast in agony, saying: 'I wish to God someone would stop that old swine howling there! *I* can't . . . I was going to tell you fellows that it would be a dam' long time before Graydon advanced *me* two quid.'

We escaped together, and found Gleeag waiting, with Lady Castorley, on the landing. He telephoned me, next morning, that Castorley had died of bronchitis, which his weak state made it impossible for him to throw off. 'Perhaps it's just as well,' he added, in reply to the condolences I asked him to convey to the widow. 'We might have come across something we couldn't have coped with.'

Distance from that house made me bold.

'You knew all along, I suppose? What was it, really?'

'Malignant kidney-trouble – generalized at the end. No use

worrying him about it. We let him through as easily as possible. Yes! A happy release . . . What? . . . Oh! Cremation. Friday, at eleven.'

There, then, Manallace and I met. He told me that she had asked him whether the book need now be published; and he had told her this was more than ever necessary, in her interests as well as Castorley's.

'She is going to be known as his widow – for a while, at any rate. Did I perjure myself much with him?'

Not explicitly,' I answered.

'Well, I have now – with *her* – explicitly,' said he, and took out his black gloves . . .

As, on the appointed words, the coffin crawled sideways through the noiselessly-closing door-flaps, I saw Lady Castorley's eyes turn towards Gleeag.

GERTRUDE'S PRAYER

(*Modernized from the 'Chaucer' of Manallace.*)

That which is marred at birth Time shall not mend,
    Nor water out of bitter well make clean;
All evil thing returneth at the end,
    Or elseway walketh in our blood unseen.
Whereby the more is sorrow in certaine –
Dayspring mishandled cometh not againe.

To-bruized be that slender, sterting spray
    Out of the oake's rind that should betide
A branch of girt and goodliness, straightway
    Her spring is turnèd on herself, and wried
And knotted like some gall or veiney wen. –
Dayspring mishandled cometh not agen.

Noontide repayeth never morning-bliss –
    Sith noon to morn is incomparable;
And, so it be our dawning goth amiss,
    None other after-hour serveth well.
Ah! Jesu-Moder, pitie my oe paine –
Dayspring mishandled cometh not againe!

The Manner of Men

'If after the manner of men I have fought with beasts.'
I Cor. xv. 32.

HER cinnabar-tinted topsail, nicking the hot blue horizon, showed she was a Spanish wheat-boat hours before she reached Marseilles mole. There, her mainsail brailed itself, a spritsail broke out forward, and a handy driver aft; and she threaded her way through the shipping to her berth at the quay as quietly as a veiled woman slips through a bazaar.

The blare of her horns told her name to the port. An elderly hook-nosed inspector came aboard to see if her cargo had suffered in the run from the South, and the senior ship-cat purred round her captain's legs as the after-hatch was opened.

'If the rest is like this – ' the inspector sniffed – 'you had better run out again to the mole and dump it.'

'That's nothing,' the captain replied. 'All Spanish wheat heats a little. They reap it very dry.'

'Pity you don't keep it so, then. What would you call *that* – crop or pasture?'

The inspector pointed downwards. The grain was in bulk, and deck-leakage, combined with warm weather, had sprouted it here and there in sickly green films.

'So much the better,' said the captain brazenly. 'That makes it waterproof. Pare off the top two inches, and the rest is as sweet as a nut.'

'*I* told that lie, too, when I was your age. And how does she happen to be loaded?'

The young Spaniard flushed, but kept his temper.

'She happens to be ballasted, under my eye, on lead-pigs and bagged copper-ores.'

'I don't know that they much care for verdigris in their dole-bread at Rome. But – you were saying?'

'I was trying to tell you that the bins happen to be grain-tight, two-inch chestnut, floored and sided with hides.'

'Meaning dressed African leathers on your private account?'

'What has that got to do with you? We discharge at Port of Rome, not here.'

'So your papers show. And what might you have stowed in the wings of her?'

'Oh, apes! Circumcised apes – just like you!'

'Young monkey! Well, if you are not above taking an old ape's advice, next time you happen to top off with wool and screw in more bales than are good for her, get your ship undergirt before you sail. I know it doesn't look smart coming into Port of Rome, but it'll save your decks from lifting worse than they are.'

There was no denying that the planking and waterways round the after-hatch had lifted a little. The captain lost his temper.

'I know your breed!' he stormed. 'You promenade the quays all summer at Caesar's expense, jamming your Jew-bow into everybody's business; and when the norther blows, you squat over your brazier and let us skippers hang in the wind for a week!'

'You have it! Just that sort of a man am I now,' the other answered. 'That'll do, the quarter-hatch!'

As he lifted his hand the falling sleeve showed the broad gold armlet with the triple vertical gouges which is only worn by master mariners who have used all three seas – Middle, Western, and Eastern.

'Gods!' the captain saluted. 'I thought you were—'

'A Jew, of course. Haven't you used Eastern ports long enough to know a Red Sidonian when you see one?'

'Mine the fault – yours be the pardon, my father!' said the Spaniard impetuously. 'Her topsides *are* a trifle strained. There was a three days' blow coming up. I meant to have had her undergirt off the Islands, but hawsers slow a ship so – and one hates to spoil a good run.'

'To whom do you say it?' The inspector looked the young man over between horny sun and salt creased eyelids like a brooding pelican. 'But if you care to get up your girt-hawsers tomorrow, I can find men to put 'em overside. It's no work for open sea. Now! Main-hatch, there! . . . I thought so. She'll need another girt abaft the foremast.' He motioned to one of his staff, who hurried up the quay to where the port guard-boat basked at her mooring-ring. She was a stoutly-built, single-banker, eleven a side, with a short punching ram; her duty being to stop riots in harbour and piracy along the coast.

'Who commands her?' the captain asked.

'An old shipmate of mine, Sulinus – a River man. We'll get his opinion.'

In the Mediterranean (Nile keeping always her name) there is but one river – that shifty-mouthed Danube, where she works through her deltas into the Black Sea. Up went the young man's eyebrows.

'Is he any kin to a Sulinor of Tomi, who used to be in the flesh-traffic – and a Free Trader? My uncle has told me of him. He calls him Mango.'

'That man. He was my second in the wheat-trade my last five voyages, after the Euxine grew too hot to hold him. But he's in the Fleet now . . . You know your ship best. Where do you think the after-girts ought to come?'

The captain was explaining, when a huge dish-faced Dacian, in short naval cuirass, rolled up the gangplank, carefully saluting the bust of Caesar on the poop, and asked the captain's name.

'Baeticus, for choice,' was the answer.

They all laughed, for the sea, which Rome mans with foreigners, washes out many shore-names.

'My trouble is this—' Baeticus began, and they went into committee, which lasted a full hour. At the end, he led them to the poop, where an awning had been stretched, and wines set out with fruits and sweet shore water.

They drank to the Gods of the Sea, Trade, and Good Fortune, spilling those small cups overside, and then settled at ease.

'Girting's an all-day job, if it's done properly,' said the inspector. 'Can you spare a real working-party by dawn tomorrow, Mango?'

'But surely – for you, Red.'

'I'm thinking of the wheat,' said Quabil curtly. He did not like nicknames so early.

'Full meals *and* drinks,' the Spanish captain put in.

'Good! Don't return 'em too full. By the way' – Sulinor lifted a level cup – 'where do you get this liquor, Spaniard?'

'From our Islands (the Balearics). Is it to your taste?'

'It is.' The big man unclasped his gorget in solemn preparation.

Their talk ran professionally, for though each end of the Mediterranean scoffs at the other, both unite to mock landward, wooden-headed Rome and her stiff-jointed officials.

Sulinor told a tale of taking the prefect of the port, on a breezy day, to Forum Julii, to see a lady, and of his lamentable condition when landed.

'Yes,' Quabil sneered. 'Rome's mistress of the world – as far as the foreshore.'

'If Caesar ever came on patrol with me,' said Sulinor, 'he might understand there was such a thing as the Fleet.'

'Then he'd officer it with well-born young Romans,' said Quabil.

'Be grateful you are left alone. *You* are the last man in the world to want to see Caesar.'

'Except one,' said Sulinor, and he and Quabil laughed.

'What's the joke?' the Spaniard asked.

Sulinor explained.

'We had a passenger, our last trip together, who wanted to see Caesar. It cost us our ship and freight. That's all.'

'Was he a warlock – a wind-raiser?'

'Only a Jew philosopher. But he *had* to see Caesar. He said he had; and he piled up the *Eirene* on his way.'

'Be fair,' said Quabil. 'I don't like the Jews – they lie too close to my own hold – but it was Caesar lost me my ship.' He turned to Baeticus. 'There was a proclamation, our end of the world, two seasons back, that Caesar wished the Eastern wheat-boats to run through the winter, and he'd guarantee all loss. Did *you* get it, youngster.

'No. Our stuff is all in by September. I wager Caesar never paid you! How late did you start?'

'I left Alexandria across the bows of the Equinox – well down in the pickle, with Egyptian wheat – half pigeon's dung – and the usual load of Greek sutlers and their women. The second day out the sou'-wester caught me. I made across it north for the Lycian coast, and slipped into Myra till the wind should let me get back into the regular grain-track again.'

Sailor-fashion, Quabil began to illustrate his voyage with date and olive stones from the table.

'The wind went into the north, as I knew it would, and I got under way. You remember, Mango? My anchors were apeak when a Lycian patrol threshed in with Rome's order to us to wait on a Sidon packet with prisoners and officers. Mother of Carthage, I cursed him!'

'Shouldn't swear at Rome's Fleet. 'Weatherly craft, those Lycian racers! Fast, too. I've been hunted by them! Never thought I'd command one,' said Sulinor, half aloud.

'And now I'm coming to the leak in *my* decks, young man,' Quabil eyed Baeticus sternly. 'Our slant north had strained her, and I should have undergirt her at Myra. Gods know why I didn't! I set up the chain-staples in the cable-tier for the prisoners. I even had the girt-hawsers on deck – which saved time later; but the thing I should have done, that I did *not*.'

'Luck of the Gods!' Sulinor laughed. 'It was because our little philosopher wanted to see Caesar in his own way at our expense.'

'Why did he want to see him?' said Baeticus.

'As far as I ever made out from him and the centurion, he wanted to argue with Caesar – about philosophy.'

'He was a prisoner, then?'

'A political suspect – with a Jew's taste for going to law,' Quabil interrupted. 'No orders for irons. Oh, a little shrimp of a man, but – but he seemed to take it for granted that he led everywhere. He messed with us.'

'And he was worth talking to, Red,' said Sulinor.

'*You* thought so; but he had the woman's trick of taking the tone and colour of whoever he talked to. Now – as I was saying . . .'

There followed another illustrated lecture on the difficulties that beset them after leaving Myra. There was always too much west in the autumn winds, and the *Eirene* tacked against it as far as Cnidus. Then there came a northerly slant, on which she ran through the Aegean Islands, for the tail of Crete; rounded that, and began tacking up the south coast.

'Just darning the water again, as we had done from Myra to Cnidus,' said Quabil ruefully. 'I daren't stand out. There was the boneyard of all the Gulf of Africa under my lee. But at last we worked into Fairhaven – by that cork yonder. Late as it was, *I* should have taken her on, but I had to call a ship-council as to lying up for the winter. That Rhodian law may have suited open boats and cock-crow coasters,* but it's childish for ocean-traffic.'

'*I* never allow it in any command of mine,' Baeticus spoke quietly. 'The cowards give the order, and the captain bears the blame.'

Quabil looked at him keenly. Sulinor took advantage of the pause.

'We were in harbour, you see. So our Greeks tumbled out and voted to stay where we were. It was my business to show them that the place was open to many winds, and that if it came on to blow we should drive ashore.'

'Then I,' broke in Quabil, with a large and formidable smile, 'advised pushing on to Phenike, round the cape, only forty miles across the bay. My mind was that, if I could get her undergirt there, I might later – er – coax them out again on a fair wind, and hit Sicily. But the undergirting came first. She was beginning to talk too much – like me now.'

Sulinor chafed a wrist with his hand.

'She was a hard-mouthed old water-bruiser in any sea,' he murmured.

*Quabil meant the coasters who worked their way by listening to the cocks crowing on the beaches they passed. The insult is nearly as old as sail.

'She could lie within six points of any wind,' Quabil retorted, and hurried on. 'What made Paul vote with those Greeks? He said we'd be sorry if we left harbour.'

'Every passenger says that, if a bucketful comes aboard,' Baeticus observed.

Sulinor refilled his cup, and looked at them over the brim, under brows as candid as a child's, ere he set it down.

'Not Paul. He did not know fear. He gave me a dose of my own medicine once. It was a morning watch coming down through the Islands. We had been talking about the cut of our topsail – he was right – it held too much lee wind – and then he went to wash before he prayed. I said to him: "You seem to have both ends and the bight of most things coiled down in your little head, Paul. If it's a fair question, what *is* your trade ashore?" And he said: "I've been a man-hunter – Gods forgive me; and now that I think The God has forgiven me, I am man-hunting again." Then he pulled his shirt over his head, and I saw his back. Did *you* ever see his back, Quabil?'

'I expect I did – that last morning, when we all stripped; but I don't remember.'

'*I* shan't forget it! There was good, sound lictor's work and criss-cross Jew scourgings like gratings; and a stab or two; and, besides those, old dry bites – when they get good hold and rugg you. That showed he must have dealt with the Beasts. So, whatever he'd done, he'd paid for. I was just wondering what he *had* done, when he said: "No; not your sort of man-hunting." "It's your own affair," I said: "but *I* shouldn't care to see Caesar with a back like that. I should hear the Beasts asking for me." "I may that, too, some day," he said, and began sluicing himself, and – then— What's brought the girls out so early? Oh, I remember!'

There was music up the quay, and a wreathed shore-boat put forth full of Arlesian women. A long-snouted three-banker was hauling from a slip till her trumpets warned the benches to take hold. As they gave way, the *hrmph-hrmph* of the oars in the oar-ports reminded Sulinor, he said, of an elephant choosing his man in the Circus.

'She has been here re-masting. They've no good rough-tree at Forum Julii,' Quabil explained to Baeticus. 'The girls are singing her out.'

The shallop ranged alongside her, and the banks held water, while a girl's voice came across the clock-calm harbour-face:

'Ah, would swift ships had never been about the seas to rove!
For then these eyes had never seen nor ever wept their love.

Over the ocean-rim he came – beyond that verge he passed,
And I who never knew his name must mourn him to the last!'

'And you'd think they meant it,' said Baeticus, half to himself.

'That's a pretty stick,' was Quabil's comment as the man-of-war opened the island athwart the harbour. 'But she's overmasted by ten foot. A trireme's only a bird-cage.'

'Luck of the Gods I'm not singing in one now,' Sulinor muttered. They heard the yelp of a bank being speeded up to the short sea-stroke.

'I wish there was some way to save mainmasts from racking.' Baeticus looked up at his own, bangled with copper wire.

'The more reason to undergirt, my son,' said Quabil. '*I* was going to undergirt that morning at Fairhaven. You remember, Sulinor? I'd given orders to overhaul the hawsers the night before. My fault! Never say "Tomorrow". The Gods hear you. And then the wind came out of the south, mild as milk. All we had to do was to slip round the headland to Phenike – and be safe.'

Baeticus made some small motion, which Quabil noticed, for he stopped.

'My father,' the young man spread apologetic palms, 'is not that lying wind the in-draught of Mount Ida? It comes up with the sun, but later—'

'You need not tell *me*! We rounded the cape, our decks like a fair (it was only half a day's sail), and then, out of Ida's bosom the full north-easter stamped on us! Run? What else? I needed a lee to clean up in. Clauda was a few miles down wind; but whether the old lady would bear up when she got there, I was not so sure.'

'She did.' Sulinor rubbed his wrists again. 'We were towing our longboat half-full. I steered somewhat that day.'

'What sail were you showing?' Baeticus demanded.

'Nothing – and twice too much at that. But she came round when Sulinor asked her, and we kept her jogging in the lee of the island. I said, didn't I, that my girt-hawsers were on deck?'

Baeticus nodded. Quabil plunged into his campaign at long and large, telling every shift and device he had employed. 'It was scanting daylight,' he wound up, 'but I daren't slur the job. Then we streamed our boat alongside, baled her, sweated her up, and secured. You ought to have seen our decks!'

'Panic?' said Baeticus.

'A little. But the whips were out early. The centurion – Julius – lent us his soldiers.'

'How did your prisoners behave?' the young man went on.

Sulinor answered him. 'Even when man is being shipped to the Beasts, he does not like drowning in irons. They tried to rive the chain-staples out of her timbers.'

'I got the main-yard on deck' – this was Quabil. 'That eased her a little. They stopped yelling after a while, didn't they?'

'They did,' Sulinor replied. 'Paul went down and told them there was no danger. And they believed him! Those scoundrels believed him! He asked me for the keys of the leg-bars to make them easier. "*I*'ve been through this sort of thing before," he said, "but they are new to it down below. Give me the keys." I told him there was no order for him to have any keys; and I recommended him to line his hold for a week in advance, because we were in the hands of the Gods. "And when are we ever out of them?" he asked. He looked at me like an old gull lounging just astern of one's taffrail in a full gale. *You* know that eye, Spaniard?'

'Well do I!'

'By that time' – Quabil took the story again – 'we had drifted out of the lee of Clauda, and our one hope was to run for it and pray we weren't pooped. None the less, I could have made Sicily with luck. As a gale I have known worse, but the wind never shifted a point, d'ye see? We were flogged along like a tired ox.'

'Any sights?' Baeticus asked.

'For ten days not a blink.'

'Nearer two weeks,' Sulinor corrected. 'We cleared the decks of everything except our ground-tackle, and put six hands at the tillers. She seemed to answer her helm – sometimes. Well, it kept *me* warm for one.'

'How did your philosopher take it?'

'Like the gull I spoke of. He was there, but outside it all. *You* never got on with him, Quabil?'

'Confessed! I came to be afraid at last. It was not my office to show fear, but I was. *He* was fearless, although I knew that he knew the peril as well as I. When he saw that trying to – er – cheer me made me angry, he dropped it. Like a woman, again. You saw more of him, Mango?'

'Much. When I was at the rudders he would hop up to the steerage, with the lower-deck ladders lifting and lunging a foot at a time, and the timbers groaning like men beneath the Beasts. We used to talk, hanging on till the roll jerked us into the scuppers. Then we'd begin again. What about? Oh! Kings and Cities and Gods and Caesar. He was sure he'd see Caesar. I told him I had noticed that people who worried Those Up Above' – Sulinor jerked his thumb towards the awning – 'were mostly sent for in a hurry.'

'Hadn't you wit to see he never wanted you for yourself, but to get something out of you?' Quabil snapped.

'Most Jews are like that – and all Sidonians!' Sulinor grinned. 'But what *could* he have hoped to get from anyone? We were doomed men all. You said it, Red.'

'Only when I was at my emptiest. Otherwise I *knew* that with any luck I could have fetched Sicily! But I broke – we broke. Yes, we got ready – you too – for the Wet Prayer.'

'How does that run with you?' Baeticus asked, for all men are curious concerning the bride-bed of Death.

'With us of the River,' Sulinor volunteered, 'we say: "I sleep; presently I row again."'

'Ah! At our end of the world we cry: "Gods, judge me not as a god, but a man whom the Ocean has broken."' Baeticus looked at Quabil, who answered, raising his cup: 'We Sidonians say, "Mother of Carthage, I return my oar!" But it all comes to the one in the end.' He wiped his beard, which gave Sulinor his chance to cut in.

'Yes, we were on the edge of the Prayer when – do you remember, Quabil? – *he* clawed his way up the ladders and said: "No need to call on what isn't there. My God sends me sure word that I shall see Caesar. *And* he has pledged me all your lives to boot. Listen! No man will be lost." And Quabil said: "But what about my ship?"' Sulinor grinned again.

'That's true. I had forgotten the cursed passengers,' Quabil confirmed. 'But he spoke as though my *Eirene* were a fig-basket. "Oh, she's bound to go ashore, somewhere," he said, "but not a life will be lost. Take this from me, the Servant of the One God." Mad! Mad as a magician on market-day!'

'No,' said Sulinor. 'Madmen see smooth harbours and full meals. I have had to – soothe that sort.'

'After all,' said Quabil, 'he was only saying what had been in my head for a long time. I had no way to judge our drift, but we likely might hit something somewhere. Then he went away to spread his cookhouse yarn among the crew. It did no harm, or I should have stopped him.'

Sulinor coughed, and drawled:

'I don't see anyone stopping Paul from what he fancied he ought to do. But it was curious that, on the change of watch, I—'

'No – I!' said Quabil.

'Make it so, then, Red. Between us, at any rate, we felt that the sea had changed. There was a trip and a kick to her dance. *You* know, Spaniard. And then – I *will* say that, for a man half-dead, Quabil here did well.'

'I'm a bosun-captain, and not ashamed of it. I went to get a cast of the lead. (Black dark and raining marlinspikes!) The first cast warned me, and I told Sulinor to clear all aft for anchoring by the stern. The next – shoaling like a slip-way – sent me back with all hands, and we dropped both bowers and spare and the stream.'

'He'd have taken the kedge as well, but I stopped him,' said Sulinor.

'I had to stop *her*! They nearly jerked her stern out, but they held. And everywhere I could peer or hear were breakers, or the noise of tall seas against cliffs. We were trapped! But our people had been starved, soaked, and half-stunned for ten days, and now they were close to a beach. That was enough! They must land on the instant; and was I going to let them drown within reach of safety? *Was* there panic? I spoke to Julius, and his soldiers (give Rome her due!) schooled them till I could hear my orders again. But on the kiss-of-dawn some of the crew said that Sulinor had told them to lay out the kedge in the long-boat.'

'I let 'em swing her out,' Sulinor confessed. 'I wanted 'em for warnings. But Paul told me his God had promised their lives to him along with ours, and any private sacrifice would spoil the luck. So, as soon as she touched water, I cut the rope before a man could get in. She was ashore – stove – in ten minutes.'

'Could you make out where you were by then?' Baeticus asked Quabil.

'As soon as I saw the people on the beach – yes. They are my sort – a little removed. Phoenicians by blood. It was Malta – *one* day's run from Syracuse, where I would have been safe! Yes, Malta and my wheat gruel. Good port-of-discharge, eh?'

They smiled, for Melita may mean 'mash' as well as 'Malta'.

'It puddled the sea all round us, while I was trying to get my bearings. But my lids were salt-gummed, and I hiccoughed like a drunkard.'

'And drunk you most gloriously were, Red, half an hour later!'

'Praise the Gods – and for once your pet Paul! That little man came to me on the fore-bitts, puffed like a pigeon, and pulled out a breastful of bread, and salt fish, and the wine – the good new wine. "Eat," he said, "and make all your people eat, too. Nothing will come to them except another wetting. They won't notice that, after they're full. Don't worry about *your* work either," he said. "You *can't* go wrong today. You are promised to me." And then he went off to Sulinor.'

'He did. He came to me with bread and wine and bacon – good they were! But first he said words over them, and then rubbed his hands with his wet sleeves. I asked him if he were a magician. "God forbid!" he said. "I am so poor a soul that I flinch from touching dead pig." As a Jew, he wouldn't like pork, naturally. Was that before or after our people broke into the storeroom, Red?'

'Had *I* time to wait on them?' Quabil snorted. 'I know they gutted my stores full-hand, and a double blessing of wine atop. But we all took that – deep. Now this is how we lay.' Quabil smeared a ragged loop on the table with a wine-wet finger. 'Reefs – see, my son – and overfalls to leeward here; something that loomed like a point of land on our right there; and, ahead, the blind gut of a bay with a Cyclops surf hammering it. How we had got in was a miracle. Beaching was our only chance, and meantime she was settling like a tired camel. Every foot I could lighten her meant that she'd take ground closer in at the last. I told Julius. He understood. "I'll keep order," he said. "Get the passengers to shift the wheat as long as you judge it's safe."'

'Did those Alexandrian achators really work?' said Baeticus.

'*I*'ve never seen cargo discharged quicker. It was time. The wind was taking off in gusts, and the rain was putting down the swells. I made out a patch of beach that looked less like death than the rest of the arena, and I decided to drive in on a gust under the spitfire-sprit – and, if she answered her helm before she died on us, to humour her a shade to starboard, where the water looked better. I stayed the foremast; set the spritsail fore and aft, as though we were boarding; told Sulinor to have the rudders down directly he cut the cables; waited till a gust came; squared away the sprit, and drove.'

Sulinor carried on promptly:

'I had two hands with axes on each cable, and one on each rudder-lift; and believe me, when Quabil's pipe went, both blades were down and turned before the cable-ends had fizzed under! She jumped like a stung cow! She drove. She sheared. I think the swell lifted her, and over-ran. She came down, and struck aft. Her stern broke off under my toes, and all the guts of her at that end slid out like a man's paunched by a lion. I jumped forward, and told Quabil there was nothing but small kindlings abaft the quarter-hatch, and he shouted: "Never mind! Look how beautifully I've laid her!"'

'I had. What I took for a point of land to starboard, y'see, turned out to be almost a bridge-islet, with a swell of sea 'twixt it and the main. And that meeting-swill, d'you see, surging in as she drove, gave her four or five foot more to cushion on. I'd hit the exact instant.'

'Luck of the gods, *I* think! Then we began to bustle our people over the bows before she went to pieces. You'll admit Paul was a help there, Red?'

'I dare say he herded the old judies well enough; but he should have lined up with his own gang.'

'He did that, too,' said Sulinor. 'Some fool of an under-officer had discovered that prisoners must be killed if they look like escaping; and he chose that time and place to put it to Julius – sword drawn. Think of hunting a hundred prisoners to death on those decks! It would have been worse than the Beasts!'

'But Julius saw – Julius saw it,' Quabil spoke testily. 'I heard him tell the man not to be a fool. They couldn't escape further than the beach.'

'And how did your philosopher take *that*?' said Baeticus.

'As usual,' said Sulinor. 'But, you see, we two had dipped our hands in the same dish for weeks; and, on the River, that makes an obligation between man and man.'

'In my country also,' said Baeticus, rather stiffly.

'So I cleared my dirk – in case I had to argue. Iron always draws iron with me. But *he* said: "Put it back. They are a little scared." I said: "Aren't *you*?" "What?" he said; "of being killed, you mean? No. Nothing can touch me till I've seen Caesar." Then he carried on steadying the ironed men (some were slavering-mad) till it was time to unshackle them by fives, and give 'em their chance. The natives made a chain through the surf, and snatched them out breast-high.'

'Not a life lost! Like stepping off a jetty,' Quabil proclaimed.

'Not quite. But he had promised no one should drown.'

'How *could* they – the way I had laid her – gust and swell and swill together?'

'And was there any salvage?'

'Neither stick nor string, my son. We had time to look, too. We stayed on the island till the first spring ship sailed for Port of Rome. They hadn't finished Ostia breakwater that year.'

'And, of course, Caesar paid you for your ship?'

'I made no claim. I saw it would be hopeless; and Julius, who knew Rome, was against any appeal to the authorities. He said that was the mistake Paul was making. And, I suppose, because I did not trouble them, and knew a little about the sea, they offered me the port inspectorship here. There's no money in it – if I were a poor man. Marseilles will never be a port again. Narbo has ruined her for good.'

'But Marseilles is far from under-Lebanon,' Baeticus suggested.

'The further the better. I lost my boy three years ago in Foul Bay, off Berenice, with the Eastern Fleet. He was rather like you about the eyes, too. You and your circumcised apes!'

'But – honoured one! My master! Admiral! – Father mine – how *could* I have guessed?'

The young man leaned forward to the other's knee in act to kiss it. Quabil made as though to cuff him, but his hand came to rest lightly on the bowed head.

'Nah! Sit, lad! Sit back. It's just the thing the boy would have said himself. You didn't hear it, Sulinor?'

'I guessed it had something to do with the likeness as soon as I set eyes on him. You don't so often go out of your way to help lame ducks.'

'You can see for yourself she needs under-girting, Mango!'

'So did that Tyrian tub last month. And you told her she might bear up for Narbo or bilge for all of you! But he shall have his working-party tomorrow, Red.'

Baeticus renewed his thanks. The River man cut him short.

'Luck of the gods,' he said. 'Five – four – years ago I might have been waiting for you anywhere in the Long Puddle with fifty River men – and no moon.'

Baeticus lifted a moist eye to the slip-hooks on his yardarm, that could hoist and drop weights at a sign.

'You might have had a pig or two of ballast through your benches coming alongside,' he said dreamily.

'And where would my overhead-nettings have been?' the other chuckled.

'Blazing – at fifty yards. What are fire-arrows for?'

'To fizzle and stink on my wet seaweed blindages. Try again.'

They were shooting their fingers at each other, like the little boys gambling for olive-stones on the quay beside them.

'Go on – go on, my son! Don't let that pirate board,' cried Quabil.

Baeticus twirled his right hand very loosely at the wrist.

'In that case,' he countered, 'I should have fallen back on my foster-kin – my father's island horsemen.'

Sulinor threw up an open palm.

'Take the nuts,' he said. 'Tell me, is it true that some infernal Balearic slingers of yours can turn a bull by hitting him on the horns?'

'On either horn you choose. My father farms near New Carthage. They come over to us for the summer to work. There are ten in my crew now.'

Sulinor hiccoughed and folded his hands magisterially over his stomach.

'Quite proper. Piracy *must* be put down! Rome says so. I do so,' said he.

'I see,' the younger man smiled. 'But tell me, why did you leave the slave – the Euxine trade, O Strategos?'

'That sea is too like a wine-skin. Only one neck. It made mine ache. So I went into the Egyptian run with Quabil here.'

'But why take service in the Fleet? Surely the wheat pays better?'

'I intended to. But I had dysentery at Malta that winter, and Paul looked after me.'

'Too much muttering and laying-on of hands for *me*,' said Quabil; himself muttering about some Thessalian jugglery with a snake on the island.

'*You* weren't sick, Quabil. When I was getting better, and Paul was washing me off once, he asked if my citizenship were in order. He was a citizen himself. Well, it was and it was not. As second of a wheat-ship I was *ex officio* Roman citizen – for signing bills and so forth. But on the beach, my ship perished, he said I reverted to my original shtay – status – of an extra-provinshal Dacian by a Sich – Sish – Scythian – I think she was – mother. Awkward – what? All the Middle Sea echoes like a public bath if a man is wanted.'

Sulinor reached out again and filled. The wine had touched his huge bulk at last.

'But, as I was saying, once *in* the Fleet nowadays one is a Roman with authority – no waiting twenty years for your papers. And Paul said to me: "Serve Caesar. You are not canvas I can cut to advantage at present. But if you serve Caesar you will be obeying at least some sort of law." He talked as though I were a barbarian. Weak as I was, I could have snapped his back with my bare hands. I told him so. "I don't doubt it," he said. "But that is neither here nor there. If you take refuge under Caesar at sea, you may have time to think. Then I may meet you again, and we can go on with our talks. But that is as The God wills. What concerns you *now* is that, by taking service, you will be free from the fear that has ridden you all your life."'

'Was he right?' asked Baeticus after a silence.

'He was. I had never spoken to him of it, but he knew it. *He* knew! Fire – sword – the sea – torture even – one does not think of them too often. But not the Beasts! Aie! *Not* the Beasts! I fought two dog-wolves for the life on a sand-bar when I was a youngster. Look!'

Sulinor showed his neck and chest.

'They set the sheep-dogs on Paul at some place or other once –